GAGG

Richard Asplin was born in 1972. He has been a stand-up comedian, guitarist, film critic, marketing assistant and underpant salesman. He lives in London with one girlfriend and two cats.

Praise for T-Shirt and Genes

'Asplin's wit means every other line is guffaw inducing'
Heat

'Fast paced and laugh-out-loud funny'
New Woman

'Sharp, funny observations'
Hello!

'Smart, stylish and highly enjoyable'
Emlyn Rees

'A witty, brilliant and irreverent read'
B

'One hysterically good read!'
19

Also by Richard Asplin

T-Shirt and Genes

Richard Asplin

GAGGED

arrow books

Lines from *Are You Being Served* © Jeremy Lloyd and David Cole
Reprinted by kind permission of the authors
Lines from *Fawlty Towers* © John Cleese
Reprinted by kind permission of the author
Lines from *Hi-De-Hi* © Jimmy Perry and David Croft
Reprinted by kind permission of the authors
Lines from *Porridge* © Dick Clemens and Ian La Frenais
Reprinted by kind permission of the authors

Published by Arrow Books in 2004

2 4 6 8 10 9 7 5 3 1

Copyright © Richard Asplin 2004

Richard Asplin has asserted his right under the Copyright, Designs and
Patents Act, 1988 to be identified as the author of this work

Arrow Books
The Random House Group Limited
20 Vauxhall Bridge Road, London SW1V 2SA

Random House Australia (Pty) Limited
20 Alfred Street, Milsons Point, Sydney,
New South Wales 2061, Australia

Random House New Zealand Limited
18 Poland Road, Glenfield, Auckland 10, New Zealand

Random House South Africa (Pty) Limited
Endulini, 5a Jubilee Road, Parktown 2193, South Africa

The Random House Group Limited Reg. No. 954009

www.randomhouse.co.uk

A CIP catalogue record for this book
is available from the British Library

Papers used by Random House are natural, recyclable products made
from wood grown in sustainable forests. The manufacturing processes
conform to the environmental regulations of the country of origin

ISBN 0 09 941685 9

Set in 12/16pt Walbaum MT by SX Composing DTP, Rayleigh, Essex
Printed and bound in Great Britain by
Cox & Wyman Ltd, Reading, Berks.

For my father

When Jasper Philips pushed open the door of the hotel room, four things struck him as being wrong.

Really, very wrong indeed.

First was the floor. It didn't go with the rest of the room at all. From what he had seen of the hotel interior so far, Jasper had expected a fancy carpet. Plush, patterned and so deep he'd have to jump up and down to see what shoes he was wearing.

What Jasper hadn't expected was paper. A4 typing paper. Hundreds of sheets of it. Some crumpled, some torn in half, some screwed up in tight white balls. It blanketed the room almost entirely, from the doorway where Jasper stood, all the way over to the second unusual aspect of the room, namely the strangled corpse by the bed.

The third thing that struck Jasper was the noise. It sounded like somebody sprinkling cat litter on a Billy Connolly LP going at the wrong speed.

It wasn't, of course. It was Angus Fisher, slumped grotesquely over a laptop computer at the dressing table in the centre of the room. Angus Fisher. One half of *the Angus & Malachy Madcap Madhouse* – an exhaustingly rubbish variety act he'd shared the bill with at the Edinburgh Festival that summer.

1

If Jasper remembered correctly, they had gone on after him in front of a disinterested lunchtime crowd and died horribly. Almost as horribly as they had now, in fact.

Head on the keyboard, bubbles of blood popped and glistened about Angus's blue lips; cold fingers clawed at a mouse-mat. Malachy lay by the bed, eyes swollen in purple sockets.

The fourth thing that struck Jasper was an American television producer.

From behind. Unexpectedly, with an aluminium baseball bat.

As the paper-strewn floor came roaring up to meet Jasper's face and the world went a funny colour, he had just enough time to decide that this producer, for all his talk and promises, probably wasn't going to offer him his own television show after all.

WEBLET'S WISEGUY WINNER SENDS MERCURY MINISERIES MILLIONS UP IN SMOKE

By PENNY LANG

HOLLYWOOD

Ailing studio Mercury Pictures may be notching another disaster on to their executive bedposts as the ratings plummet on their new period London miniseries.

Last night's FYRE (ABC 9 p.m.), part costume drama, part high-explosive actioneer, dropped from its initial 14.2/22 share to a humiliating 2.1/3 despite round-the-clock trailering.

Sked watchers report all America's eyes were over on KBL for another dose of celebrity-anchored smut, sleaze and scandal. In fact last night's Mafia edition of SEXPOSÉ – Dirty Dons (KBL 9 p.m.) scored a mammoth 19.4/32.

Meanwhile FYRE isn't being helped by reviews, which have ranged from "SHYTE" – *LA Times*, and "CRAPPE" – *Boston Globe*, to "A POX ON THY SCHEDULES, SIRE" from the *Chicago Sun*.

This comes on-top of Mercury's disastrous lumberjack/gangster sit-com WOODFELLAS that was axed from the ABN skeds last week due to record-breakingly low numbers.

Mercury's only remaining show is 'E.R. E.R. . . . OH! (ABN) which is also taking a beating from KBL, this time by SHRINK in the Friday 8 p.m. slot.

Mercury Comedy VP Don Silver, who was behind both laffers, is rumored to be in the UK working on a new unnamed project with British sitcom writer Melvin Medford.

Turn to page 2 for more on Mercury's shaky future.

Variety
Monday 25 September

On any Monday afternoon, over London's Soho, a cloud of frantic urgency hovers. It prickles the air like a coming storm.

Painfully thin blonde girls hand frantically urgent scripts to wincingly pierced cyclists. The cyclists in turn bike the scripts across open-plan offices, yelling *'Coming through!'* to rubber plants, handing them to groovily-goateed producers. The producers rush the scripts to glass-bricked boardrooms where slightly older yet just as painfully thin blonde women sip their cappuccinos and toss names of actors and directors about the table like a parlour game, while back in the painfully blonde reception areas, frantically urgent photocopiers rattle out more wincingly goateed scripts.

For it is in these tiny offices – a hundred production companies sharing the same nine square feet of crumbling W1 office space – that television is being made.

Groovily urgent, wincingly frantic and piercingly blonde television.

And it is in a small room of glass-bricks that Ben sat.

A not groovy, not blonde, not goateed and not pierced Ben Busby.

'So, Benjamin,' Mr Fleming-but-call-me-Josh began.

'It's Ben, really.'

'Right. Ben,' call-me-Josh corrected, picking up his black Duofold and hovering it over the application form. 'Impress me.' He slid lower in his leather seat and winked. 'What you gonna bring to Kathode Productions?'

With a sigh, Ben's soul collapsed in upon itself and grey despairing exhaustion consumed him.

He hoped it didn't show.

People (usually men) had been asking him this question (occasionally twice) in the same production offices (always glass) for, Christ, it had to be two years. The only thing that ever changed was the stupidity of the job-title he'd always fail to be given at the end. So far, tanned middle-aged men in polonecks had refused him the right to call himself an associate assistant script-editor; a junior concept administrator; a trainee feature compiler and, his particular favourite, an executive associate assistant trainee (pastry and cappuccino division).

'Bring?' Ben said. Call-me-Josh nodded with what he presumed was a relaxingly laid-back smile. Ben thought he'd had a stroke.

'Gosh heavens. I don't know really. I just, well, I dunno. Uhm, y'know?' Ben closed, helpfully.

It was pretty much the answer he always gave. He'd got it from a book on interview techniques his girlfriend Jacqueline had bought him. Although he was beginning to have a sneaking suspicion he might be getting the emphasis a bit wrong.

'I see from your CV . . .' Josh began on a different tack, lifting the dog-eared A4 sheet from beneath the application on his desk.

Oh, here we go, Ben thought.

This was the point he hated most. The only thing you could really see from Ben's CV were the gaps. Huge white spaces where qualifications and fabulous past jobs really should have been. It was as if someone had spilt Tippex all over his life.

'You left university two years ago?'

'That's right,' he nodded, bracing himself for the inevitable.

'And you studied . . . ?'

'Some of the time, yes.'

Josh pushed his heavy, fifties-style black-framed glasses up his nose a bit, not realising until too late he'd actually left his heavy, fifties-style black-framed glasses on a pile of scripts on the desk. He scratched his eyebrow instead.

'Sorry, English and Drama,' Ben said with a fidget.

'Right, right. And since then you . . . uhm . . .'

Ben watched the poor man's eyes flash over the gaping holes in the page in front of him, looking for something. For anything. He was lost, floundering and panicky in a great white sea of unemployability. Ben threw him a lifejacket.

'Writing mainly. I'm a . . . writer.'

'Ah. Ah, yes, I see.' Josh started breathing again, bobbing on the surface among the flotsam of small talk. 'You've got *comedy* down here as your hobby . . .'

'That's right,' Ben said, sitting up a bit. 'Sitcoms mainly. Well, *a* sitcom. My writing partner and I, Sheridan . . . he's a school friend . . . we've been kind of working on an idea for a show. If you'd like to see?' And Josh pulled an awkward expression as Ben reached down to the bag at his feet, sliding out two freshly printed pages reverently. 'We do a bit of stand-up too. I've got a gig tonight, actually – I mean, if you're interested? Do you know Guffaw-Play? In Ealing?'

Josh shied away, sliding back even further into his swivelly chair, chin now folding into his belt buckle. He watched Ben hold out the script.

'*Tailback*,' Ben said. 'It's set in a traffic jam.'

Josh made no move to take the pages. Ben drew them back slowly.

'Right, great, yeah. Then I tell ya what,' Josh said, 'why don't you just whitter on about that for ten minutes, you talentless wannabe? I'll ask some questions to pad the time out and make you feel inadequate – then you can fuck off and I'll go back to my life? Twat.'

'I-I beg your pardon?' Ben said.

'Your writing? Why don't you tell me about it?'

'Oh. Oh, er, right,' Ben said, giving his head a little shake. 'Sorry, I thought you said . . . oh, it doesn't matter.'

And so Ben Busby explained his life's ambition for the twelfth time that year to another in a long line of ageing, disinterested men in designer eyebrows. The huge retro railway-clock ticked away slow seconds on the wall as call-me-Josh said *uh-huh* and *I see* and *hey, that's just terrific,* while behind his eyes he imaged the pierced, painfully thin seventeen year old blonde girl he'd be giving the junior office-job to.

Half a mile away on a high rooftop, Ben's girlfriend Jacqueline stared down at the porn shops, electrical discount shops and the discount electrical porn shops of Tottenham Court Road and thought about giving up smoking.

Giving up a lot of things in fact.

Perched on the edge of a huge silver air-conditioning unit, waggling her shoe half on, half off, paperback hanging loose at her side, she stared out over the misty rooftops and quietly finished the absolutely last, final and never-againth Marlboro Light of her life.

In this new-found spirit (which had been on the go seriously for about an hour now), Jackie had also decided finally to give in and renew her gym membership for a whole year. None of this month-by-month nonsense. No, she'd take a big step. Certainly a bigger step than she'd ever managed in her aerobics class, anyway. She would bite the bullet, sign the cheque, lace up her new Nikes and just do it. He new life of sweaty, shiny, glowing fitness would start immediately. Well, perhaps Saturday.

Week. Saturday week.

She sucked the last yellow suck from her cigarette and held the glowing filter up to the cloudy sunlight. That was it. Last one.

She exhaled deeply.

Hmmm. No real difference so far.

'Jackie?' a voice said behind her. She spun around, attempting to flick her hair a bit in a healthy, non-smoking Timotei sort of fashion.

It was Rachel, the bouncy new girl from the pod opposite hers.

'Sorry, your phone's been going mad.' Rachel waggled a Post-it overhead like a trench surrender. 'Someone from Avatar called again.'

'Oh, what, *now?*'

Avatar were the largest entertainment management company in London. If you were a comedian and you'd appeared on telly, chances were your 10×8″ was clogging up the Avatar filing cabinets.

'Philips's Shaftesbury Theatre show has been pulled,' Rachel said. 'He won't be playing anymore London dates.'

'Shit, you're kidding? But he's on our cover.'

Jasper Philips was indeed leering his trademark leer from the cover of that week's *Out There* magazine, heading up their Edinburgh Festival Award-winners section.

'They were just letting you know,' Rachel said.

'So what are we going to do? What am *I* going to do? I've got front stalls tickets for Saturday.' Christ, she could do with a cigarette.

'I did tell them it was already printed . . .'

'Okay, I'll be there in a minute,' Jackie said flapping her paperback, Rachel disappeared back through the fire door.

Jackie sighed. This job was another on her quit list. The comedy listings for *Out There* magazine wasn't journalism. Not proper journalism. She sometimes felt she was like a man announcing the delays on the London Underground Tannoy system, who thought he was getting a foot in the door as a Radio One DJ.

She felt the cold prickle of September rain on her neck. It

dappled the paperback's pages with dirty smudges and she slapped it shut, standing up with a half-hearted groan. God wanted her back at her desk, it seemed.

It was getting on for 4.30. She had another riveting hour of telephone calls and listing-composition before she could legitimately skulk out of the office making 'miss-the-crush' noises and meet Ben and Sheridan for a coffee.

Jackie returned to her cluttered pod thinking positive thoughts.

A celebratory coffee. Because Ben would have some good news this time. Of course he would. It was only an office junior job, Ben could do that. He was bright and eager and knew more about television than anyone in the world. They would ask him when he could start and it would be cappuccinos in champagne flutes all round.

Easy, she told herself, dialling her phone with crossed fingers.

Not even Ben could fuck this one up.

'I mean, it's still in its early stages,' Ben said. 'But we've nailed the three main characters now. There's Phil, Arnie and Bob. Bob is the—'

'In here,' call-me-Josh interrupted groovily, a slinky blonde waif depositing a tray of coffees on the desk and trotting out in a horsey waft of Prada and incompetence.

'Sorry, Ben. That's great. What you were saying. A car park.'

'A car *pool* . . .'

'Great. Sounds hilarious.' Josh lit a Lucky Strike. 'You a Jasper Philips fan?'

'Oh, yeah, yeah,' he said. 'My girlfriend and I, it's our anniversary on Saturday, I'm taking her to—'

'Cool. Jasper's people are talking to us about a sitcom at the moment but I dunno,' Josh said, glad to be back to talking about himself. 'We're kicking around some concepts. He's got some idea about cheese? Talking cheese?' Josh gestured at the tray.

'You sure coffee's okay? It's just we're not really a tea kinda office, y'know?'

'It's fine, really,' Ben said, lifting the bath-sized cup of froth from the desk gingerly, scalding his fingers. 'I shouldn't really have asked for tea anyway. I've got this, well . . .'

'What?'

Ben looked at him. Could he risk it? Here? Now? No. Now wasn't the time. He'd blown too many interviews like that. He would save it, try it somewhere else. On someone else. This really wasn't the time.

'Well, I've got this thing about tea,' he said.

Oops.

'Uh-huh?' Josh said, blowing a smoke ring. He'd lost interest at this point and was happy to let Ben burble on for a few minutes. They were both well aware he was never going to get this job. Two years since university and all he had to show for it was two pages of a co-written sitcom about a carwash or something? No work experience, no contacts. Jesus, he hadn't even gone to the trouble of being thin or blonde.

'See, you order coffee in a restaurant, and it comes. Like this,' Ben said, sitting up a bit, motioning with his cup. 'Coffee. Finished. Frothy milk, chocolate sprinkles – whatever. Made by baristas, experts in their field.' He was talking quickly now, loudly. The confidence that had evaded him as he'd mumbled about his ambitions, so half-baked he could have served them in a Little Chef, was now roaring through him.

Josh, on the other hand, suddenly felt rather under attack. He would have slunk lower in his chair if he could, but it would have meant sawing a hole in the floor.

'But you order a cup of *tea*? It turns into an episode of Ready Steady Cook. They give you a cup and saucer, a bag, a little pot of hot water, little pot of milk. They're handing out sachets, spoons, napkins . . .'

Josh was trapped. Trapped in the horrible, clammy, fixed-grin world of the comedian's 'bit'. Ben had been desperate to try this little routine out for days. He and Sheridan had written it last week, shiny-fingered and sprawled on Sheridan's living room floor among pizza boxes and beer cans, arguing about whether '. . . *sachets, spoons, napkins* . . .' was funnier than '. . . *sachets, saucers, silverware* . . .'

'I, er, guess they don't know how people like it.' Josh shrugged. 'So, anyway, Ben—'

'I trust them! They do this for a living!' he said, putting down his cup with a loud clatter, gesturing wildly. 'I mean, they don't know how I like my *soup*, but they don't bring me hot water and a chicken!'

The room fell silent.

The clock tutted its disapproval.

'Mmm, heh, right, right,' Josh eased out eventually as his grin began to throb and lock. He stubbed out his cigarette firmly and began to sit up, fussing with Ben's CV.

Ben chewed the inside of his lip.

'Look, Benjamin,' Josh said, 'it's like this. You're looking for a job here as a foot-in-the-door, am I right? For your writing? This traffic cone show?' And he pointed at the script in Ben's lap.

'Traffic *jam* . . .'

'See, Benjamin,' Josh was saying, standing up, 'we get a lot of this. Out there,' he gestured through the glass bricks to where the office buzzed and clattered, 'my receptionist's a drama student. My MA has a PA in media studies. Christ, the girl who delivers the sandwiches has a PhD in comparative theatre. I don't need anymore wannabes, I'm sorry.'

'N-no, no, really,' Ben stammered. Fuck it, he'd done it again. Jackie was going to kill him. 'This?' he said, lifting the script. 'This is nothing. It's just, y'know, a thing. Really, not important. I only brought it along as a maybe kind of, well, y'know, maybe – if you *did* need a writer or something and I was *around* . . . ?'

It was over.

Minutes later, Ben's cheeks burned as he paced back out

11

through the office, past blonde, painfully thin water-coolers with BAs in English Lit'.

He'd got as far as the brushed chrome lift before a determined resolve possessed him.

Red faced and breathless, he strode back through the open-plan office and knocked lightly on call-me-Josh's door. He had to know. He couldn't waste the rest of his life.

He poked his head around the jamb, Josh peering worriedly over the edge of a coffee cup.

'I know . . . look, I know you're busy and what you said and everything. And . . . and, well, I guess you're right. About me wanting a foot-in-the-door. I'm sorry. But, well, I just need to know . . .'

Call-me-Josh put down his cup slowly and nodded warily.

'If I'd have said "a little pot of milk, sachets, saucers, *silverware*", would you have taken me on? 'Cause it's better, right? *Silverware?* Funnier. *Silverwear.*'

Two minutes later, Ben discovered that the Kathode Productions security guard had not only a PhD in French Cinema but a very firm grip indeed.

'Believe this?' Don said, motioning over his shoulder at the window. The barman stopped polishing an invisible stain from a heavy tumbler and looked over. Spots of dull rain began to tap and pink softly on the window. 'It's a hundred and two in LA,' Don said, jabbing his finger on his folded newspaper.

'The weather, sir?' the barman said, arching a single eyebrow in the manner taught in every London hotel.

'LA doesn't get weather,' Don said. 'You Brits get all the weather. We get sunshine. All day, every day. No umbrellas, no macs, no gloves, no galoshes.' He knocked back a mouthful of fiery liquid and slammed the glass down for a refill. 'Just beaches, broads and bikinis.'

'Mmm, sounds delightful, sir,' the barman said, topping up the tumbler. He thought it sounded like hell on earth.

It was like hell on earth, of course.

A bit warmer, perhaps.

The bar of the Margrave Hotel on London's Piccadilly, where Don Silver sat alone, fidgeting and cursing, is a pretty sumptuous affair, considering that beneath its frilly coasters and tinkly piano music it's just a hugely overpriced pub.

Don didn't like the place much, with its snooty barkeep and plastic flowers. Don was a party person. He liked a bar that was dark and hot and crowded and tasted of sweat and girls. He liked to drink, buy a little coke, drink a little more and buy a lot more coke. He liked to talk loudly and boorishly to preposterously breasted women for too long about stuff he didn't know about, take all his coke at once, remove his pants and fall over.

That was what Don liked.

Snooty barkeeps he hated. Plastic flowers he hated.

Rain he really hated.

The weather had been the first sign, the first little ruffle in his pampered Los Angeles feathers when he'd stepped from the company Gulfstream IV on to the bleak tarmac five days ago. The air had been spotted with a half-hearted dirty rain that had speckled his dark suit and made his Ray Bans look even more ridiculous than normal.

Standing waiting for his car, he'd watched with wonder the stalwart Blitzy British. Emerging from the sliding doors, a quick half-glance skywards to make sure there wasn't a hurricane or a typhoon roaring through, and then up went the collars, out came the 'brollie', and they scuttled on their way, being, well, awfully British about the whole thing, he supposed.

Don had managed to resist the temptation to be awfully Californian about the whole thing. He hadn't barked into his mobile phone, he hadn't had his PA sacked, and he hadn't got his lawyer to draw up papers taking the Prime Minister to litigation over Don's treatment in this country as an American citizen by some British clouds with no *goddamn' respect.*

No. Don had just turned to his travelling companion.

'Now, you sure this is a good idea?' he'd said.

Melvin Medford, the award-winning British comedy writer in whose hands Don had placed his fragile career, smiled a huge smile, like he was attempting to digest a coat hanger.

'What, are you kidding? This is perfect! Absolutely perfect. Home again. Jesus, it's been a long time. Smell that.' And he'd taken in a huge lungful of grit. 'England. Too long, old friend, too long.'

'Is the air meant to be this colour?' Don had grimaced.

easyJet

PB   A   B   C   D

PB   A   B   C   D

HALLIDAY/GORDON

Passenger

LTN

To

03DEC   STS

Date

12

Flight

S534

Security Number

8819899408

Boarding Pass - Carte d'embarquement -
Einsteigkarte - Tarjeta de embarque

Gate Number

Boarding Time

0630

'Trust me, I can feel it coming back to me now. This is going to be great.'

Don had rolled his eyes, hefted up his aluminium luggage, and the pair of them had shuffled forward towards the waiting car.

He'd hoped Melvin was right.

Because Don had made promises. Big promises. To the studio heads. To his father. To the men halfway through building his house.

He'd promised it would be fine. He'd promised they could relax.

This time he was coming back with a hit.

In New York it was noon.

The CEO of Mercury Pictures pounded and growled and sweated and gasped and ran and ran and ran and ran. Hard and fast, pushing his body forward, forward, to its aching limits. To the point, in fact, of almost spilling his drink.

Puffing and oofing, Howard Silver managed a quick look down at the red numbers in front of him. 3 *m.p.h.* He lifted a cotton-rich towel from the handrail and gave his face a pat. Clinking the ice around his whisky a little, he decided that that was enough for the day.

He podged the off button with a fat finger and the machine slowed to a halt.

He'd do another two minutes tomorrow.

Howard puffed across his cavernous office to the nearest leather sofa and dropped into its hug with the familiar haemorrhoidal howl of a sixty five year old. He bent, pulling off his tight leather brogues, releasing hot puffy feet to the cool carpet of the office.

A light knock, and a pretty young woman wafted in briskly, smelling of coffee and stamps.

'Second post, Mr Silver.'

'On the desk, Caroline, please. Those reporters gone yet?' he said from beneath his shroud, grabbing at breaths like they were high apples.

'Security has removed most of them but a Miss Paretsky from the KBL network is still staking out the lobby waiting to catch you.'

'Christ, still?' Howard sighed. He peeled the damp towel from his face, his white hair tacking on to the cotton. 'Damned hack. That woman and her goddamn' tabloid TV is everything that's wrong with network broadcasting in this country, Caroline, I mean it,' he said, unsticking himself from the leather and heaving himself to his feet.

'There's one here from Mr Dolawitz in Los Angeles,' she said, fanning the lunchtime post out on his huge cream blotter. 'Two from the board. Still nothing from Donald yet. The non-urgent mail I'll put—'

'You say Dolawitz?' Howard said. 'I'll look at that now. Go on, get out of here,' he said, and with a smile, Caroline trotted out. She paused at the door.

'And the answer's no, Caroline,' he said. 'Nobody's firing anybody. So *Fyre* dipped a little in the ratings last night? Big deal. It's new, it'll settle down. We had Miss Paretsky's damn' Mafia sex-show up against us on the other side. Frankie Corillo on death row reliving the greatest lays of his life? Jesus,' Howard grumbled. 'But don't you worry, Caroline. Everything's peachy, we'll bounce back. Now go get yourself some lunch.'

He threw his wet towel over a leather chair and took a seat behind his desk, reaching forward for the post. Which, being in the middle of his sweeping, football-pitch of a desk, he couldn't reach without getting up again. He decided to refresh his whisky as he read.

He was halfway to the bar when the phone on his desk trilled dully. Normally, with Caroline out at lunch, he'd let the machine pick up. But the reporters buzzing around the lobby had raised Howard's blood pressure a little and he snatched up the phone.

'*Mr Silver?*' a female voice said. '*My name is Diane Paretsky. I'm down in the lobby*—'

'I got nothing to say to you, miss,' he growled, rattling the ice in his empty glass. 'No comment. No comment at all.'

'*You won't confirm that your son Don's party lifestyle is costing Mercury Pictures a million a week? That his string of flops means*—'

'Miss Paretsky, let me tell you this.' Howard felt the whisky warm his head, filling him with a righteous glow. 'And sharpen your pencil 'cause you can quote me here. I have a meeting scheduled for tomorrow morning. You know who with? One Penelope Lang.'

'*Penny ... From* Variety?'

'For a series of profiles they're doing on *top* studio heads. You want me to spell that for you? *T-O-P*. Movers and shakers, Miss Paretsky. Read all about it in Wednesday's edition. Good day to you.' And Howard slammed down the receiver.

He felt the familiar tightness spread across his chest as he caught his breath.

Dammit, where were these stories coming from? Again, this morning's *Variety* was full of gossip about their supposedly 'shaky future'. He should call his brother Bernie. He was meeting with the shareholders at the bank this morning. As CEO of Mercury he would be able to shed light on the—'

The phone trilled again, loudly, shattering Howard's thoughts. He grabbed it up.

'Look, Miss Paretsky,' he barked loudly, the perching New York pigeons jumping into startled life on the ledge outside his window, flapping away over Central Park. 'If you'd take your tape recorder out of your ass for two minutes and do some actual reporting for once, you'd know that my son flew out in the company jet to London last week with England's top sitcom writer to discuss a major new project. Hardly the actions of a studio looking to cut back on its spending, wouldn't you agree?'

17

'*Why, Mr H,*' a familiar male voice said. '*Hoo-boy, you got ya haemorrhoids in a bunch, sweetie.*'

'Shifty Dolawitz,' Howard growled, his voice like a vintage Bentley on a gravel driveway. 'Jesus, can't I go a day without you agents biting my ass? What is it this time? And make it fast, I've got an empty glass in my hand.'

'*Of course, pumpkin. Just a quick questionarooni — you get my letter?*'

The offices of J. T. Stanley, the global investment bank, stood on Wall Street, chalky and imposing in the afternoon sun.

In design, much like that of the New York Stock Exchange opposite, the J. T. Stanley building had mythological figures carved in stone about its pediment, gazing out blankly across the narrow street. And like the New York Stock Exchange, it hadn't taken long for the gritty and poisonous Manhattan air to nibble and bite at these figures, causing them to deteriorate and crumble.

The New York Stock Exchange, keen that nothing about their building should project an air of vulnerability or weakness, was quick to tear down their crumbling frieze and sneakily replace it with a weather-resistant, sheet-metal copy.

J. T. Stanley, however, simply sat back and let themselves take a horrendous beating, the figures wearing down to crumbling grey lumps.

Rather aptly, perhaps, as J. T. Stanley was one of the major financiers behind Mercury Pictures.

In a small, dimly lit basement room, ten men — J. T. Stanley bankers and Mercury Pictures shareholders — were deep in financial debate.

'With you,' the dealer said.

Bernie Silver, the CFO of Mercury Pictures, looked at the dealer and then down at the fuzzy green table-top, worn and stained with years of beer and cigar ash. The fifth card had been flipped over. An eight of hearts.

Bernie was a trim fifty-five, ten years younger than his brother Howard and so far managing to evade the Silver family paunch, keeping in shape on a diet of cigarettes and anxiety, sweating off most of his body weight around race courses and card tables.

Hilliard White, the investment honcho looking after Mercury, sipped his water. His two cards lay face-down in front of him.

'I tell ya, boys,' Hilliard said, leaning back cockily and knotting his hands behind his head. He was in shirt sleeves, the morning's formal meeting now over, 'when Bernie and Howard first came to see us about starting Mercury . . . when was it?'

'Fifteen years ago,' the dealer said. 'Still with you, Bernie,' he added.

Bernie nodded thoughtfully, eyes flicking over the cards on the table.

A jack, a nine a king and now two eights.

'They were both sitting upstairs in reception waiting for me to come down,' Hilliard continued. 'I was only twenty-eight. I don't know who was more nervous. I walk across the lobby to greet them. Howard can't get up out of the chair, the fat fuck! You remember, Bern?'

A little laughter from everyone but Bernie.

'And this one,' Hilliard continued, 'is crapping his pants so bad he's brought a handful of poker chips along with him to calm his nerves. He's sitting there clicking them and flipping them, like he's in fuckin' Vegas. And he's asking us to find him – what was it?'

'Fifteen million,' the dealer said.

'I tell ya, boys, never invest money with a CEO who carries poker chips.' Hilliard smirked at his own wit.

Around the table, however, the remark fell on somewhat stony ground.

'Mighta told us that before we all sank a bundle in his studio,' an older man said with a resigned roll of his eyes.

'Damned right,' another sighed. There was a rumble of agreement about the table.

'I gotta be straight with you, Bernie,' another said. 'I'm not sure how much longer we can keep throwing money at this damned thing.'

Amid all this Bernie's mind, for the moment, was elsewhere. He plucked his soggy cigar from his lips and fanned out the two cards in his hand.

A pair of kings. With the cards on the table, a full house. Three kings and two eights.

Bernie knew there were 2,598,960 possible combinations of five card hands in a game of poker. He'd known that since fifth grade. What he'd also known since fifth grade was that catching a full house was 1-694 against. Only two hands beat it — four of a kind and a straight flush.

Bernie sipped his water.

'I'll check,' he said, laying his cards face down and sitting back.

'Yeah, me too,' the player on his left said, dragging on a cigarette. This threw the bet back to Hilliard.

'All in,' he said, and pushed his stacks forward.

There was a murmur about the table.

'Look, gentlemen,' Hilliard said, relaxing back in his chair, unbuttoning his cuffs. 'I think this morning's meeting was a good idea. We were aware that many of you felt wary of yet another round of investment. What with the . . . teething troubles we've experienced.'

'Teething?' somebody said with a sigh. 'For fifteen years? What are you, the freakin' Bee Gees?'

'Bernie's laid out the projections. Look them over, take some time—'

'I don't need any time,' a shareholder said, shaking his head. 'I'm gonna be straight with you gents, I'm not going around again on this one. I'm sorry.'

Bernie looked up from his cards.

'But . . .' he said. 'But I thought we agreed . . .'

'Jack, hey, c'mon now,' Hilliard said, shifting in his seat. 'Don't jump to any—'

'No, I'm sorry. I'm cutting my losses on this one.'

'Heyyy, slow down, slow down,' Bernie said. But despite the polite nods and handshakes upstairs, a handful of other men all nodded and growled the same message. 'Hey, look, guys. Guys, c'mon now,' Bernie said, forgetting his cards. 'It's a blip – it's just a blip. There's no need to get panicky.'

'Big fuckin' blip, Bernie,' Jack said. 'I'd 'a' got more return sticking my money in a goddamned mattress. No, that's it, I'm sorry.' And he got up, reaching for his overcoat. Suddenly everyone around the table seemed to be moving. Scraping chairs, clicking briefcases, shaking heads.

'Wait! Wait, guys, c'mon now. You haven't even looked at the projections!' Bernie began to flap and fuss with a leather binder. But all around the room men were pulling on jackets, snapping phones. 'Heyyy, it's *show business*,' he said, trying and failing to keep the desperation from his voice. 'This ain't AT&T. High risk, high returns, you guys know that. It's about confidence. Riding out the bumps. So we have a bad run – we'll bounce back! Don's in London working with the hottest new writer, Gill Kramer's gonna be the *Pilot* cover-star again this week—'

'We're sorry, Bernie.'

'*E.R. E.R.* . . . *Oh!*'s about to hit the hundred? That's *your* syndication money you're walking away from. Just a few weeks, c'mon, we discussed this! Half an hour ago you were willing to come in again! And now Jack gets cold feet . . .'

'A few weeks?' Jack said. He was shaking hands solemnly with Hilliard, moving towards the door. 'With this *Fyre* show costing, what? Four million a pop?'

'And that *Woodfellas* show getting canned?' another added, clicking a briefcase. 'What did we lose on that?'

'Jesus, guys, we're havin' a game here. Sit down, have a drink, let's talk about this . . .'

But apologies were being handed out like party bags and, slowly, half a dozen navy overcoats shuffled from the room.

'I'm sorry, Mr White. Bernie,' Jack said at the door. 'I realise the position this leaves you in. But we feel that throwing any more money at Mercury Pictures would be throwing it away. C'mon, everyone knows ABN will axe *E.R. E.R. . . . Oh*! the moment it hits the hundred. You'll have nothing.'

And they left.

Hilliard looked at Bernie. Bernie looked at Hilliard. And with crossed fingers and silent prayers, they both looked at the only investor who hadn't moved. He was still sitting at the table, peering over his cards, a cigarette smoking in his fingers.

'Uhm, Mr Lambert?' Hilliard said. 'Do you . . . ? I mean, uhmm, Bernie?'

'Mr Lambert,' Bernie took over quickly, sitting down at the table. 'Look . . . Shit, you've been in from the beginning. You have the largest stake in Mercury Pictures. If you're out too, we're all out.'

Bernie chewed his lip. The room went quiet.

'I'm out,' Lambert sighed.

Bernie closed his eyes. Hilliard ran a damp hand through his expensive haircut.

'I was waitin' for a fuckin' queen,' Lambert said, slapping his useless cards on to the table. He shook his head and stubbed out his cigarette.

'Wh-what?' Bernie said, heart thumping. Lambert threw back his drink.

'We've been partners for fifteen years, Bernie,' he said. 'I trust you. You say you can turn Mercury around, you can turn it around. Do whatever you've got to do and send dad the bill. We don't like to cut our losses. We'll stick with you.'

The atmosphere in the room visibly relaxed.

'We could be talking about a sizable investment now,' Hilliard cautioned.

'Hah!' Lambert said. 'Not as sizable as this one.' And he motioned to the skyline of chips in the centre of the table.

'And the standard net-point agreement still only applies to the back end,' Bernie added cautiously.

'Whatever, whatever. Look, we playin' cards here or what?' Bernie took another quick glance at his cards.

'I'll see you, Hilliard,' he said, sliding his stack forward and flipping over his cards. 'Full house. Cowboys over snowmen.' A roar went up from the others in a belch of stale blue cigar smoke.

'Hope that's an omen,' Lambert laughed.

'Hope it isn't,' Hilliard said, flipping over his two eights.

Howard, meanwhile, was scrabbling his creaking fingers among the mess of post on his blotter, sending most of it fluttering to the floor. He snatched up a brown envelope and fumbled with it, phone clamped underneath one of his many jowls.

'*Now I'm afraid, Mr H, and, y'know, it breaks my heart . . . I'm gonna have to ask for another million,*' Shifty was saying.

'Wait!' barked Howard, ripping open the envelope. 'Just wait a goddamn' minute.'

'*As you know, Gill Kramer, my client, is shooting the ninety-eighth episode of* E.R. E.R . . . Oh! *on Thursday night. Now that brings Mercury Pictures within an inch of the magic hundred episode mark. And we all know what that means, don't we boys and girls?*'

'You pulling this shit again?' Howard said and reached in for the letter. 'Chrissakes, Dolawitz, when's it going to be enough? I needn't remind you your client isn't the only actor in the world.'

But there was no letter.

Just photographs.

'What the hell is this?' Howard said, struggling with the glossy photographs, turning them the right way up.

'*Oh, you're absolutely right, Pumpkin, absolutely. None righter,*' Shifty said. '*Gill Kramer is not, and for everyone's sake I pray never will be, the only actor in the world.*'

'Holy Mother of God . . .' Howard whispered, staring at the glossy 10×8″ images in his trembling fingers.

'*But what Gill is, is the actor you need to keep showing up for work for the next two weeks.*'

'Is this . . . this can't *be. . .*' Howard put his hand out to steady himself, knocking the remainder of the days post to his feet.

'*You can't retire without the syndication money, you can't syndicate* E.R. E.R. . . . Oh! *without a hundred episodes and you can't shoot the last two episodes without my client.*'

Blood began roaring in Howard's ears as he stared panic-stricken at the images.

'*So we've been thinking. As Gill's going to be voted* Pilot *magazine's TV Star of the year on Wednesday, and of course he and his wife Elaine are up for the Celebrity Couple award, fourth year running, why not give your studio's only star the salary bump he really deserves? So, another million. Then Gill can keep showing up for work and everybody can get rich on syndication rights. What do you say?*' Shifty schmoozed. '*Oh, and that's per show, naturally. Howard? Howard, can you hear me?*'

Howard, sadly, didn't hear a thing.

The receiver had slipped, cracking against the desk, and was now swinging from its curling cable, slowly, like a pendulum, brushing the deep office carpet.

Shifty burbled on distantly.

Howard trembled, staring at the photographs. *No, this couldn't be.*

Two nervous pigeons returned to their grimy spots on the window ledge and flapped a little. They blinked at him.

Howard stared back, heart banging in his chest, fear etched across his face.

The pigeons took off once again across the park and told their pigeon pals to avoid the Mercury building.

There was going to be a lot more shouting before the day was through.

easyJet

Passenger: HALLIDAY / GORDON

From: LONDON LUTON

To: EDINBURGH

Flight: EZY23 Date: 06DEC Seq No. 105

Sheridan McDonald shuffled between the café tables, placed two cappuccinos on the Formica with a clatter and handed Jackie her bottle of water. She eyed their coffees enviously as Ben blew the crunch of spilt sugar on to the tiled floor. Jackie would have loved a cappuccino. No, an espresso. Oooh, yes. Two inches of that thick black treacle with a heaped ladle of white sugar and a cigarette.

She sighed, twisted off the lid of her water and tried to get excited about sit-ups.

Sheridan scraped back a chair and sat down.

'Okay?' Ben said softly, sugaring his coffee, not meeting Sheridan's eyes.

Sheridan took a couple of deep breaths and glanced about apprehensively.

It was almost five o'clock. The smeary glass counter of the sandwich bar only offered empty tin trays, speckled with parsley and crumbs but the café was still full, sweating with the rainy odour of wet denim.

Sheridan gave a short nod.

'Let's do it. From the top.'

'What are you two – oh, *no*! Not *now*,' Jackie said, the realisation clanging her hard in the face like a comedy frying-pan as she spotted for the first time on the table that familiar yellow exercise book. 'Not now, please, everyone will stare.'

She tugged at Ben's trousers under the table in anguish. '*Please.*'

'People are meant to stare, it'll be all right.'

'No, Ben,' she said, grabbing her bag from the floor. 'I'll leave, I will, I'll leave. I'm not sitting here again while you two —'

'It's a quick one, just a quick one,' Ben patted.

Teeth grinding in frustration, knuckles white around her water bottle, Jackie held her breath, closed her eyes and braced herself for the worst.

'*Well!*' Ben boomed suddenly, folding his arms and leaning back in his chair. 'I think it's just plain *unfair.*'

Other patrons glanced up from their mozzarella ciabattas at this shouty loon. Jackie attempted to slide under the table. Why? Why did they do this?

'*Oh, get away, where you get unfair?*' Sheridan said back even more loudly in his Scouse tones. 'R2-D2 didn't need a *face.* He was just a *mechanic.*'

'C3-PO got a face, why not Deetoo?' Ben countered. 'He got a *head.* But no face.'

'*Oh, not this again,*' Jackie whispered.

'Durr! 'Course *Threepio* gets a face. He's an *interpreter,* in' he? He's hangin' out with the humans. Deetoo just fixes the ships. He's working-class. A *labourer.* They don't want Deetoo mixing with the princess.'

'Deetoo's got that little shake of the head, though,' Ben said. 'Plus that slow whistle.'

'Yeah, well, like I said, he's a mechanic, in' he? It's like: *Dented your X-Wing? Phweee-yooo, s'not gonna be cheap, mate . . .*'

Ben nodded.

The three of them sat silently for a moment, the performance over. Jackie's face burned in crimson humiliation. Conversations gradually bubbled back up, something was yelled out in Italian behind the counter, the chime of loose change hitting china, and the sandwich bar bustled back to normal.

Sheridan slid the yellow A4 book over, cracking it open to where his leaky biro marked a page.

'*Are you finished?*' Jackie hissed under her breath, not even daring to look up.

'Absolutely. Went pretty well, I thought,' Sheridan said, underlining the dialogue with bold strokes.

'Tough crowd,' Ben said, slurping his drink.

It had been very early in their relationship that Ben had first, with hushed reverence, presented Jackie with a glimpse of 'the yellow book'. In a scene more akin to *Lord Of The Rings*, candlelight dancing about her small lounge, a little incense in the air, Ben had approached Jackie on the sofa gingerly, the crackly tome hugged to his chest.

TAILBACK

she'd read. Done in crooked Letraset on the front page.

A Sitcom

Had Jackie known then the level of humiliation, embarrassment and horror this book would come to bring to their relationship every time it appeared – in bus queues, on station platforms, in Charing Cross Road sandwich bars – she would just have hit Ben with it and fucked off.

'But you can't tell if it's any good until you hear it out loud,' he was saying now, all wide-eyed and apologetic.

'It's like gauging an audience's reaction, y'know?' Sheridan added, not looking up. His nose was inches from the page as he scribbled. 'To new bits.'

'*New* bits?' Jackie said, choking on her water a little. 'You wrote that a year ago.'

'No, we've changed it,' Ben said. 'It was "*What do you mean, unfair?*" But we've changed it to, "*Where you get* unfair?"'

'Better,' Sheridan agreed, nodding and scribbling.

'Oooh, oooh, Jack,' Ben said, jigging up and down suddenly.

'Did you get them?'

With a sigh, Jackie bustled in her bag for a second, producing two magazines. Ben grabbed *Variety*, Sheridan snatching the latest *Out There*, published that day.

'Jasper fookin' Philips?' he spat, holding the grinning cover star at arm's length. 'Talentless tosswipe. You two ain't still goin' on Saturday, are ya?'

'Not anymore,' Jackie said.

'What?' Ben yelped, sending cappuccino froth flying. Jackie gave him the news of the cancelled run.

'Are you serious?' Ben said, deflated. 'So what are we going to do instead? I want to take you *somewhere*.'

'I don't know,' Jackie shrugged. 'Actually, Ben . . .' She looked down at her bottle of water. Her heart gave a twinge but she pushed on. 'I'm not so sure I want to do anything on Saturday. Y'know, I'm really pissed off with work at the moment and . . . look, I know it's three years and everything but . . . let's talk about it tonight, yeah? Ben? *Ben?*'

'There!' he yelled excitedly. He was half out of his seat, jabbing the magazine in Sheridan's sweaty paws. 'There, down there!'

'All right, calm down, calm down, move your finger.'

Jackie sighed and struggled with the temptation to empty her bottle of water over Ben's head as the two boys squirmed and grinned at the sight of their names in the magazine.

They're excited. They're in print, Jackie thought, with a big grown-up sigh. That was fine.

What she wanted to talk about was probably best left until they got home anyway. Where she could hold his hand and try and explain.

Of course, if Jackie thought Ben was a little intense, a little geeky, a little odd, a glance through the window of the Margrave Hotel, Piccadilly, at the short, thin young man in Walmart khakis and a Muppet Show T-shirt pacing up and down by a bed would have had her sending Ben's CV to United International Pictures with 'Next James Bond?' scrawled all over it.

Melvin Medford skipped and paced and heel-toed, up and down, up and down, beside Don's bed, his laces untied, flapping and clicking about his ankles, eyes purple with exhaustion.

'Are you done? Hnn? Hnn? Are you? Hnn? Are you done?' he pestered.

Propped up on massive pillows, reading, Don cracked his toes a little in their $500 black silk monogrammed socks and sipped his drink.

'Hmmm,' he said doubtfully, flipping over a page.

'What? *What?*' Melvin said excitably, suddenly at Don's pillowside, flapping about the script like a startled pigeon. 'Show me!'

'Just relax, Mel. Relax, for Chrissakes,' Don said, lowering the pages to his lap. 'I can't do this with you dancing about. Go get a drink, go back up to your suite. Let me look over this properly.'

'But it's good, right? I mean, better? Y'know? Than before? Funnier, right?'

Don shot him a look.

'Sorry, sorry, I'm sorry,' Melvin said, and scuttled into a heavy, high-backed chair. He managed to sit still for a long, slow, unbearably frustrating second before his feet danced and scuffed on the carpet, his hand instinctively leaping to the scab on his face he'd been picking at, dabbing the crispy wetness tentatively. He wriggled in his chair, the antique wood groaning and creaking.

'Now where are you up to?'

'*Mel.*'

'I'm s-sorry.'

Don had first found Melvin seven days ago, hunched over a sticky table at the Comedy Store's late show on Sunset Boulevard, sipping a glass of milk and glugging vitamins. Even in this dark setting, lurking like a fungus, Don had recognised his salvation.

Melvin had all the tell-tale signs Don was looking for: mid-twenties, ghostly pale, muttering and mumbling, slack-jawed and with a back buckled from a life spent shut up alone in a room hunched over a laptop.

As he'd jabbered and stuttered on to Don about his career in England, about his awards and accolades, about his attempts to break the American market, Don could only wonder at the level of sheer geekosity Melvin displayed. Don knew that television writers tended to be on the nerdy side. In the handful of pitch meetings he'd forgotten to get out of, he'd seen them: rake thin with pot bellies, hairy shirts and odd socks, pale pocked skin and nervous tics. But Melvin? Christ, he belonged on a poster in a doctor's surgery: MOTHERS! Let Your Son Meet Women, Eat Fruit And Go Outdoors! Or He Could End Up Like THIS!

'Don, what time is it? Is it five-thirty yet? Don?'

With his nineteenth sigh of the evening, Don lowered the script again and threw a glance to the bedside where his chunky Rolex sat like a prize-fighter's belt.

'Yes, a little after.'

'Noo! It's started, it's started!' Melvin yelped, leaping up and scuttling like a bath spider over to the television set, jabbing and punching clammy fingers on the remote like it was a Playstation controller.

Don watched him. He was bent over the television, squatting, face inches from the screen, the static fizzing on the end of his nose. The picture was bubbling up from the darkness. Melvin, his face glowing in the light of the screen, began to sing along with the theme softly.

'*Ground floor perfumery, stationery and leather goods . . .*'

With a shake of his head, Don returned his focus to the script, flipping over the pages.

The three sheets were blank on the reverse.

'Is this *it?*' he spat.

'*Wigs and haberdashery, kitchenware and food — going up! Dooo doot-doot doo doo . . .*'

'This took you all night? Three pages? Of jokes about fuckin' *cheese?*'

'Shhhh,' Melvin hissed.

Don slid from the bed with a springy creak.

'Mel? Buddy, hey. We're on a schedule here, pal. We had a *deal.*'

Melvin didn't take his eyes from the screen.

'C'mon, pal. I made good my end, you're back home, staying somewhere fancy, your own suite, a bit of privacy. You're meant to be giving me something I can show my father. *I'll write you a zinger*, you said. *Fly me back to London, I got a hundred ideas*, you said. Melvin?'

Melvin, lost in his own world, bounced up and down on his haunches, singing along with sheer glee.

'Melvin? Christ, what is this shit you're watching?' Don sighed, peering at the screen. 'Did you just say, *Have a doobery?*'

Across town, Sheridan was running an inky finger down the comedy-listings page.

'''Ere we go. *"Larf A Sixpence"*. Er — *"This converted room above the King's Arms goes from strength to strength. Tonight the quirky and side-splitting northern comedy of Sheridan MacDonald—"* Quirky and side-splitting?' he repeated, frowning.

'It's what you wanted,' Jackie shrugged.

'What's mine say?' Ben asked.

'Er, where are we . . .'

Jackie felt Ben's hand under the table take hers tenderly and give it the tiniest nervous squeeze.

'*"Monday the twenty-fifth September"*,' Sheridan read. '*"Guffawplay. Another strong night at this West London haunt*

31

with the surreal Simon Morrow, topical Tim Brayley, the warm and infectious Benjamin Busby——"'

'Warm and infectious,' Ben said to Jackie with a smile. 'Thanks hon, I like that. Warm and infectious.'

'"*. . . plus an extended set from the Perrier short-listed Angus & Malachy Madcap Madhouse. MC Shmuck Berry. Doors 8 p.m.*".'

'Wait! Shit, let me see that,' Jackie said, craning her neck over the magazine. 'That's not right! Shit, that's a misprint. I asked Rachel to get it changed. Honestly, she's useless. Their manager phoned on Friday. They've quit.'

The two guys both turned slowly towards her. Silent. Reverent.

'Quit?' they said as one.

Sometimes Jackie felt that it was only her job that kept her and Ben together.

Beyond discussions about the machinations of the London comedy circuit – when the BBC were looking for new scripts, whether there were any comedy-writing courses coming up she'd heard about – they seemed to have almost nothing in common.

They bumbled and trundled on in their own little way, of course, nodding and smiling as they shared each other's news. But news got pretty thin when one member of the duo sat at home all day and never did anything more than rewrite the same two sitcom-pages week after week.

Jackie was understanding enough to make the right noises but, in truth, wasn't as convinced by Ben's ambitions as she perhaps allowed him to think she was. Most days she felt like a football widow, faking it all to keep the peace. Wearing the scarf, bringing in trays of nibbles, cheering the goals – but deep down in her heart desperately wanting to yell 'Oh, who gives a fuck?' and turn over to watch *Casualty*.

'I'm just telling you what he told me,' she said, bustling with her bag and coat. There was a sudden scraping of chairs and rattling of china as they all clambered to their feet. 'Can't take the pressure or something. Hung up their red noses and called it a day.' They squeezed and pushed their way out to the street. The rain had lightened to a spitty drizzle.

'But they were runners up at Edinburgh? They had a meeting with Channel Four?' Ben was mumbling, shaking his head. 'And now they're quitting?'

'Hey, how was the interview?' Jackie asked hopefully. 'Did they give you any hint?'

'Huh? Oh, er, not great. They said they weren't looking for wannabes, y'know?' He shrugged. 'I might have overdone it talking about our script.' He gave her hand a squeeze. 'I'm sorry. Next time.'

Jackie closed her eyes and took a deep breath. When she opened them, Ben and Sheridan were lagging behind together.

'I tried out the tea bit,' Ben was saying. 'Silverwear. Definitely *silverwear*.'

'Great!' Sheridan giggled, reaching for the yellow book.

'*Dooo doot-doot doo doo*. No, haber*dashery*.' Melvin corrected. 'Cloth, zippers, fasteners. It's like tailoring,' He settled down into a cross-legged position, rocking back and forth, a dopey grin on his face. 'I love this show.'

'Mel, buddy, seriously. It's been five days and all you've come up with is three totally unrelated scenes—'

'*Shhhh!*' Melvin hissed with a flash of fury. 'It's a draft. Just a draft.' He waved Don away, keeping his eyes on the screen as the show began. 'Give me a few more days. I told you I'd come up with something, right?'

Don sat down on the end of the bed.

'You did. But warm, okay? The Mercury execs are looking for something warm.'

'And it'll come. I'm waiting for . . . inspiration. Don't worry, don't worry.'

Melvin's eyes stayed fixed on the television.

33

Don watched him for a moment. Then, shaking his head, he got up and wandered into the stark white bathroom, splashing on the taps loudly.

'I'm hitting the tiles again tonight, buddy,' he called through to Melvin. 'Got myself a few lovely English ladies lined up.' Don had no intention of staying home watching a bunch of gay tailors interfering with mannequins. 'Not that they know it yet, of course.'

He unzipped his large black sponge bag, heavy with a clear plastic bag of cocaine. A little pick-me-up he'd scored in a thudding Soho club the night of his arrival to counter the jet-lag. He dipped and licked a wet finger like a child with sherbet, enjoying the usual shivery rush. He splashed some water on his face, grabbed a fluffy towel and wandered back into the bedroom.

Melvin hadn't moved.

Don tugged out a copy of *OK!* magazine from a pile on the bed, flipping it open. This was the only London guide he needed. His eyes slid hungrily over the society photographs: an actress, a model and a very minor royal stood flashing teeth and thigh at some club, voluminous cleavages casting shade over brimming champagne flutes.

Yes, they would do. Don made a mental note of the name of the club, then a mental note of the names of the women. Then thought, Fuck it, and just tore out the photograph, stuffing it into his pocket. He'd track them down.

'Did you pick up my magazine?' Melvin said absently.

Don slid out the new copy of *Out There* and handed it to Melvin, moving back into the bathroom.

'And I need to borrow another shirt,' Melvin called in to him. 'And socks and stuff. I didn't pack enough.'

'In the wardrobe,' Don said, emerging with a toothbrush. 'Did she just say *pussy?* What the hell kinda show is this?'

'You don't know this? *Are You Being Served?* Written by Lloyd and Croft, the guys behind *Hi-De-Hi!* and *It Ain't Half*

Hot, Mum. Pilot went out September the eighth 1972, nine-thirty, BBC1.'

'You certainly know your shit, you know that?' Don said out loud. As opposed to *you fuckin' freak* which he kept to himself. He wandered back into the bathroom.

'So you'll be staying in to work again tonight, right, buddy? Dad's expecting a first draft of something any day now. I told him about you, the stuff you'd done over here, and he's real excited. But he's not gonna stump up this five-star shit forever.'

Melvin said nothing. Nothing audible. Just the faintest muttering along with the TV show. Repeating the lines, nodding at the actors.

'Mel?' Don peered around the door.

'Yes,' he said eventually. 'I'm going to re-write those scenes. I'll need some quiet.' He looked up at Don for the first time. His face was pale, eyes sore. 'I mean it. Don't knock on the door or anything like that. I may go out later, just for a while. But when I come back, I don't want to be disturbed.'

Bit fuckin' late for that, y'weirdo, Don thought, returning to the bathroom.

FOUR

High in the Los Angeles hills, a bleached stone house balanced with terrifying precariousness on three steel struts, like an H.G. Wells Martian vehicle that had stopped off for some Kendal Mint Cake.

Despite its terracotta roof, shuttered windows and fat chalky pillars guarding the wide front door, it resembled a genuine Roman villa about as much as a Burger King salad resembles Kew Gardens.

Inside, the effect the designers were missing by a long mile was English stately home. Oak panelling, leather wing-backed chairs, ludicrously heavy tables and even heavier oil paintings had been nailed up or flung about the room with the meticulous period research of a bored removal-man. Fortunately, the owner had chosen to stop short of the absolutely genuine English Stately Home look — wisely figuring sixty bored nine-year-olds sprawled all over the parquet, colouring in pictures of Henry VIII and whining about the gift shop, would be something of a bitch to dust. On one wall of this flock-papered Disneyland *Tudorville*™, suspended from the ceiling on tensile wires was a television: a monstrous glass wall of such forehead-slapping clarity and size that every news bulletin was a booming Sermon on the Mount, every denture-cream jingle an opera by Puccini. It hung, flat and crisp, above a solid marble fireplace cluttered with wedding photos, comedy awards, statuettes and celebrity-couple-of-the-year trophies.

Gill Kramer, the recipient of all these accolades, sat slumped on a green studded-leather sofa, silk-robed, with a remote control in his hand. His chin was buried deep on his chest, pressed down heavy and hard. Harder every time he snarled at the screen. Which, due to the revoltingness of the video-tape he was watching, was most of the time.

'*And what about that* Shrink, *eh?*' the host sighed in exasperation on the massive screen. '*Is that a chat show gone nuts or what?*'

The studio audience whooped and cheered and whooped a little more. Gill watched the host prowl his little raised stage, banging out his opening monologue. Gill's hands hovered over the remote control. He was tempted to skip forward but let it go.

This was a subject very close to his heart.

'*I mean, this is entertainment now? Watching these poor tortured millionaires gripe about their childhoods every Friday night? How daddy only gave them five ponies on their birthday?*'

More howling and clapping from the whipped-up crowd.

'*But I mean it, this is a genuine phenomenon. Celebrity psychoanalysis. You've got these big names queuing up to break down in tears, live on network television.*'

A bit of whistling now. Whoop-de-clap.

'*Give your psyche a good old spin there! Oooh, five hundred dollars. You can go for an inferiority complex or parental abandonment. It's* Wheel Of Misfortune!'

The audience roared and screamed like someone had thrown a thousand volts through their tiered seating. The house band exploded into fast brassy funk, the cameras swooped. '*Yes! After the break, the host of* Shrink — *Dr Dick Trent* — *is in the house! Whoo! It's quite a night, don't go . . .*'

Gill began to spin forward through the commercials, the television flickering silently. He groaned a nervous, anxious groan, stared once again at his antique-effect telephone and let his head loll backwards like a broken doll.

Why didn't he *call?*

Gill was used to waiting for his agent to ring. And naturally, Shifty Dolawitz was used to keeping his client waiting. Like most actors, Gill was convinced this was a deliberate ploy, designed to give the impression Shifty was busy sweating over contracts and earning his ten percent, while in reality he wallowed in a diamond-encrusted hot-tub, lighting twelve-inch Havanas with Gill's $100 bills and having hopeful young actresses massage his . . .

Hold it. Gill had spotted something familiar on screen. He spun the tape backwards and pressed play.

A young man, head trapped in a filing cabinet, flailing and whining, the audience roaring with laughter. '*A double bill of* Office Politics, *afternoons on ABN,*' the announcer was saying. Gill thumbed the freeze-frame and stared back at his younger, trimmer self.

Ahhh, those had been the days.

Gill had found himself cast in the pilot of ABN's *Office Politics* pretty well by accident.

Don Silver, being creatively shiftless and inventively lazy, had side stepped the traditional wade through 10×8"s, auditions and casting agency lunches, choosing instead to turn up to a late show at The Comedy Store on Sunset Boulevard and pick the first six people he saw who could deliver a joke.

Thus Gill Kramer, a middle-aged English comedy actor who'd only been on a visitor's visa and who'd only volunteered for the open-mic spot out of drunken bravado, found himself unexpectedly inside a primetime smash-hit sitcom.

He wired home instructing his mother to sell all his belongings, cancel his dance lessons and turn down his walk-on role in The Bill. He bought a house in the hills, found an agent, married Elaine Stamford, a cosy daytime TV host, in a whirl of publicity, and never looked back.

Office Politics ran for five happy years making celebrities of the whole cast and a very smug, rich, popular couple out of Gill and Elaine Kramer.

The show's downside came however, when Don was put under increasing studio pressure to produce more hits.

Rather than spend months with writers and producers looking for original ideas, he had simply yanked out each *Office Politics* actor and spun them off into their own dire vehicle.

Five laugh-free sitcoms appeared, one by one, in a flurry of publicity. Bright, brash and eager to please, they all failed to connect with a fickle American public and were yanked from the schedules and painlessly destroyed.

But not Gill Kramer's.

Through a cunning mix of luck, luck and just plain old-fashioned luck, Gill's spin-off, *E.R. E.R. . . . Oh!* – *a simple-minded Midwest farmer joins a Chicago emergency room and brings his homespun country wisdom to the big city* – did the business. Going out at 8 p.m. every Friday night, it topped ABN's ratings for four years. Four good years. Solid, Emmy-winning, tux-sporting, pay-renegotiating, interior-decorator-hiring years.

But as Gill sat in his hilltop home, staring up at his classy Sistine Chapel ceiling, anxiously chewing the inside of his cheek, he knew that a big change was just one phone call away.

And as if willed into life, the antique phone rang its antique ring.

Gill tossed the remote to the table with a clatter and snatched up the candlestick, cursing its clumsy weight and pointless awkwardness. He spent a moment or two speaking into the ear bit and pressing the mouthpiece to his head, as he did every time it rang.

'Yes?' he barked. 'Shifty, is that you? What did Silver say? Does he understand?'

'*No, honey,*' a voice said timidly. '*No, it's me. Has Shifty not called yet?*'

'For heaven's sake! You're calling me now!' Gill ground out through clenched teeth.

'*Please don't yell, sweetheart. I just wanted to see how you were.*'

'I . . . I wasn't yelling,' he whispered, breathing deeply. 'I'm just a little on edge that's all. He should have called by now.'

'*Did you catch* The Tonight Show? *That fraud Dick Trent was on. I taped it for you in case you missed it. I could bring it over if you wanted, we could watch it together—*'

'I'm watching it now,' he said hurriedly. 'Look, sweetheart, I should really hang up. Shifty's—'

'*Did you get the flowers? They were just a kind of early congratulations thing really. The* Pilot *cover on Wednesday, plus odds-on favourite for the Couple Of The Year again. You still planning a big party?*'

'Sweetheart—'

'*And the ninety-eighth show on Thursday too, don't forget. It's going to be quite a week! They were just my way of saying—*'

'I did. I did, honey, they were lovely. Thank you. But I've got to go. Really, got to go,' Gill said, leaning back towards the table. 'I can't miss this call.'

The line went quiet.

'*Love you,*' the voice said.

'Huh? Oh yes. Yes, you too, honey, you too. I've got to go now, though. Talk to you later.'

'*Have you told your wife about—*'

Click.

Gill replaced the handset. He couldn't deal with that now.

He stared at the silent phone. This waiting was unbearable.

Ring, Gill urged. Goddammit, Shifty, *ring*.

FIVE

In Ben and Jackie's small Finchley flat, he and Sheridan were getting ready for their shows.

They both knew very well that they were never going to be the world's greatest stand-up comedians, that their names were destined never to be followed by the words, *'Extending their sell-out West End run for six more weeks!'*

But they didn't mind. That wasn't why they did it. It was merely a way of getting their names and faces about. They'd both studied enough comedy careers and waded through enough celebrity biographies to know that it was a lot more likely *Tailback — A Sitcom* would receive a warm response when it landed on television producers' desks if it was written by two established comedians rather than a couple of shuffling pale suburban nobodies.

Simply put, their plan was to get a couple of good solid routines under their belts and hawk themselves up to the Edinburgh Festival where, with any luck, a desperate television producer might spot them and ask them to write a television show. At which point, with a swift tah-dahhh, *Tailback* would be slapped down on the table.

Ben skipped nimbly around the door-frame and into the lounge where a tea-time sitcom burbled away.

'Jack,' he said, his copy of *Variety* buckled in his hand, 'you haven't heard any rumours about an American . . .' And he stopped, catching sight of the television. '*Hey!* Hey, this is a *classic!* Pinky and Perky give birth!'

'Huh? Oh, uhm, *Terry & June*, I think,' Jackie said absently. She was curled on the thin sofa, shoes off, smeary remains of her Spoil-In-The-Bag dinner on a plate next to her, glass of Château Value in her hand, flicking through a month old copy of *OK!* magazine listlessly, still in a little mood about Ben's job interview.

'The *pigs?*'

'What pigs?' Jackie said, looking up at him.

Ben looked fairly ridiculous, sporting as he was just black knee high socks and some red boxer shorts that had enough elastic in them to stop him throwing them away, but not enough for them to do their job with any real enthusiasm. He looked rather like a superhero who developed his powers by being bitten by a radioactive pipe-cleaner.

'This is *The Good Life*,' he said enthusiastically. 'Second series, I think. Pinky and Perky have a litter of pigs. Look, there's Lenin.'

'An American . . . ?'

'No, their cockerel's called Lenin. There.' He pointed. 'I thought you knew all this stuff? Geraldine's the goat, Lenin—'

'No I mean what rumour? What American?' Jackie said, teeth gritted, eyes closed.

'Hn? Oh, an American TV producer,' Ben said, dragging himself away from the screen. 'It's in here.' And waved the paper. 'Some stuff about a guy. Don Silver? Coming to London to work on a comedy show?' He handed Jackie the paper and bent forward, clattering up her dinner things. 'No one in your office said anything?'

'Never heard of him,' she said. 'Why? You and Sheridan gonna give him both pages of your show? See if he'll make you a big Hollywood star?' And she handed the paper back.

'Nope,' Sheridan said, appearing in the doorway behind Ben and snatching the paper. He too was in crappy superhero mode,

42

but without the advantage of a girlfriend to rein in his more excessive habits, he resembled perhaps Tummy Man or Captain Feet-Up. 'We ain't showing it to no one. Not yet. And Pinky and Perky is series *three*, divvy!' he added, hitting Ben across the head with the paper.

Ben rattled off, muttering, to finish getting ready.

'You really don't think we could try and show *Tailback* to this Don Silver guy?' Ben said, casually, rummaging for his trousers.

The bedroom was a tip. Clothes hung from chairs and radiators, pillows lay on the floor next to forgotten glasses of furry water and piles of unread magazines.

The bed itself was awash with A4 paper and chewed biros, the yellow notebook cracked open in its centre. Two greasy plates lay on the floor for Jackie to tread on later.

'No. Not a good idea at this stage, mate,' Sheridan said, giving himself a cold spritz of deodorant with a little yelp. 'We need a fookin' rewrite. I'm still not happy with any of it. It needs a complete going over. The whole thing.'

'*Whole* . . . ? We have *two pages!* Bob, Phil and Arnie sitting in traffic talking about *Star Wars* and being late for their meeting. How many times can we rewrite that? Jesus . . .'

'As many times as it takes to get it right,' Sheridan said flatly. He stamped into some laced-up shoes. 'This isn't some idle hobby, y'know. This is my career we're talking about. You might be happy settling for any old thing but I—'

'Any old thing!' Ben spat. 'Ohhhh, come *on*.'

They both stopped dressing, frozen half-dressed like a gay-porn photo love story.

Ben was tired of Sheridan's constant stalling. He hadn't done all this work just for the yellow notebook to languish in a desk drawer forever.

'We've rewritten that joke thirty times. Let's leave it, move on, get it finished. *Show it to somebody*.'

'We will.'

'When?'

'When we're happy with it.'

'When's that going to be?'

'When we're *happy* with it.'

'Jesus! But you're *never going to be happy with it!* Ben yelled.

Next door, Jackie pushed the door closed and turned up the volume on Pinky and Perky's squealing. It was time for Ben and Sheridan to have that row again it seemed.

In the most horrible house in the world, the most horrible phone in the world rang its horrible ring once again.

Gill lunged for it.

'Yes, yes, it's me, I'm here, I'm here,' he snapped irritably, flicking a tangle of flex away from his face like a picnic wasp. 'I hate this stupid phone! Tell me, what did Silver say? Did you tell him how unhappy I am?'

It was Shifty Dolawitz.

Gill stood up quickly, his bare feet sticky and cold on the mahogany floor. He'd been waiting for this call for two days. Fluffing his cues at rehearsals, irritable and distracted at dinner, the suspense was making him physically sick.

Shifty, however, had no intention of putting Gill out of his misery yet. He whittered down the phone about special relationships and nurturing real talent and other fawning, ten-percent-justifying gibberish.

'Just *tell me*,' Gill cut him short. 'What did Howard say? Did you make my point clear? The direction the show needs to move in to fight this . . . this pornographic *freakshow?* This macabre *carnival of crass!*'

Gill looked up at his television. Freeze-framed, a huge bearded face bore down on him with a taunting grin.

SHRINK.

In the comfy-chaired, oak-desked, cue-carded history of American chat shows, this was the big one, the season's runaway smash hit, smothering the cover of every magazine, headlining every tabloid, and spoiling lunch conversations all over the city. In fact, some LA restaurateurs were now moved to offer strict *non*-Shrink-*conversation* tables for those bored to tears by the absurd phenomena. As Gill hit Hollywood Boulevard on his way to the Mercury lot for rehearsals every morning, he was bombarded on all sides by dozens of screaming billboards, each one showing the now-familiar black leather couch and the teasing tag: *Tell me about your mother . . . ?* Shrink, *8 p.m. Fridays on KBL*, above a silver beard and bouffant framing the Outspan-complexion of Dr Dick Trent, simpering sensitively down at the commuter traffic.

With a whip of the flex, Gill walked the telephone out through the Tudor double-glazed bullet-proof patio doors on to his balcony.

On the other end of the line, Shifty bowed and scraped and told Gill that he was right and that his beloved agent had sorted it out.

'Wait, wait, *wait!*' Gill interrupted in disbelief. 'What are you *saying?* An extra *million?* This isn't *about* more money! You think the cover star of *Pilot*'s Top 100 issue needs to bicker about *money*, you greedy four-eyed twerp?! You think one half of the most popular showbiz couple in America is concerned with *money!* This is about *art!* About *truth!*'

Gill spat and roared on the balcony, his whole home trembling.

'The show's in trouble! ABN are *this close* to pulling the plug. You were meant to tell Silver about my ideas for saving it! Cutting back on the goofing around, the falling over and all the stupid surgery slapstick. *E.R. E.R. . . . Oh!* needs to get its teeth into issues, into life! That's what America wants, something real. Trent is pissing all over our ratings every damned week, giving America psychos and soul-searching, while we're emptying bedpans over each other!'

He paced around his balcony, bare ankles warm in the early

45

afternoon air, the city stretching out beneath him, sunshine winking off the glass and steel.

'God, don't you listen to *rumours?* Our head's on the block! Unless our numbers improve, the hundredth show is the last! The *last!* ABC will cut me loose, Dolawitz. Axed, fired, off to the big silver trailer in the sky. You've got to talk to Silver about turning this show around otherwise you'll be living off ten percent of *nothing*, you understand? One tenth of *zilch!* You'll have a penniless has-been as your number-one . . .'

And he stopped, a look of horror dawning across his neatly tucked face.

'You son of a bitch! That's what this is about, isn't it? Isn't it, you greedy . . . You've heard something. You *know* they're pulling the plug, that's why you're after more money. These are the last two pay-cheques I'm getting, right? *Right?!*'

Shifty protested unconvincingly.

'Shut up! Agents? Executives? Networks? You're all the same. All the fucking *same!*' And Gill tried to slam the phone down, which being an antique candlestick he couldn't do with any satisfaction.

He stood, breathless and panicky, blinking in the afternoon sunshine.

No, it couldn't be. It *couldn't be.*

The phone immediately started to ring its horrible ring again. He snatched it up.

'*Oh, honey!*' the voice cooed softly at the other end. '*I've been sitting here fretting. I'm so sorry, Gillybubs, I called at the wrong time, I didn't know Shifty was going to be—*'

'Not now!' Gill hissed, and wrenched out the wire from the base of the phone, tossing the whole thing over the balcony.

'We're off,' Ben called from the top of the stairs. 'Wish me luck.'

The sound of squealing pigs burbled from the TV in the lounge.

'Jack'?'

46

'Oh, sorry, g'luck,' her voice floated out half-heartedly. 'Don't wake me up when you come in.'

Ben thumped down the stairs of the little flat, leaving Sheridan scurrying behind. Their row still hung about them, unresolved. Sheridan slammed the door and scraffed down the weedy gravel and on to the street in the September drizzle, struggling with a broken umbrella like Dr. Who with an unconvincing robot octopus.

They trudged towards Finchley Central tube in silence.

'So,' Ben said eventually, 'are you going to let me find out where this Don Silver guy is staying or not?'

A few more steps in silence.

'You're saying I've got no balls,' Sheridan mumbled.

'No, I'm asking if you're going to let me find out where this Don Silver guy is staying or not.' Ben grabbed at some leaves on a hedge, snapping them off with a sharp yank. 'You brought up testicles, I don't know why.'

'That's fookin' rich mate, that is.' And Sheridan let out a dry laugh. But apparently not dry enough, as he proceeded to hog the twisted brolly.

'No, it's not *fookin' rich, mate*. It's true,' Ben protested. That was it. He'd had enough. Five years they'd been dancing about this point, avoiding it, ignoring it. He'd had enough. 'You're scared.'

'Fook off.'

'You're scared. You're not going to finish the show, you're never going to finish the show. You've been wasting your time and you've been wasting my time. For five years. 'Cos the moment it's finished, the moment you type THE END, then it'll be judged. And producers and commissioning editors will have to look at it and read it and tell you if you're funny or not. And they might say you're not. They might take out a little slip of BBC stationery and write "Fuck off, you unfunny scouse twat, and take your short-arse mate with you" and that'll be the end of it. So you're going to sit at your desk and rewrite the same

47

two pages for the rest of your life. You've been stringing me along all this time because you're *scared*. Well, I've had enough.'

Silence. He looked over at Sheridan who had momentarily stopped.

'Bollocks,' he said finally and set off walking rapidly, swopping hands with his umbrella to make sure it didn't shelter Ben in the slightest. Ben jogged after him.

'Fine,' he said. 'Forget it then.'

'If anyone's got no fookin' 'nads out of us, it's you,' Sheridan growled. 'I'm workin' every afternoon, every night, every weekend on this—'

'On the same three jokes!'

'While you're out with Jackie. Picking her up from work, popping round her mum's, goin' round the shops. Always something better to do than get some writin' done.'

'Oh, well, I'm *sorry*,' Ben said, not sounding particularly sorry at all. 'I'm sorry I have some sort of *life*. And a girlfriend and shopping and laundry. I'm sorry I can't go three weeks without sleep like you can, strung out on coffee and Marx Brothers movies. Jackie wants me to find a job, what do you want me to say? I've got to meet her from work and do the shopping some nights. I can't just drop everything.'

'Can't drop *anything*.' Sheridan muttered.

'Oh, that's *so* not fair. You go through it, we've written *exactly* the same amount of words. Exactly. Fifty-fifty. It's ours equally. Tailback by Ben Busby and Sheridan McDonald.'

'Sheridan McDonald and Ben Busby,' Sheridan corrected. 'Funnier.'

They reached the station and bustled through the barrier.

'Not that it matters of course,' Ben said as he dropped on to a damp platform bench. Sheridan stood a few feet away, reading an advert. 'Because we're not going to show it to Don Silver for his advice. We're going to pass up the chance of a lifetime.'

Sheridan stood brooding.

'Well, *I'm* going to try and find him. Get his address, his hotel. Talk to him, see if he'll look at our pages.' Ben pulled the copy of *Variety* from the bag at his feet and stared at the headline. 'Otherwise . . . well, otherwise what's the point? What have we been doing for five years?'

Sheridan still said nothing.

'I'll go to reception and leave him our pages. Ask him what he thinks.'

Sheridan looked at Ben with simmering rage.

'Over my dead body,' he said.

An hour later, in Howard Silver's Fifth Avenue office, the heavy velvet curtains were drawn against the world. An ugly, over-priced desk lamp threw a small pool of ugly amber over-priced light over a brown envelope.

Bernie sipped Styrofoam coffee from a Styrofoam cup. Opposite, his heavier-set, white-haired brother, face gaunt with worry, pushed an envelope across the desk towards him.

Bernie took the photographs out in a slither.

Howard, sitting back with a soft creak, said nothing.

'Holey moley, Mother of God,' Bernie said, a dark splash of coffee scalding his thigh. 'Ow, *dammit.*' He got up and began to fuss and dab at his leg. 'Christ, Howie, is that . . . ?' he spat, flapping the top photograph. 'Is that who I *think* it is?'

Howard just nodded solemnly.

It was *exactly* who Bernie thought it was.

'Jiminy Christ,' he said. 'What kind of *lens* is this guy using? Is the guy *in* the men's room with them? I mean, Chicken McFuck, you can see *everything.*' Bernie put down his coffee and flicked through the next couple of photographs, peering at them closely like he was trying to find a loved one in an old school photo. 'You got his face, you got the dealer's face. You got the cash changing hands? Hoo-boy.'

He lowered the photographs and looked his brother in the eye.

'I don't know much about this stuff, Howard, but it looks like we've gone and got ourselves two things here. Numero number uno, our boy Donald in a nightclub john, buying enough coke to keep a Rolling Stones World Tour going for, what, nearly an hour? Look at it!'

Howard, creaking like a toppling redwood, placed an ageing elbow on the desk and propped his tired head in his hand.

'Christ, is he dealing, now? 'Cos, Howie, a little root-a-toot-toot is one thing, but this amount? Got to be possession with intent to supply. He's looking at twenty years right there. They'll put him away. They'll put him away for sure.'

'Christ knows what he's doing, Bern,' Howard sighed, exhausted with worry. 'I've been trying to call him all day, he's got his damned cell-phone turned off.' He shook his head. 'And? You said we had two things?'

'Well, you said these were from Shifty? Then numero number dos — we've gone and got ourselves here a *very* good reason to do exactly what Shifty asks us to do.' Bernie tossed the photos on to the desk where they fanned out like a movie storyboard. 'Fuck! What the hell does he think he's doing?'

'The guy's a Hollywood agent, Bernie. You think there's a level to which he will not stoop?'

Howard thumbed through the photographs like a flicker-book, watching the club, the deal, the sample, the cash, all flash forward in jerky animation. He did it backwards, watching his son sneeze white powder back into a plastic bag.

'But he's never pulled this kinda shit before.'

'Maybe he was frightened we wouldn't bite this time?' Howard said, tugging a white handkerchief from his trouser pocket like a magician and wiping the sheen from his crinkled brow.

Bernie sat down.

'But you're not going to do it? Not another million? We can't.'

'I already did it,' Howard admitted. 'And made Shifty

51

promise to send me the negatives. He, of course, just kept saying, "*What negatives, Mr H?*"'

'Sonofabitch. So we're givin' Gill Kramer *three* mill per show now? Holy McMoley, we can't make that back, Howard, and you *know* it. With this Shrink thing up against him? You gotta call Shifty back, tell him . . . tell him you made a mistake, Tell him . . . I dunno.'

Bernie looked again at the glossy photographs splashed over Howard's desk. That really was a lot of drugs.

'Tell him—'

'What? Tell him what?' Howard said loudly. 'If I don't play ball, God knows who's gonna wake up and find these pictures in their morning mail. The Feds? Scotland Yard? The *National Enquirer?*'

Bernie closed his eyes.

'Plus Shifty was talking about Gill *quitting*. We can't risk it, Bernie. There are only two episodes to go before we hit the hundred. This is my *future*. We need to keep Kramer sweet.' Howard shook his head. 'On the subject of which, how was the meeting? You tell everyone about the next round of investment? They all on board?'

'Huh? Uhmm . . .'

'Bernie?'

'Everything's fine, absolutely fine, Howard,' he said quickly. 'They're looking over the projections, they're gonna let me know. One or two are a bit . . . *concerned* is all. These crazy rumours . . .'

'Tell me about it. You see *Variety* this morning?' He reached over and lifted the paper from his desk, reading aloud. 'Shyte' — The *LA Times*, 'A Pox on thy—"'

'Yeah yeah, Howie, I saw,' Bernie stopped him quickly. 'Gossip like this is half the problem. Shareholders getting hold of *Variety* and paying more attention to the fluff than the facts. They see some crap in print about 'shaky futures' and they all start jumping out the window. So, look, I've been thinking. You still got your profile tomorrow with that Penny woman?'

'Me and some cable-station guy from Nashville,' Howard nodded. 'Old and new, big and small, you know how they like to mix these things around.'

'So we give them a story to run. Positive news,' Bernie said. He drained his coffee and leaned forward. 'It's like poker. Everyone thinks we're about to fold? So we start smiling, lighting cigars, chatting away. Let everyone think we're holding aces.'

'I thought you didn't play anymore?'

'J-Just a figure of speech.' Bernie laughed nervously.

'You still goin' to the GA meetings every Tuesday?'

'Of course, of course. But look, it'll calm the shareholders down while we ride out the bumps.'

Bernie got up quickly and began to move around the office, light on his feet, clicking his fingers.

'This Gill thing,' he said, eyes flashing, 'turn it around. Announce the pay increase. Big news! *Kramer collects in massive Mercury wage windfall.* That kinda thing.'

'Right, right,' Howard nodded, sitting up a little. This sounded better. 'Uhm . . . *Studio shrugs off* Fyre *fiasco with soaring star salary.*'

'Great! *Silver shows heart of gold as Mercury millions secure . . .*'

'*. . . Sitcom success,*' Howard topped off with a grin. 'I getcha.'

'Meantime, let me have a look at LA,' Bernie said. 'See if I can't trim back a little wood on the lot.'

'That necessary? Surely if the investors are all willing to bump up their investment—'

'I know but . . .' his brother interrupted nervously. '. . . it'll look good. Efficiency, cutting down on waste. Call it stream-lining. I'll do it today.'

'Whatever,' Howard said after a moment. 'You know best.' His heavy cufflinks winked in the desklamp as he shuffled the photographs back together and slipped them away again. *Out of sight*, he hoped, *out of court.*

Bernie walked slowly over to the windows, pushing the curtains aside. He stared down at Central Park.

'If it's not one thing with Don it's another, huh, Howie?' he said. 'That kid. I know family's family but, with respect, I've always felt that his promotion was our big mistake. Sure, put him in the mailroom. Don was fine in the mailroom, he could cope with the mailroom, there wasn't much to fuck up in the mailroom. But then, President of Development?'

'Don's out,' Howard said softly.

'I mean he finds *one* hit, what, *ten* years ago?'

'Don's out,' Howard said again.

'I swear since then, if it wouldn't sit on his dick or fit up his nose, the boy simply wouldn't . . . sorry, *what?*'

The room fell silent, Howard's words hanging in the air like Wile E. Coyote over a cliff edge before they fell to the floor. The whole building shook with the aftershock.

'*Out?*' Bernie said eventually. 'Your son? You – you *fired him?* My nephew? *Out?*'

'Well, near enough,' Howard said with an apologetic shrug. 'You see the show last week? Don's big new *hit?*'

'No,' Bernie sat down. He felt the edition of Don's name to a TV show was about as appealing as the edition to a Broadway show, the words '*On Ice!*'

'*Woodfellas*,' Howard said, rattling around in his desk drawer. A shiny sheet of fax paper was now in his hands. 'I ask you. *Three Sicilian wiseguys on the run from a big mob family, hide out as lumberjacks in Vermont.*'

'Sounds . . . erm . . .' Bernie said. And he was right.

'We all held our breath. Maybe *this* would be the one that would mark his change of luck.'

Howard looked at Bernie. Bernie looked back, meeting his brother's watery eyes. Howard handed him the piece of paper.

It was a black-and-white line drawing. A cartoon. A little

smudgy from the fax, but clear enough. It was Don Silver. But Don with a Fender Stratocaster round his neck and black-framed glasses on, looking more like Buddy Holly. And he was pictured with his head sticking out of an aeroplane, the company Gulfstream IV, with *Mercury Comedy* painted on the side. Howard was in the back, screaming, although he'd been drawn to look more like the Big Bopper. The Mercury plane, with them both on board, was inches from crashing into a huge mountain.

Bernie noticed the caption below as he moved his thumb.

Buddy Silver gets behind another reliable pilot.

'Shit,' he said, which seemed to cover it.

'Was meant to run in Friday's *New York Times*,' Howard said. 'I had it pulled by a guy who owed me a favour.'

'What do you want me to say Howard?' Bernie said, inviting frankness to the table for its input. 'I've been telling you for years, with the greatest respect, your boy's a damned liability. I mean, Jesus H. Wept, he's been living on the fumes from *Office Politics* for Christ knows how long.'

'I know that, Bernie. Jesus. You sound like Marion. She thought he was out of his depth pushing the mailcart. Anyway, I went through those numbers you brought to our last meeting,' Howard continued, 'and you were right. Don has lost us over forty million dollars in failed shows over the past ten years. That dumb thing with the super-intelligent sheep running that Wall Street brokers?'

'*Ringing For Ewe?*' Bernie winced.

'Yep. Cancelled after two shows. That Godawful *Nuclear Family?*'

'With the five good-looking kooky draft-dodging brothers starting up that coffee shop?'

'In Hiroshima? Yep, failures. Every one. So I called him in, laid it on the line.'

'What are you talking about?'

'Last week. I sat him down, there where you are,' Howard

55

said, 'and I told him. He had one more chance to bring this studio a hit. And I'm not talking about some piece-of-shit show with woodchoppers or goddamn' talking sheep. A genuine hit. Something warm, something real. Something the American people would want, something they'd grow to love. Otherwise,' Howard said, bringing out his hanky once again and dabbing his glowing forehead, 'and here's the kicker. He's out.'

'Out?'

'On his pinned-back ear. Out. No job, no expense account, no car, no house, no credit cards. Out on the street. It's the only way.'

'Jesus, Howie . . .'

'Of course, he danced around the table awhile like a car salesman. *It's the networks, it's the writers, it's the guy who brings the coffee.* On and on. *You can't do it to me, Dad. But I'm your only son, Dad. I got debts, I got responsibilities.* But my mind was made up. One shot . . .' And Howard looked up to the heavens for a moment. 'One last shot at redemption. He could take a final development cheque. Drive it, drink it, crash it, fuck it, piss it up the wall, walk away, and never come back.'

'I don't believe this,' Bernie croaked.

'Or he could find a writer, work with him, develop a project. Come up with something new, something exciting. Something to make me proud.'

They two men sat in silence for a moment, lost in thought.

'So he's gone to London with a writer?' Bernie said eventually. '*Who* exactly?'

'He's *here!* Sheridan? *Hello?* Arse. *Hello?* He's *here!* Ben yelled, finger glued into one waxy ear, the feeble pub pay-phone pressed hard against the other. '*Sheridan? Hello?* Oh, cock it!'

He slammed the receiver down and rattled about hurriedly in his black stage trousers for another twenty pence.

It was nearly eight o'clock. The pub, however, was virtually empty. Two barmaids in branded polo shirts nattered by the peanuts; a pair of moustachioed locals sat on stools up the other end of the bar, a folded *Daily Mirror* crossword at their elbow, passing loud comments on the state of each other's motor cars. The juke box, well aware no one was paying it the slightest attention, got its own back by playing nine Status Quo songs in a row.

Jabbing in Sheridan's mobile number again, Ben took a moment to take in the suburban serenity and not believe it.

How, he wondered with dizzying bewilderment, could these people just *sit* there? These men. Like it was any *ordinary* wet Monday night? Like downstairs was just an *ordinary* comedy-club audience? Like this wasn't *the* most *important night* of Ben's *life?*

He wanted to shout, to jump on table, to shake these men from their quiet stupors and yell '*Don't you know who's downstairs?*' Get them fired up like some kind of comedic William Wallace.

But he didn't. If they wouldn't even nod their heads to 'Rockin' All Over The World', these men had no souls worth stirring.

Purr-purr, purr-purr. Ben waited for Sheridan to pick up. Come on, come *on!* A click.

'*Sheridan?* Sheridan, it's *me* . . . take it — *what?* . . . take it *outside* then,' he shouted over the geiger-counter static. The men at the bar continued to ignore his raving. 'Yes, yes, that's better. *He's here,*' Ben yelled. 'The American. *Silver!* He's *here!* He's downstairs . . . no, *now! Right now* . . . because his name's on the door, that's how . . . no, some guy just pointed him out. What shall I do? . . . I know what you said but . . . *Sheridan?* . . . *Hello?* . . . *Hello?* Sheridan? . . . *Arses!*' He slammed the receiver down.

His heart banged away in his chest. Possibly due to 'In The Army Now' which had just come on. But probably not.

He was here. Don Silver, television producer. *Here.*

Ben took a deep breath, grabbed his bag and ran quickly downstairs to the lavatory.

At that very moment, in New York, somebody else was getting excited about the thought of Don Silver. His devilish eyebrows, dark sparkling eyes, lascivious smile and firm jawline. Broad shoulders, snug in a dark tuxedo, drink held aloft.

Diane Paretsky slowly eased the wheel around on her editing console. The picture flicked forward frame by frame, the Martini glass glinting in the glare of popping flash-bulbs, Don's smile widening, his tongue licking his lips slowly, a cigar moving towards the damp cavern of his mouth. Diane watched as the on-screen Don silently puffed a billowing cloud of blue smoke out at her. And as he winked his trademark wink, eyelid closing slowly like a garage door, Diane jabbed the pause button. The screen flickered a little, freezing the shot.

She sat back, sipped her Diet Coke and nodded to herself.

Not bad at all.

She made a note of the digital counter and pencilled the word '*Titles?*' next to it.

What she really needed, of course, were some images of his father Howard looking troubled. Nervous, worried, on the ropes a little. But these would come.

Yes, these would certainly come.

Diane Paretsky had quickly realised that as far as modern journalism went, what mattered wasn't so much *what* was said as *who it was* that was saying it.

As a freshman at college, she'd been overwhelmed by how much more credence a celebrity-voiceovered five-second blurry documentary clip was given than, say, to a *New York Times* banner headline. It appeared that the American public didn't really believe anything had happened, from a famine to a war to a dog falling off a skateboard, until they'd heard a familiar, reassuring Hollywood voice tell them so, earnestly, touchingly, and-meaning-that-most-sincerely-lay-gennermen.

It was this nugget of valuable information, combined with the extraordinary ratings-leap shows like 60 Minutes got when they crow-barred the word 'sex' into their stories, that led her to swap her Nikon for a palmcorder, switch her degree to television media and, three years later, burst on to the scene with a series of award-winning *Sexposés* for the KBL network.

A phenomenon was born. Sex lives of politicians, firemen, cops, funeral directors and, most recently, convicted crime bosses — all were given the 'famous voiceover' stamp of quality and shoved out on Prime Time.

Diane was a hit, KBL had a winner and America couldn't get enough of it.

However, it would be the next *Sexposé* Diane had planned that would be the big one.

Her cell-phone bleeped on her editing console and she skidded back across the polished floor, snapping it open. It would be another person congratulating her on last night's show.

'Paretsky.'

'*Di? Like, hi!*'

'Oh, hey, hon,' Diane said, a big smile in her voice. The call she'd been waiting for.

It was Penny Lang, an old college friend of Diane's who had moved out to the West Coast the moment she graduated, absorbing the tan, the fashions, the attitude and, most tediously for Diane, the dialect as if she were a native Valley Girl. She was currently writing for *Variety*.

'How's the West?' Diane asked.

'*Like way out and wicky-wild-wild as ever,*' Penny said. '*Apologies for my slackitude. Though like, I hear it's Emmys all round for* Dirty Dons *last night? Hoo-boy, that was sizzling TV.*'

'Why, thank you. It did cut together pretty good, if I say so myself.'

'*How the hell d'you do it, sister? De Niro narrating? And all*' *that death-row footage of Frankie Corillo? Man, is that guy a pervert!'*

'Just good investigative journalism.'

'Well, while they're FedExing you your Pulitzer, we can play catch up. What's the scoop, Betty Boop?'

'A favour,' Diane said, attempting to hack her way through Penny's West Coast jargon.

'I see. Flavour favour?'

'No biggie. I want to interview Howard Silver tomorrow.'

'Oh, like, puh-leeese! No way, girl. I got a whole day's shopping on this road trip, lady. No can do. Anyhoo, Nancy Drew, like what was the clue?'

'I spoke to him a few hours ago at his office. He mentioned you were coming over to New York to talk to him for some profile.'

'Guilty, counsellor. Him and some cable station owner from Nashville. Or Louisville. One of those "ville" places anyhoo.'

'Oh, come on, Penny,' Diane pushed. 'You know how important this is. Next month's show — "Mercury: SLIPPERY, SILVER and HOT!" It's gonna be the best yet. I've got hours of stuff on Don. The houses, the hookers, the coke, the cars. Perversions, premiers, *Playboy* parties. But I need to meet his dad, the big man himself, face to face. I've got a hundred background questions. Early days stuff, his family, Silver Screen . . .'

'Like, double click on help?'

'Silver Screen. It was Howard and Bernie's first business. Years ago. Studio rental.' And Diane wandered over to her coffee table, cracking open a box-file, tugging out a yellowing edition of *Entertainment Week*. 'They ploughed millions into it, the whole family fortune,' she said, skimming through the paper. 'Lost it all. Declared bankrupt in 1985. Yet five years later, there they were, Howard and Bernie, all over the trade press,' she quickly fumbled for a photocopy, 'announcing a huge new studio complex in Burbank. I gotta discover who the hell they found to stump up that kind of dough: And not only that, but *keep* stumping it up.' Diane pushed her notes aside, revealing an elaborate spreadsheet, striped with coloured high-lighters. 'Nearly twenty years of losses. Flop after flop after flop. *Ringing For Ewe. Nuclear Family*. That piece of shit about the Civil-War Buddhist?'

'I'm A Yankee-Doodle Ghandi?'

'Right. Promoting Don to VP has lost the family firm millions, never mind what his extravagant party-man habits are costing. It's juicy stuff, great TV, but I gotta get his dad's side of the story.'

'*Go easy on Donny boy, hon. He still owes me dinner.*'

'Oh, Penny, no. Not with Don Silver?'

'*Oops. Guilty, counsellor. But I plead mitigating cheekbones and his new Brentwood house.*'

'Well anyway,' Diane said, leaving Penny's sex life aside, 'I'm just saying something's not right. By my reckoning Mercury have got to be hocked up to their assholes. Any other studio with this track record would have lost its shirt years ago. J. T. Stanley should be in there with packing crates and calculators, trying to get their money back.'

'*Mmm. Don looks pretty good without a shirt,*' Penny said idly. '*I think he's had a tuck but he denies it.*'

'Well, let me talk to his dad and I'll find out for you. C'mon?'

'*This is like why they call you Di Trying, right?*'

'You can still come to New York. I'll put you up for a couple of days, take you to dinner.'

'*Uh-uh, I gotta be back in LA on Wednesday. I'm covering Gill Kramer's Pilot party.*'

'Then you'll wanna tear Barney's apart, not waste your time talking shareholders with Howard Silver.'

'*Okay, Nancy Drew, you convinced me. Let me give you the details...*'

Diane made notes as Penny gave her the address of the inter-view. She said her 'see-ya-arounds', got an earful of appalling 'miss-you-alreadys' and hung up.

SEVEN

Some kind soul had dumped a bucket of WD40 on the door hinges since he was last there so as Ben threw himself into the acrid toilet, the door banged hard against the chipped wet tiles and caused the cubicles to vibrate. He began to pace urgently, with nauseous apprehension, running through his act out loud.

'Uhm . . . g-good evening, ladies and gentlemen! Uhmm, let me hear you say—'

'Busby!' a voice yelled behind him suddenly, accompanied by another fillings-rattling bang of the toilet door. He turned and a rabbi walked in.

Black hat on his head and two plaits of hair framing his face, a black ceremonial robe swept down over his sandals. He also had sunglasses on. And a cherry red *Gibson ES335* electric guitar slung around his neck on a sequinned strap.

Schmuck Berry, MC of Guffaw-Play.

'Er, hey,' Ben said, frustrated at the interruption of his pacing. He had a mile to go before he slept.

Berry strode over to the chipped white sink, swung his guitar around to his back, hoisted his robes and ran a tap, the water falling about his hands in that oh-all-right-if-we-must pub toilet manner.

'*Oy vey,* what a night,' he said, in an accent so un-Jewish he sounded like he had two foreskins. 'You been out there? Place is

heaving. *Heaving*. Everyone 'ere to see the fabled Angus &
Malachy Madcap Madhouse, ain't they? Now I gotta go and
announce they're not coming. Plus some bigshot TV producer's
sat at the bar or summink, makin' all the acts jittery. Jeez.' He
shook his head. 'No Madhouse. They'll be bayin' for blood
upstairs when they find out.' Berry stepped away from the sink
and stared at his reflection in the rusty mirror. He tugged at his
plaits to even them out. 'So, er, I'm putting you on beginning of
the next half, Benny boy, all right?'

'Sh-sure,' Ben said.

First? Oh, crikey. His stomach did a back flip. With a fumble
of belt buckle and zip, he got himself inside a toilet cubicle. He
shut the door and sat down, feet dancing nervously on the wet
tile.

'Bleedin' Yanks, think they can just click their fingers and us
Brits will come runnin'.'

'What?' Ben called out, loudly to disguise a pooey splash.

'This Silver bloke,' Berry said. 'Caught Angus and Malachy
at the Comedy Store on Saturday night, didn't he? Met them
outside and offered them their own hour-long special on ABC.
I tell ya,' Berry said, 'I've been doing this fifteen fucking years,
still can't get a gag on Radio Four.'

'I thought they just quit?' Ben called out.

'Naaah, mate. Silver's handin' out contracts like they were
bleedin' Twiglets at a housewarming. Same story with Philips,
innit?'

'Jasper Philips?' Ben said, flushing and opening the door.
The rabbi had perched himself on the edge of a sink and was
tuning his guitar with thin twangs.

'Silver was backstage at the Shaftesbury last night,' Berry
said, not looking up from his fret-board. 'Had his arm round
Philips, plying him with champagne. Dragged him off to his
hotel to talk about some sitcom contract. Jammy fucker.' he
added with the usual magnanimous, life-affirming goodwill so
prevalent among young comedians.

'Sitcom?'

Berry hopped on to the floor with a splash, gown flapping, like a Hassidic superhero.

'That's me done.' He adjusted his hat and pulled his false beard up on to his face. 'Three minutes, yeah?' And he vanished back through the doors with an echoing slam, singing his Yiddish Rock 'n' Roll to himself.

'*Oy you can do anything, a-just stay off-a my blue suede yarmulke...*'

Ben fell against the sinks, nauseous with nerves.

Could this be true? The American handing out sitcom contracts and TV specials? *Variety* clearly said he already *had* a writer?

Ben dived into his bag and yanked out the crumpled magazine, scanning it quickly.

Yes, here. '*Rumoured to be in the UK working on an unnamed new project with British sitcom writer Melvin Medford.*'

Ben chewed his lip. But Jasper? And the others . . . ?

He flashed a look at his watch.

Two minutes to showtime.

He walked over to the mirrors under the guise of checking his outfit. He straightened his tie. Then crooked it. Then straightened it again.

The sound of the club faded up, loud. A guitar chord. A round of applause. The glasses, the laughter, the boozy shouts. Chairs were being scraped, people were settling in.

Ben hunched over the sink, staring at his own terrified face in the mirror.

'*Listen to me, Busby,*' he said out loud, eyes wide. '*This is it, okay? This is it. You won't fuck this one up, you hear me? You go out there and you do it. You've got Don Silver out there. Yes, he might just be here for a night out. But maybe he isn't, y'hear me? Maybe he isn't. You don't get these chances twice. So go out there and do it! This could be the night your luck changes. But it's got to be good. You go out there and hit your marks and keep your feeds slow and bang the punches, and then, you go over to that bar and stand next to him. And if he doesn't say anything, doesn't buy you a drink – then fine. He doesn't like your stuff. Go home and get over it. But...'*

And he leaned in slowly, staring himself down like a poker player.

'... but if he doesn't respond because you fucked up a joke, or you missed a cue, or you got heckled down, or you did one of so many amateur night fuck-ups?'

He took a deep breath, his stomach flopping over, queasy green taste in his mouth.

'One chance, Ben. One chance. This could be the one that changes everything – so concentrate.'

He stood up quickly and walked over to the door.

'Calm, calm, calm,' he mantra-ed, out of breath.

He swung the door open wide. It smashed hard against the tiles and he jumped.

'A real favourite down here at Guffawplay,' an amplified voice was saying with a squeak of feedback. Ben swallowed twice, wiping clammy palms on his trousers, and moved quickly towards the small room.

'Give it *up*!' a voice yelled from a million miles away. 'For *Ben Busby!*

A burst of applause.

He pushed through the curtain and jogged towards the raised platform, snaking through the rows of chairs on a warm wave of applause.

'Thank you, thank you, everybody, good evening. Let me hear you say "*Yeah*".'

'*Yeahhh!*'

'Great. Let me hear you say "*All right*".'

'*All RIGHT!*'

'Splendid, you're in good voice. Now let me hear you say "*Get The Fuck On With It, Short Arse*".'

Big laugh.

The American at the bar closed his copy of *Out There*, took a sip of milk and turned to watch.

Yes. Ben's luck was about to change indeed.

The window of the cab was dimpled with late night rain as Don and his new companions skooshed through Hanover Square, down Regent Street towards the lights of Piccadilly.

Ordinary, Don thought, staring out into the night.

The neon blurred through the raindrops making fireworks on the glass.

Being *ordinary*.

Imagine it. No pools, no parties, no premiers. No meetings, manicures or masseurs. Just an ordinary workaday life. The grind and the gridlock, TV dinners and tired feet. Saturdays spent standing in line to hand coupons to girls at cash registers. No limos, no lunches, no leggy companions.

Ordinary.

And in LA of all places. Where the world is divided into two classes of people: those shiny, sexy, successful types who *make* entertainment — and the sagging, sweaty saps who soak it up. That's what Don would become. Not a creator. A *viewer*.

He shivered, trying to shake the feeling from his shoulders.

It wouldn't happen. No, of course not. Dad was exaggerating, piling on the pressure. Trying to scare him into shape. He wouldn't do it. Don was his son, for the love of Christ. His *only son*. Would Howard honestly risk sending his entire genetic lineage spiralling back downwards into a primordial slime of unemployment cheques and thrift-store shopping, just to make a point? Take away Don's office, his assistants, his title? Take back the car, the credit cards, his new *house?* Leave him penniless? Unemployed? On the street? *Ordinary?*

Don gave another shiver.

No. Melvin would come up with a new script, Don would fax to it his father and he'd be back in LA in no time.

He missed LA. After five days in London, he could feel

himself beginning to wilt and furl at the edges like a pot plant kept out of the sun. He needed a pick-me up, something to get his leaves shining again.

The bottles of Baby Bio curled either side of him in skintight dresses would do.

As the cab splashed through the London night, they chatted busily to each other. The pair of them it seemed were soap actresses. Famous enough to get camera bulbs popping as Don had escorted them out of the club to the purring cab, but minor enough to be giddy from the champagne he had offered them at the bar. From his talk of Hollywood, too, and the television opportunities available there for beautiful, young, open-minded English girls.

Don leaned forward and rapped a tanned knuckle twice on the thick glass.

'Hey, this is it,' he barked, the cabbie nodding benevolently and swinging the cab round in a tight half-circle with the squeak of unoiled brake pads.

'Oooh!' the girls tittered, throwing Don little playful smiles.

The hotel doorman was attempting to clear the taxi rank of a large orange delivery van. Don watched the meter click upwards another forty shillings until the orange van pulled away after some colourful and fruity exchanges and the cab slid into its place.

The doorman strode through the rain smart as a clockwork soldier in his scarlet velvet and braid and snapped open the taxi door, Don stepping out on to the wet street, unfurling the fare, the girls clacking about him in their preposterous heels.

'Good evening, sir.' The doorman bowed and passed a surreptitious glance over the bare legs of Don's companions. His eyebrow slowly cranked up like it was letting a tug-boat pass underneath.

Don, mindful of etiquette and aware that the words *nieces*

and *visiting* would stink like a week-old athletic support, ushered the girls in quickly without meeting his glance.

At that hour, the hotel lobby was liberally cast with a whole spectrum of international guests, milling and bustling. They were mostly setting out for evenings of the highest culture London had to offer. That is to say, Lloyd Webber and an Aberdeen Steakhouse.

Don was glad of the cover, pushing his new friends through the crowds towards the lift and seclusion. Sadly for him, however, the girls would have been quieter pitching snooker balls at a school blackboard with a bazooka, and pretty much the entire lobby turned to look at them.

'Oh, Mr Silver, sir?' a polished voice rang out through the crowd. 'Sir?'

Don closed his eyes.

'Mr *Silver*?' it came again. A tight, clipped English voice that smelled of jodhpurs and cucumber.

Don grabbed the elbows of his companions and whispered urgently in their ears. With the same knowing smiles and playful winks they'd been flinging about the place all evening, they stepped over to the lifts to wait. .

Nieces, Don repeated to himself. *Nieces*, that's all. *Niecey niecey nieces*.

'Ah, good evening, sir,' the Concierge oiled briskly, straightening the blotter, the pen holder, the vase on his desk top quickly as if they were parts of a child's puzzle. 'I trust you are enjoying your stay here with us?'

He was a youngish man, Don noted, with dark tidy hair and that unique, politeness-as-a-form-of-rudeness British hotel manner. It was brilliantly assured, practised and frustrating – much like being burgled by someone who does the hoovering and the washing up before they leave.

'It's just the teensiest thing, Mr Silver, if you will? Ma-haa,' he laughed for no reason known to man.

'Problem?' Don said smartly. He was eager to bundle his

companions into the lift and get started on that coke. He threw a quick glance over his shoulder to check on the girls. There, by the rubber plants, smoking long cigarettes and pouting, they were giving directions to a tourist armed with camera and map.

'Yes, item one, as it were, on the agenderette, ma-haa!' the Concierge said, riffling daintily through some crisp paperwork to be sure of the details. 'There are two suites under your name, I understand, sir? On the first and second floors? Now, housekeeping have informed me, and they are usually reliable on such matters,' a smile skimmed across his face and plunged out of sight, 'that you have asked specifically for the second suite to be left alone. Is that correct? Not, as it were, *to be touched* until further notice?'

'Problem with that?' Don said.

'Ma-haa, not at all, sir,' the Concierge laughed again pointlessly, condescension running down his face. 'It's just the, ahem, *procedure*, as it were, for assuring such *particular requirements* are met is, ah, shall we say, a tad more *complex*, so to speak.'

'What?' Don said, understandably.

'Pecuniary advances follow a certain *pyramidal scheme* . . .'

'Look, I gave 'em all a couple of bucks,' Don rolled his eyes. ''Sthat what this is all about?'

'I understand you were most generous sir. The amount of currency is not the issue here. More the, ahem, *direction* the currency was, as it were . . .'

'Oh, for Chrissakes,' Don sighed, whipping out his wallet. The Concierge busied himself with a slow blink.

'Shit,' Don said, thumbing through the empty flaps. 'Gimme a second here.'

'Back again,' Don smiled, appearing by the lobby lifts. The girls turned to him with looks of surprise on their overly made-up faces.

'We're still all right for our . . . casting session?' one of them asked.

69

'Oh, yes,' he replied, feeling the usual urge stirring within his boxer shorts. 'But let me borrow a few bucks for a second, would you?' he said, reaching for her expensive bag. 'And you, beat it!' he said to Mr Camera-map, who backed away, hands raised. 'They're with me.'

Don snapped open the flimsy bag and reached in. He snatched off a handful of notes from her purse and dropped his key-card inside, handing back the bag.

'Room 103,' he said. 'I'll be two minutes.' And peeled away across the lobby with a wink.

The girls smiled, adjusted their bosoms with a wiggle and jabbed the lift button.

As the glowing numbers descended, they watched Don hand the grubby floret of notes to the short guy behind the desk who lost them discreetly about himself with a low nod and a smile.

The Concierge in turn relaxed as he watched the girls totter into the lift and disappear.

Don watched the floor number blink its way up to the first floor and smiled to himself as it stopped.

None of them watched the guy with the camera.

None of them saw him close his map, whisper into a very small transmitter in his cuff and then duck through the rubber plants, out on to the street. And nobody saw the orange van's back doors crack open and the man with the camera climb in, fiddling with the lens.

Or indeed how long that lens was. A very, very long lens indeed.

EIGHT

The flashing red lights in Bernie Silver's rear-view mirror almost made him soil his trousers there and then. He held his breath, gripped the wheel and clenched his bottom, holding the pose for a split second, cigarette dangling from his lip.

There was a squeaky blip behind him and the light went off, the car returning to its cool darkness, with just a faint glow from the dashboard.

Bernie craned around to look over his shoulder with a soft fart. It was the seat, just the leather seat, he lied to himself. Behind him, across the dark underground parking garage of the Mercury offices, a man was unlocking his car and going home. Unlocking his car with a little handheld bleeper. Central locking.

It had just been his hazards blinking.

Bernie collapsed with a huge sigh, palms sweating against the wheel. He watched the man climb into his car and glide across the damp tarmac, bump up the ramp and away. He was alone again in the darkness.

'*Bernie?*' the voice crackled from his speakerphone.

'Sorry . . . I'm sorry. I thought I saw . . . nothing. Forget it.'

'*It's forgotten. Go on. You were saying? A reshuffle?*'

'That's right, sir, active immediately. I just put through the call to Los Angeles to confirm it. Nothing too crazy, just moving a few development assistants around, cutting back some of the dead wood. Lateral moves. Losing an assistant here, a development associate there. A dozen mid-level execs are clearing their desks. It's nothing to worry about. The main thing is, it'll save us money.'

'*Cutting costs?*'

'Y-yes, exactly sir, exactly. Less is more. Streamlining. Plus it's good to shake the staff up now and then, see who falls out. A little bit of musical chairs keeps everyone on their toes. Mr Silver will announce it officially in his interview with *Variety*. I thought as major shareholder you should know in advance.'

'*And what was this other thing? A pay rise?*'

'Er, y-yes. Yes, sir. For Gill Kramer. Again, it'll be in Wednesday's paper.'

The voice sighed, making the little speaker crackle.

'*How much is it this time, Bernie? I mean, we had this same conversation three months ago . . .*'

'It's not much, just a cursory thing,' Bernie said, clearing his throat. He was glad his car wasn't fitted with a video phone. His face was glistening with sweat, huge dark patches blooming under his arms, his tie off, slung on the passenger seat. 'It's nothing to worry about.' He sucked hard on his cigarette.

'*Worrying's not something I waste my time with, Bernie. That's why I let my Tommy look after the deals and meetings. I'm sure you know what you're doing.*'

'It's j-just important that we keep Gill Kramer on side for the next few weeks. It's a syndication issue.'

'*Syndication? What're you talking about Bernie? English please, you know I don't understand any of your Hollywood mumbo-jumbo. We'll start making some money finally, is that what you're saying?*'

'Th-that's right, sir. We can sell *E.R. E.R. . . . Oh's!* broadcast rights to other stations. Cable stations, affiliates, all over the country. You can't do it with less than a hundred episodes. Syndication's where the real money is, Mr, Lambert. That's what we've been waiting for.'

'*And about time, Bernie. About time we started to see some kind of return. Tommy tells me the meeting this morning collapsed. Your other shareholders have given up waiting? That right?'*

'I'm afraid so, sir. Cutting their losses. I pleaded with them, showed them the projections, but they wouldn't budge. I can only apologise, sir.'

'Well, that's not our style, Bernie, you know that. I don't believe in—'

A blare of car horns.

Bernie jumped, throwing a look over his shoulder. Two drivers bickered at the ramp.

'You got me on speaker?' the voice said, angrily. *'Take me off. Take me off, I hate that!'*

He blustered an apology, jabbing the button and fumbling with the receiver.

'It's okay, I'm in the car, there's no one . . . yes, yes, I understand that, I didn't mean . . . no. No, of course . . . Yes, sir . . . Yes, of course . . . and I do appreciate it, really. Things will pick up . . . Headlines? What headlines?'

Bernie squirmed in his seat, phone sliding in his clammy grip.

'No, sir, I can assure you, only rumours . . . really, you have nothing to worry . . . no, no, you're right, you did say that . . . Howard? No, he has no idea . . . absolutely none sir . . . I will . . . an-and thank you . . . hello?'

He had gone.

Bernie replaced the receiver, let his head loll back and breathed out, long and loud. What would Howard say if he knew? What would he do? He'd fire Bernie, of course he would. If he didn't kill him.

'But he doesn't know,' Bernie said out loud, starting the car. The engine was loud, reverberating in the concrete tomb of the garage. 'And as long as Don doesn't fuck it up in London, he need never know.'

As his Uncle Bernie began his battle with Manhattan's after-noon traffic, Don threw a sleepy glance at the illuminated clock by his bed. 21:26. He looked down at the long curves of the girls lying either side of him. Blonde hair tumbling over the pillow like huge scoops of vanilla ice-cream, they slept serenely. Don pursed his lips, hummed for a bit and graded them around a four. And a half.

Maybe.

For the rest of mankind, these women would have been up in the nines, but Don had been rather spoilt by Californian girls.

The Beach Boys were right, he thought, giving his warm belly a scratch. If only they all *could* be Californian girls. How much more eager they were about the whole thing. They didn't wince at Don's kinkier, more 'boisterous' manoeuvres, didn't get all coy about the wide-angle palmcorder whirring away on the dressing table or start chattering afterwards about him coming down to the country next weekend for some girl called Charlotte's wedding.

And they certainly, Don harumphed, rising from the springy mattress with a creak, thumbing off the video-camera and moving across the chilly room, didn't insist on having the damn' curtains and windows wide open throughout the whole procedure.

He clattered about with the tangle of rods and clips and began to rattle the window closed, the cold night air waking his sleeping nipples.

Don was depressed to discover how similar the real London was to the fibreglass soundstage of the *Fyre* lot back home. When he'd been shown around studio 6, the phoney cobbles, hatmakers and half-timbered buildings there had seemed impossibly ancient. Prehistoric almost. And yet here he was, here *it* was, four hundred years later. The pointy churches and cold narrow lanes.

What a horrible place, he mused. Whoever had left a cigarette burning in that East End bun-shop back in the 1600s certainly had the right idea.

The phone rang suddenly, making him jump.

He shushed the hotel curtains shut loudly and wandered over to the dressing table.

The girls stirred on the bed.

'What time is it, honey?' one murmured sleepily.

'Time you were getting your sweet little tushes in the shower,' he said, picking up the phone.

'*Donnie? It's your Uncle Bernie. What the hell's goin' on over there, kid? You tryin' to get us all busted?*'

'Uncle Bernie?' he said. Long-distance. A bad line. 'You in the car? What're you talking about? Things are going—'

'*Shut up and listen to me, I'm about to go into the tunnel. I don't know who or how or why ... well, shit, I know who. Dolawitz. That slippery bastard!*'

'Shifty? Uncle Bernie, what are you—'

'*And I know why, the greedy sonofabitch. Jesus, three million a show ...*'

'Uncle Bernie —'

'*Shut up, kid. Look, you've been caught. Snapped. Say cheese. In some men's room. Gotta be a couple of Ks. Dolawitz has the negs. I mean, you dealing now? What in hell did you think you were doing?*'

'Ohhh, crap,' Don groaned, eyes shut tight. 'How? I mean, who—'

'*It doesn't matter, we're dealing with it this end. But flush what you've got, for Chrissakes, and try and keep your nostrils on a leash, can you? Jesus H. Lawrence ...*'

'Does Dad know?'

'*He's pissing his pants, I'll tell you that right now. He thought you quit. Mind you, he still thinks I'm going to Gamblers Anonymous.*'

'You're *not?* So where *do* you go every Thursday?'

'*Got a high stakes, no-limit Hold 'Em game upstairs at Sardi's. Listen, kid, I haven't got long, the tunnel's coming up. There's been a shake-up in LA. Streamlining.*'

'Since when?'

'*About an hour ago. What with this Dolawitz thing, we gotta find some money. So we've lost a few department heads, shifted some key positions around. You're still VP, don't worry about that. But, hell, you know what this means.*'

'Nobody wants to develop the last guy's ideas, right?'

'Right. Everything old is out, everything new is in. They want short shows long, long shows short. Black actors white, white black. Hour-long shows have gotta be half-hour shows, comedies are becoming documentaries. They got a load of execs goin' nuts trying to turn a two hour special on handguns into a Busby Berkley musical number. Anyway, upshot is, they should be faxing . . . list of new department . . . ello? . . . uck, Donald? . . . llo?' And he was gone.

But across the room there was a click, hum and whirr from the fax machine. The green light winked on the top, a sheet of slippy paper shuddered its way out with a whine, a swipe of the inner blade and it dropped, curling into a warm roll on the desk.

Don lifted the fax and unfurled it.

'Hey Mr Producer?' a girl murmured from the bed. 'How was my audition?'

But he was busy scanning the fax. A memo from LA. The Comedy Development heads.

Or rather, the 'new' Comedy Development heads.

Oh, for Chrissakes, Don thought. This wasn't good.

'Hey, babes,' he said to the girls on the bed, wrapped toga-style inside the sheets. 'I gotta go.' And, without waiting for a reply, was puffing down the corridor moments later, fastening his belt buckle, heading for the lift.

Across town, upstairs above the club, Ben stood at the bar, shaking. It took a sturdy taut clench of every muscle, a tight boy-scout knot of every nerve-ending and a white-knuckled grip on the dark wooden bar to stop himself from running, screaming, whooping out on to the street to yell and dance with unconcealed glee.

So Ben clenched, knotted and gripped, and ordered a bottle of champagne with a grin on his face that was in danger of affecting the tides.

Just wait, he thought, tapping out an excited rhythm on the

bar like Ginger Baker waiting to use the lavatory. Just wait till he told Jackie. Oh, and Sheridan, of course.

Shit. He'd said . . .

No. No way, this was *their* show. Fifty-fifty. Theirs. And, for heaven's sake, Don had approached *him*, not the other way around. What was Ben meant to do? Turn this down? The biggest break of their lives?

He flipped a surreptitious look over his shoulder. The American was finding a corner table, slapping his magazines down and slipping off his huge jacket.

Hollywood.

It couldn't be, could it? I mean, *could it?*

Ben was suddenly aware of an ache about his jaw. He attempted to relax, but his smile just sprang back into shape like an executive toy. The sort of bendy, squeezy, stress-reliever a top American television writer might in fact have. That he could massage and pummel while spitballing a few gags with his co-writers. Glugging little bottles of mineral water and gazing out into the LA sunshine, before planning an afternoon of tennis lessons and parties.

'Birthday?' a voice said.

Ben looked up, his drum solo paused mid para-diddle. The barmaid was pouring out an arc of golden bubbles with a smile.

'Hn? Oh, er, no. Just . . . just some good news.'

'Hey,' Don called, pacing barefoot down the hall, belt buckle clanking. 'What the hell you doing there?'

Outside Melvin's door, a bearded man in scruffy orange overalls knelt down, whistling to himself, walkman headphones on. A battered toolkit at his side lay with jaws wide open, stuffed with gleaming metal and wire, silvery tools and equipment, like a Californian teenager at the dentist.

Don reached him and tugged at his shoulder. The workman spun round.

'Jesus Christ, guv,' he said. 'Gimme bleedin' heart failure.'

He popped his earphones out. 'Chas 'n' Dave,' he said, tapping the cassette player on his belt. '*Snooker Loopy, Rabbit, Margate.* Got 'em all. You a fan, mate?'

'What are you doing here?' Don said, and rapped hard on the door. 'Is he in?'

'Dunno, guv,' the man said, clattering about with his tools. 'I'm just redoin' this wiring. Some bloody dago cleaner tore it up wiv 'is vacuum. Got to replace the lot.'

Don pounded on the door again. Nothing. Not a sound.

'Mel!' he yelled, rattling the doorknob. 'Mel, you there? I got notes from LA.'

Still nothing.

'Sure you ain't seen him? Short guy . . . red hair . . . glasses?'

The workman shut his tool box and stood up.

'No one's been in or out of this corridor the last hour. 'Course, I 'ad me speakers on wiv' the boys givin' it some "Gertcha" so it's possible someone snuck darn 'ere. Been busy wiv me cables, though. Don't see much then, me.'

Don rattled the handle and banged again.

'Mel? You in there?'

Christ, where was he? Don looked down at the fax in his hand, now sweaty and crumpled. Of all the times for Mel to be out.

'I'll be off, mate, that's me done,' the workman said, and wandered down the corridor singing, toolbox banging against his thigh. '*Gertcha, when yer kids are swingin' on the gate, gertcha . . .*'

'Mel?'

Don listened at the door, pressing an ear against the cold wood. Nothing. Not a sound.

Where the hell was he?

Ben brought the drinks over to the table.

'To you,' the American said, raising a glass, blinking behind his thick lenses.

'Er, cheers then,' Ben said and, with a nervous shrug, threw the contents of the glass down his neck in one.

'So, Ben, what do you think? We got a deal?'

'I-I don't know. I-I mean, yes, yes, of course. I think. I don't know.' Ben knotted his brow slightly and leaned closer. 'I mean, sorry, but are you *serious* about all this? This isn't, y'know, a *joke?*'

'A *joke?*' the producer said with a laugh. Ben noticed his teeth were crooked, with one dead grey one like a tombstone in front. He pushed his lank hair from his eyes, revealing a pitted, acne-scarred forehead. 'I don't do jokes, Benny Boy. But,' and he pointed at Ben, 'my job, my vocation, my *reason for being*, is to find the guys who do. Guys like you.' He smiled.

'Gosh.'

'Er, fuckin' *gosh* is assing-well right!' the American said, which took Ben by surprise somewhat. 'Jesusing acts like you, Benny boy, are the Christing reason to goddamn I'm in this mothering business.'

It seemed to Ben that this producer must suddenly have realised he was not going to meet his quota of swearing and decided to get a week's worth into every sentence.

'You are bitchingly where the talent is at. Ass,' he finished off limply.

'Right, right,' Ben nodded. 'But, and I don't want you to think I'm not grateful for this opportunity,' he said, shrugging and bowing away modestly, 'surely in LA you've got plenty of—'

'*Warmth!*' the American barked, adding a quick, 'Er . . . godammit. I'm looking for warmth. Warmth is what the damned American people want. The whole fucking industry's looking for bitch-mothering writers who can do fucking warmth. In goddamn' short, Benjamin,' and the American folded his arms, 'they're looking for guys like you. And it's my job . . . holy crapoly, it's my duty . . . to bring you to the American people. Now.'

'You want me to come over? With you, I mean? To Los Angeles?'

'Sure!' the American said. 'Damn' sure. I'm takin' a whole bunch of you British guys back home – really shake things up. You heard of these, ah, what did they call themselves . . . ?'

'The Angus & Malachy Madcap Madhouse?' Ben said, wide eyed. 'Is that true? You've got them . . .'

The American nodded modestly.

'And Philips? Jasper Philips? 'Cos he had this West End show and his management—'

'I set him up with a Malibu beach house.' The American checked his watch. 'With any luck he'll be flying outta Heathrow within the hour.'

Ben's jaw dropped.

'So, here it is.' The American began to collect up magazines and papers from the little table like a newsreader wrapping up a bulletin. 'Let's grab a cab over to my hotel, yeah? I gotta suite at the Margrave on Piccadilly. We'll have another drink and hear what ideas you got, okay?'

Ben looked down at his empty glass, feeling the warm champagne fuzz around his head. The American hadn't touched a drop of his. 'And hey,' he added, giving Ben a punch on the upper-arm, 'there's nothing to look so worried about. You made it, kid. You made it. You'll be sipping Martini's at the Regent Beverly Wilshire in twenty-four hours. This is your big break, your own TV show.'

Ben looked down at the business card in his hand, sweaty and buckled in his eager grip.

Don Silver, it said in raised gold leaf. *Vice President – Comedy Development.* He stroked his thumb over the lettering, reading *Mercury Pictures* printed beneath. Ben's breath caught in his chest. The address . . . so glamorous, so mysterious:

20201 West Alemeda Ave, Burbank, Los Angeles CA 91505.

California. Los Angeles, California. It sounded like palm trees and swimming pools and convertibles and rollerblading girls in bikinis.

'Benjamin?'

'Sorry, sorry. It's . . . it's just so unbelievable. See, technically I'm not *actually* a stand-up comedian. Wh-what I really want to do is write.'

'Is that *so?*' the American said.

'We've, well,' Ben began picking his thumbnail nervously, 'my friend and I, Sheridan . . . well, maybe I shouldn't be telling you all this. I sort of promised . . . but I mean . . .'

Somewhere, a phone bleeped.

The American held up a finger, leaving Ben with his mouth hanging open, and began rifling through the acres of fabric in his huge suit jacket, fumbling for the phone. He flipped it out and looked at the number illuminated on the screen.

'I, er, gotta take this,' he said to Ben. 'It's, *uhm*, LA. The er, Associate Assistant Vice President of Current Comedy. It's his associate assistant's assistant. Can I . . . ?'

Ben nodded quickly, reversing off his stool.

'Hello,' the American said. 'W*hat?* . . . I'm out . . . no, just out. I'm taking a break, c-can't I take a break?'

Ben left the man to his call, throwing himself eagerly down the stairs to the toilets, flipping and flapping the little card.

'Look,' the man continued behind him, his accent began to slip a little. 'I've been doing those rewrites for hours, I just s-stepped out for a break . . . calm down, would you? . . Sh-shake-up? . . . What fax? What shake up? . . . Changes? Wh-what kind of changes?'

Across town, a man's voice. British, well-spoken but scared. Clearly very scared.

'I thought, Mr Silver, maybe a cruise ship?'

Long pause, then another voice. Less clear, further from the microphone. Probably standing.

'*No. Been done. 1959.* All Aboard. *Starring Arthur Lowe. Gimme another.*'

'Oh . . . er . . . rest . . . rest . . .'

'*Rest home?* No, *1990.* Waiting For God. *Stephanie Cole.* Another.'

'No, I meant rest . . . aurant. How about that? An all-night deli kind of thing?'

'*Deli* . . .'

'Look, Mr Silver, please, this is crazy! I can't . . . these bodies . . .'

'Delicatessen, *no. 1994.* All Night Long, *Keith Barron.* Another.'

'Mr Silver, please, Mr Silver . . .'

A loud crack, then a scream.

'*Another.*'

'Ah ah ah . . . woman. A woman . . . Jesus!'

'*Woman?*'

'A woman . . . shit, my hand . . . a woman . . . a nanny . . .'

'*No! You ever watch TV? Huh? Ever? 1980. Beryl Reid in* Nanny Knows Best. *Another* . . .'

'Mr Silver, Jesus Christ, please! I can't . . .'

'*Another!*'

'A woman in a rugby team . . . female rugby team . . .'

'*And?*'

'And . . . shit, and all the time she's juggling being . . . being feminine with having to play rugby . . .'

Silence.

'*Feminine?*'

'Y-yeah. She's the manager of a shop . . . a dress shop . . .'

'Private Benjamin *meets* Are You Being Served?' The American voice calm. Measured.

'Yes! Yes!' The English voice is excited now. Loud.

'*No. 1973.* All Our Saturdays *starring Diana Dors.*'

'Aaaaargh . . . ow, no! No, Don, no! No!' Banging, something being smashed. Screams.

The back door to the van swung open and a bearded man in rain-spattered orange overalls clambered in among the equipment, dropping his heavy toolbox to the floor.

82

The second man snapped off the tape recorder, bringing the screams to a sudden stop, slid out the horrific cassette and scribbled a note on the label. He slipped off his headphones and laid them on the console.

'Get it done?' he said.

'Doddle, mate,' the bearded man said, passing what looked like a Walkman over to his colleague. 'Bumped into Silver at the door, though. Fed 'im some cobblers about fixing a cable.'

'Suspect anything?'

'Naaah,' the bearded man said, unzipping his overall and sitting down on the bench. 'Coked out of his face as always.'

His colleague flipped open the Walkman to where the cassette would normally sit. In its place was a tiny video screen showing a grainy picture of a hotel room. Bed, dressing table, TV, a sea of white balled-up paper.

'Holy shit,' he said.

Ben slammed back up the pub stairs with Christmas morning eagerness. At the table, the American was still on the phone. Ben jogged over to the bar and ordered another round of champagne and it was all he could do just to chuckle goofily at the barmaid and slowly take the drinks to the table.

The American was hanging up the phone with a tiny bleep and a click. He saw Ben and stood up quickly.

'Here we go,' Ben said, handing him a glass. 'Another toast?'

The American took the glass and placed it directly down on the table without a thank you. Without a sip either. Or a smile, come to that.

'Siddown, Benjamin,' he said.

'I-is everything all right?' he said. The room had got a little warmer all of a sudden. Over-compensating, he presumed, for the fact that the atmosphere had got a whole lot chillier.

'Just sit down.'

Oh, no. This wasn't good, he thought. A bowling ball he distinctly remembered not eating appeared in his hollow stomach. Sit down is never good. Sit down is almost always bad. Sit down is death, it's bereavement, it's sweet tea and policemen. Ben sat down.

'I-is everything all right?'

'No. Mercury Pictures have had . . . something of a shake-up.'

'A shake-up?' Ben said. He looked at the champagne glasses sitting on the table. The bubbles pinked and fizzed quietly to themselves. They looked quite remarkably out of place all of a sudden.

'A shake-up, a reshuffle, a shift of personnel.'

The American pressed the heel of his hand hard against his forehead and grimaced, eyes tight shut.

'Mr Silver . . . ?'

'Some movement,' he said, out of breath. 'A few executives, key executives, have gone. Which means there's been a tilt of focus. It happens. Apparently, it . . . it happens.'

Ben noticed for the first time that the man had buttoned his huge jacket. Buttoned it in exactly the way a man staying put for another celebratory drink wouldn't. No, this couldn't be right.

'It's the business, Mr Busby. It's just the business.'

Mr Busby? No, wait—'

'So now there's a whole new bunch of execs looking over the situation and they feel, well, that it might need a new direction.'

Ben's voice finally came back. It hadn't even told him it was going out. But now it was back, crackly, wavering and dry.

'Situation? Sorry, I don't understand? What situation? We've just met, I don't really . . . I'm not clear what you're . . .'

'I know, I know,' the American said, nodding frantically. He picked up his copy of *Out There* magazine, closing it up with a flap. 'Bottom line is, Mr Busby, that warmth, everything warm, is *out*.'

Ben opened his mouth but it seemed his voice had only popped back to get something and had promptly fucked off again.

'Warmth. The whole warminess *thing*, y'know? Things with warmth. Warmaciousness in all forms. Gone, canned, binned, axed, red light, marching orders, off the lot, outta here. Gone. If it's warm, they're not interested,' said Silver, standing up.

'Th-that's it?' Ben couldn't believe it. No, surely not? This had to be a mistake. Phone them back, he wanted to say. Phone them back, let me talk to them, this couldn't be.

'You're no good to me,' the American said. 'I g-gotta find someone else. Y'know?' He seemed to be whimpering now. Ben just stared at him. 'Someone *quirky*, they said.' And he shook his head as if being bothered by wasps. 'Quirky is the new warmth. Warmth is too last season. The *old* execs liked warmth, but they're gone. Now we're looking for *quirk*.' And he stepped back, stumbling over the stool. 'I dunno, m-maybe . . .' And he began to flip frantically through his *Out There* magazine.

'Wait!' Ben said quickly. 'Wait a second. *Quirky*?'

In their little Finchley flat Jackie listened to the phone ring and ring.

She listened to the click and murmur of the answering machine. A beep. Then some chatter. It sounded like a pub. Another beep and then silence.

She'd listen to it later.

She placed her glass of wine on the edge of the bath, cast her eyes over her glossy magazine one more time and let it drop to the floor with a slithery thud.

She'd had enough shiny moronic advice for the evening.

She knew that eating twelve avocadoes a day wouldn't give her visibly detoxed pores in two fabulous weeks. She knew that mixing and matching vibrant pinks and cool oranges this season wouldn't put an autumn get-up-and-glow zest into her whole wardrobe. And she was pretty sure she'd be able to tick off far, far too many *nos* in the relationship-test.

She lay back, bubbles prickling her scratchy armpits, lifted her glass again with pruney fingers and thought about Ben.

Jackie loved Ben. Really, she loved him very, very much.

It was only the fact she simply couldn't stand him for more than about twenty minutes at a time that was worrying her. Couldn't stand his relentless joking. Couldn't stand his naïve optimism. Couldn't stand his laziness, his inability to get through a job interview without trying out awful routines. Couldn't stand Sheridan permanently at his side, teasing her, winding her up, bantering.

Oh, the endless bantering.

She reached for the soap and began to lather her shoulders.

Not that it had *always* been this way.

Jackie had met Ben during a very flirty period in her life. She'd been flirting with pretty much everything that moved. Interior design, Tai Chi, Feng Shui, writing children's books, yoga – you name it, Jackie had spent, oooh, almost an entire weekend convinced it would make an exciting and challenging career, and the sort of career she could do, and do well, and come home weary from, ideally to a smart white minimalist flat in town, all barefoot on nice wooden floors.

Her *Ladybird A-Z of Arty Media Careers* had brought her to a new comedy club, Krazy Ken's Komedy Kavern! (sign on the door 'koncessions two kwid' she noted grimly) one August evening with a pad and a pen and a vague idea about being a journalist/reviewer/successful media type with a smart white minimalist flat in town with nice wooden floors. Ideally she'd have skipped these rather probationary exercises and gone straight to charging about a newspaper office in a smart two-piece saying 'chief', and slamming down hard-hitting copy and threatening to 'walk' if he changed 'one goddam' word', of course, but the editor of *Out There* magazine, a short, tidy, thoroughly un-chief-looking man with a beard, had said a couple of reviews would be enough to give him an idea of her writing.

And would she mind not saying goddamn' so much. Thank you.

The evening, however, a horrendous 'open-spot' night with twelve amateur comics and approximately half that number of decent jokes, had started badly — Krazy Ken himself, about as off-the-wall as a pine shelving unit — and got rapidly worse. In fact, as comic number nine leaped desperately on to the small stage (in fact a pool-table with two planks of hardboard on it), she was about ready to pack-up and go home.

But then it happened.

'Laydeeeees an' gennermen, Krazy Ken's Komedy Kavern is proud to present act number nine tonight — Ben Busby!'

Out of her bath half an hour later, toes sudsy on the lounge carpet, Jackie topped up her white wine, setting it down atop her new *Teach Yourself Journalism* book. With the flat to herself, she had decided to make a stab at a bit of proper writing. Her eyes flicked over her computer screen.

C'mon, girls, think about it. When we're sitting around in bars, or lurching and shrieking in the back of white stretch hen-night limos, cackling away like a production of *Macbeth* sponsored by Smirnoff, we talk about men. Of course we do. Our complaints and our confessions echo about behind smoked glass all over the cities of Britain.

Hmmm, she thought. Not a bad start. She'd been in a stretch limo about three months ago and that seemed to cover the experience.

And by the time we've pinned 'L' plates to the bride-to-be's tits and cracked open a fresh box of Marlboro Lights, we'll have got on to what we might be looking for in an ideal bloke.

Yes, this was the sort of thing.

Jackie wriggled smugly in her seat, sipped a little more wine and thought about maybe putting on a little classical music in the background like a proper successful journalist might. And then she remembered she didn't have any classical music. And Ben's *STAR WARS – Original Motion Picture Score* probably wasn't quite the mood she was going for.

Ah, well. She cracked on.

We then naturally have to wade through twenty minutes of the usual monthly-mag moronicness about pecs and abs and similar nonsense before someone will say, 'Oh, and he's gotta have a sense of humour.' And we'll high-five and say 'go girl', burp and collapse in hysterics again.

Yes, without a doubt, a tickled clitoris is one thing – a tickled funny bone is a lot more difficult to come by.

As it were.

There. Good, Jackie nodded to herself. We're getting some-where. She could see this nestling in a glossy supplement, perhaps with her photograph at the top. A nice black and white shot where she had just the one chin. She sat up again.

Because if the guy you're with doesn't make you laugh, laugh until it hurts and you have to lock yourself in the bathroom and lie on the floor, tears rolling down your face, aching and aching for him to stop but wanting him to go on forever – well, then, trust me, girls, you're with the wrong fella.

Hmmm. *Trust me, girls?* Jackie stared at it for a moment. It was a bit teenage weekly. It wouldn't be the hugest step in the world from 'trust me, girls' to saying *Phwoarrr!* and telling the world which branch of Top Shop sells Burberry-style thongs.

She pulled her dressing gown around her chest a little more. Not to worry, she could trim it in the next draft. She let her fingers hover like a concert pianist over the laptop keys, and after a thoroughly professional pause, jabbed a few keys with her pruney fingertips.

So, bearing that in mind, you might be thinking that a professional comedian is the best possible of choice of partner. That you should pop-down to your nearest Comedy Club and start chatting up the acts at the stage door. A non-stop, one-way ticket to Gigglesville should await, right? Every daylight hour filled with snappy one-liners and shared, rib-aching hilarity.

Well, you'd be wrong.

Jackie stopped, hands leaping guiltily from the keys like she'd been caught stealing fresh biscuits from a cooling tray.

She read that last line again.

No, this wasn't right. She jabbed the delete key and wiped the last line away. No, she'd gone wrong, got off on the wrong track. This was meant to be a light-hearted magazine piece on life-with-a-comedy-writer. On the importance of a good sense of humour over things like excitement and passion.

That was all.

She took a healthy swig of white wine. No, get back on track, she thought, and re-read it from the beginning, fingers hanging over the keyboard, until the last paragraph.

Jackie held her breath and bit her lip.

'Well, you'd be wrong,' she typed again.

A worrying realisation leaked slowly in, like a burst yoghurt at the bottom of a carrier bag. Her fingers found the keys once again and, as if they had their own little agenda, began typing. Jackie could only sit and watch the screen as the words appeared, feeling coldness seep in.

You'd be wrong, because it's not enough. Not really. Oh, you might think it is in the early days. When your heart is full of romantic comedies – two beautiful people strolling through the autumnal New York leaves, quipping and laughing at each other.

Jackie's heart gave a horrible yearning reach as the winking cursor spat out her feelings all over the screen. But she didn't stop.

But give yourself three years of it. Three years of never being able to have a sensible conversation about anything. Three years of sighing and biting your tongue as the man in your life jabbers on, trying out his material, asking you which word is funnier, which line is stronger.
I'm sorry Ben.

And Jackie froze.
She'd done it. It was out there, in black and white.
With horrible exam-hall sickness, she got up to get her tissues from the bedroom, her head pounding with unspoken feelings.
No, she told herself, it wasn't that she wanted to be out of the relationship with Ben. She wanted Ben. She loved him.
But she'd like a slightly different Ben, she thought, looking down at her feet standing in his cold plate of half-finished lasagne.
Like the Ben she already had. The kind one, the considerate one, the funny one with the sweet nature and the soft eyes. But perhaps with a full-time job. And ambition. Proper ambition. And a career plan and a car and a selection of talented and interesting friends who knew about wine and travel and . . .
Oh, she didn't know.
She threw the tissue away and wandered back into the lounge when she saw the answerphone light winking.
Bleeeeeeeep.
A loud rumpus, chattering, shouting. Definitely a pub. Then Sheridan's excited Scouse tones.

'*Hey, Jack, it's me. I got a call from our Ben. Couldn't make half of it out, my mobile's on the blink. Said that the American prod . . .*

The message crackled.

'*. . . at Silver fellah. Said he was down at his club. If ya speak to 'im, tell him not . . . anythin' . . . we've gotta make a . . . hello? . . . oh, this fu . . .*'

Jackie's world fell silent again.

How nice it would be, she thought, capturing the quiet, to be able to have an ordinary Monday night. Writing. Alone.

Well, not alone *exactly*. Maybe some regular, handsome, *ordinary* guy coming in once in a while with an apron on and carrying a steaming wooden spoon. 'Try this,' he'd say, and she'd smile and taste something hot and garlicky and amazing. And he'd wander off back to the kitchen in his apron and his broad sensible shoulders while she, the famous investigative journalist, quickly put the finishing touches to her devastating exposé.

She settled back into her chair, rubbed her eyes and looked at her letter.

She scrolled to the top.

'Dear Ben,' she added, pressing the return key and feeling it lean on her heart.

Her goodbye letter.

'Jackie!' a voice yelled from downstairs.

She jumped as the front door slammed, vibrating her glass of wine like an approaching T-Rex.

'Jackie, you up?' Ben called, thudding up the stairs, two at a time. The hall light snapped on. Jackie quickly saved the file and closed it down.

He appeared in the doorway, breathless.

Hair tousled from the rain, jacket misbuttoned, he gripped a copy of *Variety* in one hand and a crumpled business card in the other. He held it out for her to see, an exhausted grin on his face.

'You're never going to believe what's happened . . .'

STUDIO NEWS
MERCURY EXEC CULLING
IN DOLLAR DESPERATION

THE AXE fell on thirty jobs at Mercury Pictures yesterday leaving the Burbank-based studio reeling.

CFO Bernie Silver wiped out fifteen low-level and fifteen mid-level executives from the comedy and drama divisions in a sweeping move that sources suggest is down to belt-tightening and budget cutting.

Still in London, comedy development VP Don Silver will remain in place, with all eyes on his latest venture, which Mercury hopes will bring an end to his current run of disasters.

The axe is even hovering over hospital laffer E.R. E.R. . . . OH! which will be shooting its 98th episode on Friday. Sources at ABN say the network may have to pull the Gill Kramer vehicle just weeks before it hits the big 100 as it continues to take a beating from SHRINK.

Mercury CEO Howard Silver talks to *Variety*'s Penny Lang today about the future of his troubled family studio.

See tomorrow's edition for the full story.

Variety
Tuesday 26 September

92

NINE

The Margrave Hotel's dining room was tall and dark and almost entirely empty.

This was no reflection on the breakfast, which was more or less as good as one would get in any London hotel. Underdone toast, with underdone eggs and underdone bacon with choice of either underdone mushrooms or underdone tomatoes. In fact, the whole breakfast experience was so almost-finished that it came as a surprise to Don that there wasn't a seamstress sitting opposite him, frantically hemming the tablecloth.

The room was empty because it was getting on for lunchtime and most of the guests were early risers, early eaters and early wandering-about-Regent-Street-buying-Burberry-tea-towel-ers. Waistcoated staff rattled and echoed about, and in a far corner, tucked out of the way, Don got rid of his companions.

'Our *screen-tests* go okay last night?' The women smiled, standing up and lighting long cigarettes.

'Hn? Oh, absolutely.' Don smiled back. Normally he'd have got up too, kissed them both long and hard, and perhaps given their pert asses a quick squeeze, but he had been finding it difficult to initiate any serious movement since a waiter had dropped a hotel napkin on his lap that seemed to be made of one part granite to three parts granite.

'So you'll call?' The blonder of the two women was pulling on a light jacket.

He winked and patted his empty breast pocket.

The women air-kissed him with 'mwahh mwahh' noises and tottered out.

Don relaxed a little, tapped his foot and threw an anxious glance at the Rolex hanging loose on his tanned wrist. Where the hell was Melvin?

'Sir?' a clipped voice said. A stick-thin waistcoat with a waiter concealed somewhere inside it wafted past like an epigram. 'We'll be dressing the dining room for lunch in a moment.'

Don sighed, threw back the cold coffee and checked his watch again. But before he had time for another *where the hell is Melvin?* under a shock of ginger hair and a pebble-dashing of greasy pores, there the hell was Melvin.

'Good morning, Donald,' he said loudly, scraping back a chair and knocking everything over with a clatter. He began to blink and sniff and twitch, fumbling about in his jacket pockets for little white plastic pill bottles that he rattled down on to the table, one after the other, like he was setting up a chess game.

'Milk!' he yelled at no one in particular, fussing with some more pill bottles. Clear orange ones this time.

'Jesus, where have you been?' Don said, giving him the once over. 'You slept?' Melvin stank of day-old sweat, the shirt Don had lent him crumpled and grimy.

'Working, I've been working,' Melvin said, distracted, clacking off lid after lid with a hurried twist of gangly elbows. He began to tip two pills from each bottle into his oily palm. 'Came back last night. After you told me about the shake-up?' he said. 'Thinking less warmth, more quirk. *Milk!*' he yelled again. A whole health-food store of supplementary vitamins and vitamintary supplements sat in a coloured pyramid in his open hand. 'Got a couple of pages for you to look at.'

The waistcoat appeared at their side with a jug, filling Melvin's glass. Don watched him.

'Don't you ever eat? I mean, like a meal?'

Melvin threw the whole cocktail back into his throat, pills

rattling around his teeth, glug-glug-glugging down the milk until it streamed down his chin. He banged the empty glass on the table and began fishing behind himself awkwardly like a panting teenager with a tricky bra-clip.

He brought out a clear plastic A4 sleeve that he'd clearly had half stuffed down the back of his trousers. He tossed it nonchalantly on to the table.

They both looked at it.

'Best thing I ever wrote.' And he began to gather up his pill bottles and drop them back into his baggy pockets with a rattle.

Don reached forward with nervous fingers trying not to imagine what being down the back of Melvin's trousers was like. He slid the two warm pages out carefully. Double-spaced, centred and printed neatly in Courier New.

CARPOOL

'*Carpool?*' Don said, flipping through. 'So what is it?'

Meanwhile, Ben was finding that a combination of eating cereal, hiccups and gritted teeth made one hell of a mess of one's pyjama top. But he took another great slooping mouthful, wiped the debris from his chin, hiccupped a few flakes across the table and concentrated even harder.

He wasn't looking at the clock until the bowl was empty.

Another munch, slurp and hiccup.

No way.

He'd tried Sheridan's phone thirty-one times that morning. Sloop-munch. Standing there in bare feet in the hall, jabbing redial over and over. Munch-crunch. He wasn't picking up. Crunch-munch. So Ben would leave it a decent amount of time before he tried again. Hiccup-splatter. He'd eat a leisurely breakfast and then give him another call. Munch-gulp-hiccup.

There, Ben thought, tossing his spoon into the bowl with a clatter. He could now check the time.

It had been six minutes past eleven when he'd last called. So, hell, by now it had to be at least . . .

Fuck. Ten minutes past eleven. And that was his second bowl of Ricicles.

He scurried hiccupping into the hall, snatched up the phone and hit redial.

C'mon c'mon c'mon c'mon.

Nothing.

Ben hiccupped again in frustration and trundled anxiously into the kitchen to wash up his breakfast things.

Had Don Silver made it over to the club in time last night? Had he caught Sheridan's act? Had they spoken? Had Sheridan talked to him about the show?

Head spinning, Ben dried his hands on a greasy tea-towel, wandered back into the hall and hit redial for the thirty-third time. Nothing.

Where the hell *was* Sheridan?

He moved to the bedroom. He wasn't calling again until he was dressed. Cardie *and* trainers.

The wardrobe doors were open, an odd shoe lay on the carpet. The bed was a tangle of jumpers and coat-hangers and dusty bags. The window-sill where Jackie's make-up normally stood regimented was a tumbled disarray of old tissues and bottles and empty space.

Ben pulled on his jeans. He felt anxious. A little tired. A little lonely.

He wasn't sure exactly why he felt lonely, just that he did. And when he attempted to pin down the reasons for that feeling they kept flipping, like he was looking at that old optical illusion, trying to spot the vase between the two faces.

Were the squirty, hollow nerves because the woman he loved had told him his love wasn't enough anymore? Or was it the thought of the most important meeting of his life going on somewhere without him, Sheridan and Don, feet up, sipping Martinis and chatting about networks and pitch meetings?

Ben didn't know.

He gave a yawn that became a hiccup halfway through, which succeeded in shaking him up a bit.

He sat on the bed.

Ben had been up talking to Jackie until 3 a.m. Holding her, feeling her body shake as she cried. Feeling her heart ache as she sipped tea and explained her feelings. Feeling a shoe hit him on the back of the head when he'd popped out of the room to try Sheridan's phone one more time.

What? He couldn't help it. It was important.

Ben stomped into some trainers moodily. He loved Jackie more than anything, but . . . Well, this was . . . He sighed again and mooched into the hall, buttoning his cardigan.

Jackie's mum's number was on a Post-it on the phone where Jackie could be reached for a day or so. Time for Ben to think about what he really wanted, she'd said.

The maddening thing, of course, was that Ben already knew what he wanted.

He wanted Sheridan to phone with good news. And Jackie to care.

He picked up the phone and hit redial for the thirty-fourth time.

God, where the hell *was* he?

'A car?' Don nodded, a smile slithering across his face. 'Three guys in a car.'

'It's quirky,' Melvin said flatly, and began to tap his fingers on the table quickly causing the silverware to jump and dance.

Don started nodding at the cover page again. *Carpool.* He pictured it on screen, nestling in the *TV Guide.* 'This . . . this is good,' he said, eyes flashing. 'It's . . . it's *real.*'

'Right.'

'I mean . . . I mean, that's the problem, right? *Right?* Sitcoms aren't *real.* They're a bubble, a fantasy, a never-never land.' Don began warming to the idea more and more. Melvin was on to something here. 'A make-believe world of charming drunks and kooky neighbours and wise-cracking kids. Crazy coincidences and slapstick schemes. Coffee-shops where you can always get a seat, quaint bars with no piss on the floor, gorgeous apartments with no rent hikes. Right?'

'R-Right, you're right.'

Don pictured himself in a *Carpool* baseball cap, a *Carpool* flight jacket.

'*Right*. And meanwhile, what's getting the ratings? Dick goddamn' Trent. Tears, bitterness, anguish, regret. That's what Mr & Mrs John Q. America want. Something *real*. Something they know. Gridlock. Yellin' at the traffic, bitchin' about the boss. *Carpool*!' And he slammed his flat hand on the script.

'Well, that's wh-what I was—'

'Right. It's bold, it's . . . it's ballsy, sure. But, hey, it's friendships too. It'll have that tenderness . . .'

'And quirk.'

'Right, a quirky tenderness. An . . . an off-beat timeless-ness . . .'

A vision floated in front of Don, a vision of *Carpool Season One* etched on the base of a glittering Emmy statuette. Acceptance speeches. A new dawn of modern comedy. A shining light in quality entertainment. Brave, honest . . .

'Idiosyn*classic?*' Melvin offered.

'Heyyyy, I *like* it,' Don said. He was bobbing up and down in his seat now. He hadn't been this excited since a super-intelligent talking sheep in braces and red plastic glasses running a Wall Street brokers had landed on his desk. He had that old feeling, that tingle. This! *This* would be the one. Sure the time might not have been exactly right for the Hiroshima coffee-shop, and maybe America wasn't quite ready for lumberjack mobsters.

But this? It couldn't fail. It was life. It was *real*.

'These three men are now,' Don smiled. 'They're us, they're . . . they're . . .'

'Zeit-guys?'

'That's it! That's *it*! *Zeit-guys*. In a . . . in a steaming four lane agenda-bender at the . . .'

'Intersection?'

'. . . of counter-culture and pop-propriety.'

'Exactly.'

'Oh, this is great, Melvin, this is great!' and Don held the pages out in front of him. 'And I'm sure when you've written more than —'

He flicked through.

'— a page and a half, we'll *really* have something!'

Melvin grinned.

'Who,' Don said, pointing at the cover, 'are *Sheridan McDonald and Ben Busby?*'

'What?' Melvin spat. He scrabbled for the pages, eyes wide as if seeing them for the first time. 'That's . . . oh, that's just my pseudonym. For n-new work.'

'Right, right.'

'See, if I put my name on stuff, what with all my awards, producers don't give it an objective eye. You know, Ronnie Barker—'

'Whatever,' Don said. 'Get it finished, I'll get word to Dad. You did great kid. *Grrrreat.*'

Melvin stood up sharply, his pockets rattling with pills. His chair fell backwards with a loud thud on to the floor. With a grin, he sniffed then scratched his scalp and wandered off, bumping into tables and humming tunelessly.

Don relaxed, head lolling backwards, an easy calm spreading through his body.

He was going home. With a hit on his hands, he was going home.

An hour later, Ben stepped back off Sheridan's front porch into the late morning sunshine and stared, for the sixteenth time, up at the two first floor windows of his friend's flat. Not a movement, not a flicker, not a twitch. Ben didn't quite know what he'd expected to see up there, but nothing was what he saw and it bothered him. In fact, the only movement that had come from the terraced conversion since he had arrived was from the plaster and the brick, busy crumbling and peeling and going about the business of lowering their resale value.

Where the *hell* was he?

Ben stepped up again and gave the dusty intercom its sixteenth stab until his fingertip whitened and throbbed. He could hear from deep inside the flat the nasal drone of the internal buzzer, calling out like Kenneth Williams trapped under a piano.

Nothing.

He bent down again and pushed open the letterbox for the sixteenth time, revealing a narrow 70mm Cinemascope view of the communal hallway that Sheridan shared with the woman downstairs. The usual local newspapers, yellowing and fading, a poker hand of minicab cards and pizza menus. And there, five feet away, the white internal door of Sheridan's flat.

And then Ben found himself stumbling, falling forward, getting a mouthful of slingbacks and saying 'Fuck' as the front-door swung open wide with a clatter.

'Oh my good Lord!' a figure said, bringing a hand to her mouth in alarm. Sheridan's downstairs neighbour stood framed in the doorway, shopping basket in her hand, biscuit crumbs about her mouth, wearing both a knitted navy beret and an oh-I-haven't-got-time-for-this expression.

'Hello, sorry,' he said, getting up. 'Is Sheridan about? Upstairs? I've been trying his buzzer. He should be—'

'Haven't seen him,' she said irritably. 'Heard enough of him, though. Banging about he was, last night, waking the whole street up.' She bustled down the step, forcing Ben backwards. 'Who are you? Jehovah's Witness, is it? Jehovah's *witless*, more like. D'ya hear? *Witless?*'

'What? No, no, I'm . . . sorry. Last night, you said? He was here?'

'Gone one it was. Left a cab running at the door, thumped about upstairs. Woke the cat up. Then ten minutes later, bang, crash, back in the cab and he's off. No consideration for anyone who might have to *work* in the morning.'

This confused Ben rather as the woman was clearly just going out shopping after wolfing down a leisurely custard crème with her elevenses. Perhaps the cat went out to work. He let it go.

'A cab? You don't know where he was going?'

'I don't,' the lady said, stepping out into the sunshine and slamming the door behind her, bustling off down the path, shaking her head and tutting about the modern comprehensive system.

Fuck, Ben thought, and with nothing else to do, found himself staring up at the blank windows again. Coming back late? And then scooting out again?

He wouldn't have . . .

No, Ben thought, shaking off the worry. No, there would be some perfectly good explanation.

But not answering his phone? Or his mobile? And with news potentially this big?

A cloud rolled over the September sun and Ben briefly went a little cold. A thought struck him. They had been very pissed off with each other last night. Could Sheridan have taken their row too seriously and now be in the Margrave hotel with Don Silver signing away their—'

He stabbed the intercom again quickly.

Kenneth Williams groaned.

Nothing.

Ben sighed, chewed the inside of his lip and sat down on his friend's front step. No, don't be ridiculous. He was out. He'd be back soon, that was all.

That was all.

Howard's club was pretty much like Howard himself.

It was based in uptown Manhattan, it was crumbling, old, a fading orange colour, and it made women feel uncomfortable.

Inside it just looked like every gentlemen's club in the world. Past the empty pigeon holes where bored spiders played Celebrity Squares, past the cloakroom with the identical clutch of cashmere overcoats and leather briefcases, elegant leather wing-backed staff wafted and bowed slowly with trays of whisky and port that, if they weren't vintage when they were ordered, certainly were by the time they arrived.

It was 9.30 a.m.

Howard had tucked himself, the young popsy from *Variety* and the second interviewee, Randy Garland, away in one of the dark panelled side rooms, walled with books as dusty and leathery and unread as Howard himself.

Randy Garland was the head of SEBN, the SouthEastern Broadcast Network, a small cable station, broadcasting from their Nashville base down as far as Alabama, out east to Macon, Georgia, Kentucky and Memphis. In his early-fifties, with a handsome and well-worn outdoor face, he had a clean cotton outdoor smell that conjured up hay bales and prairie skies. He was wearing a white Stetson, checked shirt under a smart sportcoat, bootlace tie and polished black boots. Howard had half expected Randy to clamber up on to the back of the chair and whip its wings, riding around the library three or four times to the twang of a banjo, shouting 'Yee-har'.

The 'profile' had been underway for about half an hour. A red leather waiter with brass studs and Queen Anne legs had deposited Howard's bourbon, Randy's beer and Miss Lang's mineral water, and left them to it behind the heavy click of the green double doors.

Diane Paretsky sat, her video-camera on a tripod over her shoulder, Howard's wide head and shoulders filling the frame, biding her time. Face to face at last, this was her big chance. She would let the whisky dwindling from his fat tumbler work its magic, then she'd hit him squarely with her questions.

If the cowboy would just shut up for five minutes, that is.

'Now y'see, young lady,' Randy twanged, 'the success of mah li'l station is down to our ability to do what yur big boys, yur NBOs, yur CBNs, cannot. That's to say, pin-point a precise audience, y'geddit? ABN an' the like are in a ratings war, tryin' to cater for the whole dang' country. Hence their over-reliance on sitcoms and them big-money game shows. Now us cable stations, we allow such luxuries as News channels for those who wanna know *what*, History channels for them that wanna know *when*, Educational channels for those who wanna know *why* – an', o' course, Movie channels for them that likes cars blowin' up an' titties.'

Diane watched Howard roll his watery eyes at this hicksville moron.

'Ah'm proud, in SEBN, to offer what I believe mah viewers really want – that's beer commercials, country music, wholesome girls with leather tassels on their nipples, and occasionally on a good day beer commercials featuring country music sung by wholesome girls with leather tassels on their nipples.'

'Mr Silver, if I may turn to you?' Diane interrupted.

'See, we got this young girl at SEBN does an evenin' cookery show, Carleen's Clam-bake Cook-out,' Randy bouldered on.

103

'Amateur, no fancy college smarts. Daddy runs a liquor store in Batesville.' He leaned forward a little. 'Now that young miss gets more fan-mail than the rest of the station put together. A' course, she does do the whole thang with her little titties out.'

Howard coughed, bourbon spraying from his nose.

'Mr Silver, you were saying?' Diane interrupted again. 'You left home at sixteen to—'

'But with respect to you, Mr Silver – *can ah cahll ya Howie?* – with respect to you, Howie, they ain't none of your Californian plastic jawbs. These are simple homespun southern puppies. Like yo momma mighta had . . .'

'At *sixteen*,' Diane continued, 'to work for NBC.'

'Correct, Miss Lang,' Howard said. He was finding this chuckling cowboy hugely irritating and the image of the cookery-girl not a little disconcerting. He hoped she didn't have a chest like his mother had, considering Howard's mother had spent the last few years of her life tucking her breasts into her knee-socks. 'Television was in its infancy, of course, but I knew –'

'And four years later, you and your brother started your first company, Silver Screen, is that right?'

Howard raised a bushy eyebrow and sent a fat palm over his waistcoat on a cigar-reconnaissance.

'Indeed, Ms Lang. You are well informed, but that's all very much in the past.' He skooched himself forward a little, the leather chair squeaking and farting in complaint. His palms returned from their cigar-search unsuccessfully for debriefing. 'What I want to talk about is the success of Mercury—'

'Silver Screen went bust after dramatic overspending, I believe?'

Howard's jowls quivered. He fixed Diane with a glare, his watery eyes shining. A light profile, she'd said. An overview.

'Real estate debts running into the millions? What happened there Howie? Your brother blow the lot on the Superbowl?'

'Now see, Miz Lang.' Randy took this opportunity to leap in, 'folks have called me exploitative. Old-fashioned. But ah say to them, if folks don't like two milky-white perky young—'

'A number of *regrettable* business decisions,' Howard interrupted firmly, his loud voice bouncing about the high ceiling, playing in the cornices. 'A few unwise investments that ultimately left the venture untenable, that is *all*, Miss Lang. And I resent the implication that—'

'*Regrettable business decisions*? I see. You wouldn't want to make a habit of that,' Diane interrupted briskly. 'However . . .

'Miss Lang, I am not—'

'Coming more up to date for a moment, promoting your son Don to VP of Comedy Development might fall into that category, wouldn't you say? Rumour is he's costing Mercury half a million dollars a week. Any truth in that, Howie?'

'Miss Lang.' Howard swallowed hard, licking his dry lips and attempting an air of off-handed confidence. He was meant to be putting rumour and speculation to rest. 'I have no idea where you've got an insane figure like that.'

'Well, let's pick a week at random,' Diane said loudly, flipping over a page in her notebook. '*Monday the fourteenth of August*, say. Forty-nine thousand dollars at the BMW dealership on Wilshire Boulevard, Beverly Hills. Twelve thousand seven hundred and fifty at Giorgio Armani, Rodeo Drive. Five thousand on something called *discreet personal services* at a place called Madam Heidi's All Night—'

'All right! Now you just wait one moment, young lady . . .'

Oh, she had him rattled now.

'I did *not* come here to discuss the private life of my family. I don't know where you've scraped up these . . . these insane and slanderous numbers, but I have absolutely no comment to make. And with *respect* I think we've strayed from the point.'

'Darned right,' Randy slid in gingerly. 'Let's talk sex-appeal. Mah clambake girl's gawn an' got herself knocked up. Got a belly like a sweaty sow. You think guys wanna see that at seven-thirty every evenin'?'

'Okay okay,' Diane interrupted. 'Let's try this. Family is

clearly important to you both. Mr Garland, you spoke of setting up your first studio with your cousins. Mr Silver, you'd agree in show business it's vital to be surrounded by those you trust?'

'Of course, Miss Lang.'

'Leaving aside your promotion of Donald from the mailroom to VP of Comedy Development, Mercury's CFO, Bernie, is your younger brother, is that right?'

Howard nodded cautiously.

'And on a scale of one to ten, how happy would you say your shareholders are about having their investment looked after by a recovering alcoholic with a gambling addiction? Three? *Two and a half?* I mean, give us a hint here.'

'Ooh, boy,' Randy whistled, slapping his thigh like the flank of a sweaty thoroughbred.

'Miss Lang!' Howard spat, shuddering like an outboard motor. 'That is simply . . . How . . . how dare you . . .'

Diane hid a smile behind her note pad as the camcorder continued to whirr softly, taking in his spluttering red face.

Across town, a recovering alcoholic with a gambling addiction was working on his heart problem.

Bernie didn't have any kind of condition or symptoms, but what he did have was good reason to fear every phone call, every ringing doorbell, every tap on the shoulder, every creak in the night. He lived like a rodent, his heart slamming away at 120 b.m.p. every second of every day.

In the chrome and clatter of a coffee shop, he threw back the last of his latte, pushed away his plate of eggs and shakily lit a cigarette. His basketball team, the New York Knicks, had won the night before – a flukey three pointer in extra time, right on the buzzer. This result put Bernie ahead in a foolishly elaborate spread-bet he had going. If his luck held, he was set to clear a cool three hundred grand, putting him a little closer to clearing his huge debt with the bookies. However, it all rested on the New Jersey Devils hockey team beating the Florida Panthers by more than two points on Friday night.

Bernie gnawed at a thumb-nail. Beyond chain-smoking and twitching, there was nothing he could do now but wait.

The TV set in the corner of the coffee shop was showing a clip from Sunday's *Fyre* – a young Samuel Pepys was swinging from Tower Bridge, grabbing Charles II from the top of St. Paul's as the roof caved in beneath him.

Another four million dollars well spent, Bernie sighed.

He turned his attention to this morning's *Variety*, sitting as it was on the counter, blackening his mood like an unopened medical report.

That goddamn' headline. Would it have killed them to put a positive spin on it? *Mercury streamlines its studio to increase efficiency*, maybe? Or, *Less is more – How Bernie Silver is spearheading a fabulous new initiative to reinvent the television industry?* Was that so much to ask?

Thank Christ the Lamberts weren't residents of Los Angeles, Bernie thought, exhaling slowly. The last thing he needed was his only remaining investor misreading the trades and coming down on him like a ton of shit.

He would have to make sure they didn't see the paper.

And, more importantly, he sighed, flipping open *Variety* and sliding out a greasy fax, that they didn't see *this*.

Bernie shook his head, sucking hard on his cigarette. Jesus, look at it. Howard had forwarded it to him that morning, asking for his opinion. His opinion?

CARPOOL
by
Sheridan McDonald & Ben Busby

It was Don's worst idea yet. Did the dumb kid *want* to get fired? Was that what it was all about? There was no *way* Howard would green-light it. Three guys sitting in traffic? Christ, it had *flop* written all over it.

Bernie sighed, tossed some crumpled bills on to the counter and stubbed his cigarette out in the remains of his eggs. God, it made Wall Street sheep look like *Upstairs* frickin' *Downstairs*.

The kid had blown it. Howard would have no choice, he'd have to let Don go.

Bernie pushed his way out on to the street towards his rusty Buick, slapped with fading bumper stickers from Atlantic City. He clambered in, checking his watch. Howard would be still talking to *Variety*, trying to put a positive spin on things, which meant Bernie had a good couple of hours. He decided to swing by a poker game in New Jersey. With any luck, a decent few hands of Hold 'Em would tide him over until . . .

'*Holy Christ on a Honda!*' Bernie screamed, jumping three feet in the air. Which is neither easy nor advisable when you're sitting in a 1971 Buick Regal. 'Ow! Ow, Jesus, Tommy.' He rubbed his head.

'Shut the door,' said Tommy, his fat frame spilling over the passenger seat.

Bernie slowed his breathing and slammed the car door, the world clunking into sharp silence. Bernie continued to rub his head. It didn't hurt that much but he figured if he played up one wound, Tommy wouldn't feel obliged to furnish him with another.

'Hey, Bernie, howsit goin'?' a voice said from the back seat, sending him jumping again. 'Lucky win for those Knicks last night, huh? You better pray the Panthers don't improved their defence by Saturday.'

'Ow! Vinnie, Jesus, would you stop doing that?' He rubbed his head and adjusted his rear-view. A younger but equally large gentleman sat in the back seat.

'Dad's pissed, Bernie,' Tommy said. 'Normally it'd be him talking to you now but he's a busy man, y'know?' Tommy was staring out of the windscreen at the mid-morning midtown traffic. He seemed even fatter than he'd been at the card game yesterday. Big and round with a profile like a boxing glove. His suit was tailor-made and expensive, yet on Tommy's huge sweaty frame, it hung like a cheap circus tent.

'Now you know,' he continued, 'Dad likes to keep as far away as he can from any . . . unorthodox business practices.'

'Unortho . . . Oh, Tommy, no, c'mon now,' Bernie said, skittering like a trapped bird.

Tommy reached into his jacket.

'Tommy!' Bernie shouted, loud in the cramped interior. His hands flew to the door, flapping and thudding for the release. 'Tommy, Jesus Christ!'

Tommy whipped out that morning's *Variety*, folded tight.

'Relax, Bernie. Christ, you showbiz people are tense.' And he unfurled the familiar front page.

'Shit. I-I can explain,' Bernie said, his mouth dry.

'You told Dad everything was in great shape, Bernie. That things have never looked better. But according to these rumours, they're gonna cancel *E.R. E.R.* . . . *Oh!* That right? That's our syndication money, Bernie.'

'It's dropped a couple of points, ABN are concerned, but I don't think—'

'Relax,' Tommy said. The car interior felt suddenly close and hot. 'We like you. And we like your shows. That *Woodfellas* thing?'

'That was fuckin' funny,' a voice chuckled from the back. 'Burnin' down the forest for insurance . . .'

'Sure. An' the talking goat?'

'Sheep . . .'

'Sure. That nephew of yours, Don, he's got talent. But see, Dad don't like being lied to, Bernie. According to this,' and he waved the paper, 'it looks like you're about to go under and take all our investment with you. See, that's not what you told us.'

'C'mon, fellahs! You're not gonna walk away from us here . . .'

'No. Like I said, we don't do cuttin' our losses, Bernie. We

109

don't believe in notchin' shit up to experience. That ain't our style. But between you an' me, Don's *next* show better be huge, Bernie. And I mean prime-time, Emmys, a hundred episodes, big-fuckin'-bucks.'

Bernie shifted anxiously in his seat, clammy hands trying to close about the fax in his lap surreptitiously.

'What's Donny workin' on now? Paper says he's in London?'

'Now? Oh, uhm . . .'

'That it?' Tommy said, pointing at Bernie's lap. He closed his eyes. Tommy reached over and slid the pages from his hands.

'*Carpool?*'

'What's that?' Vinnie asked from the back.

'It's, uhm, well, it's three guys,' Bernie croaked, 'in a c-car. It's not—'

'Three guys in a car?' Tommy nodded. He gazed out of the window. 'Hey, y'know, that's pretty funny. Cos, hey, we're three guys in a car, right? And ain't we havin' some laughs?'

The car fell silent.

'So,' Tommy said, slapping the pages back at Bernie, 'here's what ya dó. Go talk to the guys at ABN. Tell 'em they'd better buy this show.'

'*This* show?' Bernie squeaked. Oh, Christ. 'No, Tommy, look—'

'This show. I like the sound of it. And we ain't got time to sit around while the whole West Coast takes a fuckin' meetin', y'understand? This show. And no cancellations.'

'Ahem,' Vinnie coughed from the back.

'Oh, an' yeah. When they're pickin' the actors . . . whaddya call it?'

'Casting?'

'Right.' Tommy clicked his fingers. 'Get 'em to give Vinnie here a call. Vinnie's the nephew of one of my father's associates. Wants to be an actor. It'd really help my father out if you could give him a part in the show. He's been sittin' in cars his whole life, he'd be perfect.'

'Look,' Bernie said quickly, 'Tommy, I understand your position. But, see . . .' He looked down at the crumpled pages. 'This really isn't the—'

'ABN. Prime time,' Tommy said, cracking open the door. The blare of horns and roar of traffic suddenly grew loud. 'Oh, an' sign 'em to a hundred episodes off the bat. Just so there's no confusion.'

'Wait—'

'Don't let us down. See ya around, Bernie.' And the two men heaved their massive bulks from the car and waddled through the traffic.

'Oh, c'mon, Howie, level with us here. The headline hits the nail on the head.' And Diane flourished a copy of *Variety* like a chequered flag. '*Exec culling and dollar desperation.* You simply can't afford to sustain anymore of your son's losses, right? That's what these cutbacks are about.'

'We may have made a few moves to . . . to streamline our West Coast departments over the last twenty-four hours, agreed,' Howard blustered. 'But—'

Diane let him tie himself in knots a little.

'But, if you knew anything about business, Miss Lang, you would recognise these as the strategies of an *expanding* studio. A growing studio.' Howard's chest seemed to puff up like a toad's. 'A studio embracing this century boldly, with confidence, with health—'

'Oh, so your shareholders are *happy?*' she suggested playfully. 'Tell us about them for a moment? J. T. Stanley found your investors back in 1990, isn't that correct? Who *are* they exactly, Howard? They've always been a little cagey about coming forward.'

'My CFO deals with—'

'And, more importantly, how much longer are they going to stand by and watch your son snort, bed and crash every penny they've invested? He hasn't had anything approaching a success

111

since *E.R. E.R . . . Oh!* Face it, Howie, the kid couldn't find a hit if you stapled it to his monogrammed socks.'

Howard shifted and shuddered in his seat. He would set this story straight if it was the last thing he did.

'Well, I'm glad you brought up *E.R. E.R . . . Oh!*, Miss Lang,' he said boldly, Bernie's words echoing in his head. 'Very glad.'

Could have fooled me, she thought to herself, watching the old man sweat it.

'In line with Mercury Pictures' increased plans for *expansion*,' he ennunciated, nailing the last word between Diane's eyes with what he hoped was a steely glare, 'you can print that we now retain the highest paid comedian on network television. Gill Kramer, who'll be recording the one hundredth episode of *E.R. E.R . . . Oh!* next month, is on the cover of *Pilot*'s 'Hot 100' issue and hotly tipped for Couple of the Year, will be starting next season on three million dollars a show.'

'Three *million?*'

Howard forced a grin. It was the reporter's turn to look flustered.

'We are a studio, Miss Lang, who invests in our future. Print *that*.'

'But, Jesus, Howie, where's the *money* coming from?' Diane pleaded. 'Every day the coffee shops and restaurants of LA are buzzing with talk of your losses and Don's spending habits. You know he blew three million dollars on a sound-stage for his home so he could tape himself cavorting with call-girls?'

'I—'

'And one point two million moving the second floor of his new house downstairs so he wouldn't have to use the stairs?'

As Howard bluffed and blustered, waving these accusations off, shuddering and splashing whisky about the place, Bernie's words rang in his head.

These rumours are scaring investors. Tell them Mercury's in good shape, tell them we're not worried.

112

'And now a jet to London? Two suites at the Margrave? Is this a tax thing, Mr Silver?'

'It's a *talent thing!*' he roared. 'Miss Lang, playing with video-cameras and buffing your nails might be how you became a journalist.' Breathless, he spun round to face Randy. 'And waving your niece's breasts in front of a bunch of banjo-plucking hicks might pick you up an Emmy down south . . .'

'She's my step-niece,' Randy said.

'But you want to talk to me about my son? I'll have you know, miss, that far from the playboy screw-up your fancy rag has fun slandering once in a while, Don is . . .' Howard swallowed hard, '. . . the most gifted and insightful VP Mercury Pictures have ever had, and I stand by *every* decision he has made for our studio!'

'But still nothing from London? Sounds like he's stalling.'

'*Stalling?*' Howard roared, slamming his glass down on to the side table. 'Well, that shows how much *you* know, Miss Lang.' And he began to root around in the briefcase at his feet. He wouldn't have his business, his *family*, dammit, held up for ridicule by this popsy.

Howard tugged out the slippery fax pages and handed them to Diane triumphantly.

She flicked through, nonplussed.

'*Carpool?*'

'Miss Lang, you are holding there the first page of a show by one of the UK's most *successful* comedy writers,' Howard said firmly, 'commissioned by *my* son, for *my* studio, this very morning. It's gonna knock America's socks off. It's new, it's brave, it's exciting. It's, uhmm, just what it says there.'

'Idiosyn *classic?*' Diane said doubtfully. 'I'm sorry . . . *Zeit-guys?*'

'Right.'

'So you ain't goin' under? Is that what yur sayin'?' Randy added. 'Coz, Ah heard you wuz in trouble. T'be honest, miss, that's what I thought this little pairin' up was about. Out with

113

the old,' he poked a thumb at Howard, 'and in with the new,' he sat back with a wink.

'On the contrary, Howdy-*Doody*,' Howard spat, trembling with indignation, 'we're coming *back*. Bolder, bigger, brighter.'

'And this goes into production . . . ?'

'*Immediately!* he shouted.

Diane's pen flew across the page.

'Uhm . . . y-yes. Yes immediately,' Howard said, worry skittering briefly across his eyes.

Diane craned around and sighed with relief as she saw the camcorder's red light winking away. She had it, she had it all.

There was the tiniest knock.

They all looked up, Howard sweating, angry at the interruption, Randy hoping to order another beer. A waiter wafted Jeevesily in bearing a stiff brown envelope and a fountain pen on a silver tray. Howard signed for the envelope and sent him wafting back out again.

It would be the negatives from Shifty, he thought to himself, breathing deep, trying to slow his heart rate down. Bernie must have called him, piled on the pressure. Howard busied himself, all fat fingers and thumbs, popping the envelope open. He tipped it up and gave it a rattle.

It seemed to be empty.

'Whatcha got there, Howie?' Randy asked, peering over.

Howard gave it a firmer rattle, and a fat wad of glossy photographs came splashing out all over the floor.

'Oh, Jesus,' he said, flustered, heaving himself out of his chair and snatching them up.

'Here,' Randy said, bending over, 'let me—'

'No!' Howard said, grabbing them from him in a panic.

Diane spotted a photograph lying face down under her chair and quickly slid her camera bag over it in the confusion.

'Y'all right there, Howie?' Randy asked. 'You don't look well.'

'Oh, son,' Howard whispered at the trembling images in his fingers, his complexion shocked and pale. 'Oh, son, *no*.'

ELEVEN

In London a few hours later, the clock struck teatime.

The lobby of the Margrave Hotel sat quiet and empty, the majority of its foreign guests still out and about the West End, pissing off eager-to-close shop-assistants by waving travellers cheques and Tower Bridge snow-shakers. The hotel staff sipped tea and stretched their backs, the Concierge looking up from his computer and smiling at the harried young man panting before his desk.

'Sir?'

'Hi, yes,' Ben said, a little out of breath. 'I'm . . . I'm trying to get in contact with a Mr Silver. He mentioned he was staying here? American. Don Silver?'

'Indeed, sir,' the concierge said with a little nod.

Ben collapsed all over the desk in relief, upsetting a pen tidy, a brass bell, and the Concierge somewhat.

A morning of unanswered phone-calls and three hours spent on Sheridan's step feeling his bottom going slowly numb had led Ben to worry that the whole thing might have been a strangely vivid hallucination. Jackie had suggested as much last night when he'd babbled of beach houses and contracts. Maybe he'd imagined the whole thing.

But no, it was real. Silver was here.

'Do you know if Mr Silver has a guest with him? I'm kind of looking for them both. A Sheridan McDonald?'

'I understand he isn't alone at the moment, sir. Let me call his room for you. Your name?'

Ben gave the Concierge his details and explained at far too great a length the events of the night before, during which the Concierge smiled a smile as flat and sugar-free as a supermarket diet cola.

'How marvellous for you, sir. One moment then.' And he dialled the room.

Ben held his breath. This was it.

'Mr Silver, sir? Good afternoon, this is the front desk, I have a visitor here asking for you . . . Apparently you met last night? . . . British, that's right . . .' The Concierge peered over the desk and gave Ben the once over. 'Well, I wouldn't perhaps go as far as to say a "honey", sir . . .'

Ben shifted awkwardly, buttoning his cardigan.

'But . . . yes, sir . . . I'll pass that on sir, apologies for the disturbance.' And he hung up.

'Okay? Can I go up?' Ben said.

'There is no Mr Silver staying at this hotel,' the Concierge said.

'I'm sorry?'

'There is no Mr Silver—'

'But . . . but you were just talking to him?'

'Mr Silver is not staying at this hotel, has no memory of your audition, any undergarments you left behind are now the property of Mercury International Pictures and he asks you to forward any paternity charges to his lawyer. Was there anything else?' the Concierge asked, eyebrows raised.

Ben stood dumbfounded for a moment, head thumping. He looked about the lobby. All was still.

Was this a joke?

'Sir?'

'Look, there's been a misunderstanding. Don Silver —'

'Ah yes, the gentleman who *isn't* staying here,' the Concierge added unhelpfully.

'— is upstairs in his room with a friend of mine,' Ben pleaded. 'I've spent all day . . . look, I need to talk to them both. *Please.*'

'And were they both here, sir, I would be happy to inform them of your request. But sadly . . .' The Concierge shrugged. 'Perhaps you might try another hotel?'

Ben took a deep breath.

'Okay, so which room *isn't* he staying in? Can you tell me that?'

'Mr Silver currently doesn't have two suites with us, sir. And I'm naturally not at liberty to divulge the number of either of them. Might I make a suggestion?'

Ben let out an infuriated sigh.

'You could try phoning the Margrave on Piccadilly and asking to be put through to him directly.'

'But this is . . . you mean, you'll put me through if I phone?'

'*I* won't, sir, no. I've been instructed to inform you he is not residing with us in either of his two suites. But if one of my colleagues should answer the phone, they'd be happy to patch you through.'

'Fine,' Ben said, rummaging for change. 'Are they *likely* to answer the phone?'

'When their shift starts in two hours, sir, yes.'

Ben looked at the Concierge, ran through a quick imaginary fight sequence in his head which involved jamming the brass bell down the man's throat so he let out a polite 'ding' every time he opened his mouth, turned on his heel and stomped out into the warm evening.

'Oh, Jesus. No! Oh, son. Oh, son, no . . .'

A harsh buzzer vibrated through the loft. Diane jabbed her 'pause' button, leaving Howard's flustered face frozen, staring out across her apartment, and jogged to the speaker by the door in her thick socks and baggy sweats.

'Come on up,' she called, taking the door off the latch.

She wandered slowly back to her desk, rattling a pencil between her teeth and staring at the screen.

Interesting. It was all very interesting.

'Well, Scooby Dooby Doo, how the hell are you?' Penny called from the doorway as she squeezed through, armfuls of flat glossy shopping bags hooked and draped over every limb. 'Pheee-yoo-wee!' She held her purchases out like a Fifth Avenue scarecrow. 'You got some ice I can put my Visa card in?'

Penny poured herself a white wine from Diane's monster of a fridge and threw herself on to the sofa with a sigh.

'So how was Howard? You get anything?' she said, bringing flimsy tops sliding out of their tissue paper one by one and holding them all up. 'This I will *never* wear.'

'Plenty,' Diane said. 'I can pretty much confirm that when Howard and Bernie approached J. T. Stanley about starting Mercury Pictures, they were penniless. Absolutely penniless.'

'Like, *what* was I thinking?' Penny said, peering at another absurdly expensive piece of slippery fabric.

'I've been trying to get the details of their shareholders, see if they can shed any light on it, but it's all small-time venture capitalists. No one big enough to kick-start a studio of their size. Or keep it running, for that matter. You know they've upped Kramer's salary?'

'Kramer? I heard he was getting cancelled?' Penny said, peering into a shoe-box.

'Three mill' a show. It doesn't make any sense.'

'Hmmm. Fascinating, Mr Holmes. And what news of young Donald?'

'Hah! Another new high-concept half-hour with cancellation written all over it,' Diane said. '*Carpool*. Written by . . .' she scrabbled for the pages Howard had left her with, '. . . a Sheridan McDonald and Ben Busby. What happened to Melvin Medford is anybody's guess.'

Penny got up, gathering all her bags together like a game of designer Buckaroo.

'Well, Mr Garrison, your magic bullet theory?'

'Not a clue, honey. But I haven't told you the best part,' Diane said excitedly, jogging back to the twin screens on her far wall and staring the old man directly into his frozen eyes. 'I thought I had Howard on the ropes, stuttering and babbling away. But that was *nothing*,' she turned to face Penny, 'compared to what happened when one of the club staff brings him in an envelope full of *these*.' And she slid a glossy photograph from under her paperwork and handed it to Penny.

'Oh, my God!' she said, hand over her mouth. 'Is that? . . . Who is that?'

'The dead guy at the computer? I've no idea,' Diane said. 'Curtains are drawn, it's all dark. Looks like the camera had some kind of night-vision lens, though.'

'And the guy with his back to us? With the baseball bat? Is that Don?'

'Could be,' Diane said. 'It kind of cuts off the top of his head a bit, as you can see. It's not clear. But look here.' And she pointed at a bulky refuse sack bundled up against a bed.

'Jesus, is that an arm? Di, what the hell *is* this? Are there more of them?'

Diane took the photograph back.

'Well, there was no address or stamp so they were hand delivered by . . . whoever.'

'Shook him?'

'Like a dynamite enema. He threw us out of the club and started yelling for the phone, juddering away like he had a runaway pneumatic drill up his ass. Screaming for Shifty Dolawitz.'

'*Dolawitz?*'

The two women stood blinking and pondering and saying hmmm for a few moments, lost in their own conspiracy theories.

Penny broke the silence, cracking the loft door open.

'Anyway,' Diane said, dropping a Dictaphone cassette into

one of Penny's bags. 'Enjoy writing that up. And enjoy your flight.' They exchanged air kisses. 'And hey, thanks for the break. I'm gonna edit this into some kinda shape and then head out tomorrow. See if I can corner Bernie Silver.'

Penny left under her weight of bags and Diane pushed the door closed and leant against it, chewing her pencil. She should definitely take this photograph to the cops for investigation. Definitely.

And she would

Once she'd done some investigation of her own.

Don Silver had never heard the poem – *The year's at the Spring, the day's at the morn, morning's at seven, the hillside's dew-pearled. The lark's on the wing, the snail's on the thorn. God's in his heaven and all's right with the world* – but he was familiar with the sentiment.

In Don's particular case, the rightness of his world had surprisingly little to do with thorns and snails, and perhaps more with two freshly picked-up girls on the bed, coke on the porcelain, do-not-disturb signs on the doors, and a potentially Emmy winning sitcom writer upstairs churning out a hit.

Either way, Don, if not God himself, was in his heaven.

'Hey, honey, watcha doin'?' a female voice wafted in from the bedroom, coy and alluring.

'Be right out, ladies,' he yelled. 'Feel free to start without me.'

It was six o'clock in London. Don stood among the bathroom's dazzling white tile and marble, naked save his Ray-Bans and a tiny white hand towel about his waist. He checked his reflection again, close-up, powdery fingers pawing at the lines and folds. He was looking old. This light didn't help but, shit, were those wrinkles always there?

He rattled about the bottles and jars, grabbing up moisturiser, applying a liberal smear to his hands and hastily pummelling it into his face. Must stay young, he panted under his breath, must look good, must stay young. He'd be home soon. Few more days he'd be smiling triumphantly from every magazine cover on the West Coast. *Vanity Fair, Time, Entertainment Week, Pilot* . . .'

Brrrrriiinnggggg!

All five telephones about the suite burst into life together. Don jumped, slipping barefoot on the wet marble and cracking his head on the basin.

'Jesus! Ow, fuck!' he spat. Not *again.* He wiped his nose quickly and snatched up the receiver. 'Hey, look, pal, I'm not here, okay? Get rid of 'em for me. Tell 'em last night was a blast but I got two fresh young actresses who wanna try their hands at—'

'*Donald? Donald, that you?*'

'Dad?' he said nervously. No matter how old he got, he would always feel nine years old in front of his father. 'Wh-what a surprise,' he squeaked, testicles retracting back to their pre-pubescent location. 'You get the pages? I faxed them—'

'*Jesus, kid, where have you been? I've been tryin' to call you for two days.*' There was the usual echo of long distance.

'I-I've been busy. Working with Melvin, y'know? On the show. How's . . . how's Mom?' he asked, wiping the last powdery smears from the porcelain quickly, as if his father was stomping up the stairs to his bedroom.

'*Working? Working! I'm lookin' at men's rooms, I'm looking at . . . baseball bats, trash-bags . . . holy Christ, boy, what the hell you got us into now?!*'

'Baseball? Dad, what are you—'

'*Get yourself back here. I'm on a cell-phone, I don't want to say too . . . just get yourself on a plane and get back here now.*'

'You . . . you don't like the script?'

Shit! He didn't like the script. Shit, shit, shit. Don closed his eyes.

'*Just get you and your writer the fuck outta Dodge, and your asses back to LA, fast. You got a show to do.*'

121

'You *like* it?'

'Variety *are announcing . . . look, I haven't got time to explain. Just . . . for Chrissakes, keep your nose clean and don't beat up anymore . . . The airport are sending a car. You got an hour.*'

Moments later, Don rapped a tanned knuckle on Melvin's door.

'Mel?' he hollered. No answer. '*Mel?*'

Shit, where the hell could he be now? He was meant to be finishing the script.

There was a muffled click and Melvin's door cracked open six inches. His blank eyes appeared round it.

'I'm working,' he said.

Melvin didn't look like he'd been working. He was out of breath, bony chest heaving under his faded Muppet Show T-shirt. His sallow face shone with sweat. He stood in his socks on a crumpled sheet of paper.

'Well, heads up, buddy, I got good news.' Don grinned and took a little step forward, expecting to be invited in.

'Later,' Melvin said, and his face disappeared, door slamming shut behind them.

Christ, Don thought. Fuckin' writers.

'*Mel!*' And he hammered on the door again. 'Mel, we're leaving. Limo's coming in an hour, y'goddit? An hour? Pack your bags.'

Silence from inside.

'Well, I'll see you in the lobby. And take a shower, for Chrissakes.' Don hurried back down the plush corridor to the lift, buckling his belt and buttoning a shirt.

A sudden 'crack' behind him. He spun around.

Mel's head poked around the door.

'Going?' he said, stumbling out into the corridor like some blinking nocturnal mammal.

'Good news, buddy. Just spoke to Dad. He wants to green-light it. *Carpool*, by Melvin Medford, produced by Don Silver. Announced it to *Variety* already. So come on, our work here is done.' And he clapped twice, excitedly, walking backwards. 'Let's hustle. Downstairs in an hour.'

'Now?'

'What's the matter? You did it. *We* did it. Home and dry.' He reached the lift and pressed the button. The doors rolled open. 'See you downstairs at seven.'

'*The Margrave Hotel, good evening.*'

'Yes, hi,' Ben said. 'Do you have a Donald Silver . . . Don Silver . . . staying with you at the moment? *Please?*' His heart thundered.

'*One moment, sir.*' There was an aching silence. Ben's head crowded and shoved. '*Hello? Yes, sir, we do.*'

He allowed himself to breathe out, resting his forehead against the cold metal of the platform payphone. He was on his way back home. There was no way he could have sat in the hotel lobby for two hours, not in his state. Pacing, anxious, twittery. He was heading home, to wait until the Concierge had definitely finished his shift and then to try the hotel again. Speak to Don, speak to Sheridan. Find out what the hell was going on.

But he hadn't managed it.

The twisting nerves, sickening hollow fear in his guts, had grabbed him, yanked him, thrown him stumbling and lurching off the underground train on to the platform to find a phone. He was only three stops from home but he couldn't wait a second longer.

'*Although he is checking out today, sir.*'

'What?' Ben felt queasy.

'*Just informed us. I have down here that a car is picking them up in about forty minutes, sir.*'

'Them?' The receiver was suddenly cold in Ben's hand, his hair bristling.

'*Two female companions. And an Englishman, I understand. A writer.*'

'No.'

'Limousine's taking them to Heathrow, I understand, sir.'

Feet were crackling across the paper carpet. Sheridan looked up, eyes sore from the glowing screen in the dusty half-light. A laden silver tray was carried across the room, rattling and clinking as it was placed next to the laptop on the dressing table.

Bottles. Pill bottles. Orange glass, white plastic. About a dozen. Sheridan watched, his hands frozen and clammy on the damp keys as a bottle was lifted, examined.

The cap was clicked.

A palmful of white tablets rattled into a greasy palm. Sheridan struggled, wincing and straining against the bindings as filthy fingers reached towards his face, scrabbling at the soggy towelling belt in his mouth, yanking it out sharply.

Sheridan coughed, slivers of cotton caught in his throat, then swallowed, gasped huge desperate breaths, tasting a hundred air-fresheners stinging and acrid on his tongue. Jasmine Mists fought Honeysuckle Glades fighting White Flower Forests, the air was dry and chemical.

A hand grabbed him by the hair at the back, yanking his head hard. His dry throat croaked, and then gagged as the palmful of pills was shoved and stuffed into his mouth.

'Drink,' he was told, a fat tumbler of water raised to his lips. The Margrave paper doiley was still stuck to its base.

'No . . . no, *please* . . .' Sheridan croaked. The pills rattled against his teeth.

'They won't hurt you.' The glass was pushed up to his mouth.

Sweating, sore and scared, he drank.

Ten minutes later, the dusty speaker crackled.

'Hello,' Ben said. 'It's me again, sorry. Can I have a word?'

'You that Jehovah's Witless again? Hear what I said — Witless?'

'I-I . . . sorry, can I have a word? It's important.'

Trembling with rage, he let the buzzer click off and stood with his nose inches from Sheridan's peeling front door. His head reeled and stang with anger. He hadn't time to make it back to the hotel. He had to know. He wasn't going until he knew.

There was a bustle behind the door and the neighbour clicked it open.

'He hasn't been back, I don't know what you—'

But Ben pushed past her in a flurry and into the hall, grabbing at the handle of Sheridan's inner door, rattling and tugging at it. He had to know.

'Good Lord!' the woman cried. 'What do you think you're doing?'

It was locked. But still he had to know.

He stepped back and took a deep breath, placing his clammy palms on the walls to either side of him.

'Oh, no, you don't,' the woman said quickly.

'I'm sorry,' Ben said, pausing, his knee raised up somewhere near his chin. 'I'll pay for it. But I have to know.'

And he promptly kicked the door open.

'I'm calling the police!' the woman shrieked behind him as Ben pushed through the splintered Ryvita of lock and handle, thundering up the stairs.

'Sheridan!' he yelled breathlessly, darting in and out of each room. '*Sheridan!*'

But of course there was no answer.

There was no Sheridan.

And after fifteen minutes of maddeningly closer inspection, Ben ascertained there was also no fucking yellow exercise book.

In the marble lobby of the Margrave Hotel there was a great deal of excited squealing. Some fat Arabic moustaches with small men behind them were steering children out into taxis. A cluster of American kids sprawled and chewed all over the sofas, and a pair of nineteen-year-old blonde twins laughed and clapped.

'We'll just pick up your passports on the way.' Don smirked coolly behind his sunglasses. 'I hate to fly without a little,' and he peered over his shades at the matching curves, 'in-flight entertainment. You been in a private jet before?'

'Sir?' the limo driver interrupted with a polite cough, gloved hands behind his back. 'Do the ladies have any baggage?'

'Yeah, yeah, we're gonna go pick up their passports on the way to the airport,' Don said, slipping an arm about the girls' waists and following him out. A preposterously long black car purred at the kerb, taking up three taxi spaces. 'Climb on in, girls. Give Jeeves here your address.' Don checked his watch. 'I'll see what's happened to Mel. *Mel?*' he called, pushing back into the lobby.

The lift door dinged open and Melvin appeared, a bulging green holdall over one shoulder, a pale chubby young man in dark glasses over the other.

'Fuck,' Ben said, checking the hooks on the back of Sheridan's bedroom door. 'No rucksack.'

They struggled out of the lift, Melvin puffing and straining, his companion woozy and limp, legs wobbling beneath him.

'Who the fuck's this?' Don said.

'Th-this is a friend of mine,' Melvin said. His friend dribbled a little and lurched forward. Don held out his hands to catch him, getting a little vomit on them from the lad's shirt front. His chin was spotted with blood.

'Fuck,' Ben said again, slamming around in Sheridan's bathroom. 'And no shaving kit.'

'*Wh-where . . .*' he mumbled, sunglasses slipping down his nose.

'Coked up to his eyeballs,' Melvin said, sliding the spectacles back on. 'He's an actor. Been partying upstairs from us for three days. Just got a callback from Paramount. Hasn't slept, hasn't eaten. Found him wandering around. He's a wreck.'

'Looks like it,' Don said, shaking his head. The guy was out of it, big-time.

Don was of course, used to this sort of thing. The sort of depraved, disgusting, perverted sights that would send most regular people rushing to the bathroom with their hand over their mouth, or alternatively rushing to the Basildon Bond with a fountain pen and the address of the *Daily Telegraph*, left Don cold. Whereas most people would think a party had got totally out of hand if some red wine got on the sofa-covers and the dog ate a pink Pie-Piece wedge from Trivial Pursuit, so as far as Don was concerned the evening simply wouldn't have started. Not unless a film director's Lambourghini had also ended up upside down in a bowl of humous and everyone was naked and dipping their cheese and pineapple sticks into the orifices of a Playboy bunny called Candice.

So the sight in front of him that evening, while it drew disapproving tuts from the Concierge, didn't bother him unduly.

The two of them helped a stumbling Sheridan across the polished floor to the doors. Melvin handed a rucksack to the limo driver. 'Oh, careful with that,' he said.

'Bastard.' Ben said, staring at the blank desktop in Sheridan's lounge. 'And no laptop.'

'He's gone and missed his flight. He has to be at the Four Seasons Beverly Hills in twelve hours' time. Is there gonna be room . . .'

'*Wh-uhh . . .*' the young man said, the rush of street air hitting him.

'. . . on the jet?'

'Oh, Donnie?' two female voices purred from within the limo. 'These seats fold flat . . .'

Don grinned.

'Sure, sure, if the kid can party, he's welcome aboard.' He helped the stoned young man stumble into the car. 'He got his passport?'

'Shit,' said Ben, slamming the desk drawer in Sheridan's little flat.

MERCURY HIT GREEN ON BRIT GRIDLOCK GAGFEST

Continued from page 6

& Ben Busby.

This new high-concept half-hour, provisionally titled CARPOOL, set in gridlocked traffic, certainly has uniqueness on its side and what CEO Howard Silver called an "*off-beat timelessness. Instantly idiosynclassic.*"

Watch this space to see if networks will be as excited about this kooky car-com as Mercury clearly are.

The Heat Is On

Howard Silver was also keen to talk up FYRE, which he promised would come bouncing back from its critical crucifixion with fiercer flames, bigger bangs and a scorching series send-off.

All Checked Out

And of course E.R. E.R. . . . OH! As the show nears its valuable 100th episode, Howard was quick to dismiss yesterday's rumours of cancellations, announcing a huge unexpected pay rise for Gill Kramer.

However, unnamed sources at ABN say it's time to turn off the life-support and tie a toe-tag on the medical-mirth maker.

Full interview pages 35–36

Variety
Wednesday 27 September

A fat sun hauled itself through the smog, picked grit from its teeth, wiped its brow and Wednesday morning came to Los Angeles.

Mercury Pictures, Burbank — a low sprawl of studios, pink production bungalows, tarmac and golf buggies on a handful of palm-treed acres — was bustling with life. On studio 6, dozens of technicians were touching up seventeenth-century London's fibreglass cobbles, so come the afternoon and the call of 'action', Samuel Pepys would be able to deliver his line ('If you can't stand the heat, motherfucker . . .) and punch a baker through a sugar-glass window.

While on the cold floor of studio 3, at a long trestle table littered with stale doughnuts and chewed pencils, Gill Kramer was having his Wednesday morning tantrum.

'Oh, for heaven's sake, people, what the hell kind of line is that?!' he yelled, banging his fist hard on the tabletop, sending coffee splashing over scripts. There was a sudden flurry of elbows and cloths and oh-for-Christ's-saking.

Rob Coupland, the episode director at the had of the table, piped up, 'Is there . . . *another* problem?' He sighed. Rob was a short, rather intense bearded man in squeaky trainers and a chunky jumper. Short because his father was short, bearded because he thought it gave him something of the Spielberg about him, and intense because Gill Kramer shouted at him for nine hours a day plus lunch breaks.

'*Knick-Nack Paddy Whack, give the dog a bone?*' Gill read slowly. 'I'm sorry – *a bone?*' He rattled the script high in the air like he imagined a great orator might.

The rest of the cast and crew began to cough and shuffle and find hundreds of other things to look at.

'Gill, *Gill*,' Rob said through a chewed pencil, 'it's just a line. We'll take another run at it in the next draft, but time's ticking on so . . .'

'It's *nonsense*,' he snapped. 'My character would never *say* such a thing. In fact, the whole episode premise is ridiculous, just ridiculous.' He slapped the script to the table. 'Are you *really* expecting the American people to believe that Farmer McDonald would send a sheepdog across Chicago? For a *penis?*'

The studio went even quieter, the only sound now that of two dozen cast and crew members staring at their fingernails.

'McDonald *loves* that dog,' Gill exclaimed. 'He's had it since he was on the farm.'

'Gill,' Rob said, 'it's Wednesday. We go live on Fri—'

'Don't you remember, everybody? Season two, that lovely moment with the two of them? When McDonald has donated his own kidney to the poor orphan? And the orphan is trying to wake me after the operation? And I'm lying there . . .' Gill went all syrupy suddenly, wiping away a non-existent tear. Two dozen baseball caps were tugged over eyes. They all remembered, Gill having brought it up at every reading for the last two years.

'And your dog licks your face and you wake up?' Rob nodded quickly. 'We remember, we remember.'

'Emmy nomination! *Rrrright* there!' Gill slammed the table once again, spilling all the coffee he'd managed to miss spilling the first time. 'It was real! It was tragic! Touching! *That's* what the show needs.'

'But Gill, Gill,' Rob attempted to explain, 'we have that here.

Picture the scene. There's the gridlock, the ambulance won't get through. It's an emergency. You've got that great *tension*.' He hunched down at Gill's side, fists clenched. 'The dog's their last hope. He's *gotta* get through.'

'But, a *penis?*' Gill winced like a Victorian schoolmistress. 'It's cheap. Smutty, frat-house farce. Mr and Mrs America don't need *penises* shoved down their throats at eight p.m. on a Friday night.'

There was a muffled chuckle from the writers' seats that turned quickly into a coughing fit.

'But it's upbeat, it's light,' Rob said gingerly.

'Uhhh!' Gill moaned with exasperation. 'It's blinkered thinking like that that's *got* us into this hole! We're not challenging the viewer. We're not opening our hearts, baring our wounds, our souls!'

He stood, scraping his chair. He closed his eyes and cleared his throat which signalled the arrival of his character's thick, appallingly unconvincing Oirish accent.

About the table, scripts trembled in white-knuckled fists, coffee-cups froze halfway to mouths. Rob clenched his eyes tight shut, his buttocks likewise. This was going to be bad.

'*Ah, to be sure? Or not to be sure? Ain't that the question, to be sure?*'

Silence. Somebody coughed.

Gill opened his eyes. Scripts were held over faces. Shoulders vibrated with suppressed laughter.

'Jesus Christ, people!' he exploded. 'Don't you know what's going on here? They're letting us die!' And he snatched up that morning's *Variety* in a clenched fist. '"*Time to turn off the life support and tie a toe-tag on the medical-mirth maker?*" Unless we turn this show around we're finished!'

Newer crew members began to stand up; others, more used to these scenes, covered their heads against flying debris.

'I will not let my career be destroyed by . . . by *him*,' Gill raged, writhing about inside his jacket, tugging out a buckled magazine, defaced and scrawled on. 'Look at him! He's laughing at us!' And he slapped the *Pilot* 'Hot 100' edition to the table, the bearded wink of Dr Trent smirking out at everyone.

Nobody looked at it, principally because everyone had seen it already. It fluttered on every newsstand across the city. Most of the cast and crew were sitting on their copies as he spoke. Gill Kramer, pushed out to the number two spot. Dr Dick Trent, his arch ratings rival, voted most popular man on television.

'You think smutty innuendo will save us? Barnyards and bedpans? Chickens and charts?' Gill began tearing off pages of his script, tossing them into the air. 'We're finished, y'hear? Finished! I ask for new writers, new blood, fresh ideas, but no! Bernie Silver's too busy firing staff, cutting back costs. Well, we're next!'

'It's rumours, Gill, just rumours,' Rob soothed. 'If they were pulling the plug, wouldn't they send some network exec to let us know? Wouldn't Al Rosen be here? Wouldn't he?'

Al Rosen peeled off Alemeda Boulevard and bumped on to the Mercury lot.

Mickey, the waddling security guard on the main gate, gave him a little salute, raised the barrier and Al rolled his green Lexus through, parked in the visitors' carpark and hurried, *Variety* clenched in one sweaty hand, across the shady lot.

'When you say he's not here,' Al addressed Trixi in the peach-coloured front office moments later, 'do you mean not *in his office*? Or, *not on the lot*? I thought he was back from London this morning?'

'He is, sir, yes, but . . . sorry, one moment, please.' And she snatched up her ringing phone and punched the light.

'Don Silver's office,' she said briskly. 'No, Mr Tomlin, he's still not . . . some time this morning, sir . . .'

Red lights blinked on the telephone.

'Thank you.' She punched the next light. 'Don Silver's off— no, sir, we expect him any . . . CBN, I have it, thank you . . . Don Silver's office . . . ?'

Al stood fuming as Trixi jabbed her buttons and repeated the same message to every network executive on the west coast. He'd bothered to show up in person and a lot of good it had done him.

Al Rosen, a trim forty-five year old in a faded *Office Politics* baseball cap, was the Senior Vice President of Comedy at ABN, which meant he decided whether or not they were going to buy and air Don Silver's shows. The baseball cap was a favourite, a memento from the first show he'd bought from Don all those years ago, and he was never without it — the down side of this being that everyone presumed Al was losing his hair, a problem redoubled by his moustache which seemed like so much over-compensation. But Al wore his cap anyway, as a reminder of his beginnings.

And, of course, because he was losing his hair.

'. . . you and everyone else sir, *Variety* broke the story this morning, I can't be anymore . . . yes, Mr Schreiber, HBN, I'll be sure to pass that on.' And Trixi snapped the next call on hold. 'Where *is* he?' she yelled across the office. 'Has he landed yet? It's crazy.' But no one paid much attention. Mostly because, thanks to Bernie's round of firings, everyone was at home wiring their parents for more money and scouring the want ads.

'Wait — HBN?' Al spluttered, butting in quickly. 'You're talking to HBN? About what? About this?' And he held up that morning's paper. 'Oh, lordy, I *really* need to see Mr Silver . . .'

He looked again at the sweaty crumpled *Variety* in his hands.

MERCURY HIT GREEN ON SILVER GRIDLOCK GAGFEST.

The industry was going crazy.

He had heard young men in suits chattering about it in Starbucks when he'd picked up his morning iced coffee. He'd heard snatches of conversation on car phones as convertibles had purred past him on Santa Monica Boulevard. It seemed every network executive had woken up to the pitch in the paper and was clamouring for the first look at this car-based comedy.

So innovative! NBO must have first refusal . . . So daring! CBN must have first refusal!

Of course, deep down, lurking below their ulcers and decaffaccinos, they all – Bill Tomlin at WN, Connie Smith at CBN, Mickey Schrieber at HBN, and the rest – had massive doubts. Three men in a stationary car was, after all, a fairly thin premise. But then anticipating which fairly thin premise America would take to its heart next season was a network executive's job.

A job one didn't get very far in by letting *other* network executives nab first refusal of the latest thin premise.

'Sweetheart,' Al said, leaping in between calls, 'it's very urgent that Don speaks to me first. We have a relationsh—'

'Hello, Don Silver's office?' Trixi punched the line open when suddenly Gill Kramer smashed through the double doors of the office in a big flounce, a black mood and a salmon pink silk dressing gown.

'I must see Donald Silver!' he trumpeted. 'The standard of . . . Al?' He stopped suddenly. 'What are *you* doing here? Ohmigod, this is about me missing the *Pilot* cover! I was number two. I was still number two! Don't cancel me!' Gill's eyes popped and his hand went hurtling over his mouth. 'You're cancelling me! You can't!'

'Mr Kramer, really, it's fine. You have nothing to worry about,' Al reassured him, waving his hands.

'I keep telling everyone, fewer jokes, fewer laughs. America wants to see Farmer McDonald's soul, understand the suffering, the pain. Behind the dungarees and the blacked-out teeth—'

'Mr Kramer, please, please, relax. Look, let's . . .' Al steered him towards Don's empty office. '*Two minutes,*' he mouthed to Trixi, cracking open the door and pushing Gill through.

He followed him in and closed the door behind them.

*

'What can I say, Gill? It's all above my head.'

'So it's true?'

'It's just . . . well, the network heads feel——'

'You swine! You backstabbing, weak-willed snake! You . . . you . . .'

'Coochybuns!' And Al flew forward, dropping to his knees at Gill's side.

'*Keep your voice down!*' Gill hissed, pulling away, wrapping his robe tighter. 'Above your head? *Above your head?* You're ABN's Senior Vice President of Comedy, for heaven's sake! Cancelled?!' He huffed and sobbed on the chaise-longue. 'I don't believe it . . .'

'It's just, what with Shrink's ratings, the *Pilot* cover . . .'

Gill pushed him aside and got up.

'I always thought having a boyfriend on the inside would make things *easier*,' he hissed. 'But you're not even lifting a finger to stop them ruining me. *Oh, it's all above my head.* You could pull strings, talk up my ideas, give me a little support here.'

'Oh. Oh, I see,' Al said, sniffing and pouting for a moment. 'So that's what I am to you, is it? A man on the inside? After nearly ten years? Just your paid lackey?'

'Oh, don't be such a drama queen. I just meant that you of all people should be on my side about this. But no. Far be it from you to raise your voice at the network. If they want to cut me off then that's just fine by you, right? Look at you, you're pathetic with that ridiculous cap. Take it off. Everyone will think you're losing your hair.'

Al pinked, fussing with his hat.

'I am on your side, sweetheart. Don't be beastly, you know I am.'

'Pah! The moment I mention my story ideas, you yawn and roll over and start talking about an early start.'

'Gillikins, it's nothing *personal*, sweetheart,' Al said. 'The network just doesn't think . . .'

'You have to talk to them, Al, you have to talk to them.' Gill began pacing back and forth, gown flapping behind him. 'Elaine and I are tipped to be Celebrity Couple of the Year again. We're the most popular twosome in the world, they *can't* cancel me! America *loves* us! We get invited to fund-raisers, premiers, parties. She's got her talk-show, I've got the sitcom, we're the *American dream!*'

'Look,' Al said, 'relax. You've got the *Pilot* party tonight. You've been looking forward to that for weeks.'

'Party! I'm number two! Number *two! I* can't have a party!'

'Just shift the angle. Make it a . . . a *still here* party. A *can't-keep-a-good-man-down* party. A *who-cares-that-I'm-cancelled-let's-boogie* party. Show the world!'

'You think I'm old,' Gill muttered. 'You think I'm tired. You think it's time to put me out to pasture, time to forget me.'

'That's not true, coochybuns! I'm here, aren't I?'

'For *Carpool*,' Gill snarled. 'I listen to coffeeshop gossip too, you know, *coochybuns*. It's out with the old, in with the new, eh? Move over Gillykins, there's a hot new pitch in town? Well, fine.' And he stormed to the door. He turned, thunder rolling across his face. 'The party's still on, *Al*,' he sniped. 'But I don't want to see *you* there.'

Gill stood at the door, trembling.

'I'm not finished *yet*. I'll show this town. I'll show you all!' And he flounced into the hallway and was gone.

THIRTEEN

It was 3.30 in London, and an exhausted Jackie was on the roof of her office, smoking furiously. Because for once in her life she needed advice – craved advice – and her beloved magazines had let her down.

She didn't need much. She wasn't asking for a voucher she could cut out of *Marie Claire* that got her two fifty-minute counselling sessions for the price of one. She wasn't asking for three trial Valium, even if they came in their own laminated moc-croc dispenser with *Elle* printed neatly up the side in gold foil – which, let's face it, they probably would.

Just some advice would do, something to stop her feeling so mixed up and lost and confused. A general two-thousand-word feature on difficult boyfriends maybe. Or perhaps a helpful exposé on other women whose partners had taken the term 'trial separation' to mean that they could sod off to the USA with the joint credit-card. Even one of those fatuous quizzes wouldn't hurt.

Boyfriend sitting on his arse all day, trying to be all 'creative'? More interested in being with his best mate than with you? Off chasing a pipe dream of fame and fortune? Answer the questions below and check your score to see if you should forgive 'im or forget 'im!

But no. Jackie had skulked in her pod all morning, sipping Diet Coke, telephone unplugged, flipping with exhausted fingers through every glossy problem under the sun apart from hers.

She was going to have to deal with this alone.

The phone had rung at her mother's last night at around nine o'clock. She'd known it would be Ben even before she'd heard her mother's muttered advice from the hallway; '*It's him. Don't let him bully you into coming back if you don't want to.*'

The conversation hadn't gone as Jackie had planned. There was little audible heartache from Ben's end, very few tearful regrets. In fact Jackie's pointed sighs and long silences were almost entirely wasted as he jabbered frantically over the top of them like a madman. *Sheridan's gone. Don Silver! Sheridan's gone! Phoned the hotel! Limos to the airport! Sheridan's gone! Our script! The bastard!* On and on.

Jackie had closed her eyes. Hadn't what she'd said the night before meant anything? That she couldn't do this anymore? That she needed time away from all of Ben and Sheridan's crap? That she needed a more ordinary life?

She'd clenched her teeth so hard, eyes screwed up so tight, head pounding so loud, she'd almost missed the reason for Ben's call, which apparently wasn't because he wanted her back.

'Wait, wait, wait,' she said quickly. 'Back up. What are you talking about? You're going *where?*'

As Jackie smoked her cigarette, back in the Finchley flat Ben slammed about with fists full of clothes and a folding chair, struggling into the bedroom with it, clanging it against the radiator.

'*I'm takin' a whole bunch of you British guys back home — really shake things up.*' The American's voice filled his head.

Ben unfolded the chair and stood on it, yanking open a high cupboard and tugging out a small rucksack, crackly and coated with dust. Jackie hadn't really understood last night. She'd wanted to talk about them. Their future. Their problems. But Ben couldn't. Not now, not while his head raged and fizzed and whirled with the American's voice.

'With any luck he'll be flyin' out within the hour.'

And anyway, didn't she understand that this *was* for them? Tailback wasn't *changing* the subject, it *was* the subject. It was about Ben doing what he had to do.

She'd hoped a good night's sleep would have calmed him down, helped him put things in perspective.

And it had. In a way.

He punched and jammed socks and pants into his bag, cursing at the zips, running through what he would need. He moved quickly into the lounge and yanked at drawers and pulled at loose cupboards in the sideboard. It was in here somewhere.

'Jackie?' a voice came from the fire escape behind her, making her jump. She turned. 'Someone in reception for you.'

Jackie slid slowly from the aluminium air-conditioning cube, took a last drag of her cigarette and ducked back inside. It would be Ben. Full of apologies and hugs. Of course he wasn't leaving. He'd been being stupid, thoughtless. He was sorry. He would try harder from now on. Get a job in a bank. Be more dependable, more reliable.

The lift doors rolled open and she climbed in.

Sheridan would have turned up too. She allowed herself a smile.

'And how will you be paying, sir?'

'Huh? Oh, uhmm, VISA.'

The phone still wedged under his chin, Ben paced the tiny lounge, bulging rucksack on the table, hands clammy, heart slamming away.

'So that's a one-way to Los Angeles LAX, departing from Heathrow at 19.30 today. Non-smoking . . .'

Jackie would understand, Ben thought quickly. She knew

how important this was. She would understand.

'Can I take your credit card details, sir?'

In his Los Angeles office, Shifty Dolawitz gazed at the face in the glossy 10×8″ photograph. It was of a young actor, Zachary Black. Shifty guessed late-twenties, although his resumé said *early*. Brooding, lip slightly curled, hair slightly tousled, he frankly looked rather pissed off but Shifty presumed he was, like all aspiring actors, going for mysterious and/or tortured, and failing at both.

His phone began to jangle.

Thankful for a reason to postpone wading through the prom-dress padding of Zachary's flimsy CV, Shifty reached through the maze of silver photo frames on his expansive desktop and snatched up the phone.

'Okay, before we start,' a gruff voice said quickly, *'I don't want a goddarned word from you, y'hear me? Not a goddarned word.'*

'Heyy! That *you*, Big H?' Shifty sang, leaning back in his chair. He smiled, gazing out of his window into the Los Angeles sunshine. 'How *are* you? I saw that frightful hack-attack in *Variety* yesterday. "Exec-culling" indeed. I'm embarrassed. What's happened to the art of journalism? Where's the pun? They couldn'ta gone with "crew cut"? Something like that? No pride in the job anymore, Howie, no—'

'Enough, Dolawitz,' he barked. *'Button it and keep it buttoned for one goddamned minute.'*

'Why, pumpkin, you seem vexed?'

'Look, I'll cut to the credit-roll here, Dolawitz, because I guess you're a busy man. You probably got the President's daughter tied up in your garage and some shots of the British Prime Minister with a goat you gotta pick up from the twenty-four-hour photomart.'

'I'm sorry, a *goat?*' Shifty said, bewildered. 'Howie, sweetheart, I think you may have your speed-dials in a muddle. This is Shifty. If you wanted kinky barnyard phonelines, you've called the wrong—'

'*Kiss my ass, Dolawitz!*'

'Well, unless you've been on that treadmill of yours, that's a job that's gonna mean me clearing a window for three or four days, Howie, and like you say, I'm a busy bee. But I *mean* it, are you okay, Big H? You want maybe a fruit basket?'

'*Listen to me,*' Howard whispered. '*I got your package yesterday, okay? Delivered straight to the club while I was talking with* Variety. Variety, *for Chrissakes!*'

'Package?'

'*We had a deal. Instead I get more blackmail shots? This photo shit is no way to do business, you hear me? No way to do business. Girls in hotel rooms? Bodies in trash-bags? What the hell's the matter with you huh?*'

'Howard, Howard, just stop your stallions there a minute. Blackmail? What in hell are you getting your Calvins in a bunch over now? Blackmail? Oh, puh-*leese*. I called you Monday to discuss my client's salary. Standard renegotiation, that's all? There's nothing—'

'*Don't talk to me about standards!*' Howard yelled. '*I'll say it once and that's it, you hear me? I want the shots of Don and these drugs destroyed. I want these shots of the girls destroyed. The bats, the bodies, the blood, everything. Get me the negatives by the end of the day and I'll give Gill an extra hundred thou'. It's all I got.*'

'Extra hundred thou'?'

'*Okay, two hundred. But that's it. I need your goddamn' word that it stops and it stops right now, you hear me?*'

Shifty began to laugh.

'*DOLAWITZ!*' Howard yelled.

'Oh, I hear you, Howard, I hear you,' he chuckled. 'But no deal, I'm sorry. No deal.'

There was a violent explosion at the other end of the line. Howard clearly wasn't happy.

'Howard, pumpkin! For goodness' sake, hon, you'll give yourself a coronary!' Shifty soothed. He could hear the old man spluttering and coughing at the other end. 'Go lie down, play

142

golf, have a smoothie. There's no *deal*, dear man, because there are no photographs.'

'*Don't push it, Dolawitz. You think you're safe over there in La-La-Land, huh? I'm gettin' on a plane. I'm getting on a goddamned plane and, I swear, I'll be tearing ten percent out of your flabby little—*'

'I MEAN IT!' Shifty yelled. 'I have *no idea* what you're talking about! Ropes? Trash-bags?'

It went very quiet at the other end.

'Believe me, Howard,' Shifty jabbered quickly, 'not a clue. I mean, do you know what ten percent of two hundred thou' a show *is*? Nearly half a million a year. If I had pictures worth half of that, I'd walk 'em over to New York myself. I got *nothing*, you hear me?'

Shifty listened to Howard's raspy breathing.

'*You asked me if I got the brown envelope? You said it Monday, did I get the—*'

'Brown?' Shifty said. 'I never said brown, Howard dear. All our stationery is mint green. Mint green envelopes, paper contracts. Classy, y'know? Brown envelopes are *nothing* to do with me.'

'*Wait a minute . . . you swear?*'

'On my mother's condo. What's the matter, Howie? What you got yourself mixed up in? Howie. *Howie?* Howie, you *there?*'

Shifty sighed and hung up. What a start to the morning. He turned his attention back to Zachary Black's letter.

'*I am working as a bell-boy in West Hollywood at the moment, but what I really want to do is direct . . .*'

'Lunch!' Shifty cried, tossing the paper on to the desk and tripping out of his office.

It was 11.30 a.m. in New York. The fat September sun hung high over the city, dazzling the shoppers, winking off the cabs and sending a cheery glow through a certain Fifth Avenue office.

'Chill out, Al, chill out,' Bernie said, cell-phone cradled under his chin, jotting on Howard's blotter. 'Of course you're our first choice for the show . . . well, naturally everyone's interested . . . don't worry, Don will be in touch . . . any minute, absolutely. Thanks, Al.' And Bernie hung up. 'Jesus, who'd have thought it? No one's seen the script of this piece of traffic-jam crapola, no one's heard a joke, and still they're nipping at our ankles. Trixi says her phone hasn't stopped since seven-thirty.' He turned to Howard who was staring at the phone on his desk. 'Howie? This is great news. This is . . . hey, Howie, you okay? What did Shifty say?'

Howard, his grey sweat-suit blotted with dark patches, said nothing. He just breathed deeply and slowly, his memory reaching back to Monday lunchtime. Second post.

'Howie?'

'Shit,' he said, heaving himself up and waddling around to the side of the desk. He puffed down on to his knees and peered underneath. 'Aww, shit,' he said again, liver-spotted hands clawing at an envelope that had fallen out of sight. A mint green envelope.

'Whatcha got there?'

Howard struggled to his feet, tearing at the envelope, a sick feeling spreading about his insides.

'Shit. A standard contract renegotiation.'

'*What?*'

The intercom buzzed.

'*Mr Silver, a gentleman here to see you.*'

'I said, no interruptions, Caroline.'

'*Sorry, sir, he says it's very urgent. That he has a business proposition.*'

'Networks,' Bernie said. 'Gotta love 'em . . .'

'*About some photographs?*' Caroline interrupted.

The room went suddenly cold. The two men glared at each other, ashen-faced, like burglars at the sound of a key in a lock. Bernie shrugged, wide-eyed. Howard's fat finger paused over the intercom before he swallowed deep and punched it hard.

'Send him in,' he said, and patted his brow with the towel slung about his fat neck.

An excruciating pause, a click, and the double-doors to Howard's office swung open.

'Holy shit,' Howard said, clutching the desk for support. 'You gotta be kidding me. You?'

'Good morning, Don Silver's office?'

'*Trixi, it's me. What the hell's goin' on? I've been trying to get through for ten minutes.*'

'Mr Silver, at last!' she cried. 'Sorry, sir, the phones have been going crazy all morning. Have you seen the paper?'

'*Not yet,*' he crackled. '*Listen to me, get another limo over to the airport. Melvin's standing on the freakin' sidewalk, puke down his pants, twitching like he's on hot coals.*'

'Another car? I thought . . . is he not with . . .'

'*Don't think, Trixi, just fix it. I got a couple of . . . companions with me here.*' And there was a muffled giggle over the car-phone. '*We've taken the limo. Send another one for Melvin pronto, y'got that?*'

'Sir.'

'*Oh, plus he's got a guy with him. Some actor from our hotel. Make sure the limo drops him where he wants to go.*'

'Got it,' Trixi said, scribbling on her memo pad, her preposterous nails click-clacking around her biro.

'*Right, first things first. The guys still working on the house? Moving everything downstairs?*'

'They're almost done, sir.'

'*Call 'em for me, tell 'em to leave the office where it is. Melvin's gonna use it as his base 'til we get him his own place. Oh, and make sure he's got a chair, the kid needs a good chair.*'

'Yes, sir.'

'*I'm on the 405, should be home in about thirty minutes. I want*'

Variety, Entertainment Week, Hollywood Reporter, *three bottles of JD, a hot bath and a steak sandwich waiting for me.*'

'Steak sandwich . . . goddit. How are you for, uhmm, your medication? You want the usual party bag left in the bathroom?'

'*Yep, better make it . . . shit, no, scratch that! Keep it clean.*'

'Are you sure, sir? Are you sick?'

'*No. 'S just the girls got Melvin to try a little sniff on the plane, sent the guy nuts. We had to keep it out of his way, just while he's at the house. Boy can't take his stimulants.*'

Trixi jotted it all down.

'*Now, what's the scene tonight?*'

'One second, one second.' And Trixi scrabbled for her notes.

'*C'mon, c'mon, I've been back in LA for ten minutes, I need a party!*'

'Okay, okay, there's a black-tie fundraiser at the Getty Centre for—'

'*Nope. Next?*'

'Erm . . . Mickey Schrieber's having drinks at—'

'*Nope. Next?*'

'Oh, Gill Kramer's meant to be having a party, but he was in here a couple of hours ago shouting and screaming. He didn't make the *Pilot* cover, so that might be all off. Al Rosen from ABN was talking to him. He'd come in to see you.'

'*Al? Shit, what did he want?*'

'"*Carpool.*" First refusal. Everyone wants first refusal. *Variety* leaked it this morning. It's all anyone can talk about.'

The line went quiet, just the faintest murmur of female voices audible over the hum of traffic.

'Sir?' Trixi said.

But Don was laughing.

Back on Fifth Avenue, two businessmen were rather confused.

'Well, a fine mornin' to you, sir. Garland. Randy Garland, SEBN.' Howard watched as the Southerner removed the white

Stetson from his salt-and-pepper thatch and pumped Bernie's hand vigorously. 'Now, Ah don't believe we've had the pleasure although I made the acquaintance of Mr Silver here on Tuesday. How are ya, Howie?'

Howard had turned into a snowman – fat, white-faced and frozen to the spot. He watched, dumbstruck, as Randy tossed his hat on to a chair, rolled his shoulders with a groan and began strolling about the office.

'You want to explain yourself, Mr Garland?' he said eventually.

'Well, gennermen, shall we take a seat?' Randy said, holding out his palms like he was greeting chat-show guests. 'A little more businesslike, don'tcha think?'

Bernie looked to Howard for some answers as the three men settled in silently. What the hell was going on?

'Now I see, Mr Silver, you received the *items* my associates forwarded to you?' Randy began, turning his hat slowly in his lap and nodding at the glossy pile of photographs on the blotter.

Howard fixed him with as steely a glare as he could manage under a towelling headband.

'Do you mind telling me what the hell they're meant to mean?' he said slowly. He was attempting to keep a heavy lid on his rage at this hick's insolence but it was bubbling and spitting and making a mess of his worktop. It would have to blow soon.

'Well, as for the how, a little group of professionals goin' by the name of Probe-It. I don't know if they means anything to you?'

Bernie and Howard shrugged.

'*Professional Broadcast Entertainment Intelligence Targeting,*' Randy spelt out. 'Offices in London, Madrid, Los Angeles. And here in New York, of course. They probe. It's their business. Media, studios, actors, networks – you wanna know who's got their hand in the till, whose stocks are about to go nose first into the dirt – these are the boys you call. Now they ain't cheap but, as you can see, gennermen, they are thorough.'

'*Thorough?*' Howard said, breathing deeply now, capped

teeth grinding a little. He picked up a photo from the top of the pile. A suited man stood over the bloodied pulp of what looked like a high-speed collision between head and laptop computer. A raised baseball bat obscured his face.

'Now, now, Howie. They can't take any responsibility for what they might find, they're just paid to dig. Whether they come up with a handful o' diamonds or just a field o' shit ain't their concern. But, crap or crystal, they deliver. And I think you'll find, Howie —'

He bristled at the chummy familiarity of this man, with his plaid shirt and easy smile.

'— that it's very difficult to get an *in-no-cent* man,' he punched out the word, 'to be photographed doin' anything, shall we say, *questionable*.'

The room fell quiet. Randy's audacity sat fatly between them, arms folded, like a sideshow freak. Bernie and Howard could only stare.

'See, what you must understand, gennermen,' he continued with a light laugh, 'is that none of this photo nonsense was my *original* intention. Like I told you yesterday, Howard, SEBN is just a small cable outfit, just an honest, homegrown station.'

'With titties,' Howard added flatly.

'Good old-fashioned country girls who ain't ashamed of what the Lord done given 'em, correct.' Randy clearly felt this was a little below the belt. Which was nonsense, frankly, because if Howard had wanted to do anything below Randy's belt it would have taken nine strong men just to get the huge brass steer-horn buckle off.

'So what was your *original* intention, Mr Garland. *Exactly?*' Howard asked. He was tiring quickly of this hickville cornball act.

'To buy you out, Mr Silver. To buy you out.'

'Buy us?' Bernie said.

'Oh, not outright, Bernie. But a piece of you. SEBN's been lookin' to expand, start makin' our own shows, rather than buyin' them in. That's where all the real money is, ownin' the whole dang shootin' match. So I did what any self-respecting businessman would do: I investigated the market. Slipped a few dollars to these young Probe fellas — asked 'em to give me a list of who might be plum rich for the pluckin'.'

Did he make this shit up as he went along? Bernie thought. Holy Christ, he'd be bringing out a guitar and lighting a campfire around the desk in a minute, getting Howard to whip up a mess o' beans.

'And Mercury was top o'the list. There was talk that perhaps your good selves might need to lighten your load a little. Dispose of a few assets, cut back on your spending. You got this Flayme show costin' you a pretty penny, these fancy offices,' Randy threw a look about the sumptuous room. 'Been a long time since you had a hit, gennermen. Ah just thought you'd appreciate gettin' your hands on some o' the sweet stuff. So far all above board.'

'So *far*,' Bernie said flatly.

'My idea was to approach you fine gennermen and find out if you might be willing to sell an arm or two of your company to me. Straight-shootin' and simple.'

There was a knock and Caroline slid in briskly, a fresh pot of coffee in her hand.

'No,' Howard said, leaning over the desktop, 'thank you, Caroline, Mr Garland isn't staying.' He stood up with a wince. 'Be so good as to call him a cab, would you, sweetheart?' And he ushered her from the room, closing the door softly behind her.

'Now, Howie,' Randy began, but Howard spun round as fast as he could without toppling on to the sofa.

'Can it, cowboy!' he barked. 'Grab your stupid hat and clink on outta here, bar's closed. I can see where all this is leading. These investigation boys of yours — Delve or Rummage or whatever the hell they're called — they come back with a price but it's just a little too rich for you country fellahs, isn't it? We're as healthy as the day we were born, right, Bernie?'

Bernie sat quietly, chewing his lip.

'But you get greedy . . .'

'Now, Mr Silver, I can assure you —'

'. . . so these Grope guys dig a little further and find — what? My son buying a bag of flour from an old friend to use on his baking course. No more than that. So then some dumb shmuck at Poke-It gets creative. Ties up some actor, splashes some corn-syrup about, makes like Don's some crazy killer, hoping these grubby snapshots will get me to drop the price a little. Am I right? Well, I have news for you, Mr Garland. I, unlike yourself, haven't just strolled into the big city for the first time with a pickaxe up my ass to see if Fifth Avenue's paved with gold. I — what're you smiling at?'

'Well, Howie, Bernie, I can't say that did'n' cross my mind, these photographs landin' in my lap so fortuitously an' all. But it was the report from Probe-It that came with 'em that changed my mind. Turns out it weren't gonna do me no good using these photos to blackmail you fine gennermen at all.'

''Cause we don't take kindly to idle threats, Mr Garland?' Bernie said.

'No, Bernie — because Mercury Pictures ain' worth much more than a puppy's pecker anyway,' Randy said, tugging a file from the briefcase next to his chair.

Bernie looked at Howard. Howard looked at Bernie.

'Healthy as the day you were born?' Randy said, arching one wispy eyebrow. 'Gennermen, the day you were born they shoulda slapped your ass, locked you in an incubator and thrown away the key.' He flicked through the pages of figures in a manilla folder. 'You're broke, gennermen.'

Howard shot a steely glare at his brother who bobbed and gaped like a dying fish.

'Your son *Dawnald?*' Randy bent the word like a pedal steel guitar. 'Fancy cars, plastic surgery, holidays, real estate . . . Jesus, the boy's dental-work bill alone would cover my Nashville staffing costs for six months.'

'All right, that's *enough!*' Howard barked, stomping round to the intercom on his desk. He'd have this slithery hick out on the street before you could say . . .

But the ten-gallon son of a bitch was laughing.

'Fact is, I don't want your damn' studio, gennermen. You got it in a bad enough state without mah help.'

The office fell silent.

'So what *do* you want, Mr Garland?' Bernie said, tentatively.

'Well, boys, what I wanted was to call the whole damn' thing off. Blackmail ain't my style, I'm a businessman. Ah told Probe-It to stop with the whole mysterious photos thing. But then, on Tuesday, Howie here changed my mind.'

He blinked. Tuesday? The *Variety* profile? He hadn't said anything.

'*Carpool.*' Randy smiled. 'Ain't that what you're callin' it? With the three fellahs whinin' and bitchin' and chewin' the fat?'

'*Carpool?*' Howard said. His scalp began to itch and prickle under the headband.

'Oh, yes, sounds like quite a li'l show young Donald's found himself there. Just what SEBN needs to fill a half-hour hole in our schedule. See, now our l'il clambake gal has got herself in the family way, we need something new and snappy kinda at short notice.'

'You're kidding, right?' Howard? *Carpool?*' Bernie said in disbelief.

'Only asset you have,' Randy said, and smoothed back his hair with a scratch. 'Believe me, we've looked.'

'No. This is nuts,' Bernie said suddenly, the end of his tether finally reached. 'You can't be serious about this? You want us to hand over the idea to *you?* For broadcast on the fuckin' *Corndog Banjo Network* between *Hokey's Hoe-Down* and *Live Nudie Bale Stacking?*'

They couldn't lose the show. They needed the show. Bernie needed the show. He'd promised Lambert, he'd promised everybody.

151

'Ah'll have you know our nudie bale stackin'—'

'No dice, I'm afraid, cowboy,' Bernie yelled, gathering the photographs up in his arms and hurling them at Randy. 'If that means anything to you. No spurs or no damn'...' trembling, his mind raced for some western image '... cactuses.'

'Cacti,' Randy corrected.

'Shut the fuck up! Yeah, okay, you seem to have Mercury over a barrel with these shots at first glance, but you probably don't know how things work in Los Angeles. Very differently from your little cornfed barnyard down South, I'm sure. You even *attempt* to publish these shots, we'll bring our lawyers down on your head so fast your ten-gallon hat won't hold a spoonful o' bull-spunk.'

He was quite getting the hang of this.

'I shit you not, Mr Garland. Christ, even if these did hit the press,' Bernie laughed with what he hoped was a confident swagger, 'Donny would be considered a hero by Hollywood standards. Swanning around London with a nose full of sherbet, coming back with a hit pilot? Christ, he'd get his own fuckin' miniseries. You got nuthin'. Not a hell-hot hope in Hades, Mr Cowboy.'

Out of breath and red-faced, Bernie looked at the man sitting in front of him. During this last tirade, Randy had merely been straightening up the photographs in his lap and knocking them square.

Bernie watched him calmly slide them back into a file, replace his Stetson on his head and clear his throat. He reached into his briefcase once again, bringing out a fat manilla file and a dictaphone. He half stood, placing the machine upright on Howard's desk.

Howard and Bernie looked at it, standing there like a tiny monolith.

'Do the names Angus Fisher, Malachy Flynn and Jasper Philips mean anything to you, gennermen?'

*

In the *Out There* offices in London, the lift doors rolled open with a 'ting' and Jackie stepped out into the cool darkness of reception and looked about for Ben. The walls were lined with covers of past issues — famous faces from all walks of life, framed in silver, hanging behind the dense rubber plants like pro-celebrity Vietcong.

'A D.I. Watts for you, Jackie,' the receptionist squeaked, nodding at the man sitting on a sofa by the doors, flipping through a small black notebook.

'Miss Heaney?' he said, standing up. Crikey, he was tall. 'Detective Inspector Watts, good afternoon.'

'Er, hello,' Jackie said, crossing the polished floor. D.I. Watts took her hand in a firm, dry shake.

'Miss Heaney, I'm sorry for taking up your time but I have a number of questions that I hope you may be able to assist us with.'

They sat, Jackie tugging her skirt over her knees self-consciously and flicking her hair out of her eyes. She watched him riffle backwards through his notepad.

'What's this about?' she said. 'Has something happened?'

'You talk to promoters, clubs and artists and so on when you're putting together the weekly schedules here, I understand?'

She nodded.

'So you would have a good idea about, say, which comedians are playing where, who might have cancelled and so on . . . would that be right?'

Jackie nodded again.

'Would you have spoken to anyone in the last seven days about one Jasper Philips, can you recall? Or perhaps to Mr Philips himself?'

'Jasper Philips?' She thought back. 'Well, his West End run was cancelled. I got a call from his management. Exhaustion, they said.'

Watts checked his notebook.

'And you spoke to his management yourself?'

'Ye— no. No, actually, I didn't. A girl in the office took a message.'

'Okay.' Watts made some loose jottings. 'And you speak to a lot of clubs, a lot of promoters? Have any of them had any contact with Mr Philips?'

'No, not that I . . . look, what's this about?'

'We're just trying to get a picture of Mr Philips's movements over the last seven days. We were told you knew pretty much what was going on around the circuit.'

'But why?'

Watts read his notebook attentively for a moment, as if disputing a restaurant bill.

'Well, whoever your colleague thought they spoke to, Miss Heaney,' he said flatly, closing his book, 'it wasn't Avatar.'

'Then who—'

'Jasper Philips has gone missing. He's vanished. We suspect he may be in grave danger.'

'Angus Fisher and Malachy Flynn,' Randy twanged slowly, like he was beginning a campfire ballad. Bernie and Howard exchanged glances. If Randy was expecting them to join in the chorus, he was on his own. They'd never heard of them.

'A comic double act. First documented appearance June '89 at their end-of-year revue in Manchester, England. Played a few local bars and clubs. Appeared at somethin' callin' itself the Edin-burg Festival. Shortlisted for some fancy water prize. Talented boys. Bright future ahead o' them, no question there. An', of course, Mr Jasper Philips. Winner of said water prize at the Edin-burg Festival this year. Again, good career ahead o' him,' Randy continued. 'Chat shows, live appearances, video cassettes, TV. Oh, yes, all grade-A comics with bright futures. All in all,' and Randy looked down at the fat file in his lap, 'they had everythin' to live for, you might say.'

The room fell silent.

154

Randy lifted his Stetson and gave his head a good scratch, smoothing his hair down at the back. Picking up the thick file again, he got up and took a leisurely amble to the window of the office, peering out over the street below.

'Mr Garland,' Howard interrupted, 'I'm not David Letterman, I'm not booking comics, so I'm not sure what good I can be here. Where exactly is this going?'

Randy raised a white eyebrow.

'For young Donald? Downhill fast, I'm afraid.'

Meanwhile, in the balmy morning sunshine of northern Los Angeles, a black Mercury Pictures limousine swung slowly through the wide, snaking roads of Brentwood.

It rolled up a hill slowly, sweeping past lawns clipped so crisply they could join the Marines. Past the wide double garages, the No Smoking signs on each gentle bend, until it squeaked to a halt by the kerb.

Melvin skooched along the leather seat and craned his face out of the tinted window at the huge white house on Palmwood Drive. It dazzled in the sunshine, fat and white like a slice of wedding cake dropped on a country house lawn. With its impressive stone staircase and pillars, it had the aspect of a Roman villa belonging to a particularly well-to-do Emperor. But from the bustling activity outside, an Emperor who'd returned from a five-year battle to find his son had been busy with his Mastercard.

The front doors stood open. Three dusty builder's vans stood on the street, backs open, filthy tools and equipment spilling out over the lawn. About these, two dozen young women milled. Some clutched huge square shopping bags, others slithery dry-cleaning. Two or three were in skimpy starchy white uniforms, holding bottles of lotions and fluffy towels. Most were in cocktail dresses, flipping compacts like Star Trek communicators, sipping champagne and tugging at hemlines.

A young blond girl stood at the top of the steps with a clip-board.

'Okay, okay, manicurists and dieticians, you're next. Wardrobe and hygienists, we need you in the bedroom and bathroom. Grab a drink from the tray, c'mon now, we're on a deadline.'

A gleeful Don appeared in the doorway, barefoot and dazzling in crisp tennis gear and Ray-Bans, a *Woodfellas* base-ball cap perched on his head.

'Trixi, my masseuse — you got me my masseuse?'

Melvin clambered out of the limo. The air was immediately wet and warm and reassuring on his face after the car's dry air-conditioning. He slammed the door.

'Trixi, a word. Some of these are too tall. That one at the back, bring her up to — Mel!' Don called, catching sight of him. 'You made it!' He bounded down the steps. 'How you feelin'? You all right now? Jesus, look at you. Let's get you unpacked and into some clean clothes. Come on in, come on in!'

Don steered him through the cluster of girls and clouds of hairspray, up the steps, through the door and down the echoing coolness of the polished hallway. Loud disco music throbbed and pumped about the room, rattling the modern art on the white stone walls.

'Wow, th-this is . . .'

'Follow me, follow me, got to — wait! Shit.'

Three women were rattling a clothes rail full of dark suits down the hallway.

'No, I want these! These are the one's I . . . *TRIXI!*'

The blonde came scampering in, armed with notebooks and three cell-phones.

'Look after Melvin.' And he snatched the phone from her ear. 'Giorgio? It's Don. I'll take 'em all, buddy. Send the bill to the studio.' And he marched back down the hall into the sunshine.

'Sorry, Mr Medford,' Trixi cooed. 'Come this way.' And led a bewildered Melvin towards the crashing din of the lounge.

If the front porch had seemed bustling and busy, it was a hushed British Library reading room compared to this. Disco music thudded through the walls and floor. Two telephones rang and rang. A dozen preposterously beautiful women were draped over each other on rugs. A dozen burly men yelled and stomped and slammed about, snapping tape measures, draping dust-sheets, ticking checklists, scratching sweaty scalps under faded caps. Dripping in beach towels and stilettos by the drinks cabinet, the two actresses from the plane sucked olives and heaped ice from a bucket into tall glasses, and said, '*Pardon? What? Oh, I knowww!*' at each other.

Trixi guided Melvin through the deafening labyrinth and up a wide wooden staircase to a landing. In contrast, this was utterly blank. No rugs, no pictures, no furniture. He noticed the brass handles on the white wooden doors still had clear plastic film on them. Trixi clicked down the hall to the far door.

'Is this new?' Melvin asked, gazing around the hallway. There was a layer of sawdust over the banisters and floor.

'Mr Silver doesn't do stairs,' Trixi said in a half-whisper. One of her cell-phones chirped. 'Sorry, excuse me. You're in here,' she said, opening the door for Melvin and scuttling away with the phone.

'Mr Silver's . . . I'm sorry, speak up? . . . Al? Yes, yes, he's here . . . about an hour ago . . .'

Melvin peered around the room, his hands stroking the fresh surfaces. The keyboard, the monitor, the printer, the polished desktop.

He nodded to himself.

The house continued to rattle and roar about him, phones jangling, movers yelling and thudding. Don running this way and that, phones to each ear, girls laughing, skipping out of the huge patio doors to the heated pool.

So nobody paid Melvin much attention as he slipped back down the hall, creaked down the stairs, threaded his way through the deafening chatter, down the cool hall and back out into the squinty sunlight.

The limo driver quickly flicked away a cigarette and touched his cap.

'Mr Medford, sir? Shall I bring your bags?'

Melvin nodded, cracked open the back door and slid in. He slammed the door behind him with a muffled clunk. He rattled around in his greasy khaki pocket for a bottle of pills, clicking the lid and spilling a couple into his hand.

'Uhhh, mffmmuhhh,' Sheridan said woozily, from behind the sunglasses.

'Welcome home,' Melvin said, holding out the tablets.

'Bullshit.'

'Killed 'em all,' Randy said calmly. 'In his hotel suite. The one you paid for, Howie, I expect. The Margrave, on Piccadilly. Five-star, quite sumthin'. If you gotta be strangled somewhere, I guess—'

'That's insane,' Howard barked. 'Don, a killer? What the hell kind of scam you tryin' to pull, Garland? You think these snapshots are foolin' anybody? You can't make out a face, it could be anybody.'

'Insane?' Randy ruminated, turning from the window. 'Maybe. Who knows? Young man, strung out, stressed as hell. Under pressure to find a hit show. Pressure you put him under, ain't that right? Foreign country. Out of his head on drugs . . .'

'Baking powder,' Howard interjected, limply.

'Fact is, they're dead. All three. And then like *that*, he's outta there. And in some hurry too.' Randy shook his head and took what could only be described as a mosey back to his chair. 'Hotel had him down for another week at least but there he goes. Private jet. Guess you paid for that too. Am I right, gennermen?'

'Bullshit,' Howard said once again.

'Well, t'be honest, boys, that's what I thought too.' Randy opened a file, sliding out two clear plastic wallets carefully. 'Til those oh-so-*thorough* boys over at Probe bring me these. Easy there, they ain't pretty.'

They were clear plastic, sealed airtight at the top. Inside, the plastic had become a little smeared, clearly from the soggy pink card jammed in the corner of the bag. Pink in the way that an expensive white business card would become pink.

If you picked it up with bloodied fingers.

'Young *Daw*nald's card,' Randy twanged. 'Probe done got themselves a dozen like it. Blood matches that of young Angus Fisher, as do the fingerprints. Now how d'yuh suppose he managed to get that?'

'Means nothing,' Howard said, clearing his throat. But he knew it meant far from that. 'Kid coulda had a nosebleed, found the card in a bar somewhere. Any decent lawyer would have that thrown out in a—'

'Howard,' Bernie said darkly. He held out the second clear bag. Howard took it. A single $500 black silk monogrammed sock lay curled and bloodied like a dead fish. He exhaled slowly.

'So what? Laundry gets mixed up. These big hotels, who knows what goes on?'

'Yur probably right,' Randy said, strolling back around his chair and easing himself into it slowly. 'Nuthin' to worry about. In fact, here's a thought,' he said, leaning forward and picking up the Dictaphone from the desk. 'Let's have ourselves a listen, shall we? We got it all here.'

'Garland—'

Randy held one finger to his lips. The room fell silent.

He pressed play.

Ben stuffed the last of the sixteen slippy shiny in-flight magazines back into the free in-flight bag, along with his in-flight socks and all the other crappy old in-flight crapola, and shoved the lot in the pouch in front. He sat back and let his breathing slow to something less resembling a panicked hamster tied to a skateboard.

About him, families jostled and bickered, passing books and bags and blankets about anxiously like it was an Anderson shelter. Ben sat back and listened over the high, hair-dryer whine below him as the huge jet prepared for its voyage.

More and more of last night's conversation was seeping back into his head.

Jackie wanted a break. She didn't want to have to spend the rest of her life coming home to an untidy flat, a sinkful of washing up, and Ben hunched down in front of a twenty-year-old episode of Hi-de-Hi. She wanted changes. She wanted someone more . . . how had she put it? . . . adventurous. Dynamic. More of an achiever.

He snapped the little plastic handset out of the arm of his seat to take his mind off things, punching and prodding it like a baby with a bath-time activity centre.

He would show her.

Because what was this if not the most dynamic thing he had ever done? Ben thought while the plane began to taxi slowly forward.

Flying halfway across the world to realise his dream.

The whine rose in pitch. The nervous chattering and squabbling faded out slowly. Passengers exchanged glances, grins, eyes wide with nerves. The plane swept left. Those with window seats stared out at pale brown tarmac sweeping beneath them, blurring. Magazines vibrated in laps, everyone folding them away hurriedly, conscious of the sickly yellow glow of the seatbelt lights.

He would phone her from his Malibu beach house. Tell her to drop everything and catch the next flight over.

Past other planes now, huge and white and still. 'Ooohs' and 'Looks!' as children craned and strained to watch sparrows hitching rides on the warm air currents, like dolphins chasing ships.

Or even send Mercury's private jet to pick her up, he thought.

Slowing, pausing, turning. Turning again, like the pilots up front were bickering over the route.

'*America's left here, then right at the lights.*'

'*No, trust me. Go right and follow the one-way system, then left. It's quicker.*'

A rumble then a burst of speed as the huge 747 roared down the runway.

Strangers shared smiles, knuckles gripped fabric. Ears filled with glue, palms turned suddenly cold and wet, the world disappeared beneath them. Houses, rooftops, fields, clouds, white mist. Stomachs lurched like carsick childrens'. Silence. Cold air on forearms.

Ben loved Jackie. With his whole heart.

'Worst part over with,' the lady next to him said, leaning in a little.

Ben looked up, surprised. Blinking, he took in his surroundings. The conversations were bubbling up now, like after a movie. He looked out of his window.

England lay far, far below him.

'*Good evening, ladies and gentlemen,*' a voice came over the speakers. '*On behalf of Virgin I would like to welcome you to Flight 147 to Los Angeles.*'

The next time he saw Jackie, he would be the man she could truly love back.

'*And . . . shit . . . and all the time she's juggling being . . . being feminine with having to play rugby . . .*'

'*Feminine?*'

'Shut it off,' Howard said, his face white, hands cold and trembling. He had heard more than enough. 'Garland, shut it off!'

'*Y-yeah. She's the manager of a shop . . . a dress shop . . . Look, Mr Silver—*'

'Garland! Shut it off! Shut the damn' tape off, you've made your point,' he bellowed.

'*Aaaaargh — ow, no! No, Don, no! No! Mr Silver, no! Don — aaarggh!*'

'Garland!'

'*Mr Silver, please! Jesus Christ, no! Don, no! Don—*'

A tiny click and the room fell quiet, just the deep rasping breathing of Howard Silver audible, shoulders hunched, sweating on to his blotter. The men sat still. Suddenly, as if he'd just realised he'd left the iron on, Randy was bustling round.

'Well, gennermen,' he said, placing the little tape recorder back on the desk, grabbing up his case and clicking it open, 'there you have it.' He tugged out a document, sliding it across Howard's desk. 'A signature there and there, where ah've put the l'il crosses, please?'

'Wait,' Bernie said, 'signature? What the hell is all this about?'

'Oh, it's very simple, gennermen. You will make *Carpool*. Twenny . . . no, say thirty-six episodes. Sounds about right.' He smiled, giving his peppery moustache a little stroke. 'That'll fill mah little schedule nicely. Ah think the cost'll be covered quite nicely by me holdin' on to this evidence of mine and not, say, sendin' it to the FBI. The contract is just so there's no confusion. Whaddya say?'

Howard looked at Randy.

'Don't sign it,' Bernie said, up on his feet. 'And you listen to me, you sonofabitch . . .'

Howard stared at the contract in front of him, the small print swimming woozily.

'It's a lot to take in, Ah appreciate,' Randy said. 'Ah'll give you twenty-four hours. This time tomorrow Ah'll have that signed, sealed and on mah desk.' Randy's silvery-blue eyes twinkled, crow's feet deepening a little. 'Well, Ah'll bid you good day, gennermen, you have a lot to discuss, I expect.'

'You think you'll get away with this . . . this bullshit?' Howard gravelled. The intercom on his desk crackled into life.

'*A car for Mr Garland, sir,*' Caroline said politely.

'Thank you for your time, gennermen. Speak to you tomorrow, ah expect.' And, with a tip of his hat, he headed for the door with that touch of the mosey at his hips.

'Just hold it one second, Garland!' Bernie yelled, waving the envelope.

Randy, one hand on the doorknob, turned back and smiled.

'Oh, and did ah mention? What's today . . . the twenty-seventh? I need the first episode on my desk by the seventeenth of next month. Three weeks' time. Coupla cars, coupla cameras, shouldn't be too tricky. Ah look forward to seeing it.'

And with a wink, Randy left.

FOURTEEN

There was the usual maddening bottle-neck of commuters at Tottenham Court Road tube. And for once not because of the half-dozen blank-faced men and women trying to interest people in their little cards advertising the *Cambridge School of English, Ealing*, nor the thousand *Golf Sales* being advertised on a thousand placards and getting in everyone's way.

No, everyone in London was slowing down to get a glimpse of the banner headline on the *Evening Standard* vendor's stand.

In fact, Jackie was the only person to enter the station that evening who was able to walk past *TOP COMEDIAN VANISHES* without slowing down.

An hour later she clattered into her mother's house, the weight of the world on her shoulders, prepared for an evening in the company of her baggy Snoopy T-shirt, fading blue jogging bottoms and a Nicorette patch. She snapped on the television for news about Jasper Philips – maybe some new development in the case, something that might spark her memory. And as she stood there watching, remote control in hand, she felt a tiny frisson of hope that maybe D.I. Watts's strong chiselled face might appear, his name flash across the bottom of the screen. Perhaps sitting at a desk, a bouquet of microphones in front of him, giving an urgent press conference, appealing for witnesses.

But nothing.

She trundled into the dining room.

No, Ben hadn't phoned, her mum told her through a plume of steam in the kitchen. But there was a message on the answerphone. A very nice message from someone who sounded much more suitable, her mother said, sticking a fork into a boiled potato.

'Hello . . . this is, er, a message for Jacqueline Heaney . . . this is Pete . . . oh, D.I. Watts. We spoke this afternoon. I'm calling to see if you're available this evening. I understand it is very short notice but I am visiting a comedy club in Kentish Town and I was hoping you might be free to accompany me . . . professionally. If you've spoken to these promoters in the past, you might be able to fill in any gaps or . . . well . . . you have my number . . . but if you're busy, y'know, then that's . . . erm . . .'

'Much more your sort of chap,' her mum nodded, wiping her hands on a Golden Jubilee tea-towel.

Diane Paretsky stood on Fifth Avenue, being buffeted and bruised by the lunchtime crowds. The office buildings bled thousands of New Yorkers all about her, scuttling out for sandwiches and coffees, surrounding her like a fast-flowing river. Three times her silver case was kicked out into the busy street, her tripod and video camera knocked clattering to the floor as she tried to focus on her shot.

It was no good. Even when she managed to find the tiniest lull in the swarming sidewalk traffic, her viewfinder was blurry and busy, crissing and crossing with frantic lunchers, the occasional bright flare of a yellow cab flashing across the frame. Hopeless.

Diane had headed down to midtown to try and bump into Bernie Silver. His was still the voice she most needed to hear on her documentary, the swarthy gambling divorcee who knew exactly where the Mercury money was coming from. Unfortunately, the security guards in the Mercury building hadn't even let her get fully out of the cab before they were bristling through the revolving doors, on to the street, palms held out, apologising but forcing her to back away.

So she was stuck on the opposite side of the wide street, trying to get a little footage. But from where she was standing, she was getting nothing. She needed to be nearer. A little nearer and about four foot taller.

'Hey! Hey, lady! What the fuck you doin', huh? Get the fuck down 'fore I call a fuckin' cop! Hey! I'm talking to you, lady!'

'One second!' Diane pleaded, eye jammed against the viewfinder. This was better. This was much better.

'Not one second! What da fuck you doin' to my roof, huh? Somebody get a cop here!'

Balanced precariously on top of the cab, the rubber feet of her tripod squeaking against its metal, Diane shifted her weight and focused on the building opposite, the yellow roof popping and thunking beneath her.

'No, that's it, lady!' And she was aware of someone sliding her case from the roof and tossing it loudly to the sidewalk, lenses and cables clattering on to the concrete.

'Please!' she yelled, one hand held aloft. She was zooming in slowly to the doorway. 'I'm almost done!'

'You done now, bitch! Look it my cab! Hey, *officer!*'

There. Hold on the doorway. The glass, the concrete. The revolving doors, the security guards. Just three more seconds and she'd have her shot . . .

'Hey, officer . . . officer! I turn away for two minutes and this dumb bitch is climbing all over—'

Holy shit, Diane thought suddenly. Is that . . .?

Across the wide street, a familiar face under a familiar Stetson was exiting the Mercury offices, pushing through the revolving door with an alligator-skin briefcase. She reached around and wound the manual zoom sharply clockwise, the doorway in her screen lurching forward. The face was lost for a moment in the blurring crowd.

'Ma'am?' A voice below her. Different. A New York voice. Stern. 'Ma'am, get the hell off this guy's cab, wouldya? It ain't no jungle gym . . .'

There! It was him. Definitely him.

'Shut it off, ma'am. Otherwise, I gotta haul your ass downtown for damaging—'

'I'm coming, I'm coming,' she said quickly, shutting off the camera. She turned and looked down. The cop was holding out one hand to help her, shaking his head. A small amused crowd had gathered, blocking the sidewalk.

Back on firmer ground, as she busied herself packing her equipment away, the cab driver yelling and cursing at his pocked roof, the cop taking details, Diane's mind flipped quickly through the possibilities. There was only one reason a cable station would talk to a studio.

She slammed her case and flipped out her phone, jabbing through the address book quickly.

'And he said to me, "Oy! Rabbi Berry, I cannot understand your religion. You say you are Jewish? Is that right? *Jewish?* But how can that be? Surely you're either a jew or you're *not?*"'

The room exploded once again in a loud roar of a laugh.

'Anyway, oy, I'm toitally *oysgemitchet*! That's it for tonight! *Sholem aleichem* everybody! *Sholem aleichem!*'

The small crowd erupted into enthusiastic clattering applause, whooping and chuckling as the compère took his bow, his black robes flowing. After a loud chord on his guitar, he held his arms aloft and clambered, sweating, from beneath the lights to make his way to the bar.

'Excuse me?' a voice said. The compère turned. A tall man stood at his elbow. Waxy jacket, denim shirt, serious expression. 'My name is Detective Inspector Watts. I wonder if I might have a moment of your time?'

'Hey, sure, sure,' Berry said quickly, grabbing his drink. 'But

I can't give you my real name for security reasons. Social Security reasons, heh-heh! You wanna beer?'

'Not on duty, sir, thank you. Oh, but my colleague . . .' Watts said, turning.

'A white wine,' Jackie smiled. 'That would be very nice, thank you.'

'No problem,' Berry said, signalling the barman. 'You not on duty?'

Jackie breathed in, pulled her shoulders back, fixed her jaw and flashed a look at Watts, who gave her a warm encouraging smile.

'I'm an investigative journalist, assisting the police with their enquiries.'

The three of them sat at a sticky table in the upstairs bar, tucked a little out of the way. The club goers were trickling out through the pub, buzzing and grinning. Watts had his black notebook out, scribbling down every detail as Berry, still in his sweeping black comedy robes, sat nattering away, Jackie sipped her wine and nodded attentively, head tilted, attempting to look like Kate Adie via Lois Lane.

'Shit, Jasper Philips? That what this is about?' Berry asked.

'You've seen the paper, I take it,' Watts replied. 'Now according to my notes, Mr Philips was known to play here from time to time, is that right?'

'He ain't missing,' Berry said. 'Shit, I knew I shoulda called someone. Paper's got it backwards. He left.'

'Left?' Jackie interrupted. So far she'd had almost nothing to add beyond nodding intelligently every time Watts did.

'Got offered some sitcom in Hollywood, didn't he? By that bloody Silver bloke.'

The pub seemed to go very quiet suddenly. Status Quo rocked all over the world softly to themselves.

'Don Silver?' Jacked said.

'Wait! Hold on one second.' Watts was scribbling furiously. 'Who is this we're talking about?'

So Jackie told the policeman everything she knew. The article in *Variety*, the meeting, Sheridan's disappearance, Ben's flight out to LA.

'And you didn't go with him?' Watts said, placing his hand over hers quickly to interrupt her.

'We're . . . well, kind of on a break.'

'Madcap Madhouse,' Berry spoke up suddenly. 'That's another one. This Silver bloke nabbed them too. When was it? Saturday . . . Comedy Store.'

Watts was nodding and scribbling excitedly.

'Excellent, this is excellent. Don Silver, Los Angeles. This could be it.'

It was a warm summer evening. The smoked-glass doors of the pub swung closed with a squeak, the juke box, the chatter, all muting, leaving D.I. Watts and Jackie standing opposite each other on the pavement. She fiddled with her jacket buttons a little, he fussed with his note book.

'A lift home?' he said eventually, motioning towards his Vauxhall at the kerbside. 'To say thank you? These really are some very strong leads, Miss Heaney. If this Don Silver has merely shipped these comedians over to California wholesale for some kind of job, then that's the lot wrapped up as far as I can see.'

'Bus is fine,' Jackie said, hoping her pinking cheeks weren't showing in the street light.

She attempted to concentrate on his words as he explained the police's next move. How it would be a matter of contacting Los Angeles, squaring this story . . . but it was no good.

He was lovely.

There, she'd thought it. He really was. Lovely. None of that cocky Sweeney-style *look-sonny-you're-in-right-schtuck-mate* wankiness.

'You've certainly saved us . . . well, me . . . a lot of legwork here, thank you,' Watts said, clicking the top of his pen. 'To be honest, I avoid these comedy places when I can. Can't stand them. Comedians, I mean.'

'No, you're right.' Jackie nodded. 'Weirdos, most of them. Always arguing about which classic *Good Life* episode had Lenin the pig in it or whatever.'

She buttoned and unbuttoned her jacket sixty or seventy times.

'But what I wanted to stress, though,' Watts said, 'is that at the moment everything pertaining to this investigation has to remain confidential. I'm going to have to ask you to keep all this to yourself.'

Jackie nodded, bottling up her frustration. She had thought of rushing straight home, booting up the computer and dashing off a hugely exciting exposé of the Jasper Philips mystery, using her contacts, her knowledge and her first-hand experience. Cover of the *Guardian* supplement, surely?

'Does anyone else know about this Don Silver?' he asked. 'Talked to anyone?'

'No, no one.'

'Mum and Dad? Hairdresser? Mention it at work?'

'No, I haven't told anyone.'

'So it's just this Sheridan character and Ben, your boyf— your ex-boyfriend?'

Oh, wait, here we go. What a clumsy attempt, she thought. Jackie pulled her shoulders back a little and fiddled with her bag.

'Yes,' she said, trying to keep a fixed businesslike look. But the whole thing collapsed involuntarily and she found herself shuffling on the spot, her hand immediately called up on emergency hair-twiddling duty.

'That's good. I-I mean . . .' he stumbled. Quite attractively. 'I mean, it's good that no one knows about this. Do your best to keep it that way for the moment.'

And they said their goodbyes.

There was no kiss. No hugs. They shook hands. Did Jackie detect a slight hesitancy as they did so? A slight embarrassed meeting of eyes? Yes, she thought. Maybe she did.

She wandered up to the bus stop; a toot-toot and a wave as Watts's Vauxhall roared past on urgent cop business. Jackie spent the journey home thinking about how much she was missing Ben.

Or trying to, at least.

Top down, Don's Ferrari roared throatily on to Wilshire Boulevard to a chorus of car horns.

'Oh, fuck you, Mr Subaru!' he yelled at the lunchtime traffic, grappling with the wheel like a bare-chested Greek wrestler, sending his car sliding wide and deep like a scalpel through the dull squat of tin boxes. Don continued his flat-out, terrifying 80 m.p.h. drag for approximately a foot and a half before slamming to a halt behind a beige Lexus, Trixi next to him head-butting the dashboard with a yelp, dropping one of her three cell-phones. Melvin, folded into the back seat, got a mouthful of leather trim.

'Beautiful day, ain't it?' Don grinned from behind his Ray-Bans. 'Beautiful. Chew that air. Mmmm! Who's up, Trix?'

She flashed a look at the handful of phones.

'Your father's been on hold for five minutes on the Nokia, says it's urgent, I got Al Rosen on the Ericsson and the *Hollywood Reporter* on the Motorola.'

'Tell Dad I'll call him later, the *Reporter* wants an interview about London – put 'em through to Mindi, tell her to schedule something for later in the week. You better patch Al through to the hands-free.'

It had just gone noon and Don was eager to get to the studio in time to introduce Melvin to the new department heads and then go out for lunch. The LA sun burnt through thick yellow-grey clouds, torching the flat hot city. By the edge of the highway, a huge peeling billboard advertised *Fyre* – a bare-chested Samuel Pepys, diary aloft in one hand, crossbow in the other, atop a fiery St Pauls. *Feel The Burn*, it read along the bottom. *Sundays, 9 p.m. ABN'*.

The traffic crawled past it with painful lethargy.

'Hey, c'mon!' Don yelled, throwing almost his whole upper body out of the car. 'What the hell is all this?' He waved his hand at the river of cars snaking away bumper to bumper ahead of him. 'It's twelve o' goddamn' clock, for the love of fuck! Where are you all going! Can't you order-in, for chrissakes?'

His hands-free began to chirrup. He pulled down his *Woodfellas* cap a little and punched it on.

'Al, that you?'

'*Donny!*' Al crackled over the speaker. '*You're back. How was London? You and the Queen take afternoon tea?*'

'Shuttup, Al, listen to me. Trixi tells me Gill was flouncing about the lot this morning, talking about ABN cancelling *E.R. E.R.... Oh!*? What's he heard? Is this true?'

'*I'm sorry, Don. We're announcing tomorrow. The hundredth episode will be the last.*'

'Shit!' he hissed.

'Your father's still holding,' Trixi said, holding out the little phone.

'Not now.' Don waved her away. 'Listen, Al, we need to talk about this. You going to Gill's party tonight?'

'*I, er, might stop by,*' Al crackled.

'I'll talk to you there.'

'*Well, Don, hell, everything's negotiable. I mean ... maybe if I had a little sweetener? Something I could take upstairs, it might smooth things over a bit?*'

Don laughed.

'You want a first look at *Carpool* by any chance?'

'*Oh, that's very kind. Can you bring it to the party?*'

'That depends on Melvin. Mel?' And Don craned around in his seat. 'Might you have something I can show Al later?'

Melvin, folded in the back seat, knees about his chin, chewed the inside of his mouth anxiously. He shook his head.

'It's not finished,' he said, staring out at the silver snake of traffic. 'Few more days.'

'Few more days, Al,' Don said, 'but don't worry. You'll get a look. I'll see you tonight.' And he jabbed the phone, turning to Trixi. 'Next?'

'Your dad's gone, he couldn't wait. But he says you have to call him urgently. And I've got Connie Smith from CBN holding. This is the fifth time she's called.'

Don allowed himself a little smile and relaxed back in the warm hug of his bucket seat. The traffic began to purr forward gradually.

'You hear that, Mel, m'boy? Everybody's sittin' up and takin' notice. Looks like your idea has got the whole city talkin'.'

'What shall I tell Connie?' Trixi said.

Don reached for the phone.

'Let me – no, wait.' And his dark eyes flashed a little. 'Tell her to make sure she's at Gill's party tonight. Tell 'em all, Gill's party tonight.'

Trixi passed the message on to Connie and hung up.

'Are we going to a party?' Melvin said, poking his head through the beige leather seats.

'Not you, buddy. After last time? They're still hosing down the Gulfstream. Best we keep you away from the party powder while you're working. But me? Oh, yeah.'

'So you gonna give *Carpool* to ABN?' Trixi asked.

'Let me tell you something about this town.' Don smiled. 'The key word is *relationships*. Who you know, who owes you a favour, who you worked with before, whose personal trainer once had a date with whose pedicurist's sister.' He snapped his fingers quickly three or four times. 'It's what makes the world go round. *Who* y'know, not *what* y'know. *Relationships*. Now we could hand *Carpool* to Al at ABN. We have a relationship, see? They've got *E.R. E.R. . . . Oh!*, they had *Office Politics*. We're used to each other. Deals are already done, friendships already made, contracts already in place. Christ, I've got my own parking space there.'

The car rolled forward another foot and a half.

'But it's when you've got yourself a show everybody's interested in seeing that you remember the most enjoyable aspect of a steady relationship.'

'Wh-what's that?' Melvin asked.

'Cheating.'

FIFTEEN

Night eventually smothered Los Angeles, like a black satin robe thrown over a sweaty heavyweight boxer. The city slowly lit up, glowing with the strips and stripes of taillights and neon. The hills twinkled away with the glow of parties, balanced precariously on steel struts.

On one particularly revolting balcony, groups of absurdly handsome men, tanned to the colour of builder's tea and dressed in dark suits, chuckled and slapped backs and threw back fat tumblers of Jack Daniel's and said '*Hey, you the man!*' a lot. On their arms, young women dripping in impossibly shimmering frocks, hooked themselves like padded coat hangers, which was pretty much exactly what they were.

Inside, among the antiques and oak, the party continued, camp waistcoated caterers passing flaky canapés to disinterested middle-aged men returning one by one from the marble bathroom with tiny pupils and wide grins and dispro-portionately increased enthusiasm for this, their sixth identical stop-off of the night.

Seated at the white baby grand by the fireplace in a tartan tux, Shifty Dolawitz tinkled and smarmed, but within his bald head his abacus brain clicked away busily. He should have pushed for more than an extra million-a-week for Gill, he thought to himself. His client would be unemployed in two weeks' time. Ten percent of zero wasn't going to put his kids through college. He wondered if he might try and corner Don later and squeeze Mercury for a little more.

Draped over the piano lid, Gill's wife Elaine mumbled a ballad into her Martini glass.

If the culture of celebrity wives could be divided up into three categories, Elaine Kramer fell into: equally-talented-but-willing-to-take-a-slight-back-seat-to-placate-husband's-flimsy-ego.

The other two categories (#2 gold-digging-waste-of-space and, the most common, #3 well-meaning-yet-punchable-organiser-of-self-aggrandising-charity-functions-and-fatuous-causes-using-husband's-influence-and-chequebook) Elaine encountered regularly as guests on *Wake Up LA*, her hugely popular mid-morning chat show. Millions of Angelenos greeted the day with her fatuous mix of peach sofas, hairspray and moronic features. Her popularity, she knew, was largely thanks to her status as one half of the happiest couple in Hollywood.

How her ratings would fare tomorrow when she became simply that-TV-woman-married-to-that-guy-who-got-his-ass-canned she was in no hurry to discover.

So Shifty tinkled, Elaine sang, and they both smiled and secretly wished the other one would stop so they could go and find people with more clout to schmooze with.

Most of the evening's clout stood in clusters among the bubbles and powder of the party, picking over and reheating the two warm corpses of the day's gossip.

First was that of Don Silver. It seemed the prodigal schmuck was back. But what actually *was* this show of his about? It all sounded rather flimsy. Executives slid in and out of groups, bobbing like meercats. Had anyone actually *seen* a script? Apparently not. There was even a rumour floating about the balcony that only a page and a half had been written. Everyone laughed at that one.

Everyone not twittering over Don Silver was gossiping

snippily about the host of the party. Sipping his champagne with fingers shiny from his flaky canapés perhaps, but gossiping snippily none the less.

Missing the *Pilot* cover? *Jeez, that had to hurt!* And his show getting cancelled? *So over already.* And what the hell was a, '*Here's to my glorious future*' party anyway? *How in hell dare he show his face?*

Truth was, Gill wasn't showing his face.

He skulked in the kitchen, yelling at the caterers, wolfing finger-food and throwing great splashing mugs of Cheval Blanc 1995 down his neck. He knew all his guests were talking about him, laughing at him. Once in a while, one would get lost on their way to the bathroom and waft in. Air kissing with noisy mwahhs, telling him how proud they were of him, glad to see that he wasn't letting the news get him down. He would simper back through gritted teeth.

And where was Al? At his side? Telling him everything would be okay? Reassuring him that he would do everything he could to persuade ABN to rethink their decision?

Ha!

Gill refilled his mug of vintage wine to overflowing and yelled at a tray of salmon.

Al, in fact, was upstairs in a guest suite. The suite, decked in a fairly restrained gold and purple velvet with fuchsia and lime green accessories, held eight guests in total. Guests who, either because of or despite their similarities, normally wouldn't wish to spend time in each other's company.

In one armchair sat the only woman of the group, although she managed, in a terrifying display of over-compensation, to be more masculine than the rest of the men in the room put together. Opposite her, gazing at his reflection, picking a little pastry from between his teeth, stood one of six identical dull faceless men. Mid-thirties, well-brushed hair held in place with an overpriced mousse, they were all a little paunchy, with the same worried expressions, the same twitchy nerves, the same Lexus key-fobs ruining the hang of their pants.

Al sneaked a glance about the room at them. The man by the door, checking his watch nervously. The guy on the cell-phone, perched on the end of the bed. The man gazing out of the window, hands in pockets, trying to look less nervous than he actually was; another hunched low on a plush footstool.

CBN, NBO, UPC, WN, HBN and KBL.

And Al Rosen, representing ABN, *Office Politics* cap pulled down over his brow, chewing his lip and wearing out a figure of eight on the bedside rug.

Guest eight banged the edge of his credit-card down on the marble dressing table quickly as a chef cutting cucumber.

'Shan't keep you long, people. I'm sure you know what this is about and you're all eager to get back to the party.'

'What the hell is this, Silver?' Pastry-Tooth said, turning to face him. 'Trixi calls me and tells me I'd *better show up tonight?*'

'Yeah, Donald,' Al piped up. 'What do you think you're doing? I thought we had a *relationship?*'

'People, people, *people*,' he said, rubbing a finger on his gums and standing up straight. He checked his reflection in the huge mirror, turning this way and that, smoothing his chins nervously, ruminating like a poker player on which ones he could discard. 'You all saw *Variety* this morning,' he began, turning to face the room. 'You all know about *Carpool*. I don't need to tell you how big this could be, right?'

Nobody said a word, eyes flickering anxiously.

'Right? Mickey?'

Mickey Schriber from HBN jumped a little.

Shit, he thought. His skin began to prickle and sweat, a thousand paranoid thoughts flushing through him. The room was looking at him over bitten lips and chewed fingernails.

'Uhmm,' he said.

What if he said he wasn't so sure about this *Carpool* idea?

That he would need to see a script? Might Don take that as HBN not being interested? But what if everyone else *was* interested? What if it was a *good idea*? He'd be forever known as Mickey — the guy who turned down *Carpool*. He'd be humiliated. He'd be fired! He'd have to go and get a job working at his brother's hardware store . . .

'Mickey?'

'Oh, yeah. Yeah, Donny. Like you said, *The Zeit-guys*. You're right.'

A murmur rippled through the room. Suits rustled, toes clenched in loafers, palms went cold.

Shit. HBN were interested?

'It's a microcosm of the . . . the modern motorist's malaise,' Mickey added quickly.

Suddenly the room erupted as everyone leaped in with their own comments and insights. If HBN was interested, they were interested too.

'It's now. It's real. It's . . . it's really now,' NBO jabbered.

'It defines us,' CBN spouted. 'As a culture. It's a mirror . . .'

'A rear-view mirror!' KBL yelled.

'Oooooh, shit, that's a good one,' everyone said, fists clenched. 'Fuck . . . erm . . .'

'Because aren't we all in a carpool?' WB yelled above the din, wistfully. 'In our lives?'

'Yes! Boxed in?' NBC interrupted. 'Trapped between the glove-box of hope and the head-rest of memories?'

'Pinned!' UPC came in a little late. 'Between the stick shift of regret and the automatic passenger side window of loss?'

'I was about to say that!' NBO hissed.

'Yeah?'

'*Yeah!*'

'But we have a relationship!' Al screamed over the chatter.

'Okay, okay, okay!' Don said, raising his hands. 'Settle down, people. I think it's clear that there's no doubt whichever one of you gets this show, you'll clean up.'

The executives all slowly returned to calm, chests heaving, red-faced and paranoid.

'Sure, things will trot along behind, a season, two seasons later on its coat-tails. Three guys trapped in a lift, three guys stuck on a desert island, three guys in a prison cell — but this is the big one. This, *Carpool*, is setting the standard. Which is why I'm offering it, lady and gentlemen . . .'

The room held its collective breath.

Don smiled.

Across town, on a dimly lit corner of West Hollywood just off the 101 Freeway, a schlumpy and crumpled Ben Busby tinged a front-desk bell and propped himself up on the Formica with a scratch and a yawn.

The lobby was small, square and just the right side of sleazy. Also, like most things in LA, it was stuck in the fifties. In fact it seemed the whole hotel was like an ageing starlet, desperately harking back to when curves were *quite the thang*, almost proud to be a reminder of days gone by. The place jutted its hips, chewed gum, layered on the mascara and made positively no concessions to the twenty-first century. From the imitation leather couch in a lovely Tiffany turquoise to the smoked-glass mirrors, the square pushbutton phone to the framed prints of Bob Hope, it smelled of Brylcreem and bobby sox.

Ben's body, by way of coincidence, was also stuck in the fifties. Or possibly the thirties. Actually, maybe the year 2047. It certainly had no idea what the time was.

'Hey,' a voice said, the bellboy appearing from the back. A few years older than Ben, he had blond shoulder-length hair tumbling over his droopy eyes, a Hawaiian shirt covering a white vest, and a broad Californian smile. He slapped a copy of *Variety* down on the desk and rested a large steaming coffee mug on top.

'Er, yes, hello,' Ben said. 'Can I get a room? Sorry it's so late, I just got in.'

'You British?' the bellboy said, flipping open the guest register. 'Holiday?'

'Huh? Yes. I-I mean, no. British, but not on holiday.' A thought occurred to him and he flipped out the greasy business card from his pocket. 'Actually, can you tell me, where is, uhm, West Alemeda Avenue? 20201? Is that far from here?'

'*Mercury?*' the bellboy asked. 'Why, you got a deal?'

'You know it?' Ben was surprised.

'Twenty twenty one Alemeda? You got like, a pitch there or what? They are like hot, man.' And he licked a finger and went *tssssss* on the newspaper. 'Like McApple filling.'

Ben shook his fuzzy head. And this guy was a hotel porter? Jesus Christ.

'Oh. I-I'm a writer,' he said. 'Sitcom writer.'

'Shit!' the bellboy said quickly, slapping a hand on the counter and vaulting over the top excitedly, landing inches from Ben's startled frame. 'You McDonald or Busby?' And he grabbed his *Variety* from the desk, flapping about with it like it was a paper bird.

Holy fuck. Ben almost lost his balance, his head light and airy, the room swimming.

It was about his show. It was all about his show! He scanned the page.

'*Little is known of award-winning Brit-scribes Sheridan McDonald or Ben Busby,*' he read. Award-winning? That lying fuck.

The bellboy pumped his hand vigorously.

'The name's Zachary. Zachary Black, but my pals call me Zak,' he said groovily, flashing his expensive dental-work.

'Huh? Oh, sorry. Hi, Ben Busby.'

'Zak. Like, I'm ex-ZAK-ly the guy for this part!'

Ben smiled weakly. He doubted he was the first person in the world to hear that particular one. The Hawaiian shirt had been combined with some bright orange trousers, cut off messily an inch below the knee, and the largest trainers Ben had ever seen in his life. It was as if Zak was standing in two armoured cars.

'I'm an actor. Well, like, who isn't, right? But get you!' And Zak slapped him on the chest boisterously. 'Sitcom, huh? You're hangin' with Don Silver? You got a meeting?' he said, sweeping the blond hair off his face.

'Er . . . I 'spose. Kind of.' Ben couldn't take his eyes from the paper.

'That's cool, man. 'Cos like, tomorrow, it's like, I got some time off? So like, I'm thinking I can show you the way, right? Chauffeur you to the door.'

'Well, gosh, I mean, I don't know . . .'

'And in return, maybe you can get me in with you? I swear, just for an introduction.'

'Oh, I don't know. I mean, I haven't even . . .'

'Just something 'bout how I'm the funniest actor you ever saw in your life, like how your sister saw me off Broadway and had to go to hospital 'cause she like laughed her spleen out of her face, or something? Something like that?' Zak nodded and smiled and nodded a bit more. There may even have been a wink thrown in. 'Trust me, I'm a good man. Just got a call today from Shifty Dolawitz, Gill Kramer's rep? Dolawitz is the man, I'm telling you that. He is hot. Hot like Malibu gridlock, man.'

Ben stood there woozily as this insane young wannabe flapped about all over the hotel reception.

'So agreed, right?' Zak was saying. 'We'll slide over tomorrow? Say ten o'clock?'

'Huh? Oh, er, sure.'

Zak grinned his blinding grin once again, slipped his sunglasses off the top of his head and tossed them to Ben.

'Then get some zeds, buddy, see you in the a.m.'

In New York, Marion Silver, blue hair in a net, frail body in a velvet robe, bunioned feet in fluffy mules and nose out of a catalogue, stood in a dark hallway. It was late. She fiddled with the telephone flex with manicured, liver-spotted fingers and waited for someone to answer.

Howard was bent over the stove in the kitchen, messing about with hot milk and sneaky measures of whisky.

He had got in late from a meeting with Bernie and come to bed with the quiet grace of a hippo in a deck-chair, waking Marion and keeping her awake with his tossing and yanking-of-the-quilt.

'Nobody there?' Howard grumbled, splashing milk, mind flooded with the sounds of screams, the thought of cowboys and bloody business cards. It was becoming more a mug of whisky with a finger of milk. 'I gotta speak to him.'

Marion listened to the phone ring and ring until finally there was a slick West Coast click.

'*What?*' a voice snapped. There was a lot of noise going on in the background. A banging and thudding like someone moving furniture.

'Hello, Donald,' she said cheerily, 'it's your mother.'

There was a muffled shriek from the end of the line, making her jump. Another thud. And a loud crack followed by muffled yelling.

'*Help! Jesus Christ, help me, please!*'

'Hello?' Marion said again. 'Donald? Are you all right? Your father wanted a word urgently but I never get to see you these days, you're so busy with your little TV shows.'

Another helpless shout from the line. Another sharp crack like splintering wood.

'Donald, good heavens, what's the—'

'*Out! Parties!*' a voice yelled and hung up.

'Who's there? Is he there?' Howard said, waddling up the cold hall in his pyjamas with two mugs of hot milk. 'I need to speak to him, give it to me.'

Hand over her mouth, Marion hung up, shaking.

'There's someone answering, pretending to be Donald.

Making an awful racket. Really, the people he associates with out there . . .'

Howard shook his head and handed a steaming mug to his wife.

'California assholes. C'mon,' and he snapped off the light, 'I'll try his mobile from the bedroom.'

'What can be so urgent, hon?' Marion asked as they creaked upstairs.

'It's just business, dear, business,' Howard sighed. 'That new show of his. I've gotta fly out tomorrow and talk to him about it. Something's come up.'

'Oh, yes. Carpark,' she clucked happily as they got to the landing. 'From your little interview. You said the networks should start bidding. Sounds very exciting.'

Howard could think only of Randy's words. Randy's evidence. Randy's threats.

'For his sake, dear, I'm praying it hasn't got that far.'

Don was enjoying himself enormously.

The room had erupted in fury again. The gist seeming to be that this was no way to do business, they weren't gonna be jerked around, and something unpleasant about Don's mother.

'Hey, look.' He shrugged. 'What do you want me to say? Shit happens. So I'm fast tracking this one through.'

'B-but all at once?'

'Sure! Get it over with. I don't have time for all those one-by-one meetings, lunches, pitches, lunches, meetings. Notes on the dynamic, notes on the ambience. So, like I say, tomorrow. Eleven o'clock. Mercury Pictures. I want whoever signs the cheques and makes the decisions. And, hey, no lackeys, no assistants, no deputy sub-vice second-in-commands. One guy. I'll bring the writer in case you got questions, you bring your cheque books. Whoever bids highest per episode, that's it. We go to casting a week later.'

The room stood dumbstruck.

'That's it, kids.' Don grinned. 'Tell your bosses I'll see them all tomorrow. Eleven o'clock. Miss me.' And as the room exploded once again, he sailed out into the wide hallway with a smirk. Seven harried executives pushed past him brusquely on the staircase, already shouting into cell-phones and shooting him looks.

'Call for you, sir,' a waistcoat said, appearing at Don's shoulder and handing him a cell-phone. Don peered into the illuminated screen, shooing the waiter away.

'Father!' he said, jamming a finger in his ear. 'How are ya? . . . Huh? . . . Flight was great, great, what can I do—'

Don's boyish grin faded into bewilderment.

'Secure line? What are you talking about? It's a regular cell-phone . . . who's gonna be listening? Dad, what's this about ? . . . Can't you just tell me . . . Sure, lunch tomorrow's fine . . .'

He began descending the glass stairwell. Shifty was still at the piano, attempting 'Smells Like Teen Spirit'. Three or four women in impossibly voluptuous gowns turned to look at Don. He winked.

'Okay, sir,' he said. 'Tomorrow. I gotta go.' And he hung up, dancing down the final stairs, rejoining the party.

Things were going to be just fine.

KRAMER VS . . .
HOLLYWOOD???

By PENNY LANG

HOLLYWOOD Egg on the face? Not likely, when most of it was used in the flaky pastry canapés.

But the shock of the night was **Gill Kramer**'s refusal to cancel his *Pilot* cover party when he learned that boffo-beardy box-doc **Dick Trent** had pipped him to the post.

Add to that the 'shock' cancellation of E.R. E.R. . . . OH! and most Hollywood watchers presumed Gill would retreat for some wound licking.

SPOUSE WARMING

But no, the stars were out in Kramer's hilltop home.

WAKE UP LA host **Elaine Kramer** was her usual smiling self, on hand to greet the guests, each one eager to congratulate her on her Couple Of The Year nomination – how do the übercouple do it?!

PITCH-SLAPPED

But the real news of the bash was going on upstairs, away from **Shifty Dolawitz**'s piano recital as Mercury VP **Don Silver** held court in a guest bedroom with eight network execs.

It's all a little hush-hush, but we speculate that it has something to do with Don's prodigal-like return and his high-(way) concept new laffer.

Watch this space.

Variety
Thursday 28 September

Boarding Group
B

Passenger
HALLIDAY/GORDON

From
LONDON LUTON

To
EDINBURGH

Flight
EZY23

Date
13DEC

Seq No.
90

Thursday brought another warm September morning to New York. The dark reservoir of Central Park lapped at its muddy banks, lapped in turn by exhausted joggers, panting, slapping and puffing their wobbly frames about the park, fleeces and Lycra crackling and chafing.

By eleven o'clock, however, all but the slowest and fattest were showered and towelled behind their desks at work.

'How many . . .' Howard panted, puffing away in his track-suit, '. . . laps so far?'

'Er . . .' Bernie looked about the place for a landmark, two roller-bladers zipping past like Scalextric. 'See that there? That bench we just passed?'

'Uh-huh,' Howard gasped.

'When we pass it again, it'll be one.'

'Oh, Christ, Bernie, let's . . . let's take a break here.' And Howard slowed, clanging against the chain-link, bright white trainers scraffing on the path. The two brothers collapsed on a bench.

'Lord. And this is meant to beat . . . beat the treadmill, you say?' Howard panted, wiping sweat on to his fleecy sleeve.

'It's the great outdoors, Howie. The Big Apple.'

'Big Apple? You wanna see big apples so bad, I'll give you a call when I next see my proctologist.'

Their chuckles faded into a cold silence.

'I threw the pictures away,' Bernie said eventually. 'Just put the whole lot on the fire.'

'They're just *copies*, Bernie. Christ knows how many Garland's got floatin' around out there. The guy might play dumb — all that *gennermen* stuff. *Puppy's titties plump ripe for the pluckin'*. And he might dress like Howdy-Doody's colour-blind cousin — but, Christ, the guy ain't stupid.'

'I know *that*, Howie, I just didn't want them in my home any more, didn't want to be near them.'

Howard puffed a while, gazing out across the still water.

'God, what a damn' mess,' he said eventually. 'Any luck with talking to ABN yet?'

Bernie shook his head with a sigh.

'*E.R. E.R.* . . . *Oh!* is E.R. . . . E.R. Over. Come the hundred, they're pulling the plug. Their mind's made up.'

'Dammit. But . . . but we've still got syndication, right? Anyone sniffing around yet? We need that cheque, Bernie. That's my nest egg, that's my retirement.'

'That cheque'll just about pay for thirty-six episodes of *Carpool*, Howard. We won't be left with shit.'

'Christ!' he growled. The two men fell into angry puffing silence.

'You don't think . . .' Howard began. 'I mean, you don't think it's possible . . .'

'That Garland's right? Don's some coked-up psycho? Strung out, stressed as hell, under pressure? You tell me, Howie. Where Don is concerned, nothing would surprise me.'

'But come on, Bernie, we both know he's no killer, for Chrissakes. The kid couldn't get rid of a spider from the bathtub.'

'But, Howie, what *we* know isn't the issue. You gotta think about a jury. Slap this in front of twelve angry men and what have we got? A Hollywood executive with a reputation for partying? Father tells him to bring back a hit show or he's out? Foreign country? Cocaine? Fingerprints? Screaming?

Quick exits? Shit, you heard it. *Mr Silver, no, no! Don, no, no!*'

'All right, Bernie! Jesus . . .' He didn't need it spelt out. 'So what do we do? Give Garland the shows? Spend our whole damned syndication cheque and then just hand it over to John-Boy Walton with our warmest wishes?'

'Until we know exactly what the hell went on in that hotel, we gotta give Garland what he wants.'

'And we tell the trades what?' Howard spat. He began to shudder, red-faced and cursing. 'The whole industry's looking at us, Bernie. Waiting to see what we do, whether or not we can live up to my little speech. Who's gonna tell them we just decided to *give away* our top new show to the Hillbilly Hoedown station?'

'Just calm down, Howard. Just calm down or you'll give yourself a coronary.'

'Cos it ain't gonna be me, Bernie. It ain't gonna be me.'

The two men fell silent again. The morning sun winked and flashed between the leaves across the water. They were thinking about those screams.

'What did Donald say?' Bernie asked.

'Huh? He was on his cell, I didn't want to risk anyone overhearin',' Howard sighed between rasping breaths. 'I'm gonna fly over there in a couple of hours. Have lunch with them. See what the hell he knows about this whole damn' hotel business.'

'But you told him not to make any deals, right? That we've got SEBN waiting in the wings? We can't have him promising the show to Al Rosen or Connie—'

'Oh, you know what he's like. It'll be premiers and parties for a fortnight before he even remembers he's got a script,' Howard said. 'Don't worry. He won't have done anything yet.'

'Pitch? What do you mean, *pitch?*'

'To the networks, like I said,' Don replied. 'We gotta – well *you* gotta – sell them the idea. Sell them the show.'

'What, now? We're going there *now?*'

Top down, Ray-Bans on beneath a *Yankie-Doodle-Ghandi* baseball cap, as Don roared his BMW north towards Burbank in the sunshine he imagined the world was watching. Watching a young, hard-hitting, hard-nosed, hard-assed, hard-bargaining, hard-dicked hard-man begin a day of million-dollar deals.

Of course, the world *wasn't* watching. In fact the only people who paid Don the slightest bit of attention that morning were two young Mexicans, digging up the freeway with a construction team. Sipping Coke and enjoying the sunshine, one nudged the other as Don's car screamed past them.

'Hey, Pedro, tha's one for me! Bring me closer to the top, *si?*' he chuckled to his friend.

Pedro nodded. Their '*spot the tiny-dicked Hollywood asshole who'll be dead in a year*' sweepstake was certainly hotting up.

'I don't like this suit, this feels weird,' Melvin jittered from the passenger seat, squirming and itching in $3000 worth of Don's best navy wool Armani. 'Can't I go back and change? I feel more comfortable in my stuff.'

'Relax, you look fine,' Don said, whipping the car in and out of lanes.

Melvin began to wriggle and fumble, popping lids of bottles and tubs, glugging tablets down his neck with sloshing mouthfuls of mineral water.

'I still don't see why they can't just read it?' he grumbled, patting the clear sleeve on his lap, a fresh print-out of the script neatly knocked together, still warm from the laserprinter.

'What? Are you kidding me?' Don grinned, the car slowing to a halt, boxed in by the morning traffic. 'These guys ain't what you'd call readers. Unless you're talking the financial pages and the wine list at Morton's.' He gazed out at the sea of steel in front of him. 'Hey, c'mon!' he yelled. 'I got a pitch to get to here!'

'We all got pitches, pal,' a voice floated over from his left. A goateed man in a convertible Beetle, all plaid shirt and yellow fingernails, peered from over some John Lennon shades. 'Ain't you heard? Nine a.m. Thursday? It's the new Tuesday at noon. I personally got a pitch with Fox.'

'Sitcom?' Don asked.

'Fuck you. *Feature*,' the goatee said back. 'Big, futuristic Sci-Fi blockbuster.' He checked his watch hurriedly. 'Although I'm gonna be re-pitchin' it as a goddamn' period-piece by the time I get there if this traffic doesn't get a fu—'

The rest of the diatribe was lost as the writer slammed his hand on the car horn. Around them, everyone else in Los Angeles realised that this, *this* was why it was taking so long. Nobody was honking their horns enough and the air suddenly blared and squawked with the frustrated scream of motionless vehicles.

'How's it coming anyway?' Don asked Mel over the din. 'You get much done last night? I heard you bangin' about when I got in.'

'Erm,' he said, hands sliding over the plastic protectively, 'another page.'

'A page?' Don shook his head. 'So what's that, three we got now? Isn't there anything you can do to get done a little faster here?'

Melvin gazed out at the traffic.

'Maybe,' he said.

'Why, Don Silver,' a familiar face pierced the honking air. Don craned around. A black convertible E-type Jaguar purred in the gridlock beside him. Two hands in string-backed driving gloves gripped the wheel. The soft collar of a pink polo shirt flipped in the wind. 'You old Judas.'

'Gill! Good morning. How are ya?' Don said, peering over his shades. 'Great party last night. Elaine looked absolutely—'

'Oh, fuck you, Silver,' Gill spat. 'Fuck *you*.' And hurled a balled-up *Variety* at him, sending it caroming off his hair-gel and bouncing into the back seat. 'Another one bites the dust, huh? Another great Don Silver spin-off goes nose first into the dirt. Careers ruined, lives ruined, but whadda *you* care? Syndication will put another Porsche in your garage, another pool in your lawn, right? And you've got this *new* piece-of-crap everyone's getting in a tizzy over . . .'

'Relax, Gilly boy. Hey, let me introduce Melvin Medford. Mel? This is Gill Kramer, voted the second most popular—'

'You're not interested in *me* anymore, are you? No one at Mercury could give a damn about *me*! Because I'm not *new*! I'm not exciting! I'm not a-a-a steaming four-lane agenda-bender at the intersection of whatever the goddamn' hell that is.'

'Counter-culture and pop-propriety. You got a rehearsal today?' Don turned to Melvin. 'You can sit in on Gill's rehearsal today, if you like, give you a feeling of how we—'

'Oh, juuuust wait. Juuuust you *wait* . . .' Gill snarled. Ahead of them, the honking and blaring faded and the cars began to roll forward.

'Gill, buddy, what can I say?'

But Gill's E-type lurched, swung into another lane to a scream of horns, and vanished into the traffic.

'Touchy.' Don smiled, punching his car-phone speed-dial.

Across town, on Trixi's small cluttered desk, the phones were going nuts.

'Don Silver's office,' she said briskly. 'Yes, Mr Rosen, nine o'clock . . . I believe all the networks will be represented . . . I'll pass on that message when Mr Silver appears . . .'

Red lights flashed and winked on the telephone like a Jean-Michel Jarre concert.

'Thank you.' And she punched the next light. 'Don Silver's . . . oh, Mr Silver. Good morning, sir.'

Trixi slid away her pad and pulled out the *regular* book. A redhead? A brunette? Blonde sixteen-year-old twins?

'*They all here yet?*' Don yelled over the roar of his exhaust note.

'Oh,' Trixi said. She closed the book on *Luscious Lindi* –

S&M speciality and pulled out her pad again. 'We have representatives from ABN, UPC, WN, NBO and KBL, sir,' she rattled off. 'Still awaiting CBN and HBN but they've all called to confirm.'

'*Great. They waiting in my office?*'

'Er, ABN are in your office. We've had to put WN in the lobby, KBL are in the cafeteria, UPC are in the——'

'*No, no, Trix,*' Don barked. '*I need to see all eight guys at once.*'

'Eight, sir? I've signed in . . .' There was a long pause. The sound of flipping pages, '. . . seventy-three gentlemen so far.'

'*Oh, for Chrissakes. Didn't I make it clear enough yesterday? I want decision-makers only? Last thing I need are dozens of dumb Harvard schmucks in cheap suits, saying, "What do you think?" "I dunno, what do you think?" "I'm not sure, it's a gamble, let's get a team on it." Get rid of them*' Don yelled.

'Yes, sir. Eight heads,' Trixi repeated, making notes, 'in office . . .'

'No, no, here's what I want,' he barked. 'Get them to meet us in the parking lot.'

'Sir?'

'Stand them in my spot. Tell 'em . . .'

Don looked over at Melvin next to him. He was flipping frantically through the script, muttering to himself. Don smiled.

'*Tell them the next big thing is just thirty minutes away. And, oh, they should bring their calculators with them. Big ones. With space for lots of zeros.*' And he clicked off.

Trixi took a deep breath and yelled Don's instructions across the busy office. Everybody began to fluster and flurry, bustling protesting executives in and out. She punched another winking light.

'Good morning, Don Silver's office . . . no, I'm afraid Mr Silver is unavailable for at least another couple of . . . he's presenting an important pitch this morning . . . I'm sorry, Mr Busby, if you call back . . . Sheridan who? . . . Oh, I see, in

Variety. No, sir, there's been a misunderstanding. There *is* no Busby or McDonald. These are pen-names. You can't speak to ... No, they don't exist, Mr Busby, that's what I'm saying ... I'm sorry, but you can't be. He doesn't exist ... Well then, *you don't exist*, sir ...'

Trixi sighed. Her phone winked urgently.

'Well, you can, sir, but being *fictional*, I can't promise you'll be allowed into the ... not a problem. Thank you.' She sighed and punched another button. 'Don Silver's office?'

Ben hung up.

'Weird,' he said.

There was a groovy knock on the door and Zak loped in, blinking beneath his flopping fringe. Another ghastly shirt, another questionable pair of slacks. And today's trainers? Christ.

'Hey, man, you ready to roll?' He slapped his palm with a rolled-up copy of *Variety*. 'Ready to meet the man?'

'One second,' Ben said. He chewed his lip for a moment and then, with renewed resolve, continued to stuff everything he had into his thin rucksack.

'So how d'ya like your room?' Zak asked, throwing himself on to the bed with a creaky squeak. 'I got the Steve Guttenberg Lounge upstairs. Landlord like ran out of what you might call classic comics.'

'You *live* in one of these?'

The *Rough Guide* made a big deal of what the Glitz Hotel called its theme rooms, considering they were just rather standard, boxy affairs decorated with clip-framed prints and reproduction posters. Ben was in the Groucho Suite which came complete with a bathroom mirror that had a thick black moustache and glasses painted on it.

'Sure. In return for doing odd jobs. Changing linen, front desk, whatever. In between auditions an' shit.'

'Y'know,' Ben said, stuffing his *Rough Guide* into the top of the rucksack and clipping it shut, 'I called the studio. Just to check that Sheridan was there? They seem to be under the impression he doesn't exist. That he's just a pen name. That *I'm* a pen-name.'

'You spoke to Don?'

'No, just some assistant. Don's not in yet. He's giving some big pitch or something at nine.'

'I guess you'll put 'em straight when you turn up at the door though, right? C'mon, let's like saddle up, dudes.'

The pair of them fussed with jackets and clicked about with sunglasses and then headed out of the hotel, down in the clanking lift to the underground parking lot where Zak's car waited. Ben was full of squirty apprehension. He hadn't been able to sleep, stretched out and itchy on his hotel bed, air-conditioner grinding and moaning away in the airless heat.

They cracked open the tired old Ford and clambered in.

'I really appreciate this,' Ben said, fussing with a seat belt.

'Hey. 'Snothin'. Just remember who I am when you're a big star,' Zak said as the old car lurched and bumped out into the sunlight.

In New York, two worried men sat puffing on a park bench, staring out across the choppy water.

'What about the cops?' Howard said quietly. They hadn't mentioned this possibility before and he knew it was time to consider it.

'Now, don't . . . don't get crazy,' Bernie warned.

'But why not the cops, Bernie? *I* know Don's innocent. *You* know he is. This has to be some *mistake*,' Howard insisted, fat fists clenched. His face was red and shiny, framed around the neck by a fat towel, the effect being that of a cherry atop an ice-cream sundae.

'Howard, you're not thinking—'

'Send in the cops, the Feds, whatever. Get them to blow this thing open. They'll prove Don had nothing to do with those dead bodies. They'll come up with all that forensic hoo-haa, then we'll be able to tell that bastard Garland to shove his damn' threats up—'

'NO!' Bernie snapped back like a terrier. 'No. Let me go and see Garland. See if I can't reason with him.'

'But, Bernie, this is blackmail! You can't reason with people like that. I say let's go to the cops. Right now. Just stroll into the nearest precinct and—'

'Howard! Jesus, think about this for a minute, will you?' Bernie heaved himself up and walked over to the fence, staring through it, looking for answers in the thick black water. He turned.

'What do we say, huh?' he hissed under his breath. 'That some cotton-eyed Joe has framed your son for murder and in return wants our latest TV show? So, please, officer, would you mind arresting him and locking him away for fifty years? Thanks so much, you're a goddamned *gent*.

'For the love of Mike and our Lady of the freakin' Mechanics, Howie, you're not *thinking*. You think the cops'll just take our word for it? It's *murder*, Howie, not a three-month-old parking ticket. They're gonna wade in with their nightsticks and warrants, shut down the studio, shut down the office, shut down production,' he hammered on. 'You'll have British bobbies, the LAPD, the FB-fuckin'-I, all wading through every inch of our station. *Variety* will run it, the *Hollywood Reporter*, the *LA Times*, the *National Enquirer*. It'll be bigger than OJ.'

Howard furrowed his brow in angry realisation.

'No one will *care* if Don's guilty or not, it'll be lost in fuckin' gossip and rumour. All the fame-hungry crazies will come out, claiming Don killed their brother, Don ate their dog, Don took a shit in their station-wagon – all to get their fifteen minutes on *Oprah*. Every illegitimate trailer-park toddler will be a Don Silver love-child. Mud this thick sticks *good*, Howie.'

'All *right!*' he said. 'All right, Jesus. Siddown, Bernie, just sit down for a minute.'

Bernie sat down.

'So what do we do, huh?' Howard was suddenly feeling his age. He put a hand on his brother's shoulder, fixing him with watery eyes. 'You're my fix-it guy. So how do we fix it?'

Bernie sighed, blinking back at his elder brother.

'Well, first I'm gonna fly down to Nashville. Talk to Garland. Make him see sense. *Something.* You get yourself to L.A. Have lunch with Don. Ask him about the tape, ask him about that hotel room. See how much he knows. Until you've spoken to Don, we can't do anything. Now c'mon.' The two men stood. 'Let's finish this lap.'

'You're right, Bern,' Howard said. 'Maybe if you talk to Garland, make him see . . . Bern? You okay?'

'Huh? I . . . er . . . I'm fine. Fine,' he said. But Bernie was far from fine. Because Bernie was looking over Howard's shoulder.

At three approaching joggers.

Not approaching very quickly. In fact strolling would probably be nearer the mark. Crunching slowly along the asphalt, in long expensive overcoats and glistening shoes.

'Bernie?' Howard said.

'Shit, Howard, look. Fuck!' Bernie flapped, failing rather spectacularly at playing it cool, grabbing his brother around the arm and marching him away like an eager bride. 'Go. You'll miss your flight.' He threw frantic looks behind him as the three men drew near. They were whispering to each other, the fat one in the middle nodding calmly.

'Bernie, Jesus, okay, okay . . .'

'C'mon, c'mon, go. I'll uhm, I'm gonna stay here a while. Do some thinking. And, uhm, yoga.' And pushing his brother away, Bernie began to bounce up and down slowly like a drama-class frog. 'I'll call you from Nashville when I've spoken to Randy. Everything will be okay.' And he propelled Howard, bewildered and puffing, down the path in search of a cab.

Hunched on his haunches on the cold path, fingertips on the gravel, Bernie began to tremble, his heart thundering away beneath his fleecy top.

Three pairs of shoes drew level with his hands.

Good shoes. Expensive shoes. Polished.

Bernie stood up slowly like a tailor, taking in in close-up the trousers, the coats, the gloves, scarves and ties. The waft of expensive aftershave.

'Morning, Bernie,' the man in the centre said slowly. 'Beautiful day, isn't it? Good for jogging, for keeping fit. A day to be thinking about your health.' He smiled. 'You thinking about your health, Bernie?'

Tommy stood squarely on the path. His two companions steered Bernie back on to the bench and sat him down.

'I have one of those home gymnasiums myself,' Tommy smiled. 'Takes up the whole damn' basement, all these pads and levers.' He shook his head with a laugh. 'I tell my wife I'm gonna work out, dress up like you with the sneakers and pants, and I go down to the basement and I watch TV.'

The two men either side of Bernie chuckled. Then Bernie began laughing. Then laughing harder. And louder. In fact, the more the two men gripped his upper arms, squeezing, pushing their fat fingers between bone and muscle, the louder he laughed, until eventually Tommy gave an unseen signal and the men let go.

Bernie dropped gasping to his knees, breathless and white.

'You got that contract from ABN yet? For the hundred *Carpool* shows?'

'Tommy, please,' he croaked, 'Really. Let me explain the way the system works . . .'

'The way it *works?*' Tommy said, and tugged out a rolled copy of *Variety* from his overcoat pocket.

'Tommy, no, please.' Bernie made to stand up. The two men either side of him gripped his biceps again, hard, and squeezed gently. He stayed where he was.

'*"Upstairs, Mercury VP Don Silver held court in a guest bedroom wid eight network execs"*,' Tommy read. '*"We speculate it has somethin' to do wid Don's high-way laffer."*'

The four men listened to the whisper of distant morning traffic for a moment.

'It don't sound like Donny boy has got da message, Bernie.'

Bernie swallowed, shifting uncomfortably on the bench as best he could, sandwiched between the two slabs of meat in Versace.

'T-Tommy,' he began. 'Tommy, I don't know what you've read or what you've heard, but please, let me . . . *Yeaarghh!*' he yelped, the hoods' gloved hands pressing between muscle and bone. 'Oh, *Jesus* . . .'

'You think I'm fuckin' with you, Bernie? That it?'

'P-please . . .' he stuttered, almost passing out from the pain in his arms.

Tommy squatted on his haunches in front of Bernie, allowing his cashmere coat to trail on the muddy verge. He shook his head with deep regret and tutted.

'We don't have all day, Bern.'

'Tommy . . .'

'I gotta go back to Dad with a deal in place, signed on the line which is dotted. So stop wasting my time and get the deal done, Bernie. You hear me?'

Tommy blinked slowly, flicked a look at both hoods and then settled it back on Bernie, fixing him with a flat, emotionless stare.

'Hey, listen,' Bernie said breathlessly. His mind swam with thoughts of Nashville, of cowboy hats, of photographs and tape-recorded screaming. 'There might be . . . there might be a little complication.'

At some unseen signal the man on Bernie's left reached around his huge frame, turning smoothly and confidently, grabbed Bernie's left arm in two white-knuckled fists and cracked it at the elbow. Only an inch, but an inch further than it wanted to go.

Which is an enormous amount.

Bernie screamed, dropping helplessly to his knees, tears

spraying from his eyes, clutching at his bad arm with his good one, trying to hold it, push it, squeeze it, turn it. Do anything to alleviate the roaring pain.

Tommy was talking. Buttoning his coat, giving instructions to his men, but for Bernie it seemed a thousand miles away. His world swam and bucked and lurched, pain roaring behind his eyes, purple, red, angry. He tasted his own hot bile stinging his throat, he was dizzy . . . the sky, the ground, the sky, the fence . . . He was going to pass out. The ground. Tommy. The ground. The sky. Tommy's voice soft. Far, far away.

Louder now.

'Enough's enough, Bernie, and I'm sick of dis. So dis is the way it is. You bring me der contract for one hundred shows, guaranteed, ABN prime-time by *Monday morning* or it'll be more than just your arm that'll need patching up.'

'Tommy, please.' Bernie winced, eyes streaming, heart slamming away.

He gave his men a nod. They stood, twitching and shifting in their big coats, clicking huge necks, rolling beefy shoulders. Bernie remained kneeling in the mud, clutching his arm, whimpering desperately.

'Please, wait . . . Wait!' he screamed, stumbling to his feet. Mud and grit speckled his knees and hands; his face was wet with sweat and tears.

'Get it signed, Bernie. I mean it. Monday morning.'

SEVENTEEN

'Shit!' Ben said, pointing through the open passenger window. 'Shit, there he is!'

'Your buddy?'

'No, Silver. Don Silver! There, by the car!' Ben was almost halfway out of the window with excitement as Zak coughed his old Ford along the wide sprawl of Almeda Avenue.

Fifty yards away, across the parking lot littered with 4x4s and gleaming Porsches, a group of burly men huddled about a convertible BMW in their shirt sleeves, shaking hands one by one.

'Oh, like, Jee-*zus!*' Zak cursed, his car rolling to a halt. 'We got a problem.'

Ahead of them the street was gridlocked, blocked tight with identical silver Lexuses. Two dozen, gleaming and winking in the sunlight, locked in like a used-car lot. Around these identical cars, two dozen identical grey-suited execs paced and gestured and swore and paced some more and barked into phones and glugged water and tried to book the same corner table at the same restaurant.

Three or four were being turned away by a squat security guard on the gate.

Zak killed the engine and he and Ben sat still in the warm car, backs sticky against the vinyl seating. Ben stuffed the map away and looked at Zak.

'So what do we do now?' he said. 'If he's not letting *these* guys in, we'll never—'

'Confidence, Benny Boy. C'mon. And like, try to look British,' Zak said through the side of his mouth, clambering out.

As security guard on the main gate of Mercury Pictures, Mickey Thomopoulos had a fairly easy life of raising gates, ticking lists and doffing his cap. He had little to say, beyond 'morning, sir', 'morning, miss' and 'relaxation therapist for Mr Silver? The side entrance if you would, ma'am, thank you very much'. It wasn't well-paid work, which was why Mickey also had a night job providing armed security for the rich and paranoid up in Beverly Hills. The Mercury job, however, did give him plenty of free time, which was why he liked it.

Because it was within the long afternoon lull between lunch and dinner that Mickey chased his dreams. Quietly, thermos at his side, typewriter on his little desk, within the cramped confines of his pink booth.

This particular morning, however, he had barely had the chance to feed the paper into the rollers, what with the rumpus of cell-phones and car-horns and nervous executives pleading with him to be let in.

'Hullo? Good day to you, sir, pip-pip!' a voice called loudly.

Mickey put down his cup of coffee for the hundredth time and emerged blinking from his booth, adjusting his ill-fitting snug polyester trousers, his ill-fitting snug polyester blazer, and brandishing his ill-fitting, snug polyester radio.

'Help you, gentlemen?' he said.

'Now, my man. We are here for an urgent rendezvous with one Master Donald St John Silver,' a young blond man said, whipping off his sunglasses and peering at Mickey's laminate. 'Be a good fellow and let him know we have arrived . . . Mickey, is it? Well, Michael, run along now, chop-chop.'

Another young guy scuttled up behind the blond, teeth clenched in a wince.

'Names, gentlemen, please?' Mickey said, flipping out his clipboard.

'I am Master Zachary Smythe of the Londonshire Smythes,' the blond trumpeted, sticking out a pleased-to-meet-you hand. 'And this is Sir Benjaford S. Busbyworth. We are from the BBC in England, don't you know, old chap.'

Mickey slid a fat finger down his clipboard, shaking his head.

'You're not on the list, boys. No appointments, no name, no entrance. Sorry, fellahs. I'm gonna have to ask you to back your car out through—'

'I don't think you understand, Michael,' Zachary insisted. 'This is Sir Benjaford S. Busbyshire.'

'You said Busbyworth . . .'

'S. Busby*worth*, exactly. S for Shakespeare. He is the great-great-great-grandson of the finest writer in the English language. *Hamlet, Macbeth, Much Ado About A Night's Dream?* He has written the very *show* all these gentlemen here are so eager to buy: *Carpool.* Originally broadcast on the BBC under the title . . . uh . . .'

'Tailback,' his partner said.

'Tailback, exactly. Starring Benny Hill, Peter Sellers and . . . uhm . . . Princess Di, God rest her soul.'

Mickey blinked back at this insane young man in his dayglo trousers, preposterous footwear and floppy blond hair.

'You guys really from the BBC?' he said slowly, eyeing them suspiciously. ''Cos with respect, gentlemen, over here you gotta call first. You can't just show up here demanding to be seen. There's procedure, protocol. Get your office to call Mr Silver's office, get an appointment—'

'The electric telephone!' Zachary spluttered loudly. 'We have sailed over from the London coast, on the *Queen Mary*, to dock at Plymouth Rock. Spent six weeks travelling the length of this Godforsaken country, our horses fairly expiring from strain. And we are told, after a journey that Phileas Fogg made in double the time, that we should have made an *appointment*? We are from the BBC! We have been broadcasting quality programming to the Queen and her subjects since 1372. What shall I tell her, hmmm? She'll have us beheaded!'

Mickey chewed his lip.

'Well . . . okay, boys, I don't want you to get beheaded or nuthin',' he said. 'C'mon through.' And with gracious nods, the two young men scuttled through.

'But, hey,' Mickey called out, 'a favour for a favour, guys, huh?' And he grabbed his work from the booth. 'Would you have a look at this for me?'

He handed Zachary a slim wad of paper, fixed at the left edge with brass fasteners. Zachary held it up.

MAIN GATE - pilot by Mickey Thomopoulos

'I've been tryin' to get Mr Silver to take a look at this for three years. It's a comedy about a guy who works at a TV studio. Security guard, y'know? Kinda Homer Simpson meets Ted Danson kinda thing. He works on the—'

'*Main gate?*' Zachary guessed. 'Sounds delightful, my man, sounds delightful. What do you think, Benjaworth? We could put it on between the Queen's Speech and Monty Python? Leave it with us, good chap, leave it with us. Toodle-oo,' he added, and minced past the gate and off across the parking lot, his partner scuttling after him quickly.

'Sign in at reception, they'll show you to Mr Silver's office, gents,' Mickey called after them. 'And, thanks. Thanks a lot.'

'*Y'see?*' Zak whispered to Ben when they were out of range. '*I'm good. This is second nature to me. I only been around you like, what? An hour? But I already got your speech, your vocabulary, your style . . .*'

'Madam, please remain in your seat,' the stewardess said briskly, using the first-grade teacher tone she had been taught at International Stewardess College. 'And fasten your—'

'But I just need to speak to my friend, it's urgent.' She was pushing her belt aside and standing up. 'He's up the front? If I can just—'

'Please, madam, the seatbelt sign is illuminated,' the stewardess said, placing her hand on the seat in front, blocking Diane's escape.

She smiled weakly and dropped back into her seat, the stewardess waddling off down the aisle, bobbing and smiling like a nodding dog on a car's rear shelf.

Diane sat chewing a biro.

It was midday. She'd spent the morning on the phone, calling the Mercury offices on Fifth Avenue and the studio in LA, trying to piece together her key characters' whereabouts.

Howard, it seemed, was on his way to see his son on the West Coast. Diane had no intention of waiting politely while he and Don cooked up a cover-story for these photos so needed to intercept him urgently to find out what was going on. She'd got Howard's flight number from his overly helpful PA and bought the cheapest ticket she could for the first leg of his flight, thus enabling her to get on board and talk to the old man.

She checked her watch.

She had about fifteen minutes to find him, get her answers and be off the plane to avoid being stranded in Boston with no car, no cash, and no . . . *ow!*

Diane's seat jolted forward as the passenger behind kicked out sharply. She craned around to see a young child squirming and bawling against her belt. Stewardesses bustled over, dishing out *there-there*s and *brave-girl*s, the child lashing out again, knocking one of the stewardess's blue hats to the floor. Other passengers were twisting round now, pointing and mumbling. The child shrieked and bellowed, the parents adding a helpful smack across her bare legs to the cocktail of chaos.

Oh, this was all she needed, Diane thought. She looked down glumly, her eye caught by something under her seat, poking out a little.

'Seatbelts now, don't forget your seatbelts, ladies and gentlemen,' Diane said, bustling towards the front of the plane. The stewardess's hat was a little large, but nobody seemed to notice as she pushed through the curtain busily. She'd buttoned up her jacket to the neck and pulled it down at the bottom as far as it would go, covering as much of her Levis as she could. Fortunately most of the passengers were distracted by the little girl performing highlights from the *The Exorcist* at the back of the plane.

Through the curtain, into the wide aisles and legroom of first class, the hat came off, tossed on to one of the many empty seats. Diane threw off her jacket too and attempted to appear bored and spoilt and a bit lost, grabbing a glass of champagne from a trolley and wandering between the seats, humming tunelessly, looking for a familiar head of white hair.

Ah-ha.

'Why, Mr Silver, good morning,' she said, dropping into a huge seat next to his.

'Miss Lang?' Howard said, shuddering into life, stuffing glossy pictures back into a stiff envelope.

Diane reclined her seat sharply, kicking off her sneakers and holding up her champagne glass. 'Cheers!'

Howard went very pale, which was astonishing considering how pale the old man was already. He really didn't look well. His face was white and slack, mouth hanging open limply. His forehead danced with a light sheen of sweat. He swallowed and shifted painfully.

'You off to see Donald?' Diane continued. 'Ask him about this new show of his? The one you're selling to Randy Garland?'

Howard almost fell out of his chair.

'I mean, that's a bit strange, isn't it? *Variety* talking about bids coming in from all the major networks, and yet there you were yesterday, talking to a small-time cable station hick in your office. What's the story?'

'What . . . how . . .' Howard blustered and flustered, rolling about like a barrel in his reclining chair. 'I did no such thing! I have no idea what you're . . .'

'I saw him leave,' Diane said calmly. She sipped her champagne. 'Mmm, this really is—'

'He wanted to talk to me about . . . about the profile. Had I seen it, what did I think of it? He dropped by for a chat, that was *all*,' Howard ad-libbed. 'We are not selling him *anything*.' He reached for his arm-rest and began jabbing the *stewardess-call* button. He would soon have this nosey woman back in economy class where she belonged.

'Forget his hat?'

'I'm sorry, what?'

'He forget his hat? Leave it at your office? Is that why Bernie is flying down to Nashville today to see him? I called your PA. Caroline, is it? Helpful girl. She told me about your emergency trip out west, and said Bernie was booked to fly out from La Guardia this afternoon. Delta Airlines flight 6151 to Nashville International. Now unless Bernie's got some secret Tammy Wynette fetish he hasn't told anyone about, I'd say it looks like you and Mr Garland have some kind of—'

'Miss Lang—'

'Paretsky,' Diane corrected. 'Diane Paretsky. *Sexposé*.'

'*Paretsky?*' Howard whispered, realisation sucking the life from his face. He shifted in his seat, itchy with panic. He really didn't look well. Breathing fast, puffing, knuckles white on his plush arm-rests. 'You attempt to turn any of this insane speculation into anything even resembling a story, I will . . . I will . . .'

'You all right, Howard?' she said. 'Jesus, you need to relax. We're just talking, that's all. I haven't seen you this flustered since, well . . .' And she tugged an envelope from her jacket.

Howard froze, breath held, as Diane slid the photograph out.

'. . . these arrived at your club. What are they all about anyway? This Donald here?'

Howard made an instinctive move to grab the picture, but it wasn't until his hand was halfway out that he realised this was rather incriminating. So he pulled back. Then, realising what Diane might do with the picture if she was allowed to keep it, he quickly lunged out again. And then he changed his mind once more.

For a moment, Diane watched the panicky old man hokey-cokey, hand out, hand in, hand out, brain shaking all about with terrified computations and consequences.

'Yes, can I help you, Mr Silver?' a familiar voice said. The stewardess was back. Her bouffant, free of its hat, was ballooning and expanding to fill the aisle. 'Madam,' she said sternly, 'would you return to your seat?'

Diane got up, nodding and tucking the photograph away again.

'It's okay,' she said. 'I'm getting off, I changed my mind. I don't fancy LA after all.' She wandered back through the curtain to the rear of the plane. Gathering up her things, she hoisted her bag on her shoulder and strolled calmly to the exit, singing softly to herself.

'All together now, *stand by your man, waah waah waahhh . . .*'

Half an hour later, in the warm sunshine of the Mercury lot, Don watched an unusual sight. That of five hundred million syndicated dollars wandering away from him. His world, his future, his life. Just scratching its head and shrugging its shoulders and wandering back to its car.

He closed his eyes and craned his face up to the sun. He felt the warmth on his cheeks, on his eyelids, the world pulsing purple and orange. He took a long, deep breath, tried to focus, to centre, to remain calm. In out, in out, like his personal Tai Chi instructor had taught him.

He opened his eyes, exhaling slowly. He turned to Melvin, standing scratching himself sheepishly by the front of the car.

'S-sorry,' Melvin said.

'*Sorry!*' Don screamed in exactly the way his Tai Chi guy hadn't instructed him to. 'You fucking *moron!* What the *hell's* the matter with you, huh? HUH? Have you *any* idea what you just did, you talentless piece of *crap*?!'

'I didn't know what t-to say.'

'Oh, this is bad. This is bad!' Don began to pace, running a clammy hand through his thick dark hair. 'I'm out. *We're* out, you hear me? Out. It's okay for you, you can go crawling back to Weybridge-on-Rye or wherever the hell you're from.'

'Walmington-on—'

'But me? It's all over. All over. Dad'll take the job, he'll take the house, the car, everything. I'll have to leave Los Angeles.' Don stopped suddenly, the realisation clanging him in the face like a Tex Avery frying pan. 'Leave LA? I can't leave LA! My dentist is here! My decorator is here! What am I going to do? Jesus, what am I going to *do*?!' He paced again, saying 'fuck' rather a lot.

'I just thought if I told them—'

'You just thought? Oh, you just *thought*? That sort of information is not the sort of thing that gets nervous networks jumping into bed with us, Melly boy. In fact, it's pretty much a sure-fire way to have them yawning and standing up and asking for local cab firms because they don't want to *spoil the friendship!*'

'So, uhmm, what happens now?' Melvin asked softly.

'What happens now? What happens now?' Don chanted over and over. 'I'm out of the fuckin' TV business is what happens now. *Christ!*' And he threw himself against the hood of the car with a horrible thunk. 'This was the easiest fucking pitch in the world, Mel. The easiest pitch in the world! They're all standing there . . . Ted, Merv, Al . . . flapping their cheque-books, drowning in their own drool, desperate to get hold of this show.

All you had to do, *all you had to do*, was just tell them it's three guys, it's cheap and it's funny. That's it. That's all it needed. Three guys. Cheap. Funny. But, no, *you* tell them . . . aarghhh!' he wailed in frustration.

'I'm sorry . . .' Melvin mumbled.

'Oh, Jesus, we've blown it. *Blown it!*' And Don pounded his fists on the warm metal. 'This was my last chance. My last chance and we've blown it. What am I gonna tell Dad, huh? *What am I gonna tell Dad?* I'm having lunch with him in . . . fuck!' He looked at his Rolex. 'I gotta stall him, gotta fix this. Melvin, go home, just get outta here, I gotta fix this . . .' And he spun around, eyes wild and flashing.

Melvin watched him charge across the lot.

'Trixi! Trixi!' yelled Don, fumbling for his cell-phone.

Across the lot, Ben pushed his way out of reception, blinking in the sunshine. Don's BMW glinted a hundred yards away. Ben began to run excitedly.

The studio was alive with frantic action. Over by the main gate, a handful of older men were shouting at the young execs, silver Lexus after silver Lexus reversing and backing up and crunching into each other. Phones were being brandished, water bottles passed about, brows mopped – and Mickey was attempting to coordinate it all with burly movements.

There was a honk and Ben leaped to one side as a forklift rolled past balancing what looked like a charred bit of timbered wall on a palette. Another honk and two golf carts zipped by, driven by men in tatty peasants' rags, sipping Starbucks coffee cups and sporting sunglasses.

'Move!' another voice yelled, a tall handsome man in a panic rushing past him, cell-phone clamped to his ear, muttering about his father.

Ben hurried towards the car, yelling and waving as it slowly moved off.

'Mr Silver! Mr Silver! It's me, it's Ben. Ben Busby?'

The car rolled to a halt. The American stared at him blankly.

'We, er, met in London a few days ago? Good to ... er ... good to see you again,' he said, catching his breath.

The American sat still, mouth slack, hands on the wheel. A thousand signals seemed to be flashing and sparking at once behind his eyes.

'Ben! Y-yes, of course. Sorry, sorry. What . . . what are you doing here?'

This threw him rather. What was he *doing* here?

'The show? Tailba – *Carpool*. I read about it in the paper. You've got Sheridan here?'

The American said nothing.

'Sheridan? The writer? Fat? Liverpudlian?' Still nothing. 'Are you all right, Mr Silver?' This was very weird, he seemed in a terrible state. Maybe the pitch hadn't gone well?

But then suddenly, as if the puppeteer had returned from lunch and snatched up the marionette strings again, he was moving, fast and urgent. He was out of the car, scuttling quickly to the passenger side where Ben stood, snapping open the door and bustling him in. He scrabbled at Ben's shoulder, pushing his rucksack and jacket, folding it all in and slamming the door. He fussed about behind him at the back of the car, fiddling with the clips and catches of the roof, yanking and tugging it up over the top.

'Of course, of course. Sorry, my mind's on a million different things. Good to see you, Ben, good to see you. Sorry, buddy. Sheridan's back at the house.'

Ben watched him struggle and battle with the clumsy roof mechanism.

'You want me to give you a—'

'No, no, you stay where you are,' the American said, pushing him back in with a slam and a click. 'Tailback! What a show, *what a show!* he laughed. 'You tell anyone you were coming here?' He fastened one side and bustled around the back of the car.

'What? Oh, er, no. I just thought I should come over,' Ben said, wide-eyed.

The American finished snapping the roof to the windshield and threw a nervous glance over his shoulder before clambering in. He revved the engine and the car crunched over the gravel towards Mickey at the exit. 'You fly over by yourself? Didn't you bring your wife or your mom or anyone?'

'Huh? No, just me.' Ben couldn't believe it. It was true. It was all true. 'So you liked it? The show?'

'Just you. Just you. Okay, okay,' the American said, steadying his breathing. 'So tell me, what's been going on, Benny-boy? How the hell are you?'

Ben caught sight of Zak's old Ford on the corner.

'Shit,' he said quickly, throwing a thumb over his shoulder. 'Sorry. My friend, he's still up in the office. He wanted to meet you. Maybe I should let him know—'

'Don't worry about him,' the American said. 'Let's j-just get you home. Get you and Sheridan together again.'

As Ben and Mel eased their way tentatively on to Alemeda Avenue, the seething network executives huddled in packs on the wide street, tossing expletives and car-keys about in the sunshine. The only executives not deep in consultation with calculators and rolled-up newspapers were the thirty-strong team from ABN. They stood in the warm afternoon in sweaty shirt sleeves, phones against their heads, sunglasses on, wandering between the crush of traffic, gazing about the lot like lost children and repeating the same question.

'Al? Where the hell is Al?'

At that moment, Al was jogging bristly in the other direction, through the wide shady lanes between the studios.

With a nod and a '*Catching the show, Mr Rosen?*' he was waved through by a squat security guard with an ill-fitting snug polyester face, past the little golf carts and trailers as he joined busy production staff hurrying about with coffee and clipboards.

The lanes were alive with preparation for the shooting of the next episode of *Fyre* on Saturday. It was to be the big one. Taking their cue from Howard's *Variety* profile, the production team had doubled the special-effects budget. Samuel Pepys was now going to pack a full-scale mock-up of St Paul's Cathedral with dynamite, causing it to topple into the Thames, the resultant colossal tidal wave extinguishing the flames on both banks of the river. ('Surf's up!' was rumoured to be his straight-to-camera line.) Timber and powerful spotlights were manhandled from forklifts and racks of charred costumes trundled across the lot as Al clanged up the iron staircase outside Studio 3 and, checking over his shoulder like a child skipping school, ducked through into the darkness.

'Mr Rosen, good morning,' young staff in headsets whispered one by one, stepping aside to let him among the chill scaffolding, gantries and swathes of black cloth of the studio. Al moved quietly among the three hundred tiered seats dotted with crew members sipping coffee and found a place near the back.

Under the glare of the hot lights on the studio floor, burly men set up the four cameras, each monstrous thing the size of a forklift taking two men to pull it in and out. Trainers squeaked over the black floor, constellated with bits of coloured gaffer tape; dozens of people wandered about with clip-boards and headphones and pencils.

Al sat back and breathed deeply, a warm tingling smile spreading across his face. Gill would kill him if he knew he was here, but Al couldn't resist it. He loved nothing more than sneaking out of pitches and conferences to come and see his Coochybuns give a performance. The taste of the stale studio air, the smell of squeaking rubber floors, the hospital set looming life-size . . .

Al sat transfixed by it all.

'Checking up on the talent?' a female voice whispered behind him.

He jumped and spun around. A young woman in slim black spectacles, her blond hair in bunches, winked back at him from behind a notepad.

'Penny Lang,' she said, offering him a hand. '*Variety*. Not out a-schmoozing with the other networks?'

Al was flustered.

'Uhmm, no. I thought I'd just drop in. See, uhm, how the . . . uhh . . .'

'The big nine-eight, huh?' Penny said. 'Impressive. I'm doing a little piece about the mood on set. After all, just two to go before everyone's . . .' And she slowly drew a long fingernail across her neck. 'Ahem, *pursuing other opportunities.*'

Al scowled a little and tried to focus again on the rehearsal.

'Heyyy, care to give us *your* viewpoint, Mr Rosen?' Penny said, shoving a cassette recorder up Al's nose. 'I wanna talk to everyone involved. Rumour is, *you* broke the news to Gill Kramer, true? How'd he take it? Threw all his toys out the pram, I'm guessing. And Don? What about him? That's almost a hundred percent flop record now. He must have flipped.'

'Don . . . Don has other things on his mind at the moment,' Al quavered.

'You, I said out!' Don barked, slamming out of his office like a typhoon with PMS.

'But Mr Black is an actor, sir,' Trixi said quickly, getting to her feet. 'He's been waiting to see you for half an hour . . .'

'Zachary Black,' Zak began, tossing his blond locks over his shoulder like a university scarf and extending a hand and a warm smile. 'But my friends call me—'

'A cab,' Don interrupted. 'Your friends call you a cab. Get off my lot. You,' he barked at Trixi, 'once you've stopped flirting with no-talent actors, have you reached my father yet? Stalled him?'

'N-no, sir,' Trixi said, grabbing up her pad from the cluttered desk. 'But he definitely boarded the plane at JFK this morning.'

'Shit, shit, shit, shit,' Don said, flapping about.

'Er . . .' Zak interrupted limply. 'They call me *Zak*, as in—'

'As in, you're ex-Zak-tly the guy security are about to throw into the street,' Don snapped, and jabbed a finger at Trixi. You, in here. Damage control.' And he spun on his heel and flew into his office.

*

'He freezes. You believe that?' Don said hurriedly.

'Sir?'

Trixi sat in a low chair, desk diary on her lap, watching her boss try and control his panic. His usual pose — feet up on desk, hands behind his head, glugging bottled water and flicking listlessly through the trades until lunchtime — was gone. He looked haunted and hunted, like a man on the run.

'Clams up tighter than a crooked accountant's ass in a San Quentin shower block. Nothing, not a word. The eight most powerful men in network television are standing in the goddamn' parking lot and he's staring at the floor,' Don said, whipping off his jacket and tossing it over a chair. He began to pace and roll his sleeves, yelling at his modern art, at his leather sofa. 'So they figure he's nervous, right? Ask him questions, regular pitch shit. *How do you see it curving, Melvin?*" *"What's the central dynamic, Melvin?"* *"How will the characters platform, Melvin?"* Stupid son of a bitch just shrugs and says: *"I don't know. I've only written three pages."* '

Don let out a scream of frustration.

'He brought the fucking *truth* to a pitch meeting! Not, *"Good question there, Al."* Not, *"It'll curve beautifully, Merv."* Not, *"I'd be interested in your input, gentlemen."* Oh, no. He gives 'em *"I don't know, I've only written three pages."* The dumb fuck!'

Don threw himself into his chair, sending papers and pencils skittering across the desk to the floor. He covered his head with his hands.

'So then . . . so then they're pissed, right? Ted, Mickey, Bill, the lot of 'em. *"Wasting my time, Silver! Kid doesn't even know how it ends?"* *"Your father'll hear about this, Silver."* On and on. And Mel starts yelling over the top of them like a lunatic.'

'Yelling?'

'*"It's not my fault!"* he shouts. Not his fault? He's only the fuckin' writer.' Don was up on his feet again, twitchy with panic. '*"Not my fault,"* he says. Then he starts pointing out to the street. *"Leave me alone! It's not my show!"* he says. *"It's their show!"* Over and over. *"It's theirs! Ask them!"* '

'*Oh, but, begorrah! Send Shep!*' Gill cried in his appalling accent for the fifth time as Farmer Old McDonald suddenly stood on a chair in the emergency room. '*Aye, to be sure, 'tis the only way you'll beat this terrible traffic, so 'tis.*'

Clustered in a semi-circle in front of this ghastly performance were five lecterns, each one on wheels with a name stencilled on the front, open ring binders and pens and baseball caps and bottles of water covering their tops. The directors, the assistant director, the producers and technical team watched the scene on little monitors, nervously.

Their nervousness was nothing, however, compared to the nail-munching, pencil-chewing, foot-tapping and botty-churning anxiety of the eight writers huddled about their shoulders, all clutching bottled water, buckled scripts and each other.

'*M'boy knows Chicago like t'were the rollin' hills o' Donegal,*' Gill continued hammily. '*Sure, he can name every traffic light from the Sears Tower to the Navy Pier, to be sure he can now. Aye, an' he's pissed on most o' them.*'

Al watched in rapt appreciation of his beloved.

'Okay, great,' Rob yelled from his lectern, a cue for the frozen tableau of people on the studio floor suddenly to explode into frantic life, leaping up from the monitors and lecterns and on to the set in a flurry of scripts.

'Great?' Gill spat, clambering from his chair. 'Are you out of your tiny mind?' And he pushed a light meter from under his nose. 'Just get out of my face!'

Rob slunk gingerly past the sea of cameras and assistants on to the set, holding a buckled script over his chest like a shield. He knew what was coming and braced himself for the blast.

'I'm dying up here!' Gill snapped, glaring at him. He snatched off his straw hat and pushed Rob in the chest with it.

'Gill, it's still only the first scene—'

'It stinks! Sending a dog across Chicago to get a nose? A *nose?* What's funny about that?'

'B-but it was your suggestion?' Rob said, flipping back his notes. 'We agreed that a nose would—'

'This is *ridiculous!* I quit! This is shallow, soulless drivel! I *quit!* Ninety-eight episodes or not, I *quit!*' And Gill pushed past Rob, sending thirty people scattering like pavement pigeons. 'I mean it this time. Let me through, let me *through*.' Cameramen looked at producers, costumers looked at lighting riggers, and Al sat frozen in numb horror. Rob called after him.

'Gill, you can't—'

'*Watch me!* ABN want to leave me dying up there? Well, how about I take their precious syndication cheque to the grave *with me!*' And he charged off the floor.

'Heyyy!' Penny said as Al leaped up and began to tumble and hurdle over the plastic seats towards his fleeing star. 'Now *that's* a story.'

There was a light knock on Don's door.

'Not now!' he yelled. 'Jesus, Trix, Dad's relying on this to save his reputation. I'm relying on this one to save my ass. You realise what he'll do if I tell him I've fucked up? This was my last chance.'

Trixi watched her boss, jittery with nerves, pace about the room like a kid outside the Principal's office.

'Okay, so here's what we do, right? Cancel the restaurant. Get them give a message to Dad when he shows up. I'm sick, I've got a meeting, I died . . . whatever. Doesn't matter. Send him back to New York, we need him out of the way while this damn' fiasco blows over. Then get Merv and Al and Ted and Fred and everybody on the phone. No, better still, send cards to their offices. Flowers, wine, something. Tell them it was a joke. A . . . God, I dunno, a test of their commitment, experimental street theatre. Anything. Tell them the real pitch is next Monday. Put it in your diary. Then call *Variety* and the *Hollywood Reporter*. They're gonna try and run a story but we can't let Dad—'

'Mr Silver?' a soft voice came from somewhere. Don stopped, mid-panic. A young assistant had her head poked around the door jamb, a handful of 5x3" index cards fanned in her hand like a magician.

'What's this?' Don said. Trixi took them and peered at them, passing them to her boss.

'From the networks,' she said.

Don, puffing, took the cards in trembling hands and turned them over like a croupier.

'What the hell . . . ?'

It seemed Ted Cohn of ABN had gone back to his team of people by the main gate, an anxious man. As had Merv Kushnick at KBL, Mickey Schriber from HBN and the rest, jackets off, shirt sleeves rolled up, pacing and muttering.

They *had* to have it.

How *brilliant* it was, how utterly, ground-breaking and innovative. And the *pitch!* Extraordinary, frankly, just *extraordinary!*

Which? Why? How? the faceless executives all muttered in unison What *happened* out there? And the presidents, with fluttering hearts and tight throats and opening wallets, had explained.

To start in *utter silence.* Just sitting behind the wheel of a car, rocking back and forth.

Genius.

After all, wasn't this how most ordinary Americans spent their lives? Not goofing around in coffee-shops, not wise-cracking on radio stations, not downing beers and coming up with crazy schemes. Just sitting, frustrated, in motionless vehicles. It was true, it was honest, it was *real.*

And then, when they finally asked the writer about his show, what did he say? Did he dance around, wisecracking about zany plot ideas and goofy coincidences like every other sitcom schmuck? Did he baffle them with the nerdy jargon, about arcs and warmth and curves and platforms? Did he hug his precious idea to his chest and refuse to budge an inch?

We don't know? the harried but still faceless assistants all over the street all cried in unison. *Did he?*

Absolutely not! the presidents cried. He just (and there were lumps in throats and tears in eyes at this point), he just turned. And he pointed out, out to the streets, out to the men of America, out to the working men of the world and shouted: '*I* don't know what happens. It's not *my* show! *It's theirs!*'

Truly touching stuff. To dedicate the whole concept, not to the self-serving award-giving tux-sporting coke-heads of the industry, but to the ordinary working men of the world whose lives this show would finally speak for.

In his office, Don was laughing.

Gill wasn't.

'I've had enough, Al. You hear me? Enough. I quit.'

He sat in front of his huge dressing-room mirror, gown wrapped tight around his dungarees, toes curling angrily in his slippers.

'I've been humiliated. *Humiliated!*' he spat. 'Stabbed in the back by *you* – cancelling me, leaving me high and dry. Then that bastard Dick Trent steals my cover-shot! I tell you,' and Gill snatched up *Variety* from his desk, 'Penny Lang got it right.'

'Easy! Easy there, Gill, c'mon now,' Al said nervously, aware that the hack in question was in all likelihood skulking around the corridors of the studio right this minute.

'... *Most Hollywood watchers presumed Gill would retreat for some wound licking*...'

'Gill—'

'Well, she's *right*, dammit! I should be! After the way I've been treated. By this studio, my public. *You!*'

'*Sweetheart—*'

'But, *no!* Not good old Gill! There I am, up there under the lights, churning out more of this drivel. Finishing the season like a good little boy, getting ABN the hundred, making sure *everybody* gets rich. The network, the studio. Well, why *should I*, answer me that? After the way I've been treated? Why in Cosby's name *should I?*'

'Sweetheart, c'mon now,' Al soothed. He had a horrible sick feeling in his stomach about where this was heading. 'Look, we're all *relying* on this money. Mercury need it, ABN need it. We've been waiting for four years for this. And it's *my* responsibility to make sure we get that hundredth show in the can. My job on the line. Can't you do this for me?'

Gill glared at him. Al swallowed nervously and crouched down at his side, holding Gill's trembling hand.

'Why don't you hold your head up, bite your tongue and finish the series, hmm? It's only two more shows. Keep Mercury happy. Don, the network, everybody. Let 'em know you're a *team player*. They're bound to look more favourably on you afterwards. Find you another project.' And he straightened Gill's robe. 'Or alternatively, hell, this syndication deal is as much for you, Gillybubs, as anybody. You'll be able to retire on the—'

'*Arghhhh!*' Gill exploded, hurling a pot of face cream at the wall, splashing his huge photograph. 'You're all the same! Shifty, Don, you! *Retire?!* I don't want to retire! I'm an *artist!* This is what I do!' And he threw his hands in the air. 'This is my life! But ABN get two more shows out of me and I'm *finished!* No career, no Couple Of The Year awards, no *nothing*. Finished!'

'Gill, relax . . .'

'So.' He smiled tightly, pulling his gown around him. 'Here's what I'm *thinking*.'

Oh, God, Al thought, gripping the back of his chair.

Oh, yes? Penny thought, outside the door, gripping her cassette recorder.

*

Don was flipping and flapping through the cards, a huge greedy grin dripping from his chin.

'Still nothing from ABN,' Mindi said, 'but everyone else—'

'Fuck ABN! Fuck 'em!' Don laughed. 'Have you seen these?' he shouted, waving the cards over his head. 'Jesus Christ, we're back! Y'hear me? We are *back!* KBL and CBN are both offering ten million a show. NBO have come in with eleven and a half. This is nuts! Eleven and a half million? Per show? Nuts!' And he shook his head, laughing.

'Am I still cancelling lunch?' Trixi said, heading to the door.

'Are you shitting me? Get on to Spagos. Get them to move me to the biggest fucking table they've got. If they give you any shit, just read one of these to them.' And he threw the cards at his assistant.

Don wandered round to his chair and dropped into it with a happy sigh, allowing it to swivel around a couple of times. 'And make sure the restaurant has a medic standing by. Dad is gonna have a freakin' coronary when he sees those. Don Silver, golden boy. No more prodigal son.' And he cracked his feet up on top of the desk loudly, throwing his hands behind his head. 'Prodigal sun shining out of my goddamn' prodigal *ass!*'

'Will that be all, sir?' Trixi said, retrieving the cards from the floor.

'No. Get me *Vanity Fair*.'

'This month's?'

'The editor,' Don said, closing his eyes and luxuriating in his chair. 'I feel a cover photo coming on. *Silver Strikes Gold*,' he said, sending a broad hand sweeping across the room. 'Whadd'ya think? We'll get Leibowitz to shoot it. Maybe a few girls in bikinis sitting around, stroking my—'

'Donald!' a voice shrieked from outside the door, shattering the mood.

'Ha! You're too late, Al,' Don called.

Mindi was pushed aside as the door was thrown open and a breathless, red-faced Al Rosen burst in.

222

'You haven't . . . signed anything, have you?' he panted, holding his chest. His hair tumbled over his eyes, his shirt clung darkly across his chest. 'Don't sign anything, Donald, please. ABN will buy it, whatever it costs. Gill just walked.'

'*Walked?*' Don went pale.

'For real this time.' Al looked bad. It was as if he'd died on a bus going over a cattle grid, and here his ghost was, sickly and translucent, still wobbling away. 'He won't tape the last two shows. Refuses.'

'*Refuses?*' Don's jaw dropped. Or it would have done if the skin hadn't been tucked quite so tight underneath it. As it was, it opened about half an inch. Which for Don was a look of terror. 'He can't refuse. We need this hundred, Al. Everybody *needs* this hundred, he can't refuse. Shit, can he refuse?'

Al nodded.

'But without the hundred, we got nothing. *Nothing.* This was gonna pay for my house, Dad's retirement. This was our future.' Suddenly Don didn't feel too well.

'He says he'll only come back and do the last two if we *promise* to put him in a new show.' And Al slapped *Variety* down on the desk. '*The* new show. ABN have got to have it. *Whatever* it costs.'

NINETEEN

A silver BMW rolled up Palmwood Avenue slowly, past the lush, clipped lawns and whispering sprinklers in the still Brentwood morning.

Dumbstruck, Ben peered out through the windscreen, dizzied by the bizarre architecture. There was a plastic, Disneyland *Houses of the World* feel to every well-kept street. A mock-Tudor mansion followed a Spanish taverna which followed a Western ranch. Wigwams followed igloos followed brick followed straw followed wood, the effect being one of the three little pigs inviting all their cousins to come and live on the same street.

'Here we go,' the American said.

'Fucking hell!' Ben exclaimed as the car rolled to a stop.

The American was out of the car quickly, Ben hurrying to keep up, jogging past the palm trees and up the stone steps to the cool blue shade of the porch and the huge pair of studded doors. Ben's trainers scruffed on the chalky surface, his stomach flopping nervously. He wiped his palms hard on sweaty khakis.

This was it, this was fucking *it*. He was here.

It wasn't that Ben had never seen a room like it because he had. On school trips mainly. To museums and art galleries and the odd modern church. His loud involuntary gasp was because he simply couldn't get it into his head that anyone would actually *live* in a space like it. It was enormous. Cool white stone walls, a towering ceiling humming slowly with fans. A squeaky polished floor showed through the gaps between a half-dozen dust-sheets. The furniture consisted of just a huge television, two white wooden garden recliners and a drinks cabinet, each covered in a thin film of brick-dust.

His host winked on the television with a slim remote and excused himself, disappearing up the wide wooden central staircase, leaving Ben alone for a few minutes, breathing deeply, wide-eyed, trying to stop his feet from dancing. A sitcom burbled away on screen softly.

'*Mr Fawlty? The Germans are here . . .*'

'Sheridan?' Ben called out, dropping his holdall to the floor and squeaking off on the long trek across the room. He stared out through the glass wall, at the tennis court and the pool, winking in the sunshine. 'Holy shit! We did it. Sheridan? *Sheridan!*' he echoed again. '*Hello?*'

The house was silent.

The six o'clock news on Thursday 28 September would be one that Jacqueline Heaney would never forget.

Back at the Finchley flat, home from work, she threw her wet jacket on to the banisters, kicked her shoes across the hall and wandered into the kitchen, shaking her umbrella. Staring into the fridge, she noted there was nothing she could reheat. Nothing covered in foil or cling film, leftovers of fancy recipes she'd thrown together earlier in the week. She sighed, cut herself off a thick block of value cheese, poured a woozy amount of white wine into a chipped glass and trudged into the lounge in a cloud of wet hair and damp cotton.

This wasn't exactly how she'd imagined life without Ben was going to be. His sudden departure hadn't brought with it stripped wooden floors, a dozen exotic friends and a fully stocked fridge as she'd sort of hoped it might.

She snapped on the television and flicked through the channels idly.

Courtney Cox was teetering about on Channel 4, Ronnie Barker was larking about on BBC2, and two po-faced blondes with nasty brooches were dishing out the news on ITV and BBC1. Jackie eventually came to rest on one of these in a desperate wave of self-improvement. Maybe she'd watch the news all the way through. Even the financial bit near the end.

They were recapping the headlines. Going back live to an outside broadcast.

Another po-faced woman, in a red jacket that didn't suit her, was standing outside a swanky-looking hotel leaving long nodding gaps between her answers. Harsh flaring halogens lit the drizzly evening street, illuminating the ambulances, the police cars, the crime-scene tape and the constables in their hooded wet-weather gear.

Jackie watched for a few minutes, half-heartedly flicking through the *TV Guide*, when she was jolted from her daze by a sudden squeal of car brakes outside. Her palms went cold, hair prickled, adrenalin pumped and she braced herself for a crash. A horrible loud metallic scream of steel and glass.

But the crash never came. Just a lot of slamming of doors and yelling.

Jackie shook herself a little and stumbled to the window, tugging the grimy nets to one side and looking down at the wet street.

At a car, slung idly across the pavement. A burgundy car. A Vauxhall. And striding quickly up to her door, two men, only one of whom she didn't recognise.

The officer she didn't recognise made three cups of tea, D.I. Watts steered Jackie back into the lounge.

'Now, Miss Heaney, I don't know if you've been watching the—'

Watts stopped abruptly as he noticed the television, still

burbling away in the corner. It had moved to a special report. The woman in the red jacket that didn't suit her was still squinting away in the drizzly flare of the halogens outside the Margrave Hotel, Piccadilly, confirming the same sparse facts to a nodding beige jacket in the studio.

'What? What's going on?' Jackie said. She was shaking a little.

'Why don't we sit down?' he said and they both wedged themselves on to the thin sofas. Watts flicked the television off with the remote.

'If you don't mind?' he said. There was a click and a rattle from the kitchen. 'I don't know what the TV is saying but it's three men,' Watts said sombrely. 'Our three—'

'Our . . . ? I don't understand? What's happened?'

'From the list. Your list.' And he was pulling out his little notebook. 'An Angus Fisher,' he read slowly. 'A Malachy Flynn and a Jasper Philips. They're dead, Miss Heaney. Murdered.'

Jackie gasped, her hands flying over her mouth, fingertips cold on her numb face.

'Strangled,' Watts said. 'With those belts you get on bathrobes.'

'Oh my God!'

The second man entered the room with his tray of mugs and began to put them down on the coffee table. For a brief moment there were the formalities of tea. The sugar, the milk, the spoons. A little bit of mundane triviality to punctuate the numbing horror.

'We're putting time of death somewhere between three and four days ago,' Watts said as he stirred his cuppa. 'The killer was using a room at the Margrave and it seems had paid off the housekeeping staff to ignore it for a week. Generously, it seemed, because it hadn't been touched. But when none of the cleaners had seen the gentleman for a couple of days, they opened the room and found, well . . .'

The room fell quiet, just the calm tinkle of mugs and spoons.

'It seems this Don Silver has something against comedians.'

'Sorry?' Jackie said. 'Don Silver? But—'

A wave of nauseous panic rose within her.

'No! You don't think . . .' And Jackie's eyes pricked, her throat closing fat and tight, knuckles white about the cushion on her lap.

'So the cleaning staff are saying. We've put together a pretty good picture,'

'But Ben. B-but Sheridan and Ben . . .' Jackie stammered.

'We don't know.'

Suddenly the weight of realisation landed upon Jackie and she buckled like an empty shoe box. Collapsing into Watts' arms, she began to sob like a child.

Watts held her tightly.

'Trixi, goddamn you to ass, get me Dad on the goddamn' Nokia and *Variety* on the fuckin' Ericsson!'

Ben jumped a little at the voice. He had been lost in a distant world, head swimming, hypnotised by the slow throb of the ceiling fan. He'd been picturing poor Mr Fleming-but-call-me-Josh at Kathode Productions, at home in a pokey Stoke Newington studio flat with its sofa bed and lava lamp and E-Z-Clip wood-effect flooring feeling oh-such-a-big-shot.

The American bounded down the stairs loudly, cell-phone to his ear. He was no longer drowning in an outsized suit, having chosen instead to drown in absurd tennis gear. Shorts that flapped about his knees, a billowing polo-shirt, sleeves covering his thin elbows. On his head sat a *Woodfellas* baseball cap and over his shoulders a red cashmere cardigan flapped like a Superman cape.

'. . . and on the Jesus to bitchin' Motorola I want, uhmm . . .'

Ben looked at him. The American smiled back weakly.

'Er, some drugs. Lots of drugs.' He held the handset over his chest. 'You like drugs, Benny boy?'

'What? Oh, er, no. No, I'm fine right now. Thank you,' Ben said.

'Just ten kilos for me then, you goddamn' hear that, bitch? Okay, now I gotta go,' he said loudly, slapping across the floor, 'I got Ben Busby here so okay, fuck off. 'Bye.' And he stuffed the phone in his shorts.

'This is quite a place, Mr Silver,' Ben said. The American stood in the centre of the room watching the television for a moment. Not blinking. Not moving. His mouth hung a little loosely, his lips twitched, eyes glazed and distant. The television burbled on.

'Oh, prawn! That was it. When you said prawn, I thought you said war.'

'Prawn,' the American said flatly.

'Hitler, Himmler and all that lot, oh, yes, completely forgotten it, just like that.'

'Er, Mr Silver?' Ben repeated.

'And the pickled herring,' the American said. 'You'll have one of your own soon enough.'

'I'm sorry?'

'Hermann Goering, yes, yes. And von Ribbentrop . . .'

'Houses. Like this. And they'll want four cold meat salads.'

'And four cold meat salads.'

'Salads?' Ben said. This was getting confusing. 'Er . . . what?'

And then slowly, as if emerging from sleep, the American blinked, looked about him, startled, noticed Ben and then smiled.

'Fawlty Towers,' he said, motioning at the television, and then with a blink moved towards the drinks cabinet.

'Is . . . er . . . is Sheridan about? And the others?' Ben called, the American clattering with bottles and glasses.

'Upstairs. You know, everybody's sittin' up and takin' notice of you, Benny Boy. Looks like your idea has got the whole city talkin'. Oh, an' hey, sorry I didn't call earlier. It's a budget thing, y'know? Networks don't like the writing teams too big. I tried to tell them you and Sheridan worked together.'

Ben nodded.

'But four guys, that was all I was allowed to bring back, y'know? And Basil, don't forget the four Colditz salads.'

'*So that's two eggs mayonnaise, a prawn Goebbels . . .*'

'But when the studio read your show, your *Carpool* show, they said I was to get you over here right away. Looks like you saved me the trouble.' And the American smiled. 'Come on, siddown,' his host said, leading Ben to the two lawn chairs, handing him a drink. 'We had a little pitch at the studio this morning, talking about your show. Execs had a few questions, so it's a good thing you're here.'

'Well, I'm just glad to have finally—'

'Now you said you came here on your own, right? Colditz salads. No one with you?'

'Wh—? Er, yes.' Ben was finding the producer a little intense, his mind flicking seamlessly from the television to reality and back.

'Good. That's good.'

'*. . . and four Colditz salads. No, wait a moment. I got a bit confused there, sorry.*'

The American paused for a moment and then got up sharply, reaching into his voluminous shorts, bringing out a huge bunch of keys. 'That's very good,' he said distantly, and wandered over to the huge patio doors.

'*I got a bit confused because everyone keeps mentioning the war . . .*'

'So tell me about yourself,' he called over his shoulder. 'You got any family? Someone take you to the airport? Your wife? Tell them they started it, Basil. Anyone you want to tell you're here?'

'What? Oh, er, well, actually, if I can use your phone?' Ben stood up.

'*. . . Yes you did, you invaded Poland.*'

'I'd like to call my—'

Then suddenly, from above them, came a cry. Loud and

desperate, like a trapped animal, that promptly stopped with a dead thud that rattled the ceiling fans.

A still silence descended.

'*I'll do the funny walk . . .*'

The television audience exploded into tinny laughter.

'Sheridan?' Ben said.

Melvin turned and looked at him. They stared at each other. The world stood still for a moment.

'*Sheridan?*' Ben called out loudly over the TV set, his voice a little cracked. No answer.

Melvin just smiled.

'You want to go upstairs and look? Ch-check he's okay?' he said. 'Me and Basil will stay down here.'

Ben nodded and thudded up the stairs quickly.

Something was wrong. Very wrong.

At the top of the stairs was an empty landing. The same polished floor, white walls, but it had an unused, hollow feeling. The banisters were coated with clear sticky plastic. It smelled of sawdust. Ben listened for the sounds of conversation coming from a room, or the sounds of a running shower. The sounds of anything.

Nothing.

No, not nothing. He craned to hear a rattle and a clinking coming from below over the mumble of the television set. It sounded like someone washing up china.

Yes, he thought, moving gingerly down the wide hallway, something was definitely wrong.

His heart began to make itself a little more audible as he neared the first door. He called out Sheridan's name, to no response. It was all eerily quiet, like a church on a summer afternoon.

'Sheridan?' he said again, knocking on the door, surprised by the anxious dry croak of his own voice. 'Sheridan?' he said a little louder, clearing his throat.

He gripped the doorknob. It too was covered with clear

plastic. Holding his breath, he turned it. It was slippery in his sweaty grip but it caught and clicked. He pushed the door open.

'Hello?' he said. His voice echoed a little. He tasted dust on his tongue.

His fingers found a pull string which he twanged. The pull string had a price label on it. The bathroom was empty. No Sheridan, no Jasper, no bath.

Floorboards, bare pipes and a raw plaster wall, checker-boarded with missing tiles.

Ben could hear his own heart thumping. His stomach was filling slowly with liquid lead, his throat closing tight.

'Sheridan?' he said again, too loudly.

Heart banging, he scuttled out of the room and kept himself busy, throwing himself in a tight panic through the other doors on the landing. He didn't want to stop, didn't want to slow down, didn't want to think. He just wanted to see a face, a familiar face that would tell him everything was okay, that there was nothing to worry about, that he was spooking himself.

It was as Ben moved fast out of yet another hollow shell of a room back on to the landing, panic beginning to slip its hand about his shoulder, that he heard it again.

Not a cry this time. Not a trapped animal wail.

A word. Whispered.

His name.

Coming from behind the white door at the end of the landing.

Jackie had allowed herself to imagine D.I. Watts holding her. In daydreams. How he might feel, how he might smell. How safe it would be. But on her tatty sofa in her tiny flat that night in his arms, she would have given the world to open her eyes and see her beloved Ben.

'We need the exact whereabouts of Ben Busby and Sheridan McDonald, luv,' the second constable said firmly.

Jackie sat up, snotty and puffy-eyed, wiping her face and apologising.

'No, no,' Watts said. 'You go ahead,' handing her a fresh white handkerchief. 'Take your time, it's okay.'

'But we are gonna need those addresses,' the constable added. He seemed to be in a hurry.

'Ben . . .' she began. 'Los Angeles. Yesterday. I don't know exactly . . .'

'What are you saying? You two had a bust-up or summink?'

'Constable,' Watts said loudly, 'why don't you make us all some more tea?' He glared at his colleague as if he was an embarrassing spouse. The constable sighed and stomped off.

'I'm sorry,' Watts said, taking Jackie's hand. 'It's just that this is important. Might there be any way of contacting Ben or Sheridan?'

Jackie gave a shrug.

'I hoped he would have phoned. Do you think they'll be safe? I-I mean, if this man is the one who . . . Jasper and . . .' The thought of them all, lying dead, flooded Jackie's mind. The tears came again.

'You must help them!' she said, covering her face with her hands and sobbing. A terrible ache of loss and loneliness enveloped her. 'You must! He could be . . . he could be . . .'

'It's all right,' Watts said. 'We'll find them before anything happens.'

Locked.

'Sheridan? Sheridan, is that you? What's going on, are you all right?' Ben began to tug and pull at the door handle, his hands cold suddenly against the brass, his scalp itchy with panic. The door thudded a little in its frame but remained locked firm.

'*Beb,*' the voice came again from deep inside, making him jump. It was both desperate and hushed, like an angry prayer. '*Beb. Jefuff Byffe, Beb!*'

He was hurt. Trapped or hurt or . . . something.

Ben stepped away from the door and leaned over the banister. 'Don! Don, I think there's been a—'

'*Beb!*' Sheridan's voice hissed angrily. '*BO! BO! Beev! BO!*' Oh, this was wrong, Ben thought. This was very, very wrong.

The sounds of clinking continued below him over the mumble of the television, echoing up the stairwell.

Someone playing pool? Stacking chairs? Something like that.

Ben looked at the door in panic. He reached out and began to run his hands over it desperately in urgent seduction. He rattled the handle again, slipped his fingers around the door frame, his heart jumping when he touched something that fell tinkling to the floorboards.

Sheridan's muffled voice jabbered desperately on the other side of the door. Ben couldn't make out a word, but he could make out fear.

'It's all right, hold on,' he said grabbing the key from by his feet. He fumbled it in and turned it, pushing the door open.

He was in an office of some sort. That much was immediately obvious, even in the dark. Heavy curtains had been pulled to, glowing softly in front of the lunchtime sun. Ben could make out the beige hulks of a copier and a printer, feel the spongy carpet beneath him. Although there was something on it, crackly like dry leaves.

The room began to sharpen quickly as his eyes adjusted.

A filing cabinet, a wastepaper bin. The floor, covered in paper. Balled up, ripped up, written on. Hundreds of sheets.

'*Peb!*' a familiar voice hissed from behind the door.

Heart thundering, Ben reached behind him, his fingers finding the brass light switch. He snapped it on.

'Jesus Christ!' he gasped. His heart leaped into his throat, struggling with his stomach and lungs like Japanese commuters all trying to escape at once. Ben's hand flew to his mouth as if to hold them in and he jumped forward, crackling across the papery floor, to where his friend was sitting.

If you could call it that.

Sheridan's office chair was black and leather and chrome and ergonomic, fitted with levers and pads and adjustable whatnots, all presumably for optimum executive comfort. Sheridan had clearly misunderstood the manual at a fairly basic level, however, as optimum executive comfort was unlikely to be achieved with the chair flat on its back on the floor. Ben also thought it unlikely the user's guide recommended strapping oneself into the chair with tight white cotton belts or trapping oneself under a fallen desk either.

'Holy shit, what the hell's . . . I mean, what's . . . how the hell . . .?' Ben was attempting to lift Sheridan upright, slipping on the paper-strewn floor, puffing and straining against the awkward weight of the chair, his friend, bewilderment and panic jostling for his attention.

Sheridan growled and shrieked against his gag.

'Hold on, just hold on,' Ben grunted. Rather pointlessly as Sheridan clearly had no choice but to do so. He was bound fast, ankles lashed to the chair legs, his waist, chest and neck whipped to the back. His wrists, red and angry, were hand-cuffed to the drawers of his desk. When he'd tipped backwards, the cuffs had pulled at the drawers, tipping the desk over on to his knees.

A laptop computer lay upside down and open like a paper-back on the floor next to him.

Breathlessly, Ben struggled on, slipping and thudding, until, with a heavy bang the chair was upright, sending the desk tipping back with a crack against the wall.

'*Bo! Bo! Jeefuf Byffe!*' Sheridan shrieked as Ben moved quickly around to face his friend. He clawed and grabbed at the gag in Sheridan's mouth, a fat white cotton belt, balled up and shoved in, feeding it out as fast as he could with wet fingers. Sheridan's fringe was stuck to his forehead, splayed out like a spider, eyes red and rubbed. Blinking back tears of terror, Ben pulled the last of the belt free and Sheridan could do nothing for five slow seconds but gasp and suck in huge lungfuls of air, working his aching jaw round and round, Ben doing nothing but stare.

'You . . .' Sheridan managed eventually in his croaky Scouse tones. 'You took your bleedin' time.'

Ben began to fiddle and fumble with the other belts hurriedly, heart slamming away, whole body prickling with perspiration.

'What the fuck's going on?!' he said. 'What happened? Jesus . . .'

'No, please. Leave me, mate!' Sheridan said quickly in a terrified whisper. 'Leave it. Go. Just go. Get the fookin' bizzies. Now!'

Ben struggled with the belts, pressed tight against Sheridan's greasy stage clothes.

'I've got to . . . get you . . . to a . . . *fuck*,' he winced, fingernails tearing on the solid knots.

'A fook'd be nice, mate. Sound. But not now. I mean it, you gotta go. Just go, put the belt back in!' Sheridan jabbered fast. 'He'll fookin' kill yer. I mean it! Go! Just fookin' go!'

'Are you kidding?' Ben said. *Yes!* One belt free.

'Listen to me, mate, please. For the love of Lennon, listen.'

'Who did this, huh?' Ben panted, fingers working fast. 'Does Don know about this?'

'*Listen!*' Sheridan rasped as loud as he dared. Ben bounced back, surprised. Which was extraordinary, considering that as far as Ben was concerned he'd maxed out his potential for shock a good minute ago.

'Look, mate,' Sheridan croaked. His voice was dry and horrible, his mouth chapped and bloody at the edges where it had been forced open. "E's not Don. Don's the other fella. Dis guy's Melvin something or other. 'E's fookin' mental. 'E's got me 'ere finishin' the show.' And he gestured at the laptop on the floor. Reeling, Ben picked it up and stared at the glowing screen.

BOB

Can you believe this traffic?

Sheesh, what time is it?

PHIL

Eight-forty. Toot your horn.

BOB

I'm not tooting. I'm a sitter. I'm a waiter. I am not a tooter.

(EXASPERATED) God, I'm going to be so late.

'You've got Phil saying the "toot" line now?' Ben said, distracted for a moment.

'Jesus Christ! *Do me back up,*' Sheridan shrieked, almost lifting the entire chair from the floor as he writhed, eyes flashing. 'Put the gag in, put the belt on, do me back up. *NOW!*'

'I can't leave you . . .' Ben began, helplessly.

'If he figures out you've seen me like this, he'll kill us both. He'll kill us both? 'E's fookin' nuts. The only chance is if you go. Just go! Pretend you didn't find me. Door was locked, no noises whatever. Go back downstairs, tell him you didn't see anything and then get out. Get the fookin' bizzies over here now! He's got a fookin' gun. Do it. *Do it!*' Sheridan rasped again.

Ben did it. Head throbbing and bursting, blood roaring in his ears, he refastened the belt, gathered the soggy gag from the floor and rolled it up as small as he could. He held it in his trembling hands, inches from Sheridan's face.

'Shall I just stick it in your mouth?'

'Ooh, er, missus, I knew seeing me like this would turn you on,' Sheridan said, managing a painful smile. 'Fookin' pervert.' Ben held his breath and eased the gag back into his friend's mouth, teary eyes fixed on each other.

Job done, he stepped back and took a long look at his friend, trussed and sweaty among his IKEA Hieronymus Bosch Home Office range. Ben put the laptop back on the desk, eyes flickering over the rest of the page.

ARNIE

C'mon, so give her the old toot.

BOB

Why? What do you think will happen? This great sea of
traffic will miraculously just part, and we'll drive through
the middle with ease? What do you think we're driving
here? The Ford Moses?

'Ford Moses,' Ben read, nodding. 'Pretty good.' And then,
purely out of habit, he winced a little and turned to his
whimpering friend. 'Hmmm, maybe try *Renault* Moses?'

Sheridan's eyes blazed in fury. Ben apologized, crackling
across the papery floor. He snapped off the light, slid the door
quietly closed and tiptoed down the landing.

He held his breath.

The same clicking and clanking downstairs, the squeaking of
footsteps around the ground floor.

This was going to take some doing.

The sun hung high in the Los Angeles afternoon, baking the
tarmac, baking the hills and putting a smile on Don's face. He
stared out of the back window of the cab, his cell-phone pressed
to his ear, waiting for New York to pick up.

He was in a very good mood indeed. So much so that he
hadn't been able to sit still in his enormous office any longer.
After giving Trixi instructions to start organising the party to
end all parties, he had grabbed a cab and was heading home to
Brentwood for a shower, a change of clothes and a line or two to
get him in the mood for his lunch date with Dad.

And what a lunch it would be.

For the first time since forever, he was about to make his
father very proud. Slates would be wiped clean. No, he thought,
not just wiped clean. Wrapped in lead and buried underground.
It was time for a brand new slate, fresh and sparkling, still in its
bubble-wrap. A slate on which to write himself a new future.

easyJet

Passenger
HALLIDAY / GORDON

From
LONDON LUTON

To
EDINBURGH

Flight	Date	Seq No.
EZY23	22NOV	89

Boarding Group
B

Several Khan-

The dawning of a new age. An age when his father would finally be able to put his arm around his son's shoulder with pride. Stand side by side, hug, bond and shoot hoops like some kind of appalling shaving foam commercial.

There was a tiny chirrup, and a second phone in Don's pocket began to ring. Still on hold for New York, he fished it out and thumbed it open.

'Silver.'

'*It's me,*' Al Rosen said distantly.

'Hey, Al,' Don said. 'What's goin' on? You tell Gill we had a deal? Get him back to rehearsal?'

'*He's happy. I told him ABN would buy* Carpool *and give him the lead as long as he finished* E.R. E.R. . . . Oh!'

'That's great. Trust me, this pilot's gonna be the best fifteen million you ever spent. Hey, y'know, he and Elaine should come to the party I'm having at the house tonight.'

'*Wait. Gill spoke to Dolawitz. Like, I dunno, he doesn't trust me or something? Anyway, Dolawitz says no.*'

'What!' Don spat.

'*Not 'til it's in writing. He wants a contract. Mercury, ABN, commitment, salary package, everything signed in triplicate before he'll even let Gill back on to the Mercury lot.*'

'Greedy fuck,' Don sighed. 'Okay, so we'll get the legal boys on to it, get something drafted up. Meet in a couple of weeks, bang out the details.'

'*No way. It's gotta be today. I gotta get Gill back to rehearsal today. Jesus, I can't let anyone find out I let him walk,*' Al whispered. '*It'll be my ass.*'

'You haven't *told* anybody he *quit?*'

'*Shhhh! Jesus!*' Al hissed. '*For Chrissakes, Don, I'm the Senior Network Vice President of Comedy. Gill Kramer is the biggest star we got. If words gets out we nearly lost the syndication deal, my ass is out on the street. I need to get all this signed and get him back in rehearsal before anyone upstairs hears about it.*'

'Fine, fine,' Don said. 'I'm meeting Dad at Spago at four for lunch. Join us. I'll bring a contract, you bring your cheque-book, we'll get everything done.'

'*Can you bring a* Carpool *script? Something I can take upstairs?*'

'I'll get Mel on it.' Don smiled.

'*Good afternoon, Mercury Pictures,*' the phone crackled in his other hand. He snapped Al closed.

'Hey, Caroline, it's Don. Howyadoin', honey? Is Uncle Bernie there? Stick the old man on for me, would ya? I got some great news.'

'*Bernie isn't in the office, Don.*'

'Shit. You want to patch me through to his home? It's important. Deal's done, I got myself a hit.'

The cab rolled west down Wilshire Boulevard. Don caught sight of another huge billboard. Flaming orange clouds, the figure of Pepys standing atop the Tower of London, arms aloft triumphantly. *Get Ready For Uncle Sam*, it read along the bottom. *Sundays, 9 p.m. ABN.*

'*He's not there either. You spoken to him today? You hear about his accident?*'

'Accident? What're you talking about?' What had the old fool done now? Don thought.

'*He and your father were jogging in the park this morning. Bernie fell apparently. Fractured his arm. The hospital wanted to keep him in.*'

'Where's he at? Sinai? You got a number there for him?' Don reached for a pen. Here he was with the deal of his life and there was no one around to hear.

'*Well, that's the thing, Don. He discharged himself. Said he had an urgent meeting he couldn't miss. And then he got me to book him a plane ticket. He flew out from La Guardia a few hours ago. Flight 6151 to Nashville International.*'

'Nashville?' Don said, pressing his ear to the phone a little harder. 'What the hell's he doing in Nashville?'

'*Beats me,*' Caroline said.

Don hung up, leaning forward and rapping on the greasy thick glass.

'Hey, take the 405 north. Brentwood.' And the cab eased right, out of the traffic towards the intersection. Don sat back in his seat and thumbed Trixi's number.

'Hey, it's me. Get another space at Spago. Al's gonna be joining us later. Oh, an' call the legal boys, tell 'em I'm gonna be faxing over details for them in a few minutes. I want something ABN can sign . . . Yep, the deal's as good as done.' He allowed himself a smile. 'Any word from Dad yet? . . . Delayed? Jesus, where? . . . Well, when's it gonna land? I got the best news he's gonna hear all year and he's stuck . . . okay, okay. Well, find out what time and call me at home.'

Don glanced out at the sunny street signs.

'Five minutes.'

It was stage fright. Simple as that. He'd had it before, he was having it now.

Ben paced the landing urgently, as he had that dank club toilet just three nights ago. His audience was downstairs. A small audience.

His stomach flopped over as it always did, the same queasy green taste about his jaw.

He would have to go downstairs now. He'd been up here too long. The American . . . Melvin . . . whoever he was . . . knew Sheridan was up here. He'd sent Ben up to discover it for himself.

He moved to the top of the stairs and heard the TV burbling beneath him. He swallowed twice and began to creak down the stairs into the cavernous white lounge. The two lawn loungers were there, the TV, two glasses of water. No sign of Melvin, Then he heard a click and a squeak from the hallway.

'Er . . . Mel . . . Don? Don?' he said loudly, coughing over the crack in his voice. He reached the bottom of the staircase, moving quickly across the room.

'Don?' he said again.

In the hallway, he watched as Melvin pushed the heavy wooden door closed with a solid click, twisting a key once, twice around. Ben could hear large bolts being thrown in the jamb.

'D-Don?' he said, forcing a light, easy smile. 'Don, there's . . . uhm . . . no one upstairs. I couldn't see anything . . . I guess he must have gone out or something, right?'

Melvin didn't turn, didn't answer. He just moved silently over to the window and fumbled with the keys.

'Don? I mean we were gone a while, right? I guess he'll be back later. Maybe I should . . . uhm . . . come back tonight? When he's here, yeah?' Ben picked up his rucksack from the archway where he'd dumped it.

Eventually finding the key, Melvin twisted the dead lock once, twice, and then stepped away, dropping the keys into his huge pockets.

That's what Ben had heard. Not washing up. Not china plates. Melvin had been wandering methodically around the ground floor of the echoing house, from door to door, from window to window.

Locking them both in.

'I'd prefer it if you s-stayed,' he said, turning to face Ben and walking slowly towards him.

Moments later, Ben was walking quickly across the polished floor. But backwards. Which isn't easy to do.

He moved down the hall and into the airy lounge, dropping his rucksack on to the wooden floor with a thud, hands raised, voice croaking, mind racing frantically.

'Relax, relax,' Melvin was saying nonchalantly, walking down the dark hall towards him.

'*Who won the bloody war anyway?*' Basil yelled on the television.

'You tell them, Basil,' Melvin said, picking up the remote from on top of the set. 'Do excuse me for a moment, though.' And he winked the TV to black.

'I-I think maybe I should go,' Ben said. 'But I'll come back in a while, yeah?' His voice sounded loud against the high stone ceilings, competing bravely with the deafening thud of his heart in his chest. 'I-I think . . .'

He thought what? Truth was, Ben hadn't a clue. The rug on which his world had sat, warm by the fire, had been pulled from under him with a violent yank, by a violent Yank or whatever Melvin was, and Ben was utterly bewildered.

'Get any funny ideas up-stairs? Any in-inspiration for the show?' Melvin was walking slowly towards Ben, casually, like he was out taking the air after a big lunch. Not threatening, not violent.

Well, if you didn't count the gun.

As Ben's palms pumped cold sweat and his throat closed tightly, he ran through every movie gun-play scene he had ever experienced. What exactly were you meant to do?

They backed further into the room.

'I-I mean, you're the writer,' the American stammered. 'Well, what ideas you got?'

The only idea Ben had was to get something, anything, between him and this gun. Some kind of dramatic leap behind the furniture seemed to be the most obvious choice. In the few action movies he'd seen, there always seemed to be a handy desk in these situations, something solid the hero could throw himself behind. The villain would always get a shot off, of course, but it would clip the edge of the wood, sending smoking splinters into the air. The villain would then yell, '*Damn you, 007!*' or something along those lines, giving 007 about an hour in which to hunch down, run to the nearest large-heavy-steel-bar shop, purchase a large-heavy-steel-bar, return, leap out and clunk the guy with it, probably quipping nonchalantly about success '*going to his head*', eyebrows flailing wildly.

Ben glanced about him in the empty room. Yards of emptiness in every direction. The two loungers and the patio doors were well behind him, the drinks cabinet and kitchen doorway a good way in front. He wouldn't be jumping behind anything without a Space Hopper at least. If he tried running, Melvin would have an age in which to aim and fire. There was nowhere to go.

'There's n-nowhere to go,' Melvin said, just in case he was getting any ideas.

But slowly, as they edged backwards, Ben was getting ideas.

'Oh! Oh, I *see!*' he said loudly. He was going for bravado and boisterous bonhomie. He hoped his dry tremulous voice sounded better from where the other guy stood than it did in his own head. 'It's, what, like a pressure thing, right? Right? Like a test for us new guys? I *see*! Very clever, very clever . . .'

'Upstairs,' Melvin said flatly.

'You did this with all the guys, yeahhhhh?' Ben said trying to force his frozen terrified features into some kind of smile. 'Seeing how us Brits react under pressure? Being under the gun to come up with scripts, right?' He grinned. 'Pretty clever, pretty clever,' Ben bounced. It was a petrified, needing-to-shit-his-pants bounce but Ben thought it could just as easily play as a get-up-and-go eagerness. He added a *who-hoo!* and clapped his hands a little.

'Upstairs. You have a lot of work to do.'

'Huh? Oh, yeah, sure,' he said, raising his hands over his head. 'Right. *Don't shoot, mister!*' he joshed, swallowing hard. He needed to get into the kitchen. There would be knives, there would be bottles, there would be something.

'Why don't I, uhm, fix us some drinks? And then we'll talk about some more ideas, right?' he said quickly, and moved fast towards the cabinet on the far side of the room.

He was three yards from it when the voice came again, repeating the demand.

But Ben kept walking, trying to turn his rattling knees into some sort of bouncy swagger.

'Ice?' he said, busying himself noisily at the wet bar. He attempted to gather up some glasses quietly, calmly. It sounded like two milk floats colliding on an ice rink. His eyes flashed over the counter top. Shot glasses, Martini glasses, tumblers, high-balls, Champagne flutes. It all twinkled and shone. Coasters, straws, stirrers, little umbrellas and toothpicks.

And there, at his left elbow . . .

'Sorry, Don,' he said loudly, 'did you say you wanted ice?' And Ben turned rapidly, throwing his left arm out a little. He caught the plastic bucket with his forearm and it tumbled to the floor, lid spinning off like a hubcap.

'Whoopsie!' he said.

It hit the floor with a crash, water and ice splashing like stolen diamonds all over the floor, soaking Ben's trousers and splashing over Melvin's ankles. As he cursed and stepped back, gun momentarily lowered, Ben moved quickly to the archway ten feet away which he hoped led to the kitchen.

'I'll get some more,' he called over his shoulder as casually as he could.

'Wait!' Melvin yelled.

It was a huge kitchen. Absurdly big considering it was only for Don's house. Every surface was of oily chrome, with more dull reflections than an omnibus edition of This Is Your Life.

Ben pounded past the worktops with their glittering blenders and toasters, ducked beneath a rack of copper pans and skidded to the back door. Melvin would be on him in seconds.

He grabbed the handle and yanked it hard.

Locked.

Through the glass he could see the alley running down the side of the house, three or four bins and a couple of mountain bikes propped against a hedge. He pulled and slammed at the handle helplessly and then began thudding at the toughened glass with aching fists.

He heard wet footsteps squeaking towards the kitchen and lunged towards the huge white freezer, a fifties-looking monster the size of his Finchley flat.

He unclicked the heavy door and opened it a few inches. Cool plumes of icy air billowed and slithered out of the drawers.

'I can't see any,' he called, leaning in, obscuring himself from view. The cold air was freezing the sweat on his face. 'Some steaks, a lot of vodka . . . are these fish fingers?'

He held his breath as he heard the squeak coming towards him across the kitchen. Ben looked down, at the gap beneath the open door, the toe of a shoe suddenly appearing.

He yanked the freezer door wide open as hard as he could. There was a yelp and a thud as it met Melvin's nose, hard.

Ben ran.

He burst out into the cavernous lounge. If the kitchen door was locked, it meant Melvin had probably done them all. He had no choice but to try the glass of the patio. It was twenty yards in front of him at the other end of the empty lounge. He pounded hard, breathless, feet slamming and squealing on the wooden floor.

And then the sound changed a little.

Not so much a slam, more of a splash.

Ben hit the pool of ice and lost his footing, his damp trainers suddenly at eye level as he hung there, suspended in mid-air, for the briefest moment.

'*Basil, stop him!*' a voice bellowed behind him, and then a bang. A deafening bang that shook the room and echoed endlessly.

Ben landed with a crash, half on a shoulder, half on a leg that was bent and twisted under him. The pain screamed at him as he slid four or five feet across the wet floor. Scrabbling on the ice, he slipped and swayed to his feet, stumbling forward, forward, towards the wall of glass.

Another loud bang, a billow of splintering plaster and brick dust flowered into life.

He passed the two lawn chairs, fifteen feet from the patio.

Would it break? Would it hold? Would it break? Would it hold? Like a coin spinning in mid-air, the two contrasting thoughts were flipping in front of his eyes.

Ten feet.

'*Basil! Where are you? He's getting away!*' the voice bellowed again.

Five feet. The glass winked and shone smearily in the afternoon light. Behind it, the grass looked so green, so soft, so well kept.

Ben launched himself at it with a loud cry.

Would it break? Would it hold? Would it break? Would it hold? Would it break? Would it hold? Would it break? Would it hold?

And then with a *ringgggg*, the doorbell went.

Tch! Always when you're in the middle of something.

Don pressed the bell again.

Behind him, the cab rolled back down the winding hill, leaving him alone outside his own front door in the cool blue shade of the porch. His own front door was on the chain and he couldn't get in.

'Mel? *Mel?* What's going on in there?' he yelled, shouting through the inch of space, giving the heavy door a little rattle.

Ben stumbled to his feet with a bloody nose, holding his head and saying, 'That's a *hold*, then.'

Another gun shot roared through the room, sending his heart leaping in his chest. He stumbled forward, grabbing a lawn chair by the middle and heaving the aluminium frame over his head. With a mighty scream he whirled round, smashing it against the patio glass, causing a web of cracks to shriek out a little further.

Another deafening gun shot tore a hole in the plaster, just feet from the cracked glass wall.

Melvin was lying on the floor, commando-style, gun thrown out in front of him, letting rip.

'Basil! Grab him! Manuel! D-don't let him go! *Don't*—'

Ben swung the lounger up and round again, whirling it

toward the glass again with a scream, Melvin holding the trembling weapon out in front of him.

'L-let him—'

Ben let go of the lounger and it hurtled through the glass.

'Go!' Melvin shrieked and let off another sound. The bullet met the glass just as the lawn-chair did and the glass exploded beautifully, like a dying star.

The whole wall, floor to ceiling, crystallised with a dazzling *frishing* sound. The room suddenly lit up like a church as light rained and sparkled through a million shards.

'*Mel?*' Don hollered, stabbing the doorbell for a third time and holding it down. He heard it ring out, solidly, deep within his home. Through the din he heard footsteps, loud, moving quickly, and a rattle on the other side of the door. Eventually it swung open, but Melvin was already charging back down the hall.

'*Mel?* Jesus Christ, what in *hell's* going on in here?' Don said, pushing into the house, tossing his briefcase to the floor.

Melvin spun around to face him but kept moving towards the lounge, squeaking backwards. He was drowning in Don's tennis gear, like a boy on his first day at private school. Panicky and sweating, hair stuck to his forehead, he gestured frantically, the gun flashing in the light.

'I had an accident,' he panted, moving quickly through the wide stone arch into the lounge.

'*Accident?*' Don's mind spun.

He entered the lounge, taking in the debris. The upturned ice bucket in the pool of water. The bullet holes in his plasterwork.

And the gaping, jagged hole in the plate glass. About the size of the lawn-chair that lay bent and buckled on the grass outside.

'What the fuck's been going on?'

Bernie sat in the large reception area of the South Eastern Broadcast Network, rattling poker chips in his fingers and trying to enjoy his headache. The receptionist, under a startlingly huge bouffant of over-teased blonde hair, face loitering about at the bottom somewhere, stopped chewing gum and smiled a perfect white smile at him once in a while. She would ask him if his arm was painful, Bernie would say no and was there a chance that Randy was off the phone yet? She would say no and then silence would descend once again on the soft carpeted area.

Silence, as long as you didn't count the Patsy Cline being pumped through invisible speakers, hidden in the ceiling and behind the glugging water cooler.

Bernie was pretty sure there was one in the girl's hair-do, but couldn't be certain.

He didn't like Nashville. He'd only clambered from the plane an hour ago but in that sixty short minutes, he'd decided he was never ever coming here again. On the cab ride across the city, through streets full of pick-up trucks and fat-necked men in baseball caps, it had seeped in on him — that good ole' self-righteous uh-thank-a-you ma'am homeyness.

And everywhere the *music*: *Yur listening to KMW point nine, honest-to-gud'ness country boys singin' the best twangy schmaltz about their gurls who've dun gawn. Non-stop and back to back and rightly getting' awn yur tits.*

'Ah-weh-*hellll*!' Randy smiled, standing up, pushing the white brim of his Stetson from his eyes. 'What a-happened to you, Bernie? Been wrestlin' steers again?' He gestured at the sling.

Bernie sighed as the door clicked closed behind him.

The office was about as foul as he'd imagined it would be, decorated in a style that made Graceland look like an exercise in Swedish minimalist restraint. The desk, the walls, the rugs, the paintings. Anything that could have been made of leather or suede or snakeskin, had been. And then trimmed with a little gold. Occasionally in the shape of a cactus.

'Those FBI boys, they can be a little rough,' Bernie said carefully. 'But it's nothing.'

Randy paused, momentarily. FBI? Bernie didn't dare look at his face, he was playing this one very cool. But he knew the connotations would slowly be swimming through Randy's head. Giving him just a little something to worry about.

'Ah see,' Randy said slowly, and then sped up, as if the subject was forgotten. 'Well c'mon, siddown siddown,' he said, pulling out a brown leather swivel chair with steerhorns on the back. Bernie sat with a wince. His arm began to throb angrily and he took a sweaty moment to reach for some painkillers, spilling them awkwardly into his hand. A little too awkwardly? Possibly. But Bernie knew he would have one chance and one chance only. Randy glugged some water from the cooler by the window and handed him the paper cup. 'You awlright, Bernie?' he said, clinking back around the desk to his own steerhorned chair.

'Just aches a little,' he said, the memory of Tommy and his burly thugs refreshed for a brief moment.

'So. You got mah contract for me?'

'Look, Garland, listen to me — it's all over.'

'Our li'l clam-bake gal is beginnin' to bloat out like a hog. Three weeks' time she won't even fit in that l'il denim g-string o' hers. Ah'd like to be able to announce Monday that we got ourselves a replacement show, Bernie. So let's have it.'

'Are you listening to me?' he said, heart hammering away. He threw back a little more of the cold water. 'It's over. Your blackmail plan? It's over.'

Randy smiled, head tilted.

'Oh, you didn't fly all this way in your condition to give me a loada bullshit, Bernie.' And he reached into his suede-covered in-tray and pulled out a sheet of paper. 'Just hand over the contract an' stop your horsin' aroun'.'

'Garland—'

'Now, Ah been havin' some ideas 'bout this l'il car show of ours.' And he began to scan the page. 'Howsabout it ain't a car but a pick-up truck? An' it ain't stuck in traffic, but stuck in the mud? Three good ole boys, stuck in a field. Maybe a pig in the back for the kids? Put him on a lunch box or—'

'Garland, I'm here as a professional courtesy, one television guy to another. The FBI wanted to send a team of trigger-happy suits down here but I said, no, let me go down. Talk to him. Reasonably.'

Randy looked up from his notes, stared Bernie in the eye then sat back, fingers laced across his chest, chin raised a little. He said nothing so Bernie pushed on. It was poker. A straightforward bluff. No matter what you have, play like you're holding aces.

'Those murders in London? The bodies? All faked. These Probe investigators? They're a scam operation. They get actors, photographers, cook up stories about the companies they investigate. Feds have been watching them for two years.'

Randy didn't make a sound. Nor a movement. Just listened.

'Back in February, they set up a phoney insurance office in Philly to catch 'em. Hired Probe to investigate some theft. They came back with plenty: tapes, photographs, fingerprints, the lot.'

'A scam?' Randy said flatly.

'Clever guys. Bureau contacted Howard and myself last

251

night to tell me they'd picked them up, snooping around our accounts. Planting false transactions. You've got nothing, Garland. You've been had.'

The room went quiet. Bernie had played his hand. Pushed all his chips to the centre of the table. It was now a simple waiting game. Bernie's cards were face down on the baize, it was up to Randy to decide how to play it.

'Bullshit,' he said.

Bernie blinked back at him slowly. Took a sip of water. Easy now, it was times like this that separated the men from the boys. He just had to hold his ground. A card player would often throw out remark like that. Or laugh. Or shake their head. But all the time, they were watching for that flicker, a flash of worry from Bernie.

He always smiled right back at them.

The pain in Ben's side stabbed again and again, harder and more pinched. As the hill levelled out, his sprinting slowed to a flat slapping jog and he fell gasping against a *No Littering* sign, pressing the cold metal of the post to his cheek.

Thankfully he still had his passport, his travellers cheques, his wallet, guide book, a handful of change and his address book safely zipped up in his rucksack.

The only downside to this being that his rucksack was still sitting in Don Silver's huge cool lounge with shattered glass and a psychopath.

His chest ballooning and contracting hard, heart smashing against his ribs like a quarterback, Ben stumbled out of the road and over the lush grassy bank in front of one of the houses. A huge place. Huge and stone and pink.

He stepped on to the covered porch, out of the sunlight, his chest still burning, his breath slowing gradually. He jabbed the bell next to the studded oak doors and waited in the still silence.

Nothing.

He tried again. He could hear the sound of the bell inside echoing against what sounded like wall to floor tiling. Still nothing.

Then, from beside him, like a curious wasp, a buzz in his ear.

Ben turned, catching the flash of something a few inches away, like sunshine on a speeding car. He squinted and suddenly it pulled into focus. A black lens, in the tree by the door, nestling deep within the leaves. With another buzz, the lens turned clockwise, adjusting focus.

'*Please leave this property immediately*,' an automated voice crackled behind him, making him jump.

It was tinny and authoritative and coming from a metal grill in the opposite tree.

'Hello, excuse me?' he said into the grille with a cough — trying to sound as little like a sweaty maniac as possible. 'Hello?'

'*Please leave this property immediately*,' the voice snapped again. '*You are trespassing*.'

'Look I know, I know,' Ben said. He stepped off the porch and backed on to the tightly cropped lawn, shielding his eyes and staring up at the shuttered windows on the first floor. Not a sign of life. He stepped back in. 'Can you call the police? My friend is hurt, he's been kidnapped. In a big house over the hill there. Please, he has a gun, can I just——'

'*Leave this property immediately*.' No 'please' this time. '*Dogs patrol these premises. They will be released in ten seconds*.' The voice clicked off.

'Please!' Ben yelled. 'Someone, hello?' He banged on the door hard with his fist.

And then he stopped. There was a clanking 'whirr' and the sound of a gate opening somewhere.

Or a kennel.

'*Five* . . .' The grille spoke again calmly. '*Four* . . .'

Oh, for fuck's sake. Barking began somewhere to his left behind the thick shrubs.

'*Three* . . .'

Leaping over the lawn and throwing himself down the street, Ben left the two, the one and the ravaging hounds far behind him.

'You know what a wire is?' Bernie said. 'You seen them in movies? When the Feds get a guy to go to a mob meeting with a microphone strapped to his chest, while they're sat in the next room with headphones and tape machines?'

Randy smoothed his moustache a little.

'Well, sometimes, see, the guy they're trying to trap is too far away from the microphone. Gets muffled. What they really need is a way of getting the mike out the front. In the open. Without it being spotted, of course.'

Bernie saw Randy's eyes flick. Almost imperceptibly, but he saw it. Down. And then back up.

'Trouble is, most mob bosses are wise to that sort of thing. Why they call them wise guys, I guess. They're not going to trust some guy they hardly know, wandering into the meeting with, say, oh I don't know ... an arm in a sling, for example,' he said. 'They'd be on to him in a second. No, apparently, the Feds only use the arm-in-a-sling wire when they've studied the target and are absolutely certain he's too dumb to notice anything out of the ordinary.'

Randy glared at Bernie, eyes flashing. Your call, Mr Garland.

'Ah ain't said a word,' Randy said softly, a slight dryness to his voice. 'Not that it matters none, this is bullshit anyway ...'

'Well, that's up to you, Mr Garland,' Bernie said. 'If you're happy with a word like '*blackmail*' sitting around on FBI tape waiting to be played in court, as I say, that's up to you.' Bernie leaned forward a little. Randy leaned in a little too, like two grandmasters over a chess board. Bernie had him. He could taste it.

'When this goes to trial,' he whispered carefully, 'it'll all come out. Who Probe have worked for, who they've dealt with.

But between you and me, Mr Garland,' and Bernie slipped his good hand over his cast, 'the Feds have fucked up a little. Swooped in too early. You're an innocent victim. You haven't actually profited from the information they supplied.' He paused for a long second. 'Yet.'

Randy licked his lips and bent in a little closer.

'They can't charge you with anything. It's up to us whether we bring a case. Now we have no desire to have our name dragged through the papers, and I'm guessing you don't either. So if you'll just agree to forget Probe, forget Mercury, forget *Carpool*, then we'll forget you ever came to see us.'

The two men sat in silence for a moment. Bernie took a sip of water, trying to appear as relaxed as possible.

Would he fold? Please, let him fold, Bernie prayed. Over a thousand card tables he'd been in this terrifying position. Waiting, aching, for the other player to throw his cards in. Breath held, buttocks clenched.

'Fine,' Randy said finally. 'Forget it.'

Bernie attempted not to explode with relief. He just nodded slowly.

Randy got up, rolling his shoulders a little. He stared out of the glass in the rear door, out into the sunny parking lot. When he turned back, a look of black anger was rumbling across his face.

'Wires. Jesus . . .' and he shook his head. 'Okay, boys, get yerselves in here. Ah'll give yuh what you want,' Randy said loudly. The room fell silent. 'Hello?' he called again, leaning over the desk, pushing his face close to Bernie's cast. 'Are you receiving me?' And he tapped three times on the plaster like he was testing a microphone.

Which, of course, he wasn't.

'There's no, uhm, there's no speaker,' Bernie said nervously. 'They can hear you, but they can't say anything. It's one way.'

'But they're next door, right?' Randy said, standing up straight. He walked across the office and threw open the door.

Some Patsy Cline wafted in from reception. He turned and walked back in. 'C'mon, boys!' he yelled. 'Ah'll get you all some coffee, give you a statement and we'll call the whole thing off!'

Silence.

Bernie began to feel a little sick.

'Ah got photos, recordings, all right here. Whatever you need. . . . Hello?'

Nothing.

Randy glared at Bernie and then spun around, marching out of the office and through reception. Bernie heard the front door swing open, a cool breeze dancing through, the sound of the afternoon traffic.

It was all very quiet in the office. The music was still playing, Patsy explaining she was crazy, crazy for feeling so lonely.

And she wasn't the only one.

Randy was back. Laughing. With a slow nod, he turned to face Bernie who sat glugging water and panicking in his swivel chair.

'Pretty smart, Bernie.' Randy grinned. 'Pretty damn' smart. Wires. Philadelphia stings? But no vans, no tapes, no suits, no nothing.' He looked down at the cast. 'Broke your arm, right?'

Bernie closed his eyes.

Fuck.

Officers Walsh and Dorfler sat sipping coffee and chewing gum in their patrol car on Sunset Boulevard.

Both from New York, they had transferred to LAPD together six months ago. They told colleagues it was for the weather and the women, but secretly both harboured desires to be spotted in action and offered their own television show. So far there had been few developments on this front despite their spending most of their days circling major television studios at 80 m.p.h. with the sirens blaring, taking squealing corners and yelling the contact number of Walsh's acting coach over the Tannoy.

'Did y'see *Sexposé* over the weekend? "Dirty Dons"?' Dorfler said, flipping through *Variety* surreptitiously. 'Had that Corillo guy on death row talkin' about his girlfriends and shit?'

'Fuckin' perverts those wiseguys,' Walsh sighed through a mouthful of gum.

'And y'know my brother's on the force back east? Well, his team was in charge of getting' the film crew in and out of the secure wing to shoot it, makin' sure they were safe.'

'He get spotted? He got a deal lined up?'

'No, no. Point is, he says the producer never got Corillo to sign no release. As far as he was concerned, he was bein' interviewed for some psych report for the justice department. He spilled his guts thinkin' it was gonna buy him some leniency. Next thing y'know, it's all over prime-time. The guy's pissed.'

'And stuck on death row? What a way to spend your last thirty days,' Walsh said. 'Great show though. That De Niro commentary? Classy.'

'Say, you wanna go do a couple of laps around Paramount? I put the extra squealey tires on?'

'Sure thing,' Dorfler said, and they started up the car, rolling forward, when suddenly there was a figure in front of them, stepping out.

Dorfler slammed the brake and punched the horn. The figure, a young man, leaped backwards, tripping on the kerb and landing on his back.

'Oh, Jesus, thank you!' he gasped from the sidewalk and clambered up quickly, stumbling towards the door. 'Please, you've gotta help me.'

Walsh and Dorfler shared a slow, doubtful, sardonic look, incorporating no smiles and lots of eyebrows.

'You wanna watch where you're going, sir,' Walsh drawled with minty-gum breath, pointing at the messy steel knot of street signs opposite. 'Wait for the *walk* sign,' And the car began to crawl forward.

'No, wait, *wait!* You don't understand! You've got to help

me!' the young man cried, clammy hands on the door-frame. 'It's my friend. It's Sheridan . . . they've got him trapped up at this house, this big white house . . .'

'You want to step away from the car, sir?' Walsh said slowly. They slowed the patrol car to a halt, engine idling. 'Tell me from the beginning what the problem is?'

'Okay, okay, I'm sorry,' said Ben, standing up, regaining his breath. 'My friend and I, Sheridan, that's him . . . I'm Ben,' he panted, 'we're from London. Well, no, he's from Liverpool. But see, we wrote this sitcom. Well, the first episode. It's these guys, just sitting in a car . . .'

'Ohhhhh, you're a *writer*?' Dorfler nodded dryly, sending a smile over to Walsh. 'A scared writer in Los Angeles, whatever next?'

'You said somebody had someone in a house?' Walsh said, pulling out his sunglasses and cleaning them. 'Trapped, was it?'

'No, a car . . . trapped in a car,' Dorfler pitched in. 'A white car, didn't he say?'

'No, that's the show we wrote,' Ben said again. 'There are three guys on the show. Only one guy is trapped – Sheridan, up in the hills, in Brentwood.' And he gestured feebly over his shoulder.

'So the other two guys . . . ?' Dorfler said, frowning a little, confused.

'This car's in Brentwood?' Walsh said, holding his sunglasses up to the light. 'And where are the keys to this car? Have you called a breakdown truck?'

'What? No—'

'Sir, sir, if you don't mind?' And Walsh shushed Ben with a raised hand. 'You're from out of town, we understand that. We see a lot of angry writers, a lot of frustrated actors, running around claiming Hollywood is out to get them.' The police car revved a little.

'Wait, no, wait!' Ben said, placing his hands on the warm metal roof. 'A gun, he has a *gun!*'

'Sir, this is Los Angeles. Everybody has a gun. Your buddy's trapped in his car? We're not a breakdown service. Unless you'd like to report a crime—'

'He's pretending to be a producer . . . he's in his house!' Ben was flailing now, the car rolling forward. 'No! He stole the script, it's our script!'

'Then I suggest you find a lawyer,' Walsh said.

'Yeah, and a second act,' Dorfler added, shaking his head as the car pulled forward on to the intersection. 'Trapped in a car? Where's the dynamic? The tension? Doesn't curve.'

'Warm though,' Walsh chipped in, picking up his coffee.

'Oh, I don't question the milieu, but it's so static. I can't see any of the major networks picking it up. Maybe mid-season . . .'

And Ben yelled after the police car as it squealed a little and bumped around the corner, peeling into the late afternoon traffic.

Don's home, meanwhile, was understandably in chaos.

Had he the sort of neighbours who took an interest in what was going on in their street, he would have had them all piling out of their houses, hands on their hips, complaining about the noise. As it was, the three catering trucks, four motorcycle couriers and the news team were able to disperse themselves all over the wide street without so much as a twitch of a neighbour's bullet-proof, laser shielded, twenty-four-hour security-guarded net curtain.

Backs of trucks thrown open, trailers down, dozens of men in white jackets and checked trousers hefted chilled silver platter after chilled silver platter up Don's wide stone steps. On the clipped grass verge, Trixi signed courier's clipboard after courier's clipboard, dozens of Jiffy bags cradled in her arms, while Carol Sawyer, the host of Entertainment Today, chatted excitedly to the nation via her small camera-crew.

'*The breaking story all over Hollywood,*' she smiled enthusiastically, '*is that in the mansion behind me here, comedy*

VP Don Silver is preparing a party for the writer of his hot new hit Carpool, *which rumour has it has been bought by ABN for a record breaking fifteen million dollars a show...'*

Through the cool echo of his hall, voices yelled and hollered as trolleys of food and drink were rolled through the cavernous lounge to the clattering kitchen. The whole building chattered and thudded and clanked with activity.

Don was talking into his phone to 'Pendleton Security', waving young waitresses in with his other hand.

'He had a tantrum, you know these writers. Threw some furniture, let off a couple of rounds. We've all done it . . . No, there's no need, Jack, really. Just the big window . . . being done as we speak.' He threw a look at the two men clattering about with brooms and plywood at the end of the room.

Wandering back down the staircase, Melvin sat himself down on the bottom step. His laces were loose, slithering across the polished wood, pale bony knees pressed together. He was muttering to himself, just by way of a change.

'Hey, pal,' a sound engineer yelled at him, bare-chested in baseball cap, record-deck under his arm. 'This yours? My guys nearly fell over it.' And he dropped a rucksack at Melvin's feet with a heavy clunk. Melvin looked down at it, leaning forward and inching the zip open slowly, reaching in. A map, a guide book, a soft leather wallet. He let it fall open, a credit card clattering lightly on to the wooden floor. Melvin picked it up.

'Just reset the alarm . . . thanks, Jack,' Don said, and snapped the phone shut. 'Okay, that's that. You,' he barked at the sound engineer, 'get that plugged in anywhere. Get some music on in this place, we're having a paaarty!'

He was in a very good mood.

'Trix?' he yelled over the din.

She wobbled into the lounge, struggling with armfuls of padded envelopes.

'What the hell's this?' he said, sliding one from under her

arm. He read the label. *To Melvin Medford. Hand delivered. From DTA, Dolawitz Talent Agency, Olympic Boulevard.* 'Already?' Don laughed.

'There are three more bikes still outside.'

'Give 'em to Mel, it's his call. Mel?' Don called.

Melvin was still on the low step, bony knees about his ears, flicking through a guide book to LA.

'Mel, m'boy, we're in business. Back at the TOP!' Don yelled with a laugh.

Melvin said nothing.

'Look, I'm sorry I yelled at you back there, I guess I didn't see what your pitch was going for. Thought you were having some kind of breakdown. Forget it, doesn't matter. I forgive you, because you, old Brit pal of mine, are a fucking genius. We are big. And I mean *big!*'

Trixi began to tear open the Jiffy bags and stack up the spec scripts on the stairs next to him.

'How far is West Hollywood from here?' Melvin said, nose still in the book.

'What? Four, five miles, something like that. But did you hear me?' Don laughed again, throwing his arms wide, almost smashing a delivery man in the face. 'We're a goddamn *hit*. I had Al Rosen from ABN all over me, practically had his head in my pants.'

'I n-need to go out,' Melvin mumbled.

'Out? Whaddya mean, like to celebrate?' Don yelled. 'Sure, it's all arranged! We got a late lunch at Spago at four. You'll meet Dad, talk to Al, I'll schmooze around the tables. Then it's back here for girls and dancing. Hell, you've earned it, buddy. But, hey, *no coke, right?*' he added in a preposterously obvious whisper. '*Not after last time*.' And he clapped his hands loudly with a bark of a laugh. 'Jeez, when Dad gets here and I tell him about this, the old man's gonna dance a fuckin'—'

'Mr Medford?' a female voice came floating through the din. Don turned. A two-man camera crew were picking their way gingerly through the debris, a pretty reporter holding out a microphone. 'Mr Medford? I'm Carol Sawyer. You're live on Entertainment Today. Care to comment on these rumours of your new success?'

'Huh? *Live?* Oh, er, sure, sure. Uhmm, *good afternoon, America,*' Don grinned at the camera with a slick wink. 'My name is Don Silver, currently VP at Mercury Pictures, and the man behind me is young Melvin Medford, the hottest writer in television today.' He guided the camera through the lounge to the stairs. 'You see him here, surrounded by literally hundreds of spec scripts, each one from a writer begging to work with this man.'

Slowly, Melvin turned, staring at the single black shark-eye of the camera.

'No team,' he said flatly. 'It's my show. I write it. Just me.' He stood-up, looked down at the guide book and then back up at the lens. 'Do you know where Franklin Avenue is?'

'It's Ben!' Jackie yelled, staring aghast at the two policemen in her flat. They exchanged quick glances, Watts getting up quickly, moving towards the telephone.

'Ben! Ben, oh, Jesus, where *are* you?' she said, receiver pressed hard against her ear to screen out the long-distance echo. 'Hotel? Which one? It's not safe, Ben. Something's happened. Don's killed them . . . Jasper, Malachy, everyone! They're dead . . .'

Her voice trailed off.

She was exhausted. From the hour, from the worry, from the bathful of sweet tea sloshing inside her.

Watts was there beside her, lifting the phone from her trembling hands.

'It's okay, let me talk to him.' The constable led Jackie, a snotty whimpering wreck, back to the sofa.

'Tell him to come *home*,' she said. 'Tell him to come home *now!*'

Watts was on the phone, telling Ben to stay calm, listening to his story, answering his questions. *I'm sorry*, Watts said, over and over. *I'm sorry.*

Jackie was sipping Tesco value brandy and blowing noisily into tissues by the time he rang off.

'Is Ben okay?' she said through red, tear-sore eyes.

Watts took a deep breath and let it out slowly, composing himself.

'It seems Mr Busby and Mr McDonald have had something of a run-in with our mysterious subject,' he said.

'Oh, God!' Jackie gasped, her face paling into translucence, hands over her mouth.

'Mr Busby was able to escape and is currently holed up in a West Hollywood hotel. Mr McDonald is still with the American.'

'Has Ben called the police?'

'Not yet. In fact, it was very lucky for us that he thought to phone you first, Ms Heaney. The last thing we need is three cars worth of ill-informed, gung-ho LAPD storming in. Silver's lawyers would tie the whole thing up in knots and it'd be months before we got him back on British soil.'

'So what's Ben going to do?' Jackie sniffled. 'Just sit in his hotel?'

Watts turned to his colleague.

'Call the Yard. Have them contact LAPD and explain what's going on.' Watts handed his notebook over briskly. 'It's only lunchtime over there. Have them go to this hotel and ask for Ben Busby. I've told him not to move on any account, just to stay put and wait for the police to pick him up.' Watts turned back to Jackie and sat down close to her. He took her hand. 'We'll bring him home. He'll be quite safe.'

Jackie exhaled deeply and closed her eyes.

He'll be quite safe, she said to herself, and allowed the tiniest smile of relief on to her face.

Watts moved out of the room to talk to his colleague. Jackie, blinking blearily, thumbed on the television, finding a late news broadcast.

The hotel murders were still the top story. The po-faced woman, her red jacket still not suiting her, was still standing in the drizzle repeating the details over and over.

'...*A spokesman for the Metropolitan Police has told the BBC that the identities of the three victims are impossible to ascertain at this stage, given their condition. Their only hope is a laborious DNA scan that could take up to a week to produce any sort of result...*'

Jackie blinked, brow furrowed. A thought scuttled through her head but didn't linger.

'... *Police are anxious to speak to anyone who may have information regarding the identities of the victims...*'

'But ... Detective Watts?' Jackie called out, a little confused.

He appeared in the doorway, looked at Jackie then at the TV then back at Jackie.

He sighed an *ah, well* sort of sigh and promptly slapped her very hard in the face.

The shock and the pain froze Jackie for a good second, like a toddler preparing for tears. Watts, using his tremendous body weight, threw a hand over her mouth and toppled her yelping on to the sofa. She felt his hot breath on her terrified face, the coarse waxy chaffing of his Barbour jacket against her chest, his knees hard on her thighs. She held her breath in a silent scream.

'Not a *sound*, you hear me.' Watts glared at her, the whites of his eyes burning inches from hers. 'You even blink loudly, I'll break your neck.' He pressed his forearm against her throat, causing Jackie to gag. She tried to struggle, to flail and bite and tear, but Watts was almost completely over her, crushing her ribs, his wide forearm pressing hard against her throat.

They lay frozen silently like lovers.

'Not a sound,' he whispered.

Jackie's heart hammered, her head swam. Watts leaned in a

264

little harder. She felt her throat closing up and purple and white stars danced and flickered in front of her eyes.

The constable crept in softly. Talking. Not to her, into a phone.

'*It's London Two, stick Steerhorn on,*' he hissed. '*And get a fackin' move on, love.*'

'Remind him he isn't covered for this strong-arm shit. This is a one-off,' Watts said to his colleague softly. Jackie felt his breath on her cheek, sticky and cold with tears.

'*Steerhorn? London Two. Can you talk?*' he said. '*Well take it outside then. Jesus . . . Have all the evidence located and collated . . . as we speak . . . hold on.*' And he covered the phone. 'He wants it delivered.'

'Delivered? Oh, for fuck's sake, give it here.' And Watts took the phone. '*Steerhorn? London One. No can do, moving the package is not viable, repeat, not viable. Unable to leave London. We will hold it here until . . . no, I'm telling you, I can't do it, I'm needed here until at least . . . I am listening, and I'm telling you . . . Shit!*' he said, grinding his teeth. '*Okay, but no fucking about. This is the last thing, you goddit? I need to be back here with the full balance settled by midnight Saturday . . . well, make sure you do . . . Right, see you 0800 tomorrow.*'

Watts closed the phone and turned to look at Jackie.

Her head screamed and burst in confusion.

The constable moved to the window, peering out gingerly.

Watts said something about *the stuff*, and began to pull up Jackie's sleeve roughly.

She had to *do* something. Terrified, she first tried to squirm out from under his heavy body and slide to the floor.

Failing that, she tried to twist her exhausted frame away as she felt something cold wiped on her upper arm.

Failing that, she attempted to kick and wriggle and bite as the needle pricked her.

Failing that, she just tried to stay conscious.

Failing that.

Bernie sat in Randy's office, eyes flicking over the leather trim, the suedette covers, the gold cacti. Through the speaker hidden in the Stetson on Randy's hatstand, KMW.9 piped out more honest-to-gud'ness country boys singin' the best twangy schmaltz about their gurls who've dun gawn.

He was definitely never coming back to Nashville.

The door cracked open behind him and Randy moseyed back in.

'Sorry about that, Bernie,' he said, snapping shut a little cellphone. 'Bit o' business.'

'Mr Garland,' Bernie said. His arm had begun to throb again. 'Mr Garland, let me level with you. I didn't fall. My arm was broken. Broken by a very unhappy Mercury Pictures shareholder.'

'Should serve pastries at yur AGM,' Randy said with a smirk, dropping into his chair and hauling his ridiculous boots up on to his desk. 'Keeps their minds off yur spending. Good t'see yuh, now. Mary Jane'll call you a cab back to the airport if you—'

'This shareholder isn't a happy man,' Bernie pushed on. 'He represents a group of people. Powerful people.' Bernie was staring at Randy, at the hat, the moustache, the bootlace tie. But his mind was on Central Park. Tommy. The reservoir. The threats.

'He has asked me to sign this show to a major network. Wants it in writing by Monday. These are not men who like to negotiate, Mr Garland. And not men who take kindly to threats.'

Randy chuckled.

'Bern, sounds to me like you been watchin' too many o'those *Sexposé* specials on FOX. You got a violin case up yer ass or something?'

'If this deal doesn't go through, they'll take the money out of me. Piece by piece. And then they'll come looking for you.' Bernie leaned forward, breathing quickly. 'This is bigger than you think, Mr Garland.'

There was a loud knock on the door. Bernie almost jumped

into the ceiling fan. It was pushed open. A huge blonde bouffant floated in, the receptionist trotting in briskly beneath it with a memo.

'Mary Jane, Ah said I wasn't to be—'

'Ah know, sir,' she said, 'but this is kinda urgent. It's Carleen.'

'Clambake Cook-Out Carleen?' Randy said angrily, snatching the memo. '"*Dear Mr Garland*",' he read aloud, " '*you have been like a father to me . . .*"' And his voice faded into a snarl as he read on.

Bernie looked at Mary Jane. She shook her head at him, biting her bottom lip.

Randy sighed and dropped the paper to the desk.

'Well,' he said. 'Ah'd better let you go, Mr Silver. Seems our schedule has been bumped up a little. Young Carleen's husband came back. They've had somethin' of a reconciliation. He'll give up mule wrestlin' if she'll stay home an' keep house. Carleen wants her young 'uns t'know his daddy so she's gawn.'

'*Gawn?*' Bernie said.

'Gawn. Left. Skedaddled. No farewell show, no teary goodbyes. Gawn. Which means you better tell Dawnald to shift his ass. Ah'm gonna need that pilot episode a little earlier than we discussed.'

'You said we had three weeks.'

'Hmmm. No, better be Monday mornin'.'

Bernie looked at him.

'Monday . . . *this* Monday? That's less than four days.'

Randy smiled.

Bernie hauled himself up. Was he serious? Four days? He had to be kidding.

'Ah'm sure you'll think of some way t'do it. Thanks for droppin' by now.'

'But . . .' Bernie said, rooted to the spot, mouth flapping silently.

'Time's a wastin',' Randy said with a wink. Bernie stumbled dizzily from the office.

Randy closed the door behind him with a grin.

TWENTY-ONE

Ben sat alone on the end of his hotel bed, shaking.

The afternoon traffic hissed past the windows, heading west down Franklin Avenue. The air conditioner gave a cough and a clank. He closed his eyes, hoping that the dream would end when he awoke. That he'd be warm in bed next to Jackie. Or bent on their bony sofa. Or be naked, upside-down in a ditch off the M6 on his wedding day – anything apart from here.

He cleared his throat and opened his eyes to the light.

Melvin had killed them all, Angus, Malachy and Jasper. That's what the policeman had said. Killed them all. Strangled them. Left them in a hotel room.

Ben got up, wandering dizzily into the glare of the bathroom, and ran the cold tap.

How long before the police turned up? He felt sick, squirty, exam-room nerves. The British policeman had said they would send LAPD over. For Ben to sit tight. Not to do anything, not to go anywhere. Just wait. How long ago had that been? A minute? An hour?

He splashed cold water on his face and moved, dripping, to the bathroom window, gazing out on to the sunny street for the thousandth time. No cop cars. No policemen. No SWAT teams in flak jackets leaping about with visors and weapons.

The phone rang, wrenching the afternoon quiet in half.

Ben moved quickly out of the bathroom to the bedside, lifting the heavy handset.

'Hey, dude, you cool? It's like, me. You got a visitor down here in the lobby.'

Ben almost collapsed on to the bed in relief.

'Already? Thank fuck! Tell him I'll be right down.'

Out of his room, Ben crossed the chipped terracotta tiles quickly, past the drained, stained swimming pool, towards the rusty lift. His heart felt the wrong size for his chest. Huge, pressing, aching against his ribs.

He jabbed the lift-call button and heard the groaning clank as it heaved itself up the shaft.

It would all be okay. It would all be okay.

He would tell his story to the police. Hopefully not the two gum-chewing coffee guys from the car. He would explain the whole story. They would take details. Call for back-up. Reality would be put on hold, the lights would dim, the curtains open and then the movie would start. With sirens and cop cars and gun-fire and rescues and then Ben and Sheridan would be able to go home. Home. To England, with its cups of tea and tube trains and Bank Holidays and cold beaches. He would see Jackie again.

This whole thing would be over.

He stepped into the lift and pressed the button for the lobby, the rusty metal doors heaving themselves together with a bored sigh.

It shuddered down the shaft with a painful slowness and gradually trembled to a halt with a soft ding.

Ben could hear voices behind the cold steel doors. Zak was talking animatedly.

The doors rolled open slowly.

Zak stood behind the counter, sipping a take-out cappuccino, sweeping his hair from his eyes, and nodding at the visitor.

Ben's rucksack was on the floor, resting against the reception desk.

The back of a tall, broad-shouldered police detective, in the neat black uniform of the LAPD, cap tucked under his arm, side-handled truncheon on his belt, gun on his hip and mirrored sunglasses clipped to back pocket, was unfortunately completely absent.

The back of a short figure, drowning in white tennis gear three sizes too big, sadly wasn't.

Ben froze.

The door-close button was an arm's stretch away. If he moved, the metal walls would pop and buckle.

Teeth gritted hard, he willed the doors to close.

Quickly. Please.

'This is like, about his friend, right?' Zak was saying chattily. ''Cos it was like, woahhhh, man, y'know? When he got back here? I was out the back and I heard him come in. Shit, like, he looked Brody bad, man. I mean, he was shakin' like Scheider.'

'Brody?' the visitor said.

'Brody? Chief Brody? *Jaws*, man. Spielberg, '75. Roy Scheider. *We're gonna need a bigger boat.*' Zak shook his head and let out another in a long line of *woahhh* noises. 'Ben's like on the phone, shaking. Shit knows what happened over there. Says some guy had a gun? Had his buddy tied up? Man, he told me he was gonna hide in his room until you guys got here. I'm on lobby stake-out.' And he snapped his fingers, pointing at the door. 'For anyone suspicious.'

'You w-want to try his phone again?' the visitor asked. 'Or maybe you could just let me know what room he's in? I just need a few moments, I have his th-things here . . .' And he bent down to pick up the rucksack from the floor.

Zak lifted the receiver and then jumped a little, catching sight of Ben standing stock still in the lift. Zak smiled.

'Hey!' he said cheerily, phone halfway back to the cradle.

But Ben was shaking his head, mouthing *no, no, no*, over and over in terrified silence, somehow trying to curl himself into the metal of the lift wall. He was pointing, jabbing furiously at the visitor. *It's him!* he mouthed in terrified silence. *It's him!*

'Uhmm, hey!' Zak repeated, even louder but with an anxious waver. He brought the phone back to his ear. 'Uhm, Ben, hi there.'

The lift doors dinged, clanked and began to roll closed noisily. Eyes flashing, the visitor turned.

'*WHAT!*' Zak screamed, clearly panicking. The man turned back to face him. '*Not the window ledge, Ben!*' Over the visitor's shoulder the metal doors were rumbling together. '*That's a goddamn' three-storey drop! Don't do it!*' Zak placed his hand on his cheek hammily, throwing back his head and dropping his jaw. '*He's goin'! He's goin'!*' he yelled at the visitor. 'You gotta stop him! Room sixteen! *Room sixteen!*'

The short man spun on his heel, white trainers screeching, grabbing the rucksack and turning to the lift, reaching out for the call button.

'No!' Zak yelled. 'The stairs, man! Take the stairs!' And the visitor hurled himself up the stairwell.

'*Jesus Christ! Ben!*' Zak sobbed down the phone loudly. '*Think of the kids, damn you! Think of the kids!*'

After a moment, Melvin's footsteps echoing away, the lift dinged and the doors rolled open again.

'Like, what the hell's goin' on, man?' Zak blurted.

'Think of the kids?' Ben said, creeping out gingerly.

'It's improv, honey, what can I say?'

'You gotta get rid of him,' Ben jittered, scurrying around the desk to the back office. 'That was him. The guy with the gun. Melvin.'

'*Him?*'

'Him. When he comes down, you gotta—'

'*Okay okay, shhhh!*' Zak hissed. He began to take huge actory breaths, in and out, shaking his arms. 'Stay back there. I'm finding my character. Mi-mi-mi-*miiii*, la-la-la-*laaaah . . .*'

*

Don was in the bath when the call came.

He didn't hear the phone at first, his mind being on other things. The fabulous spread he was about to enjoy with Al and Mel and his father. How cool he looked, reflected in the dazzling mirror tiles and spotlights on his bathroom ceiling. What he might wear in four years' time to the *Carpool* one hundredth show wrap-party. How much longer Carol Sawyer from Entertainment Today could hold her breath.

Her perm floated up to the surface of the water like blonde seaweed, her manicure around his microphone.

'Mmmm,' Don said.

Ringgg, the phone went.

'Fuck it.' Don said.

He clambered dripping out of the bath, Carol taking the opportunity to return to the bubbly surface and massage some feeling back into her jaw.

'Shall I stop?' the cameraman said, peering up from behind his lens. The boom man sighed, lowering the fluffy microphone pole to the towel rack.

It had been too much for Don's ego to resist, having his frolics recorded by a professional news team.

'Take five, boys, I'll just be a minute,' he said, grabbing the handset from the wall and wandering into the lounge. 'Silver?'

It was his Uncle Bernie. He sounded miles away, yelling frantically over the blare of car horns.

'Jesus, what in hell's the matter? You okay? Caroline said you had a fall?'

'*What? No, no, I didn't, that's just what I told the hospital. Listen to me, kid, you spoken to your father?*'

'Dad? Not yet. His plane was delayed. I got lunch with him at four. He's gonna flip at the news, I tell ya, Uncle Bernie. *Uncle Bernie? You okay?*'

There was a desperate keening moan coming from the phone.

'What the hell's the matter?'

So, two thousand miles away, Bernie took a deep breath and tried to explain. Don paced his lounge naked, wandering among trays of canapés and champagne glasses, dripping on to the wooden floor. Bernie didn't have time to go into detail, neither did he have time to keep stopping, so a dumbstruck Donald could say '*b-b-but*' like a second-hand outboard motor while he punched out the basics for his nephew. All in all, considering, Don took it like a man.

'IS THIS A JOKE? *MONDAY!*'

'*Donny, listen to me*—'

'ARE YOU OUT OF YOUR FUCKING MIND? *MONDAY!* FOR FUCKING *CABLE?!*'

Just not a very well-balanced, happy man.

'I GOT *ABN* SITTING IN FUCKING *SPAGO* WITH A *FIFTEEN-MILLION-DOLLAR CONTRACT!*' Don yelled, stomping around the room. 'THEY'VE *GOTTA* HAVE THIS SHOW! THEY DON'T GET THIS, KRAMER *WALKS! WALKS!*'

'*Donny, calm*—'

'WE LOSE THE SYNDICATION, UNCLE BERNIE! YOU HEAR ME? MY HOUSE, MY CAR, DAD'S RETIREMENT ... HOLY CRAP, UNCLE BERNIE! AND WHAT DO I TELL *AL?* WE'RE JUST *GIVING CARPOOL AWAY?* WHAT THE *FUCK'S* GOING *ON?!*'

'*We don't have a choice here, kid. It's ...it's complicated. You gotta trust me.*'

'FUCK YOU!' Don bellowed, upsetting a tray of crudités with a clatter. 'You explain to me *exactly* what you've gotten us into here, Uncle Bernie.'

'*Kid*—'

'I mean it. I'm listening. From the *beginning*. What photographs? Photographs of what? And who the *hell's* Randy fuckin' Garland?'

*

273

Half an hour later, by way of contrast, Gill Kramer couldn't have been happier.

Top down, squealing along the twisting narrow lanes of Griffith Park in his E-type Jag, he felt young and alive again. That buzz of excitement, that tingle of giddy apprehension. He *was* young again. Back in London, seventeen years old, a student at RADA. Scarves, coffee bars, workshops and auditions. When it was all fresh and new. When the world's stages had lain before him like . . . well, he didn't know. Like something he was going to be able to conquer. Yes, he thought, taking a fast bend, the wind in his wig, something like that.

A new show. He was going to be in a *new* show. He slapped the steering wheel with excitement. It had been so long. Five years of *Office Politics*, then four of *E.R. E.R.* . . . *Oh! How* he looked forward to it. The new friends, the new dressing rooms, the little pre-show drinks and presents.

He checked his watch. It was half-past three. Thirty more minutes of unemployment and then Al, his sweetheart, would be signing the contract and *Carpool* would be his. *Carpool.* It would be fantastic. He would schedule meetings with the writer to talk about his role, to see where it could be given brevity, weight, darkness . . . everything he had missed over the last six years of pratfalls and punchlines.

Bumping across the intersection with Western Avenue, Gill grinned and began humming chirpily to himself.

Yes, half an hour of unemployment and he would be back where he belonged.

Unemployment. The word crawled over his skin like a greasy beetle. He shivered and tried to put the thought from his head, to enjoy the lush greenery, the LA sun flashing through the trees, but the thought scuttled over him again.

Just the idea of it made him feel queasy. His name being crossed from address books, his glossy 8×10″ torn in half. People boxing up his costumes, his dressing room key, his last script, all to be sent to one of those parasitic memorabilia stores on Hollywood Boulevard.

A cold knot of panic seized him. He *needed Carpool*.

If Al fucked this up, it would be over. By 4.30 p.m. he would become a trivia question, a where-are-they-now? A name that people throw in to celebrity gossip, deliberately to get an eyebrow-raising 'Holy shit, remember *him?*' By 7 p.m. he'd be kitschy nostalgia. A rare collectable. Seen smiling on the covers of old *TV Guides*, sold in polythene bags at collectors' fairs.

No, Al said it would all be fine. He had promised. Gill gave himself a shake and allowed himself to breathe again. This was merely a transition. A short dip in the antiseptic foot-bath of has-been-ness, which would allow him to splash about forever in the Olympic sized swimming-pool of celebrity.

His mind was so flooded with relief he almost didn't see the short figure in tennis gear come dashing from a hotel doorway and tear out in front of his car.

'He's gone,' Zak said.

'What did he say?'

Ben sat nervously behind the reception area, in a small brown office where a thick layer of dust battled a large framed poster of Laurel & Hardy for who could dominate the room. The dust was slightly ahead on points.

'Nuthin',' Zak shrugged. 'Just came runnin' down the stairs and out the door. Didn't think much of room sixteen, it seemed.'

'What's in room sixteen?'

'Nuthin'. Been empty for weeks. Just a lot of pictures of Chevy Chase.' Zak pulled up a sagging armchair. 'You want to explain what the hell's goin' on? I mean, the whole thing. From the beginning.'

So Ben, punctuated by deep breaths, a handful of 'no way, mans' and the most revolting cup of tea he'd ever had in his life, explained what was going on.

*

'No way, man!'

'Yes, way, man.'

'But like, no wayyyyyy, man!'

'Uhm. Yes. Yes, like, yeeeeeeeeees way. Uhm, man. Sorry.'

'*That* dude? Dawson's *Geek*? Close Encounters of the *Nerd* Kind? *He* tried to kill you? *Him*? Holy shitoly.' And Zak shook his head. 'You think Silver's in on it?'

'In on it?'

'Sure. I mean, he hasn't had a hit in four years. They're runnin' on fumes, man, everybody knows it. He's gotta be desperate for a hit. Desperate. Trixi said he was pretty stressed out.'

'Trixi?'

'His assistant. I met her at Mercury this morning while you were out in the parking lot.'

'Yes, but there's desperate, y'know, and there's *desperate*, for heaven's sake!' Ben said, putting down his cup of hot tea-style drink. 'I mean, you're a desperate actor right?'

'Right.'

'Some stuttering loon comes wandering into the lobby, rings the bell and says, Hi, Zak, my name's Melvin J. Psychopath. If you fly me to London and put me up in a swanky hotel, I'll dress up as a top executive and go around theatres murdering everybody, so eventually they'll will be so short of actors they'll have to give *you* a part. Deal?' Ben shook his head. 'What would you say?'

The room fell silent. Ben watched Zak slowly nod, working the idea around his head.

'Would it be a lead part?'

'Zak?'

'Sorry, man. But like, yeah. Don would say like, "No way dude, you're crazy." And like, call the cops.'

'Of course he would,' Ben said. 'Talking of which . . .' He stood up, anxiously checking his watch.

'LAPD are on their way, right?'

'That's what the policeman said on the phone. He told me just to wait.'

Guilt was gnawing away at Ben's heart. He had shoved the gag back in his friend's mouth, turned and walked away. Leaving Sheridan in the hands of that lunatic.

'Then we wait, man,' Zak said. 'It'll be cool. LA's finest will show up soon and they'll wrap up the whole thing. Now relax. Let me make you more tea.'

Don meanwhile was a mass of panic. A lengthy, incense-plumed mass, in the full Latin with hymns and a half-time baptism. He smashed back into the bathroom in a whirl of flailing arms and genitalia, Carol Sawyer letting out a shriek. Slapping and slipping across the wet tiles, he began to fumble with the video equipment around the cameraman's chest, finding the eject and yanking the tape free.

'B-but, Donny baby,' Carol whined from the bath. 'What's happened?'

He cracked the cassette open and began yanking out the ribbon of tape in huge florets, eventually dropping the tangled mess into the foam.

'Out! Everybody out!' he yelled, moving quickly across to his bathroom cabinet, rattling through jars and bottles and packets frantically. 'Calm, calm, calm,' he repeated over and over. 'Must relax, must be cool.' Pills and lotions tumbled into the sink with a clatter. 'Must stay out of jail.'

'Donny? Honey?'

'Calm, calm, calm,' he muttered. 'Stay out of jail. Stay out of jail. Must stay out of jail.' With a handful of foil packets and plastic bags in his fists, he slammed back out of the bathroom.

He stood naked in his huge kitchen, blood roaring in his ears, water roaring into the sink, throwing glass after glass of it down his neck, each glass joined by a handful of pills.

He swallowed some Valium to catch the Librium, he'd swallowed the Librium to catch the coke, he snorted the coke to catch the Thorazine, he swallowed the Thorazine to catch the Lorazepam. (He didn't don't know why he swallowed the Lorazepam. Perhaps he was high?)

Prison. Murder. Evidence. He couldn't believe it.

But Uncle Bernie! he had yelled. *I never met a Jasper or a Malachy or an Angus!* Uncle Bernie didn't care. *Shut the fuck up, not on a cell-phone,* he kept saying. *I'm on my way to LA. I'll explain it all in person. But if you don't have the show for SEBN by Monday, you'll be in front of the grand jury for triple murder by Tuesday.*

Don threw the rest of the water over his face and stood dripping like a madman for a moment, chest heaving. What was going on he had no idea, but he didn't have time to worry. Focus, he had to focus.

Script. He needed a script.

He bustled quickly from the kitchen, across the lounge to the stairs. Melvin was still out, but maybe he had something in his room. A rough draft, an outline, something Don could use.

He pounded up the stairs two at a time. He was two steps from the landing when the doorbell rang out through the house.

He was halfway to Melvin's office door when it rang again.

'Fuck it!' he yelled, spinning and thudding back down the stairs.

It was Trixi.

'I've just heard the news,' she said, 'I thought I'd . . . thought I'd better . . . uhmm . . .' and tailed off, biting her lower lip sheepishly. Don looked down. Trixi put some coffee on, Don some pants.

'Right, okay, we can do this,' Don said breathlessly.

It was five minutes later and they were in his kitchen, Don in his robe, marching and pacing and running clammy hands through wet hair. Forty-six urgent plans of action all stood along his mental touchline, blowing on their hands, jogging on the spot, stretching and bending, waiting to be called forward.

'First, get a call to Spago. Tell Al it's all off. No deal. Something's come up, a change of plan, whatever.'

'But doesn't this mean Gill won't finish *E.R. E.R. . . . Oh!*?'

'Just . . . just get word to him,' Don blustered. 'Second, call the lot. Talk to someone in production. I'm gonna need a studio for Saturday night.'

'Saturday night, right,' Trixi jotted, click-clacking away, her nails playing merry hell with her shorthand. 'That might be a problem sir. Most of the production crew are putting together *Fyre*. We're kinda short of space and manpower.'

'Shit, shit, shit,' Don winced. 'Okay okay, uhmm, tell 'em to clear out the *Woodfellas* set on studio five, it's been sitting idle for three weeks. Tell 'em I'm gonna want to be in there, full dress rehearsal, Saturday afternoon. That gives them forty-eight hours. It's an easy set. A plain family station wagon. Bit of tarmac underneath, bit of sky behind them. Just sitting in traffic. Piece of fuckin' piss. Write it down.'

'Fucking piss . . . got it.'

'Then get publicity on the case. I need an audience. Three hundred gag-hungry Angelenos. For Saturday night. Curtain up seven o'clock.'

Trixi's pen was flying.

'Now where's Mel? I gotta break the news. He said he was going where?'

'Franklin Avenue. Didn't say why.'

'Shit. Find him. Get him back here. Tell him we need a finished draft by the morning. He's got seventeen hours to get it written, polished and on my desk. Which leaves me to worry about a cast.'

Trixi looked up from her pad.

'You mean . . . ?'

Don nodded solemnly.

'We did it before, Trix'.'

She swallowed nervously, took a deep breath and wrote two words on her pad, underlining them twice.

'Eight o'clock?'

'Front row.' Don nodded, chin firm. 'Tonight.'

'Right away,' Trixi said, and moved to the phone on the wall by the fridge. 'Sir? What's going on, sir?'

'What's going on, Trixi dear, is that the deal has gone belly-up. No ABN, no CBN, no XY fuckin' Z. Uncle Bernie's signed over the *Carpool* rights to—'

And he stopped. Stared at her anxious face.

'Wait. What do you mean, *what's going on?* You said you'd "heard the news". That's why you're here. You'd *heard the news.*'

'No, I meant the news about your *father*, sir. I just wondered if you needed some flowers sent.'

'Flowers? What the fuck are you talking about?'

'Oh, gosh. It's Mr Silver Senior. He had a heart attack on the plane, sir. He's in hospital.'

TWENTY-TWO

The telephone was already sitting among the thick linen and sparkling glasses when, at four o'clock, Al was wafted towards his table. The doors stood open to the terrace, a warm Los Angeles breeze whispering across the leafy courtyard. Outside, diners chatted and laughed to the accompaniment of the trickling stone fountain.

'Mr Silver's table,' the waiter said, pulling out Al's chair and tucking him in. 'You are the first to arrive. Can I get you a drink?'

'Yes. A bottle of champagne,' Al said with a smile. 'Your best champagne.'

'Very good, sir.' The waiter nodded. He made to move away but Al caught him, motioning at the telephone quizzically.

'Oh, you have a call, sir.' The waiter smiled. 'Just this moment.' And then he disappeared to fetch the drinks.

Al sat among the tinkling chatter for a moment, looking at the handset. It would be Gill, he thought to himself. Checking up on him. For heaven's sake, he'd only been there five seconds.

Have you got them to sign yet? Have they agreed my fee yet? You better not screw this one up, Albert. On and on.

He sipped some water. This was going to have to stop. Yes, Gill was the big TV star and Al was just a humble VP. But he didn't want to feel like the lackey anymore. Once he'd done this deal he'd have to start making changes. Try and get the relationship on a more equal footing. Maybe even try and persuade Gill to leave Elaine.

'Hello, Al Rosen speaking,' he said, trying to keep as much impatience from his voice as he could.

But it wasn't Gill.

The call didn't take long, and two minutes later Al was sitting quietly at his table, staring at the cutlery.

Could you kill yourself with a fork? he wondered. Just grab it and plunge in into your chest? He picked it up, prodding the cold steel tines. Not long enough. Perhaps in the throat?

Yes, a sharp stab in the neck would do it.

He looked around at the busy restaurant. The other diners paid him no attention, enjoying as they were paying enormous amounts of money for large exotic pizzas and salads, sipping water and laughing young successful Los Angeles laughs. The words *deal*, *relationship* and *pitch* all floated above their heads like they were brands of beer printed on table umbrellas.

'Al!' a big voice boomed behind him. 'I saw you sitting there. Waiting for someone?'

Al looked up at the large man whose fat sweaty hand was leaving a grease spot on his shoulder.

Could you kill a President of ABN's Entertainment Division with a fork? he wondered idly.

'Been hearing some worrying things, Al,' Jack Weinstein said, easing himself into a chair with a creak. He had a napkin tucked into his tight collar, smeared with the greasy remains of something he'd paid a fortune for and missed his mouth with completely. 'Rumour was Kramer walked off the set halfway through rehearsal this morning. What the hell's going on over there, Al? He not taking the axe too well? You gotta keep him under control.'

'What? Uhm, I don't know, that's the first I've heard,' Al said quickly, twisting his napkin in his lap.

'We need these hundred shows, Al, you know that. This is

what the four years has all been about. He walks before the hundred, we're all in trouble. And when I say all, I mean, of course, *you.*'

'R-right. Yes, of course. I'll, uhmm, talk to him, find out what's going on. I'm sure it's just a misunderstanding.'

'It's down to you to keep Kramer happy, Al, you know that. At least till we have the hundred in the can. Find out what his goddamn' beef is and get it fixed. I'm trusting you with this. Oh, and how did you get on with Silver? You get a bid in for this Car Lot show?'

The waiter was back, clanking and rattling about with a shiny ice-bucket on three long legs, setting it up next to the table busily.

'What's this, *champagne?*' Jack said. A wide grin stretched across his ample face. 'Good news?'

'Uhmm, well.' Al's hands were clammy. 'We still have some d-details to iron out.'

'Good man!' Jack chuckled, his mammoth frame wobbling the table. 'I'm hearing great things about this one, Al. A quirky zeitgeist, I hear. Or a ziety quirkgiest? Something like that. Sounds great.' He heaved himself up. 'Say hi to Don when he gets here,' he said, and placed his fat hand on Al's shoulder again. 'Do this one for the team, Al, and we'll talk about your future.'

There was a loud *pop*! and the waiter whooped a little, gaily, glugging the champagne into Al's glass.

'You got any bigger forks than this,' he asked with a nauseous sigh.

Trixi spent the next hour on the phone, calling everyone from the Beverly Hills hospital, to let them know Don was on his way over, to the production manager of *Fyre* to let him know Don would be requisitioning his carpentry team for some emergency set-building.

Being a good-natured and conscientious sort, she also

remembered to call one Zachary Black, the handsome young actor she had met that morning, to postpone their date. And being a self-conscious paranoid sort, she took his frankly upbeat reaction to this blow-out very personally.

It was, of course, nothing personal.

'Ben, man,' Zak said, loping in like a bundle of clothes on a heavy soil washing cycle. 'The plot, like, thickens, dude.'

'Was that the police?' He was up on his feet.

'You better siddown,' Zak said, and threw himself into an armchair, legs and arms hooking over it like a spider-monkey. 'That was Trixi. I was meant to be takin' her out tonight. She dug my laid-back Zak-Attack, man.' He winked revoltingly.

'Congratulations.'

'But like, she's blown me out. Don's got her workin'. It's all systems go on *Carpool*, dude. They're shootin' Saturday night.'

Ben lost control of his eyebrows and his jaw passed some time with his socks.

'*Saturday?*' he said eventually. 'Saturday, like today's Thursday, Friday, *Saturday?*'

'Don's going nuts, man.'

'But why? What's the hurry?'

'You tell me, dude. Everyone's in a flap.'

'Has Sheridan written it all?' Ben's mind was reeling. 'I don't understand. Who's going to be in it? Do they have a cast?'

Zak was shaking his head and smirking.

'They will do soon,' he said. 'And it's given me an idea.'

Gill's new, more modern and yet equally revolting telephone was ringing as he led Melvin from his E-type Jag into his Naff-Type Home. Gill ignored it, deeply enchanted as he was by the youthful creativity, the artistic integrity and the instinctive talent prevalent in his own voice.

'– so I suppose, what I'm trying to say, Melvin dear, is that *Carpool* is my chance ... well, *our* chance ... but mostly *my* chance, to say something about the human condition. To hold out man's soul, bloody and raw, and say, *I am your voice. I understand the humble struggle of Earth's children.'*

They moved beneath the chandeliers down the panelled hall to the huge lounge. Melvin gazed about him at the oil paintings and statues. The phone continued to ring revoltingly. Gill continued to whitter on.

'After all, what is a freeway but a passage? From A to B, from the cradle to the grave. And what is a car *upon* such a freeway? A life. A solitary life. Moving, slowly, towards the inevitable?'

'But they're not moving,' Melvin said, gazing up at the huge television screen. He turned to his host who had the back of his hand over his brow and his eyes closed. 'That's the point. They're stuck.'

'Stuck! Yes!' Gill gasped. 'And is mankind not stuck? After all, what is a freeway but an asphalt ribbon of love? And what is a car *upon* such a freeway but a human heart? Stuck forever. Trapped between the suburbs of regret and the downtown office complex of possibility?'

The revolting ring continued to echo about the house.

'The glovebox of hope, forever cradling the streetmap of . . . Goddamnit, who *is* that?' Gill spat, breaking his tableau. 'Melvin . . . Melvin, dear boy, I'm so glad I ran in to you. But please, do excuse me. Help yourself to a pick-me-up.' And he waved at a tray of refreshments on the mantelpiece. 'I'll just get rid of this caller,' and he wafted into the kitchen. Melvin sniffed and then squeaked across the room with a shrug.

On the mantelpiece, two dozen awful photographs smiled out from two dozen awful silver photo-frames. Gill and Elaine on their wedding day. Gill and Elaine in chunky knits by a log fire. Holding hands on a beach, simpering around a Christmas tree, ice-skating arm-in-arm around Central Park. Melvin picked one up at random – Gill and Elaine cutting a huge anniversary cake – noticing that this shot, like all the shots, had been cut from a celebrity magazine.

His eyes swept over the three heavy awards, mounted on

marble plinths. Three pairs of frosted glass hands, fingers interlaced, wedding bands picked out in white gold.

Reader's Vote – Couple Of The Year.

Melvin's eyes eventually fell upon the refreshments.

The tray was silver, sparkling with crystal tumblers and champagne flutes. Two bottles of malt whisky glowed in the afternoon sun. And in the centre sat a mound of white powder. A huge mound. Melvin half expected a flag in the top and a moat around the base lined with seashells. He picked up the little silver straw and licked the end. Blinking quickly and licking his lips, he rattled the tray over to the coffee table and sat down with it, picking up the TV remote from the sofa.

He clicked on the television. Voices and colours faded up. A theme song.

'. . . *join in the fun in your blue suede shoes. On the Holiday rock, holiday rock. Hi-de-hi-de-hi-de-hi-holiday rock . . .*'

He smiled.

He knew this one.

In the kitchen, Gill slammed the door to drown out the television and snatched up the telephone.

'What? . . . *Oh, Al!*' he cooed. 'How are you, sweetheart? How's the deal going, all signed and sealed? I have the writer with me now . . . No, found him wandering about on Franklin Avenue. We're having a little drink, a little coke, discussing my changes to . . .'

Gill's excited grin began to waver and collapse slowly like a bouncy castle at dusk.

'Problem? . . . What do you mean, *problem?*'

It was about twenty minutes later that he finally slammed the phone down on what was now very much his *ex*-boyfriend. He'd heard about as much snotty grovelling and as many toadying apologies as he could stomach.

He stared at the brushed chrome handset, sleek and modern on his tiled wall. With a wail of rage he yanked the whole unit from the wall, stomped out of the kitchen, passed Melvin and threw open the patio doors, hurling the damned thing off the balcony to join its ancestor.

Breathless, he gripped the cold steel of the railing and stared out across the city's hazy afternoon, the wind whipping through his hair.

Unemployment.

The word smothered him like a wino's greasy blanket. He fought it, beating and flapping against its oily grip, but it was no good. It surrounded him, tight and sticky. Out there, across the city, the word would be out. Hundreds of celebrities would be crossing his name from their address books.

Gill felt sick. A sudden desperate urge gripped him, to hurl himself from the balcony. Right now. To break himself on the rocks and shrubs below. Prostrate, arms wide, like Christ. That'd show them. That'd show them all.

He took a deep breath through clenched teeth and closed his eyes against the horror.

No, he told himself, trying to focus. No. Dammit, he wasn't beaten yet.

He spun around, letting the creeping feeling of failure fly from him like Wonder Woman's handbag, and charged back into the house.

'Melvin? Melvin, listen to me,' he said quickly, approaching the green leather couch. He had an idea. The television chattered away at full volume, some ghastly sitcom. 'Melvin?'

He would get this writer on his side. They were friends now, he would listen to him, help him persuade Don to change his mind.

'We're friends, right? We understand each . . . oh, holy Christ!'

Holy Christ, *indeed.*

The whisky bottles were on the coffee table, two inches of amber liquid left in the bottom of them both. They stood, like telephone boxes on a snowy London pavement. The part of the snowy London pavement was being played convincingly by the cocaine. It was everywhere. On the table, on the tray, on the floor, on the sofa, a great plume of it splashed down Melvin's shirt front, accompanying the huge wash of vomit that sprawled across his chest.

Melvin sat slumped, head lolling, silver straw between his fingers, dribbling on the couch and muttering to himself.

'Miss Cathcart . . .'

'Melvin? Oh, Jesus, Melvin? Can you hear me?' Gill flapped. 'Oh, don't die. Don't die, Jesus, don't die!' He grabbed the coke-smeared remote from the tabletop and thumbed off the television. He knelt down and took Melvin's hand. 'Melvin? Melvin, it's me, Gill. If you can hear me, please don't die. It'll look bad, Melvin. They don't give Couple of the Year to people who have dead writers on their couches. Melvin. *Melvin?*'

'Go go go . . . to the holiday rock,' Melvin mumbled, eyelids twitching. 'Miss Cathcart. I want . . .'

'You want . . . to throw up? To stand up? What? Help me here Melvin?'

'I want . . . to be a yellowcoat . . .'

He was babbling.

'Melvin, Melvin, listen to me.' Gill squeezed Melvin's hand, limp and clammy. 'Melvin? Look at me. I need you focused. We have to talk to Don. *Melvin?*'

After an age, Melvin rolled his heavy head up and stared, blinking, at his host. He was white. Vomity bubbles popped about his mouth.

'Melvin, listen to me. What day is it? Do you know? What is the day today?'

'Chris Morris,' Melvin said, licking his lips. 'Rebecca Front, Steve Coogan. First shown, January the nineteenth, 1994 . . .'

'What?' Gill said. 'Okay, shut up forget that, forget it. What is your name, do you know your name?'

'Mel . . . Starring Melvin Medford.'

'Good, good. And . . . and your parents' names?'

'June Medford. And Terence. Terence Medford. I miss them. . .'

'Okay, Melvin. June and Terence. And where were you born? Can you remember that?'

'Walmington,' Melvin said. He seemed to be sobering up a little, pupils zooming in and out. 'Walmington-on-Sea.'

Gill laughed.

'Ha-ha, very good. Seriously, Melvin. You and your mum and dad? Where did you grow up.'

'Walmington-on-Sea,' Melvin said flatly. 'Uncle Arthur works at the bank. He's a chief clerk.'

Gill looked at the writer, blinking on the couch like an owl.

He stood up. Thought for a moment. An idea shuffled uncomfortably in the darkness at the back of his mind and stepped tentatively into the light.

Gill chewed his lip and took a slow, long, pondering lap of the room.

He returned to the sofa, grabbed the remote and winked on the television. A studio laugh burbled up. A man in sideburns stood by a swimming pool judging a holiday-camp beauty contest. Closing credits ran across the screen.

'Melvin?' Gill said, pointing at the TV. 'Have you been there? On holiday, as a boy?'

Melvin looked up at him and nodded.

Gill smiled, eyes twinkling.

'Tell me about being a boy, Melvin,' he said. 'Tell me absolutely *everything*.'

TWENTY-THREE

Eight o'clock came, and on Sunset Boulevard the news was out, running amok across the Californian night like a monster in a 1950s B-movie. *RKO Pictures present! In Technicolour! The horror! The terror! The Rumour That Ate Los Angeles!*

The warm evening was being wrenched apart by the deafening scream of trapped car horns blaring and gnawing as the traffic piled on top of itself, every car attempting to get as close to the doors of the club as it could. The parking lot was overflowing, the street was overflowing, traffic frozen in both directions, backing all the way down to Santa Monica Boulevard. A dozen motorcycle cops stood about on the sidewalk like a Village People tribute audition, shaking their heads, unable to squeeze their fat motorcycles between the traffic.

The cars were scraping each other, jamming each other's doors, but that didn't matter. Hundreds of eager comedians were clambering out of their sun-roofs. Other latecomers, actors and agents, stuck at the back of the gridlock, punched their horns and screamed '*Do you know who I am?!*' out of their windows. Whumping loudly above, a helicopter was lowering agents one by one down thick ropes to the roof.

Inside the dark club it was like a stock market crash, with waitress service: the black wooden tables and chairs tumbling and drinks crashing to the sticky floor, hundreds of eager performers piled and squeezed up the thin stairwell, past the wall of fading faces winking out from their 10×8″s, dragging barking agents and squealing publicists in tow. Behind the toughened glass in the booth, a squat grumpy man was yelling himself hoarse. "*Names, please! Get in line and give me your names! No name, no shot. Settle down there, Jesus Christ!*" '

'Er, like, hi, man,' Zak said nervously, nose pressed against the greasy glass. 'It's Zak. Zachary Black.' The queue bumped and shoved behind him.

'Black,' the gruff man repeated, scribbling the name on an index card. 'Zachary. Representation?'

'Oh, uhm, Dolawitz. Shifty Dolawitz.'

Behind him an elderly man in a cheap wig and a purple crushed velvet tuxedo bartered with a younger comic over material.

'You got anything in like a *fat-wife* kinda thing?'

'Sure, Pops,' the young man said. 'Can give ya, "*My wife is so fat, when she dances, she makes the band skip*"? Hundred bucks.'

'Okay, okay, good,' and the old man began thumbing out greasy bills. 'Any more?'

'Mr Black,' the man in the booth was saying. He handed Zak an index card. 'You got two minutes. Hand that to the guy on the mic before you step up. Got ya down for around 9 p.m. Miss your call, you miss your shot. *Next!*'

Don, who at that moment should have been in the front row of the Comedy Store with contracts and a pen, was running late. Sitting, technically. Next to a bed, sipping what the machine had called 'coffee' and listening to another machine go 'bip'.

It was one of the hospital's private rooms, away from the echoing antiseptic wards and the clattering trolleys. The hospital had tried to make the private room seem like home, as all hospitals do, with dull wallpaper, flowers and inoffensive watercolours. But it missed, as all hospitals do, by a wide mile.

It would only look like home if home was a cheap hotel room. And a cheap hotel room you were sharing with a second-

hand life-support-machine salesman. The little black rubber
accordion puffed in and out wheezily. Lights winked. Drips
dripped. Don sipped his thin drink.

The machine went 'bip' again.

The last time he had seen his father had been in New York,
when Howard had called him in and yelled about ratings and
budgets and last chances. That had been been his familiar
father, all sweat and shirt sleeves.

This father he didn't recognise. Dripped up and pale beneath
a green blanket, eyes closed, mouth open a little, he seemed like
a waxwork, an animatronic special-effect version of his dad. An
exhibit at SICKWORLD (Adults $10, Kids $5. Under 5s go
FREE!). A dusty exhibit that might open its eyes and turn its
head with a feint whirr of internal levers and gears.

There was a clatter and a chatter outside the door suddenly.

'He's in here, right?' Bernie said, cracking open the door in a
fluster of overcoat and worry, carrying the weight of the world
on his shoulders and the terror of blackmail in his sling. 'Don!
Hi, kid. Jesus! Jesus, look at this.'

'You heard,' Don said, giving his uncle a gruff slappy hug.

'Trixi called me. I just got in minutes ago. What are they
saying?' And Bernie peeled off his overcoat carefully around his
throbbing arm. 'He gonna be okay?'

'Stable,' Don sighed, four hours of fretting, gnawing and bad
coffee written across his face. 'Mild heart attack. Happened on
the plane over Colorado.'

'Jesus, Paul and Mary,' Bernie sighed. He looked terrible. He
looked over his shoulder quickly, as if to check they were alone.
'How's the . . . uh . . . how's the pilot coming? Your boy got it
written?'

'*Jesus Christ!*' Don hissed. 'The *show?* Dad's lying here with
tubes sticking out of his ass and you want to talk about the
show?'

'Look, kid, it's compli—'

'Don't "kid" me, Uncle Bernie. Don't start with the "kid"

thing.' Don was shouting. 'And don't say "sonny boy" or "scamp", and don't ruffle my hair and give me ten cents for a goddamn' comic book. I wanna know what the hell's going on?'

'Donny, Jesus, calm down, would ya? Your father's resting here . . .'

'Dying here, Uncle Bernie. My father, your brother, is *dying* here. Look at him. Whatever it is you've cooked up, this is what it's done to him.' And Don gestured at the array of hardware and screens and drips.

As if in acknowledgment, the machine went 'bip' again.

'I want you to tell me what's going on? No bullshit, no window dressing, just tell me the truth. You said this Garland guy has the skinny on me about London, some bullshit murder story? And that's why we gotta give him the show? The guy's talking shit! Look, we'll call the cops, tell 'em what he's up to . . . ?' and Don fumbled in his jacket, tugging out his phone. He flipped it open.

'No!' Bernie cried, snatching the phone from his nephew.

'But the guy has nothing!'

'Nothing?' Bernie said. '*Nothing?*' He tossed Don's phone into a bowl of fruit and tugged out a Dictaphone from his own coat. He held it up to Don's face and waggled it. 'This sound like nothing, your honour?' He pressed play.

As the tape spooled and Don tried not to pass out, Bernie explained about photographs and bloody fingerprints and shareholders and exactly why they couldn't go running to the police. While in a West Hollywood hotel, Ben was going running to the police.

'*Hold, sir*,' the operator said, then almost immediately somebody barked, '*LAPD?*' as if he'd got them out of the bath.

'Hello. Uhm, I don't know where to start, really . . .'

It had been five hours. Five long hours since Jackie's tearful voice.

Five hours since the kind British bobby on the phone had

said, 'Leave it to us, Mr Busby.' Five hours since, 'We'll contact the LAPD from this end. Just stay put for the time being.'

It had been the longest five hours of Ben's life. And for someone who usually watched BBC1's Children In Need, that was certainly saying something.

Zak had left for the Comedy Store on Sunset Boulevard an hour ago with a hastily scribbled copy of Ben's stand-up act to wave about. He was to try and keep Melvin destracted, leaving Ben to lead the cops safely to Sheridan.

But it was an hour later and Ben was still alone at the hotel.

'*Hold up a second, sir, just hold up there,*' the cop interrupted. '*Brentwood kidnapping? This sounds familiar.*'

'Oh, thank God,' Ben said, collapsing into a puddle of exhausted relief all over the desktop.

'*Let me . . . er . . . let me pass you over to another officer.*'

There was some shouting. And then what sounded like a laugh.

'*Heyyyy, if it ain't Mr British Jaywalking Sitcom Man,*' a familiar voice drawled. '*Pip pip, old fruit.*' There was a roar of laughter in the distance somewhere. '*You got yourself a show business lawyer yet, Mr British Jaywalking Sitcom Man? Or you still wasting our time?*'

Oh, for fuck's sake, no.

'*This is an emergency line only, sir. Not a twenty-four-hour helpline for embittered artists.*'

'No. Look, you don't understand,' he pleaded.

'*But you're in luck, buddy. I got a second act for ya. I was thinkin' about it in the car. You got these three guys right? Trapped in a car? In Brentwood wasn't it?*'

'Listen, *please!*'

'*Comedy cop,*' the voice said. There was a distant groan from behind him. '*Ahh, shuddup, fellahs, this is my big break here. Comedy cop, see? Gives them a ticket. Now technically I'm a cop, but I've been in acting classes for six months now. Had a couple of callbacks—*'

Ben hung up.

Breathlessly, he dialled Jackie's number. It was 3 a.m. in London. She'd be there.

Eight rings, nine rings. Ten.

A minute later, Ben was slamming up the narrow stairwell to the first floor, past the empty pool and into his room.

He grabbed his greasy denim jacket from the bed and stood looking quickly about him.

How exactly did one pack for a rescue?

He rattled around the empty wardrobe pointlessly for a moment, tugging at the stubborn drawers, twanging into the bathroom, heart pounding. He knew he didn't have much time.

Failing to find a complimentary set of wire cutters next to the coffee-maker, a Corby grappling hook or indeed a black balaclava and glove set tucked under his Gideon bible, Ben was out of the room, hurling himself down the stairs to the lobby a minute later, pulling on his jacket.

He clattered about behind the lobby desk, rummaging through Zak's faded *Variety*s and dried up biros, until – ah-ha!

Throat tight and breathing fast, he threw open the petty-cash box, peeling off about fifty dollars in grubby notes, stuffing them into his pocket.

Of course, if he'd been able to plan this, he'd have liked to have been a bit more sexy and dynamic about the whole thing. Purred silently up the hill towards Don's Brentwood home in a silver Aston-Martin with swivelly number plates and an ejector seat. Or zipped down a wire silently from a helicopter in a black jumpsuit. Something a bit more fitting a rescue.

But even in Hollywood sadly, life wasn't like that, Ben thought, grabbing up the phone from the reception desk and plucking a cab number from the corkboard.

Back at the hospital half an hour later, Bernie sat staring at the floor, his feet aching in tight brogues on the peach carpet. He was deep in a desperate yet rather one-sided conversation with his brother.

'I played Don the tape, showed him the pictures. The kid nearly lost his lunch, Howie. . . Guess you were right all along. It ain't him . . . Don says it can only be this Melvin guy. The writer? So hell knows what we do now . . .'

Bernie sighed.

'Don wants to go to the cops but I've told him . . . shit, we can't afford an investigation, Howie. There are things that . . . things you don't know. . .'

The machine sadly went 'bip'.

'God, I hope you can hear me, Howie,' Bernie said, his voice cracking.

'Y'know, I don't think he can,' a voice said.

'Jesus Christ!' Bernie started, almost slipping from the chair. 'Oh . . . oh, Jesus, wait.'

'How you doin', Bern?' Tommy said from the doorway, slipping off his leather gloves.

'Shit! Tommy, look, this ain't a good time . . .'

'You know my father?' he said, waddling into the room. Bernie went very pale and tried to scrabble to his feet as a group of men followed Tommy in, settling themselves in position like fat skittles.

The two goons responsible for Bernie's broken arm rested fat gloved hands on his shoulders and eased him back into his chair.

Tommy and another goon threw looks down the corridor before shutting the door quietly. Vinnie, sweating in his double-breasted silk, took the corner of the room.

And finally Tommy's father took his place at the end of Howard's bed, peering at the charts like a consultant.

Mr Lambert was a short man. Not circus short, but certainly a good head shorter than average. However, he was the proud owner of a good head of dark hair, a walk-in wardrobe full of expensive suits and a walk in mouth full of expensive dental work. He was pushing sixty but had worked a rich dark tan into his crow's feet. Surrounded by his men, he resembled a satsuma in a bowl full of oranges.

He spoke slowly and softly because he could.

'How you been, Bernie? How's that arm of yours? I'm sorry Tommy had to do that. You'll be aware that I deplore violence. But Bernie, in my experience, as reminders go, an arm in a sling beats a Post-it on the fridge.'

'It, uhm, aches a little. Now and then,' Bernie said. 'N-not so bad, Mr Lambert.'

'Not so bad, I see.' Lambert nodded. Bernie half expected him to whip out a stethoscope and ask him to lift his shirt up, he had such a gentle, soothing manner.

Well, for a violent criminal anyway.

'You know what a guy in Chicago once told me?' Lambert said, replacing Howard's chart on the end of the bed. 'Years ago this was. Little tip for you, Bernie. For all of you.' And the five goons all cocked their heads to one side as far as their fat necks and tight white collars would let them. 'The best way to take your mind off an old nagging pain like that?' Lambert looked about the room. 'A brand new one. Oh, yes.' He nodded.

At this, Bernie threw his head back violently, wrenching his neck hard and yelping. Not something he'd normally do. But it seemed to be the done thing, considering Sonny, the goon behind him, had gone to all the trouble of grabbing Bernie's thin hair in a tight fist and pulling very hard. Flailing, feet dancing on the carpet, he heard a soft *snik*, like a cigarette lighter behind his ear.

'Oh, yes, that'll do it. Your arm will seem like a distant memory, Bernie.'

The hairs that weren't being yanked from his scalp were suddenly prickling as something flat and cold was placed against Bernie's exposed neck. He swallowed, his Adam's apple just nicking the blade. He held his breath.

'I'm getting very tired of show business, Bernie,' Lambert

sighed. 'Very, very tired. Truth is, I'm only in this mess because of young Vinnie here.'

'Uhh, Vin*cent*, Mr Lambert. I prefer Vincent.'

'Vincent. Fancies himself as a bit of an actor, y'see. So I figured havin' you in my pocket, Bernie, might help him out. Vinnie has an influential father, you see, Bernie. A good friend of mine. And keeping Vinnie happy keeps his father happy. We understand each other?'

Bernie croaked, which Lambert fortunately took for an agreement.

'But it hasn't exactly worked out, Bernie, has it? Your shitty little outfit has been more trouble than it's worth from day one. The very textbook definition of a bad investment.'

Bernie, as it happens, was at that moment the very dictionary definition of **pants** *pl. n.* **1. shitting your.**

'My boy Tommy tells me that not twelve hours ago you promised him that you'd get a contract signed for this Carpark show by Monday. ABN, prime-time, a hundred shows. Get things back on track. You remember that, Bernie? In the park?'

He nodded as best he could without opening his throat all over the carpet.

'So then why did Vincent immediately follow you not to ABN, but down to *Nashville?* Watch you going in and out of some cable station? Hmm, Bernie?' Lambert said.

'Uhh . . .' he squeaked. His left arm throbbed in the sling, his right arm hung loose at his side. There was an emergency button on the wall above him. All the private rooms had them. With a quick movement, he could bring his good hand up and hit it, bringing a dozen doctors running to the room.

Howard's machine made an apologetic 'bip'.

'See, Bernie, I could ask you what all this is about. Waste each other's time with some back and forth. Who this Randy guy is. What you were doing in Nashville. But you'd only lie, right? Right? Like you lied to Tommy this morning?'

Bernie, paralysed with terror, the cold blade pressing harder against his throat, shut his eyes. If he hit the button, would they kill him? Or would they just panic and run? His good hand flexed and clicked at his side, unseen by the edge of the bed. The button would be just above his shoulder. If he was fast, he would hit it.

'So look on this as a friendly reminder. No more screwing around. Whatever you think you've got cooking down in Nashville, just forget about it. Call it off. We want to read about the deal in Monday's press. Now, you going to remember that? Or shall Sonny give you a more permanent reminder?'

Bernie pulled away quickly with a yelp. His scalp screamed and his eyes prickled with tears as he slammed his fist hard against the red button on the wall.

The room remained horribly quiet.

Barry Manilow began to burble 'Can't Smile Without You' tinnily from the headphones above Howard's bed.

Bernie peeled his fist from the 'radio on' button.

Lambert shook his head and began clicking his fingers, giving orders briskly.

'Vin*cent?* You want to be in showbusiness? Go find Don Silver. Make sure the boy isn't doing anything foolish. Tommy? This Gill Kramer character . . . He doesn't walk away from this studio unless *I* say so, you got that? We're counting on this syndication money. Find him. Take Sonny here with you. Explain our situation. And I don't want any of you boys calling me until you have *good* news, y'got that?'

The goons all grunted in the affirmative.

'No excuses. I'll see you back at the Beverly Wilshire when you've got something to report. Now let's go.'

A terrified Bernie watched them shuffle out of the room.

Howard went 'bip'.

In the small comedy club, the crackly PA system pumped New Orleans jazz from the low ceiling speakers, inaudible over the chaotic din. The backstage area was packed like a commuter-

299

train, stinking and sweaty, spilling out among the tables and chairs as comics jostled and elbowed, glugging water and comparing running-orders, trading spots, buying jokes. Everyone was minutes from their big break, muttering their material, pacing and stumbling in tiny circles.

An anxious Don pushed through the throng to a vacant table at the front, eyes wide, sweaty and jittering.

'Sir? Sir, are you all right?' Trixi asked, pulling out a chair for her boss.

'Where . . . where is he? Is he here? Melvin. Is he here?' And Don hunkered down at the table, throwing worried glances about the heaving room. 'You haven't upset him, have you?'

'What? No. No, he called, he's with Gill. They're both on their way over. Jeez, can you like, *believe* the response here, though?' she said, motioning about the room. 'Three hundred comics on the line-up and they're still queuing round the block . . .'

'Trixi, shit, listen,' Don said quickly, heart fluttering.

'They've all heard that you're selling it to some southern cable station but I don't think anyone believes it. Not after ABN offered fifteen—'

'*Trixi!*' Don hissed, pulling in his chair. 'Listen to me. It's . . . it's too complex to explain now but . . .' Don's head still swam with Bernie's story. The photographs. The tapes. 'Look, if we don't get this show in the can and down to Nashville by Monday morning, I could be in a lot of very deep shit. Multiple homicide, death-row, showering with other guys kind of shit.'

'*Sir?*'

'I can't . . . I can't say much more. Just that we're in a hurry.'

'Gotcha,' Trixi nodded, promptly leaning over the back of her chair. '*Okay, okay!*' she yelled at the room. 'Hey! We've got a sitcom to cast here. Let's get this thing going, we're running late. First act, you're up! C'mon, move!'

'*Trix!*'

The whole room murmured as one, heads darting, craning to

300

see who would be first to put their career on the line. A ripple of applause washed through the room as a young guy pushed his way to the stage.

'No, no, *wait*!' Don writhed in panic. '*We gotta wait for Melvin. We can't upset Melvin.*'

'But sir, there are over three hundred comics—'

'I *know*, but . . . but . . .'

Don's inside's gnashed and writhed. It was all too much.

Trixi handed him the comedian's index card.

'*Hey, everybody, how's it goin?*' the comic began, unhooking his microphone. The room whooped.

TWENTY-FOUR

'Here,' Ben whispered, tapping on the glass, the cab rolling to a crunching halt in the still evening. The engine idled a while, ticking over, while Ben sat in the back seat, listening to his heart beat and trying to think of reasons not to get out of the car.

'Call it forty bucks,' the cabbie said.

Ben passed him a fistful of notes and, after an awkward minute of smiling limply in the rear view mirror, nodding and saying, *home, eh? Tch!'* finally clambered out of the cab, shutting the door softly.

Not a sound. No dog barking, no passing traffic. It seemed even chirruping crickets couldn't afford the rent in this part of town. Ben looked up at the square stone house, glowing a soft blue in the street light. Cool dark lawn, wide stone steps, heavy front door, hushed as a church.

He allowed himself the quickest glance to left and right but the street was deserted. Just big ugly quiet house following bigger, uglier, quieter house for silent miles in every direction.

'Y'okay, pal?' the cabbie asked. He was still at the kerb, window wound down, watching Ben suspiciously. And who could blame him. He didn't look like the sort of person who lived here. And standing looking up at the house with his knees trembling, he wasn't exactly playing Lord of the Manor either.

'Heh? No . . . uhm . . . no problem. Uhh, thanks then?' Ben said with a weak smile.

The cab driver nodded. The cab driver smiled. The cab didn't move.

Ben swallowed hard and rustled quickly over the damp lawn, up the stone steps to the dark seclusion of the porch and the thick oak doors. He patted his pockets, as if searching for his keys, and awaited the sound of the car pulling away. He patted his pockets again. And again.

After an unbearable age there was a squeal as the cab peeled away in a wide U-turn and rolled off down the wide hill. A minute later, Ben was utterly alone.

He looked over the huge studded doors quickly. Thick and heavy. He touched the cold black metal of the keyhole. He didn't have what he needed to pick the lock — namely a hairpin, gloves, a black polo-neck and thirty-five years' professional lock-picking experience. But that was okay. That wasn't his plan.

Stepping off the porch, around a stone pillar, he moved quickly along the front of the house in a sort of bent crouch, twigs and branches crackling loudly beneath his trainers, hands cold against the stone, feeling his way along to the—

Ow! Shit.

Ben winced, dropping to the earth, heart thundering. He'd trodden on something, hard and flat. Fronds of vegetation wet and chill about his hands, he picked it up from the ground, trying not to rustle overtly. He tilted and squinted at the blue wooden placard, about six inches square, planted in the bushes.

Protected by Pendleton 24hr Armed Security, he read.

Crivens!

He looked up quickly and peered out through the shrubbery at the wide dark street. No movement, no sound. No squeal of tyres, no wail of sirens, no thump of helicopters. Not even a friendly, 'Oy, mate, clear orf!' Nothing.

Throat tight and stomach rolling, he scurried along behind some palms until he reached the far left of the house and a black iron gate, covered in steel mesh. Feeling suddenly exposed, expecting a gloved hand on his shoulder any second, Ben reached up his hands, to grip the cold iron. He heaved himself up, landing on his stomach, legs flailing wildly, and then hauled his legs over, landing with a crunch and an *ooof!* and the light balletic grace of half a dozen broken umbrellas. He lay still, rubbing his bruised areas and awaiting the sirens and dogs.

Nothing.

So far, so good.

Up on to his feet and bent over like Richard III at a Fun Run, Ben crunched down the side alley between the high hedges and the cold blue stone. Past the litter bins and mountain bikes by the kitchen door, and finally on to the vast lawn at the rear.

The grass still crunched with fragments of glass. The buckled lawn chair had been thrown across the tennis court. He looked over the shattered pane of Don's towering patio doors and knelt down.

Fuck it.

The hole he had made had since been patched up with a large sheet of wood, nailed to the window frame. Ben shaded his eyes with his hands like blinkers and pressed his nose against the glass, peering into the familiar darkness. The lounge now seemed to be filled with trolleys of food and drink. A large sound system was set up against one wall. But there at the back was the archway to the kitchen. The drinks cabinet, the ice bucket back in place, the wide staircase.

He swallowed hard and checked his watch. The illuminated face glowed red in the night. It was just after nine.

What was it Zak had said? They'd taken over the eight o'clock show? Don and Melvin would be hours yet, surely. Ben squeezed the button on the side of his watch to turn the red illuminated dial off. It took him three or four good hard squeezes before he realised: he didn't have an illuminated dial.

He moved his wrist back and forth slowly, a red dot glowing on his pale skin. A bit like a broken security beam.

Exactly like one, in fact.

Across town, Al Rosen sat in the darkness of his office on the ABN lot, staring at a letter.

Eventually, he pushed it aside and went back to playing with his balls. Sadly, with a resigned listlessness and a feeling that this might be the last time he ever saw them.

Holding one in his fingertips, he let it go and watched it click-clack click-clack back and forth against the others. As they chattered into silence, he reached for the cold steel gyroscope next to it on the desk and set that spinning. Then, at a nudge, a tiny silver man on a tightrope wobbled across a thin wire.

Executive toys, the catalogues called them. Toys for executives. To help executives unwind. Pendulums and puzzles, gadgets and gizmos, every Christmas and every birthday Gill had got another one engraved for Al to place on his cluttered oak desk. To remind him of Gill and to help him think. To help him relax in times of trouble.

They weren't helping.

But then, Al mused regretfully, they never really had. They'd been useless when he'd been an executive. No reason to think they'd start working now he wasn't.

He lifted his resignation letter and read it through once more.

It was crisply worded and succinctly put. Paragraph one apologised for failing to keep Gill Kramer in *E.R. E.R.* . . . *Oh!*, costing the network millions of syndication dollars. Paragraph two apologised for trying to cover this up. It closed by apologising for letting *Carpool* be snapped up by a cable station.

Just sign it, Jack Weinstein's Post-it on top of the letter read, *and get the hell out of my building.*

Al hurled a squishy leathery ball at the wall, listening to it give an unsatisfying metallic, '*Ow! Go take on the day!*' before dropping to the carpet with a thud.

Losing out to *cable*. What a legacy, he sighed. Probably one of these huge new corporate owned stations. Had to be.

Al hunched over his solid silver miniature golfing set, flicking the tiny ball all over his blotter.

Hell, what did it matter who got the show? He scored a quick birdie with a tricky in-off his desk-tidy and wiped a hot tear from his moustache.

He'd been fired by letter and dumped by telephone.

Gill had left him. Just like that. Not hinted at it, not danced around it, not slammed a kitchen cupboard and hoped Al got the hint. Just left. If Al couldn't get Gill Kramer a simple lead role in a simple new sitcom, then he clearly didn't think much of their relationship. No *Carpool?* No Gill. And that was that.

And Al had known from Gill's voice on the telephone that this wasn't like other fights. Al wouldn't be able to send over a sonnet tucked in a fruit-basket and be welcomed back with a hug and opera tickets. No, this was the big one. No more Gill Kramer. The man Al loved, the man Al adored. The wonderfully kind, talented, considerate man who had been Al's life, his whole world, for almost ten years. The end.

So Al sat, forty-eight years old, unemployed, gay and alone.

Playing with his balls.

Some cleaning staff gave a yell from outside the door, making him jump, knocking his tiny pool table and the miniature I-Hate-Mondays punch-bag from his desk.

Al rubbed the tears from his cheeks and pulled his *E.R. . . . E.R. Oh!* baseball cap down. A voice outside was saying, '*In here, right?*' and the door was pushed open.

They didn't look like cleaners, Al thought immediately, as the two huge men rolled in, squeezing themselves through the doorframe. They had no dusters or sprays or overalls. What they did have however were a set of gargantuan shoulders, an expensive shiny suit and an unpleasant sneer each.

'Albert Rosen?' the first man said casually, standing in front of the desk, picking up Al's toys one by one and peering at them like he was killing time in an antique shop. The second man squeezed himself into a black leather armchair with a loud farting noise and picked up a back issue of *Variety* from the coffee table.

'Wh-what is it I can do for you, gentlemen?' Al said. He had no idea who these huge guys were, but he knew that if they were kind, understanding, easy-going fellows who wanted to put Al at his ease, they were making a lousy job of it.

'Mr Rosen, my name is Tommy an 'dis is Sonny,' the man at the desk said, turning Al's tiny silver cricket bat in his fat fingers. 'We'll come right to da point here. We rep-er-re-sent,' he said, giving the word about sixteen extra syllables, 'a shareholder of Moicury Pictures.'

'I-I'm sorry?' Al said, trembling a little. '*Moicury* . . . ?'

'Pictures. Dat's right. We need to talk to a Gill Kramer. He here?'

'Gill?' Al said, a tremor in his voice that he tried to cover with a cough. 'Why, er . . . why do you need to see Gill?'

'*Why* we want him ain't none of yur concoin, pal,' Tommy said, the friendliness nipping out of the room for a moment. 'Yur concoin is wid telling us if Gill Kramer is here in da building or not?'

'Well, uhm, you see, the thing is, Gill Kramer is my . . . well, a personal friend of mine,' Al wobbled. 'I'm sure you gentlemen understand, I can't be seen to be handing out Gill's private whereabouts willy, as it were, nilly.' He swallowed and snatched a pen from his desk tidy. 'B-but if you want me to pass on a message . . .'

'Heh! It's like anudder fuckin' language wid these Hollywood guys,' Sonny interrupted loudly from behind the paper. 'I mean, what da hell is *hittin' green* on a goddamn' *gagfest?*'

'Shuddup, Sonny,' Tommy snapped. 'Look, Mr Rosen, my father has aksed us only to speak to Mr Kramer himself. Which we need to do as soon as possible. So if he's such a poisonal friend, why don't you just be a good boy and tell us where he's hidin', huh? None of us wants no trouble here, am I right? It's too damn' hot for dat.'

'Tr-trouble?' Al quivered.

'Sure. I mean da last thing I need right now is to waste half an hour of everybody's time slowly pushing dis cricket bat,' which glinted in the lamplight, 'into your ear, inch by inch, you screaming and bleedin' all over your fancy desk, until you tell me where we can find him. The *shareholder* we rep-er-re-sent is very keen dat *E.R. . . . E.R. Oh!* should stay on duh air. He'd like Mr Kramer to *reconsider*. So, like I say,' and Tommy looked again at the sliver bat turning in his hand, 'where is he?'

'I-I don't know,' Al gulped. 'Really, I-I don't know. I-I sp-spoke to him earlier this evening, and he said he was . . . uhm . . . going away.'

'Away?' Tommy said, and put down the cricket bat, picking up the heavy steel gyroscope instead, tapping its sharp point slowly.

'Honestly. He's a big star, has homes all over the world,' Al said, almost wetting his pants. 'By now he could be in Paris? Or Alaska . . .'

Tommy looked at Al. Flat, unblinking, a hint of a sneer around his jaw.

Al held his breath.

'Shit,' Tommy said with a sigh. 'Hey, Sonny,' and he turned away, kicking his partner's shoe.

'H-heh, lissen tuh dis,' Sonny read. ' "*Dat young miss gets more fan-mail dan duh rest of duh station put together. She duz duh show with her little titties—*" '

'Sonny, lissen, we got a problem here. Dad ain't gonna like it. Looks like Kramer's flown da coop.' And Tommy began to whisper with his colleague.

Al couldn't make out what they were saying. But then his mind was suddenly elsewhere.

He was thinking about titties.

'Wait!' he shouted, scuttling quickly around his desk 'What did you just say? Can I see that?'

Sonny handed him the paper. As the hoodlums watched, Al scanned the article.

Well, slap me twice and call me Judy, he thought.

SEBN. The station Don had mentioned on the phone. It was that dumb cowboy with his titties and his tan-mah-hides. Al *knew* he'd heard of them before somewhere. He couldn't believe it. *They* were getting *Carpool*? SEBN? That tiny one-horse outfit down in Nashville?

A hint of a plan scuttled past his eyes like a fox in headlights.

'We'll see ourselves out,' Tommy said, buttoning his jacket. Sonny hauled himself out of the chair breathlessly.

'Wait!' Al said quickly, the idea freezing with a screech. 'Guys, wait a moment. I . . . I might have a way of helping you out.'

The two thugs in the doorway looked at him.

'You want Gill to come back to the show, right? Well, like I say, he's a personal friend of mine. I might be able to track him down, talk him into coming back. That'd help you out with your dad, right?'

The two thugs exchanged dumb looks.

'Now if I was to do this for you,' Al said slowly, returning to his desk and clinking out a bottle and three tumblers from his desk drawer, 'might you do something for me?'

'Keep talkin',' Tommy said.

Al handed out the drinks.

'Do you . . . uhm . . . do you like country music?' he asked.

'Mr Silver?' Jack called, rapping loudly on the studded door with his nightstick. 'Mr Silver? Sir? Pendleton Security, you there?'

'Anything?' the second guard called. He was flashing a torch down the narrow alley. A few bins, a couple of bikes. Nothing out of the ordinary.

'No answer,' Jack said. He unclipped his radio from his heavy belt and squelched the channel open. 'This is Pendleton three-zero. Me and Mickey are at four-seventy-seven Palmwood. No initial signs of entry, over.'

'*Receiving you, Jack. Silver called in a broken window this afternoon. Could be a late alarm response, but you better check it out. Send Mickey round the back, go inside and give the place the once over. I'm neutralising from this end now, over.*'

'Received,' Jack said and began to fumble for his ring of keys.

'*Oh, and Jack,*' the voice crackled. '*Take it easy. Try not to kill anybody this time.*'

'Hey, it's called armed response,' he said, unclipping a holster and hauling out a huge handgun. 'I'm armed and I respond.' He pulled the hammer back with an uneasy click. 'Anyway, Mickey's the guy you should worry about. Liable to bullshit the guy to death.'

'I heard that,' Mickey hissed from the gate. 'And it's not bullshit. Zachary Smythe and Benjaford Busbyworth from the BBC said they'd look at my script. I told you that Mercury Pictures gate job was the way in, Jack.'

'Mickey, take your typewriter outta your ass and take a look round the back. And be careful. I mean, if *you* get shot, who's gonna let Gill Kramer's car in and out?'

'Hardy fuckin' har.'

The two men rattled around with their keys, opening their respective doors. Pushing them wide, they edged forward: Mickey scuffing down the left side alley past the bikes and bins towards the rear of the house, Jack in through the front door, squeaking down the wide hallway in the darkness, gun outstretched.

'*Just gimme an excuse, punks,*' he whispered. '*I'll take your fuckin' heads off.*'

Ben, crouching down in the right-hand alley, held his breath.

At the sound of the guards entering the house, he quickly heaved himself up on top of the gate, dropping down again on to the damp grass. He caught sight of a large blue van parked diagonally across the wide street, *Pendleton 24hr Armed Response* lettered upon the door in gold. Heart slamming away, breathless with nerves, he scrabbled through the bushes and up the stone steps to where the huge front door stood ajar.

Wincing, braced for the haunted-house creak, he quietly eased the heavy door open another foot. At the far end, through the stone arch, Jack was checking the lounge for intruders. Flashing his long Maglite over the trolleys and trays, Ben watched him snaffle a couple of canapés, wipe his mouth on his sleeve and spit a few flaky crumbs about the room.

'*Stick your head out, motherfucker! Gimme some target practice . . .*'

Ben lowered himself to his belly silently and, breath held, began to slide his way down the hall.

Jack sighed and unclipped his radio.

'Mickey, status report, over?' The radio crackled a response. 'A swimming pool? Okay. But anything suspicious, over? . . . Look, Mickey, you're not selling me the goddamn' place. Frankly I couldn't give a hairy ass if he's got a wine cellar and a panoramic view of the ocean making this an ideal investment opportunity. We're looking for a frickin' break in, over.'

Heart thumping, Ben lowered his head and squeaked forward another three feet like a crocodile. He was now about twenty feet from the archway.

'Footprints? On the ground where . . . ? Hold on, stay where you are, I'm comin' to you, over.'

Ben held his breath. Jack's squat figure waddled past the archway with a sigh, gun held loosely in his right hand, torch up at shoulder height. Ben hunched his shoulders, ready to move fast. Jack's footsteps changed as he moved from the wooden floors of the lounge to the tiled kitchen.

Now.

Teeth gritted, wincing at every squeak, Ben got quickly to his feet, hunched over and low, and began to scuttle as quickly as he could down the hallway in the darkness. In the lounge, tall and airy, cluttered with trestle tables and speakers, Ben kept going, hunched over, up the staircase as quickly as he could, flumphing into a curled ball at the top.

He held his breath and listened.

A click and a clatter from the kitchen and a cold breeze swept through the house.

Sounds of men scuffing around outside.

Ben looked up quickly to the landing. Half a dozen closed white doors.

One familiar one.

Please, he thought to himself. *Please, Zak. Don't let Melvin leave.*

Ben had nothing to worry about on that count. From where Zak was, he could see Melvin perfectly. He'd watched him arrive in a woozy state with Gill Kramer. Watched him stagger dizzily through the tables to Don and Trixi at the front of the club. Watched Gill join Shifty Dolawitz at a rear table.

Yep, from where he was, he could see just about everybody.

'Uhmm, hey. Er . . . how . . . how y'all doin?'

He swallowed, licked his dry lips and squinted out into the sweaty glare. A dark sea of faces stretched infront of him, sitting, standing, staring.

'Uhmm, my-my name's Zak.'

Ben's crumpled notes were clenched in his clammy fist. Heart banging loudly, he glanced down at them, the words swimming. He stuffed them into his pocket and looked again at the shuffling crowd.

'I . . . er . . . I didn't think I'd actually be, y'know . . . Shit. Th-that they'd make me come up and . . . uhmm . . . well. Here goes, I guess.'

He licked his lips again, unclipping the warm microphone and flipping out the flex.

'L-let me hear you say *yeah!*'

*

312

In the hot darkness of the club, tucked away at a rear table, Shifty Dolawitz sucked an olive and watched the stage.

'I recognise this guy,' he whispered, motioning with a cocktail stick. 'He sent me his picture. Zak something, did he say?'

'Jesus, Shifty,' Gill hissed from behind a laminated menu, 'aren't you listening? This is important!'

'You like the way he looks? I like the way he looks. Got like a soulful kinda surfer kinda thing. What do you think?'

'Shifty!' Gill said, grabbing his sleeve. 'I'm talking about Medford? The so-called hot English writer.'

'Like a Brando meets Malibu Ken. And the crowd like him too. Feel that warmth. He's got something, no doubt about it.' Shifty snatched Gill's menu and dropped it to the floor. 'Whoops! Let me get that.' And he disappeared under the table.

'Shifty! Would you stop doing that? Shifty, this is important!' And Gill followed him under the table.

Beneath the table, in the darkness, it was surprisingly busy. Flapped open on the floor were three fat directories, bristling with Post-its and curling corners. On top of these, Shifty had opened a huge desk diary. He was whispering into his cellphone.

'Black. Zachary Black . . . Yes, find his letter and bike over the standard agreement. I want him signed before Don gets his hands on him. The kid's got something . . .'

'Got something?' Gill spat as Shifty blipped off the phone. '*I've* got something. I've got Don Silver and this whole fucking studio by the balls. Are you listening to me? I had Melvin up at the house. He had a little too much to drink, took a noseful of coke, started blabbering.'

'Ah, yes, Melvin,' Shifty said, 'that reminds me . . .' And he began to flip and flap through his directories. 'Writers . . . writers,' he muttered. 'Did he mention who his representation was? The kid's got a future, it's time he and I were in business . . . writers, ah, here we are.'

'You won't find him in there,' Gill said. 'That's the point! The boy's a fake. He's no writer. He's crazy. Deluded. Nuts.'

'Odd. There's no Medford listed . . .'

Above them, the room burst into riotous applause.

'Listen to that! That's my boy!' Shifty said, eyes flashing with potential future earnings. They scrabbled upright. Gill banged his head hard on the table, but his yelps were lost in the audience's cheers. Zak was a hit, the room was going wild. Shifty clapped and whooped.

The only people not smiling were at the front table.

'What . . . what do you th-think, pal?' Don asked tentatively over the din. 'He on your maybes list?'

Melvin blinked a few times silently. Don sat trembling, breath held.

'I've heard it before,' Melvin said quietly. 'The routine. I've heard it before. But . . . I like it.'

'*Great!* Good choice! Terrific! Absolutely!' Don cried, nervous sweat pouring from him. 'Whatever you want, buddy, heh, okay? Trixi, make a note.'

'Sir? Are you okay?'

'F-fine, no problem.' Don smiled weakly, eyes wide, muttering under his breath, '*God, please don't kill me, please don't kill me.*'

Zak took a bow and stepped from the stage. The MC, sitting at a keyboard below, tinkled a snappy piano riff and leaned into his microphone.

'That was act thirty-six, Zachary Black. And now,' he did a little roll of the low notes to build up excitement, 'the Comedy Store is proud to present, from ABN, the one and only – Gill Kramer!'

The crowd went wild with applause.

Gill just went wild.

'What!' he spat. Shifty grinned back at him, nodding towards the stage and handing him an index card. 'What have you done? *Audition?!*'

'Gill, honey, c'mon now,' Shifty said. Heads began to turn towards the back of the club. The agent beamed back at them. 'Look, you walked off *E.R. . . . E.R. Oh!* which means you're out of work and I'm out twelve million a year in commission.'

'I don't *audition!* I'm Gill Kramer! *Audition?* At this . . . this *amateur hour!'* Gill glared at his agent.

'Then what are you doing here?' Shifty cried. 'Meet me at the Comedy Store, you said.'

'Yes! So I could tell you . . . God, haven't you been listening?' The place was still thundering with applause.

'This Melvin Medford, this writer? I don't know what he's told Silver but I swear this show isn't *his.* The kid's *nuts.* No *way* he's some top British talent. He can't tell real life from—'

'Last call for Gill Kramer!' the MC said. 'We don't have a lot of time here? Is there anybody . . . ?'

'You don't understand!' Gill pleaded. 'He's made it all up! His parents, his home town, his awards. He let it slip out . . .'

'*Uhhh, hey,*' a new voice broke loudly over the din of the club. All heads turned. Someone had got on stage. A fat guy in a tight shiny suit. '*Hey, like ex-cuse me here? This is uhhh, this is da Comedy Store, right? Wid like, the jokes and shit?*'

'Who's *this* guy?' Shifty said, turning away from Gill and fixing his eyes on the squat man at the microphone.

'Shifty!' Gill spat angrily.

'Er, excuse me? *Cousin Vinnie?*' the MC said from beside his piano. The audience laughed. 'If you're up next, I'll need your card before you start?'

'Fuck you, pal. An' the name's Vincent,' Vinnie complained over the applause. 'Shut the fuck up! My name is Vincent. Sheesh, why does does everyone insist on callin' me Vinnie? Whaddo I look like? Some kinda gangster?'

The place went wild.

Shifty dived under the table for his directory and phone, leaving Gill fuming.

This guy was *great.*

'Sheridan? Sheridan, it's me!' Ben whispered, face pressed close against the cold door. 'Sheridan, are you there?'

'*Beb?*' Sheridan said faintly from within.

He was alive. Ben almost collapsed on the floor with exhausted relief. He reached up to the door frame for the key.

Or rather, to where it should have been.

'Shit! Sheridan, there's no key! Where's the key?'

Suddenly the still darkness was wrenched apart by a deafening wooden banging from downstairs. Then an equally loud, '*Ow! Fuck!*' and a slightly softer, '*Sorry, Jack.*'

Ben slammed his hand against the door. He only had minutes. Once, twice. It shuddered and stayed firm. He tried his shoulder, calling out all the while in a frightened voice.

'It's all right, hold on,' he said, and took a step backwards, a deep breath, placed a clammy palm on the wall beside him, raised his knee up to somewhere near his chin and kicked the door open.

Or tried to.

It banged loud, hard, and stayed firm, sending a vibration volt up Ben's leg and shaking the landing. Would the guards be able to hear it from outside? It was awfully loud.

Leaning back a little further, knee a little higher, closing his eyes a little tighter, his leg still buzzing from the shock, he planted his second kick firmly just below the door handle.

With a crash, the lock snapped, the door splintered open and Ben lost his balance, stumbling into the gloom.

'*Beb!*' Sheridan cried desperately. Ben stood upright, feet slipping on the papery floor, and snapped on the light. Breathlessly, he scrambled across the room to the desk where the laptop sat glowing, its screen filled with words. The yellow notebook lay cracked open at its side, a pile of pages scattered on top of it.

He yanked the balled up towelling belt from Sheridan's spluttering mouth.

'Da bizzies? Did ya bring da bizzies?' Sheridan coughed. 'Are dey here or wha?'

'*Shhhhhh!*' Ben hissed. '*It's just me,*' and began tugging and fumbling quickly with the tight belts around Sheridan's chest and neck. There seemed to be dozens more then he remembered.

'Just you?' Sheridan said. 'Awww, bleedin' 'eck, mate! Whad 'appened? You were meant to bring da bleedin' cavalry!' He writhed and twisted, wrists still shackled to the drawer handles.

'*Shut the hell up!*' Ben whispered, fingernails tearing frantically at cotton. Some of the white belts crackled with coppery dust. It smudged on his fingers. 'Shit, what's this?'

'He didn't . . . didn't like da *Ford Moses,*' Sheridan said.

Ben looked up and noticed for the first time the horrific purple bruises on his friend's temple. Swollen and yellowing, there were three wide dark scabs running through the middle of them.

'It only hurts when I blink,' Sheridan said.

'Okay, okay,' Ben said. 'Listen, Melvin's at the Comedy Store but there are armed guards wandering around outside. We need to get you out of this chair and out of here.'

'When's the psycho due back?'

'I . . . fuck it . . . I don't know. But I've got someone keeping him there. We should be okay.'

Zak was standing, reeling and woozy, in the chill darkness of the parking garage next to the club, his whole world spinning and shouting and ringing like a fairground. Cheers and laughter roared in his ears, lights and applause, a sea of smiles. He had never felt anything like it. The rush, the buzz. He trembled with racing exhilaration, hands and knees shaking, cold sweat drying on his face.

'There you are!' Trixi said with a grin, jogging across the tarmac towards him. 'That was a great show, honey, a great show.' She kissed him on the cheek. 'You're a big hit. Hey, you okay?'

'Yes, yes,' Zak said, trying to focus on her face. Trying to focus on the envelope being pressed into his hands.

'Tomorrow morning, eight a.m. We'll send a car.'

'I'm s-sorry? What?' Zak said. His head was still on stage, bathed in the spotlight.

'That's the usual contract, plus the first three pages of the script. Melvin should have the whole thing ready for the read through tomorrow.'

'I got a part?' Zak croaked. 'In the show? A proper part? No way? Way? No? No way? Me? No wayyyyy? Way?' Zak said over and over for about a month.

'You're gonna be a star! C'mon, come meet everybody.' and Trixi steered a dizzy stumbling Zak out of the garage and back into the throbbing club. 'Comic called Vincent something . . . does like a fat wiseguy thing. He's great!' Trixi chatted away busily as they walked but Zak didn't take in a word.

He couldn't believe it. No more hotel lobby, no call-backs. He'd done it. A sitcom.

'You'll have to excuse Mr Silver. He's in a weird mood tonight. Kinda jumpy. Keeps laughing out of context, asking Melvin if he's okay.'

'*Melvin?*' Zak said. The name sounded wrong to him. Definitely wrong.

'Edelman. He's gonna be playing the third role. Insists on it. Between you and me, not exactly movie-star looks but hell, it's his show. Don just wants to keep him happy.'

They pushed through the crowds, up the stairs and ducked back into the sweaty room. Clambering on to the stage was an elderly man in a cheap wig, a purple crushed velvet tuxedo and capped teeth.

'*Thank you, thank you,*' the old man began, unhooking the microphone. '*Y'know, my wife is so fat, when she dances, she makes the band skip?*'

'Y-you said Melvin? Where, uhm, where is he?' A cold feeling sank within Zak's stomach.

'*Yes, it's true, and her teeth are so crooked, when she smiles it looks like her tongue is in jail...*'

'Can I get you a drink?' Trixi asked. But Zak had gone pale. His brief glimpse of stardom had been pushed aside. He began to look quickly about the club.

'*And fat? Boy, when she ran away, they had to use all four sides of the milk carton. Yes, it's true...*'

'Is he still here? Melvin?'

'*I told her to haul ass last week. Took her three trips. Yes, it's true...*'

'No, he left. He's got the script to finish.'

'*But she's not only fat, she's short. You can see her feet on her driver's licence. Yes, it's true...*'

'Home? Shit, when? When was this?'

'*Hey, shut up, I got a hundred of these. My wife isn't the sexiest woman in the world either, I'll be honest. I called her up for phone sex and I got an ear infection...*'

'Ten? Fifteen minutes ago? Is there a problem? Zak? Zak, wait!'

'*Hey, c'mon, c'mon, where you going? Hey, what's the rush? I haven't told you how ugly my wife is. You know, I took her to a haunted house once? She came out with a paycheque...*'

It was no good, Sheridan was trapped. The handcuffs around the drawer handles pinched about his wrists. The knots in the belts were fat and tight, Sheridan's terrified sweat fusing them into dozens of hard cotton balls. Unless they could somehow get the whole chair apart, he was going nowhere.

'Slide me backwards,' he whispered. 'The drawers should come all da way out. Quick.'

'Okay, okay.' And Ben began to move quickly back and forth between the chair and the drawers, the chair and the drawers, easing Sheridan back slowly, sliding the drawers open inch by maddening inch, Sheridan hissing in frustration.

Eventually they slid free, hanging from Sheridan's wrists like two gargantuan charm bracelets.

'Now quick, get us out on to the landin'.'

'The landing?' Ben whispered. 'Sheridan, there are two guys out in the garden with torches and guns—'

'Then you'd better get a bleedin' move on!' he hissed. 'I ain't gonna be here when that bloke gets back. He's fookin' crazy, mate. C'mon, shift me out to the landing. I've got an idea. *C'mon!*'

So with Sheridan's idea being better than Ben's total lack of one, he stacked the two drawers on top of each other on Sheridan's lap and got behind the chair as quietly as he could. He heaved it forward, a little bit on the left, a little bit on the right, across the paper towards the door. It was a slow process.

'Your head all right?' he asked, wincing at the sight of the wound.

Sheridan nodded as best he could.

'Six pages he got out of me,' he said, 'y'know that? That crazy fuck!'

'Keep it down mate, for Chrissakes,' Ben whispered, edging the chair though the door out on to the still darkness of the landing.

'He was like, *not funny*, then BANG. *Not funny*, BANG. Side of the head. Six pages.'

Ben peered over the banisters. Downstairs was dark and still. A breeze still swam in from the open front door, whipping the dustsheets and sending party balloons skittering across the polished floor. The guards were nowhere to be seen.

'Further down,' Sheridan urged, Ben obediently dragging the huge chair along the landing. 'I need to . . . *SHIT!*'

'Shhh!' Ben rasped in alarm. He could hear two distant voices below them in the dark. The soft crackle of a radio. 'This isn't the time.'

'No! *The book! The six pages. It's back in the room!* Go and get it!'

'Sheridan! Jesus, the fuckin' guards are—'

'Get it!' Sheridan spat, wrenching round in the chair. 'Next to the computer! I ain't leavin' them behind.'

Ben let out a frustrated groan before squeaking back down the landing as fast as he could. In the office, he snatched up the open book and squeaked back to where Sheridan sat trussed. He dropped the book into one of the drawers stacked on his friend's lap.

'Our fookin' life's work that,' Sheridan whispered. 'Now turn me around, like. Put my back to the stairs.'

'What are you—'

'Quick!' Sheridan ordered.

Ben shifted the chair around as best he could.

He couldn't take his eyes off the bruises on Sheridan's head. He looked down at his face, sweating and scared.

'My fault,' Ben said softly. 'Talking to him in the pub? Sending him to your gig? This is all my fault.'

'Fook it,' Sheridan said. 'Six pages in two days? Fookin' worth it, mate.'

They shared a smile.

'Now, push.'

'Push?' Ben whispered. 'Push wha— Oh, no, Sheridan! Jesus Christ, you'll kill yourself. They'll hear!'

'I can do it by meself but it's easier if you help. Look, mate,' Sheridan hissed, 'you said it y'self. The belts aren't coming off, we'll have to take the chair apart. Otherwise I'm gonna be stuck in this fookin' chair the rest of my life like the fookin' Corbett De Sade. Push! Once I'm outta this, we can leggit.'

Ben swallowed, bent down and grabbed two sturdy steel chair legs. He hauled them six inches from the floor.

'Ready?'

'*Wait!*' Sheridan hissed suddenly. Ben stopped. 'Corbett De Sade? Whaddya think?'

'Very good,' Ben said, wrenching the chair legs up, the weight suddenly disappearing as gravity took hold and it tipped back, back, back.

Sheridan yelped a rollercoaster yelp in the darkness.

The chair smashed down on to its back and began to judder down the staircase, Sheridan wobbling and yelling. The drawers tumbled from his lap, tangling in the banisters, and the whole chair tipped over again on to its side, splintering the wooden rails and falling, falling, spinning fifteen feet on to the polished floor below. Sheridan screamed. It landed with an earthshaking crash, wood and metal spinning across the floor, the back of the chair wrenching away from the seat with a great crack and crunch and rip of fabric. Ben, hands over his mouth, held his breath.

After a horrific moment's pause, with a clank of metal and a thud of wood, Sheridan appeared from the tangle, bloodied, dizzy and smiling. Handcuffs swung from his wrists, the splintered remains of drawer handles dangling. He stepped out of the loops and twists, picking up the yellow book from the floor.

'Got it!' he yelled.

And then a gun went off.

Below Ben, the world erupted into chaos. Torchlight flashed about the cluttered room, Sheridan lurched from the tangle of rope and chair and began to slam dizzily across the floor towards the archway and the hall. Trolleys tipped, trays flipped and speakers crashed over as he flew. Jack let off round after round, bullets roaring in the room, flat bangs shaking the world.

'*STOP!*' Ben screamed.

Sadly, that was about as far as his plan went.

'Just . . .stop,' he added limply. The torchlight swung about the room.

'Who's there?!' Jack called, radio crackling, firing another deafening shot that tore past Ben's head.

Jumpy and sweating, he began to thud angrily down the

stairs. He took deep breaths, swallowed and prayed to God the guards had never actually met their employer before.

'Get some lights on in here,' Ben shouted, remembering to add a quick 'er, goddammit' to the end in a broad Californian accent. There was a scuffle and a clatter and a click and the room burst into blinding light.

'Who the fuck are you, pal?' Jack said, heavy handgun levelled at Ben's eyeline.

Ben could see him clearly now. He was in his late-forties. Stocky and squat, pudgy cheeks and hands. The blue polyester uniform was stretched across his wide stomach, a stomach that seemed to think there was something interesting going on in the shoe area, as it was leaning over his belt eagerly for a bit of a look. The torch looked heavy and standard. The gun was fat and black and gun-looking.

'Ahh might ask you thurr same question!' Ben said angrily, accent coming out a bit twangy. He knew from his experience with Zak at the gate of Mercury Pictures that this acting lark seemed to be entirely based on confidence and brusqueness. The louder and ruder you seemed to be, the more likely people were to believe you. 'You Pendleford guys! Ahh mean, Jesus.' Ben shook his head in a *sheesh-am-I-sick-of-this-shit* sort of way.

'Pendel*ton*,' Jack said. The gun was lowered slightly. Not much, but slightly.

'Yeah, like ah give a fuck,' Ben said. 'Christ, you gonna pay for the holes in mah wawl?'

Jack looked over at the chipped plaster. Then back at Ben.

'Mr *Silver?*' he said.

'Elementary my dear Livingstone, I presume,' he said. 'You mind telling me why I bother paying for twenty-four-hour armed security when firstly, the slightest breeze sets those lasers . . . uhh, those cock-damned lasers . . . off in the garden? Uhh . . . yard. In the yard?'

Oops.

'An' . . . uhm . . . secondly, why it takes you ten goddamn' minutes to drive all the way to your asses over here? I-I mean, haul over here? Your asses? Ten minutes to haul your asses over here?'

Jack blinked back at him. The gun twitched. Up a little? Down a little? Ben couldn't tell.

'And thirdly, when you do finally arrive, you start shootin' the place up before even finding out if I'm home. Here. On the . . . uhmm. . . range.'

'Mr Silver, jeez, I apologise. I'm sorry, sir.' Gun and torch were slipped quickly back on to Jack's fat belt. 'I knocked on the door, I guess you didn't hear me or—'

'I was rehearsing!' Ben shouted. 'Er, goddammit,' he added. 'I don't know if you read the papers, but I got a brand new show going in front of the cameras on Saturday. I got my lead guy here, er, Sheridan McDonald . . . sberg . . . stein. Sheridan McDonaldsbergstein. We're doing the torture scene, a very intense scene. And you come in blowing holes in the wall? This guy's an actor! He's sensitive! Eight months he's been preparing! Physically, mentally. Now I gotta go right back to the beginning. Jesus . . .'

'Mr Silver, like I say, I'm sorry,' Jack said over and over, shrugging away, standing the trolleys back up, picking flaky pastry canapés off the floor.

'Just go. Get outta here,' Ben said.

'Sure. Sure thing, Mr Silver,' Jack nodded. 'Mickey? Hey Mickey? Let's go.'

'Mr Busbyworth?' a voice said.

Ben felt a little sick all of a sudden.

'Hey, it's, uh, Benjaford Busbyworth, right?' Mickey said excitedly. He waddled through the kitchen archway. 'It's me, Mickey Thomopolous, from Mercury Pictures?' He held out a fat hand to shake.

'Uhm . . .'

'You remember? *Main Gate*? My show? Jack,' Mickey said, waddling forward, 'this is one of the guys I was tellin' you

324

about? From the BBC. Him an' this other fellah, your pal, what was it?'

'Uhhm, gawsh, gee old uhh fruit . . .' Ben said, trying to drift his American accent a few thousand miles east surreptitiously. He sounded like a character from Get Yur Ass The Hell Outta Here, Jeeves.

'You ain't Silver?' Jack said slowly.

Ben smiled limply.

The three men stood awhile in the lounge. Looking at each other. Blinking. Eventually Ben said, 'Fuck it,' and made a dash for the hallway.

'Mr Busbyworth!' Mickey hollered after him. 'Wait! Wait, did you like the script!'

Ben slammed down the dark hall and whooshed out into the chill night air, leaping the stone steps and stumbling on to the cool wide street. The Pendleton van was still slung across the road. He passed it breathlessly, voices yelling behind him. A hundred yards away in the blue darkness, on the brow of the hill, Ben could make out Sheridan. Bouncing and beckoning frantically. His friend. Waiting for him, calling, urging him on.

Ben ran, chest screaming, trainers slapping an echo on the cool tarmac.

'Go, Sheridan! Go! Run! I'll catch you up! Move!'

But Sheridan stood his ground, waving him forward. 'Come on, mate!' he screamed. 'Come on, move it!' like he was on the terraces at Anfield.

Far behind him, Ben could hear Jack and Mickey arguing. A gun fired loudly, shaking the sky. And again. Doors slamming. The sounds of an engine.

'That's it, come on!' Sheridan said, grinning and jogging backwards like a coach, willing his friend to run, run. He disappeared slowly over the hill until Ben could just see his head and his hands waving. Then he disappeared.

Seconds later, Ben himself breathlessly reached the brow of the hill and began to pound down the other side. Sheridan was near the bottom where it levelled out at a junction. They were getting away. They were doing it, they were getting away!

Then suddenly Ben was dazzled, throwing his hands over his face. Sheridan was thrown into silhouette as a car appeared at the bottom of the hill, headlights screaming.

'Sheridan!' Ben yelled.

'I got it I got it!' he hollered, spinning around and hurling himself towards the approaching car holding his hands aloft, pleading for the driver to stop, to help.

The car lurched to a sqealing halt, Sheridan yelling *thankyou*s and *please-help-use*s in a desperate, exhausted voice.

'Tell him to call the police!' Ben yelled. Sheridan waved and Ben saw him lean into the window of the BMW.

A silver BMW.

A flash. Then a bang. Loud, echoing endlessly into the sky, bouncing off houses and asphalt, floating away forever. Sheridan stepped away from the car suddenly, holding the yellow book against his chest. Waiting. Waiting.

Ben screamed his name.

Sheridan looked down at the book and dropped to his knees. Just like that, as if the puppeteer had cut the strings. He toppled forward but Ben didn't hear him fall. His ears were suddenly full of engine sounds. A roaring in front as the BMW let out a shriek of tyres and tore up the hill. And a roaring behind.

He spun around in terror, light pouring over the hill as the Pendleton van hurtled towards him.

Frozen to the floor, his feet solid and heavy, Ben held his breath. Then jumped left. Sharply. Off the street. He could hear dogs barking somewhere. Face down on the wet grass, he heard a huge revving scream behind him. A sharp stab of car-horn. The screech of tyres. And a horrific smash of steel and glass exploding all over the street.

Ben stumbled to his feet. The car had skidded, spinning its back end round, causing the van to pile into the rear door and trunk. Which meant the driver's side door was bent, but still useable.

Melvin was quickly out, blank face illuminated by the van's single remaining headlight. With a bellow of anger he let off deafening round after deafening round at the lawn, the bushes, at the sky.

But Ben, drenched with panic and terror, scratched and scrambling through bushes and brambles, was gone.

STUDIO NEWS
ER ER UH-OH! AS CARPOOL
CASTING COMPACTS CAREERS

Photos and story by
PENNY LANG

In a week more full of gossip than the hotel breakfast table at a watercooler-salesmen convention, I can report this one from the horse's mouth.

E.R. E.R. . . . Oh! Star **Gill Kramer** walked *off* the set of rehearsals for his ninety-eighth show yesterday making it clear to ABN he would NOT be returning to complete his 100-show contract.

TOP OF THE POOL

Kramer, who with wife Elaine is tipped to be **Celebrity Couple Of The Year** winner *again* on Monday, insisted the show would disappear, and with it millions of syndication dollars, unless a role could be found for him in the latest Mercury laffer CARPOOL.

PERFECT PITCH

Sadly, however, ABN were in no position to help as **VP Don Silver** signed the gridlock gagfest to Nashville cable station **SEBN** in a shock move.

ABN VP **Al Rosen** was unavailable for comment, but a spokesperson announced Rosen will be moving on to "pursue other projects."

UNKNOWNS

In typical Silver style, the coveted CARPOOL roles were decided last night in a late-night gag-off at the Comedy Store on Sunset. Two unknowns will join scribe Medford in the three leads. Rehearsals begin today.

SILVER SICK

Finally, out thoughts and prayers are with Mercury CEO Howard Silver who suffered a mild heart attack on a flight to LA yesterday and is recovering in Beverly Hills.

Photos page 5

Variety
Friday 29 September

328

Diane rolled her rental car down the sunny street, eyes flicking between the numbers on the dusty office buildings. Her Nashville guide book was riding upfront with her on the passenger seat, while her sticky underwear was riding up places it shouldn't.

She was aching and tired.

After talking to Howard on the plane yesterday, the only flight south she'd been able to get had given her exactly not quite enough time to go home, shower, change and get back to the airport refreshed and ready to go. So she'd sat at JFK, squirming and fidgeting and decramping her numbing buttocks, attempting to force the shiny hard plastic seat into a shape even vaguely resembling a human ass, (vaguely resembling anything, in fact, that wasn't a medieval buttock-deadening device), and thought about what she knew.

Mercury Pictures was broke, thanks for the most part to Don Silver blowing million after million on bad pilots and all-over body waxing. His father Howard, however, was in some kind of denial, announcing bigger budgets and pay-rises while CFO Bernie Silver cut back half the staff in LA. Add to this the blurry photographs of Don in both London and remarkably compromising positions, secret meetings with cable stations and Bernie flying off to Nashville at the drop of a Stetson, and Diane was sure she was close to unearthing enough for this *Sexposé*, two follow-ups and a miniseries.

She slowed at a junction, squinting into the bright morning. She should be close by now.

'Excuse me,' she called to a man in a baseball cap. He was sipping a take-out coffee and leaning next to a panel van on the corner.

'Yes, love?' he said. British.

'Hi. I'm looking for the SEBN offices? You wouldn't know . . .'

The man gestured across the street to a squat yellow bungalow with a preposterous gold Cadillac gleaming in the driveway, a cactus painted on its door. Diane waved a thank you and pulled her car in next to it. Licking her teeth and wiping greasy hands on her jeans, she checked her makeup, grabbed her bag and tripod, and hauled herself out.

'Good morning. Penny Lang for Randy Garland, please,' Diane said to the bouffant at reception. Above her, from the ceiling speakers, Roger Miller was dolloping out a syrupy spoonful of 'King Of The Road'.

'Mr Garland is currently in a—'

There was a slamming sound and a yelling from behind a closed door. A door which was promptly hurled open, Randy Garland striding out, boiling behind his moustache. He moved quickly to the front door and peered out through the blinds.

'Aww, Jesus, no,' he said, lifting his Stetson and scratching back his hair. 'No, no, no, I can't have her here . . .'

'Mr Garland, with respect. That is not Probe-It's concern . . .' a clipped voice followed him from the office. A tall handsome Englishman stepped out, clutching a black leather file. 'Now I need to be back in London by midnight. If you had read the brochure you would have—'

'Jeez McCreeze, what am I s'posed to do with her?' Randy said. 'Huh?' He turned, spotting Diane a little too late. 'We can't . . . shit.'

'Uhmm, a Miss Lang for you, sir?' Mary-Jane said.

The reception area went very quiet. The water cooler gurgled its amusement.

'Miss Lang?' Randy said slowly, creeping back across the carpet. 'Wh-what are you doing here? This ain't rightly a plum time for—'

'I do apologise,' Diane said as sweetly as she knew how. 'I understood you were able to clear your diary for Bernie Silver yesterday? I just presumed . . .'

'*Bernie?*' Randy said.

Reception went quiet again. The water cooler held its breath.

'Mr Garland?' The Englishman coughed.

'Oh. Er Miss Lang, this is uhm, a *courier* o' mine, Mr Watts. Just droppin' off a van load of *film* to the studio here. Er, *yes*,' Randy said weakly, testing out each word one by one. 'Unfortunately ah have nowhere to ahem, *store* that much film as such. So, ha-haa, he's gonna have to take it away again. Now, er, Miss Lang. Come on through. Mary Jane, some coffee, I think . . .'

'Mr Garland,' Watts said brusquely, 'the *film* belongs to you now. I cannot return to my offices with it. You did ask specifically for it to be brought to you immediately, which was done at great inconvenience and expense—'

'*Yes*,' Randy snapped back through gritted teeth. 'But if you recall, Mr *Watts*, my original request was that everythin' pertainin' to this particular . . . uhm . . . *production*, be labelled up and stored safely *for when Ah needed it*. Which you, sir, agreed to do. Ah see no difference in lockin' up a few feet of film, *just for a few days!*'

Reception was saved from its third unsettling silence by Billy Ray Cyrus who'd begun to warble above them about his achy breaky heart.

'Miss Lang, join me in my office. Mr Watts? Go getchaself a cup o'coffee or sumthin'. I'll speak to you in a few moments.'

'Mr Garland, if I'm not back in London—'

'In a few goddamn' moments, goddammit!' Randy yelled, arms flying, his white hat tumbling to the carpet.

'Delivery problems?' Diane asked casually, clattering about with her tripod and setting the camera running as Randy settled himself behind the desk.

'Not at all, Miss Lang,' he twanged. 'Everythin's just dandy. Ah enjoyed yur profile by the way.' And he motioned to it, framed on the wall next to an embroidered quilt of Willie Nelson. 'Now to what do ah owe this pleasure?'

'Bernie Silver's visit yesterday,' Diane said, fixing him with a flat stare. Her fingers curled over her bag. She had Bernie's flight details, the videotape of Randy leaving the Mercury building, all ready to spring on him the moment he tried to deny—

'We were just ironin' out our deal,' Randy said with a smile Diane didn't return.

'Deal?' she said from behind freshly knotted eyebrows.

'Sure. Hammerin' out the details.'

'A . . . a *secret* deal?' Diane said, hopefully. She'd travelled eight hundred miles to hear this.

'Hardly,' Randy said, and slipped that morning's *Variety* from his in-tray, handing it to her.

She began to chew the inside of her cheek, eyes scanning the page. She hadn't had a chance to read the paper.

'Was there anything else, miss?' Randy smiled.

The camera recorded the long silence as Diane studied at the story.

'Miss Lang?'

'Why?' she said. Something didn't seem right. 'I mean, why you? It says here that Don pitched to eight networks yesterday. Eight networks much bigger than your little outfit down here. Why has he given it to you?'

Randy licked his lips and smoothed down his moustache

carefully, eyes twinkling. He got up and peered out of the window, across the rear parking lot and into the sunshine for a moment. He turned around.

'The deal between SEBN and Mercury is a meetin' of hearts an' minds, Miss Lang. Our number one concern is *great television*. Howard knows Ah am a man of mah word, he knows Ah am committed to quality broadcastin'. So he brung his little *Carpool* show to—'

And Randy stopped. He looked at her.

'You *fly* down here from New York this morning, Miss Lang?'

'Yes,' Diane said slowly. Where was this going?

'So you *weren't* in Los Angeles last night?' Randy pointed at the paper in Diane's hands.

'No,' she said, looking again at the paper. 'No, this is the first I've heard of . . .'

Photos and story by Penny Lang.

'Ah,' Diane said.

Two minutes later, Mary Jane was slamming the door and Diane was crunching back across the baking gravel to her car. All that way, she thought. Eight hundred miles chasing a hunch that everyone else in America had managed to get hold of by picking up a paper over breakfast.

She tossed her bag and tripod in to the back seat of her Ford and clambered in, cursing. *Studio sells sitcom to cable.* Not exactly the sexiest story in the world. Dammit, all she had now were the pictures of Don in London and the mystery share-holders. That was going to take a major celebrity voiceover if it was going to pull in the ratings.

She started her car.

It was time to pay a visit to J. T. Stanley on Wall Street. See if she couldn't uncover some dirt there.

The sun glinted on her cracked wing-mirror. She twisted it once, twice, until the road was visible behind her.

The man in the cap was still by his black van. He was talking to Watts, the handsome courier. Diane couldn't make out a word but they seemed pretty disproportionately pissed off with their load, consistently flapping their arms, pointing at the SEBN building and thumbing towards the rear of the van. Diane watched them for a moment.

The man in the cap was lighting a cigarette and yelling something. He snapped his Zippo shut and tucked it away in the pocket of his jeans.

Now why would a courier delivering film to a television studio, Diane thought, sliding a little lower in her seat, have a gun tucked in his belt?

'Beep beep! Comin' through!' a voice called. Two men pushed a large clothes rail, slithering with costumes in plastic bags, across the plastic cobbles. Don stepped back to let them pass, taking the opportunity to drown a handful of Thorazine with a mouthful of Pepto Bismol and to tread ankle deep in a large pile of replica horse crap.

'Oh, for fuck's sake,' he said, lifting out a sticky loafer.

'No can do,' Jerry said, pencil between his teeth and two behind each ear. 'I already told your Trixi, I'm stretched as it is.' He began to wander off, yelling at his crew.

Jerry, a burly bear of a man, was the construction coordinator on *Fyre*, and was having quite a morning. It was 9 a.m. and he had already been on the studio floor for five hours, supervising the building of the interior of St Paul's Cathedral, the setting for tomorrow night's recording. He was surrounded by the smell of glue and timber, the clank of scaffolding and the spray of sparks from saws and blowtorches.

'Outta the way!' another voice yelled, Don leaping to one side into some more replica turds as a forklift buzzed through, laden with fibreglass skeletons in scorched rags.

'Jerry! Shit, Jerry, listen to me,' he said anxiously, scuttling after him through the cool studio, under tarpaulin,

334

between lights and backdrops. 'Just give me *four* guys, then. Or *three*? It's a simple set. Half a dozen cars, a stretch of freeway . . .'

'Can't do it.'

'Jerry—'

'I *can't do it*. I got instructions from New York.' And he tugged a Mercury Pictures memo from his back pocket. 'Look at this. *In light of Mr Silver's announcement in Variety . . . an expanding studio . . . growing . . . bold, confident, healthy . . .* Everything's gotta be bigger. Budgets, blasts, bangs.' Jerry shook his head and motioned to the huge dome above them. 'Come nine o'clock tomorrow night, this whole baby don't blow and blow big, I'm out on my *ass*.'

Don squirmed anxiously.

'Sir? Sir?' Trixi's voice hollered over the din as she came ducking and dodging through the debris clutching a fat package. 'Sir, just got these back.' And she peeled out a yellow flyer, still warm from the printer. Don took it.

'*Admit One*. CARPOOL. *Starring Melvin Medford, Zak Black, yadda, yadda* . . . Looks good, Trix'. Get a couple of blondes on Sunset handing 'em out.'

'Holy shit,' Jerry said with a laugh, reading over Don's shoulder. '*Tomorrow night?*'

'That's what I'm saying, Jerry,' Don said, and slugged another mouthful of Pepto. 'This is serious. I can't tell you how serious, but it's serious. I'm in deep shit here.'

'Hey, Jerry?'

A tanned construction worker in scratched goggles appeared between them, wiping sweat from his face, clutching a buckled blueprint.

'Jerry, these plans you got us followin'? I showed 'em to my kid over dinner last night. He done some project in school. Er, apparently, dey got this Chris Wren guy to rebuild the cathedral *after* the fire.'

'*What?*' Jerry said slowly.

335

'The one you got us doin' didn't get built till 1710. We . . . er . . . we built the wrong cathedral, Jerry.'

He gazed about the cavernous studio, at the scaffolding, the pillars, the huge dome, and began to breathe deeply.

'I'll . . . I'll get out of your way,' Don said, chivvying Trixi out of the studio quickly.

'So what do we do, sir?' she said, scuttling behind Don as he charged across the warm tarmac.

'I don't know, I don't know,' he said, panicky. He drained the last of his Pepto and thrust the empty bottle at his assistant, wiping his mouth. 'First, get me a crate more of this shit. Plus plus plus,' and he began to empty his pockets, handing Trixi empty foil wrappers, 'more of these, extra-strength if you can get 'em. More of these and a shed load of these, maximum strength.' He popped the last of the pills out and threw them down his neck. '*Calm, calm, calm, stay out of jail, stay out of jail,*' he muttered, breathing deeply. 'Okay, okay, update. Where is everybody? Everybody here?'

They climbed into a little white golf cart parked in the shade of studio 6. Don turned the key, wrenched it into reverse and slid it out, spinning the wheel and buzzing through the lanes. Trixi was flipping through her clip-board.

'Cast and crew are waiting for you in studio five.'

'Okay. You . . . uh . . . seen Melvin yet?'

'Not this morning,' Trixi said. 'Oh, and Bernie's still with your father at the hospital.'

'Dad? How's he holdin' up?'

'Bernie said he's still sedated. They're doing tests. But Bernie wants you to call him. Something about an idea to *save our asses.*'

'An idea? What idea?' Don said. He swept the cart wide around a corner towards studio 5.

'That was all he . . . *MR SILVER!*' Trixi screamed, and there was the scuffing thud of arms meeting plastic. Don slammed the cart to a halt, Vinnie wide eyed and flustered sprawling

336

across the little white hood.

'Mr Silver! Jeez, I'm sorry, sir, I didn't see you there,' he said, brushing his clothes down. Don hardly recognised him out of his Italian suit. He was in a peach polo shirt, khakis and gleaming loafers, a sweater over his shoulders and sunglasses on his head. 'I got lost. These stoodios, dey don't make no sense. Stoodio eight, stoodio two . . .'

'That's fine, Vincent, that's fine. Jump on, we're heading that way.'

So Vinnie clambered on to the back of the cart and they buzzed off across the lot.

Don dropped his voice a little.

'Trix, get a call through to Uncle Bernie. Find out what this plan of his is.' Don chewed his lip for a moment. 'He really said it would save our asses?'

She nodded.

'Okay, okay, patch him through to me as soon as you can. And let's hope he's right. 'Cause without a set we got no show and we're all in serious shit.'

Vinnie piped up behind them.

'Uh, Mr Silver? You sayin' dat you needed a set built? Construction guys? Dat right? 'Cos my dad knows hundreds 'a guys in the trade. Builders, carpenters, whaddever y'need. You want maybe I give him a call?'

'Shit, *seriously?*' Don said. 'You *know* people?'

'Sure,' Vinnie said with a helpful shrug. 'Whatever. The least I can do, Mr Silver. After you gave me this shot. Leave it with me. I'll give him a call.'

Don pulled the cart into the shade and they piled out.

'That'd save my life, good man.' And he slapped Vinnie's sweaty back as they all clanged up the little flight of stairs and ducked into the coolness of the studio. A long trestle table was surrounded by three dozen people, milling about and shaking their heads and checking their watches. Nervous chatter floated about among the gantries and rigs.

'Okay, people!' Don called with a clap, his voice echoing. 'Good to see you all!'

'We got a script yet?' a costume assistant asked.

'Melvin ain't showed,' another sighed.

'Heyyy, don't worry,' Don blustered, moving quickly about the table, grabbing a pastry, slapping shoulders, winking, good-to-see-ya-ing. 'It's all under control, relax.'

'We've only got six pages,' the floor-manager whined.

'It's okay. We had a little trouble up at the house last night. There was a break-in.' Don took a seat. All eyes were on him. 'Melvin's a little . . . shook-up this morning. 'Snuthin'. Let's get started, he'll be here. C'mon, top of p-page one.'

Chairs scraped, crew groaned and everyone settled in.

Don shot a look at Trixi.

Get me Uncle Bernie. he mouthed silently. *Now.*

In Nashville, Watts was crossing the street, jogging through the traffic towards the SEBN building. Diane, hunkered down in her seat, peeping over her door at the rear-view, watched him scurry past and throw himself irritably back into the office.

She watched Baseball Cap in her mirror for a few more moments. He finished his cigarette and flicked it into the traffic, taking an amble around to the rear of the van again.

Diane reached into her bag and tugged out her video recorder, checking the tape and switching on, focusing tight on the rear view mirror. She began to whisper a commentary.

'*Two men. British,*' she said, eyes never leaving the van. '*One tall, Watts. The other in baseball cap. Armed. Watts is in with Garland. Some disagreement. Baseball Cap is opening van doors . . . Only a little . . . Seems to be talking to the film in the van . . . flashing the butt of his gun about . . . pointing . . . talking some more . . . closing the doors . . .*'

Diane watched Baseball Cap lock the van and wander back to the cab, swinging the keys on his finger casually in the sunshine. She felt the familiar tingle of intrigue and excitement, her journalistic instincts prickling like hair near a television set. After nearly twenty-four hours of wild goose chasing, it looked like something was definitely rotten in the state of Nashville.

Diane thumbed the camera off and sat up. She started her car and reversed out on to the street slowly, crossing the lanes to the other side of the road. She clunked her car into gear and began the slow crawl past the van, eyes scanning the shiny black surface. It looked pretty ordinary at first glance.

Apart from the paper taped over the rear windows.

She took the first right at the corner and bowled the creaking Ford around the block, mind racing. What was it Watts had said? Something about it belonging to Randy now? He couldn't return to his offices with it, and Randy had said he wanted it stored safely for a few days?

Diane pulled the car back on to the busy street. She would take a look at this troublesome 'film' for herself.

She pulled back on to the sunny street. The black van was a hundred yards away, parked at the kerb. Diane slowed her car gradually. Of course, she could be wrong, she thought for a moment, a large stretch of road opening up ahead. The van might be completely innocent.

Ah, well, she thought, slamming her foot down. The Ford hurled itself forward with a screech, Diane bouncing in her seat as she powered towards the van. There was a very simple, if rather noisy, way of finding out.

She braced herself, closed her eyes and lurched her wheel to the right.

The crash was loud. Much louder than she'd expected.

A smash of glass from the lights, a wrench of metal from the van doors.

A muffled female scream from inside.

Eyes blurred, head buzzing, Diane clambered out, apologising over and over. Baseball Cap was climbing out quickly.

'Oy, love, what the fack you fink you're doin'? Get away from there, hoy! Get away!' he said, flapping his arms.

339

'Gee, I'm sorry,' Diane simpered, moving to inspect the damage. The fender was hanging loose, there was coloured glass at her feet. One rear door of the van was buckled inwards, hanging open a couple of inches. There was the thud and shuffle of movement within. 'I had a wasp, I swerved, I'm so sorry...'

'Back off, back off!' he said, hands out. 'Shit, just forget it, awlright? Forget it, it daan't matter. Fack,' he said nervously. He was sweating and cursing, running his hands over the warm metal, glancing over at the SEBN building. 'Just be on your way, darlin'. We'll forget awll abaat it.'

'But really, my insurance—'

'*Just fack off!*' he yelled, spinning around. He had a furious look in his eyes, like a trapped animal. He yanked back his jacket to reveal the gun. 'Y' hear me, luv? Get back in ya motor and naff off aat of it.'

Diane backed away, hands aloft, apologising over and over. She climbed back into her car quickly, turned the key and began to reverse away with a screech of metal. Baseball Cap leaned against the buckled rear doors, muttering out of the side of his mouth.

Diane crunched her gears and pulled away. Faster this time. Much much faster.

She bowled around the block, heart thundering, palms wet against the wheel. Skipping the lights at the last junction she pulled the car around, back on to the street. Less than thirty seconds had passed.

Baseball Cap was stepping out from behind the van and walking along its side towards the cab door, reaching for a radio.

Nearer, faster, nearer, faster.

He was halfway to the door.

Diane gritted her teeth, punched her hand down on the horn and slammed on the brakes.

The car skidded forward with a squeal. Baseball Cap turned, mouth gaping and pale hands flying out. They thumped on to the Ford's crumpled hood. The wing clipped his shin and with a yell he tumbled backwards, the car bumping over his leg.

There were shouts. A groan. People were wandering out of shops on to the street, traffic slowing. But Diane was out, scurrying around to the van.

She flung the buckled rear door open.

Inside thirty or forty document boxes were stacked, each one taped up and labelled. A couple had fallen over, the cardboard lids ripped and bent. A manilla file and some floppy disks were scattered on a faded mattress. And upon this mattress, pale and petrified, a young woman lay trussed. Her clothes and hair said early-thirties, but her face was that of a child. A snotty, scared child, lost and alone and wanting her mummy. She had a handbag at her feet, a rag stuffed in her mouth and plastic fasteners tight about her ankles and wrists. Diane clambered into the van, tugging out the gag.

'Oh, Jesus, what's happening?' the woman said woozily. British.

'You're coming with me,' Diane said quickly, grabbing her bag and helping her slide, still bound, along the greasy mattress and awkwardly out into the sunlight.

The street was now alive with onlookers. Pointing, calling, saying *Hey!* a lot. Some had gathered about the man on the road who lay puffing and groaning and shouting about his leg.

Diane bundled the woman into her car, slammed the passenger door and bustled round to the driver's side. She climbed in, reversed fifty yards in a plume of rubber, yanked the wheel and U-turned into the traffic. Horns blared and screamed.

As did Watts and Garland, appearing outside the SEBN building suddenly, pointing and yelling.

But Diane was away.

They put a good mile on the clock before Diane's heartbeat slowed down enough for her to speak.

'Questions,' she said, glancing over at her passenger, wrists bound in her lap on top of her dusty bag, head lolling. 'Who are you and who were they?'

'I have . . . I have no idea who they were,' the woman croaked. 'They told me they were policemen.'

'Wait, wait,' Diane interrupted, fishing for her camera. She jabbed it on and placed it on the woman's lap. 'Talk into that.'

'My name's Jackie,' the woman said, peering out of the window. They passed under a sign. Nashville Airport two miles. 'Shit! Is this . . . we're in *America*? Ohmigod, Ben . . . Don Silver, he's . . .'

'*Silver?*' Diane repeated excitedly. Hoo-boy.

'You . . . know him?' Jackie said.

Diane smiled a broad investigative journalist's smile and double-checked the red light on the side of the camera. It was recording.

'Now then. Why don't you tell me *aaaaaall* about it?'

'Because it's yur darn' fault, that's why! Now *git!*'

'My colleague has just had his bloody leg broken by that woman, I'm not dropping everything to go chasing some journalist halfway across—'

'You'll drop whaddever the damned hell Ah tell yew t'drop, boy!'

Back in the SEBN office, negotiations were more crunchy than smooth. On the street, an ambulance was busily loading the Probe-It employee on to a stretcher, causing him to wail a frankly unnecessary amount of 'blimeys', 'Jezus Chroists' and 'fack, that 'urts'es. Watts was at Randy's desk, having a thin finger pointed at him.

'Ah wuz given to believe you Probe-It boys were professionals. Ah mean, that's what the name means, right?' Randy opened up the black leather folder on the desk in which Watts had presented his account. '*Professional* Broadcast Entertainment Intelligence Targeting? Professional? Not *Pathetically undertrained* Broadcast Entertainment Intelligence Targeting? Maybe you should change your name.'

'We're not changing anything, Mr Garland. For one thing, that would spell Pube-it, which is hardly the—'

'Look, boy, fact is you wuz hired to do a jawb.'

'Yes, and we took this investigation as far as it—'

'But the only thing you bring me is this Melvin Medford story. Some fruitcake goin' round the place butcherin' stand-up comics. Like that has anything to do with the price o' chickens. So, we get together and cook up this blackmail, pin the murders on young Dawnald, sure. See if we can't get our hands on their show. But may I remind you, Mr Watts,' Randy's voice had gone all teachery now, 'for blackmail to work successfully, the party doin' the blackmailin' must have all the evidence *in their possession.*'

'Mr Garland—'

'Dammit, if this damned Paretsky woman and this British girl go squealin' to the cops the whole story'll be out. Melvin'll be arrested, the show'll be cancelled an' I'll be left sittin' here holdin' mah pecker.'

Watts stood quietly fuming.

His boss had been right. They should never have taken this job.

From the first moment they'd greeted Randy Garland, sitting in the dark reception area of Probe-It's discreet offices, wearing a bootlace tie and rotating a huge white Stetson in his fingertips, his boss had wanted to refuse his business. With all his irritating Southern homespun wisdom about *seeing a job through* and *doing a job properly* and *how running a TV station is like leading a mule to drink* or whatever the hell it was. Investigation wasn't an exact science. It was full of dead-ends and missed chances and bad breaks. Randy didn't understand that. He wanted all the information harvested and tied up and trimmed down and stored away for the winter like Probe-It were just out plucking ears of corn.

But Watts had pushed. He hadn't worked for the company very long and saw this as an opportunity to prove himself. Difficult work, high-level surveillance. New York, Los Angeles, Nashville, London. It would get him off the probation list and into his own office. Head of department even.

Well, it's your job on the line, his boss had said.

'Mr Garland,' Watts hissed. 'The deal *was* I should neutralise the situation in London, which I have done. I bring you anyone who knows too much about *Carpool*, which I have done. Your end of the deal is settling your account so I can get back on the plane. I have to be in London by midnight for another job and I have no intention of blowing that because of you. Your account with us so far currently stands at seven hundred and fifty thousand dollars—'

'An' you won't see a red cent—'

'*Mr Garland*—'

'Not a *red cent* till those dames are silenced and silenced good. Ah don't give a damn about yur other jawb. Yur a professional. Start actin' like it and finish the goddamn jawb you started. Now get the pig-fuck outta my office and get on with it, you limey sonofabitch!'

Watts chewed some silent curses into his lip for a moment, closed his file and marched out of the office.

An hour later the *Carpool* rehearsal disbanded, ostensibly because there was only a finite number of times everyone could listen to the same six minutes' worth of jokes without running a serious risk of their fixed grin finally locking and paralysing the lower half of their face.

But in reality because no one could possibly concentrate with Don pacing, glugging, twitching, muttering about jail and leaping a foot in the air with a petrified yelp every time there was the slightest noise.

Everybody took five and stretched their legs. Don took tranquillisers and went to his office.

344

*

'*Uncle Bernie?* Where is he? Anyone seen Uncle Bernie?'

Don and Trixi bustled into the crowded reception area, crowded due to the three peculiar men standing about the pot plants.

'Mr Silver?' one of them said gingerly. He was dressed in a peach leotard over a grey sweatsuit, a peach fleecy headband matching his legwarmers. His two companions were dressed in different yet equally laughable garb. 'Mr Silver? Matthew De Paul. I'd just like to thank you for this second chance, really,' he gushed, hand on his heart. 'It means a lot.'

'Yes, yes, absolutely,' his companions said, bustling forward, tripping over each other.

'My pleasure, fellas, my pleasure,' Don said, pushing past them. 'Who the fuck are you? Trixi? You said Uncle Bernie was here? Who are these guys?'

'*Us?*' Matthew De Paul said, hand flying to his chest. 'Well, we're . . .'

'*Donald!*' a voice burst from behind Don's office door. '*Get in here!*'

'So for now we've only got six pages,' Don explained.

They sat in the quiet of his office, among the leather furniture and modern art, Bernie smoking furiously and clacking poker chips with one hand, the other throbbing uselessly in its sling.

'Melvin was meant to deliver the rest this morning but after last night . . . Uncle Bernie?'

'Huh?' he asked, distracted by the sports pages on his lap. The New Jersey Devils were making changes to their forward play. 'What happened last night? You okay?'

Don brought his uncle up to speed.

He had returned from the Comedy Store at 3 a.m. after the auditions, ready to collapse into bed, only to find a street full of broken glass, a house full of policemen, a sofa full of security

345

guards and Melvin full of tears. The security team's story was that Don's alarm had been tripped sometime around 9 p.m. by two intruders. The Pendleton team had attempted to apprehend these young men but they had escaped, getting halfway down Palmwood on foot before being intercepted by Melvin, returning home from the club. According to Melvin, the first intruder had pulled a gun and attempted to hijack the car, leaving him no choice but to shoot in self-defence.

'They reckon the second guy grabbed the dropped gun and escaped with it into the bushes,' Don said with a shake of his head.

'You buy that?'

'Who the fuck knows, Uncle Bernie!' he yelled.

'Look, relax, relax,' Bernie said, folding his paper. 'I'm fixin'—'

'*Relax!* You got me sleepin' under the same roof as a bat-wielding homicidal maniac. We can't call the cops 'coz some cowboy's got a bag of evidence that says *I'm* a killer. Plus *you've* gotten us all tied up with some mystery shareholders who don't want the Feds snoopin' through our accounts. Dad's in hospital. I got no set, I got no script, but I gotta have a show in the can in three days—'

'Jesus, kid, keep your voice down,' Bernie shushed. Don sat shaking in his chair, blinking wide-eyed panicky blinks.

Bernie lit a cigarette.

'Look, I think I mighta cracked it, kid.'

Don looked up at his uncle, hope splashed across his face.

'I had a visit from some associates last night at the hospital after you left.'

'You been there all night?'

'Yeah. Some of the orderlies like to play dice. I lost a bundle on—'

'Uncle Bernie . . .

'Right, right. Anyway. Some shareholders paid me a visit.'

'*Who*, Uncle Bernie? Who have you—'

'Shut up kid, just listen to me. They want this SEBN business over, like we all do. They want *Carpool* sold to ABN, like we all do. Gave me until Monday. They were very . . . persuasive.' And an itch passed Bernie's throat. 'They gave me an idea.'

'To save our asses?' Don said.

His uncle hauled himself off the edge of the desk and staggered over to the door. His arm throbbed in its sling.

'Guys?' he said, peering about the door. The three men in reception sprang lightly to their feet and pranced perkily past him into Don's office. 'Oh, Trixi?' Bernie said. 'Have you called costume? Got them to—'

'On their way, Mr Silver.'

TWENTY-SIX

'An on our leff' here, you know da feeelm *Titaaanic*? You know dat feeelm? Well, da house here on da left belong to da star o' dat feeelm, Lenny Di Caprio. His fren' call him Lenny.'

The bus load of tourists all went '*Ooooh!*' obediently and threw themselves against the glass, leaving greasy nose spots and finger marks as they peered out at the sixteenth identical twelve-foot wall and the sixteenth identical twelve-foot gate, complete with obligatory barbed wire, cameras and warning signs. The Mexican's little speaker gave a crackle.

'Next stop on da right, you know da feeelm *Dunston Checks Eeen*? You know that feeelm?'

The bus began to chug up the narrow winding lane, high hedges on either side, the chattering group of tourists exchanging golly-gees and mercy-mes and well-I-never-dids. Everyone was enjoying the morning tour, which was in truth little more than 'security systems of the rich and famous'.

And then, without warning, the Mexican suddenly yelled out and the bus braked, hard.

Ben waved his aching arms above his head, tripping across the dry road, hair full of hedge and heart full of terror. He scuffed across the warm tarmac and rapped, panting, on the side door of the bus.

A hiss and it folded open. He hauled himself aboard, sweating and gasping.

'Thank . . . thank you,' he wheezed. 'I need . . . I need to get to the police,' he said. The man behind the wheel just peered at him. Ben heard a faint whisper and turned.

Fifteen black shiny lenses stared back at him along the length of the bus, each topped with either a baseball cap or a headscarf. Lenses winked, lenses whirred. They all watched.

'You seeet at da back? We drop you near when we go circle?'

Ben nodded and the doors hissed behind him as he swung, gripping the cold steel poles, towards the back of the dusty bus. The whirring lenses panned across, following his movements as he dropped exhausted on to a torn vinyl seat at the rear, head lolling backwards.

The bus coughed into life and began to climb the hill.

'You awlright there, fellah?' a man said, leaning over the back of his seat. Ben looked up at him wearily.

All right? Jesus, where was he meant to begin?

Ben knew that only a handful of the richest, most powerful people got to spend their nights up in the Hollywood Hills. It was a sign one had arrived. Made it. Hit the big time.

But then Ben was also aware that part of that successful feeling meant having perhaps a house up there with you.

He had no idea how far he had run, branches and thorns scratching at his hands and face. Dogs barking, sirens wailing, he had slapped across dozens of wide, quiet streets, sprinted around the edges of at least five swimming pools, climbed nine chain-link fences and pounded uphill for a good two hours until Melvin was miles behind him. He had eventually collapsed, dropping to his knees among prickly desert shrubs and dust.

Los Angeles, shimmering and purple spread out below him, a hundred miles in every direction, lights winking and glowing. A cool night wind whipped through the dust, drying the sweat upon his face.

He was six thousand miles from home. Lost, trapped and alone.

And Sheridan was dead.

The tears didn't come for a good while. A cueball seemed to be lodged in his throat, his eyes were stinging. He was snotty and trembling. But eventually they did come.

He wanted Sheridan back. He wanted Jackie back. He wanted to be home. He wanted everything but to be here, on this scrappy, crappy hill in this scrappy, crappy city. He listened to sirens and dogs, the distant sigh of traffic.

He'd slept, waking hours later to a burning sun, eyelids orange and fuzzing.

Ben blinked away the memory and peered out of the bus window as it crawled up the snaking lanes. The palm trees, the dark shadows, the streets, hedges and gates. How different it all looked now. The busload of tourists pointed and oooh-looked and smiled at the bizarre novelty of it all, just as Ben had just three days ago when this had been a much kinder world.

'I mean, up until that point, I was convinced he was a regular policeman,' Jackie said, hurrying along after Diane.

'Until the TV told you the real police hadn't a clue who the bodies were . . .'

'. . . and he almost broke my neck, yes.'

'Jesus Christ, have we stumbled over something . . . *there!* Quick!' Diane said, and began to bustle off with inappropriate excitement. Bleary-eyed, Jackie had little choice but to follow her, aching and complaining across the stark flat echo of Nashville airport's check-in lounge.

She caught up with Diane in one of the many internet cafés that are sprinkled about international airports by people who believe jet-lag, hot water and electrical equipment are chummy bedfellows. Diane was already at a terminal, flicking and clicking with a mouse eagerly.

'What are we . . . ?'

'Gimme those discs,' Diane said, not taking her eyes from the monitor.

'*What?* No! What are you *talking* about? We need to find the *police*,' Jackie said. This was all too much. Her eyes flicked and darted over every face, jumping at every thump and hiss of the automatic doors. There was a pale, sickliness to her skin that for once wasn't the fault of the terminal strip-lighting.

'C'mon!' Diane said, clicking her fingers.

With an exhausted sigh, Jackie reached into her bag and pulled them out.

'This all you got?' Diane said, popping open a case and pinging out the shiny disc, sliding it into the tray. 'You couldn't get a ring-binder up your blouse or a box of slides in your panties?'

Jackie shook her head. God, she needed a cigarette.

'I was lucky to grab those. When we took a corner the boxes collapsed on top of me. I slid these through a gap in the bottom of one. But there must have been hundreds of files and photos, all sorts.'

Diane was pulling down boxes and clicking on icons and opening files, eyes wide, breath fast, muttering.

'What are you *looking* for?' Jackie said, chewing her lip. She didn't want to be here. This wasn't safe.

'I . . . have . . . no . . . idea,' Diane said, clicking and dragging. 'Maybe something that'll tell us who the guys in the van . . . *wait!*' She stopped. A window was open on screen listing dozens of files.

:[8]_p02.6	hOWoffi_25.09	16KB GIF image
:[1]_p01	mELbirt_06.75	19KB GIF image
:[8]_p02.1	mELpsyc_10.81	12KB JPEG image

On and on it went.

'What are they?' Jackie said, peering over her shoulder.

Diane double clicked on the first file: hOWoffi_25.09. After a pause and a whirr, the screen went blank and then slowly, feeding down from the top, a photograph juddered open.

An elderly man on a treadmill in an office. Shot through a long lens from a building opposite it looked like . . .

'Howard Silver,' Diane said. 'CEO of Mercury Pictures. Don's father.'

She closed it and clicked open another. Again, a picture juddered down the screen.

'A birth certificate?' Jackie said, and Diane nodded. It had been scanned in, fairly low-res, but the details were clear.

'*Melvin Edelman. Willingboro, New Jersey, June first, nineteen seventy-five,*' Diane read aloud, whipping her mouse across the mat.

'We should go,' Jackie said anxiously. 'We need to go. Find a policeman. A cigarette machine. Diane?'

'Hold on,' she said, tongue poking from her mouth, clicking away furiously. '*Mel psyc eighty-one* . . . Holy shit! Look at this.' And her eyes scanned greedily over the screen. '*Department of Psychology, intermediate evaluation. Edelman, Melvin. October eighty-one* . . .'

'Diane!' Jackie pleaded, tugging at her sleeve. 'Please! Ben could be in terrible danger.'

Diane quickly flipped her mouse over the list of files, sending them all to print. The machine next to them began to hum and clatter, sucking in sheets of paper one by one.

'You got any money?' she said briskly. 'A credit card?'

'What? Er y-yes, probably . . .'

'Pay for this lot,' she said, motioning at the printer stuttering out the images, 'and meet me by the American Airlines desk. I'm gonna check what time the next flight to LA is.'

'What? Wait! We can't just . . .'

But Diane was gone.

On the Mercury lot, three men were shaking Don's hand and gushing modestly.

'Mr Silver, an honour, really,' Matthew said. 'Good to see you again.'

352

'Absolutely, dear sir,' the fatter man added, removing a crimson fedora. 'Alistair Grant. It's been too long, really.'

'Ed Clift,' said the last, scooping a dark lock of lank hair out of his eyes broodily. 'And I mean that, man.'

They sat. Bernie shut the door. Don threw back a palmful of Lorazepam and stared at these three rather intense men.

This was never going to work.

'Has another network picked it up?' Matthew said excitedly, hands to his face. 'Is that what this is about? Is it?'

'Matthew,' Bernie said. 'Guys—'

'Ohmigod! I knew it! I knew it!' Matthew shrieked.

'Cool,' Ed nodded, failing to hide his glee behind a Brando-esque scowl.

There was a brisk knock and the door was pushed open, two kids in T-shirts wheeling in a clothes rail draped with suits in slithery bags.

'I gotta call my mother, I gotta call my mother!' Matthew flustered reaching for a cellphone in his satin bum-bag. 'She said I should quit. Come back to Kansas. I said, Mom, I said—'

'Guys,' Bernie said, raising his palms. 'Matthew, relax a moment. That's . . . that's not it. Nobody's picked it up.'

The three actors stopped their fidgeting, mouths opening a little.

'We're not bringing *Woodfellas* back. I'm sorry.'

They held the dejected tableau for a moment.

Bernie slid himself from the edge of the desk and took a walk around to the clothes rail. He tugged the hangers apart and looked over one of the suits. The boxy shoulders, the broad stripes, the white handkerchiefs.

'Guys,' he said, turning around, 'how are you all fixed for a show tonight? Cash in hand, a few hours' work?'

They all exchanged glances.

'I . . . er . . . got a couple of call-backs,' Ed lied. 'KBL wanna talk to me about a movie.'

'Err, yeeessss, it's a little short notice,' Alistair coughed, reaching for his battered satchel. 'My agent has set up a . . . a thing. But, you know,' and he began to flick noisily through an empty diary, 'I could move things around . . . Tomorrow?'

'Tomorrow's cool,' Ed nodded, he too not wanting to appear in any sense *too* available.

'What are we talking about?' Matthew asked.

Bernie chewed his lip, flicking a look at Don. He raised a pair of doubtful eyebrows and unscrewed his Pepto Bismol. This was never going to work.

'It's . . . it's a spin-off,' Bernie said. 'A little improvisation. Like a role-play kinda thing.'

'Uncle Bernie,' Don interrupted, 'there has to be another way.'

'A *Woodfellas* spin-off?' Matthew said, thumbing through the clothes rail. 'So we're still gangsters?'

'Right,' Bernie nodded, looking over the three flouncing actors.

This was never going to work.

'I still don't get it. Why don't Mercury, this guy, this—'

'Listen, Jackie, listen to me,' Diane said, fizzing tonic water into her plastic cup. 'Let's think about what we know here, right? Howard Silver tells his son to find a big new hit show right? Then Don arrives in London with this Melvin guy. It's all over the trades, Don's found a hit writer, etc, etc, they're gonna bring back some big new show.'

'But according to that lot,' Jackie said, motioning to the stack of print outs on Diane's tray, 'Melvin isn't a writer. He's just some kind of—'

'Precisely.'

They had been in the air for almost an hour, due to touch down at around 1 p.m., Los Angeles time. Jackie had a freshly purchased Los Angeles travel guide open on her flip-down tray and the thinnest finger of warm, winky white wine in a plastic cup. The air was dry and dusty, their ears filled with glue. Only the throb of an exhausted headache kept her awake.

'Do you think this Don Silver fellow knows about all this?' Jackie said.

'Now I'm guessing Don is as in the dark about the real Melvin as everybody else,' Diane said. 'At least, I hope he is.' She thumbed through the wad of psychiatric reports, police profiles and juvenile detention centre records.

'So what? This Melvin bloke goes out to these clubs, tells everyone he's this big producer, and gets them to go back to his hotel where he kills them? Then why not Sheridan?'

'Because he wanted his script. This *Carpool* show. He brings Sheridan to LA, ties him up in Don's house and gets him to finish the script.'

They sat for a while, listening to the bubble of chatter in the aeroplane. Diane's mind kept flipping between complex conspiracy theories and images of her Emmy acceptance speech for her *Sexposé*, 'Mercury: SLIPPERY, SILVER and HOT!'

Jackie just felt sick and achey.

Yes, she had craved a break from her life. Yes, she'd wanted nothing more than some excitement to puncture the cycle of Eastenders and microwave meals. But kidnapping and murder? Shouldn't she be easing herself into this sort of thing more slowly? Maybe reading a couple of travel guides first? Buying some new trainers?

'Any luck with the guide book?' Diane said.

Jackie flipped it open to a corner-marked page in the budget accommodation section.

'If I know Ben and he's anywhere,' she said, eyes flicking over the hotel description again, 'he's here. If not . . .'

'We'll find him,' Diane said.

In Los Angeles, the Celeb-O-Tours bus continued its stop-start wind through the lanes and laser-shields of Brentwood, Ben

dozing on the back seat. While high above them, a black convertible E-type Jaguar roared through the hills, an expensive
toupé blowing in the wind, a tiny mind reliving a recent
nightmare.

*Did you see Gill Kramer at the Comedy Store? Walks out of
E.R. E.R. . . . Oh! in a tantrum and twenty-four hours later he's
crawling back to audition . . .*

*Three million a show he was on when he quit. Three million!
He won't get that again. . .*

Gill who?

'No!' Gill yelled at the world as he lurched the car through
the narrow winding lanes. 'No, no, NO! I'll show you, I'll show
you all! I'm Gill Kramer! Gill fucking Kramer!' he yelled, and
pounded and revved up the hill, screaming against the noonday
sun.

Screaming against the fear. Against the truth.

Show business was finished with him. Finished. It had dined
well on his talents and gifts but he was now lying, picked and
greasy, on the side of the plate with a cigarette butt sticking out
of his ass and a napkin over his head.

He wrenched the car off the snaking street, bumping up the
private road towards his hilltop home.

No. If he was going down, he was taking them with him. He
was taking them *all* with him.

'What's going on here? Who in God's name are you?' Gill
yelled, tossing his driving gloves across the lounge. 'And turn
that filth off!'

In Gill's lounge two spindly men with bleached hair and
sunglasses were sliding furniture about, tangling with shiny
photographer's umbrellas and sucking in their cheeks. Three
young women fussed and flapped with make-up boxes, light
meters and armfuls of revolting drapey fabric. All five had
clearly got some sort of bulk discount at their local body
piercing mart.

356

On Gill's mammoth television screen was a repeat of Dr Dick Trent, nodding sensitively and saying 'hold that feeling, focus on that feeling' to a member of the British royal family, who was lying on a leather couch, sobbing and whimpering and promoting their new book.

'Oh, at *last!*' one of the young men called out poutily. *'Ms Kramer! Hubby's home!'*

'What? What is all this?' Gill fumed.

'Gill darling, where have you been? You didn't come home last night,' Elaine said, wafting through the doorway in a silky robe, kissing her husband lovingly. 'I told you we had the magazine shoot this morning. Go grab a shower, quickly.' She turned her attention to the photographers. 'I thought one or two on the balcony?'

'Photographers?' Gill spat. He had private ranting and fuming to do.

'Celebrity Couple Of The Year, sweetheart. We did it. Fourth year running.' Elaine wriggled smugly. 'C'mon, hon. Our public demand pictures.'

'Now? I thought this was all next week?'

'Yes, *officially* it is,' Elaine tinkled, plumping up cushions and adjusting unread books on tabletops. 'But they always do the shots in advance for the fashion spread. You know *that.'*

'Right,' Gill said flatly after a deep breath. 'I see.'

'C'mon, it's just what you need. Get back in the public eye before you become a laughing stock. I mean, really, darling, would it have *killed* you to have taken the audition?' Elaine rearranged some photo frames on the sideboard into a less pleasing arrangement. 'This way, we get to show everyone. Unlucky in showbusiness, but lucky in love.'

Gill stood at the drinks cabinet, teeth gritted, fists trembling.

'Did it ever occur to you, wife of mine,' he hissed through gritted molars, *'why* I might not have auditioned? That it might be possible I had a *very good reason* to steer clear of Melvin Medford and his *hot* new show?'

'Shush now, sweetheart,' she laughed. 'These young people have a job to do. They don't want to hear about your—'

'*Bedroom!*' he yelled, grabbing Elaine's elbow and marching her, giggling and flapping, across the room.

'Couples m-must always make time for intimacy!' she squawked to the crew. 'Write that down!'

Moments later, Gill slammed the bedroom door in barely contained fury and turned to his wife who stood by her dressing table, brushing her hair with long strokes.

'Listen to me. I have reason to believe that Melvin, Mercury's golden boy, *didn't* write this show as he claims.' Gill's eyes flashed manically. 'Reason to believe he *isn't* who he says he is. Reason to believe that beneath his fancy story is something a lot more sinister.'

'What are you whittering about?'

'He sat out there,' Gill said, 'yesterday afternoon, and told me his life story. Parents were Terence and June Medford. Brought up in Walmington-on-Sea. Dad worked for Sir Dennis Hodge, Uncle Arthur worked in a bank. Another uncle in Slade Prison for housebreaking. Went to school at Fenn Street Secondary Modern.'

'So what are you—'

'These people, these places? They *don't exist*,' Gill said loudly. 'It's all TV shows. *Terry & June*, *Dad's Army*, *Porridge*, *Please Sir*. I remember them all from when I was a boy. The kid's whole autobiography is a page out of the *TV Guide*! He's nuts!'

'So he's a little confused,' Elaine said, dismissing him. 'He's a *writer*, they're all a little peculiar. Now are you going to have shower because—'

'A writer?' Gill laughed. 'Ha!' he added. 'He's no more a writer than . . .'

He stopped for a moment, unable to think of anyone he had ever met in Los Angeles who wasn't writing something. A sitcom, a movie, a book, a treatment.

'Erm . . . well, he's not a writer, *that* I know.'

'And have you thought to ask anybody? Don or Al? I mean, what does Shifty say about all this?'

'Oh, those *fools!*' Gill flounced, throwing his head back and slamming about the bedroom. 'Shifty? Tch! He doesn't care, none of them care! They're all too busy chuckling over their cigars and adding up their percentages. But I'll show them. Oh, I'll show them,' he said with a hungry smile.

'Gill, now wait a—'

'I'll go to the papers with it. *New Mercury Show A Sham! Hit Writer A Fraud!* They'll eat it up!' Gill was dancing about the room, eyes flashing, dental-work glinting. 'It has everything. Hollywood executives, agents, writers. Lies, deception, theft, fraud. They'll never recover.'

'Look, they're all waiting,' Elaine said, straightening her robe and moving to the door. 'Let's talk about it later, hmm? I'm sure there's a very simple explanation. Now chop-chop.' And she wafted out.

Gill took a deep breath and began to heave open the wardrobe doors, mind racing.

He would do it, he thought excitedly. He would sell his story. The truth behind Mercury Pictures. A story of lies, betrayal, theft and corruption. Who would he sell it to? *Entertainment Week? Variety? Pilot?* No, no good, he thought, licking his lips. The trades were written solely by industry bastards for industry bastards.

He tugged out a suit, noticing for the first time the answerphone winking by the bed.

He crossed the room and jabbed the little button. The machine rewound and clicked a half-dozen times before letting out a long harsh beep.

No, Gill had to tell America. Every home and every housewife. Every—

'*Hi, yeah,*' a young female voice crackled, interrupting Gill's plans for world domination momentarily.

'This is Jasmine Tannenbaum calling from KBL, leaving a message for Gill Kramer? Hi, I'm a production assistant on Shrink. We had a meeting this morning and there's a rumour flying around that you've quit show business? I don't know if it's true, but the thing is, Dr Trent is very excited about it. He wants for you and Elaine to be his special guests live on Saturday night, tell us your side of the story? We all think it would be a great show, celebrity couple talking frankly, your childhoods, the secrets of a happy marriage, the whole bit. You'll have the whole country watching. Anyway my number here at the studio . . .'

Jasmine rattled on with her details.

Gill stood over the machine, smiling to himself.

TWENTY-SEVEN

An hour later, a moustachioed Mexican was clearing the lumpy mess from the back of his tour bus.

'Hey? Ma fren'? Ma fren', we heeeere.'

'What? Where . . . where are we?'

'We back at the pick-up. You okay? You still wan' maybe I call da cops?'

Ben shook himself, blinking and stretching. Had he dozed off? No. He'd just sort of slipped into a dull trance, watching sunny lowrise sprawling street after sunny lowrise sprawling street flip hypnotically past out of the window. Denim jackets and disposable cameras were clambering off the bus out on to the pavement where a faded and peeling sign for Celeb-O-Tours hung above a scrappy, single-storey building.

Ben checked his watch, plucking a little bit of hedge from the strap. It was almost two o'clock. He hauled himself up dizzily and made his way out on to the bleached street, glancing around for some clue to his whereabouts. A sign for Gower Street hung across the intersection. Ben's head swam a little, pulling in and out of bleary focus. He was just a couple of streets from his hotel.

Heart pounding in his chest, breathing fast, he slipped from the chattering crowd and began to stumble quickly up the hill. In two minutes he would be with Zak and a phone.

*

He clattered through the wire framed door into the still coolness of the lobby.

'Zak? Zak, you there?' he called. The place was deserted. Panic began to rise, bulging and bursting like a holiday suitcase, Ben doing his best to press down hard on the lid. He thought back. The last time he had seen Zak had been yesterday when he had sent him off to the Comedy Store to babysit Melvin. Could something have happened? Could Zak have confronted him? Threatened him? Could Melvin have—'

'Zak!' he called again, making himself jump.

'Hey, Mr Shouty?' a voice replied suddenly. 'He's not here.' There was a rustle of paper, footsteps, and man appeared from the back room, peeling cucumber slices from his eyes. He was middle-aged but fighting it like a rabid mastiff in a pit. His orange face had been pinned and pulled and folded back like a canvas tent, and his teeth looked like he gargled Tippex. 'Zak's gone. Left. Hitched himself to the wagon of stardom and rolled outta town.' And he threw down that morning's *Variety* on the desktop, folded back to page five.

'What? Left? I don't . . .' Ben read the caption under the photo. 'Holy *crap!*'

Above. Late night gag-off winner. (L-R Zachary Black, pictured here with his agent Shifty Dolawitz and producer Don Silver).

'He's at rehearsals as we speak,' the man said, shaking his head. 'Looks like I'm in need of a new bellboy. You got a job?'

'What? Uhmm, yeah. I-I mean no. No, sorry, I'm just a guest here,' Ben said, the world lurching and spinning. Zak had got a *part?* This was insane.

'A guest?'

'Ben Busby. Room—'

'Busby? Wait, wait, wait, you got messages.' And the man began to flap about with a large flat book. He slapped it open on the desk. 'A guy came looking for you an hour or so ago.'

'A guy?'

'Didn't leave a name. Short, glasses, bad skin.'

'Oh, shit,' Ben said, his legs buckling like slinkies. 'Wh-what did you tell him? Is he st-still here?'

'Told him you weren't around. He got kinda pissed off. Started yelling and screaming about the place. Then like *that*,' the man snapped his fingers, 'he just walked out. Weird. He a friend of yours? You gotta weird friend.'

'Fuck,' Ben said, chewing his lip and swallowing hard. 'I need to call the police.' And reached for the phone, dialling quickly.

'And then there were two girls, you just missed 'em,' the man said casually. 'But again, I said you weren't . . .'

'Girls?' Ben said.

'*Emergency?*' a voice crackled at the end of the line. '*What service, please?*'

'A Brit and a New Yorker. One had a video camera. Brit kept asking for a cigarette. I told 'em they'd got the right place but to try later. Sent 'em to the coffee shop around the – *hey!*'

But Ben was leaping the steps and clattering out of the door.

It had to be! It had to be!

He tore into the dry sunshine, hurling himself around the corner, slamming into two bodies coming the other way.

They all shrieked.

Shrieks that immediately dissolved into gasps and muffled hugs and sobs.

Diane busied herself quickly as the two Brits collapsed into each other's arms in desperate hungry kisses, scrabbling with her camera, peering into the viewfinder.

'Perfect! Oh, this is *perfect*,' she cried, framing the couple's desperate embrace, circling them slowly. '*Our two heroes unite at last. Their longing, their lust, uncontrollable. Desire rising, the danger exciting them, arousing—*'

'All right, all right,' Jackie said as they unglued themselves and got suddenly very British about it.

'I . . . I don't understand?' Ben panted. 'Wha—? I mean how . . . ?'

Jackie tugged her guide book from her bag and flipped it open.

For those on a budget and with a fondness for comedy greats, the Glitz on Franklin Avenue is a must. $29 per night gets you a bed in the Groucho Suite and a complimentary drink in the Aykroyd Lounge.

'The great detective,' Ben smiled as Diane gathered up her gear and they pushed back into the hotel. Up the stairs, across the tiles, still hugging all the way to Ben's room.

Diane made instant coffee and for the next hour, under a large photograph of Groucho Marx, the exhausted threesome all dumped out the details of their recent lives, like the contents of an old handbag. Picking through, tossing away and putting together some kind of sense.

Some kind of story.

Some kind of plan.

'No, I'm sorry, but I don't even know why we're talking about this. We call the police. End of story. Ben?'

'Uh-uh. I say wait,' interrupted Diane. 'We don't have enough yet. We could blow the whole thing if we do this too quickly. We wait, we piece all this shit together and then go straight to the top. I guarantee KBL will pay big.'

It was an hour later. Jackie sat up on the bed, propped against the vinyl headboard, hugging a thin pillow to her chest. Ben was at the little desk, sitting backwards on a chair, tapping his feet and flicking through the Melvin Edelman files.

Diane, being dynamic and frankly a bit more American about the whole thing, was up on her feet, pacing, trying to get the tight-assed Brits to see things her way.

Jackie, unfortunately, wasn't having any of it.

'But Sheridan is *dead*, Ben barely escaped alive and I've been dragged halfway across the world! Let's just call 991 or 919 or whatever the hell it is and—'

'And tell them *what?*' Diane said, throwing her arms in the air like a Jewish mother. 'What are we going to tell them? Melvin Medford is actually Melvin Edelman? *So what, lady?* He shot Sheridan? *We know that, lady.* Melvin stole Ben's script? *Prove it, lady.* We got nuthin'!'

'But—'

'Nuthin'!' Diane yelled again. 'No one's gonna take us seriously. That's why we gotta do this my way. Trust me, honey, I've been doin' this a long time. We need to get it on tape. Confessions, evidence, proof. Edit it all together, snappy graphics, music, a famous voiceover — gotta have a famous voiceover.' She was pacing again, giving Jackie a slight headache. 'Someone sexy, a bit sleazy but sombre. Add some class. We'll think of someone. But my main worry is it just ain't sexy enough yet. It's grubby, but it ain't *filthy*, y'know? I need something . . .'

She clicked her fingers, eyes flashing.

'Hey, you two aren't . . . well, y'know. You don't like it a bit . . . ?'

Jackie looked at her.

'No. No, okay, you're British. Bad call.'

The room fell quiet, bar the clanking wheeze of the air-conditioner. Diane paced and thought.

'Look, I'm sorry, but this is nuts,' Jackie said eventually. Because she was scared. And tired. And thought someone ought to point out to this woman that this wasn't in fact a late-night Channel Five eroto-drama. 'And I know you think we're being all uptight and unadventurous and British about this, and I know we look like we'd much rather have a cup of tea than chase criminals across rooftops and dangle from helicopters the way Americans do three times before breakfast, but Sheridan was murdered. And when somebody is murdered, you call a policeman. It's not sexy or exciting or dynamic. But it's what you do.'

Diane and Jackie shared a look. They both wanted very different things. Neither was about to budge.

'Ben?' Jackie appealed.

He sat back, shaking his head, a print out in his hand.

'Have you *read* half this stuff? Who this guy *is?*'

The women nodded solemnly.

'Shit! I mean, surely if we just go to the police right now, tell them what happened—'

'They'll never *believe* us,' Diane implored again. 'Which is why we need *footage*. Like adding De Niro's voiceover to the "Dirty Dons" *Sexposé*. It gave it weight, it gave it—'

'Okay, okay, but it'll all be over right?' Ben said. 'Finished? Melvin will be charged, there'll be a big investigation . . .'

Diane nodded grudgingly.

'Well then, what happens to our script?'

The room went quiet. Even the air-conditioner couldn't quite believe this one.

'The idea. Our jokes. Our characters.' he said. '*Carpool*. It just becomes evidence, right? They'll lock our yellow book in some filing cabinet somewhere and that'll be that. Five years of work, all Sheridan's fear and blood and sweat, what he was *killed* for – it will have been for nothing?'

The women nodded.

'No,' Ben said. 'I want it back.'

Jackie looked at him. He lowered his head, a little embarrassed, but somewhere written across his eyes, a fierce, trembling determination.

'The show. Our script, our work. We need to get the script *back* somehow. *Then* we go to the police or the TV or whoever.' He sighed heavily. 'For Sheridan's sake. So this hasn't all been for nothing.'

'Well, okay then,' Diane said a few minutes later, handing out three fresh coffees. 'We talk to Don Silver. We find him, sit him down and tell him everythin'. On tape, of course.'

Ben and Jackie exchanged worried looks.

'See,' Diane said, beginning her pacing anew, a look of shiny excitement in her eyes, 'I've been thinking. Don is kinda the central character to the story, right?'

'I wish you'd stop calling it a *story*,' Jackie said, sulkily. Diane really wasn't doing much to change her view of Americans.

'So he's the guy we go to with what we know. We find him, tell him what we got. Tell him we want Ben's show back.'

Ben and Jackie thought about this. It still seemed awfully *Mission: Impossible*.

'And why will he give it to us?' Jackie asked.

'Because if he doesn't . . .'

'Yes?'

'Well then, the next time he sees us we'll be on *Sexposé* in front of two hundred million people, pinning him to a triple homicide.' Diane clapped her hands and grinned. It seemed she had it.

'We give him the choice. When I break this story it can either be *Sex-Crazed Silver In Multiple Margrave Murder Conspiracy Cover-Up*, or if he helps us, *Inspirational Executive Innocently Embroiled In Medford Massacre*. It's up to him. He's a TV man, he'll know I can cut this any which way I want.'

'And in turn,' Ben said, 'I get my show back.'

'And I get an exclusive interview,' Diane beamed, clapping her hands again.

The room went quiet, bar the sound of two British people worrying. Diane naturally would have preferred it if they'd have both jumped to their feet, leaped into their spangly superhero tights and jumped into their spangly superhero car, but from two uptight Brits a polite silence was about the best as she could hope for.

The jangling of the phone by the bed made everybody jump.

Jackie gripped the pillow tightly, holding her breath. Diane thudded across the room to the bedside table. She snatched up the handset.

'Hello?' she barked.

Ben looked at Jackie aghast. Crikey, these American ladies were confident.

'Who is this?... *Zak*?'

'Shit!' Ben yelled. 'Send him up! Send him up!'

So Diane sent him up, sent him up.

A minute later, the two women were shaking the hand of the preposterously blond and floppy young actor. Ben was thankful he left his 'I'm ex-Zak-tly' line in its box on this occasion, then leaped from gratitude to surprise as Zak proceed to throw himself at Ben in an enthusiastic gruff bearhug, which involved copious quantities of back-slapping and a lot of saying 'man'. Ben, gulping and embarrassed, eventually wrestled himself free.

'It's great to see you, dude,' Zak panted, dropping into the turquoise vinyl armchair, throwing one leg over an arm and slumping low. 'I thought Melvin had got you.' He tugged out a bottle of mineral water from his large trousers and had a glug.

Hugged and glugged out, he explained the night's events.

'But like, what we failed to take into account is like, Don really dug the stuff, man,' he explained eventually. 'I like, totally blew them away up there. He offers me a part in the show. In *Carpool*. Well, what there is of it.' And he reached behind him and tugged a buckled script from his pocket, handing it to Ben.

He held the wad of paper in his hands reverently, mouth slightly open, eyes fixed upon it. With visibly trembling fingers, he flipped over a few pages. All typed, all spaced, all formated.

'So like, Don gives me this role, the Phil role.'

'Got some good lines, Phil,' Ben murmured.

'No screen test, no call back. Right there. "You got the part, kid. Be at the studio by eight a.m. tomorrow."'

'Did he tell you why it's all being rushed?' Diane interrupted. 'Anything about Randy Garland?'

'Just what it said in *Variety*. That he's done some deal with a cable station. Nobody knows why.'

'Okay, go on,' Jackie urged.

'So like I'm thinkin', woahhh, a major part in a sitcom? No wayyy. And I get a little, y'know, kinda overexcited 'bout tellin' my mom. The I remember what the hell I was meant to be doin' there! So I run back into the club to find Melvin, but—'

'He'd already gone,' Ben said, looking up from the script.

'What could I do, man? What could I do? So I come back and you're not here. No you, no Sheridan, no cops, nuthin'. Mornin' comes around, six-thirty, still nuthin'. I figure maybe the cops have picked everybody up? Y'know, maybe your plan went . . . well, to plan.'

The room went a bit quiet. Nobody looked up. Zak was beginning to realise that the solemn looks and the glaring lack of Sheridan in the room meant it probably hadn't all gone to plan.

'So I go over to the Mercury lot this morning for rehearsal, shit knows what I'm expectin' to find. Maybe the place closed down, maybe crawlin' with cops. But nuthin'. Everyone's sittin' around the table, chowin' down on like pastries and coffee an' shit. Don shows up like nuthin' happened.'

Jackie put her hand on Ben's and gave it a squeeze.

'Don says that like, there was a shooting at the house?' Zak looked about the room at the pale faces. 'Sheridan right?'

'We were trying to escape,' Ben nodded.

'I'm sorry, man.'

'There was nothing you could have done. Really,' Ben said, and meant it.

The room went quiet.

'So like, who's this Randy guy?' Zak said, attempting to gee everyone up a little. 'What's the deal with the cable thing?'

'I'd better make more coffee,' Diane said and for the next hour, from beneath his sunbleached eyebrows, Zak provided all the impressed *woahh*s, respectful *duuude*s and *like-no-wayyy-mans* of disbelief that their Probe It/Randy Garland story required.

Flopping all over the vinyl chair, shaking his head and scooping back his fringe, he cast a glance about the stuffy room. At the coffee cups, the Draylon and the tired, scared faces.

'And so like, *that's* the plan?' he said.

They all nodded wearily. Apart from Diane, that is, who nodded with an upbeat New York feistiness.

'That's the plan,' she said, clicking her fingers.

'So how we gonna do it, man?'

The room fell quiet, the air-conditioner burping its doubtfulness.

'We have no idea,' Ben admitted.

'We need to get Don on his own, away from everybody,' Diane said. She was up on her feet and going through her bag, checking cables and connections and battery packs. 'Zak, you saw him last. Did you overhear anything? Anywhere he might be going? Any clues about his schedule?'

Zak shook his head.

'At the moment his schedule seems to be nine-till-twelve, run about the place gluggin' Pepto, popping Thorazine and yelling. Then lunch, followed by an afternoon of cocaine, panic and looking for Melvin. Plan is still to shoot the thing tomorrow night, but we still only got half a script and they're only just startin' on the set. A load of Vinnie's pals were showin' up in pick-up trucks when I left, unloading paint and timber. Don's goin' crazy over there.'

'And he didn't mention any restaurants or parties? Nowhere we might be able to corner him?' Ben asked, chewing his lip.

'Nuthin'.'

On the bed, Jackie furrowed her tired brow and tried to concentrate.

And then promptly gave up.

'Oh, look, we don't know,' she said, tossing the pillow across the room. She was well aware this was a touch on the defeatist side but she'd had enough. 'None of us is from this world, we don't know about producers or parties or premieres. You'd have to be editor of *Vanity Fair* even to have the first clue. We should just call the police—'

'That's it!' Diane said. 'Of course!' And moved quickly to her bag, rummaging through leads and lens caps, finally tugging out a fat address book.

'The cops?' Zak said. 'But I thought like, the whole point was we weren't going to—'

'I don't know anyone at *Vanity Fair*,' Diane said, hurrying to the phone, clamping the receiver under her chin and riffling through the book, 'but I've got the next best thing.'

And half an hour later, as Diane had promised, the next best thing knocked on the door in a flurry of fake-fur, lip-gloss and carrier bags.

'Well, Scooby Dooby Doo, how the hell are *you*?' Penny said to Diane, tottering into the small room.

Ben and Jackie could only watch dumbly as this preposterous Valley Girl tossed her bags on to the bed and tottered over to the mirror, adjusting her make-up with a thin pinky. She had on striped barber's-pole leggings and a purple minidress, neither of which co-ordinated in the slightest with her giant orange earrings.

'Zachary Black,' Zak said, coolly extending a hand. 'But my friends call me Zak. Like I'm—'

'Ex-*Zak*-tly the guy I met at the Comedy Store last night,' Penny finished for him. 'I snapped your smile for my scoop. Congratulations!'

'Shit, you're right. Good to see you.'

'So you've been a star for almost eighteen hours now,' she said, pulling a tiny Dictaphone from her bag and thrusting it under his nose. 'How's Madam Celebrity treating her newest offspring? Burnt yourself out yet, sweetheart?'

'Penny, look,' Diane interrupted. 'That's . . . well, *Carpool* is one of the reasons we needed to talk to you. We need your help.'

'*Carpool*? Don's four-lane agenda-bender in the shop already?' And Penny clicked off her tape machine. She pulled

371

out a small bottle of mineral water, tucked her huge shades away in her bouffant and sat down, kicking off her platform heels.

'In a manner of speaking,' Jackie said. 'Y' see—'

'Well, c'mon, gang. Like I ooze for news.'

'Well—'

'You said you had some scheme? You needed my help?'

'Y-yes, we—'

'Lets see cats out of bags chowing down on spilt beans, people.'

Eventually, Penny shut up long enough for them to explain the situation.

'Well, my little sleuthing chums, you have a whole clutchbag full of options,' she said, nodding, orange earrings clattering about her shoulders as Diane wrapped up the plan. She had a fat Filofax on her lap and was slithering painted nails through the pages.

'Okay, so it's Friday, he might be at the gym tonight. That's in Beverly Hills. He has a protein shake and his pecs buffed while his personal trainer reads him the trades. But, hmmm, I don't know.' And she shook her head. 'He hates to work out when he's stressed and I hear he's *stressed*. Word is he sent everyone on *Carpool* home, told 'em to come back tomorrow.'

'What he said,' Zak agreed.

'Trixi's under instructions to bike out scripts around tonight, *if* young Melvin can come up with anything.'

'Where is he?' Ben asked nervously.

'Locked himself up in Don's house to work, they say. And Donny was last seen heading off to the Beverly Hills Hospital.'

'To see his father?'

'Like, I guess,' Penny said. 'But he's got good old Uncle Bernie with him, plus a bunch of actors, so like, your guess is as good as mine. Maybe they're doin' some after dinner theatre to cheer the old man up. Sure beats a bag of grapes. Either way, it looks like the gym's a rain-check.'

The room sighed collectively. She flicked back and forth in her diary. 'You know what I would suggest?' she said. 'I mean, if you're serious about this?'

'Go on?' Diane said.

'You want him alone. You want him relaxed. You want him vulnerable. Plus, you want to have a camera on him without him freakin' out?' Penny said. 'Well I happened to have lunch with *Entertainment Today's* Carol Sawyer who knows a little about those circumstances . . .'

'What exactly are you suggesting?' Jackie said apprehensively.

TWENTY-EIGHT

Two hours later, night fell in Los Angeles.

Penny and Diane and Zak all glugged bottled water and nodded and high-fived and said 'cool' a lot as the preposterous plan was ironed out. Ben and Jackie meanwhile exchanged anxious glances across the hotel room and made tea together that nobody drank, while muttering '*youbelievethisIcan'tbelieve thisyoubelievethis . . . ?*'

In Burbank, on the Mercury lot, the floor of studio 5 clanked and buzzed and heaved as construction workers beavered away late into the night, putting together the set for *Carpool*: welding cars, splashing paint, hauling tarpaulin and scaffolding about under the harsh lights.

While in Don Silver's Brentwood lounge, among the foul art and leather furniture, a television burbled away happily to itself. A re-run of an early *E.R. E.R. . . . Oh!*, Gill's accent and antics echoing hollowly about the walls.

A telephone rang in the darkness.

After a dozen lonely rings, a click and a whirr, a long beep shrilled through the house.

'*Hey, er, Mel . . . Mel, you there?*'

Nothing. Just the faint tinny chaos on screen as Gill Kramer horsed about unamusingly with a stethoscope and a tractor.

'*Mel? . . . Shit, uhmm, okay, you're not there. That's okay, that's okay. I'm just letting you know, I'm at the hospital with*

Dad. He's still under. Doctors say it'll be another few—'

The voice faded. A muffled conversation in the background.

'Yes, I can see the goddamn' signs but this is an important call. I'll be two minutes ... Mel? Sorry, some doctor breathin' down my—'

Another muffled row.

'I don't care! My phone's fuckin' with your equipment? Well, your gown's clashin' with my loafers, so I guess we're both fucked. Now back off ... Mel, hi, me again. Uncle Bernie's here too. He's kind of workin' on a, well, a plan kind of thing, to buy us some time ... n-not that you need time. I mean, your work's g-great, y'know? Great. Terrific. Rehearsal today? Hilarious, I mean it. You killed 'em ...'

The line dropped into a sickly silence.

'Shit. Uhhh ... b-by which I m-mean, y'know, it was funny. You didn't kill them ... Oh, Jesus. Anyway ... uhh, it's nuthin' for you to worry about. Some actors down in Nashville ... But look, that aside, we're gonna need those pages, old pal. We go live tomorrow night, seven o'clock, so we really need to get some pages out to the cast by tonight, okay? I mean, if that's all right? No pressure, but ... uhm ... a teeny bit of pressure actually ...'

In the darkness, the little spools on the tape rotated slowly. On screen, Gill was chewing an ear of corn through a hole in his surgical mask.

'Okay. Well, that's it. I was just checking up on you ... shit! In. Checking in, I mean. I'll be sittin' with Dad for the next few hours in case he wakes up. I don't know when I'll be—'

The tape whirred on in silence for a moment.

'... look I gotta go here, my signal just shut down some guy's iron lung or something. Call Trixi when you're finished, she'll send a bike to get 'em. Okay? Take it easy ... please.'

A click and the machine fell silent.

Once more, the only sound in the huge house was the tinny bubbling laughter from the television set.

That, and the sound of fingernails being munched at an upstairs desk.

The office was in a bad way.

It looked like an infinite number of monkeys had got together with an infinite number of typewriters and someone had slipped them all an infinite amount of cocaine just to loosen them up. Paper was everywhere, covering every surface. The desk sat agape, drawers yanked free, upended, splintered and scattered.

The room flickered and strobed crazily, the only unbroken lightbulb fizzing and spluttering in the ceiling.

And amid this debris, bent over the flickering computer screen, the glow reflecting on his thick spectacles, sat Melvin.

Breathing quickly, heart hammering, throat closing tight.

Once in a while, teeth gritted, he would take a deep breath, sit up and turn to the chair next to him.

'Wh-what do you think?' he would say, his trembling hands hovering over the keyboard in anticipation. 'Any . . . any *ideas?*'

The room would go quiet, his head would thud and throb, teeth grinding and gnashing.

'Any j-jokes? Anything?'

But in the world of writing partners Melvin had so far 'collaborated' with, this empty chair was proving the least co-operative.

Blinking back tears, he rolled his chair away over the papery carpet and swopped seats. He tried addressing his next questions to his recently vacated space.

But still nothing.

Breathing a little faster now, he got up and crackled about the room, yelling out questions, rattling a pencil between his teeth. But still nothing.

The soft burble of the television downstairs. The faint hum of the computer. The fizzing pop and crackle of the swinging bulb.

The chair said nothing.

With a rising panic, Melvin scratched his thin scalp and blinked hard.

Sixteen pages.

Sixteen more pages.

He crackled across the floor and threw open the door, head pounding.

Peals of laughter filled the empty hallway, floating up from below him. Voices.

Gill Kramer.

Laughter.

Melvin began to pace the landing, sweating and frantic, a crumpled sheet of paper stuck to his sneaker. He yanked the page free and stared at its gaping whiteness.

More laughter.

Damp fists clenched, nails biting his palms, Melvin moved in teary panic back to the office, laughter filling his head. He snatched up the aluminium bat from the desktop, sending a pile of paper splashing to the floor and, teeth mashing hard, swung it wide at his writing partner.

The chair still said nothing beyond a loud crack. Melvin swung again, again. The chair splintered and tumbled, the desktop cracked, the screen went 'bang' in a fizz of glass and sparks.

Gill was laughing.

They were all laughing. They knew. Of course they knew. Gill had told everyone.

Men would come. Like before. Men with caps and coats and firm grips.

They would find him. Like they found Uncle Norman. Like they found Godber and Lukewarm and Jock.

No. No, they couldn't. They couldn't. Melvin stood panting in the office among the debris. He looked down at the bat in his hand, flinging it suddenly away with a clatter as if electrified.

No, it would be okay, it would be okay. He would do the work. He would do the work, he would write the pages, he would give them to Don. Don would be happy. His parents would be happy. Everything would be okay, everything would be okay.

He focused woozily on the desktop. The smoking splintered shards of the computer, the brittle plastic shell smashed and charred. The chair at his feet, ripped and bent.

Gill was laughing.

Head screaming, Melvin pushed out of the office, down the empty hall to the stairs. He could hear the laughter below him. That happy wave of love and friendship. Heart slamming, armpits hot and prickly, he began to descend the stairway.

The voices got louder. The laughter louder.

It would be all right. Everything would be all right.

The stairway was cold and hard as always. The banisters felt smoother than he remembered. No roughness, no splinters.

His heart began to slow.

Down the stairs, one by one into the darkness.

It would be all right.

The basement had changed. It didn't smell the same. That tang of cleaning fluid, and cat litter, the dust and stone, they were all gone.

Melvin blinked hard and tried to focus his throbbing head in the darkness.

'Mom? *Hello?*' he called, moving down the stairs.

It was bigger then before. The ceiling higher. Full of furniture and pictures. The washing machine had gone. The dryer. The concrete floor was gone. The dark stains, the bare pipes.

'H-hello?'

But the television still burbled away, throwing dancing shadows and laughter about the room.

'*Ah, begorrah, to be sure!*' Gill's voice said. He hooked his thumbs in his dungarees and winked beneath a frayed straw hat. '*Intensive care unit's brimmin' over with bonnie wee babas, so tis . . .*'

'Hey, Gill,' Melvin said. 'It's me.' He stood staring at the screen, mouth hanging loose, head racing to catch up.

He looked down for his mat, for his sandwich, for his milk.

'. . . *Ah, it be a good thing that I were already here, so it be, to be sure . . .*'

'I was upstairs. W-working,' Melvin said, his face glowing in the flickering blue light of the screen. He pressed the heel of his hand to his temple hard to dull the pain. It was his new friend. Yes, his new best friend. Who he'd drunk with and chatted with. Melvin smiled a little. It was good to see him. There was laughter echoing about the basement.

No, not the basement. He wasn't at home. This was . . . this was somewhere else. Don. Don's house. Yes. Melvin gazed around the room. The ceiling fans thumped hypnotically above him. He blinked twice and edged towards the couch, not taking his eyes from the screen.

'*I be just back from the market, so I be,*' Gill said with a grin, revealing a blackened tooth.

'Uh-huh?' Melvin said. 'I've . . . I've got some writing to do. I'm a writer now.'

The room echoed with laughter.

'N-no, really,' he said. The laughter redoubled. His head stung again and he blinked hard to dull the pain. 'I can show you. It's n-not finished yet, I need a little help with the end. Do you want to see? I like to have someone sitting at the desk with me.'

But Gill wasn't interested it seemed. He was marching about the ward, pulling back curtains, revealing anxious mothers in their beds. The room then exploded into tinny hysterics as Gill wheeled a huge chrome milking machine into the ward.

'*Feedin' time,*' he said, doffing his straw hat, the laughter redoubling again.

Melvin pointed at the screen, rocking a little on the couch.

'Hey, I've seen this one, Mom. I've *seen* this one!' he said excitedly. 'When you hook them all up to the machine! Mom!'

'*Now this shouldn't be too cold, ladies. I've had the chickens sittin' on it for a half-hour,*' Gill said, waving a gleaming nozzle. '*Who's first? Now don't be shy, we got a lot to do here!*'

'A lot to do,' Melvin repeated, nodding slowly, blinking behind his thick lenses. His head still throbbed a little. 'A lot to do,' he said again. Sixteen pages. Sixteen blank pages.

The room crackled with loud laughter.

'Shut up!' Melvin said, getting up and backing away from the flickering screen. 'I can do it! I can do it!'

But Gill was busy, fussing with bedclothes and shrieking mothers.

'*Some help here, let's have some help.*'

'I don't need any help,' Melvin said, memory flashing suddenly with the faces of Jasper Philips. Of Angus and Malachy. Blue, lifeless faces.

Men would come.

Like for Uncle Norman.

. . . You are a habitual criminal who accepts arrest as an occupational hazard, and presumably accepts imprisonment in the same casual manner . . .

He needed help. He needed help.

The jeering laughter rattling around his head, Melvin moved fast, stumbling through the darkness to the telephone in the hall.

'I can get help, I can get help,' he muttered over and over. 'Don has friends, Don knows people. I'll let them help. It'll be okay. Sixteen pages. We can do sixteen pages. Don. I'll ask Don . . .'

He stared down at the telephone, wiping his hands on his greasy khakis, heart slamming hard.

Call Don. Get help. Write the pages. Read the pages. Laughs. Happy. Everything okay.

Melvin screamed as the telephone shrilled into life in front of him.

Head spinning, he reached for it. Then backed away. Frozen

to the cold wooden floor, he could only stand and listen as the phone rang over and over.

His mouth was dry, his head throbbed.

A dozen rings. A click and a whirr. A long shrill beep.

A woman's voice.

'... *achine. It's his machine... What? Shit—*'

A click and then silence.

Melvin stood staring at the machine for a long time, breathing deeply.

Thinking.

He didn't know how long he waited before the phone rang again.

A long shrill beep.

'... *o, you do it. No. You. I'm not... ow!... Er, h-hello. Hi. Uhm, hi, hi. Is that, uhmm, I mean, hey. Hey, Dan? What does that say – Danny Boy... Donny Boy? Donny? Hello. Hi, this is, uhmm... Christ.*'

Another voice. Male. Muffled.

Familiar.

Mel's mind moved slowly, recognition sparking.

The woman was back.

'*Er, Tiffany D'Amour here. Hello, how are you? I'm well... No, wet. I'm wet, I mean. Uhmm, wet with anticipation to ... er meet you... What? ... What? I can't hear ... Oh, and I'm an actress. A young actress. A young sexy actress. Who loves it ... what? I can't say ... dirty. Yes, I quite like it dirty. Well, grubby. Oh, oh, baby, yes! Yeah, rather. Yeahhh. And, uhm, so on.*'

The man's voice again. Melvin knew that voice. Then the woman again.

'*Are you around maybe? I would love to audition for a part. A big part. I want a really big part. Mmmm, er, y'know. A part? By which I mean, well ... a penis, I suppose, let's face it ...*'

Melvin listened to the English voices in the hallway. On and on they went.

Eventually it clicked off and he was alone again.

381

Blinking slowly, biting his lip, he wandered slowly back into the dark lounge.

'It's okay, Gill,' he said, 'thanks.' And shut off the television.

The world fell very quiet.

'I've got all the help I need,' Melvin said, and with a contented sigh, wandered upstairs to bed.

FOX ROCKS WITH KRAMER-SHAMER COUCH GROUCH

By PENNY LANG

HOLLYWOOD

Viewers tuning in to KBL tonight at 7 p.m. will see history in the making.

After slugging it out ratings-toe to ratings-toe for the past season, **Dr Dick 'Shrink' Trent** will finally get to face his foe head-on.

Tonight's edition, a live one-off one-hour special, will see none other than E.R. E.R. . . . OH! star **Gill Kramer** and his wife WAKE UP LA host **Elaine Kramer** take to the famous black couch and reveal all.

Insiders say that the *Pilot* no.2 and rumoured fourth-time recipient of Celebrity Couple Of The Year Award, plans to dish the dirt on the networks, studios, writers and executives that he feels were the cause of his fall from grace on Thursday (see last issue, Ed.).

All eyes will be on KBL tonight for what could become the showbiz story of the season.

Other news: Mercury CEO **Howard Silver** is still reported to be recovering after his heart attack on Thursday.

Visited by his brother and Mercury CFO **Bernie Silver** and his son **Donald** until late last night, the Beverly Hills doctors describe his condition as stable.

Regretfully this means he will miss the recording of his son's new high-concept laffer CARPOOL which goes before a live studio audience tonight.

APOLOGY

Due to last night's extended news broadcasts and coverage of the Frankie Corillo prison-break, Friday's Neilsen audience ratings will be printed in Monday's edition.

Variety
Saturday 30 September

TWENTY-NINE

The Mercury Pictures limousine lurched and swung its way through the Brentwood streets, the early Saturday morning sun flashing and splashing over its mirrored windows like paparazzi cameras.

Inside, among the mahogany and miniatures, tucked in neatly with her back to the capped driver, Trixi flapped and fussed with the morning's papers, picking out the highlights for her anxious companions. Anything to take their mind off the lack of Paddle Marts at their current picturesque vacation retreat of Shit Creek (pop. 2)

'. . . it goes on to say he "*plans to dish the dirt on the networks, studios, writers and executives that he feels were the cause of his fall from . . .*" '

'A cigarette, Uncle Bernie, you got a cigarette?' A sweaty Don twitched behind his Ray-Bans. He slid a Marlboro from a packet almost as crumpled as he was, snapped his oily Zippo and let out a tired up-all-night '*Jesus*'.

'The *LA Times* is mostly this prison break in New York,' Trixi continued. 'Apparently a helicopter—'

'But you're *sure?*' Don interrupted for the nineteenth time as the car rolled north. 'I mean, there wasn't a message or a package or a fax or, I dunno, *something?*'

She shook her head.

'Shit. Then that's it. We're fucked,' he announced to the limo interior. He lit another cigarette, found he had one in each hand and then stubbed them both out. 'Fucked. Christ, I could do with a beer.'

'We'll be all right, we'll be all right,' Bernie said, rattling three poker chips between his bony fingers anxiously. 'Trix, anything . . . er . . . anything in there about last night's hockey game? About the Devils?'

'There wasn't a *courier?* Or a cab or . . . ?'

'I called the house like four times. Every time I just got the machine. He wasn't there.'

'Great. Fucked.'

'Donald—'

'We got six pages of script we gotta pad out to twenty-two minutes in front of a live studio audience *tonight*. Great. Just great. It's a good thing Dad's the way he is. At least he won't be there when Mercury finally goes down the—'

'Relax, kid!' Bernie said, the long car rolling to a halt by the grassy kerb. 'Look, the *Woodfellas* boys are catching the 09:10 from LAX to Nashville. If all goes to plan—'

'*If* all goes to plan. And with respect, it's a fucking shaky plan and a fucking big *if*, Uncle Bernie. I can't sit back and do nothing in the vague hope your guys pull it out of the bag. We need to get the show in the can tonight and my psychopathic scriptwriter has fuckin' vanished.'

The three of them sat in the awkward silence for a moment, waiting for the driver to take the hundred yard stroll down the side of the car to let them out.

'Fucked,' Don said, unlocking the door himself and clambering out into the warm morning.

'Melvin?' he called out cautiously, creeping down his stone hallway. 'Buddy? Y-you home?' His sticky suit clung to his sweaty frame, his back and shoulders twinged. 'You got . . . er . . . you got maybe a new page or two for me? Or one? Whatever, no pressure.'

The lounge was empty save for the tables of untouched party food, curling and dry on parsley beds next to stacked trays of spotless wine-glasses.

'*Melvin!*' he called again in the still silence. '*You here?*'

There was no response.

'Oh, that's great,' Don said, 'just *great*.' He moved quickly across to his drinks cabinet and began to clink and slam about with glasses and pill-bottles. 'Then as this is my last day as a free man, I may as well have a drink.' He twisted his aching back once again. 'Hey and Trix! Call my . . . Jesus, call my masseuse. Christ, those hospital chairs! Ten grand a day and they can't afford Philip Starck?'

'Don, Don, would you try and relax? Everything will be all right,' Bernie said unconvincingly, scuttling in behind him, fussing with the sports pages.

'Relax? Y'know, Uncle Bernie, I don't think I will. I figure there'll be plenty of time to relax on death row. Y'know? In the few brief minutes I can snatch between warden beatings and shower rapes?'

'Donny—'

'He's not here, Uncle Bernie. I got no script,' Don muttered, all fingers and thumbs with a silver snuff box and straw on the marble counter. 'No script, no show. No show, evidence to the cops. Evidence to the cops, jail for me. And unless you're planning on pulling a Frankie Corillo and busting me out with a helicopter, it'll be a zillion volts up m-my—'

'Don, c'mon now, kid.'

'Jesus, I need to relax. Look at me, I'm shaking.'

Moments later Trixi appeared from the kitchen, cell-phones jammed under her chin, tottering in with a fresh pot of coffee.

'Okay, okay, like don't panic,' she said, laying the tray on the table, sitting everyone down. She ran through the status report. 'The set's almost finished. These friends of Vinnie's apparently haven't stopped. They worked right through. You've got your cars, your tarmac, your freeway. They're just giving it a lick of paint. Candi and Mindi have put all the invites out there, we should have a good three hundred crowd for seven o'clock.'

'Not that there'll be anything for them to see,' Don said, putting down the whisky and cracking open the little box of cocaine. He began to tap a line out on the tabletop twitchily, muttering and blinking.

'And there was this from Melvin. I checked his office upstairs. It's like a real war-zone. This was stuck on the door.'

Don snatched the note. It was written in a childish scrawl. He read it aloud.

'HELLO DONALD. HOW ARE YOU? WILL BRING FINISHED SCRIPT TO STUDIO FOR REHEARSAL LUNCHTIME. SORRY SO LATE.'

'He's finished it?' Bernie said. 'The crazy fuck *finished it?* On his own?'

'Looks like it,' Trixi said.

'TRY AND RELAX. EVERYTHING OK. MELVIN. P.S. CHECK YOUR MESSAGES.'

'All sixteen pages?' Bernie said. 'You think he's serious?'

'Messages?' Don said. 'What messages?'

After an evening of planning and a night of exhausted sleep, across town in a stuffy hotel room, Diane Paretsky was getting the measure of her compadres.

'What are you? B? 32B, something like that?'

'Oh she's bigger than that,' Ben piped up from the dressing table.

'Yes yes, I think we're managing all right Ben, thank you,' Jackie muttered. 'Look, look this is ridiculous, he's never going to go for it.'

'Uh-uh, tuft be.'

'*What?*'

Diane removed the sewing needle from her mouth.

'I said trust me, he'll go for it. Now look, try mine,' she added impatiently, 'we don't have all day here,' and immediately flung her arms awkwardly behind her back as if grappled by an invisible wrestler. Two quick clips and, ta-dahhh! Diane had yanked her bra from her shirt-sleeve like a bunch of magician's flowers.

'That'll never fit,' Jackie said, taking the flimsy item. Diane was a very slight woman with very little up her jumper and Jackie allowed herself a moment's irritation that Diane *sans* brassière was as indistinguishably perky as Diane *avec* brassière.

'You're meant to be Tiffany D'Amour, a desperately kinky and slutty wannabe actress, for Chrissakes,' Diane said, grabbing up the rest of the clothes from the bed and pushing Jackie towards the bathroom. 'The more you're spilling out, the better. If Don gets a glimpse of you and your look ain't screaming come-fuck-me-now-on-a-rubber-mat-big-boy then he's goin' to be outta there before you got the lens cap off. Try it all on and get yourself out here so we can have a look.' And she shoved a protesting Jackie into the bathroom, slamming the door.

'Talking of which,' Ben said, chewing his lip and holding out the video camera, Spanish instruction manual open on the desk, 'sorry, how, uhm, how *do* you get the lens cap off?'

They both jumped as the hotel room door was shoved open by Zak, dripping in a thin Glitz Hotel towel with a picture of Joan Rivers on it.

'Like, problem, kids,' he said. '*Serious.*'

'What?' Diane said.

'I just . . . *woah!* Holy Hooker, Batman!' he said, suddenly startled. Ben and Diane turned.

'Jesus Christ,' Ben said.

'Fantastic.' Diane smiled. 'No really, you look great.'

Jackie stood nervously fidgeting in the bathroom doorway, chewing her lip.

'Ow, this bra is . . . ow!'

Her trainers had been swopped for Diane's little heels. The legs of Diane's tights had been cropped about the mid thigh, the elastic from the waistband sewn around their tops to act as rudimentary hold-ups. Most of Jackie's skirt had been cut away, the thin hoop that remained hemmed to an inch above the stockings. She wore Diane's white blouse, unbuttoned halfway down, revealing two pale breasts bulging and straining against the tiny bra.

'Jesus Christ,' Ben said again.

'I look like a cheap tart,' Jackie said, with a wiggle, tugging at her bra and hem self-consciously.

'No, no, not cheap at all,' Ben said. 'Reasonably priced, say.'

'Ben?'

'Competitive?' he added, and then shut up.

'These tights keep falling down and the shoes are pinching and I'm doing these buttons up for a start,' Jackie added, fastening her blouse.

'Ah-ah-ah! No you don't,' Diane said quickly, leaping off the bed and beginning to tease up and tousle Jackie's unruly hair, patting her hands away from the buttons. 'It's all or nothing. Let me do your make-up, c'mere.'

'But the wires are digging in . . .' Jackie winced, pulling at the bra. 'It's barely holding me in, I feel ridiculous. Really, Diane, I mean it. I can't go out like this.'

'Well, that's it. You ain't goin' out at all,' Zak said, loping in and shutting the door behind him. 'There's a guy sitting in a black van out there, watchin' the front.'

Jackie went pale.

'Watts?' she said.

'I said, there's a guy,' he repeated slowly. 'In a van. Out on the street—'

'No, I mean . . . it doesn't matter,' Jackie said.

'I'll take a look,' Diane said. 'Show me.' And Zak led her out of the room and across the courtyard to his window.

Outside the hotel, inside the cab of a rented panel van, among Styrofoam coffee cups and greasy burger wrappers, a tired and angry Englishman was being yelled at.

389

'*Well, that's not what* he's *saying, He says you and Smith just turned up on his doorstep with her unannounced. For Christ's sake, Watts, what's going on over there?*'

'Just turned up?' Watts said, face scrunched up in bewilderment. 'I don't know what he's talking about. He told us we had to—'

'*He hasn't paid for delivery,*' the phone spat. '*And I need you back here.*'

'I know!' Watts cried. 'I told him that. I don't know what he's talking about!'

'*And then he says you just let her go?*'

'I didn't *let* her go,' he said, eyes tight, back teeth clenched in frustration. He was sweaty, confused and furious. Having traced Jackie through her credit-card transactions in Nashville, he'd followed her and the journalist to LA, reasoning they were probably heading for Busby's hotel. So it was outside there that he'd sat and had been sitting for the last twelve hours, silently running Randy Garland torture scenarios through his foggy head to stay awake.

'*So you have her?*'

'Well, n-no, I don't *have* her . . .'

'*So you let her go? Jesus, he's right. You won't take any responsibility for your screw ups. That's so amateur!*'

'She escaped! She had help,' he protested. 'Some journalist. Smith got hurt. He's in hospital.'

'*So we're a man down? Shit! What a mess.*' Watts could hear his boss's ulcer expanding. '*And what was giving Garland a discount all about?*'

'What? Discounts? What are you—'

There was a buzzing about Watts's belt suddenly as his pager jolted into life.

'Wait, sir, hold on,' he said, snapping it from his belt and peering into the dull screen. His boss ranted on regardless.

'*. . . offering to chase after her, get her back for no extra charge?*'

Telling him he doesn't have to pay unless he's one hundred percent satisfied? We're not Allied fuckin' Carpets!'

'I never said that!' Watts cried. A message from Garland scuttled across the screen.

KEN TURDS . . .WHERE THE PIG-FUCK IS SHE YOU USELESS SACK OF CHICKEN TURDS? . . . WHERE THE PIG-F

'Leave it to me, you said. Simple surveillance you said. Give me a chance, you said,' his boss jabbered on.

'He's lying!' Watts spat, jabbing his pager off and pitching it hard against the dashboard. 'I never—'

'But he hasn't signed off on the invoice.'

'He wouldn't!'

'Jesus. . .' his boss sighed again.

'Sir, I—'

'Wait, I'm thinking.' There was the hissy crackle of his boss's deep breathing. *'Where's the rest of the package? The files?'*

'I've left the hard-copies with Steerhorn,' Watts said. 'I've got copies on disc here.' And he threw a glance at the aluminium case open on his passenger seat. The two missing disks he thought it best not to mention.

More irritated crackling.

'Sir? Shall I pull out?' he asked hopefully, starting the van. He wanted nothing more than to pack up and come home, tell Garland where he could stick his—'

'No. You have to find this Heaney girl,' his boss said brusquely. Watts closed his eyes in despair. *'Otherwise we're saying goodbye to seven hundred and fifty thousand dollars. It's your fuck up, get it fixed. Then get back to London.'*

'But—'

'Just get it fixed!'

'Yes, sir. Is the jet still at Nashville?'

'Are you fucking joking? I've pulled it out. It's not hanging around for you with the motor running like a fucking minicab. Just get back however you can and come straight to

the office. We need to have a talk about your future with this company.'

'What?' Watts spluttered. 'But Steerhorn's just trying it on!'

'I'll see you in London.'

'Sir? Sir?'

But the line was dead.

'Fuck,' Watts spat out loud, his knuckles white about the phone. Teeth gnashing hard, he slammed the handset to the dashboard with a crack, punching and slamming the steering wheel, yelling and cursing loud inside the cramped cab. *'You dumb cowboy hickville Stetson cactus eating lying banjo fuck!'*

Zak and Diane returned an agonising minute later.

'It's him,' she said flatly. 'You can see from Zak's window. He's sitting in a van, yelling to himself and throwing things. Looks a tad antsy.'

'Oh, Jesus,' Jackie said, sitting on the bed. Her stomach flipped over, colour and life spiralling from her like someone had pulled out the plug. 'What are we going to do?'

'Is there a back way out?' Diane asked. Zak shook his head.

'You make a move out the door, he'll grab you, man. There's no way like, any of you are leaving.'

The room fell into a defeated silence, broken finally, rather surprisingly, by someone other than Diane.

'Well, I'm not sitting here all day,' Ben said firmly. 'You've got a car collecting *you*, Zak, right? Taking you to the studio?'

'Fifteen minutes,' he nodded.

'Fine. Then we'll have to hitch a ride with you.'

'But, Ben,' Jackie said, '*getting* to the lot isn't the problem. The problem is, the moment that front door opens, he'll be on to us. This guy doesn't muck about, trust me.' Her head was full of thoughts of black gloves and syringes and cold van floors.

Ben chewed his lip. He looked down, thinking hard.

The camera instruction manual was still in his lap, explaining the finer details of the '*foco completamente automático y micrófono direccional*.'

He smiled.

'Phone directory,' he said. 'Pass me the phone directory.'

'So what time are our guys landing?' Bernie muttered.

He sat folded up on the leather couch, knees about his ears, smoking furiously and checking his watch. The sports pages lay open on the table.

'Around three,' Trixi said, freshening up the coffees.

'Three. Three. Okay, that's good,' he said, cigarette bouncing between his lips. He began to clack and click his poker chips on the table again, running the plan through his head. 'Airport to the studio . . . bada-bing. As long as they don't fuck around we should be . . . oh, I don't fuckin' believe it. Devils lost. Sixty three to nine. Sons of bitches! Sons of bitches!'

'Er, Mr Silver, what are the *Woodfellas* guys *doing*, exactly?'

'Hnn?' And Bernie turned to her, face pale and drawn. 'Oh, it's . . .' He ran a shaky hand through his hair, forgetting it held a cigarette, and yelped, setting himself on fire a little. 'It's complicated.' He brushed ash from his thatch.

'Okay, okay, we're in business,' Don said, appearing back through the archway, swinging his car keys on one extended finger in a disproportionately chirpy manner. 'So I'm, uhmm, going out for an hour.'

'*Sixty-three to nine?*' Bernie muttered. '*Jesus!*'

'Uncle Bern'?'

'Wha—? Oh, you headed over to the lot, y'say?'

'Er, in a while,' Don said, his mind elsewhere. 'I'm, uhmm, well, Melvin said he'd have scripts by lunchtime, right? So there's nuthin' much I can do until then. Heat's off, show's goin' ahead, I might just, uhh, y'know.' And he straightened his belt buckle.

'What was the message?' Bernie said. 'Who was that?'

'Huh? Oh, no one, 's'nuthin'' Don waved, adjusting a small stirring in his Armani trousers and whistling absently. 'It's just been a few hours since I . . . exercised,' he said limply. 'My back, oooh, it really . . . oooh, y'know? Must be all this stress. I'm gonna get someone to, uhmm, take a look at me. All over, y'know?' And he began to back down the hall, flipping out his phone.

'You all right, kid?'

'A good, y'know, stress-busting workout to . . . uhm, anyway, be back. I'll see you on the lot, okay?'

Bernie and Trixi nodded.

'Okay, great,' Don said, breathing into a cupped hand and sniffing hard. Fresh enough. 'Trix, hold my calls.' And he spun about, heading to the street.

'Is this your regular masseuse?' she called after him. 'Will she give you an invoice? Don . . . ?'

'*Buenos días, señor. ¿Queria volver a pintar su camión urgentemente, verdad? ¿De color rosa?*'

'What? Say again, mate?' Watts said, rolling down his window and whispering as discreetly as he could manage over the morning traffic. The man in the overalls and missing tooth pushed his greasy cap out of his eyes and blinked back at him, gesturing to his oily pick-up.

'*Sin problema, sin ningún problema. Tendremos que llevarlo al garaje, ¿vale? Déjerne sujetar aquí el cable de remolque.*' And he began to unhook his winch, pawing and fussing over Watt's bumper.

'Look! Look, mate, get your hands off the van, all right? Hoi, leave it! Fucko offo? Shit.' And Watts climbed out quickly into the squinty sunshine. 'I didn't call you. Me no call-io for machanico, *sí? Comprende?*'

Across the street, in the cool darkness of the hotel lobby, Zak peered out surreptitiously through the toughened glass.

'What's going on?' Diane whispered.

The rest of the Scooby Gang were all hanging back by the lift, squeaking and fidgeting: Ben, squirty with nerves, the video camera in a bag slung over his shoulder, the tripod under his arm like a rifle; Jackie, wobbling on her heels and cowering under her preposterous back-combed bouffant, clacked and clicked and attempted to chew her nails without removing all sixteen layers of lip gloss.

'He's like, out of the van, flapping his hands. About as distracted as he's gonna get, man.'

'Any sign of our limo?'

'Uh-uh,' Zak said, checking his fat surfer's watch. 'He's runnin' late.'

'I don't like this,' Jackie said, squeezing Ben's hand hard.

'The mechanic's . . . shit! He's getting back in the truck.'

'Fuck it.'

'Wait!' Zak called as from the 101 underpass a black car loomed out of the shadows and purred up towards the kerb. 'We're in business,' he said.

'Look, I mean it, mate. I didn't make any emergency call! I don't need your help. Look . . . look here!' And an agitated Watts bustled back round to the cab, climbing in and starting his van with a healthy rumble. '*See?*' he yelled over the engine. 'Work-o fine-o. *ME NO CALL-O!*'

'*¿No quiere que lo lleve al garaje? Sin problema, señor, sin ningún problema. Podemos pintar el camión aquí mismo.*' And the mechanic heaved a rusty tool kit out from his van and clunked it down on the tarmac.

Somewhere a car door slammed.

Watts turned.

Across the street, a black limousine idled outside the hotel. The chauffeur wore a confused expression beneath his cap as a young blond man bustled out loudly with a cheery 'Yo, Jeevesy' and clambered in.

'Shit, shit, shit,' Watts said, climbing out of the van, hunching over, trying to peer into the mirrored windows. 'Wait! Hold it!' But the limo revved and slowly swung out into the traffic.

'*¿Rosado? ¿verdad? ¿Rosado?,*' the mechanic yelled, clacking a spray-can, pointing at the large pink stain on the side of the truck, running in thick rivulets down the warm metal.

'WHAT THE FUCK ARE YOU DOING?' Watts screamed, the limo pulling off and losing itself among the traffic. Horns blared. Watts leaped out of the road. Head spinning, he stood, snatching panicky breaths, watching the limo disappear. He swung round and focused again on the hotel.

Nothing. No movement. All quiet once more.

'You guys hangin' cool down there?' Zak said, stretched out on the wide back seat as the car swung south down Western Avenue.

On the floor of the limo, bits of pavement and grit still sticking to their grubby knees, Ben and Jackie lay quivering, Ben clutching the camera-bag to his chest, Jackie with a mouthful of velour.

'Hey, pal,' Zak called to the driver. 'Mercury Studios, right?'

'Yes, sir,' the driver replied.

'We need to drop my buddies off in Beverly Hills first. Regent Beverly Wilshire.'

'No problem.'

Diane was back at the window.

Below her, on the sunny street, Watts continued to flap and yell at the mechanic. It had only taken them three calls with the directory to find a native Mexican mechanic willing to tow a panel van away for an emergency re-spray. From the look of things, the mechanic had obviously not let Watts's refusal to be towed to the garage deter him from his artistic endeavours.

Job done, she allowed herself to breathe once again and jogged quickly back to Ben's room.

He and Jackie were away. Collecting a juicy confession, outlining their demands.

Zak was off to rehearsals. Leaving Diane . . .

Well, leaving Diane.

She sat on the bed. She sat in the chair. She paced. She pondered. She fidgeted. It was all out of her hands for the next hour. She could do nothing but wait. But it wasn't in her nature to sit still. She was a do-er, a go-getter. She wasn't *British*, for Chrissakes.

She got up and moved to the desk.

The stack of print-outs was still there, ordered and organised as best she could, the disks sitting beside them.

She looked at them for a moment, thinking.

She licked her lips.

It was worth a try.

'This is completely insane, right? I mean, it's not just me?'

'No, you're right. It is completely insane. I have no idea what the hell we're doing. We're going to get ourselves killed.'

'Right, right, just checking. Thought it was me.'

Satisfied with the status of their predicament, Jackie pulled her blouse about her chest a little, wiggled her crushed toes as best she could in Diane's cramped court shoes, and they stepped out of the car.

'Like, g'luck, man,' Zak said.

The white-gloved doorman slammed the limo door, tapping once on the roof, and it slid off into the traffic towards Burbank. He heaved open the doors of brass and glass and Jackie and Ben stumbled through into the hushed darkness of the hotel lobby.

It was four minutes to nine.

Inside all was cool and quiet, a wide circle of the darkest polished wood, broad desks to left and right. Ben's trainers squeaked loudly and inappropriately, Jackie clacking ahead with a wobble, although it was debatable whether or not anyone could hear these noises over the slamming of their hearts.

'Remember, I'll be right behind you,' Ben whispered in a hushed voice that sounded deafening in the polite stillness. He squeezed Jackie's hand. 'I'll loiter down here, wait for him to arrive and follow him up. Five minutes and I'll be knocking on the door. It'll be okay.'

She nodded, taking the camera equipment from him busily, but Ben could see the fear in her eyes. They gripped each other's hands quickly and tightly, squeezing them white.

'Don't be long,' she said, giving him a quick kiss on the mouth, and then, tripod under her arm, she clacked across the polished floor to the desk. Ben took a deep breath, smiled limply at the Concierge's arched eyebrow and stepped back to the archway near the bar to watch.

'Good . . .' the slim receptionist behind the desk said to Jackie with a smile.

Jackie looked at him. *Good?* she thought? *What was good? How was anything good? Did he mean—*'

'. . . morning . . .' he added eventually with a slow blink.

'Huh? Oh. Oh, yes, good morn—'

'. . . madam,' he finished softly. It was as if his batteries were running down. 'And what . . .' he began. Jackie cut him dead.

'Hi, yes, hello. I just . . . uhmm . . . need a room, please? Just a regular room.'

The man smiled and turned creakily to his computer. He began gently to stroke the keyboard, achingly slowly, with alternate fingers. Jackie glanced about her. The doorman was carrying bags across the lobby like an adolescent sloth. As someone used to London's beep-beep eagerness to get things done and get home, for heaven's sake, it was very strange, as if the whole hotel was underwater. She correctly reasoned that this wasn't because the staff were lazy or stupid. More because if the meeting you were on your way to was the sort that could start without you, then frankly, sir you were staying in the wrong hotel.

Jackie gave out the necessary details, shivering a little as the air-conditioning goosebumped her cleavage and the tops of her legs. She tugged what there was of her clothes about herself a little.

'Ah, no, Miss D'Amour,' the man creaked. 'A misunderstanding. You're here to see Mr Silver, is that right?'

'What? Oh . . . uhm . . .' Jackie flustered. They knew about this? But how could—

'If you would like to follow me?' And he wafted, as if on a cushion of air, from behind the desk and slowly across the lobby towards the lifts.

Jackie followed, heels clacking noisily, shooting Ben a look. He mouthed a discreet *five minutes* and stepped back out of sight.

Heart thumping, the bag and tripod slippery in her grip, Jackie watched the dial above the lift slowly turn in a you-weren't-in-any-hurry-sir-were-you? sort of Beverly Hills way, until, with a polite ding, the doors slid aside. They stepped in amongst more dark wood and mirrors.

'I'm sorry, I'm a bit confused,' she said, the lift gliding upwards.

'Mr Silver always holds his, ahem, *auditions* in the same suite,' the man explained.

'Oh. Oh, right, I see,' Jackie said. She swallowed anxiously, shifting from throbbing foot to throbbing foot. She tried hard to feel like an investigative journalist. Undercover, about to break a huge story. Risking life and limb for her copy. But she caught a glimpse of herself in the smoked-glassed mirrors and just saw a podgy thirty-year-old British woman dressed like a King's Cross streetwalker.

A bell dinged at the ninth floor and the lift came to rest. The doors rolled open to reveal the pale carpeted hallway.

'This way, please,' the man said, leading her down the soft hallway, beneath solemn chandeliers. They reached a white door.

'And y-you'll just send him up when he gets here, will you? I mean, he'll know where to come?'

'Oh, Mr Silver's been here for ten minutes or so already,' the man smiled. 'He likes to have time to, shall we say, prepare himself.'

He knocked sharply.

'*Yep!*' a voice called out from within.

Not far from the Regent Beverly Wilshire, Bernie Silver was stuck in a cab in morning traffic and very unhappy about it.

'Jesus H. Corbett! *C'mon!*' he yelled, leaning out of the side window.

'Hey, you believe them Devils last night?' the cabbie drawled. 'Jeez, I lost a bundle.'

'Just keep your eyes on the road, pal,' Bernie sighed, anxiety gnawing away at his stomach.

Of course, Bernie was pretty much always unhappy about being stuck in traffic. Normally because it meant there was a card game somewhere that was starting without him. Or, worse, a shareholders' meeting, where everyone was using the hold-up as an excuse to huddle around the coffee and Danishes, comparing losses and discreet exit strategies.

But this morning it was neither of these that had him lighting his fortieth cigarette and spilling ash all over the ratty cab seating.

Howard was awake.

He'd got the call just twenty minutes ago. Grouchy and woozy, Howard had apparently jabbed the alarm button and brought all the nurses running. Where was he? he'd demanded to know. What was he doing here? What were all these tubes? And what was making that goddamn' blipping sound?

Bernie had piled into a cab immediately. He had to talk to his brother before anyone else did. Who knew what Lambert might say if he swung by the hospital for one of his chats?

'Let's go! Let's go here!' he yelled again out of the window, his arm giving an angry throb.

Over the honk of traffic and the roar of Bernie's ulcer, his cell-phone chirruped a thin, half-hearted chirrup. He reached in and flipped it open.

'Yeah?' he said, cigarette ash tumbling over his tired suit.

'*Hello? Hello, Mr Silver?*'

'Where are you? You all set?'

'*Absolutely. I've had my hot water and lemon, I've made little good luck gifts for Grant and Ed. Although why I'm wasting good raffia on that Ed Clift, Streisand only knows!*'

'Matt—'

'*Mr I-was-Joey-Zasa-in-The-Godfather-Part-III–On-Ice. Oh, and if I hear Grant's Pacino story one more time, I swear I'll—*'

'Matt, shut up a second! Is everything okay?'

'*It was just a quick thing because they're calling our flight. In the notes you've given us, which are just wonderful, bless your heart, Grant's got the line – "Look pal, we got instructions not to leave dis crummy place till you agree to drop dis blackmail shit, capisce?"*'

'Right,' Bernie sighed. The traffic began to crawl forward.

'*And I come back with – "So eider youze can hand it over to me an' da boyz here, or we can take it outta your ass, piece by piece." Now would anyone have a hissy fit if he and I traded there? It's just Grant's had a cap fitted on a back molar and it's playing merry Christmas with his "capisce".*'

'Whatever . . . look, whatever,' Bernie said, the cab bumping left, rolling towards the clipped hedges of the hospital entrance. 'I don't care. Call me when it's done.' And he snapped off the phone.

Moments later, Bernie was leaning over the front desk in the reception area of the hospital.

'Howard's not here? Whaddya mean, not here?'

'What I say, sir. He's no longer with us.'

'No longer with . . . He *died*? You called me to tell me there'd been a change in his condition. You call *dead* a change of condition? Jesus . . .'

'No, sir,' the orderly said patiently, consulting the large ring-bound book on her cluttered desk. 'I mean he's no longer with us in the sense that he checked out.'

Bernie still didn't understand.

'Howard Silver was collected about fifteen minutes ago.

They signed the papers, took him away. We advised against it but there is nothing we can legally do if—'

'Who?' Bernie said quickly. 'Who took him? His wife? His son Don maybe?'

An agitated Bernie watched the woman riffle through her paperwork. Howard was gone? Last night he'd been unable to breathe without a roomful of pumps and gadgets and a machine going 'blip'. And now he was up and about?

'Ah, here we go,' the orderly said. 'A Silver. A Mr Bernie Silver. His brother. They left together, a whole, group of them, in fact.' She looked up and smiled a helpful smile.

Halfway across Franklin Avenue a heart was thumping nervously, hands were prickling, breath was quick, and the owner of all these things was moving quickly and silently across the street. Diane was about five yards from the back of the black van, moving in a crouching sort of run, like she was late for the osteopaths. Oncoming traffic slowed a little before whipping past her as she made it, breathless, between the parked cars on the opposite kerb.

She didn't have long. She whipped in and out of the cars towards the rear of the rented van.

Watts was still out of the cab, around the front, yelling at the Mexican. The pink spray-paint smear was still on the side of the van like a huge unwanted lovebite.

Diane reached the warm metal doors. Eyes clenched tight, a silent prayer, and Diane pulled. The metal screeched as it caught against the flooring and the door swung open. She peered into the gloom.

No boxes. No documents. No beige files with HIGHLY CONFIDENTIAL – TOP SECRET stamped on them in red ink, which she'd sort of hoped there would be. Just a sports holdall of some sort.

Shit.

Diane climbed into the back, pulling the door behind her.

The same tiny squeak as it nudged the floor and she was alone in the darkness of the baking hot shell.

Breath held, every movement a howling scream and crank of metal, Diane edged across the floor. Her hands slid over the warm metal until she fumbled with the bags canvas straps.

. . . which she promptly dropped, quickly spinning around, arms flying, stumbling against the side of the van with a dull clang. She tripped and thundered back towards the doors with an utter lack of stealth.

Because she figured, once you've heard the words 'Number-o telephon-o in the back of the van-o. Hold your horses, I'll have a look', you've pretty much had it, stealthwise.

Diane had a thousand thoughts at once. Thoughts about escaping, about fighting, about hiding, about all sorts of things.

None of them did her any good.

'But if they take the respray charge off my credit card . . .' the voice said, louder now. There was the all-too-familiar screech as the door was thrown open. Diane stood frozen in the sunshine like a deer caught in headlights.

'. . . then I'm coming after . . .'

Watts stopped.

'Well, well,' he said. The Mexican behind him smiled.

Diane waved back limply.

THIRTY-ONE

'Er, hello? Hello? Mr Silver?' Jackie said, creeping into the room.

She had that rollercoaster feeling. An hour ago, in the hotel room practising her walk and talk, there had been giggles and kidding and nervous larky fun. Now she was clanking and rattling up, up, up. The playful atmos was fading away and everyone was shutting up and gripping the sides tighter and wishing they hadn't come. Gritting teeth, closing eyes, whimpering and saying little prayers.

'Hello? Is anybody—'

'Miss D'Amour? Come on in, sweetheart, come on in. You're the first.'

'The first?'

'I'll just be a minute, help yourself to a pick-me-up, whaddever,' the voice floated out from behind smoked-glass double-doors at the other end of the room. 'I tell ya, this is just what I needed. I'm havin' quite a week. Quite a week.'

Jackie had never seen a room like it.

No kettle, no cigarette-burnt duvet, no framed print of Chevy Chase. It was huge. Huge and creamy and soft and luxurious, and it enveloped her like a thick warm bath towel. Everything that wasn't the deepest and heaviest polished oak was gold. Everything they couldn't get in gold was a luxuriously rich cream colour. And everything that wasn't available in cream, gold or oak had long since been removed as it frankly lowered the tone.

Heart thumping, she placed the tripod down by the low polished table. There sat six bottles of Champagne and six flutes in a pool of cold water on a silver tray. Neat white powdery lines of what was presumably the pick-me-up lay to one side.

She moved slowly into the room, past lush rubber plants and Regency furniture. The curtains were drawn, the fat bedside lamp glowing. In any other circumstances she would have wafted about the room playing at being Julia Roberts. The huge double bed, however, stripped down to the mattress and wrapped in a wipe-clean black plastic sheet, brought her concentration roaring back.

'Mr Silver?' she called, unzipping the bag and fishing out the camera.

There was the soft skoosh of a running tap from the bathroom.

Fumbling quickly, she attached the camera to the tripod, peering through the viewfinder, and wiped her clammy hands on the focus.

The running water stopped. There was a click of a switch and the smoked glass double-doors swung open.

'We've got about an hour,' Don said, appearing in the door-way, rolling his shoulders. He noticed the video camera and smiled wryly. 'Heyyy, you read my mind, l'il lady. Hope you gotta wide angle on that thing.'

Jackie was startled but tried not to show it.

Diane had stressed how important it was going to be, when meeting Don Silver for the first time, to hit the right note. Not to seem cowardly or nervous, just business-like and blunt. Sit him down, roll the camera and tell him everything. Melvin, the Margrave, the murders. Explain how this was his one chance to clear his name before the scandal broke all over network television.

Jackie had said she would try.

But then, when she'd rehearsed it in her head, she'd pictured it a little differently. They were sitting down, for one. Face to face. Oh, and Don was always wearing trousers.

He stood in the doorway, sporting a leather jockstrap and a smile. His richly tanned body, broad shoulders and suspiciously tucked tummy had been lathered in some kind of oil, giving him a shiny, slippery sheen like he'd just climbed out of a bath of baked beans to present a cheque to Comic Relief.

'Mr Silver, I sh-should explain,' Jackie said quickly. She checked the camera. The little red REC light glowed softly. Jackie stood up a little straighter and tried to compose herself. 'I am n-not an actress. That's not why I'm here.'

'Good.' Don moved quickly across the carpet to his drink. He looked tired and stressed. He handed a glass to Jackie who was too startled not to accept. 'And I'm not a television executive.' He smiled and touched glasses with a wink. 'If that's the way you wanna play it.'

'Mr Silver,' Jackie repeated. She threw a look at the door. Where was Ben? Surely he'd have put two and two together by now and asked for the room number?

'Look, my name is Jacqueline Heaney. I'm . . . I'm a journalist. My boyfriend Ben is a writer.' She threw another agonised look at the door. 'A comedy writer. He and his friend wrote a script—'

Don paid no attention, glugging his drink and bending over to take a line of coke. Jackie winced a little, twisting the camera away to edit out the hairy close up.

There was a noise outside the door.

'Oh, thank God,' she said. 'Ben will explain the—'

The noise shrieked and laughed and whooped in exactly the way Ben wouldn't.

Don lurched upright with a shudder. He turned and gave Jackie a wide eyed grin.

'Come on in, girls!' he cried, clapping his hands, pupils

zooming in and out crazily, and the door was thrown open noisily.

Four young women tumbled in with giggles of glee among dollops of blonde hair, fur coats and curves. With whoops and whistles of '*Donny boy!*' and cheers of '*Paaaarrrtayyy!*' coats flew about the room revealing waxed thighs and willowy shoulders. Four sets of unbelievable breasts bobbed about the room like eight bald ballroom-dancing dwarves.

'Grab a drink, girls!' Don sang, doing a little dance. 'Let's make movies!' And he crouched down behind Jackie's camera, drooling all over the focus. The women began to cavort and contort in pornographic parabolas. 'Better go out with a bang, ladies. This could be my last day of freedom.'

The girls on the bed gave a chorus of pouty '*Ahhhhhs*'.

'Mr Silver!' Jackie protested. 'My boyfriend is the writer—'

'Sweetheart,' he said, appearing from behind the camera, reaching for her blouse buttons in a business-like manner, 'tell him to leave his CV with the Concierge on your way out. We have an arrangement. Now I got a show to rehearse in a few hours which is gonna be a major fuckin' headache. No one's seen a script yet, the writer's out of his frickin' tree. But if it don't get done, it's San Quentin for your host. So I need a little relaxation, a little—'

'Mr *Silver!*' Jackie shouted, pushing him away quickly. 'Listen to me. I'm not a casting-couch starlet, I did not come up here to party with you. The phone message was to get your attention. I don't fancy you, I don't want a part in anything of yours, and I don't want your part in anything of mine, okay? You have to listen to me. This is important, it could be your only chance. *Lives are at stake!*'

The mattress squeaked to a bouncy hush.

The room went quiet.

Don just blinked.

'You are kidding, right?' he said, wiping his nose with a sniff. 'I mean, this is a joke?'

Jackie said nothing. The video camera whirred.

'You're *serious?*' He looked down at his oily physique and posing pouch. 'You don't *fancy* me?'

'No, sir, I still have no record of a Miss D'Amour, sir, not on our current guest list.'

'But you just showed her in!' Ben said for the fifth time. 'I saw you! You walked her over to the lift! Miss D'Amour? Or Heaney? Jacqueline Heaney? Meeting a Don Silver?'

'No, sir, still no Mr Silver either, sir, I'm afraid sir. Again, sir, are you certain it was this hotel, sir?'

Ben glowered back at the open and helpful face of the receptionist. A warm, welcoming face, full of West Coast hospitality and a frankly pathological discretion. It was what you paid for, presumably. Along with the dark wood and the word 'sir' inserted twelve times into each sentence.

Ben leant in a bit and tried to give a knowing twitch of his eyebrows. He had a tap-of-the-side-of-the-nose manoeuvre stored behind glass for emergencies but he was hoping it wouldn't come to that.

'Look, I arrived with her ten minutes ago. She's my girlfriend? She's upstairs with Don Silver . . . *auditioning.*'

The receptionist didn't even flinch.

'I'm worried about her. I'm meant to be up there too but everyone I ask keeps telling me they've never heard of them. I just need the room number. *Please?*' Ben tapped his nose.

The receptionist smiled an understanding smile, looked slowly at his computer then back at Ben.

'Sir,' he said, rather unsurprisingly, 'I have no record of a Miss—'

'D'Amour or Miss Heaney or a Mr Silver, right?' Ben interrupted. 'I know. Fine.'

The receptionist gave a little nod and glanced over his shoulder.

'Are you two together?'

And before Ben had a chance to say no, a voice behind him said, 'Yes.'

A very familiar voice.

Ben froze, feeling the breath warm and sweet on his neck. His stomach lurched, his legs giving an Elvis buckle, hands draining cold. His eyes flashed wide but the receptionist took little notice. He didn't even blink when Ben winced and gave a grunt, arching his back as something hard metal was pressed against it.

'Thank you, gentlemen,' the receptionist said and wafted off slowly.

From behind him, over Ben's shoulder, a hand appeared holding a large coloured VIP ticket, trimmed with gold. It wafted on to the polished desk. Ben held his breath.

Admit One

VIP #07

CARPOOL

Starring Melvin Medford, Zak Black and Vincent Corillo.

Written by Melvin Medford. Produced by Don Silver.

Saturday 30 September, 7pm

Mercury Studios, 2021 West Alemeda Avenue, Burbank, Los Angeles.

'Shall we go?' the voice said softly. 'Lots to do.'

'Right,' Ben squeaked through the fat wad of fear stuck halfway down his throat.

He swallowed tightly and moved slowly away from the desk, the metal at his back shoving him hard, out, through the dark lobby towards the car-park, Melvin's scuttling footsteps behind him.

*

The machines weren't going 'bip' anymore.

'No. No, no, no, don't be gone, Howie, *don't be gone,*' Bernie muttered in sweaty panic. But the hospital room was empty.

Arm banging angrily, face slack and haunted, Bernie rushed back up the carpeted hallway.

'It's a mistake, it has to be a mistake! Of course it's a mistake, just a mistake. Please, Jesus, let it be a—'

'Woahh, there!'

Bernie slammed into a doctor coming the other way in a fuss of clip-boards and stethoscopes.

'Hey, pal,' Bernie flustered. 'The room at the end there . . . old guy, white hair, probably saying goddammit a lot—'

'Mr Silver, that's right. Minor coronary condition. His brother came and discharged him. You can ask the orderly at the front desk—'

'I know, I know. But did you see the man who signed him out? Did you actually *see* him?'

'His brother? Yes. Well, there were a group of them really. I did explain that Mr Silver's recovery was only partial. Yes, he was awake and able to respond but we would have preferred—'

'What did he look like?' Bernie said firmly, gripping the doctor's arm and fixing his gaze. 'Can you tell me what he *looked like?*'

'Well, there wasn't much of a resemblance. Broad gentleman. Wide neck. Dark hair, shiny suit. Is something . . . excuse me, is something . . . wait is everything all . . . ?'

Jackie was in the lift, rolling down to the lobby, the physical sinking sensation the exact opposition of her mounting anger and fury. Where the hell was Ben? Where the fucking hell had the stupid thoughtless bastard got to? She looked at herself in the mirrored wall, hair collapsing over her face, make-up smudged, blouse bunched and rucked up under her breasts. She looked like a Panda from the rough end of the cage, who would suck off a gibbon for a stick of bamboo.

411

Thrown out. *Thrown out!* By those silicone slappers. '*Yur getting*' in the way, honey. If you ain't here to party, shift yur flabby tush! Hush your mouth, Donny likes the silent, straddling type.'

She hadn't had a chance to get a word out before they'd hurled her equipment into the hallway and slammed the door.

Great plan.

The lift doors gave a polite ding and rolled open on to the hush of the lobby. Jackie pulled her shirt closed and clacked out of the lift. Quickly she scooped off her noisy heels and jogged, barefoot and silent across the polished wood to the desk.

The receptionist looked up.

'Good—'

'Oh, don't start that,' she said. 'Have you seen a guy? A British guy? Short? Dark hair? Denim jacket? Waiting here?'

The receptionist nodded slowly.

'Left a few moments ago.'

'*Left?*'

'A few moments ago. They left this on the desk if that's any help.' And he handed Jackie the flyer.

She took it.

'Wait a minute. *They?*'

'He and the other gentleman. Spectacles. Red hair.'

Jackie gazed at the flyer, the cold claw of nausea gripping her stomach tightly.

VIP #07. Admit One. Carpool. *Tonight. 7 p.m.*

Shit.

He had Ben. Melvin had him. Just like he'd had Sheridan.

Jackie checked her watch.

The show was on in a little under ten hours. Melvin had Ben.

And she was stranded here. In an expensive Beverly Hills hotel. Dressed like an immoral panda.

Christ, where was a *Marie Claire* problem page when you needed one?

*

412

'I get *no* benefits, ten poxy days' holiday a year, a crappy pension,' Watts moaned. 'And all *this* fackin' aggro? I don't know why I do it. Don't know *whyyyy* I do it. Why *do* I do it? Tell me that, eh?'

From her position as kidnap victim, crouched in a corner of the van's dusty rear, leaning against the back of the passenger seat, Diane gave a shrug. Watts waved his gun about and whittered on.

He seemed to have a lot to get off his chest.

'I've gotta sit in here with you, waiting for Heaney to get back. Meanwhile that banjo fuck Garland will be bending my boss's ear over some shit, pinning it on me as always. Well, that's fucked my six-monthly appraisal in the arse, hasn't it? Fuckin' wanker. *Wanker!*' And Watts lashed out, clanging the side of the van with his gun, making the whole shell ring.

They had been in the back of the van together for a good half-hour. Diane had made a futile escape attempt of the 'Gosh, what's that behind you?' variety to start with, which had just succeeded in annoying Watts even more and getting Diane a smack in the face. Since then, they had slipped into their roles of captive and moany son-of-a-bitch.

'*Should never have taken the job,*' Watts muttered to himself over and over. '*Never should have taken the job.* Let me tell you, the next time I see that bloody Randy Garland . . .' And he waved his gun about a bit. 'Cactus-munchin', banjo-pluckin' son of a bitch. I'm gonna take that bloody Cadillac of his, drive it right up . . .'

Diane had stopped listening.

She flicked her eyes about the dusty van. It was fairly ordinary, the back empty bar the holdall. As Watts whittered on, she slid a hand across and pulled back the zip.

Clothes. Watts's travelling bag, she presumed.

She sighed and slumped a little lower.

'But *no*, they believe *him*, don't they? That hay-bale-haired, hillbilly, pig-molesting, spur-clanking . . .'

413

Diane leaned forward a little, surreptitiously peering through the thin gap between the front seats.

Her heart leaped.

A silver case lay there. Shiny, new, with a combination lock.

Of course. Up front. Safe. Where Watts would be able to keep an eye on it while driving.

She licked her lips and began to edge silently across the—'

'Don't even think about it,' Watts said loudly, making Diane start.

He was looking at her, the gun resting on his forearm, pointed at her chest.

'Over,' he said. 'Move.' And Diane slid herself across the dusty floor of the van, away from the seats, leaning against the warm metal side.

'That's better. I'd have no hesitation in shooting you, Miss Paretsky,' he said. 'Not that I'd waste a bullet on Garland. Ooooh, no. I'd string him up by his balls, take one of those steerhorns off his chair, sharpen it good. . .'

Diane closed her eyes and prayed he'd just shoot her.

In the lobby of the Regent Beverly Wilshire, Jackie's mind raced, flipping and flapping through her mental Rolodex.

God she knew that guy from somewhere.

The guy in question was by the desk with three companions. Two burly thick-necked men in square-shouldered suits and overcoats. Another shorter, slighter man was doing the talking to the receptionist, removing leather gloves, murmuring softly. The two fat-necked men towering behind him nodded and glanced about furtively.

The man she recognised stood among them, hunched over in a long overcoat. Long, but not long enough to hide the bottom of some stripey pyjamas and paper hospital slippers. He gave an uncomfortable little moan and a spluttering, watery cough, causing the few other guests milling about in the dark lobby to glance over.

His broad companions huddled about him protectively.

Jackie, skulking by a far pillar where she had been since the group arrived, watched the men waddle liftwards slowly.

Shit! It was *him*.

She watched them call the lift, climb in, and the doors roll to very slowly. The arrow on the wall above began to sweep upwards slowly, stopping at the eighth floor.

She hoisted her camera bag and moved quickly across the lobby, jabbing the call button for herself. During the agonising wait she buttoned her blouse to the top as best she could, tugging at her skirt hem and stocking tops self-consciously, trying to get them to meet.

Who the well-dressed men in the suits and coats were, she had absolutely no idea.

But Howard Silver she recognised from the files she and Diane had opened at Nashville airport. She stepped into the lift quickly and hit eight.

Howard Silver, she thought, her mind whirring. What did they know about him? The CEO of Mercury Pictures. Brother to Bernie and father to Donald.

Well, she thought, watching the lights. Five, six, seven . . . If his son wouldn't listen to her story, then she had no choice but to go a step higher.

With a lift-door *ding*, Jackie found herself once again in a pale corridor.

There was nobody about.

She hurried down it, slowing at the corner and easing her head around.

There, at the far end of a cross corridor, was the group of overcoats, one fiddling with a keycard. Howard was coughing and complaining weakly.

The door was opened with a click and they moved inside.

Breath held, Jackie moved after them down the soft carpet. The rest of the hotel sat silently in the warm morning.

She reached the white door and listened.

'NO! Cover this! COVER THIS OVER! I NO WANT PINKO VAN-O, CAPISCE? Jesus . . .'

As Watts yelled at the poor Mexican, Diane, alone in the back of the van, took a moment to think.

She hammered on the metal sides.

There was a scuffing and a crunch and Watts threw the back doors open.

'What? What do *you* want?'

'I speak a little of the language,' she croaked. 'You want me to explain it to him?'

Watts looked at her, hunched timidly by the wheel arch. He looked at the Mexican, scratching his head beneath his greasy cap, shrugging.

He sighed.

'All right,' he said crossly. 'Oy, Pedro? You come listen? Here? Listen?' And he waggled his ears in a charming display of international diplomacy.

The Mexican appeared in front of the van doors, a pink spray-can in his hand. He was having a very confusing morning.

'*Hola.*' Diane smiled. '*¿Ve a este señor? ¿El señor aquí?*' And she pointed at Watts.

'*¿Sí?*' the mechanic nodded. He saw him.

'*¿Dijo que a usted y a su familia les gusta hacer cosas con los conejillos de Indias? ¿Comprende? ¿Los conejillos de Indias?*'

The mechanic started visibly.

'That's right,' Diane nodded. She gave Watts a smile. '*Dijo que es una tradición familiar suya. Dijo que su madre tiene una tienda de animales domésticos en Guadalajara y que le gusta follar conejillos de Indias pequeños.*'

The mechanic stuck out his chin and threw a dark look at Watts. A family tradition, eh? How dare he. He'd never even

416

been to Guadalajara. Never mind have a mother who ran a pet-store there and liked to fuck guinea pigs.

'What are you saying to him?' Watts interrupted slowly.

'I'm explaining that where he comes from, rental vans might all be pink, but here we like them black.'

'Right,' Watts said. He turned to the Mexican and gave him a thumbs up. 'UNDERSTAND?'

The mechanic smashed him in the nose with the spray can.

Diane leaped from the back of the van in the confusion and grabbed the gun from Watts's belt as he lay shrieking on the hot tarmac, clutching his face.

'*Váyase a la chinada, cabrón inglés!*' The mechanic yelled, kicking and punching the writhing Watts. '*¿Hablando asi de uni madre? Vayase a la chingada!*'

Diane moved fast, hurling the gun over the fence into a garden and running around to the front of the van.

Watts's yelling gradually subsided and then stopped abruptly.

The Mexican, his family honour avenged and all thoughts of pornographic pet-store shenanigans over, wiped his bloodied knuckles on a rag.

'*Va a amanecer con un grave dolor de cabeza, ¿verdad?*'

'A *very* serious headache, absolutely,' Diane said, reaching into the van and lifting out the silver case. 'In more ways than one.' And to a blare of horns, threw herself across the street and away.

MICKEY
Are you kidding? That was my wife!
FRANK
(laughing) Oh! That's a good one, Mickey! Hoo-boy, you're a laugh riot. Your wife? Ha-haa! What a guy!
MICKEY
Hey, I got another, these two nuns . . .

'Mickey!' a voice yelled.

In his little booth, Mickey Thomopoulous stopped typing midflow. He cursed and hauled his portly frame from his chair, taking a glug of coffee and grabbing up his clip-board. Couldn't he be left in peace for two minutes?

He waddled out of the door into the morning sunshine, squinting on to Almeda Avenue.

It gleamed back at him, dazzling and bright.

The street was heaving, backed up for hundreds of yards, the air thick with the taste of baked asphalt and gasoline. A half-dozen delivery trucks idled, each one blocked and locked by a half dozen actors and executives in low-slung sports cars and boxy 4×4s, dozens of red faces leaning out, bare arms gesturing.

'Big day, huh?' Mickey yelled, approaching his precious gate, clicking the top of his pen. 'Okay, bub, *Fyre* or *Carpool*?'

'*Fyre*,' the truck driver drawled from behind his shades. 'I got two hundred kilos of replica seventeenth-century horseshit plus half a bun shop.' And Mickey ticked him off, waving him through.

'Studio six, thank you. Okay, *Fyre* or *Carpool*?'

'*Carpool*,' the next driver said. 'I got half an off-ramp and the front of a Lexus.'

'Studio five, thank you. Keep it moving. *Fyre* or *Carpool*?'

'You tell me, pal. Someone ordered St Paul's Cathedral?'

'Studio six, follow the signs. Okay *Fyre* or – oh! Oh, Mr Medford. Sorry, sir, go right on through, right on through. Oh, and *good luck for tonight!*' Mickey yelled after him. 'Okay who's next? *Fyre* or *Carpool*? Keep it moving. . .'

Melvin slid the BMW gingerly through the parking lot, flattening a flower bed and tearing up some shrubs, finally coming to rest diagonally across three spaces.

He climbed out and wandered around to the trunk, sliding his palm across the warm metal, pausing for a moment over the single bullet hole. He felt the sharp panicky breaths puffing through it before snapping the lock and lifting the trunk open.

Ben lay there, crumpled like a ventriloquist's dummy in its suitcase. He blinked and squinted behind his hand.

'*R-rise and shine, campers. Hi-de-hi,*' Melvin said.

Ben said nothing.

'Now I still got this,' Melvin reminded him, turning the dull Beretta, heavy in his hand. 'And it's g-going in here.' He tucked it awkwardly into his khakis. 'We're going to take a-a stroll to the production bungalows across the lot there.' Melvin stepped back. 'Out.'

Ben didn't move, hypnotised as he was with terror, drenched with panic.

'Out!' Melvin repeated loudly.

Ben winced, clambering from the trunk, unlocking his clicking joints.

'Ow, Jesus!' he said, twisting his buckled spine.

'*Language, Timothy,*' Melvin murmured, and they began their slow walk in the sunshine.

It was quarter to ten.

THIRTY-TWO

As the Saturday morning sun winched itself slowly into the smoggy sky, on the side of a hill, in the most horrible house in the world, an interview was delving deep. Very deep. Right through the foam and bubbles, all the way to the plug-hole, in fact.

'What can I say, Dick? It's Hollywood,' Gill said, his booming RADA voice echoing off the wet bathroom tiles. 'The business of show. Whatever the price, whatever the cost, whatever the damage to human hearts, to human souls, Dick. Yes. Human *souls.*'

Gill's pruney pink hands clutched the razor in front of him like a microphone.

'It's of no concern to *them*. Locked away behind concrete in their ivory towers made of glass, the *show's the thing*. Nothing must harm the show. Nothing must harm the ratings, the advertising. I woke up, Dick. I did. I woke up and realised that this was a *sick world.*'

Gill practised a solemn pout in the shaving mirror.

'A sick, twisted, *ugly* world where ideas are stolen, lives destroyed and crazy people — yes, *crazies*, Dick — can be crowned kings.'

Oooh, yes, he liked the sound of that.

'Crazies, Dick. As kings.'

Gill lowered his microphone under the water and allowed

himself to sink a little lower, the warm bubbles tickling his latest chin. He closed his eyes and took deep aromatic breaths.

Tonight's appearance on *Shrink* was going to go down in television history. Of this, Gill had absolutely no doubt. It would become legend, like Elvis, like JFK. *Where were you*, people would ask, *when Gill and Elaine Kramer did their* Shrink *interview?* Every newspaper would carry the story, video tapes of the show would change hands for hundreds of dollars. The floor crew at KBL would become denizens of chat-shows, discussing their feelings and experiences of actually *being there*, as it happened, on the fateful night.

'Bitter, Dick?' Gill continued his imaginary interview, head resting on a pink cashmere pillow, candlelight dancing across the ceiling tiles. 'About being made to audition for *Carpool*? Absolutely not, Dick, no. I'm well aware the gossipmongers and tattle-whores of this town have put it about that this is the case, but what the world fails to realise, is that *Carpool*, as a show, is a lot more than it seems.'

Oh, yes, Gill grinned. That'd get Dr Beardy Trent up on his hind legs. They'd have to hose the drool off his tweed waistcoat. *More than it seems, Mr Kramer?*

'Well, Dick, much has been made of the mysterious writer of *Carpool*, as you know. A Melvin Medford. He is quite the Mercury golden boy at the moment.'

A hush would descend over the studio audience. Dick would lean in a little. Executives all over America would be calling each other up. 'Turn on *Shrink*. Are you watching *Shrink*?!' The ratings would go through the roof, the world poised to hear the truth.

Oh, it was going to be quite a show.

Of course, there was the little matter of *proof*, Gill thought, sitting up a bit and reaching for a moisturiser. But that didn't bother him. Once the story was out there, it would take on a life of its own. Proof would emerge. Justice would emerge. And then, triumphant, Gill would emerge!

He threw his arms wide, puffing out his dripping chest, knocking a number of expensive hair-treatments on to the floor.

Emerge anew! As the biggest, brightest, boldest, bravest—

There was a knock on the bathroom door.

'What is it? I'm busy in here!'

'Sweetheart? Can I see you for a moment?' Elaine cooed.

Gill sighed.

He clambered dripping out of the bath, grabbing a towel about his waist. He clicked open the door in a plume of steam and came face to frond with a huge bouquet of flowers.

'Shit,' he muttered.

'*Another* one,' Elaine said from behind the flora. She dumped it on the hall table where four other similar baskets sat in a neat row, plucking out the latest card and reading aloud: ' "*Everything's going to be okay. Trust me. A.*" And with a kiss. You want to explain *this* one?'

'Honey—'

'We're about to go on live television and reveal to the world how to enjoy a happy ten year marriage! Who is *this?*'

'It's a fan, darling. Just some fan,' Gill soothed. 'An anonymous well-wisher, passing on their good luck for tonight, I expect. Nothing to worry about.' He took the card and dropped it into the bin, giving her a loving peck on the forehead. '*Relax.* Go see to lunch. I'll be out in a moment.'

Elaine gave her hubby a reluctant squeeze and tottered off down the hall in her mules crossly.

Gill fished the card from the bin, held it to his chest and sighed.

'What else would he be doin' here? It's gotta be to plug this KBL lady.'

'No. No, I can't believe that,' officer Dorfler said, shaking his head.

'But why else come to LA?' Walsh said again. 'The guy has

his men blow the roof of the high-security wing, tear-gas, a frickin' helicopter, for cryin' out loud? And twelve hours later he's spotted on Sunset?'

'*Rumoured* to be spotted.'

'What're you sayin'? He's just achin' to see Disneyland one last time before they fry him? It has to be her,' Walsh nodded. 'You know what these wiseguys are like about honour an' shit.'

'Shut up. Lemme call this goose-chase in,' Dorfler sighed, snatching up the radio with a squelch. 'Hey, this is eight Lincoln thirty to despatch, come in, over.'

'*Eight Lincoln thirty received, over.*'

'Yeah hi. This is Dorfler. We're heading west on Franklin. No sign of Frankie Corillo or his men. Looks like another crank call, over.'

'*Received, over.*'

'We're gonna swing by Sunset, do another sweep of — *wait!*'

Dorfler pointed though the greasy windshield at a figure hunched over on the sunny pavement.

'Pull over,' Walsh said.

The patrol car rolled to an easy stop at the kerb. Walsh gave the siren a short whoop and the two officers jammed their coffee cups on the dashboard and clambered out.

'Miss? You okay, miss?'

'Oh, thank God!' Diane swooned, clambering to her feet, half a brick in her hand, sweat shining on her face. On the pavement lay Watt's aluminium case, dented and bashed from where she had pound-pound-pounded it but still locked tight.

'This your case?' Dorfler asked easily.

Diane, a wild flash in her eyes, looked at the two cops carefully, then at the case, then smiled.

'Miss, I — *hey!*' Walsh yelled as she lunged forward, grabbing at his sidearm with both hands. Dorfler fumbled for his gun but Diane had already whipped Walsh's out, pointed it at the case and blown two large holes in the locks with two flat bangs.

'Jesus Christ! Drop it! *Drop it!*' Dorfler yelled, weapon out.

''Sall right,' she said, handing the gun back to a flustered and not a little embarrassed Walsh. 'It's a good thing you guys showed up. Listen to me, this is important.' And she knelt down, flipped open the smoking case, checked the contents and slammed it shut.

Walsh and Dorfler exchanged bewildered looks.

'My name's Diane Paretsky and I'm a producer at KBL and I haven't got any ID on me but you're going to have to believe me because it's important,' she jabbered quickly. 'For reasons far, far, far too complicated to explain now but totally sound nevertheless, I'm planning a major episode of the *Sexposé* series and it involves Mercury Pictures and a murder and a kidnapping and it's got sex and drugs and violence and, all right it doesn't have any sex really but I have a young British girl pepping the whole thing up for me now but the upshot of all this is, I need your help.'

Walsh blinked. Looked at his partner. Looked back at Diane.

'*Sexposé*? KBL? You did that "Dirty Dons" documentary with De Niro and Frankie Corillo? That's *you?*'

'That's me.'

'Miss,' Walsh said, 'we have reason to believe you could be in great danger—'

'Don't start with that,' Dorfler shook his head. 'Corillo didn't bust outta jail because of this—'

'*Corillo?*' Diane spat. 'He busted out?'

'Last night.'

She slammed on her mental brakes, changed gear and backed up a couple of blocks, head pounding.

'We think he may be—'

'*You,*' Dorfler argued. '*You* think.'

'Look, I can't worry about that now,' Diane rattled quickly, 'listen to me. The new show needs to end with Melvin Edelman being arrested with sirens and flashing lights and shoot outs and handcuffs and the whole bit, which I need to get on film, live, as it happens, and I need LAPD to do it, and it's got to be tonight. Mercury Pictures. Tonight.'

'Melvin . . . ?'

'Who? Arrest him for *what?* Miss—'

'See, that's where you gotta trust me because I don't actually have any proof at the moment. See Jackie's getting it on tape with Ben and Don but they haven't shown up yet so I got nuthin' but their word for it, but you gotta believe me because it's important and I haven't time to argue with you.'

'Are you nuts?'

'No.'

'You want us to drag a load of cops over to the Mercury lot to arrest some friend of yours, guns, sirens . . .'

'And lights,' Diane added. 'Flashing lights. It's a great visual. Oh, and one of those big spotlights too if you have it. This guy is dangerous. You might want to bring a SWAT team.'

'On whose authority? *Yours?*'

Diane smiled weakly.

'Oh, you gotta do better than that, lady. I mean, hell, if you got De Niro to show up and tell us he was dangerous, well, that'd be one thing. But you? You're nobody. Where's your authority? Your . . .'

'Gravitas,' Walsh added, holstering his weapon. 'Don't you know nuthin' about TV?'

From the patrol car, the radio squelched again. Dorfler stepped over and pulled it out.

'This is eight Lincoln thirty, come on in, over.'

Walsh attempted to calm Diane down as she flapped and pleaded with them.

'Walsh,' Dorfler said, hanging up the radio and cracking open the door. 'Walsh, we gotta go. Corillo's been seen.'

'You kidding?'

'Wiltshire Boulevard, let's move.' And Dorfler climbed in.

'Miss?' Walsh said. 'We gotta go. An', hey, you want anyone to take you seriously, get a celebrity to back you up.'

'But—'

'Walsh,' Dorfler called, stabbing the horn. 'Let's go.'

'Help you, miss?' a slow voice gravelled.

Jackie froze, her ear still to the hotel room door. A hairy hand appeared from above her and plucked up her camera bag from the floor.

She turned slowly, still crouched, coming face-to-knee with two pairs of trousers. Dark and pinstripe, they hung expensively over highly polished wine-coloured alligator slip-ons.

'Uhmm,' Jackie said, which was all she could think of for the moment. She stood slowly, passing the knees, the jacket buttons, up past a silk scarf, a couple of wide ties around wide necks, and finally their faces.

The man with her bag didn't look like the sort of man you asked for your bag back from, so she said nothing.

The man with the gravelly voice had the looks to match. He looked about Howard's age but managed to wear it in a completely different style. He was taller, wider, heavier – just bigger all over. He was pale. Not ill pale but like he didn't get out very much. Narrow eyes hid under bushy brows; white hair was slicked back up top. His skin was pocked, his features craggy and worn like an antique leather sofa.

This face had seen a lot. And very little of it upset him anymore.

If his name wasn't something like Luigi Lambino or Knuckles Tagliatelli, Jackie thought, swallowing hard, then it really—

'Mr Corillo!' a voice said loudly.

She spun around. In the suite doorway stood one of the overcoated gentlemen, hands held out.

Corillo? The name was oddly—

'Come on in, please, come on in. So good to see you. Who's, uhh, who's your friend here?' he said, gesturing at Jackie.

'Why don't you tell me?' Corillo grumbled, and before Jackie could speak, fat hands were bustling her into the hotel room.

This room was considerably larger than Don's, but pretty much the same for all that. The same pale walls, the same gold and oak thrown exquisitely about the place.

In a dark cabinet, a large television was on. A very short, neat, dark-haired man sat in front of it, flicking through the remote.

At a table in the centre of the room slumped Howard Silver, flanked by the second overcoat. He looked bad. Bad and sick and frail. He was still in his thin paper pyjamas, a little surgical tape flapping beneath his nose. He coughed unpleasantly.

'. . . *and just breaking here on the KBL morning news*,' the TV burbled, '*LAPD are on full alert as a tip off has come in that escaped Chicago crime boss Frankie Corillo has been seen—*'

'Turn that damned thing off,' Corillo said, moving into the room, peeling off his gloves. 'Jesus a guy can't blow his nose on the West Coast without a live on-the-snot report.'

Corillo? Jackie's head thudded. She knew the name. *Corillo*. It gnawed away at her. She watched the short man mute the television, leaving it flickering away, and pace quickly over to the new arrivals.

'Mr Corillo,' he fawned. They exchanged slappy hugs. 'Good to see you, sir, so good to see you. You look well. I trust everything went to plan?'

'Fuck off, Sammy,' Corillo said flatly.

'Of course, of course. Who . . . uhmm . . . who's your charming guest?' Sammy pointed at Jackie.

'You gotchaself a goddamn' eavesdropper,' Corillo sneered. 'I don't know what kinda security you call this.'

'We got a camera here,' Corillo's goon said, tossing Jackie's bag to the table.

All eyes fell on the nervous, half-dressed woman trembling by the door.

427

'My n-name is Jaqueline Heaney,' she said, attempting a confidence she missed by three time zones. 'I have no idea who you gentlemen are,' she lied, 'and I don't want to know. I just need to talk to Mr Silver.'

Howard looked up, grey skinned and tired. Jackie pushed on urgently.

'It's about *Carpool*. It's not what it seems . . .'

Nobody said anything but the room bristled, like a wind over dry crops.

'My boyfriend is in terrible danger. The writer is a killer, he has Ben now. Please, we have to stop the show. I've tried talking to Don but he won't believe me. You need to help me stop the show. Please. You're the only person who can do it.'

'Not the *only* person,' Corillo said.

Jackie looked at him. He stared back flatly.

'Take a seat, miss.'

'There's no time! We need to stop him, we need—'

'*Siddown.*'

THIRTY-THREE

Mickey Thomopoulous spent the rest of the morning in his pink booth clacking out his script, heaving himself up irritably every five minutes to raise the gate for cast and crew.

On studio 6, burly carpenters put the finishing chars and scorches to the interior of the pre-1666 St Paul's Cathedral while actors wandered about clutching hot water and lemon in one hand and buckled scripts in the other, rehearsing the final nine o'clock *Fyre* conflagration. '*Pat-a-cake pat-a-cake, baker's man. You murdered my wife, punk! Thy shit hitteth the fan...*'

Carts buzzed through the shadowy lanes, vans and fork-lifts hauled props and equipment, the morning air alive with caps and coffee and clip-boards.

Which is why no one paid particular attention to the quiet group of pink production bungalows on the far side of the lot, sitting low among lush plants, sprinklers whispering.

Why no one heard the windows close, the shutters fasten, the doors lock.

Why no one heard the bang.

Ben screamed a loud '*Jesus Christ!*' and tumbled, gasping, from his chair on to the peach carpet, holding his leg, eyes tight.

'Not funny,' Melvin said. He remained seated at the desk,

peering at the script on the screen, Don's gun still warm in his lap. 'That's n-not funny. Write it again.'

'Oh, Jesus, Jesus,' Ben panted from the floor, mouth dry, head spinning. 'Jesus fuck, you *shot* me . . .'

'That line: "Deetoo just fixes the ships. He's working-class"?' Melvin pouted. 'Not funny. Again.'

Ben sucked in short panicked breaths, hand sticky on his leg, head banging on the floor.

'But . . .' he pleaded in agony, the world woozy. This had to stop. 'But then Phil says, "*Deetoo's got that little shake of the head though, plus . . . plus that slow whistle . . .*" Oh, Jesus.' His head swam. 'It's like, "*Dented your X-wing? Phweee-yooo, 'snot gonna be cheap, mate . . .*"'

The room went quiet save for the soft throb of the ceiling fan and the soft hum of the computer and the soft seep of blood through cotton.

Melvin looked at Ben, writhing and spluttering.

'"Dented your X-wing?"' he said flatly, turning and looking back at the screen.

'*Please*,' Ben gasped, reaching up to the table-top. His leg screamed at him. 'Please trust me, X-wing's *funny*. X-wing's *always* funny . . .'

But Melvin shook his head and began to jab the delete key quickly.

'No, that d-doesn't work. You're not trying.'

Ben watched his words on screen running backwards, being sucked away to nothing. His head lolled back, thudding on the floor.

'Get up. Try again,' Melvin said. 'Now.'

'I *can't* . . .'

'NOW!' Melvin bellowed, shoving the gun in Ben's pale face. It trembled in his thin hands. 'Move! You have two hours to get this d-done. And funny.'

The world lurching and tumbling, Ben hauled himself up, sucking in air through gritted teeth. He dropped, limp, back into the office chair, leg throbbing and searing.

'Right. Right, okay, g-good,' Melvin said, suddenly sitting up, brisk and business like. 'Now this is *my* sitcom so it needs to be funny. Like me, like on TV. Funny things happening.' He gestured at the keyboard. 'Make them say something *funny*.'

Exhausted, breathing hard, Ben placed his sopping hands over the keys, crimson smears shining on the plastic.

He looked up at the empty screen, pulling in and out of focus. In the gaping white space, the cursor winked hypnotically at him.

Funny. Say something *funny*.

The word, his word, his oath, his life. It seared through his head, blinding and raw, sizzling, branding behind his eyes.

Funny. What's so *funny?*

His mouth was dry, his hands cold.

A long minute passed.

The pain in his thigh remained solid. The gun pressed to it remained cold. The page remained empty.

'I . . . I'm not sure—'

'Ten seconds,' Melvin said helpfully, placing the gun barrel to Ben's temple. He cocked it with a loud click.

Oh, Jesus.

Ben's heart began to thump, hard and loud. Under the desk, his feet began to bounce on their balls, knees banging under the desktop.

'Wait, wait!' he said, hands clammy, fingers twitching and flicking like hummingbirds.

'*Nine.*'

Oh, Jesus.

Funny. Come on. Funny. Something funny. Anything funny. Red noses, banana skins, custard pies, baggy trousers, wallpapering.

'*Eight.*'

No. No good, that's clown funny. *Vaudeville* funny. Come *on.* This is sitcom. Sitcom! he yelled inwardly, as if he could scare his sense of humour into focus. Sitcom funny. Scenes. Set-ups. Structure. Story. Sitcoms. Sitcoms. *Sitcoms.* Oh, come *on!*

'*Seven.*'

The cursor blinked on the empty page. His beloved cast of characters sat impatiently in traffic. Picking their noses, biting their nails. Waiting. Waiting for something hilariously side-splitting to say. They looked at him from within the car, raising bored eyebrows.

Well? C'mon, Mr Funnyman, let's have it. Oh, and it's six seconds, by the way.

Please, he whimpered to himself, a dull sick ache rolling inside him. *I need you now.*

That part of him, that magical spark he could let off the leash, to zip like lightning between words and ideas and possibilities – spotting connections, linking memories, wiring thoughts. The little spark that busied itself in conversation, on stage, almost without his knowledge or control.

Wake up! he yelled. There are three men! Sitcom men! Three sitcom men in a sitcom car! In sitcom traffic! Come *on!*

He writhed and jigged in his seat, creaking and bouncing.

'*Five.*'

He was panicking. He was panicking, head spinning and flashing. Oh, god. Oh god.

Calm. Don't panic, *don't* panic. *Don't panic!* Don't panic, Mr Mainwaring, don't panic! *Stupid boy, Pike.* We're doomed. We're *doooomed!* Rodney, you plonker . . . He's from Barcelona.

'*Four.*'

Listen very carefully, *I shall say this only once* . . . I'll get you, Butler. Everybody out! *I'm free!* Nice one, sunshine. Well, thank you very much, Jerry. Lovely boy, lovely boy. Oh, *Juuune?* Mmm, Betty. Only Sonia! *Norm!* Yessss, Miss Jones. More power! Power to the people. Would you believe? I don't *belieeeve* it. Heyyyy, nanoo-nanoo, smeg head. Hi-de-hi, sweetie darling.

'*Three.*'

Three. Three.

Ben's head spun and pounded, his hands trembling over the keys.

Three? *Three Up, Two Down*, BBC, starring Micheal Elphick? *Three Of A Kind*, BBC, with Lenny Henry and Tracy Ullman and David Copperfield? *Three Live Wires*, ITV, with Michael Medwin and Bernard Fox. Three men in a car. *Car fifty-four, where are you?* You're stuck in traffic. Three men, stuck in traffic. Three men.

'*Two*.'

'TWO!' Ben repeated, eyes tight shut, heart slamming. 'Two's company. *Two Ronnies*. Two to tango. Tea for two. Tea . . . TEA!' he screamed, mind tumbling into place suddenly, his hands flying to the keys. His damp fingers slapped and slipped about the keyboard.

'*One*.'

Ben's hands leaped from the keys and he twisted away, ducking from the gun in a panic.

'Done?' Melvin said calmly. He blinked and turned, looking over the lines on the screen.

Ben held his breath.

'Hot water and a *chicken?*' Melvin said.

'Sachets, s-spoons,' Ben said. 'S-Silverwear?'

Melvin looked back at him. 'Hmmm,' he said. '*Then* what?' And raised the gun again.

Across town, Jackie sat anxiously on an over-stuffed Regency sofa in an over-priced hotel room, watching five broad men circle the desk and each other warily, puffing out their suits, clinking their drinks and cracking their wide necks. It was as if a group of Alpha-male gorillas had raided the dressing-up box from a production of *Bugsy Malone*.

'Now, Howard, you know Lambert here very well,' Corillo said. 'A valued shareholder in your little studio, I understand.'

Howard looked up from the desk, then over at Lambert. They stared flatly at each other.

'But you're probably asking yourself who *I* am.'

'I watch TV, Mr Corillo,' he growled. 'I know who you are. What does a two-bit mobster want with—'

'*Mobster?*' Corillo laughed. 'Howard, nobody but you Hollywood guys calls us *mobsters* anymore. Not that we mind. We need you TV types to keep dressing us up with spats and spaghetti sauce. The violin cases, burnin' everything down for the insurance? Helps the myth. But we ain't packin' tommy-guns and I ain't here about a case of moonshine.'

'Then what do you want?'

'What I *want* is to be down in Mexico, Howard. I am wanted in twelve states after all.' Corillo sighed a pissed-off sigh. 'But no, instead I'm in this godforsaken place, sortin' out Lambert's mess.'

'Mr Corillo,' said Lambert, scuttling forward apologetically, 'Mr Corillo, I'm *handling* this, really. Bernie's under control, you've got nothing to—'

'*Bernie?*' Howard croaked.

'Bernie has a deadline. He knows—'

'See, Lambert's a fuck-up, Howard,' Corillo interrupted. He looked over at the little man, squirming away in his waistcoat. 'He does his best and he fucks it up.' Corillo walked slowly across the thick pile towards Lambert. 'Although he's well-meaning, I'll give him that.' He rested his huge hands on Lambert's shoulders.

Lambert quivered, blinking up at his boss, eyes darting nervously.

'Thinking about young Vinnie, like that. Lookin' out for him. My boy, the actor? I appreciate that Lambert, don't think I don't.'

'Th-that's all I was trying to do, Mr Corillo, just give your son a helping—'

'Yeah, shut up now,' he sighed and turned back to Howard.

'I guess it's my fault, putting too much faith in people. I shoulda just left him doing what he's good at – talking slow and unleashing his sadistic kids. Hey!' And he looked about the room. 'Where are they? Sonny and Tommy?'

'I sent them after Kramer, Mr Corillo, sir. They're tracking him down, getting him back on board like you wanted. They spoke to a guy at ABN. Think he might be hidin' out in Alaska?'

'*Tracking him down?*' Corillo said with exasperation. 'The man's on a live chat-show tonight with his wife, Lambert, for Chrissakes! They coulda tracked him down with a goddamn' *TV Guide*. Jesus!'

Corillo shook his head. Did he have to do *everything?*

'But this is all water under a very large bridge now, Howard. Bernie's had all the second chances I'm gonna give him.' He addressed the room. 'Two things I have no time for gentlemen . . .'

The assorted goons cocked their heads

'. . . second chances and cutting losses. If something ain't workin' how you want it to work, get it fixed or get it outta there. Don't ask twice, it's a sign of weakness.'

Corillo clicked his fingers and his accompanying goon stepped forward, handing him a brown envelope. He unwound the string from the lip and slid out some documents, marked with little Post-its. The goon moved around the desk next to Howard.

'And if an investment ain't payin' off? Do what you gotta do.'

'Look, Mr Corillo,' Howard said, sitting up as best he could, rustling in his pyjamas. 'We're businessmen, you and I. I don't know what it is that Bernie's got himself into here, how you're tied up in this, what he's promised you, but we can talk about it . . .'

'Oh, it's gone past that now, Howard,' Corillo said, looking over the documents and checking his watch. 'Wayyyy past that now.'

*

435

'Pick it up, pick it up, pick it up!'

Shades on, radio playing, car whipping north on the 101 freeway, Don listened to his speakerphone ring and ring. The lunchtime sun beat down on the city adding a hazy sparkle to the traffic, making the air a particularly rich shade of yellow.

Don was in a much less anxious mood now. Bordering on relaxed, even.

He wriggled in his bucket seat and adjusted his trousers. This morning's hotel 'casting session' had been just the thing to ward of the creeping fears of failure, unemployment, jail and murder. He'd just needed to unwind. Chill out. Put things in perspective.

Everything was going to be okay.

Uncle Bernie's plan would take effect in a couple of hours, making Randy Garland a worry of the past. Gill Kramer's appearance on that evening's Shrink would give the flouncy old ham a chance to get things off his chest, which meant a few well-placed calls in the morning to congratulate him on his celebrity couple award would be enough to woo him back to *E.R. E.R.* . . . *Oh!* and a sweet syndication deal. Infact, the only real worry was—'

'*Hello? Don Silver's office.*'

'Trixi, it's me. Give me an update. What's going on?'

'*Everything's fine, sir, all on schedule. The construction guys are just sweeping up, Zak and Vinnie are on set with the director and costume girls. Everyone's just waiting for the script.*'

'And do we have one? Melvin said lunchtime. Have you seen him?' Don asked, holding his breath.

'*He's in one of the production bungalows, putting the finishing touches on it now.*'

'On his own? I mean, just him? He doesn't have any . . . just him?'

'*As far as I know. Are you all right, sir? You sound anxious.*'

'I'm fine, I'm . . . I'm fine,' Don sighed happily. 'Tell Melvin I'm on my way over.'

*

Trixi hung up, spun her swivel chair and peered out across the sunny lot to the cluster of pink bungalows.

The shutters were down. The windows closed. The doors shut. Sprinklers hissed about the ferns.

She didn't want to disturb him. She'd pop over later.

Inside one of the bungalows, Melvin peered at the computer screen.

'And then what?' he said.

'Uhmm . . .'

'Ten seconds,' he said, raising the gun again.

There was a loud rap on the door.

Howard looked up from the documents in front of him.

Across the room on the fat sofa, a petrified Jackie crossed her fingers tightly.

The police. Please be the police, she prayed over and over. The police, Ben, Jeremy Beadle. *Anybody.*

At a nod from Corillo, one of the thick goons waddled to the door and peered through the spy-hole. He stepped away, licked his fat lips and cracked the door open.

Jackie's heart flopped over and sank, hope slipping away like a fun-fair balloon as a thin sweaty moustachioed man with a cigarette and a sling tumbled into the room.

'Bernie,' Lambert said. He was back at the television, flicking through the muted channels. 'Glad you could join us.'

'Holy shit on a slide rule!' he exclaimed, eyes darting over the tableau. 'Howie! Jesus, Howie, are you all right?' And he scuttled as fast as his sling would carry him over to his brother, wheezing at the desk. 'Howie, Howie, answer me! Jesus, what have you done to him? You bastards said I had till Monday! *Monday!* I have everything under control!'

'We've just been talking,' Corillo said.

Jackie watched as Bernie's brain slowly clanked and cranked through the situation. He looked over at Lambert, around at the assorted goons, then down into the eyes of his brother.

His face went grey.

'Oh,' he said eventually. 'I . . . I can explain, Howie. I can explain.' He dragged hard on his cigarette, fumbling for another.

'Then I think we'd all like to hear that, Bernie,' Corillo said slowly.

'Indeed,' Howard gravelled, not taking his eyes off his brother.

'Mr Corillo, sir,' Bernie dithered, 'what have you done? What have you told him?'

'Bernie,' Howard began.

'Explain from the beginning,' Corillo said. 'Starting around, say, nineteen eighty-five?'

'Nineteen . . . Oh,' Bernie said. He took a final drag on his cigarette and stubbed it out, eyes darting nervously.

'That was it, Lambert, right? 'Eighty-five?'

He nodded from by the television.

'We lost Silver Screen,' Howard said, his voice like a volcano stirring in its sleep. He looked at his brother. 'You were playing a little fast and loose with the company accounts. You promised to give up gambling.'

Bernie chewed the inside of his cheek, swallowed hard and tapped out a fresh cigarette.

'I tried, Howie. Y'know I did, you saw I did, I tried.' He clicked his lighter. 'But the debts kept piling up, the bills got bigger and . . . and, shit, I thought, just one win, just one big win. That'd put us back up there. Buy us Silver Screen back. Be like the old days.'

Howard said nothing.

'You never saw a run of bad luck like it,' Lambert put in from across the room. 'Every month he'd come by and see Tommy or Sonny. Every month he'd make his bets – horses, boxing, football. Every month he'd lose it. *Next month for sure*, he'd say. *Next month for sure*. Hey, Bern, shame about the hockey last night. Those Devils, huh?'

'Perseverance like that, it'd be admirable,' Corillo said, 'if it weren't so damn' stupid.'

Bernie examined the carpet like a guilty schoolboy.

'Sorry, Bernie, you were telling us?' Corillo said.

'I wound up racking up a bit of a debt. What with the interest and everything. So Tommy and Sonny come and pay me a visit. *Explain* things to me. They give me a week to find the money. So I . . . well . . .'

'When exactly are we talking here?' Howard said.

Bernie examined the carpet once again.

'I see,' Howard said.

'Oh, your brother can put together quite a business plan, Howard,' Corillo said. 'Especially if the guy he's talking to is something of a *fuck-up.*'

Jackie watched Lambert stew and squirm and scowl in his waistcoat, going back to pretending to watch the television. This Corillo, whoever he was, was clearly very much in charge.

Corillo. The name itched and scurried in her head. She'd heard it *somewhere.*

He continued.

'Bernie sits Lambert down and makes a little . . . presentation. *You're a businessman, you don't want to hurt me, what good am I to you in hospital? You want to see your money? Come in with me on our new venture. Think long term. An investment.*'

The meaning of all this began to seep slowly in.

'Now me?' Corillo continued. 'I'm old-fashioned. A traditionalist. Drugs, guns, prostitution, gambling. Maybe a restaurant or two to keep the money clean. But Fuck Face over there gets all excited.'

'I thought—'

'Shut up!' Corillo yelled. One of the goons stepped up, grabbed Lambert by his thick hair and slammed his nose against the television screen. He collapsed, wailing, to his knees.

'You're pretty much the cause of this damned mess. Thinkin'

you're Steven fuckin' Spielblatt. Ownin' a studio, some big MGM mogul, chewin' a cigar, going to the Emmys . . .'

'*For you*,' Lambert quacked from behind his bloodied hands. '*I did it for you*.'

Howard looked at his brother.

Bernie smiled weakly.

'Bernie shows Lambert numbers, flashin' around that paper of yours – *Vanity* or *Verruca* or whatever the hell you call it.'

'*Variety*,' Lambert quacked helpfully from behind a bloodied hanky.

'Right. Of course, what Fuck Chops over there doesn't put together,' Corillo spat, 'is that investors don't make *shit* out here. Investors get *screwed* out here. Oh, they put up the money, sure. Wined and dined for the money. But what do they see at the end of it? Cash? No, they see goddamn' *points*. Net "points", whatever the fuck they are.'

Corillo snapped his fingers again and a copy of *Variety* was handed to him. He flicked through it noisily.

'Resids? Front end? Back end? Above the line? Below the line? Angels? Pimp fees?' He shook his head. 'Mean anything to *anybody?* Jesus, you guys have got accountants that make my boys look like Bailey Building and Loan! We're getting paid off in "net points", right? Percentages of the "net profit"? You agreed to *this?*'

Lambert looked up sheepishly and shrugged.

'Which is what's *left* after *everybody else* has been paid! After the *actor* has his million and the *actress* has her million and the *director* gets his million and the *producer* and the *caterer* and the fuckin' guy who hoovers the *trailers*, and the *key boy dolly gaffer*, and the fuckin' *best grip rigger loader* – and after you *morons* have spent another *sixty million* on fuckin' *advertising* something that only cost half of that to fuckin' *make!*'

Corillo tossed the paper to the desk.

'You have *any* idea how much this damned studio has cost us? *Millions!* Millions *upon* millions! And for *what!*'

The room fell silent.

'Well, I've had enough. I've had enough of Fuck Pants over there screwin' everything up, bringin' me *your* excuses. It's the networks, it's the sponsors, it's the writers ... on and on! I've had enough. We gave you a deadline, Bernie.'

'I-I know, Mr Corillo. It's under control. I'm just waiting for some associates—'

'*Associates?*'

'Th-they have a meeting in Nashville w-with—'

'A meeting?' Corillo spat. 'A damned meeting? You've had twenty years of meetings, Bernie.'

'Mr Corillo,' he squeaked. 'Mr Corillo, wait. I agree th-things have been a little bumpy, but in just a few hours—'

'Twenty years, Bernie. It's time to pay the check.' Corillo reached for a fat fountain pen and twisted the documents on the desk around to face him. 'You and Howard are going to sign here.'

'What ... what is this?' Bernie lifted the documents. 'Oh, shit.'

'You'll never get away with this,' Howard growled.

'Yes, I will, Howard,' Corillo said coolly. '*You* wouldn't get away with it because you've never done it before. You'd fuck it up somehow and go to prison for a thousand years. Same as you, Bernie. You're businessmen. When businessmen try this, they fuck it up. But I am a professional, gentlemen. This is what our people "do". I will get away with this. I've got away with this before. I'll get away with it again. The studio will go up in a big bang and they'll write out a cheque.' He held out the pen. 'To me.'

'But, Mr Corillo, please . . . please listen to me,' Bernie begged.

'Sign it.'

'Mr Corillo—'

There was a scream.

Bernie and Howard spun around.

On the far sofa, a goon had a terrified Jackie trapped, his fat arm about her neck. A handgun was pressed to her temple.

'Sign,' Corillo said.

THIRTY-FOUR

In Burbank, in the corner of a small room in a pink bungalow, a chrome fan whirred, rotating back and forth slowly. Fluttering the pages on the desk. Cooling the sweat on the faces. Drying the blood on the carpet.

'*Four.*'

'And . . . and, shit, and . . . wait, wait . . .'

'*Three.*'

'Window!' Ben yelled from the floor, eyes tight shut. 'There's a tap on the window! The steamed up window.'

Melvin blinked once. Twice. He lowered the gun and turned to the screen, jabbing out the words with a greasy finger.

SFX – Tap on window.

Ben lay back, listening to the whirr of the fans, the clicking of the keyboard. How long had he been there? He had no idea. Sunlight poured through the blinds. The pain in his leg had levelled off to a continuous sharp throb that screamed at him whenever he moved. He licked his dry lips and breathed slowly.

There was a thump on the outside door and a muffled voice.

'*Melvin? Hey, Mel, buddy? You there?*'

'It's . . . it's a policeman,' Ben wheezed, head woozy and swimming.

'No,' Melvin said. He sat still for a moment. 'No, it's Don.' He checked his watch. Eleven-thirty.

'No . . . no, I mean tapping,' Ben gasped. 'Tapping on the window. A cop, a traffic cop. . .'

'*Mel? Hey, buddy? It's time! You ready to roll?*'

'He says . . . he says, "*Licence and registration, please.*" Then you fade out on that.'

Melvin tapped it out quickly.

Across the room, the laserprinter began to hum, whirring and stuttering out the final page.

'*Mel!*'

He got up and scurried over to the office door. He turned, waved the heavy gun at Ben and then moved away down the hall.

Ben lay back, breathing deep, his head throbbing, listening to the soft voices.

If he could just haul himself up. Haul himself up, grab the computer monitor, heave it to the door, run down the hall and crash it over Melvin's head, he'd be fine.

He slid his leg a quarter of an inch to the left.

Nope. That was enough for one day.

A voice was getting louder. Melvin's voice.

'. . . putting the final touches,' he said, clicking open the door quickly and moving fast across the carpet to the printer. Ben watched him woozily as he slipped out the page, knocked it together with the pile on the desk, all the while calling to Don down the hallway, 'I th-think you'll like how it develops. There's a joke about coffee and, well, I w-won't spoil it.'

Melvin scuttled over to where Ben lay, his pale face pulling in and out of focus over him.

'See you after the break,' he said, and Ben watched as the butt of the gun rose up towards the ceiling fan.

And then came down again.

Outside the Glitz Hotel, Franklin Avenue, a black panel van sat parked at the kerb in the sunshine. Perfectly ordinary-looking, if you didn't count the large pink spray stain on the side.

Or the man, lying half under the van at the rear, face down on the baking tarmac, a dented pink spray-can next to his head.

The figure groaned and shifted and craned his head, waking up woozily. His face was bloodied and scabbed, flecks of tarmac stuck to his pitted cheek.

'Uhh, hello?' Watts said. Hands out, he stood up groggily, steadying himself.

He took a few breaths, blinking hard, the morning's events wandering drunkenly up to meet him. He looked up the street in the sunshine. Over at the hotel. At his van. The spray-can.

'Shit,' Watts said. 'Shit,' he said again.

She'd gone.

They'd all gone

With a sinking, hollow feeling, he moved to the front of the van and opened the door. The case of discs was missing.

'Shit,' he said again. 'Shit, shit, shit!' And slammed the van door hard.

'Fuck,' Watts added, by way of a change, and kicked out at the tyre. That felt good. He did it again. Then at the side of the van. It rang out with a dull clang and hurt his foot, but it felt good. 'Fuck, fuck, fuck,' he yelled, kicking and punching the vehicle hard like a toddler. 'Fuck arse shit bollocks wank bugger arse bollocks arse fuck . . .'

Cars cruised past, slowing down, honking, but he just continued to slam and bang about the van, swearing and spitting about packages and discs and *damned cactus-eating cattle-fuckers*.

'More coffee here!' Diane yelled excitedly, waving her Styrofoam cup in one hand, her other flicking and clicking her mouse about wildly. She was sat at one of the handful of terminals in the *Hollywood Copy Stop* on Sunset Boulevard.

Catering to the million dreamers with greasy screenplays in their rucksacks, its windows were splashed with garish paintings of films and cameras and lights. Presumably, Diane thought, to distinguish it from the *Hollywood Script Shop* next door and the *Hollywood Screenplay Repro Mart* — *just 5 cents a page!* opposite.

She had a stack of warm printouts to her right, a broken silver attaché case open to her left and her cell-phone cradled on her shoulder. Diskettes and CDs littered every surface.

'*Are you outta your mind?*' her boss at KBL crackled on the other end of the line. '*An hour? Tonight? You gotta be kidding. No way.*'

'So *half* an hour then,' Diane pleaded, slotting in another disk, clicking open windows, dragging down boxes feverishly. 'This is huge, Bob. I mean it. Huge.' Tongue poking from the side of her mouth, her deodorant struggling desperately to hang on to its advantage, she clicked, opened and scanned down the list of documents.

:[1]_p08.3 bERNgamb_14.10 13 JPEG image
:[5]_p011.4 bERNshar_04.10 12KB GIF image
:[5]_p011.7 bERNbuic_26.10 18KB GIF image

'*I don't care, I can't do it,*' Bob said. '*Diane? Hello?*'

'What?' she said, her concentration being yanked back and forth.

'*I said, I can't*—'

'You *can*! You're the senior VP of KBL News, for Chrissakes. Get in there and clear me a slot. I mean it, this is huge.'

'*I don't have a slot to give. We've got Gill and Elaine Kramer on* Shrink *from seven till eight, which has pushed back* The Simpsons *which has pushed back* The X-Files . . .'

Bob rattled off his tight schedule as Diane, sent her documents to print excitedly, flipped out the disk and snapped in another. She clicked it open.

:[3]_p08.3rANDmeet_27.10 images/audio_aud.mPEG
:[5]_p011.4 rANDoffi_28.10 12KB GIF image
:[6]_p011.7rANDoffi_28.10 images/audio_aud.mPEG

'. . . and even if there was, I can't just throw a bunch of your hunches out there, you know that. Unless . . . unless you got more shit on Corillo? Jesus, Di, is that what this is about? You should have—'

'Corillo? No, no, no, that's dead and buried. So he bust out, who cares? He's soooo last weekend. This is something new. It's Hollywood, it's scandal, it's . . . holy shit!'

'Diane?'

'They've got everything!' she said, gazing at the screen, blinking in disbelief. 'Everything!'

She began to clatter through the attaché case hastily, pulling out disks and cases, reading labels, her heart thudding.

'Did you hear he's been seen here in LA?'

'What? Who?'

'Your guy Corillo,' Bob said. 'This morning, at the airport. Cops are going crazy. They figure there's some big wiseguy meet goin' down somewhere. Now, hey, you bring me some more on Corillo, I'll give you the top story on the eight o'clock. Diane?'

But she wasn't listening. Her nails clicked through the disks, eyes resting on a familiar name. She slid out the case.

'Wait, Bob . . . Holy shit, what's this?'

She snapped out the disk and slid it into the machine.

'What? What have you got?'

'Wait!'

Diane could barely position the little arrow over the **File** icon, her hands were trembling so much. She clicked and dragged and opened, the list of files spilling out on screen. Stomach in her throat, chest thumping, she opened the top file.

'Diane? What's going—'

'Ohmigod,' she said. 'Ohmigod. Ohmigod. This . . . this is . . . ohmigod.'

'Diane!'

'I'm coming over!' she yelled. About her, scruffy writers looked up from their warm screenplays and hole-punchers. 'I'm coming right over. I got an idea. Shit, you're gonna love me! Give me an hour.' And she hung up.

'Hey!' she yelled. 'Hey! Some help here!'

A large goateed man waddled over.

'I need duplicates made of all this,' she said, slapping her hand on her print-outs. 'Right now.'

She began to clatter her disks back into the case haphazardly. Ohmigod. Ohmigod.

'Will you be wanting them bound? We have a special offer on—'

'*NOW!*'

THIRTY-FIVE

On the floor of studio 5, the trestle table was scattered with the debris of the bored and tired: empty water bottles with the labels picked off, chewed pencils, cell-phones, doodled scripts and dry muffin crumbs.

Zak sat, baseball cap pulled down over his head, licking his lips, picking his fingernails and sighing an anxious, '*Oh, maaan.*'

He watched the crew wander about the studio, check their watches, stare up at the gantries and kick at bits of gaffer tape on the floor; Rob, the director pace and wave his arms and glug bottled water. Zak's co-star Vinnie waddled slowly about the set that still hung with the warm smell of paint and timber — peering into the cars, running his fat hands along the hoods, squinting at the backdrop.

It was ten minutes after midday.

Someone would be in soon to tell them it was all over. To tell them the show had been cancelled. To tell them to all go on home, Melvin had been arrested, Don was in custody, the whole thing was—

'*Great!* This is *great!*' a voice echoed loudly about the studio. Everyone turned. Don stepped out of the dazzling sunshine, ducking into the dim studio, flipping through what Zak thought looked worryingly like a script.

Melvin scampered behind him like an eager puppy.

Like, oh Christ, Zak thought.

'People, people,' Don said, striding over. 'We finally have it!' and he waved the fat script over his head. 'Trixi's making copies, we'll start the read through in five minutes. Good to see you all, good to see you. Help yourselves to muffins.'

Zak could only watch as the crew began to pick up their pace, chattering, scuttling, scraping chairs, pouring out fresh coffees.

'Er, Mr Silver?' he said nervously, eyes darting.

'Zakky, m'boy! What's — *heyyyy!* Check *this* out!' And Don slapped the script on to the table, wandering with arms out-stretched to the wide set.

Suspended from twelve steel cables, a huge backdrop hung across the width of the studio. Twenty feet high and a hundred feet long, made of heavy canvas, it had been skilfully painted to resemble a packed freeway on a summer morning — the familiar East Hollywood skyline, the hills, the road signs, the off ramps. And stretching from almost life size at the front to distant smudgy impressions in the distance, the cars — three lanes of gridlocked cars, tightly packed and gleaming.

In front of the backdrop were the front-halves of three real cars. Cut right down the middle, from the front they seemed complete — a radiator, a hood, front wheels, a windscreen and two front doors. But everything beyond that had been removed, leaving just painted wooden supports.

'Youse like 'em, Mr Silver?' Vinnie called across the cold echo of the studio floor as he squeezed himself into his chair, 'Dad did us proud, am I right?'

Zak watched Don nod, gazing about the set.

'These are beauties,' he said. 'So we'll have extras in the halves back here and the main cast in this fella, right?'

'Right,' the director said, consulting his clipboard.

The 'fella' in question was an old dusty red five-door Ford, positioned centre-stage between two hatchbacks. It was perfect, right down to the grubby windshield, bumper stickers, dents, bent aerial and snapped wiper.

'It's great, it's j-just great,' Melvin grinned boyishly, eyes flashing with excitement, scuttling back and forth, thumping over the stage. 'It's j-just how I wanted it.'

'Scripts, sir,' Trixi announced stepping into the studio with a document box, handing them out to everybody as they took their seats and started flicking rapidly through.

Zak took his copy and cracked it open, raising it to shield his face and peering over the top.

He watched Melvin, hands stuffed in his pockets, skip and squeak innocently about the studio floor.

He watched Rob flick a red pen about his script.

He watched as Don called Trixi over, craning to hear what was being said.

'*You get hold of Uncle Bernie yet? What's the news from Nashville? I don't like being alone with Melvin here . . .*'

Zak leaned over as far as he could, aching to hear.

'Okay, okay,' Don said, patting Trixi's behind and sending her fussing off with her cell-phone. 'We got seven hours to get this read through, learned, on its feet and blocked. Let's take it from the top, all the way through. Best of luck, everybody. *Act one. Scene A. Fade in. Interior of a family car, early-morning. A typical dull car owned by a typical dull American guy . . .*'

Across town. Another television studio. Another empty set.

No cars this time. In their place a dark, rich carpet on a raised platform. A glass-topped coffee table, complete with plastic flowers. A row of antique looking bookshelves made of the finest fibreglass. A green, wing-backed leather armchair and two long black leather couches.

Diane chased Bob across the echoing floor, weaving between cameras, stepping over tape marks and cables, waving her silver case.

'Forget it,' he said, hooking a set of headphones around his neck. 'It's too risky. Too many *what-ifs*, too many *yes-buts*, too many *Jesus-I-never-thought-that-would-happens*. This is live television.'

'I *know*,' Diane said, ducking under a camera and following him up through the empty tiered seating. 'Jesus Bob, that's the goddamned *point*. It's live. It's as-it-happens. That's how this thing is gonna *work*.'

'I can't do it,' he said, marching up the stairs away from her.

'Bob—'

'It's too risky.'

'Bob, *listen* to me,' Diane said, grabbing at the cable that hung from his phones and pulling hard, Bob stumbling backwards, gagging, clip-board flying. '*Listen to me*! We don't have time to debate this. *This* is the only way I can do it and *you're* the only person who can help me. I need an answer now. You in or out?'

'Diane,' he coughed, untwisting his larynx from the headphones. 'I'm out. You know if I could help you I would. But does it have to be tonight? This is gonna be KBL's biggest show of the *season*.'

'That's why it *has* to be tonight,' Diane urged. She bent down, unstuck the tape that held her attaché case shut and began tugging at the contents. 'Every television set in America is going to be on this,' she continued. 'Every journalist, every cop, every judge, every politician. Mr & Mrs America and all the little America juniors. They'll *see* him say it. They'll *hear* him say it. And they'll *believe* him. If I've learned one thing in this crazy business it's that without a famous face to back you up, nobody gives a damn.'

Bob chewed his lip.

'But . . . but, if he doesn't *go* for it?'

'He'll go for it! He'll be making TV history. It'll be like Armstrong landing on the moon, shooting JFK and pushing Rodney King into a crater. Right here, live, in front of *millions*. *Your* network.'

Bob gazed over the studio set in the darkness.

'I don't know . . .'

'Bob, I understand. You're worried. If he doesn't go for it, you'll be left with a gaping hole in your show,' Diane said, sliding one arm over his shoulder, the other holding out a handful of printer-paper. 'That's why I thought you might want a look at these.'

He held out his hand, tentatively.

'They're genuine, they're unambiguous and they're yours.'

'Ohmigod . . . you weren't kidding. Is this . . . ?'

'If we have a deal.'

A trembling smile slithered over Bob's face.

'But you have to make a decision. It's quarter to one. If we're going to do this, we've got to do it now.'

'Jesus, Diane, yes. If these are genuine? Yes. Let's do it. I'll call down. Tell 'em you're on your way.'

'Great!' she shrieked, slammed her case shut and hared up the stairs towards the exit. 'And give me a crew who can keep up!' she yelled, disappearing through the double doors.

Bob sat down on one of the audience chairs and exhaled deeply, gazing over the studio.

This was gonna be quite a show.

In an eighth-floor suite in the Regent Beverly Wilshire, an elderly man was behaving like a toddler. Sitting on the floor in his pyjamas, he was slap bang in the middle of a big sulk, and not only because it was time someone came along and took him to the toilet.

The reason he was unable to go the whole hog and suck his thumb was because one wrist was handcuffed to the leg of a heavy writing desk, the other to the wrist of his younger brother. A younger brother who was having not so much of a sulk, as a full-blown panic attack.

'Howie? Jesus, Howie, listen to me! Can you reach around? Howie? Can you move your arm at all? Howie? Howie, for Chrissakes, we gotta get out of here! *Howie?*'

There was no response but Bernie knew his brother hadn't gone anywhere. He could still feel his bony spine pressed hard against his own.

They were in the centre of the huge suite, both bound tightly at the ankles. A thick cord went around their waists, binding the bases of their spines together hard, their necks likewise, which meant every time one nodded, the other was in great danger of choking to death.

'Howie, for Chrissakes, I said I was sorry. We don't have time for this sulking shit. You heard what Corillo said, he—'

'Sulking?' Howard's voice rumbled behind him. 'Oh, I'm sorry Bernie, I didn't mean to sulk.'

'That's okay, Howie, that's okay. But now we need to focus here. If you can reach around—'

'I realise that this isn't the time for sulking. This is the time for *breaking your damned head open!*' his brother bellowed, before collapsing into a hacking splutter.

Across the room, in his jacket, still tossed over the silent flickering television, Bernie's cell-phone began to chirrup for the fifth time.

'Howie, c'mon now. That'll be *Don*. We need to try and get out of here.'

'*Mobsters!*' Howard moaned like a wounded bear. 'Goddamn' wiseguys! I mean, how could you? Still gambling, Bernie? All these years. Years!'

'*Howard!* Jesus, Joseph and Marybeth Lacey, we don't have time for this!'

Howard stopped wailing, his voice fading to a gravelly rasp. The phone stopped ringing.

'Shit, didn't you hear Corillo? What he said? *The studio will go bang!* We have to stop him getting on to the lot with a damn' bomb!' And Bernie began huffing and fighting at the bindings. 'Maybe . . .' and he looked around, the rope scraping his Adam's apple 'if you pull the desk . . .'

'What else don't I know, Bernie?' Howard said slowly. 'While I've been in hospital, what the hell's been going on?'

'Howie, can you pull the desk?' his brother puffed. 'If we both slide our asses across together. After three, Howie? One, two—'

'Bern? Did . . . did you go down and see Garland?' Howard puffed, straining at the ropes. 'Speak to him? Talk him out of this insane blackmail?'

'Howard, *concentrate*. I'll fill you in later but we have to try and reach my phone.'

So on the count of three the two men slid six inches across the carpet. Howard heaved as hard as his fat wrists would let him, but the desk failed to budge.

'I tried to tell Garland,' Bernie said, wincing at the memory of his feeble FBI bluff. 'He wouldn't listen. Son of a bitch even brought the deadline forward. Told me I'd better bring him the pilot of *Carpool* by Monday or he'd send the photos and tapes of Don to the cops.'

'*Monday?*' Howard spat. 'We've got *two days?*'

'His cookery girl packed up her titties in her old kit bag and fucked off outta Dodge,' Bernie said. 'How's that desk coming?'

'Hasn't . . . gaahh!' Howard winced. 'Not a damned inch. Thing weighs three tons.'

Across the room, Bernie's cell-phone called out pitifully once again.

'Shit,' he said. 'Wait. Unless . . .' And he began to crane around the room, Howard coughing and gagging behind him as the bindings bit into his fat neck. 'Sorry, but I got an idea. This room's gonna have . . . there!'

Behind the mini-bar against the wall a few feet away, Bernie could see a pale wire running up, up to the top among the jars of pistachios and complimentary playing-cards.

'Can you reach it?' Howard said.

'Not a hope. Unless I can kick the mini-bar over.' And Bernie

454

stretched his aching legs out as far as he could, feet flailing in their bindings.

'And have you spoken to Don?' Howard said, as behind him his brother twisted and yanked and thudded. 'Does he know about these photographs? What's his story?'

'Wait . . . Howard . . .' Bernie puffed, red faced. He was kicking out at the mini-bar, causing it to thud and rock. A tray of glasses on the top began to jog towards the edge with every kick.

'I told . . . Don . . . everything,' Bernie said. 'He said he . . . knows nothing about . . . the comics . . . in London.' Bernie kicked and thudded. 'Here we go . . . almost . . . there . . .'

The tray tipped over and crashed to the carpet. Bernie continued to kick, the phone beginning the same slow path across the top.

'So who killed these comics?' Howard said.

'Medford,' Bernie puffed. 'While Don was partying next door. But either way . . . fuck it, either way . . . all the tapes and . . . photographs pin . . . it . . . on . . . shiiiit!'

There was an almighty crash as the mini-bar toppled over, the door flying open and glasses and bottles shattering, spilling out in a deafening explosion of wood and glass that shook the room.

Howard and Bernie sat, hearts lurching as the din subsided.

'Well, that oughtta bring someone running,' Howard said.

'We're on the eighth floor,' Bernie sighed. 'No one's going to hear a thing.'

'Can you reach the phone?'

As the mini bar had toppled, naturally everything on the top had been sent spinning across the carpet. The phone, however, being attached to the wall by a wire, hadn't been allowed to fall too far. The handset had gone tumbling across the carpet, but the main body was three feet away.

'Feeling limber?' Bernie said over his shoulder.

'Not since I was twenty-one. What you got in mind?'

Bernie knew the body of the phone was out of the reach of his hands, tied as they were. But if he could roll on to his side, his face would be about level with the buttons.

With a great puffing and wincing, the two old men, still back to back, began to lower themselves inch by inch, down on to one side towards the phone. Their creaking hips and thighs and spines roared in complaint.

'You said . . . Don's making the show?' Howard groaned. They had moved about six inches. 'Are you kidding me? Ow, Jesus, my hip!'

'Recording tonight. S-Seven o'clock,' Bernie puffed, face crimson and wet. 'Then we take it to Garland for Monday in exchange . . . in exchange for the evidence. Unless . . .'

Inch by inch they struggled until, just under halfway down, gravity took over. They both gave a *Woahhh!* like they'd tipped over the brow of a roller-coaster and rolled over, thudding on to the carpet.

They lay there for a moment, sweating and puffing. Bernie looked up in the hot silence. His face was an aching three or so inches from the buttons.

'Unless?' Howard gasped.

'Lean your head back, Howie,' Bernie said. 'As far as it'll go.'

'Unless *what?*' he said.

'Well . . .' Bernie said, craning his own head forward towards the telephone. 'I had an idea. I . . . a little further . . . I sent some guys down to talk to Garland. Y'know, threaten him?'

'Guys? What *guys?* We talking *muscle?*'

'Erm,' Bernie said, 'kind of. Look, Howie, I'm almost there. Move your head a little so I can reach the keys with my nose.'

Howard duly cricked his neck back, allowing Bernie to position his nose an inch nearer the numbers.

'Errrrm?' Bernie said

'What?' Howard spat.

'Erm, what's the front desk? One? Or nine? Or hash star or something?'

'How the hell should I know? Just hit any number.'

'Yeah, but I don't want to get some Filippino in house-keeping.'

'Nine. Try nine,' Howard said. 'Quickly! Corillo could be halfway to the studio with a crate of TNT.'

Bernie took a desperate lunge forward, almost breaking Howard's neck, and slammed his nose down on the keypad.

'Ow! Jesus!'

'Well?' Howard said.

Bernie lay still, his face throbbing, and tried to make out the faint mumble coming from the handset lying two feet away on the thick carpet.

'*Welcome to the Regent Beverly Wilshire automated Room Service line. Please have your menu open and type in the number of the meal you wish to order.*'

'Shit!' Bernie yelled. 'I don't want to order a meal! Shit! Somebody!' he yelled, but the phone continued to burble its yummy list of lunchtime platters.

'Well, whatever you order, they're going to have to bring up, right? So hit anything,' Howard said.

Bernie lurched to hit another button.

'*Thank you. You have ordered item six-five-six. Lobster. Please allow one and a half hours for this item. Please hang up the phone. Please hang up the phone. Please hang up the phone . . .*'

'Why? What do you think will happen? This great sea of traffic will miraculously just part, and we'll drive through the middle with ease? What do you think we're driving here? The *Fiat Moses?*'

'Okay, okay, that's good,' Rob interrupted, 'hold it there.'

The cast and crew all dropped scripts to the table and stretched and groaned. It was two o'clock and they were in the second full read through. Curtain up in five and a half hours. Cameramen were scribbling shot numbers over their scripts, costumers pencilling details and ideas.

'Melvin,' Rob said, pushing his *E.R. E.R. . . . Oh!* baseball cap out of his eyes. 'That line there, the Moses line. Can you punch that up for us?'

'P-Punch?'

'Give us something else to play with? Just so we can pencil in another option if it doesn't get, y'know, if it doesn't get a big *crack* there.'

Melvin blinked nervously behind his lenses, eyes darting.

'But . . . b-but that's the joke. M-my joke.'

'Sure, sure.' Rob smiled. 'But y'know, that gag's got a six-line feed. It maybe needs a bigger payoff? Something we can try in the second take?'

The table went quiet again. Nobody moved.

'No,' Melvin said flatly. 'No, the script is written. It's funny. It's d-done.'

Rob bit his lip, slid back his chair and got up, squeaking around to Melvin.

'Okay, everyone, uhmm, take five here,' he said. Around the table, chairs were scraped back and everyone hauled themselves up to stretch legs and refill coffees.

At the other end of the table, an anxious Zak cast a nervous look about the studio and kicked his co-star under the table.

'*Vinnie,*' he hissed under his breath. '*Vinnie. Pssst!*'

'What?' Vinnie said, looking quickly over each fat shoulder.

'Relax, man,' Zak whispered. 'Like, act cool. I need your help, dude.'

'What? What youse sayin'?' Vinnie asked, leaning closer.

'I can't . . . like, I can't say much here, man,' Zak said softly, bringing his script up to his mouth. 'But you gotta trust me. Melvin's like, a psycho.'

Vinnie just stared back at him.

'He's crazy, man,' Zak pressed. 'He's a killer. There's some seriously fucked-up shit goin' down, dude, and, like, it looks like it's down to us to stop it. There were a few of us. We had a plan, but I dunno what's goin' on, man . . .'

Vinnie shook his head.

'We gotta do the show,' he said softly.

'Dude!' Zak hissed. What was wrong with him?

'No. Dis is my big chance. I can't let my father down. Da show stays just as it is.'

'But it ain't safe, dude! Melvin's like some—'

'As it is,' Vinnie repeated sternly, and sat back in his chair with a creak.

'Every line!' Melvin yelled suddenly, making everybody jump and turn. 'No! The script is *f-finished!*'

Rob stumbled back a step, shielding himself with his buckled script.

'Relax! Relax, Mellykin, not *every line*, sweetheart,' he said. 'What we've got here,' and he clenched the script, 'is a *work in progress*, right? You with me? How it looks on the page is one thing, but when we get it on its feet, when we have three hundred people out there,' and he motioned to the bank of empty seats, 'it becomes an *organic form*. I like to have alternatives to hand.'

Melvin began to breathe fast, blinking quickly, panicky, the script folding and curling in his white knuckles.

'*Alternatives, alternatives . . .*'

'Mel, darling, relax,' Rob soothed. 'Okay. Okay, everybody,' he called, clapping his hands. 'Let's pick it up and rattle through. Then we'll try it on its feet.'

As everyone settled back into their seats, Zak stared at Melvin from behind his script, watching his eyes flashing with something. Fear? Anger?

Something.

'Where are you taking me?' Jackie said as calmly as she could.

'Just relax, Miss Heaney,' Lambert told her. 'We'll be at the airfield in a half-hour.'

'*Airfield?*' Jackie said, wide-eyed.

'Horrible place, LA. Don'tcha think?' Corillo interrupted idly, sipping his drink and watching the warm Los Angeles streets whip past the tinted glass. 'The weather's fine and they keep the streets clean and everyone smiles the whole damn' time but, I dunno,' and he shook his head, 'I don't like it.'

Jackie looked over at the pair of them, sitting back in the pampering leather cushions of the limousine, fat crystal tumblers of something expensive in their hands. Her eyes flicked nervously over the shiny mahogany trim of the car. The velour floor, drinks cabinet, strip lights . . . and she found herself momentarily elsewhere. Six thousand miles away, sipping white wine in her poky lounge and tapping out a little article about hen nights and blokes with a sense of humour.

It seemed a long time ago.

'Warm and sunny. Every day, warm and sunny. Beaches, malls, warm and sunny. It ain't good for a person, Miss Heaney. Breeds a certain type of brattiness. Human beings need conflict, they need trouble, difficulty, stress.' He sipped his drink. 'Builds *character*.'

'Wh-where are we—'

'Mexico,' Lambert said flatly. 'Just for a few days.'

'Me-Mexico?' Jackie stammered, winded. *No.* This couldn't *be.* 'Mr Corillo, please, you have to listen to me, *please*.'

Lambert sipped his drink, Corillo just kept staring out of the window, the flat streets flipping by.

Jackie's mind pounded with panic. She needed to get to the studio. Ben was in terrible danger. Melvin probably had him tied up with a gun to his head at that very moment. She needed to get to him. To help him. She couldn't let this hoodlum, whoever he was, drag her all the way to—'

'I mean, look at the Silver kid,' Corillo continued. 'Everything the sonofabitch could have wished for. Education, looks, money, big-shot TV job.'

Abruptly, Jackie was slapped hard in the face.

Stunned, she blinked hard and shook herself. The two men hadn't moved. Corillo jabbered on.

She blinked again.

The slap was her memory returning, finally arriving at the forefront of Jackie's mind like the cavalry at the brow of the hill.

Corillo. TV. *Of course!*

'Now stick a guy like that in New York or Chicago,' he whittered on to himself. 'Rain, traffic, noise. Kid might not have turned out to be the complete waste of space that he is. But, Jesus, spoon-feed someone like that sunshine and Martinis every day for ten years and you see what he becomes?' Corillo shook his head. '*Ringing For Ewe?* I mean, Jesus.'

'*Mexico!*' Jackie blurted suddenly. She had an idea. Or half an idea, anyway. Ish.

'For a few days,' Lambert said. 'You'll be perfectly—'

'No I *understand*, it's fine. You have to hide out. You can't be seen. After the embarrassment, the humiliation, sure, sure, I understand, say no more.'

Corillo looked at her through narrowed eyes.

'Th-the documentary, I-I mean?' Jackie explained innocently, heart thumping. 'Diane Paretsky stitching you up? Conning you, making you look like some . . . I dunno, some pervy old letch in front the whole country?'

He breathed deeply.

'I'm surprised you haven't tried to kill her since you're in town a-and everything. After she told the world about your h-habits,' Jackie pushed on, frantically trying to recall Diane's talk of her last show. 'The costumes . . . the *nappies*, was it?'

'*Lambert*,' Corillo growled under his breath.

'Sir, we can't, the cops—'

'Hell,' Jackie continued, 'if someone outsmarted *me* like that—'

'Out*smarted?*'

'Then Mexico is pretty much where *I'd* want to hide my

461

face.' Jackie smiled sympathetically. 'Yep. I'd sit in a dusty cantina drinking warm beer for the rest of my life, absolutely. I mean, what's the alternative? Waste half an hour looking for her at, say, oh, I dunno, Mercury Pictures? Which, hey, is where *I'd* be if I were her. No, I think you're doing the right thing.'

'*Lambert?*'

'Sir, we haven't time. The plane leaves—'

'Outsmarted? That what they're saying? Turn this car around.'

'But—'

'*Now.*'

'Gill, sweetheart? Another courier for you.'

'*Shit!*' he cursed under his breath. Didn't Al realise Elaine was home? These constant gifts were getting more and more difficult to explain. 'Just m-more fans, I expect, darling. Forward these to one of your charities or something.'

Gill was in his sumptuous Art Deco bedroom, wrapped in a fluffy towel, picking suits from his mahogany wardrobe, looking for a tie and shirt combo that said both 'passionate-artistic-soul' and 'innocent-tortured-victim' while not ruling out 'quality-light-entertainer-available-for-immediate-work'.

'It's not flowers, hon,' Elaine said, tottering in. 'It's marked urgent, for your attention?'

Gill took the envelope from her.

'Can you bring me my juice mix?' he said, peering over it. Elaine tottered out.

There was no return address. Just his name and URGENT written in marker pen. He flipped it over.

Best of luck with your interview tonight, read a scrawled message.

Gill lifted the lip and shook out the contents. A thick wad of paper came tumbling out, splashing over the bed. What on earth was all this?

He snatched up a sheet at random and began to read.

*

Ben opened his eyes.

A ceiling fan he had absolutely no recollection of fitting thumped slowly above him.

It was warm. It was quiet.

He closed his eyes again.

Sometime later, he opened his eyes once more. The ceiling fan continued to whirl softly. Nothing else moved.

He shifted his right arm a little. An itchy quilt he had absolutely no recollection of buying rubbed against his bare elbow. He shifted his head against his surprising lack-of-pillow.

The same. Hard and stiff, like office carpet.

Office carpet.

His head pounded. He blinked, which didn't help. He reached up slowly and touched his forehead.

Yowzers!

Pain stabbed him sharply between the eyes. His fingers shone with coppery blood.

Shone. Shining. Sun.

He blinked.

Sunlight he definitely had absolutely no recollection of even being available to order in England was pouring through the blinds. He moved his leg.

Ahhh, yes.

It was all coming back to him now.

'H-Hello?' he squeaked, weakly.

Nothing.

'I'd, uhmm, like to complain about this studio tour.' He licked his dry lips and tried to steady his breathing. 'I have it on good authority that at Universal you get to see the house from *Psycho* and the shark from *Jaws*?'

The room remained quiet and still.

'Frankly, the Mercury getting-dumped-in-a-car-and-shot-at experience just doesn't compete. I mean, where's your gift shop?'

Quiet and still.

Ben slowly began to panic.

Slowly began to move.

Slowly, gradually, the pain dancing about between his head and his thigh, having much more fun than he was.

And then quickly, at the sound of a door slamming.

He blinked fast, heart thudding.

Must get up. Must get out. He hauled himself up on to his elbows, wincing, and peered down woozily at the remains of his leg.

Crivens.

His thigh was a black mess, khakis splattered and caked in blood.

The door of the office cracked open.

'Awake, I see?' Melvin said.

Ben looked at him.

He was in large sunglasses and carrying clothes in clear plastic bags, as if he'd just popped in on the way back from the dry-cleaner's. He laid the bags on the desk and approached Ben, peering expressionlessly at his leg.

'What's . . . what's happening?' Ben croaked tremulously, Melvin towering over him. 'Did . . . did they like the script? Are you done? Can I . . . can I *go? Please?*'

'*My* script?' Melvin said. 'It went down v-very well. Mostly.'

'*Mostly?*'

Oh, that wasn't good.

Ben let his head fall back with a thud. There was a soft rustle of plastic.

'But I need you . . .'

Ben almost laughed.

'Like this?' he said, gesturing at the sticky mess on the carpet.

'You'll m-manage. It's just across the lot.'

There was more rustling.

'And don't worry about how you look. I've g-got something to help you blend in,' Melvin said. 'See?'

Ben raised his throbbing head slowly and peered at the costume on the hanger.

'Right. Great,' he said. His head thudded back on to the floor. 'C'mon.' Melvin smiled his dead-tooth smile. 'Upsy-daisy.'

Ten minutes later, the door of the production bungalow cracked open and a figure who looked a little like Ben stumbled, wincing, down the steps into the sunshine of the busy lot, his little black shoes clicking, buckles winking in the sunshine.

About him, golf carts hummed and zipped past, paying him no attention. Crowds of actors in similar seventeenth century garb bustled about, laughing and shouting in sunglasses and pantaloons, clenching buckled *Fyre* scripts and coffee cups. The air banged and clattered with carpentry and the smell of warm timber.

'Straight on towards the s-studios,' Melvin whispered behind him, closing the door and pushing him forward with the hard muzzle of the gun.

The *Fyre* costume was exactly three sizes too small and about five hundred rediculitres units too ridiculous. The buckled shoes pinched Ben's feet. The white polyester hose prickled and itched his thin calves. The heavy black fabric of his knee-length breeches did its best to disguise his leg wound while underneath his brass-buttoned doublet, complete with white cuffs and collar, he was pouring with sweat.

Melvin had tried pulling down the tall, buckled Puritan hat over Ben's purple bruise but, being far too small, it just sat tight and high on the top of his head like a flowerpot.

A white golf cart buzzed past them, carrying four men dressed identically to him, each chattering away on mobile phones.

'Follow the signs. Studio five,' Melvin hissed.

So, wincing and mincing in his tight little outfit, Ben made his way gradually through the bustling lanes towards the *Carpool* studio.

Staff called out to Melvin cheerily as they went, wishing him luck for the show. Actors and stuntmen in their buckled shoes and tunics nodded at Ben, smiling. All the talk in the shady lanes was of *Fyre* and *Carpool*, of scripts and schedules, of costumes and casting.

Ben's heart thundered.

His leg screamed.

He kept walking.

'Here,' Melvin said finally.

They had reached the towering pink hulk of studio 5. Up the iron staircase and ducking into the cool darkness, they moved behind the tiered audience seating, past the scaffolding and through a door into the backstage area.

Nobody paid them much attention as Melvin pushed and shoved Ben down a peach-painted corridor lined with cast photographs and rubber plants.

'Just sh-showing him to the *Fyre* set,' Melvin said loudly as they pasted production staff hurrying up and down the corridor.

'In here,' he said, and pushed Ben into a small dressing room, softly furnished with mirrors and pink overstuffed sofas.

'Keep g-going.'

Ben, panic rising through him from the buckles on his shoes to the buckle on his hat, clicked into a spotless bathroom. Tiles gleamed and shone, mirrors reflecting the ceiling spotlights.

'Please,' he squeaked finally, the word fat in his throat, thoughts raging. 'Please, Melvin, whatever you're thinking of doing—'

'Kneel down,' he said. 'There. B-By the toilet.'

Ben did so, sucking in breath and yowling, grabbing the towel rails as his leg screamed at him.

'Cuff yourself,' Melvin said, tossing some prop department handcuffs to the tiles with a clatter.

'Look . . . ow, look,' Ben winced, fussing with the cold steel and the porcelain and his elaborate lace cuffs. 'Melvin. Can I call you that?'

Melvin looked down at him, kneeling and cuffed in his little outfit, blinking up feebly from the wet floor.

'Melvin . . . *Mel.*' Ben risked gingerly. 'This isn't going to work. My girlfriend? Jackie? She was at the hotel. She was expecting me. She'll find the flyer you left behind. She'll be on her way over. She'll bring the police . . .'

'Bob's going to ask me for new lines,' Melvin said, Ben's word's glancing off him harmlessly. 'I'll excuse myself, c-come back here, and you give me the joke. Understand?'

'*What?*' Ben said, a hollow feeling spreading about his insides. 'No, listen, Jackie—'

Melvin raised the gun and pressed the cold muzzle to Ben's forehead.

'I ask for a new joke, you give me a new joke,' he said. That dead-toothed smile flickered across his face and died like a candle in a storm. 'I'll be back in a while,' he said, stepping away towards the door, the gun shaking in his hand.

'Melvin, I know all about you,' Ben said suddenly. Desperately. 'About your childhood. About your family. I read some stuff.'

He said nothing.

'I . . . I *understand.* Really.'

He looked at Ben for what felt like an age.

'You *understand?*' he said softly. 'I don't want you to understand,' he said finally, his voice wavering. 'I want you to *laugh.*'

And he left, locking the bathroom door with a sickening *click.*

Half an hour later, a white *KBL NEWS* van could be seen lurching out of the busy afternoon traffic on Pico Boulevard and attempting a wide U-turn to a glorious fanfare of angry horns and yelling.

'Here you go,' the driver shouted, bumping on to the pavement and slamming on the brakes, sending pedestrians scattering like pigeons.

In the back, clattering and thudding among the equipment,

Diane Paretsky grabbed up her bag and threw herself on to the sunny street with an excitable, '*C'mon, let's move!*'

Two young men, one with a hefty camera on his shoulder, the other with a furry microphone on a pole, both in requisite faded denim and goatees, stumbled out of the back doors after her.

'We can't . . . can we?' the cameraman said, peering up at the building. '*Here?*'

'Move!' Diane yelled, halfway up the stone steps, tugging sunglasses from her hair and buttoning her jacket quickly.

The inside of the police station was pretty much as expected. Stained, peeling linoleum covered the floor half-heartedly, the smell of disinfectant hung about like it had nowhere better to be — much like the petty thieves, the homeless, the drunks and the addicts who littered the place. A constant loud clatter and chatter echoed through the high-ceilinged hall — the shuffle and slam of typewriters and desk stamps.

'Excuse me, officer?' Diane said loudly over the din, elbowing through to the raised front desk. 'Officer, my name is Diane Paretsky, producer of *Sexposé*. I need to talk to the most senior guy in the building and I need to talk to him right now.'

'You're going to have to wait, miss,' the squat officer behind the desk said, waving her away. 'Everyone's in the incident room.' Phones rang and rang throughout the hall. 'We got everyone from Northridge to Newport Beach callin' in, tellin' us they seen Frankie Corillo workin' at their local Denny's. We ain't got time for members of the public to—'

'Okay!' she yelled, spinning on her heel. 'Bring her in, boys, bring her in!'

The two-man news team clattered through the doors, the boom mic hoisted high.

'Okay, on me in three, two, one . . .'

'Hey!' the squat officer yelled. 'Hey, you can't bring that in—'

'*It was here,*' Diane said to the camera, gesturing to the bustling precinct, '*that the LAPD claimed to be quote – "too busy" – unquote, to assist in what will surely come to be known as one of the most shocking stories to come out of Hollywood in recent years. Doughnut-scoffing clock-watchers such as the officer seen here behind me chose to ignore the plight of—*'

'Okay, okay, that's enough!' he said, appearing at Diane's side, arms flapping, brushing greasy sugar from his tie. 'Shut that thing off, pal. You got thirty seconds. What the hell do you want, lady?'

Diane was scribbling a note quickly.

'You got a TV in this place,' she said, not looking up.

'A TV? Sure, down in the canteen. What—'

'Then listen to me. Whatever you're doing, I want you, your chief and your best men watching KBL tonight, seven o'clock, you got me?'

'KBL?'

'*KBL. Tonight. Seven o'clock.*' And she handed him the details on the note. 'Load your weapons, start your engines, polish your caps and . . . I dunno . . . get some celebratory doughnuts on the stove or sumthin'. This is a one-shot deal and you're gonna have to move fast. Tonight. KBL. Seven o'clock. You're gonna want to see this. C'mon, fellas.' And she began to bustle her crew back out on to the street.

'Hey, look, lady,' the officer called after her, waving the note. 'I dunno who you are or who the hell you think you're dealin' with here,' and he pushed through the doors on to the sunny steps, 'but we don't take orders off dames in the street, cameras or not, y'understand me? We got a major mob boss out there somewhere, who none other than Robert De fuckin' *Niro* called "*a perverted bloodlusty sociopath*". So with respect, little miss nobody, we'd prefer to take our orders from—'

'Oh, you won't have to take *my* word for it, Officer . . .' and Diane peered at the fat man's badge '. . . *Muldoon.* Just be watchin'. Tonight at seven. Let's go.' And she and the crew left

Muldoon standing alone on the precinct steps, squinting after them as they piled into the van, the note fluttering in his fat fingers.

In make-up room number 1 of the KBL studios, a young girl was busy with Dr Dick Trent's hair. Washed and blow-dried, she was brushing it backwards from the temples, causing it to puff up and shine beautifully in its trademark sheen. She snapped the top from the huge can of lacquer and began to hiss a fine film of hairspray all over it from above, acrid clouds stinging the air of the small room. She bent down and examined the front view in the large illuminated mirror.

Perfect, as ever.

There was a sharp knock on the door. She checked her watch. Three o'clock. She opened the door.

'Ready?' Dr Trent said, peeking out sheepishly from beneath his Lakers baseball cap. The girl nodded and he scuttled in, shutting the door behind him. He settled into the chair and whipped off his cap, the gleaming pink dome shining beneath like the hood of a freshly waxed VW Beetle. The girl began carefully to lift the toupe from its stand when there was another sharp rap on the door.

'Oh! Er, uhm, one moment, one moment!' Dick flustered, and quickly tugged on the wig, pulling it straight. The make-up girl snatched up the brush and began to finish off the finer edges. 'Er, enter!' he called with a nervous fidget.

The door opened and a young production assistant squeezed in, a clip-board pressed against her chest.

'Jasmine dear,' Dick said, 'how's everything going?'

'Dr Trent,' she said excitedly, 'we need you upstairs. Something's come up. Big.'

'With the show?' he said, his eyes never leaving his reflection, checking his chin, smoothing his beard. God he was a handsome fellow. He peeled back his top lip and gave his gleaming teeth a lick. 'Shit, Mercury haven't taken Kramer *back*, have they? Dammit! The whole point of the interview is that his career's over.'

'It's not Mercury.'

'Elaine then?' And Dick fumbled for the wad of pink 5×3″ index cards in his top pocket. 'Don't tell me her ratings are up? God, the whole *angle* is that we surprise them both with the *Couple Of The Year* award but it's tinged with regret and despair as they realise, right there in front of the nation, that the party is *over*.'

The assistant snatched the wad of questions and tore them in two, tossing the pink tatters so they rained down among the sprays and mousses and discreet adhesives on the dressing table.

'Jasmine! I hope you have a very good reason for—'

'Upstairs in five Dr Trent, if you would.' She grinned. 'You're not going to believe what we've got.'

THIRTY-SIX

One hour later early evening oozed over Los Angeles.

On the Mercury lot, in his little pink booth, Mickey peered into his tiny mirror like a fat budgie, adjusted his clip-on polyester tie, hoisted up his polyester trousers and, with a lick of his lips and a check of his watch, picked up his clip-board and waddled out into the fresh air.

It was five 5.30. A cool dry breeze played through the palm trees which bowed and rustled gently. It was a lovely calm evening.

Always a special time for Mickey.

Showtime.

'Good evening, ladies,' he said to the women in the first car idling at the gate. *Carpool,* is it?' And took their flyers and checked off the numbers with a polite nod. 'Thank you. Follow the signs, audience parking on your left here, then it's studio five which is round to the right. Enjoy the show.' Mickey ticked his clip-board and beckoned the next car forward. 'Good evening, sir, your flyer, please? . . . *Carpool,* thank you. Follow the signs. . .'

As one by one, carload by carload, the public began to arrive, the lot began to crackle and bubble with excitement. Car doors slammed, hands were rubbed together and groups of friends 'ooohed' and 'ahhh-ed' and pointed and craned as they scuttled through the lanes of a real live television studio. Everyone was

in a good mood, nobody letting the magic be spoiled by the fact that from the outside, Mercury Pictures, like all television studios, resembled little more than an ugly industrial estate. *Look!* There was a little golf cart buzzing past. *Look!* There was a forklift carrying a palette of props and technical whatnots. *And there!* People with coffee!

As the public were steered into queues by more men with polyester machine-washable radios, inside studio 5, the place was alive with activity and preparation.

On set, two young women snapped Polaroids for continuity, adjusting wing mirrors and windscreen wipers, scurrying back and forth with costumes swathed in plastic. At each of the five wooden lecterns set between the audience and the cameras, producers, assistant producers, line producers and assistant directors flapped with scripts and checklists and bottles of water. Bob, the director, beard especially trimmed and Spielbergian, nodded thoughtfully and paced up and down.

Backstage, in make-up, two girls had Melvin and Vinnie strapped into their chairs, tissues stuffed in their collars, finding new combinations of sprays and powders and creams to slap and pummel into them. Melvin and Vinnie sat in silence, flicking through the scripts in their laps, breathing deeply.

There was ninety minutes to go.

A costume assistant poked her perky blonde head around the door.

'Mr Medford?' she sang. 'I have your jacket.' And she rustled her plastic bag. 'I tried to leave it in your dressing room but it's locked?'

'Just, uhmm, just h-hang it on the handle,' Melvin said and the woman disappeared again.

He reached under his script and felt for his dressing-room key in his pocket.

'Do either of you know where Zachary is?' Melvin's make-up girl mumbled, her mouth full of hair grips. 'Time's getting on.'

'Haven't seen him.' Melvin shrugged.

'Maybe on the studio floor? I thought I saw him wid Mr Silver,' Vinnie suggested.

'Look, Zak kid, shut the fuck up, okay? I don't have time for this shit.'

'But, Mr Silver, sir—'

'The curtain goes up in an hour and a half and the show goes ahead as planned. I don't care what the hell you think you know or don't know, you hear me?'

Don was in his shirt-sleeves, a bottle of Pepto Bismol in one hand, a palmful of sedatives in the other, and he really didn't have time for this. There was no word from Uncle Bernie yet about the *Woodfellas* guys in Nashville. No clue whether or not they had tracked down Randy and wrestled the evidence from him. Plus, apparently, his father was no longer in hospital but nobody could quite pin down exactly *why*.

All Don knew was that the show had to go on.

'But, Mr Silver, sir . . . please, man, you gotta listen!'

Zak had dragged Don off the floor of the studio and under the scaffolding beneath the audience seating. Footsteps clanged and thudded above them as the public shuffled in one by one, muted voices laughing and calling.

'No, *you* listen. For reasons far too complicated to go into now,' and Don closed his eyes in concentration, 'this pilot, your pilot, *Carpool*, has to be shot and in the can by tonight. Otherwise it's possible I'm going to jail for a very long time.'

'Mr *Silver*—'

'And I'd rather not, y'understand me? I'd rather not. I like fresh air, I like cocktails, I like parties, I like girls. And as much as I like sex in the shower, I like being the one who decides whether or not I'm gonna have it. So I need your ass back out there in make-up right—'

'Oh, you *NEED?!*' Zak shouted, his voice echoing about the cold metal. 'You *need?* Man, like Melvin *needed* Angus Fisher?

And like, *needed* Malachy Flynn and Jasper Philips, right?'

Don's face slowly began to drain from its usual over-ripe Satsuma tan to a more stunned but equally carcinogenic burnt umber. Quivering, he grabbed at some cold scaffolding to stop himself dropping to his knees.

'Wh-what? Where did you hear those names?'

'Same place the world is gonna hear 'em any day now. You know the *Sexposé* shows?'

Involuntarily, Don began to shake.

'You've had Diane Paretsky on your tail all week. She's cuttin' it together like, as we speak, man. *Sex-Crazed Silver In Multiple Margrave Murder Conspiracy Cover-up*. She's got it all. You, your father, your uncle, Melvin, Randy. She's gonna blow the whole story, man. KBL primetime — "*Mercury: SLIPPERY, SILVER and HOT*".'

Don continued shaking, the seating above beginning to rattle disconcertingly. This couldn't *be*? Everybody *knew*? It was *out there*?

'B-but I'm *innocent!*' he vibrated. 'I-I didn't *do* anything!'

'Oh, she knows, she knows. That's why you got an opportunity to clear your name.'

'*Cl-clear*? Where? When? I'm there, I'm there!'

'Eight hours ago,' Zak said. 'The girl at the hotel? With the camera?'

'Ohhh, *fuck*.' Don began to pace and fluster, realisation flooding his mind. '*Sexposé*? Ohh, that's it, I'm going to jail. I'm going to jail . . .'

'We gotta call the cops, Mr Silver. We gotta stop the show.'

' "SLIPPERY, SILVER and HOT"? Oh, that's clever. Dammit, that's clever. Shit, I'm going to jail.'

'Mr Silver!?' Zak barked, attempting to snap him from his daze. 'It'll show you're innocent, it'll look good. "*The moment I found out the truth, your honour, I called a halt to the whole thing.*" Y'know, when you're up on the stand?'

'On the *stand*?' Don quavered, grabbing Zak's arms. 'I can't go on a stand. I can't. Dad . . . the business, I . . . I . . . No n-no way . . .'

'Mr Silver, we have to stop——'

'*No!*' he said, trying to focus his spinning mind. 'No, we can't. We stop the show, Melvin'll smell a rat and fuck knows what he's liable to do then. The kid's nuts.'

'I know.'

'You *know?*'

'I've seen like, reports. Some investigators? They've been tailin' you all for months.'

'Jesus. *Trixi!*' Don yelled like Fred Flintstone, pacing and fussing with his Pepto Bismol, glugging and splashing it down his neck. '*It'll be all right, it'll be all right,*' he muttered.

'Mr Silver?' she said, appearing through the tarpaulin, phones tucked strategically. 'Still no word from your uncle.'

'Nashville?'

'Nothing.'

'Shit. Look, I gotta talk to Uncle Bernie before we do *anything*, find out if Randy's out of the way.' And Don took Zak by the shoulders. '*Then* I'll get the cops. You speak to Paretsky, you tell her that, okay? I didn't do anything, I'm innocent, *I* got the cops.'

'Goddit.'

'You . . . you keep everything ticking along here. Don't let anyone suspect anything different. Especially Melvin. The kid's——'

'Nuts. I know.'

'So go, go! Make-up, costume,' and Don steered him out from under the scaffolding. 'Trixi, call the hospital. See if anyone knows where Uncle Bernie is.'

'Sir.'

'*Oh, and what the hell happened to my father!*'

Traffic had begun to back up on Alemeda Avenue as more and more guests arrived for the recording.

Halfway back, purring quietly, a black limousine sat patiently in the queue.

'We here?' Corillo growled.

'Sir, I really must stress, this isn't a good idea,' Lambert slithered over beside him, pouring himself a drink shakily. 'We don't *know* that this Paretsky woman's here. Plus the LAPD, the Feds, everyone's looking for you . . .'

'Nobody's looking for me here,' Corillo said, jaw flexing, teeth grinding a little.

Jackie, folded up on the opposite seat, her blouse pulled closed and skirt tugged down a little, said nothing. She hadn't spoken for about half an hour.

The gangsters saw nothing strange about this, familiar as they were with the solemn resignation with which many met their fate – tied to chairs in bleak warehouses, tied to lumps of granite on darkened docks. They just presumed that Jackie had realised there was no escape, no way out, no gallant knight about to ride in and pluck her out of the sunroof, and that she was quietly awaiting death.

Whereas in fact, staring out of the tinted window across the flat parking lot at the huge pink studio complex, Jackie was quietly awaiting her opportunity to run.

At the gate, Mickey approached a green Lexus which idled quietly. The moustachioed driver had an *Office Politics* cap pulled over his face and was thumbing a tiny cell phone anxiously.

'Good evening sir, *Carpool*, is it?'

'What? Oh, uhmm, y-yes . . .'

'Mr Rosen! Good to see you, sir. Straight on through, you know where you're going.'

'Th-thanks, Mickey,' Al said absently and rolled his car through, thumbing down his telephone messages.

Nothing.

Still no word from Gill about the flowers.

Still no word from Tommy and Sonny at SEBN.

He chewed his lip, parked his car and scurried across to studio 5 anxiously.

Inside, the gathering audience members chatted loudly, calling to each other, swapping seats and pointing at the television screens suspended above them featuring clips from past Mercury sitcoms.

Gill Kramer pulling up outside the familiar hospital doors on a tractor.

A talking sheep in braces, hopping out of a yellow cab on Wall Street.

Three men in snap-brim fedoras pulling axes out of violin cases and swiping away at a thick tree trunk.

The audience nudged and chuckled.

The warm-up man stepped up suddenly and began to try and whip the cold crowd into crazy shrieking banshees. Off stage, heart thundering, Zak watched him pace frantically, introducing the crew one by one, continually asking the audience to give things up like he was a primary school priest during Lent. *Give it up for the director, ladies and gentlemen*, and *Give it up for our producer, ladies and gentlemen*, over and over.

Zak checked his watch.

Don would be back with the police soon. Please, let him be back with the police soon.

Corillo's limousine rolled forward in the queue towards the gate.

Ben had to be in that studio somewhere, that Jackie knew. Melvin surely wouldn't have had time to drag him at gunpoint back to Don's house to beat the last few pages of script from him. He would have had to bring him here. And she was figuring there would be no way Melvin would let Ben out of his sight. Not before the filming began.

She flashed a look at her watch.

'Oh, we've plenty of time, Miss Heaney,' Lambert said, noticing her. 'Doesn't start for nearly an hour.' He motioned at all the cars and the excited queues. 'Looks like quite a turn out.' And he nodded to himself.

'And for your sake,' Corillo pointed a thick, branch-like finger at her, 'this Paretsky woman better be here.'

'Okay, Zak, make-up. C'mon, we're runnin' late here.'

An assistant steered him off the studio floor, down a busy corridor towards the make-up department.

'Melvin? H-Have you seen Melvin?' he asked anxiously.

The limo bumped up the ramp. The driver's window whirred down, a fat face appearing in its place.

'Evenin', sir,' Mickey said. 'Beautiful car, if I may say so. Welcome to Mercury Studios. You here for *Carpool*?'

'Three,' the driver said, throwing a thumb at the back.

'Three,' Mickey smiled, squeezing his fat face through the window. 'You're so far back, almost didn't see ya. You got a ticket for me, please?'

Jackie passed her sweaty flyer forward and Mickey took it. He raised his fat eyebrows.

'Ahhh, *VIP number seven*,' he said. 'I do apologise. I have special instructions for that. One moment.' And he flipped through his clip-board.

'What's goin' on?' Corillo growled quietly. Lambert threw anxious glances about the car.

'Yes, here we go. Number seven. You're a guest of the writer, madam. This way please, this way.' And Mickey stepped up smartly, cracking open the limo door.

'Wait! Wait one second,' Corillo said quickly, but Jackie snatched Mickey's hand and dived out of the car.

'*Grab her!*' Corillo hissed.

Lambert dropped his crystal tumbler, sending it spinning and splashing to the carpeted floor.

'Oh, you dumb – stop her! *Stop her!*'

Corillo's driver unclipped his belt and heaved his fat body out of the car, but Jackie was away, pushing past Mickey and clacking across the warm tarmac as fast as her heels would carry her.

'Miss!' he called. 'Excuse me, *miss?*'

'Jesus, if you want something done . . .' And Corillo clambered over Lambert, attempting to haul himself from the car.

'Sir! Shit, sir, *wait!*' Lambert cried, grabbing his boss inappropriately and tugging him back inside. '*Sir, you're wanted in twelve states. You can't just go running around Burbank waving a gun about!*'

Corillo landed with a 'phlumph' back inside the leather interior, red-faced and puffing.

'You're gonna have to move this vehicle,' Mickey said to the driver, holding up a fat palm as behind the limo horns began to toot and honk impatiently. 'Audience parking to your left, follow the signs for studio five on the right.'

'Sir, we should get going,' Lambert said, mopping the bourbon-soaked floor with his bloodied hanky. 'The plane is waiting.'

'Paretsky *first*,' Corillo snarled, leaning forward and banging on the glass at his driver. 'Find her, and then find Heaney. *Move.*'

'Vinnie, c'mon, you're done, let's get you out of the way.'

He hauled himself from the make-up chair, tugging tissues from his collar, and was pushed and bustled down the busy corridor towards the studio floor. The assistant checked her clipboard.

'Where's Melvin? You seen him? He should be backstage by now . . .'

Breathless and panicky, Jackie moved quickly, past the parking lot towards the towering studios.

'*Ben!*' she hollered, her voice floating away among the palms into the warm Californian evening.

She passed little golf carts, huge flats of painted scenery, silver trailers. Dozens of people milled about the lanes dressed in peasants' costumes, tunics, doublet and hose, smoking cigarettes and flipping cell-phones.

'Ben!' she called again, moving fast from lane to lane between the huge pink studios.

A harried production assistant poked her head around the door of the costume department.

'You seen Melvin anywhere? . . . What? *Make-up?* I've just come from make-up . . .'

'*Ben!*' Jackie shouted.

She had her shoes in her hands, her stockinged feet springing across the tarmac. Past more carts, more vans, a fork-lift truck, private parking spaces. She turned into another dark lane.

'*Ben!*'

'Jackie?' a voice said behind her.

Her heart exploded. She spun around, terror suddenly hauling all the air from her body.

'We need Melvin on set, you haven't seen . . . *costume?* No I've just come from costume.'

The assistant sighed and hurried off down another corridor, calling his name.

Where the hell was he?

Melvin slammed a hand over Jackie's mouth hard before she could scream, pushing her back, stumbling into the shadow of studio 6.

'Good to m-meet you at last,' he said softly, pinning her trembling to the cold steel wall.

She felt something metallic press against her exposed belly and gasped.

There was a *click* beneath her.

'Shall we go?' Melvin said.

'What're you talking about, missing?' Rob flapped from behind his lectern. 'We need him on set. Aww, Jeez, I don't need this. Check his dressing room.'

'I have,' the assistant explained. 'It's locked.'

'Then get a key. C'mon, curtain up in twenty minutes.'

A blast of cold air enveloped Jackie as she was pushed through the fire door into the half-light of the huge hangar. Her feet felt damp and clammy as she was shoved across the cold concrete floor. The air smelled of timber and paint. She could make out shadows and shapes in the gloom.

Pillars. Arches. Pews. Statues. Scaffolding. What looked like a huge stained-glass window, propped up on a steel trolley.

Melvin shoved her forward.

Around her the massive building was in eerie silence. No, not silence. Over the thud of her panicked heartbeat, Jackie could make out two quiet voices. Coming from the other end of the studio, where she could just see spots of dazzling light between the sets and swathes of black fabric.

'*Goddammit, Pepys! I won't let you do it! I don't care how little is left of this damned city, it's too dangerous!*'

'*If you can't stand the heat, Mr Mayor . . .*'

As the voices continued, Melvin guided Jackie further and further into the darkness, stepping over palettes and paint, past fat lights on tripods, between ropes and chains hanging from the grid of gantries high above them.

He eased her through between two wooden flats, picking up a toolbox from the floor and a Polaroid camera from a lectern marked 'Continuity'.

They were on the set of a huge cathedral, a sweeping dome

three stories above them. The air was cold and wooden and dusty, like a DIY warehouse. He moved her up three steps to the altar. Thick, taped-down cables ran all over the polished wooden parquet flooring, plus other cables made up of dozens of thin wires lashed together every five feet snaked up pillars and around pews and lecterns.

Their footsteps echoed softly.

'Keep g-going, back there, all the way back.'

The voices continued.

'I'll see you fry, Pepys.'

'Yeah? Like you did this city, you sonofabitch? My diaries tell it all. All! You've been taking kickbacks off that bakery for years, Mr Mayor . . . .'

Jackie got around the back of the altar, putting her hand out to guide herself in the half-light, only to realise that what looked like crumbling seventeenth-century stone was merely timber, painted and aged.

There was a strong smell of glue. Or something like glue. A powerful, chemical, petrol smell.

Waving the handgun, Melvin bade a petrified Jackie sit and peel her stockings off. He balled one of them up and fed it into her mouth, causing her to retch and gag. He wrapped the second stocking around her head three times, four times, knotting it tight at the front, keeping the first gag in place. Mouth forced open, eyes wide, sniffing and snotty, Jackie was pushed back, neck cricked, inside the hollow altar.

The chemical smell was stronger. It made her head thud. Inside the dark wooden shell she was surrounded by pipes and silver foil and clear bottles of pink liquid taped up and labelled, with dozens of wires running out through the timber floor.

'So, your honour, your Pudding Lane bakery was insured for a pretty penny, I'll wager?'

Melvin grabbed a roll of duct tape and lashed Jackie's pale wrists and ankles together, finally cuffing her to one of the thick scratchy timber supports.

'Ha! A pox on you, quill boy! You can't prove nuthin'. You're a two-bit hack and the King knows it.'

Her head spun and pounded. What was he going to do? What was this crazy fuck going to *do?*

Melvin stepped away and gazed over his handiwork. Then, blinking anxiously, he disappeared, returning a few agonising seconds later with the Polaroid camera.

THIRTY-SEVEN

'I'm just *saying*,' Ed slouched moodily at the back of the bus, licking a thumb and rubbing some dirt from his spats, 'when I was Joey Zasa in *The Godfather Part Three On Ice*, we were given real handguns, that's *all*.'

'Yes, you mentioned it,' Matthew pouted, running a moisturised hand lightly over his neck, peering into a small mirror. 'Y'know, the sooner we do this and get the hell out of Hickville, the better my glands will be. I think I'm having an allergic reaction to Kenny Rogers.'

'Had three days' weapons training. I can't do it without a *real* gun. It's something about that weight.'

Next to him, Alistair was adjusting his fedora.

'Did we decide I was trying the *"can it, toots"*, line? *Can it, toots*,' he repeated with a sneer. '*Nyahhh, can it, toots*.'

'Less Bugs Bunny, sweetheart,' Matthew said, snapping his mirror closed and slipping it into the breast pocket of his zoot-suit.

'Right, right. Uhmm . . . *"So eider youz can hand over da Moicury file to me an da boyz, here"*,' Alistair practised loudly, ' *"or we can take it outta your ass, piece by piece."* '

'And Bernie said if he puts up any resistance, we're to mess the place up a bit. Knock over a chair, crumple up one of his throws, something along those lines. Then we call Bernie and we're back to LA.'

'And you sure it doesn't say we should have guns?' Ed whined. 'On *The Godfather Part Three On Ice*, we had guns.'

'Okay, people, okay,' Matthew said, peering out of the window at the sunny street. 'Nearly there. Focus, focus, focus.' And they all began their preposterous breathing exercises.

'Mi mi mi mi mi mi!'

'HMmmnnnwwooaaarrrrrRRRR!'

'*Moicury, Moicury, Moic* – I do apologise, but is there a problem?'

A fat necked man in a plaid shirt raised a couple of wiry eyebrows at the three men at the back of the bus. He opened his mouth but no words came.

'I don't see that there's anything to stare at,' Alistair said huffily, adjusting his cufflinks.

The bus rolled down the wide busy street, past Nashville's record stores and guitar shops, past the pick-up trucks and station wagons, each one pouring syrupy country music from their radios. A huge amount of gruff-voiced earnest men, it seemed, were 'missin' their gals' and 'wannid 'em back so bay-ud'. Fat tanned elbows hung over the edges of the open windows, baseball caps and Stetsons pushed back on fat, gum chewing heads, engines idling.

'Urgh, this place!' Matthew remarked. 'That music, those clothes! It's no wonder all of country music is about wives leaving their husbands. If they'd just lose the rhinestones, try maybe a simple Gap twill—'

'What y'all doin'? Like some fancy dress kinda thang?' the stranger said, scratching his head beneath its cap. The other people on the bus were all watching the three out-of-towners curiously.

'We are *actors*,' Alistair explained, tightening a loose spat. 'From Hollywood,' he added.

''Sthat right?,' the stranger said, nodding. Other people on the bus exchanged looks. '*Hollywood.*'

The bus rolled to a halt with a squeak.

'Hey!' the driver called through a mouthful of gum. 'Hey, Crapfellas? SEBN's just across the street there.'

The passengers chuckled and watched as the three men flustered down the aisle to the door, piling off the bus on to the busy afternoon street in their enormous padded shoulders.

'Well, it's not as big as I'd thought it'd be,' Alistair said, eyeing the squat SEBN office on the other side of the road through the gaps in the slow rolling traffic. 'Is that his car, there?'

They all looked. Indeed, outside the office, slung at forty-five degrees was Randy's gold Cadillac, just as Bernie had described.

They crossed the busy street, Alistair preparing himself, shrugging his shoulders like Jimmy Cagney. Well, Jimmy Cagney doing a Tommy Cooper impression.

'Okay, people,' he said as they took deep breaths outside the office door. 'Let's make it real. We're real mobsters, we've come real far, and we're reeeeal angry, okay? Now, everybody – break a leg in there. Remember, not too fast. And just bloody enjoy it.'

'Outta the way! Outta the wayyy!'

Braided busboys and be-capped bellhops leaped in all directions as Don's car roared down the wide courtyard next to the Regent Beverly Wilshire. He slammed the brakes into a hot rubber squeal, the car sliding to a crumpled smash against a startled Ferrari and its panicked owner, glass and chrome splashing all over the street in a hiss of steam. Pepto Bismol all over his shirt again, a bottle of Thorazine upended into his lap, Don was out, tossing the keys to a parking valet sprawled in a pile of Louis Vuitton on the warm tarmac. He pushed past into the hotel.

'Mr Silver, sir. Back so soon? We—'

'My uncle,' he shouted at Bobby behind the front desk. 'The hospital booked him a cab, said it was bringing him here. That right, you seen him? Bernie Silver? Moustache, worried-looking?'

'A *Bernard Silver*, you say, sir? One moment, sir.' And with geological briskness, Bobby glided his hands over to the keyboard and began tapping in the name gently.

Don gritted his teeth in frustration. Come on, come *on*! He had no time for this graceful servility. He had to get to the police, but not before he'd talked to his Uncle Bernie. Had he heard from the actors in Nashville? Were they in the clear with Randy?

Bobby tapped away slowly, humming a Cole Porter tune to himself.

'Ah, apparently your uncle did arrive, as a guest of a Mr Lambert.'

'*Lambert?*'

'He left with some other gentlemen, but your uncle is still here as far as we know. Room eight-thirteen. Would you like me to call up to—'

But Don was gone, sprinting across the lobby. He leaped into the lift as the doors were rolling shut.

'Help you, gennelmen?' Mary Jane said perkily as Ed, Alistair and Matthew rolled into the small reception area. Garth Brooks was being sincere and heartfelt from the ceiling speakers.

'Nyahh. Hey, doll-face,' Matthew said, 'we's here's to seez Randy Garlands.'

'I see. Well, I'm afraid he's . . . uhmm . . .' And Mary Jane looked dubiously at the three men. Legs apart, shoulders back, violin cases under their arms. 'He's, er, not here.'

'*Nyahhh, can it, toots*,' Ed said.

'Heyyy!' Alistair scowled, jabbing him in the ribs.

'Not here, eh? Dat seems very *convenient*, right, boyz?' Matthew said.

'What is this?' Mary Jane said. 'Like a Ganstergram or something? Do you sing?'

'Well, *I've* done a little dinner theatre,' Alistair said, forgetting himself for a moment. 'But . . . oh, uhmm, can it, toots.'

'We ain't here's to be messed around, none, sweet-cheeks,' Ed said. Reaching into his belt, he pulled out a nickel-plated snub-nosed revolver, weighing it loosely in his hand.

Alistair and Matthew glared at it. Then at Ed.

Suddenly there was a sound from behind the reception desk. Ed jumped, startled, and let out a round from his gun, the flat flash-bang shaking the building, the gurgling water cooler exploding in a splash all over the room.

'Jesus Christ!' Matthew shrieked.

'Shit! Uhmm, sorry,' Ed said, water lapping about their ankles, dripping from the furniture. 'I guess da goirgle made me jumpsy a little.'

'He's not here!' Mary Jane whimpered.

But then from behind the office door came the sound of a scuffle and the slam of a desk drawer.

'Oh, really?' Ed said, pushing past the other two and moving to the door.

'*Where the hell did you get that gun!*' Matthew hissed, pulling at his sleeve.

'Shhhh,' Ed said, listening at the office door. There was definitely someone inside making a very bad job of moving around quietly. 'Off a guy in the bar at the hotel. I told you I needed one. Now, back up.' And he pushed Matthew and Alistair away.

Gun loose in his hand, taking deep breaths and muttering, 'Eastwood, think Eastwood', eyes narrowing a little, Ed stepped back and kicked Randy's office door open.

'*Garland!*' he yelled, thrusting the gun out in front of him.

'*Garland!*' Tommy yelled back at him, leaping up from behind Randy's desk and letting off a loud round, sending the doorframe splintering.

Matthew and Alistair screamed.

Ed fired, involuntarily, hitting a very confused Tommy in the chest, sending him spinning backwards into the chair.

'*Sonofabitch!* Al, it's a *set-up!*' Sonny yelled into a cell-phone, pushing aside the suede-covered filing cabinet he was crouched behind and letting rip with a stubby sub-machine gun.

The tiny office exploded in a long hot roar of flying lead and flat bangs and splintering plaster.

In the Regent Beverly Wilshire, the arrow in the lift touched eight and the doors rolled open.

'Why, Dawnald!' a grinning man cried in the hallway. 'What brings you here?'

Randy Garland stood beaming by the lift. He had on a crisp white Stetson and a white suit, a sequined star on each lapel. He smoothed his moustache and pumped Don's hand.

'Randy Garland, Randy Garland. Good to see ya, kid. Ah'm an old friend of yur father's.'

'Mr . . . Mr *Garland?*' Don said, stepping dizzily out into the hall. 'What are y-you . . . ?'

'Well,' Randy said softly, 'as you may know, yur li'l show is bein' handed over to me for mah li'l station down in Nashville. Ah whuz gonna wait down there for it to be sent over, but ah thought, hell, why not come out west and see how it's getting' along? Ah whuz just gonna head over to Mercury now. You fancy joinin' me?'

Tammy Wynette warbled mournfully about 'standing by her man' as a trembling Mary Jane emerged from behind the reception desk, peeled her hands from her ears and stumbled into the smoky remains of the office.

There were holes over the walls, in the furniture. Glass shattered, shelves hanging loose, paper floating softly to the floor.

Five men lay dead, sprawled on the floor, blood oozing into the soft green cactus motif in the centre of the brown suedette carpeting.

A cell-phone lay by the desk, crackling and popping.

She lifted it to her ear.

'Tommy? Tommy it's Al, what the hell's going on? Tommy? You there? Has he agreed to give up the show? Tommy?'

'You son of a bitch,' Don said quietly. He said it again a little louder. 'You son of a *bitch*.'

'Well, good to see ya, boy. Say hi to yur pappy for me.'

'Wait. *Wait!*' he yelled, shoving his hand between the lift doors. They tinged and rolled open again. 'You! Y-Y-You . . .' But rage and bewilderment and hatred and what-the-fuck's-going-on-ness all tag-team wrestled on the tip of Don's tongue. His mouth hung open stupidly to give them room.

'Guess ah might see ya over at the stoodio? You take care now,' Randy winked, leaving Don standing agape in the sumptuous silence of the corridor as he tipped his hat and the doors rolled shut.

The lift juddered and began to drop slowly to the lobby. Randy checked his appearance in the dark mirrors, pouting a little, straightening his bootlace tie, pulling back his shoulders. Yep indeed, every inch the country gent.

He whipped out a white rhinestoned cell-phone from his preposterous holster and speed-dialled the number.

'Watts,' the voice crackled.

'What the fuck's goin' on, boy? Where in the name of Roy Roger's truss have you been? You got them girls in your possession yet?'

'No. They're still in the open.'

'Jesus mothering Christ, boy!' Randy spat. 'What the hell are you tryin' to pull, huh? Ah mean, answer me that, would ya? Would ya answer me that? These women are jus' out there, wanderin' about the streets? Jesus motherin' Christ! They could be talkin' to the cops, the feds, Oprah freakin' Winfrey? Yur organisation's a freakin' joke, Mr Watts. A freakin' joke. Now listen to me. Ah'm here in LA to collect the parcel from Mercury.'

'I know where you are, Mr Garland.'

'You *know*?'

'*I am in surveillance.*'

'That's frickin debatable,' Garland sneered. 'Seems like you couldn't trace a missing person with tissue paper and a coloured fuckin' crayon.'

'*You're staying at the Beverly Wilshire.*'

'Damned right, boy. Got myself an eighth floor suite. Y'know how? Because ah'm about to take delivery of the biggest damned show of the year, that's how. An' the only li'l thing that's standin' in mah way are a bunch of dames runnin' about the place squawking to the damned cops. Dames that you shoulda taken care of by now. Now you find those girls, an' I mean right now. No fuckin' tea breaks, no games of freakin' cricket, no poppin' down the Mall to say hi to The Queen, pip-pip, old freakin' fruit, y'hear me, Watts? Get that fuckin' scone outta your ass and drag them bitches back to Nashville. This TV show gets made or I'll drag your sorry ass behind my steer, ten times around the ranch, y'hear me?'

He hung up.

That was better.

The lift dinged and he strode boldly across the dark lobby, unaware of the stares and pointing of the other guests.

Jesus, that guy was an amateur, Randy sighed to himself. If he spent a little less time checking on his employer and a little more time finding these women, then he might not be in the—'

'Cab, sir?'

A smartly dressed doorman in white gloves greeted Randy with a nod and click of his fingers. A yellow cab rolled forward in the rank and the doorman snapped the rear door open, Randy climbing in briskly.

'Mercury Studios, Burbank,' he said, and settled himself by the window.

A window that was suddenly blocked by the black van that rolled up next to the cab and stopped, engine idling.

A black van with a large pink stain on the side.

Its driver's window was rolled down.

Randy looked up in alarm.

'Scone up my ass?' a familiar voice said.

The doorman just presumed it was a car backfiring, but the cab driver screamed, the black panel van already pulling away into the evening traffic.

THIRTY-EIGHT

'Okay, live in ten, nine . . .'

'Cue camera one.'

'. . . seven, six . . .'

'Cue credits.'

'. . . four, three . . .'

'Speed.'

'. . . one.'

'Aaaaand, roll credits.'

A finger punched a button on the sweeping console and two of the five screens in the darkened control booth blinked into life with the familiar opening credits and classy Mozart theme music.

'To Dick in six, five, four . . .'

The lights swept on to the plush stage, revealing the glass-topped table, the bookshelves. The studio audience began to applaud. A spotlight faded up illuminating the beautifully bouffant silvery hair of Dr Dick Trent. He looked up from his notebook, a fat fountain pen poised in one hand, and smiled over his horn-rimmed glasses at the blank eye of camera one.

The applause faded to quiet.

'Good evening, America,' he said. *'Welcome all, to this, a very special edition of* Shrink.'

And it was welcome *all*, indeed.

Across America, millions of volume controls on millions of

remotes in front of millions of televisions were being pumped. TV trays rattled, settees and chairs squeaked, cushions were plumped and millions hurried quickly in from kitchens with beers and sodas.

The two reasons that this was a 'very special edition' of *Shrink* stood in the wings of the KBL studio, nervously shifting their weight, hands clasped tightly, fingers linked in a white-knuckled grip. A security guard stood solemnly to one side beneath a red light; a make-up girl fussed and flustered with tissues and a brush.

A padded brown envelope was tucked under an arm.

'*Our first patient tonight,*' Dr Trent read from his autocue, '*is known across the world not only as a daytime television host, but as one half of the most successful marriage in Hollywood. She greets us all every day on Wake Up LA with a smile and a warmth that have made her a genuine friend to millions.*'

Backstage, Elaine gripped her husband's hand a little tighter.

'*Our second guest first came to our attention as the bumbling assistant in Mercury's* Office Politics. *And as the well-meaning but occasionally misguided Farmer Old MacDonald in* E.R. E.R. . . . Oh! *he entertained us all. But surely it's as the husband to his loving wife that he truly captured America's hearts.*'

Gill adjusted the package under his arm.

Dr Trent then furrowed his brow a little sincerely.

'*It was, therefore, something of a shock . . .*'

'Cue montage,' Bob whispered in the control booth and the screens flickered to a shot panning across various tabloid headlines: *Kramer Career Buys The Farm* and *E.R E.R . . .Uh-Oh!*

'*. . . when it was announced by sources at ABN that he would be leaving this top-rated show . . .*'

'Here we go, places everybody,' Bob whispered.

'*. . . on the eve of its ninety-eighth episode. Not only that, but he failed to land a rumoured lead role in the new Mercury sitcom*

Carpool. *All this in the same week that he and his beloved wife Elaine have been nominated as Celebrity Couple Of The Year for the fourth year running.'*

The audience's applause swept up like a wave. In the wings, the security guard stepped to one side. Gill took a deep breath.

'To talk about that, their past and their future . . . ladies and gentlemen . . . Gill and Elaine Kramer!'

The couple stepped out under the hot squint of the studio lights, the applause redoubling. They stood a moment on the top step, smiling at the sea of faces. The cameras glid about the polished floor like a ballet.

Gill squeezed the envelope under his arm.

Yes, he was ready to talk to America.

Verily Ben's ye olde lamentable predicamente meanwhile, was ryghtly causing him muchly crapping of his doublet.

Kneeling by the toilet, hands looped and locked about the fat porcelain base, he puffed and pulled and panicked. The black puritanical robes were caked with sweat, pinching tight under his arms, around his neck and knees, the tiny hat cutting off all the blood to his brain. He'd spent half an hour kicking at the toilet, seeing if he could get it off the wall. He'd spent another half an hour yelling and clattering his aching buckled feet on the tiles.

For a while, exhausted with fear, he'd tried sitting back and trying to find the bright side.

Moments later, however, he was back, slamming and yelling and flushing the toilet and trying to get free.

He was stuck. He was going nowhere.

There was the sound of a slammed door in the outer room. He held his breath.

The bathroom door was unlocked with a click and Melvin pushed his way in, locking it behind him and crouching down to Ben's eye level.

'Hello ag-again,' he said, the gun held absentmindedly at his side. 'You ready?'

'Look, Melvin,' Ben said, licking his dry lips. His heart was bunching about his throat, eyes on the gun. 'Mel, please, look, I-I'll do it . . . I'll do it.'

No reaction.

'B-but it might take a few minutes, y'know? To come up with n-new jokes. I can't just . . .'

Melvin looked at him, then sighed, closing his eyes softly.

'No,' he said, and pressed the gun to Ben's head, pushing the hat up a little. 'When Bob wants a new joke, you'll give me a new joke.'

Ben almost threw up with terror.

'Or . . .' and Melvin slid back the hammer with a dull click.

'But . . . b-but . . . but if you kill me, y-you'll be on your own,' Ben skittered, sweat spraying from his hands, his back, his forehead. 'You need me alive, you can't kill me. You need me alive!'

Melvin blinked twice and stood up. He unlocked the door.

In the distance, the muted sound of a flagging warm-up man was faintly audible.

'*And, ladies and gentlemen, playing Arnie, the backseat driver, give it up for Vincent Corillo!*'

Melvin smiled distantly, fumbled in his jacket and pulled out a Polaroid. He looked at it and then handed it to Ben.

Ben focused on the photograph of the figure in cuffs, terror across her desperate face.

'Oh, Jesus.'

'*And, ladies and gentlemen, playing Phil, please, give it up for Zachary Black!*'

'It stinks in th-there,' Melvin said. 'The timber. It's all been coated in this gel stuff. Sticky. Helps it burn.'

'Burn?'

'*And finally,*' the warm-up man shouted, '*the writer, creator and star of tonight's show . . . without whom one of this would be possible . . . from England, playing Bob — Melvin Medford!*'

The audience cheered and whooped and clapped.

'Those pink bottles there? Kerosene. All wired up. It's f-for the big scene. They're shooting it as we speak. It's going to b-be quite something.'

'No! Jesus, no.' Ben squirmed, tearing and thrashing against the chains.

'*Melvin Medford, everybody!*' the warm-up repeated. '*Melvin?*'

'They spent all morning setting it up. Of course, m-maybe they'll go through the set one more time and recheck it all. Then they'll find her.'

'No, please! No . . .' Ben twisted and slammed. 'Where is this? Where *is she?!*'

'But then, maybe they won't.'

Melvin left.

Ben, mad with horror, stared at Jackie's desperate face.

'*Melvin? Hey, buddy? Where the hell . . . heyyy! There he is, lay-gennermen! Melvin Medford!*'

In the studio, a huge cheer went up as Melvin took to the stage.

In the Regent Beverly Wilshire meanwhile, a sweaty Don Silver banged and kicked at the door to an eighth-floor suite.

'Uncle Bernie?' he hammered. 'Uncle Bernie, is that you?'

'Ahem, excuse me, sir?' a voice said behind him. A white-jacketed young man with a silver room-service tray stood waiting. 'Lobster for eight-thirteen?'

'Open it up,' Don ordered, 'open it up!' And the waiter slid out his key card and clicked it through the lock.

'Jesus Christ, what the fuck's going on?' Don cried, stumbling in.

Howard and Bernie were still tied back-to-back in the middle of the room, lying on their sides in a puddle of melting ice and broken glass, the mini-bar face down on the carpet. The television flickered silently.

The waiter bumped the trolley through the suite.

'For the, ahem, happy couple?' he said, placing the leather wallet on a side table and reversing out with a low bow.

'Who did this, for Chrissakes?' Don exclaimed, hurrying forward and busying himself with the shackles, the men issuing moans and yelps of alarm as their aching limbs were bent and manhandled. 'Dad? Dad, are you all right? Was this Lambert? Uncle Bernie?'

'It's . . . gahh! Easy, kid! It's out of Lambert's hands now,' he said, easing his sling, rubbing his wrists. 'Frankie Corillo's stepped in and taken charge. We're in the big league.'

'Corillo? From *Sexposé*? The guy on the *News?*'

Don helped the old men up carefully.

'Sonofabitch is pulling an insurance job. He's gonna torch the damn' studio. Had me and your father sign the whole thing over to him a few hours ago.' Bernie clicked and cricked across the room to his jacket, wincing. 'Talked about planting explosives. Doing a grand job.'

'Explosives?' Don said, head reeling.

'Some time tonight,' Bernie said, pulling his jacket across his throbbing sling gingerly. 'We gotta get going. Get word to the lot.'

'Give me your phone, son,' Howard said, breathing heavily, staggering upright in his paper pyjamas. His face was pale and drawn. 'I'll call Mickey on the gate. See if he's noticed anyone suspicious, get him to frisk anybody coming in he doesn't know.'

'Holy Cannelloni!' Bernie said, staring at the television. 'Is that *Kramer?*' He snatched up the remote and thumbed the volume.

'. . . *never really thought about it, Dick. I suppose I just wanted to see my mother smile, even at that age. And if I could do that, with a song or a joke, if I could bring a little of God's light to her life . . .*'

On screen, Gill was lying back on one of two black leather

couches, fingers laced over his chest, eyes closed in a pool of dim light. His wife lay next to him.

'...*I loved to see her smile. And maybe you're right. Maybe my life has been one long show, for her, up there. On a cloud, the best seat in the house...*'

'Shit,' Bernie said. He had his cell-phone out and was flicking through the display quickly. 'Nothing from Nashville.'

'There won't be, Uncle Bernie,' Don said. 'Garland's *here*.'

Bernie looked up.

'*Here?*'

Moments later, the three men left the room together and rustled down the corridor, Don slowing down to let his sickly father keep up, Howard trying to speed up to catch his anxious son, Bernie stuck in the middle smoking a cigarette.

'So what do we do, Uncle Bernie?' Don said as they reached the lift. 'Where are we going?'

'We're going to jail, kid,' Bernie said, snorting out blue smoke from his nostrils. 'Unless Garland takes *Carp*ool with him on Monday.'

'Even if he doesn't,' Don said.

'What?'

And he quickly explained what Zak had told him at the studio.

'KBL knows it all. Paretsky. She's blowing the whole thing wide open.'

'Shit. When?'

'Who knows?'

'Then we gotta talk to her,' Bernie said, puffing away madly. 'Cut a deal. This can't get out in the open.'

They fell into a sickly silence, watching the lift sign sweep up to eight.

'Where's Melvin now?' Bernie asked, brain rattling quickly.

'On set. I left him shooting the show. As far as he's concerned, nothing's changed.'

The lift doors rolled open. The three men piled in, Howard snapping Don's phone shut.

'Mickey says there's no way anyone got any explosives through tonight. He's been on the gate, everyone checks out. No alarms, no warning bells, everyone's frisked and patted down. He's guessing Corillo's putting the frighteners on us.' He took a deep breath and wiped his paper sleeve on his shiny face.

'How you feeling, Dad? You okay?' Don asked, the lift doors rolling open to the polished hush of the lobby.

Or rather, where the polished hush used to be.

The place was alive with clatter and chatter, dozens of people standing about, running about, faffing about. Policemen and paramedics in rustling coats crackled radios and hollered at each other, statements were being taken, sirens whooping on the street, red and blue lights flashing through the glass doors, dancing on the polished floor.

'What the hell . . .' Don said, the three men weaving their way over to the desk. 'Bobby, what's going on?'

'A shooting,' he said, swallowing great shocked sobs, hands to his face. 'A guest! The old Southern gentleman, murdered . . .'

Don exchanged a wide-eyed look with his uncle.

'*Who . . .?*' Bernie whispered.

'. . . *gives a shit?*' Don said excitedly, pulling him away. 'Don't you see? Randy's out of the way! *Carpool*'s back on the market!'

'What? What are you talking about, son?' Howard spluttered.

'Dad, you gotta talk to this Diane woman at KBL. Stall her, threaten to sue, whatever. I'll talk to Al Rosen at ABN, tell him the show's his if he wants it. And Uncle Bernie?' Don said quickly. 'You need to tell Corillo to call off his explosives. After twenty years, his investment is about to hit paydirt.'

'If I can turn to you again, Gill. Leaving aside your role as a loving husband, your two most famous *fictional* roles are both men very much at odds with the world around them,' Dr Trent said, crossing his legs and waggling his fountain pen.

'Yes. Yes, I suppose so.'

'Worlds that neither of them created yet both are forced to try and survive. How much did a feeling of resonance, of identification, motivate you to take on these characters? Are there personal issues that draw you to roles of this nature? Take your time.'

Gill took a deep breath and lay quiet for a moment, hands folded across his chest, closed eyelids warm from the studio lights. He was enjoying this enormously.

Across the podium, Elaine had garnered 'ahhhs' and light applause from the audience with her simpering and sniffling about love and trust, but it was Gill who had them eating out of his palm.

They had 'ooh-ed' and 'awwed' at tales of his struggling childhood. How he had performed at Christmas in front of the relatives, unable to distinguish between the sounds of laughter and the words, 'I love you, son.' Oh, the audience had gasped at that one, and Dr Trent had had to ask them to restrain their passionate applause.

Yes, he was enjoying this enormously. How interesting he sounded, how deep and complex his psyche. He'd really had no idea he was this fascinating.

But anyway, he thought quickly, back to the question. What had Trent wanted to know? About his choice of roles, was it?

'Well,' Gill said with a perfectly measured solemnity, 'I am drawn towards darkness. Instinctively. Comedy is darkness, I have always felt. It does not come from the happy place. Not from memories of sunny childhood holidays, but from fear. From an emptiness, from a void in one's heart, in one's soul.'

Oh, yes, this sounded great. He could feel the audience sigh with him.

'Comedy comes from a desire to be loved, I think. It's a dark, hollow thing, full of despair and pain. The characters I play must all have that darkness, that feeling of being alone in a cruel world.'

'A cruel world,' Dr Trent repeated, smoothing down the glue on his beard subtly. 'And do you see your own future in these bleak, desperate colours?' he said, peering over his spectacles. 'You are a hugely popular star, as we know, but I'm talking *professionally*. What are your thoughts now show business has, as it were, taken against you?'

Gill allowed himself a small smile.

Here we go.

THIRTY-NINE

'*Okay, places, everybody,*' the director yelled. Studio 6 fell quiet. '*This is a take. Stand by effects.* Jerry?'

'Stand by,' he nodded. A few feet away in chipped plastic goggles, he stood at his black console in front of an array of tiny red bulbs and switches. He began to click each one from 'stand-by' to 'armed'. The bulbs lit up one by one.

'*And, speed!*'

'Fyre, *episode twelve, scene one one four, take one.*'

'Aaaaand . . . *action!*'

'So, my liege, your Pudding Lane bakery was insured for a pretty penny, I'll wager?'

'Ha! A pox on you, quill boy! You're a two-bit hack and the King knows it.'

'Oh, come, come. Bakery insurance fraud? What was it? Did you *knead* the *dough*?'

The appalling dialogue echoed again among the gantries and rigs.

Fifty feet away, huddled in the stinging darkness of her timber confines, Jackie closed her eyes and let her head loll against the foil and wires wrapped about the rough wooden supports. The cold cuffs bit into her wrists; her buttocks felt numb on the damp wooden floor. Her jaw throbbed, the stockings balled up tight in her mouth tasted synthetic and sweaty. She was scared. Very scared. Every time she shut her eyes, the pale glassy face of Melvin floated over her.

Please, let Ben come, she prayed. Let Ben – *JESUS!*

There was a skull-rattling bang.

Jackie lurched, cracking her head against the wooden frame, heart leaping, hands cold.

The air filled with bright heat and the icy taste of synthetic smoke, the sound of timber clattering around the floor, the soft crackle of nearby flames.

'*Aaaaaand . . . cut! Print! Excellent, everybody. Well done, well done.*'

Chatter and clatter and applause faded upwards over the sound of the fire.

'*Okay! Time's pressing on, people. Jerry? The altar? All good to go?*'

'When you are,' he said.

Jackie opened her eyes.

'*Okay, positions. Scene one one five . . . good, good, let's keep the pace up.*'

Across the lot, in Melvin's small private bathroom, Ben took deep breaths and tried to focus.

From the distant laughter in the studio, it seemed his last rather hurried replacement line, about Phil's life being a bed of roses – expensive and full of cat shit – had done the job.

But it was a momentary reprieve. Melvin would be back again soon, waving the gun, gritting his dead tooth and demanding more. Ben should be thinking about the script. About new lines, new set-ups, new come-backs.

But his mind raged, his eyes poring over the snapshot. Jackie was chained to some kind of scenery, that was all he could make out. Trapped, hurt, frightened. Because of him.

It was all because of—'

Ben sat up.

He listened.

Nothing. No audience laughter. No actors' voices. The recording had halted again.

Shit!

Panic crawled through him as he heard the outer door click and a fumbling with the bathroom latch.

'We're g-going again,' Melvin said. He was red-faced and puffing, rolled up script in his hand. 'I need a new exchange for Arnie and Bob. To show how he's getting on his n-nerves.'

Ben stared at him as he flicked through the script.

'Nerves?' Ben said.

'As it stands, we've g-got, Arnie saying, "*Bob, can you slow down a little. I feel a little sick.*" To which B-Bob replies, "*Slower? We've moved ten yards in twenty minutes. Is the G-force burning you up, Mr Aldrin?*" ' Melvin lowered the script. 'Give me something n-new.'

'I . . . I don't *know*,' Ben flustered, his head whirling. 'I — I—'

His head pounded with thoughts of Jackie, trussed and terrified.

'C'mon,' Melvin said, licking his lips.

'If you've hurt her. . .' Ben said, jaw fixed, eyes flashing.

Melvin raised the gun once again.

Across America, Gill continued to open his heart.

'Well, what can I say, Dick? It's Hollywood. The business we call show. Whatever the price, whatever the cost, whatever the damage to human hearts, to human *souls*, Dick. It's of no concern to them. Locked away behind concrete in their ivory towers made of glass, the show's the thing. Nothing must harm the show.'

Gill paused.

'Go on,' Dr Trent said with a practised sincere nod.

'I woke up, Dick,' and Gill suddenly sat up, making Dr Trent jump a little, Elaine jump a little, the audience jump a little, and the editors in the control booth start legging it about in a panic.

*

'Bob! Bob, he's sitting up, Kramer's sitting up.'

'Stay with him,' Bob shouted. 'Stay with him. This is what we expected, people. Keep it together, keep it rolling.'

'And I realised that this was a sick world,' Gill said.

'Sick?'

'A sick, twisted, ugly world where ideas are *stolen*,' he said loudly. 'Stolen. Lives destroyed and crazy people – yes, *crazies*, Dick – they can be crowned kings.'

He stood up, causing everyone to jump all over again.

'Sweetheart?' Elaine said, looking anxiously at Dr Trent, at the floor managers. What was he *doing?*

A murmur of unease rippled through the studio, crew and audience alike.

All over America, forks stopped halfway to mouths, hands stopped halfway to popcorn.

This wasn't right.

'Mad people, Dick,' Gill said, louder. 'The insane are trumpeted as artists, crazies as kings! You ask me if I feel bitter about missing out on *Carpool?*'

Cameras slid in across the shiny floor, over cables and tape.

'*Stay with him,*' Bob said into his headset, eyes fixed on the monitor. '*Stay with him.*'

'Penny?' a voice said, poking around her bedroom door. 'Penny, you gotta come down and catch this. Gill Kramer—'

'I'm catchin' it, I'm catchin' it!' Penny said, naked on the end of her bed, the portable television flickering away. Next to her, ignored, an equally naked young actor gazed at the ceiling, smoking a joint. Penny scrabbled on the side table for a pen and paper.

'*I'm well aware that the gossipmongers of this town have put it about that this is the case,*' Gill continued on screen. '*But what the world fails to realise is that* Carpool, *as a show, is more than it seems . . .*'

*

In his Beverly Hills home, Shifty Dolawitz looked up suddenly from the contract in his lap, gazing at the television. Gill was moving back to the coffee table on the raised platform. Under a velvet cloth sat the freshly engraved Celebrity Couple Award that Dr Trent was to 'surprise' them with at the end of the show. But Gill didn't reach for that. He picked up the fat brown envelope behind it instead.

'*And the man behind* Carpool?' he said slowly.

The studio audience watched in rapt silence.

Gill untucked the lip of the envelope and slid out a wad of documents.

'*What's this?*' Dr Trent said.

Across town, a phone rang. A fat hand snatched it up.

'Muldoon,' the officer answered.

'*Everybody watching?*'

'Uhh, not exactly,' he said, glancing around the empty precinct canteen at the greasy Formica, the dull chrome and the drinks machines. A small corner television hung suspended from the ceiling, burbling away. 'Frankie Corillo was spotted in Burbank, the whole department—'

'*But—*'

'I told the Chief your story, miss. He said he didn't have time to pay attention to every nutcase that thinks they—'

'*Then you'd better get your Chief in front of a TV right . . .*'

On screen, Gill Kramer was peeling off a sheet of paper.

'*. . . now.*'

'*A report has only today come into my possession,*' he was saying. '*Put together by Probe It, a team of professional investigators, and unearthed by Diane Paretsky of the undercover documentary show* Sexposé.'

'Drop it,' Bob said in the control booth, at which the editor at his console punched a button. A picture of Diane flickered up on to every screen in the booth and every television in America: a serious, grainy black and white shot she'd had done, holding a microphone, with a passionate and earnest look she'd managed to fake quite convincingly.

'It's yours, Hilliard,' the dealer said. 'Hilliard? Hey, c'mon, turn that thing off. We playin' cards here?'

'Huh?' Hilliard said. The portable set in the J. T. Stanley basement burbled away. Hilliard plucked his soggy cigar from his lips and tossed in his cards. 'Oh, I fold,' he said, watching the screen.

'*A report on one Melvin Medford, the so-called award-winning British writer behind* Carpool. *Can you get that? Any of you? Can you see that?*' And Gill held up a laser-printed photograph.

'But you won!'

'Shhh,' Hilliard said. 'Something's happening here . . .'

'Camera two, focus,' Bob said into his headset, and on the screen in the booth the image lurched forward crazily, blurring and sharpening into a picture of three young men on a London street.

'*Taken last Saturday night outside the Margrave Hotel in London,*' Gill said clearly. '*Medford's on the right here, the two young men with him are Angus Fisher and Malachy Flynn, two British comedians.*'

In the Shrink studio, the audience were shifting and murmuring.

Something was clearly not right.

In his home, Shifty watched as Gill peeled off two more similar photographs, announcing them as Melvin with Jasper Philips and Melvin with Sheridan McDonald.

He then held up a newspaper front-page.

'*Today's headline in London,*' he announced.

'Shit!' Shifty said, and looked down at the draft of Melvin's contract in his lap.

'Jesus Christ!' Muldoon exclaimed.

Not taking his eyes from the screen in the canteen corner, he picked up the phone from the desk.

'Get the Chief down here,' he said. 'Get him down here now!'

In the studio there was a huge rushing sound, like an aircraft taking off, as the audience gasped as one, threatening to suck Dr Trent's toupé from his head.

'Bob?' the booth technician said. 'Bob, what are we doing? We staying with this?'

'*The first three comics*,' Gill was saying flatly, waving the paper. MURDERED MEN IDENTIFIED it read in stark black letters. '*All strangled. Melvin clearly didn't find what he was looking for.*'

On the studio floor it was chaos, cameras out of focus, zooming in and out crazily. Technical crew with headphones and clip-boards were visible in the corners the screen, shrugging and making 'keep-rolling' hand gestures.

'Is this *live?*' Chief Sherwood barked, marching into the precinct canteen moments later, throwing his arms around. 'Muldoon? What's all this about? The phones are going nuts. You knew about this?'

'Sir . . .'

'*The fourth comic, Sheridan McDonald, one of the real writers of* Carpool, and Gill flapped a police report, '*Melvin shot dead when he tried to escape him . . .*'

In New York, Marion Silver sat in her pink reclining armchair in front of the television, embroidery ignored on her lap, hot milk going cold on the side table, jaw hanging loose as Gill continued.

'*. . . outside the home of Mercury producer Don Silver here in Los Angeles two nights ago.*'

'Oh, son,' she gasped.

'Camera two, get closer!' Bob yelled.

'I'm there, I'm there,' the voice in his headphones buzzed. On the monitor, the image of Gill grew sharp.

'Four innocent men,' he intoned solemnly, *'brutally tortured and murdered, just to bring this supposed "hit" new show to Mercury Pictures.'*

Shifty Dolawitz lifted Melvin's contract from his lap, tore it neatly in two and tossed the pieces into the air. Easy come, easy go, he thought to himself with a sigh.

'So much for their new star Melvin Medford. Or rather,' and America watched as Gill held up another photograph.

A picture of a young boy. Six, maybe seven years old. Freckled, a ginger crop, thin sallow face, a faded Muppet Show T-shirt. Smiling, a dead grey tooth at the front, but no joy in the face. No childish glee or scamp mischief in those eyes.

'Melvin Edelman. Born June first, 1975, Willingboro, New Jersey. Mother killed in a coffee-shop robbery in 1980. Currently at large and, if there are any cops watching,' Gill finished with a flourish, *'wanted on nine separate counts of murder.'*

Of course, thanks to Diane, there were plenty of cops watching.

In the chaotic briefing room, two officers frantically plugged in a portable television set. Holsters and caps were grabbed from sticky table tops, coffees splashed and spilled as officers began to bustle about the place, eager for instructions.

Chief Sherwood bouldered in with a bark and a slam.

'Sir? What's the plan, sir?' Muldoon asked.

'Keep it *down!*' Chief Sherwood yelled at his men. 'There's a *celebrity* talking!'

'Shall I put out an—'

'*Shhhhh!*'

'. . . *Melvin Edelman. As we speak,*' Gill snarled on screen, '*is recording the show he's being celebrated for. The show that everybody wants. The show that cost these men their lives! Wandering free on set at Mercury Pictures.*' And he hurled the armful of documents into the air, reports and photographs and testimonies raining down over the set.

'That's *it!* Mercury Pictures, you heard the man!' Sherwood yelled, chairs scraping, guns loading. 'Let's go! Muldoon? Get an APB out. Move it!'

'Sir, everyone's hunting for Corillo, there's hardly—'

'C'mon, let's go, let's go, let's go!'

The phone was ringing. Muldoon snatched it up.

'*Believe me now?*'

'Jesus, ma'am, okay okay we're on our way, what are you tryin' to—'

'*Oh, this is just the beginning.*'

Moments later, car radios all over LA squawked into life.

'*Despatch to all units, all units respond, over.*'

'*Again!*' Officer Dorfler yelled. '*Round again!*' And he grabbed the roof of the patrol car for support as they squealed around another wide corner. Walsh was at the wheel, cap and sunglasses on, hurling the vehicle around the Disney Studio, siren screaming, oblivious to the story spilling out across the country.

'*Despatch to all units, all units respond, emergency, over.*'

'Shit!' And with a screech Walsh took another screaming corner, grabbing up the radio. 'This is eight Lincoln thirty, come on in, over?'

'*Investigate code nine, code nine, Mercury Studios, West Alemeda, over.*'

'Mercury?' Walsh said, eyes flashing.

'Err, this is eight Lincoln thirty to despatch,' Dorfler yelled, snatching the radio from his partner. 'That's affirmative, on route, over.'

'Eight oh thirty roger, be advised. Subject Melvin Edelman, male, red hair, glasses. Highly dangerous. Use caution and await back-up, over.'

'This is it. This is it!' Dorfler flapped excitedly, slamming down the receiver. 'It's three blocks east of here.'

Walsh threw the car into a squealing U-turn and they roared up the quiet evening street, siren shrieking.

'Mercury Pictures! Casting directors, producers . . .' he said excitedly.

'Better believe it! They can fuck caution,' Dorfler said, hunched over the dashboard. 'And fuck back-up too. Whoever got offered a miniseries waiting for *back-up?*'

'Lip balm!' Walsh shouted. 'Where's the lip balm!'

'Ladies and gentlemen, ladies and gentlemen, if we could have some *quiet*, please.'

The three hundred gasping and gossiping audience members 'shushhhed' each other and settled down quickly. Above them, the control booth was in uproar.

'Dick looks shaky, Bob. He's signalling, what'll I tell him?' an assistant director asked through the speaker.

Bob pushed past the crowds gathering in the booth, all staring at the little screens, and snatched up the headset quickly.

'Patch me through . . . patch me through now! Dick? It's Bob. Get Kramer calmed down, we're still live.'

He watched the monitor. Dr Trent expertly eased Gill back to the couch, sitting him down next to his loving wife.

'That's good,' Bob said. 'That's good, you got the next question?' He yanked the headphones from his head. 'Okay, okay, let's have some hush. Some *hush!*'

'These are some allegations, Gill,' Dr Trent said in that slow easy voice of his.

'Well, yes,' Gill said. 'I thought it important that the world know the truth.' He was a little red-faced and puffing, but he'd done it. Damn it, he'd *done it*. The world knew the truth. ABN? Mercury? They'd never recover. He'd shown them. He'd shown them all.

'The *truth?* Indeed,' said Dick, stretching the word out as long as he could. 'Indeed,' he said again, and looked at Elaine then back at Gill. 'Truth. Honesty. Integrity. Important things, Gill. Especially in a marriage.'

'Absolutely,' Elaine nodded, squeezing her husband's hand, glad to be getting things back on track. Her fans hadn't tuned in to get some scandalous vengeful diatribe, they wanted heart-warming stories of love and Celebrity Couple Of The Year acceptance speeches. She flicked a quick look at the award, still blanketed under velvet on the low table.

'Which is why I think, Gill,' Dick said, easing forward and lifting the heavy trophy, 'this would be an excellent opportunity . . .'

The audience sat up a little, excitedly. Elaine squeezed Gill's hand again.

'. . . for you to tell Elaine, and indeed the world, about your ten-year relationship with Al Rosen.'

Gill froze.

The studio fell into silence.

Elaine looked at her husband.

Two hundred and fifty million homes descended into hush.

'Al Rosen'. Dick nodded calmly. 'Your gay lover?'

Two hundred and fifty million TV dinners were spat over two hundred and fifty million TV trays.

Across town on the Mercury lot, oblivious to it all, there was a broad laugh and Rob the director stepped up on stage.

'Okay, and hold it there. Thank you, everybody. Check the gates.' And a dozen people scuttled on to the set with make-up and light meters as the *Carpool* studio filled with warm applause.

The cast climbed out of the cramped car and began to groan, stretching their legs and rolling their shoulders.

'Excuse me, excuse me, coming through . . . pardon me,' a gruff voice muttered as the two men in overcoats shouldered past assistants and assistants' assistants, sending clip-boards and coffee flying at the rear of the studio.

'She's not *here*,' Lambert whispered. 'We've checked every studio, every dressing room. Mr Corillo, sir, the plane. We can't just—'

'*Vinnie!*' Corillo hissed across the studio floor.

Looking up from a powdery make-up brush under the hot lights, Vinnie caught sight of his father. His smile faded. He excused himself and trotted quickly across the studio floor, ducking under the camera and over to the audience.

'Dad?' he whispered. 'Mr Lambert. What're you . . . what're you doin' here? I thought I whuz meetin' you at the airfield . . .'

'No time to explain,' Corillo growled. 'You seen that KBL woman around? Word is she might be here?'

Vinnie shook his head dumbly.

'What about this other one?' Lambert asked, casting a surreptitious glance about the studio. 'Heaney? British? Done up like a hooker?'

'I ain't seen nuthin',' Vinnie said. 'We been on set here the whole time. Doin' the show?'

Corillo checked his watch.

'Dammit,' he snarled, and began to button his coat hastily. 'Is it all set?'

'*Two minutes, Vinnie!*' Rob called across the floor.

'Uhh, Dad?' Vinnie piped up hopefully. 'This is a pretty good show, y'know? I'm getting some good laffs. An', hey, I been thinkin' . . . Maybe, I dunno, you might not . . . I mean, you won't maybe—'

Corillo fixed his son with a firm stare.

'Vinnie,' he whispered, 'this is business.'

'But, Dad, hey, c'mon—'

'Vinnie?' Corillo said firmly, pointing a leather gloved finger. 'Is it set?'

'Nine o'clock,' he sighed.

'Heyyy, you friends of our star there?' the warm-up man

interrupted loudly, leaning over the rail and pushing a microphone into their faces. 'Giving him a bit of moral . . . heyy, you look familiar to me . . .'

'Fuck you, faggot,' Corillo said politely, and, exchanging a tiny nod with his son, bustled Lambert out of the studio.

'Oh. Oh, okay. Okay! Uhmm, who's in from outta town? Anybody?'

On the *Shrink* stage, a huge video screen was lowered silently to the floor from the gantry above.

The audience sat in stunned silence.

Elaine, her hands over her mouth, wide-eyed and hyperventilating, threw panicked, tearful looks about the floor. This couldn't . . . he couldn't . . . they couldn't . . .

Gill sat on the couch, dumbstruck, gazing up at the banks of studio lights.

He tried to speak but could only mouth the air, blinking, his world flopping and spinning and lurching like some kind of fairground ride. He held on to the side of the couch with cold hands to stop himself being thrown into space. He wanted to be sick. He wanted to go home. He wanted his mom.

'Your *gay lover*,' Dick said again, in case one of the two hundred and fifty million viewers had missed it the first time. 'You and Al are very much in love, I understand. A little house in Malibu, trips to Paris . . .'

'You . . . you said,' Elaine managed to squeak, choking, 'it was for your performance! The separate bedrooms . . . so it didn't affect your performance!'

'I . . .'

'Ten years!' she shrieked and leaped up, wrestling the crystal trophy from Dick Trent, smashing it to the floor with a sob and hurling herself from the studio floor in a flurry of tears.

'*Sweetheart! Sweetheart . . . I can explain!*' Gill called after her.

'Stay on Gill,' Bob yelled from the booth. '*Stay on Gill!*'

'Ten years indeed, Gill,' Dick continued. 'But like so many

people in Hollywood, perhaps you've let your world get turned back to front?' And he touched Gill on the shoulder. 'Let's focus on that, shall we?' He eased his dumbfounded subject back until he lay on the couch again, blinking tearily up at the lights. 'Setting your emotions aside while you worry about your career? About money, awards, success?'

Gill turned and looked at him, eyes shining with tears.

'But Gill,' and Dr Trent leaned in, touching his shoulder, again. 'what is money, success, your career, *for* if you cannot share it with that special person?'

In the booth, all eyes were on the screen. There was a close up of Gill Kramer, bottom lip trembling. It was clearly all too much for him, the emotion, the loneliness, the lights. He was overcome. Overcome and overwhelmed.

'*Listen to your heart, Gill. What does your heart tell you?*' Dick said. '*Ambition? Television? Fame? What is this if you're not true to your heart?*'

All over America phones rang. People ran squealing in and out of kitchens and dens: *Are you watching? Are you watching! I know! I know!*

'If you could speak to Al now,' Dick Trent said tenderly, 'if you could speak to Al, what would you say to him? The man you rejected, spurned, whose gifts you threw back in his face just because he was unable to hand you the fame you thought so important . . . would you like to speak to him?'

Gill paused, blinking back tears, biting his lip, then nodded.

'I'm sorry, Al,' he sniffed. 'My darling, I'm so sorry . . .'

'Oh, we can do better than *that!*' Dick announced, standing up and walking towards the huge screen now lowered to the studio floor, one finger pressed to his ear.

'On your signal,' Bob said from the control booth. 'Okay, everybody. . .'

'Because we're going *live*, ladies and gentlemen. *Live*, right now, to a special on-the-spot edition of *Sexposé*!'

The studio audience gasped.

'What?' Gill said, sitting up, still fussing with a hanky.

'Live from Burbank,' Dr Trent said excitedly. '*Can you hear me, Diane?*'

In the booth Bob cut direct to the live feed coming from the KBL News van and Diane's bright face, lit in a flare of halogen, smiled into two hundred and fifty million homes.

'Thank you Dick! This is Diane Paretsky. You join me live for this very special edition of *Sexposé*: "Mercury – SLIPPERY, SILVER and HOT!"' And Diane stepped to one side, allowing her two-man team to focus across the Mercury parking lot and on to the sprawl of studios and bungalows visible in the near distance, lights glowing in the dusk, panning across the scene.

Heart thumping, Diane took a moment to breathe deep and pull her shoulders back. This was it. This big one. Two hundred and fifty million people watching her.

She cleared her throat.

'Here at the famous Mercury Pictures Studios in Burbank, California, you will witness the dramatic finale to the most shocking story of sleaze, of sitcom and of scandal ever to come out of Hollywood.'

'*Great*,' Bob's voice crackled in her ear-piece. '*Let's have the recap. We're with you, we're with you . . .*'

'For those just joining us,' Diane continued, 'comedy star Gill Kramer has just this moment revealed his love for one man – *this* man, Al Rosen, ex-VP of Comedy Productions at ABN.'

On two hundred and fifty million television sets the screen flickered and a photograph appeared: a black-and-white image of Gill and Elaine Kramer leaving Mann's Chinese Theatre after a premiere. Behind the couple, looking sheepish, tugging at an earlobe, Al Rosen.

'Great,' Bob said from his control booth. 'Back to Diane.'

'*. . . a man currently sitting in the studios behind me, oblivious* to the live, life-shattering confession of his lover. *Sitting watching a sitcom recorded. A sitcom written by Brits Ben Busby and the late Sheridan McDonald, but stolen by one Melvin Edelman. Revealed tonight by Gill Kramer himself to be a multiple murderer . . .'*

And slowly, Diane began to tell the whole story. In the booth, on her cue, Bob cut in shots of all the Probe-It documents Diane had brought him. Photos, cuttings, transcripts, reports.

America sat and listened.

'What the hell kept you?' Corillo snapped, as Vinnie squeezed his huge frame into the back of the limo at the other end of the lot. Lambert hunched up a little to give him room to sit down. 'We've got a plane waiting.'

'Sorry, Dad . . .' Vinnie panted. Still in his stage clothes, he was breathless after his hasty waddle from the studio, sweat oozing through his thick orange make-up. His face looked like a large novelty candle. 'I had to wait to sneak out. Th-they're only halfway through . . .'

'All set?' Corillo said flatly.

Vinnie nodded.

'But—'

'Then let's get out of this fuckin' place.'

The driver flipped the headlights on, peeled the limo back slowly and swung it round towards the exit gate.

'. . . *which we believe SEBN were going to use to blackmail Mercury Pictures with,'* Diane continued. '*So follow me,'* she said eagerly, backing away across the street towards the gate, beckoning the camera on, '*as we try and enter the studio to confront comic-killer Melvin Edelman and, if you're still with me, Dick, surprise Al Rosen with a word from his beloved.'*

In the *Shrink* studio the audience bounced and jiggled in their seats, exchanging excited glances. Gill and Dr Trent stood, arms

about each other's shoulders on the podium, eyes on the big screen.

'We're still here, Diane. Gill? Gill, you okay?'

He nodded, sniffing back happy tears.

'Great. But Diane,' Dick said, finger pressed to his ear, 'if Edelman is who Gill says he is, mightn't he be dangerous?'

'*Don't worry, Dick,*' Diane smiled breathlessly, camera bouncing, '*because if I've timed this right...*'

'Here! Here! Pull in! Try and get a good *screeeech*,' Officer Dorfler shouted, gripping the dashboard as Walsh swung the patrol car on to Alemeda Avenue, past Diane and the KBL truck, bumped up the ramp and slammed to a halt at the main gate booth.

Living rooms across the country burst into whoops and cheers, backs were slapped and people yelled joyfully out of windows.

'You're getting good at that one,' Dorfler said, breathlessly inside the patrol car.

'T. J. Hooker,' Walsh said.

'Ahhh, the master.'

Walsh wound down his window as Mickey waddled over, flapping his clip-board and pointing.

'Heyyy,' he said, 'what's going on here? And who are you?' He waved at the approaching camera crew.

'*Sexposé,*' Diane called out authoritatively, dragging the puffing crew behind her, microphone extended.

'Excuse me ... Mickey, is it?' Walsh said. 'We're sorry to take up your time but we have reason to believe there may be—'

He suddenly noticed Diane and the camera crew jogging towards the car.

'*Miniseries!*' Dorfler hissed quickly.

'Uhmm ... we're, uhh, coming through, pal,' he barked instead, in a totally unnecessary cop-drama drawl. 'You got a 'goddamn' psycho on the loose. Move your ass!' And threw a stern, no-nonsense, sign-me-*please* look at the camera.

'Okay, let's all relax here,' Mickey said. 'I ain't authorised to let just any TV crew through, cops or no cops. I gotta radio this one . . . Jesus, what the hell's going on?'

Four other patrol cars came wailing on to Alemeda Avenue, lights whirling, tyres screeching, slamming to a halt all over the wide street. Officers poured out like spilt treacle, running low over the lawns, guns out, bums out, radios squawking.

In the booth at KBL, the editors were whooping and cheering, high-fiving and generally getting overexcited.

'Diane?' Bob yelled into his microphone. 'Diane, stay with it, this is great! Stay with it.'

The camera panned across shakily, following Chief Sherwood as he led a group of men over to the gate. He introduced himself to Mickey.

'We have something of a situation here, Mr Thomopoulos. Have you seen a man trying to leave in the last half-hour? Short? Glasses—'

'Hey, can we go? We just want to go,' a thick voice asked.

They all turned.

A long black limo sat idling at the exit. The driver, a thuggish gentleman with heavy brows, was pointing a pudgy finger at the gate.

'One at a time here, fellahs, huh? One at a time,' Mickey said. He turned back to the cops.

The limo driver shook his head, buzzed up his electric window.

'Sorry, officers, but look, I gotta ask. Are you all for real?' Mickey flapped his clip-board at the array of cop action, the camera crew, Diane's flushed face.

'We're real and live on every TV in America, Mickey,' she grinned. 'You wanna be a star? Let us in. We got the biggest arrest since Frankie Corillo and the showbiz love-story of the decade to wrap up here! Let's—'

Suddenly, in a scream of rubber and smoke, the limo driver hurled his car forward, ripping the gate off its hinges with a smash of metal and bumping down the ramp.

'Hey! Hey, my gate!' Mickey hollered. 'Stop him!'

'Holy Shatner!' Walsh yelled, slamming his car into reverse and spinning backwards, sending Diane and the crew diving out of the way. He yanked the wheel hard to the right, the patrol car whipping around, colliding with the front of the limo in a roar of steel and glass.

'Oooh!' Dorfler nodded. 'Good move.' And they clambered out, sucking in their bellies and clenching their jaws, pouting moodily. Diane focused on them as they moseyed over to the long car, giving it plenty of hold-its, what's-the-hurry-there-fellahs and why-don't-we-just-relaxes.

'Like I was saying,' Sherwood said, 'we're looking for a young man. Could be very dangerous. Ginger hair—'

'Er, Chief?' Walsh called. 'You better come and take a look at this. Ma'am?' And he motioned for Diane's crew to approach.

'We're here for Edelman. I don't have time for—'

'No, really, sir?' Walsh said with a smile. He had the back door open and his gun drawn. 'This you gotta see.'

Diane bustled forward, easing down a little, and zoomed in on the back seat of the limo.

Frankie Corillo blinked out at America, closed his eyes resignedly and sighed.

In the control booth, Bob went wild.

In the *Shrink* studio, the audience went wild.

America, as a whole, pretty much lost it.

FORTY-ONE

It was just after eight o'clock.

The sick yellow Los Angeles sky darkened to purple, like a smoker's fingers slammed in a car door. A cool dry wind whipped though the dusty palm trees, the city's pale neon clipping the edges of the tatty fronds.

And pushing through the chewy atmos, like a cold spoon through butter, a buckled BMW whined and coughed its way north, honking at the Saturday evening traffic.

'Al, c'mon, pick it up, pick it up,' Don wailed, phone clamped under his chin, one hand on the wheel, the other cranking down the window to get some fresh grit and fumes in the car. 'You got hold of Corillo yet Uncle Bernie?'

'Still ringing,' Bernie said next to him, and took a quick worried look at the half-hearted glow of his dying cell-phone before jamming it back under his chin. His useless arm throbbed in its sling.

In the rear passenger seat, a sickly Howard pressed a third phone to his ear, trying to reach Diane at KBL.

'How far do you think Corillo's got?' Don asked his uncle anxiously. 'The airport?'

'Lord only – hello?'

'*Who. . . this?*'

'Mr Corillo? It's me, it's Bernie. Bernie Silver.'

Don could barely bring himself to listen. He stared out at the traffic and concentrated on Al's phone, ringing and ringing.

'*I'm a little . . . -ied up here . . . ernie.*'

'Mr Corillo, you can call it off,' he said quickly. 'The bomb . . . you can call it off. There's been a development, a change of situation.'

'*I can't talk now, Bernie.*'

'Mr Corillo?'

'What's going on?' Don said urgently. 'What's he saying?'

'There's all this noise, people shouting. Sirens. Keeps cutting out. *Mr Corillo?*' Bernie yelled into the phone. 'Mr Corillo, *Carpool* is back on the market. The Nashville deal is off. So the show is ours to sell as we wish. You can call off anything you might have planned.'

'*Oh, I'm . . . -orry Bernie. But . . . -at's going to be a bit diffic- . . .*'

'Difficult?' Bernie said.

'*Hello?*' Al suddenly said in Don's ear. '*Tommy? Tommy, that you? What happened to Randy? You talk to him?*'

'Al, hey, it's me, it's Don Silver. Where are you?'

'Mr Corillo?' Bernie yelled over the hiss.

'*-ings have been . . . -ut in motion,*' Corillo crackled.

'Mr Corillo!'

'*I've got to go. Some . . . -ice men in caps want me to . . . -ang up the pho- . . . See you around, Ber- . . .*'

And the line went dead.

'Al, listen to me,' Don was jabbering. 'The deal with SEBN is off. It's too complicated to explain. You want *Carpool?* It's yours. But I need an answer right now.'

'*Don? I . . . But . . .*'

'Al? This is a once in a lifetime—'

'*Yes! Yes, I'll take it! Whatever it costs!*' Al laughed delightedly.

'Okay, okay, I'm on my way to the studio. I'll see you in a half hour,' Don said, watching a freeway sign flip past overhead. He hung up.

Bernie was shaking his head and dialling once more.

'I'm calling studio security again,' he said. 'Get them to go over every inch. He said it had been put in motion . . . Shit! Voicemail. We'll have to put our foot down. Jesus, kid, can't this thing go any *faster?*' he barked, watching little hatchbacks and 4×4s glide past casually.

'I busted up the suspension pranging that Ferrari,' Don said shaking his head. 'This is the best we can do. Dad?' He flicked a look in the rear-view. 'Dad, you okay back there? You got hold of Paretsky?'

'Nothing,' Howard said, coughing. 'KBL's switchboard is jammed. Jesus, kid, c'mon. Step on it.'

'I am!' Don said. 'She's not used to all this weight.'

'Like the Buick,' Bernie mused idly. 'She isn't actually a heavy car, y'know? It's big but it's all chassis. There's nothing really to it . . .'

Don's mind drifted back.

'Wait! Shit, Uncle Bernie, say that again?'

'What? The Buick's essentially hollow. . .'

'Shit! Of course. Of *course!*'

On the closed studio floor on the Mercury lot, still oblivious to the night's proceedings, the audience were getting restless and what remained of the cast were getting tetchy. The warm-up paced in front of the seating, chattering on, trying to keep the tired faces smiling, while on the floor among the monitors and props, the cast and crew huddled under the burning lights, hissing.

'But we *have* to finish!' Melvin stomped. 'This is *my show*. My show! We can't just . . .' And his voice trailed off as everyone gazed at Vinnie's empty seat in the prop car. 'Oh, where *is* he? He's spoiling *everything*!'

'There's no sign,' an assistant said, hurrying on to the set. 'Nobody's seen him.'

'Maybe we can fix it in the edit?' an idiot suggested.

'This ain't Star Trek, dude,' Zak said floppily. '*Woah, where's*

Arnie gone, man? Oh like, he must have beamed up at that last intersection?

'Well, we're not stopping,' Melvin hissed, gazing out at the sea of faces in the audience, shuffling, muttering, watching. 'This is *my* show.'

'Then think of something,' Rob said. 'You're the writer. Fix it. We've got eleven more pages to shoot.'

The place fell quiet.

Melvin stood twitching, staring at the floor, picking his face.

'Er, are we ready to go?' the warm-up man called.

'Wait, let me . . . I need to use the bathroom,' Melvin said, pushing through the crew in a fluster.

'Again?' Rob yelled after him. 'Boy, does that kid need a nutritionist.'

'Jerry . . . Jerry, poppet, can I double check this?' Samuel Pepys said, flicking through his fat script. He stood on a clear polythene sheet on the steps of the altar while three of the effects crew kneeled at his buckled feet, painting the back of his costume with a thick gloopy layer of fire retardant. Among the clatter and chaos, smoke machines foofing great billows of cold white smoke about the set, Jerry emerged, rolling his pyrotechnic console across the concrete floor, dozens of cables trailing.

'What's up?' he said.

'Fifteen minutes, everybody!' the director yelled. *'C'mon now. And where's my latte? Who's got my latte?'*

'Jerry, am I right that I say – *"My writings speak the truth, dough-boy! One day history will know what you did to this city! It's all in here!"'* And then I wave the book above my head. Then he fires the crossbow, yadda yadda yadda, I duck, bada-bing, grab him by his checked trousers and say – *"Pat-a-cake, pat-a-cake, baker's man. You murdered my wife, punk! Thy shit hitteth the——"'*

'Bang,' Jerry nodded. 'Right there.' Pepys scribbled notes on his script as Jerry explained, 'The whole lot goes up. We're coating you with the C19 anyway, but you'll be clear. We've squibbed the glass, the floor, the lecterns, the altar. You'll hear the fucking bang in Bel Air.'

Outside, Walsh and Dorfler moved quickly through the deserted lanes in the darkness, guns drawn, gazing up at the huge pink buildings, followed by a panting Diane and crew.

'Ladies . . . ladies and gentlemen, you are about to witness a . . . a unique event in show business history . . . that is, if we can find it . . .'

'Studio *nine* . . . studio *twelve*,' Walsh was saying. 'Whassat? Studio *two*? Jeez, you could spend your whole life wandering around this place.'

Dorfler hurried after him, throwing concentrated looks up at the studios and the occasional soulful one at the camera, sucking in his cheekbones and waving his gun theatrically.

'Studio *seven* . . . studio *five!* There!'

The pink building stood wide and looming in the fading light.

They reached the bottom of the iron staircase and squelched their radios.

'This is eight Lincoln thirty to main gate, come on in, over?'

Diane and the crew bustled around them, zooming in on the action. Bob's voice crackled encouragement in her earpiece.

'*Eight o-thirty roger, this is Sherwood, what you got?*'

'We're at the studio, Chief,' Dorfler said, looking about the quiet lane. 'No sign of anybody. There's a red light on outside.'

'Means they're filming,' Diane explained to the people at home.

'*Eight o-thirty roger. Hang back,*' Sherwood crackled. '*I've got three units dealing with Corillo here. Stay where you are and await back-up. We don't know what to expect from this Edelman. Over.*'

'Receiving,' Dorfler said and clicked off. 'We stay here.'

'*Diane!*' Bob yelled in her ear. '*We're live! You can't just stand there! You promised me an arrest!*'

And Diane knew he was right. The world was watching. The world was waiting.

'Let's go,' she said, pushing past the cops and dragging her crew clanging up the staircase.

'Hey, lady, wait! *Wait!*'

'You can wait wait!' she hollered. '*Sexposé* has a story to do!'

In front of two hundred and fifty million television sets, a great cheer went up. This was it.

This was *it*.

In the tiny bathroom, Ben's heart made a bid for freedom as the door was thrown open.

Melvin stood in the doorway, tugging the gun from the back of his trousers.

He looked bad. Or rather, *worse*.

'What's . . . what's going on?' Ben said. 'Why has everything stopped?' His whole body ached, his head pounded. He had been kneeling on the cold toilet floor for what felt like days, heart thundering. All his adrenalin had been spent a hundred times over. He was a wreck.

'Emergency,' Melvin said, sliding in quickly, not even bothering to shut the door. He had a wild panicked look about him, continually checking over his shoulder, breathing fast. 'Arnie's gone.'

'*What?*'

'We've lost him. It's j-just Bob and Phil left in the car. What do we do?'

Ben shrugged, cowering a little.

'What do we *DO!*' Melvin bellowed, smashing the butt of the gun against the tile above Ben's head. He was sweating and blinking, licking his lips.

'I-I don't know!' he said. 'Maybe . . .' But he hadn't a clue. He was exhausted. Terrified and exhausted. 'Is Jackie all right?'

'What? Focus! *FOCUS! We don't finish this show, you'll never see her again!* Now what do we *do?* We have to finish, it has to finish. It has to end *properly.* With the credits and the clapping an-an-and *you have been watching* and tune in next week an-and . . .'

'I don't know!' Ben whimpered. The gun was in his face. His mind was empty, like a staff training-room during a lunch break. A handful of empty chairs, a few empty coffee cups and a plain flipchart with the word TERROR written across it.

'Come on! Something funny!' Melvin gnashed, pressing the gun to Ben's head.

'I . . . I can't think of anything funny!' he screamed back.

Melvin looked at him, eyes flashing.

Ben held his breath.

Then, as if a cool breeze had whispered past, a strange calmness seemed to descend over Melvin.

'Then what . . . then what good are you?' he said.

He stood up straight and fired twice. Two loud flat bangs to Ben's head.

'Shit!' Walsh yelled, the shots echoing loud about the studio.

'What the hell!' Rob shouted from his control booth.

'Al!' Gill screamed on the *Shrink* floor, hands over his mouth. Dick gripped his shoulder tightly.

'Ohmigod!' Diane chorused, head bursting with images. Melvin dead? The cast and crew dead? Ben and Jackie dead?

And not getting *any of it* on camera?

Internal demons raging and squabbling over morality and ratings, she dragged her crew through the flats and slats of the cold studio, yelling, '*Sexposé*! Coming through! Make way!'

Dorfler and Walsh shoved past her, pushing through the swathes of heavy fabric into the studio.

'Wait!' she yelled. '*Wait*'

'Nobody move!' Walsh cried, tripping, rolling on to the squeaky floor, gun flailing.

A moment passed. He lay on his back, puffing, gazing up at the lights. Nobody moved.

Walsh sat up.

The three hundred strong audience sat silent in a frozen petrified tableau. The crew stood among the cameras and cars, hands over their mouths, eyes wide, saying nothing.

'Where is he?' Walsh said. 'Edelman? Where is he?'

'*Edelman?*' the director.

'You're live on KBL!' Diane shouted inappropriately, bustling in behind the policemen, microphone waving.

All over America, transfixed viewers watched the shaky camera pan around the still studio, the two officers, guns held out in front, moving quickly and cautiously and cinematically forward across the squeaky floor.

Nobody else moved. Nobody said a word.

'Where is he? Where is he?!' Walsh yelled. '*Edelman!*'

'*Al?*' Diane joined in. '*Al Rosen?*'

In the bathroom, a tall black hat lay on the wet tile.

Two charred holes in the front of it.

Ben sighed, heart pounding, flopping back against the wall. There were noises coming from the studio. The audience was murmuring.

Then silence

Then a huge cheer and a whistle. A thundering rumble as the audience got to their feet in a standing ovation.

What the hell was—'

'*Mr Rosen! Mr Al Rosen, come on down! You're live on KBL!*'

Ben went cold.

Holy shit, he knew that voice.

'*DIANE*' he yelled excitedly, his voice slapping back at him

531

a thousand times from the tiles around him. '*DIANE! IN HERE!*' And he began to slam and rattle and pound against the porcelain.

'Live? Live, I-I don't understand, I-I don't . . .' Al mumbled, stuffing his cell-phone away, stumbling down the steel steps.

'It's okay, Mr Rosen, let me explain. Ladies and gentlemen, *ladies and gentlemen*,' Diane shouted over the din She was in the centre of the studio floor. Around her, cameramen, script supervisors, associate producers, all stood about, shaking their heads and shrugging. 'My name is Diane Paretsky from *Sexposé* and we are *live!*'

The two-man team turned to sweep over the excited crowd who whooped and cheered and yelled and waved and said 'Hello, Mom!' frantically into the camera. Diane put her arm about Al's shoulder.

'We have a very special message of love for you, Al,' she said, handing him a set of headphones. 'A very special message indeed. Gill? Gill, can you hear me?'

Al went white.

The studio dropped to a hush.

'*Sweetheart?*' a tremulous but familiar voice crackled.

'*Okay, places, everybody. This is a take. Stand by effects. Stand by baker. And speed!*'

'Fyre, *episode twelve, scene one one five, take one.*'

'Aaaaand . . . *action!*'

Walsh and Dorfler meanwhile were spinning, jiving and slinking through the make-up and dressing rooms behind the studio floor, guns drawn, radios squelching.

'So when we find Edelman, do we take him down?' Walsh whispered.

Dorfler shook his head.

'Off camera? Are you nuts? You give chase, try and get him to run back this way, and I'll steer him back into the studio. Couple of forward rolls, couple of good hold-it-right-there-assholes, give the camera crew a chance to focus. Then it's blam blam, nice and loud, everybody screams, cuffs, right to remain silent, and we're guest slots on morning TV for the next two—'

Dorfler stopped.

Down the corridor, someone was yelling.

'*Oh, coochybuns!*' Al said, his tearful face filling the video-screen. '*Of course I'll marry you! Of course!*'

In the *Shrink* studio, the three hundred-strong audience stood, hands over mouths, tears in eyes, hugging each other and applauding. Gill stood in front of the video-screen weeping, hands reaching out to the face of his sweetheart. Dr Trent stood beside him, heart bursting with love, pride and ratings.

All across the country, families cheered and hugged and clinked beer cans and agreed that, yep, this had been the best goddamned show yet.

'Diane? Are you there?' Dick said over the din, his finger in his ear, interrupting the flood of emotion for a moment. 'Diane? What of Melvin? Do the police have him? Is he there? *Diane?*'

Walsh and Dorfler reached the dressing room door, pushed it open and moved through into the bathroom, where a small seventeenth-century peasant, handcuffed to the lavatory, was screaming and flailing.

'*IN HERE! HELP ME! HE'S GOT HER TRAPPED!*'

Walsh smiled.

'Dorf? Come see this.'

Dorfler peered around the door.

'Holy shit, it's Sunset Boulevard guy. What are you meant to be?'

'*Please!*' Ben panted, wrists raw and red, tight little costume soaked through. 'Please, Melvin has my girlfriend! He's chained her up somewhere! Please . . . It's going to blow!'

'Can't you go *anywhere* without people chaining up your friends?' Dorfler sighed.

'*Please!*' Ben said. 'There's no time! Get me *out of here!*'

Walsh knelt down and examined the cuffs.

'Keep an eye on him,' Dorfler said to his partner. 'I'll find something to cut these with.'

'Wait! Wait, no. Better if *you* keep an eye on him. I'll go.'

'No. Me. Let me go. You—'

'*I'll* go,' Walsh said.

'*I'm* going. You stay and look after—'

'Don't be crazy, *you* stay.'

'No, *you* stay.'

'Oh, just *say it*,' Walsh snapped. 'You just want to get back to the studio, flash your gun about and pull your shoulders back and pout at the casting directors. Just 'cause I got to do the fancy floor roll and the *nobody move* bit.'

'Well, that seems fair.'

'Oh, grow up!'

'Okay, so we should both go?' Dorfler said.

'*Gaahhh!*' Ben screamed in frustration. 'Will somebody just get me out of this fucking *toilet!*'

A few minutes later, a BMW hauled its way, growling and scraping, up Alemeda Avenue, coming to a slow coughing stop at the kerb, steam hissing from the hood.

'Go, just go!' Bernie said, flopping back in his seat and thumbing the cigarette lighter.

'We'll catch you up,' Howard croaked from the back, wheezing.

Don left them both behind, throwing his door open, heaving himself out and hurling himself across the street to the gate.

The whole studio was alive with activity.

There was a TV News van and half a dozen patrol cars parked casually about the street, blue and red lights flipping and whirling, exciting the night. Groups of policemen huddled over the roofs and hoods, radios squelching, ducking from car to car. A huge black LAPD truck stood by the gate in a pool of coloured glass next to the buckled hulk of a limousine. Four men in suits were slapped up against the side, arms spread, a dozen officers surrounding them.

'Officer!' Don yelled, breathless and waving, shirt tails flapping as he pounded towards the pink booth.

'Woah, woah, slow it down, pal,' Muldoon said, raising his hands. 'We can't let you in there, buddy, we got a possible murder suspect loose somewhere in—'

'Melvin? Yes. I know.' Don nodded quickly. His chest was heaving, snatching breaths. 'But there's ... but there's ...

'Frankie Corillo?' Muldoon said. 'We know, we have him in custody sir,' motioning to the limo at the main gate.

'Yes, but ...'

'You okay, sir?'

'But he's planted explosives. Corillo. There's ... there's a bomb.'

'A *bomb?*'

'A bomb. Studio five ... In one of the cars ... Set for nine o'clock ...'

Muldoon checked his watch. It had just hit eight thirty.

'Trust me, officer,' Don puffed, 'you gotta get everyone out of there.'

'Shit. *Chief!*'

'That's it!' Walsh said, snapping the metal of the cuffs with the wire cutters.

Ben stumbled upwards, his leg screaming, his other joints joining in with a few back-up vocals.

'We ... ow, fuck, we gotta find him!'

Dorfler was on the radio.

'Edelman's given us the slip, sir. We're moving out on foot to sweep the studios. He can't have got far.'

'Don't let him get away. There's another unit rolling to you. Sweep in twos north to south, and keep this line open?'

'C'mon,' Walsh said, and the three men headed down the corridor.

Applause and cheers floated out from the studio floor to greet them as the heavy curtains were tugged aside and a two-man camera crew pushed through, followed by Al Rosen and finally, bringing up the rear with a constant commentary, Diane Paretsky.

'*Yes, viewers, it's been quite a night. Al Rosen and Gill Kramer, now officially engaged. We're heading out to where Gill will hopefully be arriving by car in a few minutes' time. We are still waiting to hear from the LAPD regarding the whereabouts of multiple murderer—*'

She spotted the three men.

'*Ben! Ben!*' she cried, yanking the camera around. '*Ladies and gentlemen at home, this is Ben Busby, co-creator of* Carpool. *Ben, an unbelievable ordeal for you. Tell us, how are you feeling? And what are you wearing?*'

'He's got Jackie,' Ben stammered, wide-eyed and panicky. The camera crew followed him, out through the metal door, clanging down the stairs into the cool night. 'We've got to find him,' Ben said, hobbling off across the wide lane. 'We *have* to find him.'

On the *Fyre* stage, a balsa-wood door was kicked from its hinges. Silhouetted in the doorway, in wide trousers and a singed chef's hat, an actor cackled.

'*Fee-fi-fo-fum, I smell a diarist! Run, Pepys, run!*'

Jerry double-checked his console, flipping the switches from *test* to *armed*, lights clicking on one by one.

Leaving the cops and camera crew behind, Ben took a corner breathlessly between two huge studio buildings, buckley shoes clacking on the dry tarmac, leg stinging.

'*Melvin!*' he yelled, 'Melvin, where *is she?*'

Another dark, deserted lane.

'*Melvin!*' he yelled again, pounding into the darkness, foot-steps echoing, confusing him, making him spin and twirl. The place seemed deserted. He could hear sirens somewhere in the distance. Shouting. Hear Walsh and Dorfler running some-where, searching the lanes, Diane's voice jabbering her live commentary.

Chest heaving in his tight tunic, Ben reached the end of the lane. It opened out into a wide dark street. A large silver trailer squatted like a metallic slug against the side of the studio, a forklift truck beside it and half a dozen Mercury golf carts in personalised spots.

'Melvin!' Ben yelled at the night, spinning and twisting.

A crank and a whirr.

He spun again, dizzily. There was movement up ahead in the darkness.

'*Melvin?*'

Ben approached slowly, shoes scuffing, leg screaming, heart thudding in his ears.

A golf cart slid out from the fleet with a high-pitched buzz straight up ahead, little pink rear lights glowing, a short man at the wheel. He turned and looked at Ben quickly, his glasses flashing, before crunching the gears and whizzing off, away across the studio.

'Melvin!' Ben began to limp after the cart, shoes pinching and biting. 'He's here! Here!' Ben screamed to anyone who could hear him. '*Here!*'

But Melvin was away, taking a fast right and disappearing out of sight.

'Details?' Chief Sherwood barked.

The men were huddled at the main gate, faces illuminated red and blue, red and blue in the darkness. Officers scuttled around them busily, the air whooping and wailing with distant sirens.

'Corillo,' Don said, getting his breath back. 'He's had my father sign all insurance policies for this place over to him. He's going to take out studio five,' he checked his Rolex, 'in about twenty-five minutes.'

'And you *know* this?'

'As sure as I can be.'

'It's true,' Bernie said, appearing among them, pushing through the cluster of cops, cigarette dangling from his tired, sallow face, Howard dragging along behind him, paper pyjamas fluttering in the night breeze.

'Who's this?' Sherwood sighed.

'I'm his uncle. I'm the CFO of this place. Corillo told me the whole thing. Nine o'clock, this place goes bang.'

Sherwood took a deep, slow breath.

'You, Muldoon,' he said, 'get the bomb squad down here. Now! And I want this place closed off. A perimeter fence. Send in three units, pull everybody out. And I mean everybody. That Diane woman from KBL, the whole lot. Now c'mon, move.'

'Yes, sir.'

'Mr Silver, what more can you tell us about this explosive?'

Don sighed.

'It's in the prop car,' he said. 'The red Ford on the set. The sonofabitch has had it there for days.'

Ben took a deep breath and turned the key quickly clockwise, the green light winking on. He gripped the wheel in sweaty hands and gave the little gear stick a yank, swung the wheel and stomped on the accelerator, the cart whizzing out in an arc. Another clunk of gears and it whipped off.

He hummed along, reaching the corner where he'd lost Melvin, and took a right, whipping between two studios, hunched over the wheel.

'Melvin!' he hollered. '*Melvin!*'

He was nowhere to be seen.

Foot to the floor, speedometer flirting dangerously with double figures, Ben reached the end of the narrow lane and burst out into a wide crossroad.

Flicking a quick look to left and right, he buzzed onwards, cart bumping and bouncing, heart slamming away.

'*Where is she?!*' he screamed into the night. '*What have you done with her?*'

He was zipping down a narrow alley, past trailers and palettes, when Melvin's cart flashed just ahead of him, zipping right to left and out of sight.

Ben leaned forward, pedal flat to the floor, yanking the wheel, almost tipping over as he swung around.

'Melvin!' he yelled.

Two pink tail-lights buzzed ahead.

Ben's hands were wet on the wheel. He shifted and slid on the vinyl seat. Studios and stairways whipped past.

The cart in front took a left, disappearing from view behind a trailer. Seconds later Ben took the same turn, nipping down a narrow lane littered with steel tripods and gantry parts, weaving in and out.

Melvin took another left at the top, heading back the way he'd come, so Ben slammed on the brakes, the little buggy pitching to a halt, Ben oof-ing against the steering wheel.

Crunching the gear, grabbing the little wheel firmly, he craned his neck around and stomped his foot down, sending the little cart humming backwards, picking up speed, faster and faster. Ben held his breath, every twitch of the wheel sending the cart reeling and lurching crazily until he burst back out into the open by the trailer. He turned left, rolling along, staring into the gloom up ahead.

Two little headlights emerged from the right about two hundred feet away and stopped.

'*Melvin!*' Ben yelled into the darkness.

And then, with a mounting high-pitched hum, Melvin's cart buzzed forward. His teeth were gritted, eyes wide behind his thick lenses.

Ben gripped the wheel, his tight shoe hovering over the accelerator, and flashed a quick look at the gear stick. Forward would take him directly into Melvin's cart. The combined speed of the two probably scratching the paintwork a little bit. Reverse would have Melvin chasing him, bearing down on him hard and furious.

He heard a cry. He looked up and the little cart was thirty feet from him, Melvin screaming, feeble headlights straining to dazzle.

Twenty feet.

Ten.

Ben blinked hard.

He let Melvin get five feet away from him before Ben simply stepped out of his cart.

Melvin's eyes widened and he took his hands from the wheel as one cart ploughed into the other with a surprisingly feeble and thoroughly unsatisfying crunch of plastic and rubber.

The impact, however, was enough to bounce Melvin out of his seat, causing a much more satisfying crack of head-on-thick-plastic-roof. Ben, without thinking, grabbed Melvin's shirt and heaved him from the cart, the pair of them tumbling to the floor.

'*I've got him!*' he yelled. 'He's *here!* I've *got him!*'

'You hear that?' Diane said, holding up a hand. The camera-crew bumped into her clumsily.

They all fell silent and listened.

'What?' Dorfler said. He was flashing his torch over a gleaming silver trailer.

Suddenly his radio crackled into life. He snapped it up.

'This is eight Lincoln thirty receiving, go ahead sir.'

'What? That the Chief?' Walsh said. 'What's he saying?'

'*For those just joining us,*' Diane said, facing the camera, '*We are live here at Mercury Studios, Burbank, where police are hunting down one Melvin Edelman, loose somewhere in the dark lanes of the studio lot. Loose, armed and highly dangerous. My name's Diane Paretsky and you're watching* Sexposé.'

'Wait . . . Shit, change of plan!' Dorfler said. 'We got an evac'. Studio five . . . Possible explosive device. We gotta get everybody outta there and on to the street.'

'*Explosive?*' Diane said for the sake of her viewing millions. 'What about Edelman? He's still runnin' about this place somewhere.'

'Nope,' Dorfler said, clipping his radio back. 'Civilians first. Studio five, c'mon let's move.'

Beneath Ben on the cold tarmac, Melvin began to kick and wrestle dizzily.

'*NO!*' Ben screamed through gritted teeth, heaving him up, rolling with him across the ground. Ben slammed him hard by the shoulders, Melvin's skull knocking on the ground.

'Where is she?' he spat, saliva flying. 'What have you done with her, you crazy fuck?!'

Melvin winced, eyes tight shut.

Ben heaved him up for another slam.

'St-studio six! She's in studio s-six!'

'Six?' Ben said, clambering up. The world spun and lurched in the darkness as he gazed up at the huge buildings around him. 'Studio twelve? And studio . . . studio three? Where's six? Where's SIX?' he bellowed, but Melvin just lay, woozy and groaning, on the freezing ground.

Ben began to run.

'*My writings speak the truth, dough-boy!*' Pepys cried, hauling his leather diary from his satchel and holding it triumphantly aloft, the flickering fiery light streaming through the stained glass, smoke curling around his knees. '*One day history will know what you did to this city! It's all in here!*'

'Stand by FX,' the director whispered into his headset.

'This way, ladies and gentlemen. Quickly, please, this way. Quick as you can, thank you.'

Walsh had the warm-up man's microphone, Dorfler and half a dozen other officers clearing the chattering audience and the bewildered crew from the studio.

Diane and her crew had positioned themselves at the bottom of the iron stairs, thrusting the microphone at everyone who passed with a, '*Diane Paretsky*, Sexposé – *any comment?*'

'This has been great!' a young man said, pulling on a baseball cap. 'Gun-fights, arrests. . .'

'Live video-link gay TV executive reunions,' his pal chipped in.

'Is it going to be like this every week?' a young girl said, zipping up her jacket. 'Can we get tickets again?'

In the stone archway, flames licking behind him, with a wrench and a '*fwaangg!*' the baker fired the dummy cross-bow.

Pepys ducked, theatrically.

In the darkness, off stage, Jerry flipped the squib on his console and the back of a spring-loaded arrow snapped out of a hidden groove in the large wooden lectern.

Pepys yelled, hurling himself forward, feet echoing on the boards of the set, and dived at the baker, slamming him up against a padded pillar.

'Stand-by FX,' the director whispered.

Jerry placed his gloved hands over the red 'fire' switch.

'*Pat-a-cake pat-a-cake, baker's man,*' Pepys snarled.

'And go FX!'

'*You murdered my wife, punk . . .*'

Jerry flipped the switch.

'*. . . thy shit hitteth the fan . . .*'

There was a sudden yell.

'*STOP!*'

Then a sudden bang.

The breakaway lectern exploded in a bright flash of flame and smoke, lightweight timber clattering to the floor. This fired the squib within the front three pews, compressed air sending them spinning upwards. Another flash, bang and a sheet of flame shot roofwards with them.

'JACKIE!' Ben yelled, pushing through the flats, a great wooden wall yawning and groaning as it fell. The cast looked up. The crew covered their faces.

'STOP!' Jerry yelled.

A little hobbling Puritan in doublet and hose charged screaming up the aisle.

'*JACKIE!*'

Like a firework display, the squibs in the pews fired the next bang, which fired the next bang and the next, all timed to perfection. The lectern opposite exploded in another flash-bang. A breakaway plaster statue to the right of the altar pitched forward and smashed on command in a plume of dust.

'JACKIE!' Ben yelled, hurling himself up the steps to the altar. '*Help me! Somebody, help me!*'

Jerry pushed his console aside and burst on to the set, aware of the loaded props and rigged sets in every corner.

'It's here, it must be here!' Ben said, reaching the altar, heart pounding. He circled it quickly. 'Jackie! Jackie, where . . . JACKIE!'

'Holy shit!' Jerry said, reaching the back of the altar.

'*Mmmffb . . .*' Jackie said, gag stuffed hard in her mouth, face striped with tears.

Ben kicked and tore at the prop, Jerry on his knees frantically tearing out cables, wrenching out wire from the pink kerosene bottles, disarming the pyrotechnics. With a crack and a yelp of pain, Ben kicked the breakaway support, the top of the wooden altar, the whole shell splitting and collapsing in on itself.

Above them there was a great chime, a beautiful ear-splitting shatter, as the stained sugar-glass window exploded, flame machines sending a huge wall of fire up behind them.

Amid the crackle, the heat, the chaos of smoke and fire and falling timber, the little Puritan heaved the buxom wench from the flames, stumbling down the aisle in a hard flurry of hugs and fast kisses.

'What's . . . what's happening?' she said eventually, breathless and sniffing. Around them, the last of the rigged props fizzed and sparked in the darkness. Ben held her against him. He didn't want to let her go. He never wanted to let her go.

'Shit, man,' the director said, wandering over across the cables and tape of the floor. 'You two are like, on fire.'

Ben and Jackie unplugged and untangled themselves from each other, out of breath.

'Sorry,' Jackie said, pulling her blouse closed. 'It's been a while.'

'No. I mean, you're on *fire*,' he laughed. 'Somebody?'

'Holy shit,' Ben coughed, waving away thick black smoke.

Jerry let rip with an extinguisher, dousing the pair of them with icy foam.

FORTY-TWO

'Edelman?' Chief Sherwood yapped into his radio. 'Any visuals on *Edelman?* Anybody, over?'

The radio crackled and popped in the negative.

Sherwood tossed his handset on to the hood of his patrol car with a clatter.

The studio was in chaos.

Two dozen black and white patrol cars ringed the perimeter, lights flashing, reflecting on windshields, on doors, throwing a purple glow over the street. Officers reeled yellow and black tape crookedly between posts and palm trees, yelling, shouting, pushing an eager public back behind the line.

Whisper had become rumour had become spectacle and most of the three-hundred strong audience were still hanging about on the street, waiting to see the studio go bang – rubbing their hands, stamping their feet, pointing and 'oooh-ing' and 'ahhh-ing' like it was a local firework display. Anyone who'd thought to start selling toffee apples would have cleaned up.

'*Mercury Studios, Burbank, California,*' Diane said in her most solemn TV tone, flicking her hair and pulling back her shoulders. Her crew focused, the woolly mic bobbing above her head. '*Home of such disasters as* Woodfellas, Ringing For Ewe *and* I'm A Yankee Doodle Gandhi *has tonight become home to an event even more terrifying than the ratings of those three shows put together. Here,*' and Diane began to lead her crew through the buffeting crowds towards the main gate, '*a crowd who had come for an innocent evening's entertainment have been plunged into a hellish nightmare of psychopaths, gunfire and arson.*'

'This is great!' someone said loudly from the crowd.

'I'm calling my mom, getting her down here to watch.'

'Shit! Keep rolling.' Diane scowled. '*Uhmm, here we see Chief Sherwood who is heading up the police team. Chief Sherwood – what can you tell us about what's going on here?*'

Sherwood turned from his briefing, his colleagues scattering in a burst of '*yes, sirs*'. He squinted into the halogen glare of the camera's spotlight.

'*Can you confirm there is a bomb?*'

'We have a visual on the explosive. A large quantity of C4 has been rigged to a timer beneath a prop car in studio five. We believe Frankie Corillo had his men place it there yesterday under the guise of building a set, using his son Vincent as cover.'

'*And have you managed to evacuate?*'

'We have confirmation studio five is clear, a team is clearing studio six as we speak. Now I'm gonna have to ask you to step back behind the tape here. The bomb squad are on their way, we have only a few minutes, please.'

'*And what of Melvin Edelman?*'

'I have no information at this time,' Sherwood said, three or four officers joining him, pushing back the chattering crowd.

'*And Ben Busby? And Jacqueline Heaney? Have they been located? Chief Sherwood? Chief Sherwood?*'

'Through here,' Ben said, leading an exhausted, barefoot Jackie down a dark silent alley between the studios, past a battered golf cart and a forklift truck. 'We'll go in the back way.' And they clanged up an iron staircase.

'Diane? What happened to Diane? And Zak? Are they okay?' Jackie said. She was dizzy from the explosive fumes, tired and scared, and just wanted to be safe at home. Home, where sirens and explosions were kept safe, locked behind glass, on Saturday night telly.

'I guess we'll find out,' Ben said, hauling open a side door and slipping into the studio. 'Hello?' he said.

The place was deserted.

Utterly.

No audience, no crew, no warm-up, nothing. The lights were still on, burning hot and high, but the lecterns and cameras and bank of monitors all stood abandoned, as if he and Jackie were on the Studio Tour at Marie Celeste Pictures Inc.

'Hello?' Ben called again, leading Jackie by the hand, stepping over fat snaking cables. The cars all sat, warm and bright, under the lights.

'I don't understand,' he said, checking his watch. 'It's only quarter to nine, where did everybody go?'

He looked over the cameras. The white film canisters from their tops were missing.

'I don't understand, where is everybody . . .'

'Th-they're not on anymore,' a familiar voice said.

Ben and Jackie froze. The studio fell quiet.

Gripping each other's clammy hands, they turned around slowly. Ben in his tiny smouldering Puritan costume, Jackie all goosbumps and smudged mascara, to face Melvin.

'They got c-cancelled,' he said, dressed in his stage clothes with a simple handgun accessory.

Outside, a great cheer burst from the crowd, whooping and clapping as a limousine wheeled on to Alemeda Avenue, weaving between protesting policemen and patrol cars, pushing into the crowd.

'*You getting it? You getting it?*' Diane cried over the din, her camera man nodding greedily, zooming in as the rear door heaved open, sending onlookers tumbling, and a tearful Gill Kramer emerged blinking into the chaos, with Dick Trent.

'Al? Al?' Gill cried. 'Where's Al?'

The cheers redoubled as Al Rosen, his baseball cap tumbling, halogen lights gleaming on his bald head, struggled through the crowd and collapsed into his lover's arms.

Behind them, Dick Trent produced a surprise *Celebrity Couple Of The Year* trophy from the car and the crowd began to rain down a confetti of torn up *Carpool* flyers over them, cheering and applauding.

'Oh, it's a g-great line-up for Saturday nights this season,' Melvin said with a smile, his grey tooth flashing. Ben and Jackie stood still, eyes flickering between Melvin's gleeful face and the gun that wavered and bobbed as he spoke. He was moving slowly about the studio floor. *'At six o'clock it's the all new Melvin Show with everyone's favourite funnyman, Melvin Meedleford. Meedford. M-Meddleman.'*

'Melvin—'

'Join in the laughs as Melvin m-meets up with a top Hollywood producer and pretends to be a famous writer! Then, at six-thirty, Everybody Loves Melvin. Hapless Melvin M-Med-Medman has his family in st-stitches when they visit London for the f-first time and stay in a swanky h-hotel.'

'Mel?' Ben said gingerly.

Jackie squeezed his hand hard to stop him but Ben pressed on, ignoring the twinge of foreboding in his insides.

'Mel? These . . . uhmm . . . sound like great shows. Family shows, right? For all the family?' he said, thinking quickly.

'Something for all the f-family!' Melvin beamed.

'But, uhmm, I can't help noticing you h-have a gun,' Ben said, his heart banging hard. 'That's a bit odd for a family show, isn't it? A gun? Do we . . . do we need that?'

Melvin blinked hard, eyes suddenly darting about.

'Ben, *don't*,' Jackie pleaded as they backed across the squeaky floor.

Melvin peered down at the heavy weapon in his hand.

'It'll slay ya,' he said, looking up at them with a dull grin.

'*It'll kill ya. I murdered 'em out there.*' And he fired once, a loud flat bang into the air. A spotlight above popped and cracked into darkness with a fizz.

Jackie screamed.

'*Knocked . . . 'em . . . dead.*' Melvin smiled, lowering the gun to face them.

'*And that's . . . yes, that's Don Silver, VP of Comedy Development here at Mercury,*' Diane narrated over the wail of distant sirens. '*With his father and his Uncle Bernie. Let's see if we can get a few words with them about their horrifying ordeal.*' And she pushed her crew between the buffeting crowd and the limousine. '*Excuse me,* Sexposé, *coming through . . .*'

The three men were by the car, shaking hands with Al and Gill boisterously. Don held a large silver tape canister under his arm.

'*Mr Silver? Mr Silver? Diane Paretsky. You're live on KBL.*'

'Miss Paretsky,' Don smiled. 'And good evening, America.' He winked at the camera.

'*Mr Silver. With Corillo back in custody and your name cleared of these murders, can I ask you how you're feeling? And what will become of* Carpool *— the show that started this all?*'

'Funny you should ask, Miss Paretsky . . .' Don beamed.

Ben and Jackie backed away a little more quickly across the squeaky floor as Melvin chattered on, swinging the handgun to and fro, ducking under the cameras, wheeling the lecterns along absently.

Ben's panicked eyes ran over every surface. The cars, the monitors, the chairs, the cables. Something. Trying to think of *something.*

'Oh, it'll slay ya,' Melvin said again, smiling. 'It slayed *her.*'

'Her?' Ben said.

'*He* did. He slayed her. *Tonight on WGBM Local News.*

Three killed in coffeeshop hold up. He killed out there tonight. Tore the place up.'

Ben let go of Jackie's hand quickly, sliding behind her, swopping sides. They continued to walk backwards in a wide circle under the lights, between the gleaming cars.

'They said Mom was happier now,' Melvin said, his left hand up at his cheek, picking at his face. 'Looking d-down. Watching. Like TV, I guess? Smiling. Happier.'

He blinked hard.

'You'll love the new show at seven! It's The Edelmans! They're one big happy f-family. There are n-no frowns or fights or basements. No one gets cross or hurts anyone. No-one gets locked away. No, just the love and laughter of T-Terry and June and their little Melvin . . .'

As Melvin chatted manically on, Ben realised that the balance of power had shifted the tiniest fraction. What had started as Melvin walking towards them and them backing away, had now somehow switched to them walking backwards slowly, causing a distracted Melvin to follow.

Ben squeezed Jackie's hand and they began to turn, widening the circle, backing off the front of the stage towards the cameras.

'Heyyy,' Ben said to Jackie suddenly. 'Terry and June. You know *them*.' And he gave her a big pally nudge.

'What?' Jackie said, face pale and terrified.

'What?' Melvin said, blinking quickly.

'Terry and June Medford,' Ben said through a fixed grin, staring at Jackie, eyebrows flailing and signalling wildly. 'Melvin's parents? I think Jackie knows them. Right, *Jackie?*'

'Uhmm . . ?'

'Talk to him, ask him,' Ben egged her on, slowly steering Jackie backwards through the cameras to where the lecterns stood around the bank of monitors. *'Talk to him.'*

'Er . . . shit, uhmm, yes, yes,' Jackie said, exchanging a wide eyed pleading look with Ben, her knees quivering, heart slamming. She had no idea what he was trying to do. 'Uhmm, that's right,' she said. 'Terry and June. They had pigs didn't they? *You*, I mean. Didn't you?' she said, mind desperately raking through the hours of sitcom drivel Ben had made her sit through. 'Two pigs?'

'*No*,' Ben whispered, but it was too late.

Melvin raised the gun, his hand shaking.

'NO!' he bellowed. 'T-Tom and Barbara had p-pigs. They were our *other* neighbours!'

'Y-yes! That's it,' Jackie stammered. 'And a-a-a cockerel? They had a cockerel called . . . *Marx?*'

'NO!'

'*Lenin!*' Jackie shouted, blinking back terrified tears. 'I-I-I mean Lenin! A-And a goat called Geraldine? And the pigs. Uhmm . . . *P-Pinky!* Pinky and *Perky*. Series th-three . . .'

'You . . . you know them?' Melvin said, breathing returning to normal.

'Oh, y-yes, kind of,' Jackie said, heart slamming, backing away. 'You're . . . er . . . not so d-different, you and Ben.'

And Ben and Jackie stopped, bumping into the bank of monitors at the edge of the studio.

'What . . . what do you mean?' Melvin said flatly, the muzzle of the gun lifting slightly.

'Well . . .'

'Uhmm,' Ben said, hands reaching behind him slowly.

'*Everybody back! Behind the tape! Everybody! Move back behind the tape!*'

With less than eight minutes to go, the bomb squad had arrived.

Four gleaming black LAPD vans, sirens shrieking, burst their guts all over the studio, a torrent of black-clad men in masks, flak jackets and boots pouring out like oil on water. The public 'oooh-ed'. The public 'ahhh-ed'. The public 'shit-man-we're-all-gonna-die-ed'. Behind the crowds, wheeling around on to Alemeda, came two fire trucks, lights dazzling in the clear night air, klaxons shaking the people, the palms, the world.

'Can't do it,' the bomb captain was telling Sherwood firmly. 'No time. We can only prepare the place for the blast. Okay, people, listen up! I need three E-teams, I want blankets, I want jackets—'

'Wait, dude!' Zak said, pushing through into the huddle. 'Ben and Jackie, man? Like what about Ben and Jackie?'

'Who's this?' the bomb captain barked.

Sherwood shrugged.

'Zachary Black, sir,' he said, extending a hand. 'But my friend's call me Zak. Zak, like I'm ex-Zak-tly the guy—'

'Black, I'm sorry. Time's run out. Anyone still in there is staying in there. We got seven minutes. I can't risk sending officers in. Safest thing for you is to get one of these on,' and he shoved a jacket against Zak's chest, 'and get behind a car.'

'Like, but—'

'Okay, E-teams with me, let's get this crowd *back!* Move it, move it, *move it!*'

'Laughter, I mean,' Ben said, swallowing hard. 'Jokes. Telling jokes. At home. It . . . it was important. Keeping everyone happy, everyone smiling. Keeping the bad stuff away.'

'The bad stuff,' Melvin said darkly.

Out of the lights, the studio was cold, the air smelling of paint and timber. Backed up against the console, Ben continued shakily.

'Being the one. The one with the joke, th-the one with the line, with the voice, whatever. It was important, right? To get that noise in the house, that charge? So for a minute, just for one minute, everything was fine. Everybody was happy.'

'Everybody happy,' Melvin nodded. 'Everybody was always happy in the basement.'

'Sure they were!' Ben said, trying to force an easy smile, eyes on the gun.

He was sweating, panicked and dizzy. Behind him, he fumbled on the console. It had to be here, where was it, where *was* it?

'If D-Dad was at the office or-or-or running the hotel? If M-Mom was working behind the bar with Sammy or-or-or with Louie and Latka at th-the cab rank. We would laugh t-together . . .'

Ben's hands slid further over the switches. Not there, not there . . . *there!*

He gripped it and prodded Jackie in the back.

'*Take it,*' he whispered out of the side of his mouth, not moving his eyes from Melvin.

'*Wha—*'

'Uncle Fletcher, Gr-Grandpa Bilko, Cousin Clinger. We'd g-gather round . . .'

'*TV announcer,*' Ben hissed. '*On my signal.*'

'*What are you talking about?!*'

'After school was the happiest. Before Aunty Connie came home. Just me and Lucy an-and Ricky and Ethel . . .'

'*Introduce him. His show, coming up next, on my signal.*'

'*No! No Ben, I can't . . .*'

'So!' Ben said loudly. Melvin jumped, the gun twitching upwards. Ben elbowed Jackie away. 'Do you miss them all?' he continued boisterously. 'Uncle Latka and Second Cousin Basil and Aunty Frasier and Grandma Tyler Moore? All your friends from the basement?'

'Stay back,' Melvin said nervously, extending the gun a little. 'All those happy faces?'

'They . . . they're not r-real,' Melvin said, blinking hard. He pressed the heel of his hand against his temple. 'Stay back.'

'They miss you. It's been a while, hasn't it? But hey, did you think they'd miss your show?' Ben said. 'Your big night?'

His chest thumped, his throat felt tight, feet cold and cramped in his stupid buckled shoes.

He turned around quickly to face the console.

553

'Hey! Keep still!' Melvin yelled.

Sticky labels were plastered over the front, under every switch, over every dial.

Ben held his breath and hit VT Playback.

Everybody jumped as suddenly the room exploded with the crackling wash of TV laughter.

'Wait . . . w-wait . . . stop!'

On the console in front of him, Ben watched the screens flicker into life. Clips of comedy shows. The same images flickered on the two dozen television screens hanging above them from the steel gantries.

Melvin looked up, stumbling backwards. Tinny laughter, jokes, voices, echoed about him on every side.

'Farmer McDonald? Flossie? Mr Luigi? You all here to see The Melvin Show?' Ben said loudly. 'It's about to start!' He threw a look over at Jackie, standing anxiously by a lectern. '*It's about to start!*' he yelled at her.

Jackie pulled the warm-up's microphone from behind her back.

'Uhmm,' she said, startled as she heard her own voice boom from every speaker.

'Gill?' Melvin said softly, peering up at the screen. 'You . . .'

'Uhmm! Th-that's right!' Jackie stumbled, Ben egging her on frantically. 'Coming up after the break, the first in a n-new series of The, er, The Melvin Show.'

Jackie's voice echoed and bounced about the high ceilings.

Melvin stared at Ben.

Cold with terror, Ben gave as big a grin as he could manage and clapped his hands.

'That's it!' he cried. 'You're on!'

'Wh-what?' Melvin said, lowering the gun an inch.

'Come on, come on, everyone's going to tune in! We've got the cameras, the set, everybody's waiting. Can't you hear them?'

Laughter roared about them.

'In this episode, Melvin is . . . is locked,' Jackie said quickly, 'in a car on the freeway.'

'Locked in a car!' Ben cried, slapping his thigh. 'That's genius! Genius, Melvin. C'mon now, quick!' And he hurried forward.

Instinctively, Melvin backed away, stumbling against the warm metal of the red Ford.

'With just two minutes to go here, everyone is braced for the explosion. The LAPD have pulled everyone back from the edge of the studio, they've closed the streets. All we can do now is watch and wait. This is Diane Paretsky for Sexposé . . .'

'That's it, that's it!' Ben shouted, positioning himself behind one of the huge cameras, arms flapping. 'In the car — I need you in shot. That's it, quickly!'

Melvin, bewildered, hurried backwards, the laughter, the voices, the announcements clanging about his ears.

'And now, on ABN, pull up a chair, unplug the phone, put the cat out and settle down on your basement mat for The Melvin Show!'

'Dan dat dahhh! Dan dat dahhhh!' Ben sang tunelessly, heaving the camera around the floor.

In the car, sweating nervously, eyes flashing between the flickering monitors and the single glassy lens of the camera, Melvin sat still, holding his breath.

'Okay, we're gonna pan out!' Ben hollered, pulling the camera back gradually. He reached out to the console on his right, wrenching up the volume slide, the sound of voices, of jokes, of laughter, roaring, distorting, deafening from every speaker.

'Okay, and on you, Melvin in five . . . four . . .'

Ben slid the camera back further, further, grabbing Jackie's hand, pulling her with him.

'Three . . . two . . .'

They slid back, back, the camera cables tightening, lifting from the floor.

'One . . .'

The camera rolled to a halt at the back of the studio, among the swathes of black cloth.

'*Cue Melvin!*' Ben hollered, grabbing Jackie and pushing her out, through the cloth, tumbling breathlessly into the silence of the corridor.

Melvin sat in a very quiet place for a moment.

Hands clammy on the wheel, he blinked through the windshield, peering at the studio, at the world, through the familiar square sheet of glass.

He liked the world behind glass.

Everything was funnier behind glass.

Laughter, rippling, washing, crashing about him like waves.

He steadied his breathing and smiled. The flat glass eyes of the four cameras stared back at him.

Was he on?

Melvin leaned forward a little, peering further into the nearest camera eye, to see if he could see anybody.

Maybe someone sitting at home, on their mat, in the damp, in the dark, waiting for his friends.

He waved at them, clearing his dry throat a little.

'Hello,' he said softly. 'I'm Melvin.'

The laughter redoubled, echoing about him.

He smiled.

The bang was bigger than everybody expected.

Even behind toughened shields and blast blankets, hands over heads, flat on the tarmac, it shook the world. A great roar, tearing the night in two, the sides of the studio bellowing, billowing, buckling. A ball of fire belched from every door, every seam, the roof launching itself into the night sky. Cranes, steel, gantries and beams splashed like

556

toothpicks, the heat of the blast flashing against everyone's cheeks.

But the building didn't collapse.

It stood frozen against the purple night.

And then it fell. Slowly, painfully slowly, wrenching and roaring and screaming like a dying beast, through a thick sea of black smoke, yawning and crashing to the ground, the earth trembling and juddering.

And then, as if it had changed its mind about the whole thing, it stopped again.

And gradually began to rise.

The smoke sucking inwards, disappearing, the walls folding together, upwards.

And then, once again, it stopped.

Diane looked at it, chewing the inside of her lip.

Hmmm.

And then it collapsed again, faster this time. Too fast. The smoke puffing out, the walls slamming to the ground as if stomped on from a great height.

It slowed to a more regular speed. The smash and tangle of the walls and equipment collapsing, the crunch of brick and rubble, then finally to just a slow constant crackle. And then gradually the studio disappeared as figures appeared in front of it. Shapes and silhouettes. Standing up, brushing themselves down. Gasping for air, hugging and dazed.

Diane picked up a pencil and jotted down the counter number.

Sirens somewhere wailed like abandoned children, suddenly drowned out by a sharp ringing.

'Fuck it,' she said, jabbing the pause button.

On screen, the frozen shadowy figures, the flames, the smoke, the debris, all came to a gentle stop.

Diane grabbed her Diet Coke and skidded the office chair along the rubber floor of the dark editing suite. She grabbed up the phone.

'*Like, Pulitzer Prize for Miss Paretsky,*' a voice said. '*Would you like to sign for it?*'

Diane grinned.

'Where are you?'

'*Like, reception?*'

'Come on up.'

She stood up, stretching her back with a groan, glancing up at the clock.

It was 11.30 p.m.

She swigged her Coke and wandered back to the screen, rubbing her tired eyes and stacking her carefully labelled tapes into teetering *to-do* piles.

'Like, I'm ready for my close up,' a voice floated in.

'Penny,' Diane said and they exchanged hugs. 'Good to see you, hon.'

'Moët and mozzarella, the supper of kings.' Penny flapped in in a clashing whirl of earrings and heels. 'How's the big story? What you got so far? I am literally all ears.' She fussed with napkins and paper cups. 'Heyyy, this it? This here?' she said, pointing at the frozen explosion flickering on the monitor.

She jabbed the play button and began to peel open the foil on the champagne bottle.

Diane collapsed into a swivel chair and tried to massage the day from her weary face.

On screen, as the smoke billowed and bloomed, the fire crackled and roared, two figures, a man and a woman, could be seen hauling themselves up from the tarmac, stumbling forward, holding hands and running. The woman tripped, the man caught her, kissed her, held her, the studio behind blowing outwards again in a bright ball of fire, throwing the embrace into silhouette.

Penny glugged out some celebratory bubbles into the paper cups.

'Well, Nancy Drew, here's to your exclusive and the highest ratings of the year.'

'Hey, hey, enough!' Diane cried as the champagne glugged and frothed all over the console. 'I can't have all that, I gotta work.'

'Work? Like, hello?' Penny said. 'We're going *out*. You're the girl on the spot. People want to meet you. The whole Mercury thang is *big news*, honey.'

'Can't do it. KBL want all this stuff cut together for an extended morning news special. I got all these to get through.' And she sifted through the stack of tapes.

'You're not coming to the *partaayyy*?'

'*Party?*'

'The *partayyy*,' Penny corrected. 'Don's do? His digging-of-shins? He's throwing the Brentwood place open.'

'Tonight?'

'He's celebrating.'

'That two and half hours ago the family firm went up in smoke?' Diane queried.

'Oh, keep *up*, sister. A little less time *taping* life,' Penny said, tapping the teetering pile, 'and a little more time *living it*, please. He's done the deal with ABN. Rosen's bought *Carpool*.'

'No way!'

'Concept, script, the lot. For ABN. He's giving the lead to Gill as a wedding present. They're reshooting the pilot for next fall's schedule.'

'Are you *serious? Rosen?*'

'Al's back at ABN,' Penny said. 'Promoted no less. President of Comedy Development. Did the deal two hours ago.' She flapped a slice of pizza at the monitors. 'Hell, think of the ratings. *Carpool*'s the show at the centre of the biggest showbiz scandal since JFK spiked Monroe's malt with industrial *Weedol*.'

Diane sipped her champagne, getting a noseful of bubbles, and peeled off a slice of pizza.

'And Kramer's gonna star, huh?'

'It'll be the biggest show of next year, honey. Also starring one Zachary Black and some unknown Shifty Dolawitz is raving about . . . Mickey somebody? Thomopou-something? Whatever.'

They munched and slurped in silence for a moment in the flickering glow of the monitors.

'And who's gonna write it?' Diane chomped through a mouthful of greasy mozzarella. 'I mean, this is a big gig. ABN prime-time fall schedule?' She licked a shiny finger. 'Anyone we know?'

SEVEN MONTHS LATER

BIGWIG HANGS HAT WITH STUDIO SPLASH AS LEXUS LAFFER IS LIT AND WEBS HELM HOOD HAILERS

By PENNY LANG
HOLLYWOOD

There are a handful of surprises awaiting audiences this autumn as the webs wheel out their fall skeds this week.

UNWISEGUYS

A case of déjà-you-talkin'-to-me as not one, not two, but five networks have commissioned big budget miniseries based on the life of executed mobster Frankie Corillo.

ARK ANGELS

Other major projects for next season include a new period epic from ABN.

In a follow up to last year's FYRE, which was controversially revisited recently by historians at UCLA and hailed as 'stunningly accurate' and 'an eerily astute snapshot of seventeenth-century London' – ABN have announced their new period twelve-parter FLUDDE, starring Gill Kramer as Noah and unknowns Martin Walsh and Roger Dorfler as sons Shem and Japtheth. Kramer can also be seen topping ABN's fall skeds in the long awaited jam-joker CARPOOL.

VROOM WITH A VIEW

It's troubled past behind it, the static steering sitcom comes to ABN's Thursday nights, also starring Zachary Black (from NBO's THE NAME'S ZAK!) and Mickey Thomopoulous (scribe behind BAFTA winning MAIN GATE for the BBC).

Series creators are credited as Sheridan McDonald and Benjamin Busby

FAREWELL

The show is the first from the relaunched studio, previously known as Mercury Pictures and owned by CEO Howard Silver.

It is with a heavy but healthy heart that we announce his retirement.

The founder of the Burbank-based outfit, Howard suffered minor cardio problems last fall and has handed over the reins to his brother Bernie.
Finally, all eyes are on former Comedy VP Don Silver, who Bernie assures us will be seen in "a challenging new role."

Variety
Friday 16 May

EPILOGUE

A fat sun peeked sheepishly through the trees around Central Park, peering through the branches, gazing between the leaves, embarrassed. Over the last few months it had become a little conscious of its own shape as it watched over a trimmer Howard Silver pounding away healthily on his treadmill through his uptown bedroom window every morning.

It hung back behind the trees self-consciously and waited for some clouds to roll over.

Howard jogged briskly, pink-cheeked, a book in his left hand, once in a while checking his speed and glugging from a bottle of water.

Downstairs the dog was barking, the front door slamming, Marion coo-ing and fussing about in her tracksuit.

'Send him on up!' Howard shouted, jabbing off the machine, slowing to a stop and patting himself a little with a white towel. He speared a prune from the bowl on the table beside him and folded the corner of his page.

'Howie?' Bernie said, knocking lightly on the bedroom door and coming in. 'Good morning to you. Hey, look at this. How you getting on with having that thing at home?'

'Great, Bern. I'm up to a solid 6 m.p.h.,' Howard said sweeping damp hair from his shiny brow. 'What about you? Still patched up?'

Bernie sighed and gave a little laugh, tugging a box of nicotine patches from his khakis.

'I'm down to ten of these a day. Of course, I'm rollin' them up and smokin' them. You see *Variety*?'

'I told you, Bern, I don't read that stuff anymore,' Howard said, easing himself across the thick carpet to the bed, puffing off his trainers. 'Had Marion cancel my subscription. It's cleared my ulcer right up.'

'So what you reading?' Bernie said, motioning to the book. Howard handed it to him. 'Heyyy, you *bought* it?' And he began flicking through.

'Thought I'd see how we came out,' Howard said. 'So what's the news?'

'Huh? Oh, they're just announcing the moves, the name change. Talkin' of which,' and Bernie reached into his jacket and pulled out a heavy sheet of paper. 'Picked this up this morning. Whaddya think?'

Howard took the sheet and unfolded it.

'Terrific.' He smiled. 'Did *Variety* mention young Don?'

'Just that he'll be seen in a new role, "to be announced".'

Howard smiled.

Downstairs, the dog began barking again. The door slammed.

'That'll be him,' Howard said.

There was a thud-thud-thud up the stairs and Don appeared at the doorway in Ray-Bans, a crumpled suit and loafers, a book tucked under his arm.

'Hey, Dad. Uncle Bernie,' he said. 'Jesus, I'm fried. What's goin' on? Any coffee about?'

'You got one too, huh?' Bernie said.

'Huh? Oh, yeah, sure,' Don said blearily, fishing the book out. *Kramer Vs Kramer – The Gill Kramer Story. By Penny Lang.*

'Hell, thought there might be a movie-of-the-week in it. Plus I wanted to see how I came out, naturally. I've been at the launch party up town all night. Dolawitz was on piano doing

"Livin' On A Prayer". He told me to tell you that he heard our insurance cheque has cleared. Wants to set up a lunch to discuss Kramer's salary.'

'Sonofabitch!' Bernie laughed.

'Whatcha' got there, Pop?' Don asked. Howard handed the crisp new stationery to his son.

'Heyyy, look at this. *Phoenix Pictures*,' he read, admiring the fiery new logo. 'CEO Bernie Silver.'

'It's all over the paper,' Bernie said, handing his nephew a rolled-up *Variety*. 'Page four.'

Don took it, flicking through quickly.

Howard and Bernie exchanged looks.

'Here we go,' Don said, dropping to the bed with a stifled yawn. '*Corillo, yadda yadda. Fludde yadda yadda.* Carpool, *retirement, yadda yadda.* . . wait, a new role?' And he looked up. 'What new role?'

'Your uncle and I have been talking,' Howard said, putting his hand on Don's shoulder. 'It's something more suited to you, son. Where you have the experience.'

'What? *What?*' he said excitedly.

'The mailroom,' Bernie said. The bedroom fell quiet. The dog barked downstairs.

'*Mailroom?*' Don's father and uncle looked at him. '*Mailroom,*' he said again, turning it over in his head. 'Like it, that works,' he said, standing up.

'You do?' Bernie sounded surprised.

'Sure. It's blue-collar, it's ensemble. What are we thinking? Kind of an old-school Bilko thing? A crazy gang of guys working in the basement, mixing up the mail, trying to get ahead? No, no, I like it, I like it.' And he began to pace. 'It's *Cheers* but in an office. You'll have the go-getter, the sarcastic one, the dumb one, the lazy one, the snob . . . I can see it. *Mailroom.* Has anyone else heard this idea? Who's pitched it? Shall I set up a lunch?'

Howard smiled.

'That's not exactly what we mean, son.'

On any Monday afternoon in the hills of Los Angeles you can hear sprinklers hissing and whispering about the ferns and shrubs. The soft lapping of water as tanned young men in shorts skim private pools with long nets. Ice crackling and tinkling in crystal pitchers on glass table-tops. The quiet thump of ceiling fans in cool white homes.

And it was in one of these homes, high in the hills, that Ben sat.

'So,' he began. 'Tell me what you're going to bring to *Carpool*?'

The young writer perched on the edge of the white sofa shrugged.

'Bring? Gee, uhh, I dunno. Uhm, y'know?' he closed, helpfully.

'You worked at Phoenix before, I see,' Ben began on a different tack, lifting the young man's CV from the table. 'Back when it was still Mercury?'

'Uh-huh.' The writer nodded. 'I was an executive associate assistant trainee in the pastry and cappuccino division.'

Ben smiled.

'Which you took as, what, a foot-in-the-door? For your writing?'

The young man nodded.

'I do a bit of stand-up too,' he said. 'I've got a gig tonight, actually . . . I mean, if you're interested? At the Comedy Store?'

Ben nodded, getting up.

'Great. Then I'll drop by and see you there. I'll buy you a drink afterwards and we can talk more about you coming to join us. Okay?'

The young writer grinned a huge grin.

'I . . . I really appreciate this, Mr Busby. I know how busy you are, running the show an' all. But really, all I want is a chance.'

They shook hands.

'Call me Ben.'

Across the hallway of the house, Jackie sat at her laptop in the cool cream lounge and thought about giving up yoga.

Giving up a lot of things, in fact.

In this newfound spirit (which had been on the go seriously for about an hour now), she had also decided finally to give in and cancel her Pilates instructor. She wasn't enjoying it as much as she'd dreamed she would. All that bending and stretching and arching and flexing in the middle of the afternoon. Plus all the talk of nutritionists and dieticians in the juice bar afterwards. Christ, it got on her tits.

No, she'd cancel. It'd give her and Ben more time to spend together. What with all the hours he spent on the show, plus her script deadlines, they were only managing to collide once in a while, usually in the bedroom.

Not that there was anything wrong with that.

She looked up and smiled as Ben appeared in the stone archway of the cavernous room, holding a steaming wooden spoon.

'How did it go?' she asked. 'Was he any good?'

Ben nodded.

'I'm going to swing by the Store tonight and catch his act, but I get a good feeling about him. Doesn't drink tea. Doesn't like the way it's served in restaurants. Anyway, taste this. Too much garlic?'

Jackie tried the sauce on the end of the spoon, blowing on it, smacking her lips.

'Mmm, that's good.' She returned to her laptop. 'I'll be in in a second. Let me just finish this scene.'

Ben squeaked back into the plume of cooking smells.

'Hey, don't your team mind you interviewing new writers at home?' Jackie called through.

'We're the creators,' he said over the slosh of draining pasta. 'They let us do what we like. Did you read in the paper about the other Corillo shows going into production?' He poked his head back through the arch. 'You're going to have some competition. Not that you've anything to worry about. HBN are right, people are only going to want your version. On the spot, eye-witness account that it is.'

'Hope so,' Jackie said, fingers clicking over the keys. 'Although I had to talk them out of calling it *Jackie Heaney's — The Frankie Corillo Story*.'

Ben went back to busying himself with sauces and chicken.

Jackie appeared in the kitchen, barefoot, holding her glass of water.

'You . . . you said "we" again,' she said tenderly. '*We* are the creators. They let us do what *we* like.'

Ben looked at her.

'Still miss him?' she said

Ben nodded.

They held each other for a while.

'So what *are* HBN going to call your show?' Ben said eventually as they clattered heavy china.

'Hnn? Oh, I suggested *Unorganised Crime*.'

'*Unorganised Crime?* Hmm,' he said.

'What?'

'No, no, that's . . . that's good.'

'Oh, don't start. Puns in office hours only now. We agreed, remember?'

'You're right, you're right, I'm sorry. We agreed, I take it back, I take it back. Absolutely. No puns.'

Jackie raised an eyebrow and wandered to the fridge for more wine.

'*Mob's Your Uncle*? It's funnier.'

'Ben?'

'Uhmm . . . wait, wait! Mafia, hoods, wiseguys, rackets . . . Or, hey, *What's That Racket?* Geddit? Racket? Like *racket?* Geddit?'